the Cheetah Girls

the Cheetah Girls

Livin' Large!

Volumes 1–4

Deborah Gregory

JUMP AT THE SUN

HYPERION PAPERBACKS FOR CHILDREN
NEW YORK

Printed in the United States of America
First compiled edition 2003
3 5 7 9 10 8 6 4 2
This book is set in 12–point Palatino.
ISBN: 0-7868-1789-5
Library of Congress Catalog Card Number on file

Visit www.cheetahgirls.com

Acknowledgments

I have to give it up to the Jump at the Sun peeps here—Andrea Pinkney, Lisa Holton, and Ken Geist—for letting the Cheetah Girls run wild. Also, Anath Garber, the one person who helped me find my Cheetah Girl powers. And, Lita Richardson, the one person who now has my back in the jiggy jungle. Primo thanks to the cover girl Cheetahs: Arike, Brandi, Imani, Jeni, and Mia. And to all the Cheetah Girls around the globe: Get diggity with the growl power, baby!

Contents

Introduction

Once upon a rhyme, there were two beautiful, bubble-icious girls named Galleria and Chanel who were the best of friends and the brightest wanna-be stars in all the land. One night, they looked up in the sky at all the real, glittering stars and dreamed of a place where they, too, could shine forever. Under the spell of the moonlight, they made a secret pact that they would find this place no matter how long it took, no matter how hard they had to try. Then they would travel all over the world and share their cheetah-licious songs and supa-dupa sparkles with everyone who crossed their path.

But it wasn't until Galleria and Chanel banded together with three other girls and unleashed their growl power that they discovered the jiggy jungle: that magical, cheetahlicious place inside of every dangerous, scary, crowded city where dreams really do come true. The jiggy jungle is the only place where every cheetah has its day!

The Cheetah Girls Credo

To earn my spots and rightful place in the world, I solemnly swear to honor and uphold the Cheetah Girls oath:

- Cheetah Girls don't litter, they glitter. I will help my family, friends, and other Cheetah Girls whenever they need my love, support, or a *really* big hug.

- All Cheetah Girls are created equal, but we are not alike. We come in different sizes, shapes, and colors, and hail from different cultures. I will not judge others by the color of their spots, but by their character.

- A true Cheetah Girl doesn't spend more time doing her hair than her homework. Hair extensions may be career extensions, but talent and skills will pay my bills.
- True Cheetah Girls can achieve without a weave—or a wiggle, jiggle, or a giggle. I promise to rely (mostly) on my brains, heart, and courage to reach my cheetah-licious potential!
- A brave Cheetah Girl isn't afraid to admit when she's scared. I promise to get on my knees and summon the growl power of the Cheetah Girls who came before me—including my mom, grandmoms, and the Supremes—and ask them to help me be strong.
- All Cheetah Girls make mistakes. I promise to admit when I'm wrong and will work to make it right. I'll also say I'm sorry, even when I don't want to.
- Grown-ups are not always right, but they are bigger, older, and louder. I will treat my teachers, parents, and people of authority with respect—and expect them to do the same!

- True Cheetah Girls don't run with wolves or hang with hyenas. True Cheetahs pick much better friends. I will not try to get other people's approval by acting like a copycat.

- To become the Cheetah Girl that only I can be, I promise not to follow anyone else's dreams but my own. No matter how much I quiver, shake, shiver, and quake!

- Cheetah Girls were born for adventure. I promise to learn a language other than my own and travel around the world to meet my fellow Cheetah Girls.

the Cheetah Girls

Wishing on a Star

For Sabie, the original
Miss Cuchifrito.
And Toto, too.
I miss you both.

Chapter 1

Toto must think my toes are dipped in Bark-B-Q sauce, the way he's trying to sneak a chomp-a-roni with his pointy fangs. I have just painted my toenails in a purply glitter shade called "Pow!" by S.N.A.P.S. Cosmetics and am lying on my bed with my feet dangling to the winds so they can dry.

"Guess what, big brother, you're gonna have to get your grub on somewhere else," I coo to the raggedy pooch with dreadlocks whom I love more than life itself. "I, Galleria Garibaldi, supa divette-in-training, cannot afford to have Toto-tugged tootsies."

Mom isn't sure what breed Toto is, because she and Dad adopted him from the ASPCA before I was born. But when all the hair-sprayed ladies on the street stop and ask me, I say that he is a poodle instead of a "pastamuffin" (that's what I call him). It sounds more *hoity-toity*, and trust: that is a plus on the Upper East Side, where I live.

I stick the bottle of nail polish in my new cheetah backpack. I hold up my hands, and it looks like a thousand glittering stars are bouncing off my Pow!-painted tips. "Awright!" I tell myself. "This girlina-rina is gonna get herself noticed by first period, Toto. High school, at last!"

Tomorrow is my first day as a freshman at Fashion Industries High School, and I'm totally excited—and scared. I figure it can't hurt to make a big first impression—but painting my nails is also a way to get my mind off being so nervous.

I'm real glad Chuchie is coming over for dinner tonight. That's Chanel Simmons to you—she's my partner-in-rhyme (aka Miss Cuchifrita, Chanel No. 5, Miss Gigglebox, and about a gazillion other names I call her). We've known each other since we were in designer diapers. Chuchie, her brother, Pucci, and her mom, Juanita, ought to be here any minute, in fact.

Chuchie's going to Fashion Industries High, too. Thank gooseness—which is my way of saying thank you. She's about the only familiar face I'll be seeing come tomorrow morning.

Chanel is a blend of Dominican and Puerto Rican on her mother's side, Jamaican and Cuban on her father's side—and sneaky-deaky through and through! She lives down in Soho near my mother's store, Toto in New York . . . Fun in Diva Sizes. It's on West Broadway off Broome Street, where people are a lot more "freestyle" than in my neighborhood.

Down there, you can walk on the sidewalk next to a Park Avenue lady, or someone with blue hair, a nose ring, and a boom box getting their groove on walking down the sidewalk. Up here, hair colors must come out of a Clairol box. It's probably written in the lease!

"Galleria?" I hear my mom calling me from the dining room. "You 'bout ready, girlina? 'Cause your daddy's getting home late, and I'm not playing hostess with the mostest all by myself!"

"Coming, Momsy-poo!" I shout back. But I

don't move. Not yet. Plenty of time for that when the doorbell rings.

Thinking about Chanel has put me in mind of my music. I start singing the new song I have just finished writing in my Kitty Kat notebook: "Welcome to the Glitterdome."

I have to get my songs copyrighted so no one will bite my flavor before I become famous—which is going to happen any second. I have a drawer full of furry, spotted notebooks filled with all the words, songs, and crazy thoughts I think of—which I do on a 24-7 basis. I will whip out my notebook wherever I am and scribble madly. There is no shame in my game.

I pick up my private notebook, on which my name—Galleria—appears in peel-off glitter letters, and turn to a blank page. I start writing notes to myself and working on the "Glitterdome" song some more.

What I love the "bestesses of all" (as Chanel would say) is singing, rhyming, and blabbing my mouth. It's as natural to me as dressing for snaps (that means, for compliments). I can make up words and rhymes on a dime. Not rap, just freestyle flow. I also spell words "anyhoo I pleez"—as long as they're different from other people's spelling.

The doorbell rings. "Galleria!" my mom shouts. "You'd better wiggle you way over here. The 'royal' family has arrived!"

I slip into my cheetah ballet flats and hurry to get the door. Tonight's a big night for Chanel's mom, Juanita: She's introducing us to her new boyfriend. He's some kind of mysterious tycoon or something, whom she met in gay Paree, aka Paris, France, no less! From what Mom tells me, Juanita thinks he might be her ticket to the Billionaire's Ball, if there is such a thing.

"She met him in Paris, and he supposedly owns half of the continent or something," was how Mom put it. "She's trying to get him to marry her—so we've gotta make a good impression."

Well, okay. I guess I know how to make a good impression. Hope he likes purple glitter toenails, 'cause I am me, y'know? Like me or don't, I'm not fluttering my eyelashes like Cleopatra!

"Chuchie!" I say as I open the door. "Wuzup, *señorita?*" We do our secret handshake greeting—which consists of tickling each other's fingernails—and give each other a big hug.

Juanita looks like a glamapuss. Poly and Ester must have been on vacation. She's still as thin as she was when she was a model (unlike my mom, who is now a size-eighteen, class-A diva). Right now, Juanita's wearing this long, flowy dress encrusted with jewels, like she's the royal toast of gay Paree or something. Like I said, it looks good on her, but it's kinda weird if you ask me.

"Hey, Galleria!" she says. Then she steps sideways so I can see her new boyfriend. "This is Monsieur Tycoon," she says, laying on the French accent.

"Pleased to meet you," I say, offering my hand. But he doesn't take it. I guess over there they don't shake a girl's hand if they don't know her. "His Majesty" just smiles this teeny little smile and nods at me.

"Come on in, y'all," I say, and they do, Mr. Tycoon last of all. Juanita gives me a little wink as she passes and I can tell she's happy and nervous all at the same time. Pucci hugs my waist.

I look at Chuchie, and she rolls her eyes at me. I bite my lip to keep from giggling and wonder how Chuchie's managing not to giggle herself. She's always the first to lose it, not me. But that's because she's met the tycoon before.

He's good-lookin', all right, with a big black mustache and black eyes that make him look like he's an undercover spy. And he's wearing a pinstriped suit that's probably hand-sewn every stitch of it! He comes in and looks around the place, nodding like he approves. I'm so glad he thinks we're worthy of his royal highness. *Not*. I mean, I am not used to being scrutinized, you know? I wonder how my mom is going to react.

"Bon soir," Mom says, flexing her French and gliding into the room from the kitchen, six feet tall and looking every inch the diva she is—still ferocious enough to pounce down any runway. The tycoon gives her a little bow and puts his hands together like he's praying, but I think it's because he's impressed.

"I hope you're all hungry," Mom says. "I've been in the kitchen all day, whipping up a *fabulous* feast."

I know she's fibbing, but I stay hush-hush. Mom *always* goes down to the Pink Tea Cup for dinner when she wants to serve soul food. Their stuff is greasy but yummy.

Me and Chanel give each other looks that say "We've gotta talk!"

"'Scuse us for a minute?" I ask the grown-ups. "I want to show Chanel my new cheetah backpack."

"Go on," Mom says. "We'll call you when dinner's served."

We hightail it into my room and shut the door behind us. As soon as we do, Chuchie explodes into a fit of giggles. "I can't take it anymore!" she gasps.

"Is he for real?" I ask. "Shhh! He'll hear you laughing and get insulted. You don't wanna mess things up for your mom!"

"She is so cuckoo for him!" Chuchie says.

"Chuchie, you're gonna be a royal princess one of these days, and I'm gonna have to bow down and throw petals at your corn-infested feet every time I see you."

"Stop!" Chuchie says again, dissolving into another fit of giggles. When she's finally done, she says, "Seriously, Bubbles. I'm worried about Mom. I mean, his 'His Majesty' is so weird. I'm not even allowed to talk when he's around! He thinks children are supposed to be seen and not heard." Chuchie calls me Bubbles because I chew so much bubble gum.

"Children?" I repeat. "Miss Cuchifrita, we're in high school come tomorrow! We are not children anymore!"

"Tell me about it! Are you ready for the big time?"

"Ready as I'll ever be—I've got my nails done (I flash them for her), my new backpack, and attitude to spare. How 'bout you, girlita?"

"I guess," she says, not sounding too sure of herself. "It's gonna be kinda strange not knowing anybody else but each other."

"Hey, we don't need anybody else," I tell her. "We are the dynamic duo, yo!"

Me and Chanel have been singing together since we were six, but not professionally, because Chanel's mom does not want her to be a singer. A talent show here or there is "cute," but after that she starts croaking.

What Juanita doesn't know is that me and Chuchie made a secret pact in seventh grade. We are going to be famous singers despite her (or maybe to spite her) because we can't be models like she and my mom were.

My mom is a whopper-stopper six feet tall. I'm only five feet four inches. Juanita is five feet seven inches. Chanel is five feet three inches. Do the math. We're both too short for the runway sashay. (My mom was a more successful and glam-glam model than Juanita—and sometimes I think that's why they fight.)

Unlike Juanita, my mom is pretty cool with whatever I'm down with. She wanted to be a singer really bad when she was young. She had the fiercest leopard clothes, but she just didn't have the voice. Then she went into modeling and sashayed till she parlayed her designing skills.

The only reason *I* haven't become a famous singer yet is because I don't want to be onstage by myself. Being an only child is lonely enough. I would go cuckoo for Cocoa Puffs, for sure. With Chuchie around, it's like having a sister. Like I said, we are the dynamic duo, bound till death. But, still, there's something missing—and I'm beginning to think I know what it is.

"You know what, Miss Cuchifrita?" I say. "I think we need to find us some backup singers and make a real girl group."

"Yeah!" she says right away. "Girl groups always become famous. Look at the Lollipops. They were finger-lickin' large."

"Or the HoneyDews," I say. "Their bank accounts are ripe with loot."

"Or Karma's Children, or The Spice Rack Girls!" Chuchie adds. "They are not even supa-chili anymore, but they once were, and that is what counts."

The kids in junior high school used to say that I look like Backstabba, the lead singer of Karma's Children. That is probably because I'm light-skinned (dark butterscotch-y) and wear my hair kinda long in straight or curly styles. (My hair is kinky, but I straighten it.) I don't think we look alike. I have bigger hips and tommyknockers (that means boobies). I also wear braces.

Karma's Children are four fly singers—Backstabba, Greedi, Peace, and Luvbug—from Houston and they must have instant karma because they had a hit record right out the box, "Yes, Yes, Yes." From what I can see, you don't have to have a lot of lyrics to be large. The Spice Rack Girls had a hit song with even fewer words—"Dance!"—and they live in a castle, I think, somewhere in Thyme City, Wales, which is far, far away from the jiggy jungle.

"Hey, if we get in a girl group, we could travel all over the world, singing," Chuchie says.

"We could go to London," I say, getting in the groove. "Drink Earl Grey tea with the queen."

"Yeah, and shop in the West End district." That's Chanel for you. Her idea of geography is knowing every shopping locale worldwide!

"We could go to Paris, too," I say. "Eat croissants with butter—not margarine!"

"Yeah, and shop at French designer saylons," Chuchie adds, stretching the long "a."

"Like Pouf," I say, "where they sell the *très* fiercest leopard-snakeskin boots. Then we can go to Italy to see all my aunts and uncles on my father's side."

"And shop at Prada! That's where I'm headed. 'Prada or Nada,' that's my motto for life!"

Chuchie picks up my hairbrush and starts singin' into it like it's a microphone—doin' Kahlua and Mo' Money Monique's "The Toyz Is Mine." I pick up my round brush and join her, both of us bouncin' on the bed as we sing and do our supa-dupa moves in perfect har-mo-nee.

Chanel kinda looks like a lighter version of Kahlua—with the same slanty, exotic brown eyes, and oodles of long micro-braids falling in her face.

When we're done, we both dissolve in giggles. Then I roll over and say, "We're gonna do it, Miss Cuchifrita. Alls we gotta do is find the rest of our girl group."

"Uh huh. But where we gonna do that?" she asks me.

"I dunno," I say. "But one thing is for sure: It's gonna happen." We give each other our secret handshake and a fierce hug.

That's me and Chuchie: always hatchin' big dreams together. At first, we wanted to open a store for pampered pets—and now we have a game plan for becoming starlets. And you know what? One day, they're all gonna come true. Trust me.

"Hey! What are you two 'high school' girls doin' in there?" I hear Mom calling. "I got din-din on the table and I know you don't want cold pork chops and black-eyed peas!"

"Coming!" we both yell.

"I'll page you later," Chuchie says as we go to join the grown-ups. "We can 'dish and tell' later."

"You got it, girlita," I say. "'Cause I know I won't be able to sleep tonight. I'll log on when I get your page, and we can hog the chat room all night long."

Chapter 2

It's 10:45, and Chuchie, Pucci, Juanita, and Mr. Tycoon are long gone. Mom is cleaning up in the kitchen. My dad walked in about half an hour ago, and he's waving a piece of corn bread in the air as he talks. Talking with his hands comes with his heritage. Signore Francobollo Garibaldi is Eye-talian—from Bologna, Italy—but he loves soul food. I guess it comes with lovin' my mom.

Dad runs the factory in Brooklyn where the clothes are made for Mom's store, Toto in New York, and sometimes he gets home real late. Like tonight.

I give him a kiss, or *un bacio*, as he calls it, and say, "I got school tomorrow and I gotta get my beauty sleep, okay?"

"Okay, *cara*," my dad says, kissing me back. "Luv ya. Just make sure your skirt is longer than twelve inches!" He smiles at me and gives me a wink. *Cara* means "precious one" in Italian. That's my dad for you: behind me all the way, as long as I keep my knees covered!

I get washed up and get into bed, knowing Mom will be coming in to say good night any minute. She never misses. Sure enough there's a soft knock at my door, and she comes in and sits by my bed.

"You have a good time tonight?" she asks.

"Uh-huh. I guess," I say. "Mr. Tycoon's kinda different, though."

Mom laughs. "I know what you mean, sugah. You and Chanel didn't say two words the whole time, but I bet you were kicking each other under the table!" Mom knows us too well.

"Yeah." I giggled. "Better kicking than talking—I got the feeling he wouldn't like it if we did!"

"You're right about that," she says. "But Juanita's crazy 'bout him, so we've just gotta play along and hope she gets what she wants—and likes it when she does."

"Uh-huh," I say.

"You ready for school tomorrow? Just don't roll up the waistband of your skirt!" she says.

"Okay," I say, and fake a yawn. "G'night, Mom."

"Good night, baby. Don't be scared, now—stay fierce. Show 'em who you are, and they'll love you just like I do." She kisses me on the forehead and goes out, shutting the door behind her.

Mom is so cool. When I am rich and famous, I am going to buy her the one thing she wants more than anything else: Dorothy's ruby slippers from *The Wizard of Oz*. Mom is a *serious* collector. She wants whatever nobody else has, or almost nobody. There are only five pairs of ruby slippers in the whole world, and the last pair was auctioned off at Christie's for 165,000 duckets. I will find the anonymous mystery person who has bought the ruby slippers and buy them for Mom as a surprise.

Mom has seen *The Wizard of Oz* more times than I care to remember. She boo-hoos like a baby every time, too. I don't know why it makes her cry. It makes me laugh.

There is something Mom isn't telling me

about her family, but I'm not supposed to know that. She never talks about them, and I don't have any relatives on her side.

In the living room, there is a very old, gray-looking picture of *her* mom, a brown-skinned lady who looks sad. She says her mother died a long time ago, before I was born. Chanel says my mom is a drama queen. I think she is just larger than life. Diva size.

I have a lot of ruby slipper stickers, which I have put on my school notebooks and dresser drawers and my closet doors in my bedroom—the "spotted kingdom." I also have ruby slipper cards. I keep them in the leopard hat boxes by the bed.

Inside the ruby slipper card, it says MAY ALL YOUR DREAMS COME TRUE. I keep one pinned on my busybody board and open it sometimes because it gives me hope that my dreams will come true, too. I don't want to let my mother down and live in this bedroom forever.

My Miss Wiggy alarm clock reads 11:00, and suddenly, my beeper is vibrating on the night-stand. Got to be Chanel. I roll over, hop out of bed, and log on to the Internet on my swell Ladybug PC.

Toto is hunched on his front paws and staring at me with his little black beady eyes. My poor little brother can't accept the fact that he is simply a fluffy pooch. Toto is fifteen, (which is 105 in human years), and he sleeps in my room, in his very own canopy bed, with a leopard duvet. "Oh, Toto, you always make me smile," I tell him as I type my greeting to Chuchie.

"Chanel, Chanel, you're so swell. What are you wearing tomorrow, *mamacita*, pleez, pleez, tell?"

No answer. Hmmmm . . . she beeped me, but she isn't in the chat room. That's strange. There is plenty of cyber action, judging by the number of on-screen entries. Everybody must need a 'Net break since it's back-to-school "D day" for anybody under eighteen with a brain.

"Oh, if I only had a brain, I wouldn't feel so lame, and I'd jump on the A train when it rained, because there'd be no shame in my game . . ." I hum aloud while plotting my next move.

"My name is Dorinda," flashes on my computer screen. "I'm pressing my khaki boot-cut pants right now and shining my Madd Monster shoes. I'm wearing a black sweater, right. Do you think it will be too 'that' to wear a tube top underneath it?"

Oh, this girl is mad funny, I think, cracking up as I type a response. "Hi, my name is Galleria. September is the time for the belly button to go on vacation and the brain to come back in full effect. Unless you want Serial Mom to corner you in the girls' room and cut off your top with a rusty pair of scissors, you'd better leave the 'boob tube' at home! Where are you going to school, anyway?"

"Galleria, the Joker, thanks. Tomorrow's my first day at Fashion Industries on Twenty-fourth Street. I'm going to major in fashion design! Guess I can't 'cut' class. Ha. Ha."

Hip-hop, hooray. This girl is going to the same school I am, even though our majors are different!

"I'm gonna be checking for you, girlita. I'm there tomorrow, too, or I'll be a T square. I'm majoring in fashion merchandising and buying—I've got a passion for fashion but can't cut my way out of Barbie's cardboard wardrobe. I leave that to my mom. She's a majordomo dope designer. You scared about going to high school?"

"No. I'm cooler than a fan, baby. Well, okey-dokey, a little," Dorinda replies. "It's farther away from my house than I'm used to traveling in the A.M., if you know what I'm saying. And it'll take away from the time I used to spend helping my mom get everyone ready for school."

Another entry flashes on my screen. "Hey, Bubbles! Let's wear our leopard miniskirts with berets, but with a different-colored turtleneck. Which do you want to wear, red or black?"

Chuchie is finally in the house. "Gucci for Chuchie! No diggity, no doubt. You're late. This is Dorinda and she's going to be in the house with us tomorrow. Where you been?"

"Pucci lost one of his Whacky Babies—Oscar the Ostrich. That beaten-up thing was his favorite, too. *Ay, caramba*, I was so glad that he finally fell asleep on top of Mr. Mushy. Now he'll be crying when he wakes up tomorrow and sees he's got a crushy Mr. Mushy, but I'm not moving him!"

Pucci is Chuchie's younger brother. He is nine, pudgy, spoiled to death, and has the biggest collection of Whacky Babies stuffed animals in the jungle. I call him "Eight

Ball" because his head is shaven clean like a pool ball.

I type back, "Ooh, that's cold, Chanel No. 5. Dorinda is majoring in fashion design. Ain't that dope?"

"Cool, Miss Dorinda. Where do you live?"

"116th and Lenox Ave."

"Uptown, baby, you gets down, baby?" Chuchie writes.

"I try. I can move. I can groove. I'm gonna take dance classes at the YMCA on 135th 'cause I'm in the Junior Youth Entrepreneur Leadership Program there, so I get classes in everything for free."

"We got skills, too. We take dance and voice classes at Drinka Champagne's Conservatory on Saturdays. You think you got more skills than us?"

"No! I'm not flossin'."

"Correct, *mamacita*. Me and Galleria sing, too. What you know about that?"

"Nothing. But I think I can sing, too—a little. I would like to, anyway. I'll check for you two tomorrow and show you!"

"Bet, Dorinda. Bubbles, don't try to get out of it. What color top are you gonna wear? 'Cause you better not wear the same color as me, *está bien?*"

"Bubbles? That's funny," Dorinda types.

"Chuchie calls me Bubbles because I love to chomp on gum. Something I cannot do in public because my mom says it's tick-tacky," I type for Dorinda. "I'll wear the red top with the black scribble, okay?" I type to ease Chuchie's mind.

"Dorinda, where did you go to junior high?"

"I went to Wagner," Dorinda types back.

"You really are a hoodie girl, huh?"

"Guess so. It was two blocks from my house. Easy breezy on the traveling tip."

"That's cool. It could be worse."

"Word?"

"Word. At least you don't live in the suburbs!" Chanel types, proud of her snaps. "Galleria is a boho because she is so 'that,' and I'm a Dominican bap, I guess, and proud of it. We'll see if you can hang with us!"

What does she mean by I'm so "that"? I'll fix her. "You're a burp!" I type back. "Boougie, undone, ridiculoso, and princess-y to the max. Don't deny it."

"Don't let me read you from cover to cover or you'll never recover, Secret Agent Bubbles, okay, *mija?*" responds Chanel. "I'm going to wear the black turtleneck top with the leopard skirt, so you can go ahead with your red top." I can just see her giggling. She is a majordomo gigglebox and can't be stopped.

"Maybe we can be a crew. You never know," I type for Dorinda's assurance.

"Let's meet outside the cafeteria at 12:00 sharp. But we're not going in. I don't want to get food poisoning my first day of school. You know what we'll be wearing, so you can't miss us!" Chanel signs off.

"See ya and I'm tryin' hard to be ya!" Dorinda retorts.

This girl is quick. Maybe she *can* hang with us, I think, as I sign off, "Powder to the People!"

"Powder to the People!" is a joke between me and Chanel. I'll tell Dorinda about it tomorrow. For now, I log off and get back into bed.

Toto is lying on the floor now with his nose pressed to the floor.

"Toto, watcha thinkin'?" Cheez whiz, I wonder what it's like to be a dog. One thing is for sure. They don't have to get up at the crack of dawn and go to school.

In the darkness, my fears dance around like Lotto balls. So I sing out loud to all the twinkle-dinkles like me, trying to sparkle in this crazy place called the Big Apple. A real deal jungle. We don't have the grass and trees, but we do have some of the animals.

"Twinkle-dinkles, near or far,
stop the madness and be a star.

Take your seat on the Ferris wheel,
and strap yourself in for the man of steel.

Welcome to the Glitterdome.
It's any place you call home.

Give me props, I'll give you cash,
then show you where my sparkle's stashed.

Glitter, glitter. Don't be bitter!
Glitter, glitter. Don't be bitter!
Glitter, glitter. Don't be bitter!"

I drift into sleep, and I'm sure the fears have all been chased away. Not by my singing, but by Toto's snoring, which is louder than the backfire from the Cockadoodle Donuts truck that passes by our street at four A.M. every morning. My songs are my secret weapon, though, for shooting straight to stardom. . . .

Chapter 3

Mr. Drezform, our new homeroom teacher, has trouble pronouncing my last name, like all the other teachers I've had since kindergarten. "Galleria Gareboodi?"

"Here!" I yell out, smiling and raising my hand in the air like I just don't care. "It's Galleria Gar-i-bald-i."

This boy in front of me turns around and heckles me. "Gar-i-booty!" he says, and laughs. Then *everyone* else in the class turns to look at me.

"*What?*" I ask, challenging him. "What's your name, yo?"

"Derek," he says, still smiling.

"Derek what?"

"Derek Hambone," he says. "The new brotha in town—from Detroit."

"Derek *what?*" I ask. "Did you say Hambone?" Now the class is laughing at him, not me. "Hah! You'd best not be laughing. Your last name sure ain't no Happy Meal."

I snarl and squint my eyes. He turns away, busted. Now I'm looking at the back of his head, which has the letters "D U H" shaved into it. "Duh?" I say to Chanel, mouthing the words without sound. "What are we on—*Sesame Street?*"

Derek is featuring a red, blue, and white Johnny BeDown shirt with matching droopy jeans covered with logos like a roadrunner map. Johnny BeDown clothes aren't made by the Joker, if you know what I'm saying. You have to shell out serious duckets for them. They just *look* like the homeless catch of the day.

There are three things I hate. 1. Cock-a-roaches. 2. Math tests. 3. Wack-a-doodle clothes. The first I can't avoid unless I move out of New York City. The second two are *kinda* like roaches because they're everywhere.

I, Galleria Garibaldi, will never dress like every-body else. I write this in my freshman notebook using my purple pen. It's true that I get my animal instincts from my mom, but I have my own flavor, 'cause I'll wear cheetah prints in hot pink or lime green, and Mom sticks to the old-school ones.

I remember I was only four years old when she bought me my first furry leopard coat with a matching hat. My father nicknamed me Miss Leoparda because I wore that coat to pieces. I also had a stuffed leopard animal named Cheetah Kat, which I took with me everywhere. And Toto now has seven leopard coats, thanks to me.

As for Chuchie, her taste in fashion runs to berets. She is wearing one today, with her braids hanging down into her face.

"Gimme one of your pens," she groans. "Mine stopped working." Chuchie must own about fifty of these French pancakes (that's what I call them). The beret she is wearing today is black with a gold-braided edge. Her mom brought it back from Paris. Chuchie is sitting next to me, drawing silly faces in the margins of her notebook and giggling quietly.

Attendance is taking a long time, and my mind wanders to Dorinda. We're meeting her at noon, outside the cafeteria. I wonder what she'll be like. . . .

Mr. Drezform blows his nose, causing Chuchie to giggle real loud, and Derek Hambone turns around and grins at me, giving me a big wink. Heavens to Bootsy—Derek has a gold tooth in front!

Chuchie dissolves into giggles, and I give her a hard elbow to the ribs.

"Hey, Derek," I say, "what's with the haircut?"

"Oh, you mean the letters?" he asks, giving me his goofy, gold-tooth smile again.

"Yeah."

"It's my initials," he explains proudly. "Derek Ulysses Hambone."

I bite down hard on my lip to keep from losing it completely. "You know, Derek, it also stands for something else."

"It does?" he asks, clueless. "What?"

"Figure it out, *scemo*," I quip, using the Italian word for idiot.

"Okay, I will," he says. "And *shame* on you back—even though, you know, you are cute." Another goofy grin, and he turns away again.

Great. Just what I need on my first day in

high school: a fashion disaster with a geeky smile and a gold tooth who *likes me*.

I can tell it's only a matter of time till he asks me out. Someone call 911, please.

"It's time for *lonchando*," Chanel says as we wait outside the cafeteria for Dorinda.

"I've got an idea for our Kats and Kittys Halloween Bash," I tell Chuchie. The Kats and Kittys Klub, which we belong to, does all kinds of phat stuff, and me and Chanel had been talking about the Halloween Bash ever since the Fourth of July. "We should throw it at the Cheetah-Rama, where Mom goes dancing. What do you think?"

"*Está bien*. I forgot to tell you. I saw those girls from Houston on Sunday down in Soho."

"What girls?"

"'Member the twins who were at the Kats Fourth of July Bash? What were their names?"

"Oh, I don't know. You're the one who was talking to them," I say, feeling a twinge of jealousy. She's talking about those wanna-be singers who showed up and sang when nobody asked them to.

"Aquanette and Anginette Walker," I mumble.

Of course, I do remember, because I remember everything.

Despite my flinching, Chuchie adds, "They can sing. They said they're coming to the Kats meeting on Friday. They moved here to go to LaGuardia Performing Arts High. That's where we shoulda went."

"We didn't go because you were too scared to audition, 'cause of your mother, remember?" I point out.

If Chanel didn't go, I wasn't going to audition by myself, but yeah, I'd wanted to go there, too. I wonder if the twins had to audition to get into LaGuardia. Or maybe they had "connects." They sure had the nerve to floss by singing at the Fourth of July barbecue grill, with the mosquitoes flying in their hair.

"True. They can sing," I say.

"And they can eat, too. The one in the red top ate seven hot dogs," Chanel says with a grimace.

"Which one has the name like the hair spray?"

"I can't remember, but they both had on a lot of that," Chanel says, giggling. "I thought maybe the one in the red top and white shorts had a television antenna up in that hairdo, it was so high."

Dorinda waves as soon as she sees us. I see she has taken my advice and is wearing a black turtleneck top with the khaki boot-leg pants. "Hi!" she exclaims, all excited. "I'm really, really *hungry*."

She is so tiny and pretty. I mean munchkin tiny. She doesn't look like a freshman at all. (She looks about twelve years old. For true.) She is also about the same color as Chanel—kinda like mochachino—and her hair is corn-rowed in the front, then the rest is just freestyle curly. From what I can see, she doesn't have a weave, unless it's an *unbeweavable* one, as Mom would say. Mom can "spook a weave" from the other side of the tracks. And I don't mean the ones in the subway, hello.

"Oh, word, I get to feel even shorter now," says Dorinda, squeezing between me and Chanel. "And I'm wearing heels!"

"We're three shorties," giggles Chanel, trying to make Dorinda feel better. Dorinda is even shorter than us. I feel so much taller with her around. I could get used to this.

"Here comes Derek," I mumble under my

breath. "Don't look at him," I plead with Dorinda.

Derek dips down the hallway and smirks in our direction as he passes. "Hey, Cheetah Girl," he hisses, winking at me. "I'm workin' on that puzzle you gave me." Mercifully, he keeps going.

Dorinda doesn't miss a thing. "Who's that?" she asks, squinching up her little nosy nose.

"That's Derek Hambone from our homeroom class."

"He's got on enough letters to teach Daffy Duck the alphabet," Dorinda says, chuckling.

"You are funny." Chuchie giggles. "You should see the way Galleria was looking at Derek in homeroom."

"Oh, don't try it, *señorita*," I counter. "Duh!"

"*Cheetah Girl*—that's kinda cool. You two are definitely blowing up the spots." Dorinda chuckles, fingering my cheetah backpack and reading the metal letters on the straps. 'Toto in New York'? What's that?"

"It's my mom's boutique—Toto in New York . . . Fun in Diva Sizes—down in Soho," I say. I notice that her tapestry backpack with happy faces is fly, too.

"What street is it on?" she asks me.

"West Broadway, off Broome Street," I tell her. "My mom makes these and sells them in her store."

"Really?"

"Really. She's a dope designer. Nobody makes clothes in diva sizes like she does. See how fat his stomach is?" I add, patting my backpack's paunchy stomach, "and the straps are leather, not pleather, like they put on the cheesy backpacks they sell on Fourteenth Street."

"How do you know it's a he?" Dorinda asks, her slanty brown eyes getting even slantier. Definitely Cheetah material.

"'Cause he eats more." I laugh, stuffing my textile design book into his fat paunch, then zip it up.

Dorinda has intense eyes, which she now focuses on Chuchie's cheetah. "You got one, too, huh?"

Chuchie nods her head and grins. "Whatever Secret Agent Bubbles gets, I get."

"You wish, you bumbling bourgeois detective!"

Chuchie hits me with her backpack.

"Oh, that's the top you said you were gonna wear," Dorinda says, turning to me. "What's it say?"

"Powder to the People. Grace is on the case. Will is chill. Sean is a fawn. I'm Fierce, You're Fierce," I say, pointing all over my top. "Whatever supa-licious things we come up with. Me and Chanel marked up a lot of tops this summer and sold them at our lemonade stand."

Dorinda really looks impressed.

"People were loving them. Bubbles's mom made them in bigger sizes and sold them in her store, too," Chuchie chimes in, bragging about our designing bite.

"Diva sizes," I say, correcting Chuchie.

"*Lo siento, mija*. I'm sorry!"

"My mom says there are no large sizes, just sizes that are too small!" I explain.

"I want to do some," Dorinda says.

"You gotta use black fabric marker so it won't wash off in the washing machine. But you can't put it on synthetic fabrics like polyester," I explain to her. "You could write on that with a blowtorch and it would bounce off."

Dorinda giggles ferociously. "That's funny.

How long you two been best friends?" she asks.

"Oh, this dish rag? I've known her since we took our first baby steps together. Both our mothers were models back in the day," I explain.

"Were they, like, in *Essence* magazine?" Dorinda asks me.

"My mom was. But the only modeling Juanita ever did was for *Chirpy Cheapies* catalogs, and Chanel has a lifetime supply of those wack-a-doodle-do clothes to prove it." I giggle.

"Yes, my mother was the diva of the discount catalogs, I confess, but it paid the bills, and now I got skills, okay?" Chanel snaps her fingers in Z formation."My mom just wrote a book," she tells Dorinda. "She went all over Europe and Japan to write about the history of Black models since back in the day."

"Really?" Dorinda is hugging her books to her chest as we walk outside, cross the street, and slip into Mikki D's.

"Uh-huh. It's called *They Shoot Models, Don't They?*" Chanel says. "Get it? Photographers take pictures of models with cameras."

"Word. I got it."

"I just wish she would hurry up and get the money for it so she could give me some," Chanel whines in her best Miss Piggy voice as she orders from the Mikki D's counter clerk.

Chuchie is a shopaholic waiting to happen. Even I know that. Even worse than me. Getting ready for high school has left us pretty busted, though.

"These twenty-five duckets a week ain't stretching very far at the S.N.A.P.S. counter," Chanel says with a sigh.

"They are definitely drizzle duckets."

"What's that mean?" Dorinda asks.

"It means, 'If it rains, we poor!'" I giggle. "Stick with us and you'll learn a lot of words."

"I want to be a writer, too," Dorinda says. "I read a lot. My mom says I should open a library so I won't have to go there all the time."

"You go just for fun?" Chuchie asks in disbelief.

"Yeah. I take out books all the time. You should see how many books I got under my bed!"

"Like what kind of books?"

"You know. *Sistah's Rules. Snap Attacks. I'm Fierce, You're Fierce.*" She giggles, making fun of us.

She is mad funny. I didn't want to ask

Dorinda how much allowance she gets, because that would be rude. Our moms pay the bills for our cell phones, beepers, bedroom phones, Internet service, blah, blah, blah, but there are still so many other things that we want but we just have to "cheese" for it.

Chanel, of course, is much nosier than I am. She will ask anybody, anything, anytime—while she bats her eyelashes and acts all cute. "How much do you get?" she asks Dorinda, biting into her hamburger.

"For what?" Dorinda responds.

"For allowance, *mamacita*."

"Oh, I don't really get allowance. But I work at the YMCA Junior Youth Entrepreneur Leadership Program three nights a week, so I make about twenty dollars. If I was sixteen, at least I could get my working papers. That's how I could make some real bank."

"What classes you taking?" I ask Dorinda, changing the subject. I don't want her to feel like she can't hang with us just because she doesn't have duckets. Me and Chanel aren't with that.

"Sketching. English composition. Textile design. Biology. Computers—I love that. I'm gonna learn new technology applications like cyber rerouting and building databases."

"Computer nerd. You go," Chuchie smirfs. I have to laugh. Chuchie only uses the computer to get on the Internet and do her homework, otherwise she could care less about it.

"At least I got the dance class I want," Dorinda continues. "Dunk the funk. That's the move. I've had enough modern for a while."

"I heard that, *señorita*. We're taking it, too! What period you got?"

"Seventh."

"We're in the same class! That's dope," Chuchie exclaims.

Suddenly I remember something. "Check out this song I wrote last night," I say excitedly. And then I sing it for them:

"Twinkle-dinkles, near or far,
stop the madness and be a star.

Take your seat on the Ferris wheel,
and strap yourself in for the man of steel.

Welcome to the Glitterdome.
It's any place you call home.

Give me props, I'll give you cash,
then show you where my sparkle's stashed.

Glitter, glitter. Don't be bitter!
Glitter, glitter. Don't be bitter!
Glitter, glitter. Don't be bitter!
There's no place like the Glitterdome!"

"I like it, Bubbles!" Chanel says, then starts harmonizing with me. "There's no place like the G-l-i-t-t-e-r-d-o-m-e."

She is always down for bringing on the noise. There is nothing we love doing more than singing together—and Chuchie is better at putting music and melody to words than I am.

"Glitter, glitter. Don't be bitter!" Dorinda suddenly belts out, hitting the notes higher than even Chanel does.

"You *can* sing, *mamacita,*" Chanel coos.

Chanel is like my sister, but I didn't choose her. We were bound together by lots of Gerber baby food and our diva mothers. Dorinda is different. She is just *like* us, and we only just met her!

"You should come with us to Drinka Champagne's Conservatory on Saturday,"

Chanel says excitedly. "That's where we take vocal lessons."

"How much is it?" Dorinda asks nervously.

"No duckets involved, Do'," Chanel counters. "We're on special scholarship."

"Do'. I like that," I remark, pulling out my Kitty Kat notebook. "Do' Re Mi. That's your official nickname now."

"Okay." She giggles, then scrunches her munchkin shoulders up to her ears. "I'm Do' Re Mi. My sister is gonna like that."

"What's her name?"

"Twinkie. She's nine."

"Like my brother, Pucci. Maybe we can hook them up," Chanel heckles on the mischief tip.

Then she gets an idea. "Oh, Bubbles, you know what would really be dope? Bringing Do' Re Mi to the Kats and Kittys Klub!"

"What's that?" Do' Re Mi yuks.

"Me and Bubbles belong to this 'shee, shee, boojie, boojie, oui, oui' social club—'for empowering African American teens!' Chanel chimes in, imitating the Kats president. "Before, they let us come for free because our mothers were members. Now we have to pay membership fees, but we can go by ourselves—finally!"

"How much does it cost?" Dorinda asks.

Clearly, Dorinda is all about the *ka-ching, ka-ching*. She is so smart. I really like her.

"It's about six hundred dollars, or is it six hundred fifty dollars a year for us till we're eighteen?"

"I think it's six hundred fifty dollars now."

"But don't worry, Do' Re Mi. We got you covered. We want you to sing with us, right, Galleria?"

"Uh-huh," I say. Chuchie doesn't make a move without asking me first. That's my girl-ita! "We're getting together a girl group, like The Spice Rack Girls, only better."

Dorinda brightens. "Awright! Where we gonna sing?"

"I don't know. We'll figure it out," I say. "We were thinkin' of singin' at the Kats and Kittys Halloween Bash. My mom's already makin' us Halloween costumes, anyway. I bet I can get her to make one for you, too."

"What does *your* mother do?" Chuchie asks Dorinda on the nosy tip.

"Nothing," she answers nervously. "She stays at home."

"How many brothers and sisters you have?"

Chanel asks, fluttering her eyelashes. Nosy posy just won't quit.

"Ten," Dorinda says.

"That's a lot of kids!"

"I know. But they aren't really *her* kids. I mean, she's a foster mother—and she's our mother, just not our *real* mother."

For once, Chanel stopped batting her eyelashes.

"Really? Are they your 'real' sisters and brothers?"

"No, but she's nice, my foster mom. She lets me do what I want, as long as I help her and stuff."

"You gonna come with us Friday, right?" Chanel says, not waiting for an answer. "We're on the party committee and we get to help plan all of the events."

I can tell she really likes Do' Re Mi. She is acting like a big sister. Just the way she acts with Pucci, her little brother. I wonder where Do' Re Mi's real mother is.

"You know we're the Kats, not the Kittys, right?" I say to amuse Do' Re Mi, then do the handshake wiggle with Chanel.

"I heard that. What's that you two are

doing?" she asks, extending her hand, too.

"Do it like this," Chanel says, showing her. The three of us wiggle our fingertips together. "All right! We got growl power, yo!"

I can see it coming. Now that we've found Dorinda, all our dreams are gonna come true. All we need now is another backup singer or two, and we'll be ready to pounce.

Chapter 4

With seven dollars in my cheetah wallet until Monday, there is only one filling solution before the Kats and Kittys Klub meeting: the Pizza Pit on Eighty-fourth and Columbus. When we step to the cash register to pay, much to our dee-light, Do' Re Mi makes a donation into the collection plate. "I got it," she says, giving the clerk $7.85 for our pizza slices and Cokes. "You're definitely crew now," Chanel says, giggling to the ka-ching of the cash register. One thing about Dorinda: She is generous with her money, even though she's got to work for it herself. I've never known anybody like that before.

We walk to the back of the Pizza Pit so we

can sit away from all the mothers with road-runner kids. The last time we sat up front, one of them threw a Dino-saurus Whacky Baby right into Chanel's large cup of Coke and knocked it over.

Chanel is sitting facing the entrance. "Look who just walked in," she says, talking through her straw, then quickly adds, "Don't turn around yet!"

It's too late. I already have—just in time to catch the grand entrance of those fabulous Walker twins from Houston. They are about the same height and size, but one of the twins is a chocolate shade lighter than the other. You can tell they're not from New York. The lighter-skinned of the two has on a hot pink turtleneck with a navy blue skirt. The other one has on an orange coatdress with ivory on the side. They look sorta church-y—at Eastertime.

"Heh, y'all. How y'all doin'?" one of them says. The twins are kinda friendly in a goofy sort of way, and their Southern accents just sorta shout at ya, "Y'ALL, we in the house!"

"Wuzup? You two coming to the Kats meeting?" I ask them, knowing full well they ain't here for a lobster cookout.

"Yeah, we're going over there. What we talking about tonight?"

"It's time for general elections. And we have to begin planning our next event. Me and Chanel are on the party committee. What committee are you on?"

"Volunteer services. We wanna plan something for a Christmas drive at a church or a women's shelter."

"We're planning to throw a dope Halloween bash," I counter. "Y'all missed our Christmas party." All of a sudden, I notice that I am trying to talk like them.

"Is that right?" one of the twins asks with a smile. She has nice lips—what we call juicy lips. Her eyes are big, too, like Popeye's.

"What's your name?" Dorinda asks her.

"Y'all, forgive me. I'm Aquanette," exclaims the twin with the pink acrylic nail tips. Okay, pink acrylics tips means Aquanette, I tell myself so I don't forget who's who. I wonder if Aquanette puts the rhinestones on her Pee Wee Press-On Nails by herself.

"You belong to Kats, too?"

"No. I'm just visiting. I'm Dorinda. Dorinda Rogers."

"They got good slices?" Aquanette asks Dorinda. She can't help but notice how quickly Dorinda is eating her food.

"Don't ask me if they're good. I'm just hungry," Dorinda says, smiling at her. Dorinda is s-o-o nice to everybody.

"We'd better order. We'll be right back," Aquanette says.

Anginette, it turns out, is the more vocal one in the ordering department. "Can we get a slice with anchovies, extra pepperoni, mushrooms, and sausage?" she asks the counter guy.

Chanel giggles at me, looking down at her pizza and kicking my Gucci loafers under the table.

"Watch the Gucci, Chuchie! It's leather, not pleather—like yours!"

Recovering from her laugh attack, Dorinda politely says to Anginette, who has returned with two slices and a Coca Cola, "I hear you two can sing."

"Yes, ma'am. You, too?"

"Well, sorta. I haven't been in any talent shows or anything, like Galleria and Chanel, but they're gonna take me to Drink some Conservatory with them for vocal classes."

"You mean Drinka Champagne's," Chanel says, cutting in. "It's the bomb for vocal and dance classes."

"Dag on, they got everything in this town," Anginette says with a tinge of know-it-allness in her voice. "That's why we came up here to go to LaGuardia, 'cause they have the best vocal department in the country."

My first thought is, okay, was that supposed to be a one-up, two-down? My second thought is, she'd better not come for me or I'll read her like the Bible.

"We wanna be backup singers in a group," Aqua explains earnestly, slurping up the cheese from her slice.

"Forgive my sister. She hasn't eaten in five years," giggles her unidentical half. "Actually, we came up here because there ain't enough room in Houston for Karma's Children *and* us!"

Aqua is definitely the funny one. Karma's Children still live in Houston even though they're now famous.

"How old is Backstabba now?" Aquanette asks Chanel.

"They try to say she's eighteen, but I heard she's just sixteen. They still have a tutor who travels with them on the road, so it must be true, 'cause she ain't finished high school."

"I like Jiggie Jim," Angie says. "That falsetto voice, all that screeching—'Aaaaah got to know where you stand, gi-r-r-l,'" she sings, then gasps, "it just gives me goose bumps!"

Hmm. Angie is quite theatrical once she gets her pepperoni quota. She sure isn't biting off her twin sister's flavor.

"Jiggie's groove is cool, even though his voice is a little too high for me, if you know what I'm saying," I counter, smirking, "and I personally am not into guys who wear black sunglasses—at night, thank you."

"I heard there's something wrong with his eyes," Chanel offers, trying not to smirk. "His left eye doesn't talk to his right one."

We all howl. Chuchie *loves* to invent fib-eronis.

"Are you Spanish?" Anginette asks Chanel, whom she obviously finds amusing.

"Dominican, *mamacita*, and proud of it," Chanel says.

"You can call her Miss Cuchifrita," I offer bitingly. "She's going to give out *piñatas* around midnight."

"One week of Spanish and you ready to do show-and-tell," gasps Chanel, batting her lashes at me. "You know what a *piñata* is?" she asks the twins.

"Nope," say Anginette and Aquanette like a chorus.

"They're animals made out of papier-mâché and glue, then stuffed inside with candy," Chuchie explains. "When you hit the *piñata*, all the candy falls out!"

"Oh! I know what they are," Angie says. "They have them in the Santa Maria Parade in Houston."

"Are you Spanish, too?" Aquanette asks Dorinda.

"Nope, I don't think so."

"Is that right? You are so pretty. Ain't she cute, Angie?"

"Thank you," Dorinda says matter-of-factly. "Actually, I don't know my family. I live in a foster home."

Oopsy doopsy. That should keep our Southern Princess of Extra Pepperoni chomping quietly for at least a few minutes.

"We came up here to live with our father," Anginette says, trying to rescue her sister from putting another *"piñata"* in her mouth. "Our mother is a district manager for Avon, so she travels all the time. Our father felt we weren't being properly supervised since they got dee-vorced."

Their mother is an Avon lady. No wonder they're so nice. I am not gonna tell them that I only like S.N.A.P.S. Cosmetics. They've probably never heard of it.

"What does your dad do?" Do' Re Mi asks them.

"He's the senior vice president of marketing at Avon. He was my mom's boss. That's why he moved up here. They got any hot sauce here?" Aquanette asks, turning to her sister.

"Nope," Anginette answers.

"Well, then, gimme yours," Aqua says.

Out of Anginette's purse comes a bottle of hot stuff. We all burst out laughing.

"So it's like that?"

"Y'all laugh, that's okay. If our mother saw us, she would start some drama," Aqua says, pouring the Hot Texie Mama sauce on her slice.

Okay, this is hee-larious.

"They don't have this in New York, girls, so you have to bear with us. We is homesick!"

"Our mom won't let us use hot sauce because it's not good for our vocal chords. Our father don't say nothing, though," Anginette says, waiting for the bottle to come back her way.

"I didn't know that. See, Bubbles, you eat all that hot stuff. I'm glad I don't," Chanel says, acting all mighty.

"We're not supposed to drink soda, either, but I love it," Aquanette adds, slurping her Coke.

"Chanel drinks enough soda to do Coke commercials," I counter. These girls don't even drink Diet Coke. "Is it bad for your voice, too?"

"Yup. Y'all sing in a choir?"

"No, but we go to Drinka Champagne's Conservatory on Saturdays, religiously. We take voice, dance, and theater."

"Y'all should come up to Hallelujah Tabernacle on One Hundred Thirty-fifth and Lenox. We sing in the junior choir on Sundays."

"Well, I'm usually getting my pedicure at that time," I say, giggling. Aquanette has on too much white lipstick. Against her brown skin, it looks like a neon sign, I think, as both Chanel *and* Do' Re Mi kick me under the table from opposite sides. I am gonna make both of them polish my Gucci loafers, I swear.

"What's y'all's range?" I ask, imitating that cute Southern drawl. Okay, so I am jealous. They sing in a choir, which means they can raise the roof off Jack in the Box.

"Mezzo, mostly," offers Anginette.

"Mezzo, too," adds Aquanette. "The gospel stuff is cool, but we want to sing pop, R and B-style music."

"So do we," Chanel says, nodding her head.

"Well, let's sing together sometime. Y'all can come over to our house!" Aquanette screams. "What y'all doing tomorrow night?"

"Well, we sure aren't going to the movies, because the duckets have run out," I say with a sigh.

"Nah, y'all can't be as broke as us. We are more broke than a bad joke! We need to make some money, doing *something*."

Now she is speaking my language. "Last summer, me and Chanel sold lemonade right on Second Avenue and Ninety-sixth Street near the big Duckets 'R' Us Bank, and we made some serious bank. How much did we make last summer, Chanel?"

"Lemme see. About four hundred dollars.

We may have to dust off my Mom's Tiffany pitchers and set up shop again, I swear," she says, giggling.

All of a sudden, I get a brainstorm. "Hey, y'all—we should perform at the Kats and Kittys Halloween Bash. You know, like charge admission. There's five of us—shoot. We could put on a show, we'd be, like, The Black Spice Rack Girls! And wear costumes with, like, spice leaves hanging off or something. I'd pay five dollars to see that!"

"Five dollars? How 'bout twenty-five dollars?" says Do' Re Mi, egging us on.

"Oh, my G-O-D, girl, that's a good idea!" yells Aquanette.

"My mom can *make* our costumes," I offer, bragging about my designing mom once again. She is gonna kill me. No, she'll probably charge me. But I'll worry about that later. "Last year, over one thousand Kats and Kittys came to our Christmas party. And they came from all over the country."

Okay, so I am exaggerating. But they did come from New Jersey, Philadelphia, Connecticut, Westchester, and even D.C., aka Chocolate City. There are over a hundred Kats and Kittys chapters across the country, but New York is the dopest one, and we throw the "dopiest dope" parties. Everybody comes to jam with us.

I'm not sure yet if I like these girls, but I know a ka-ching when I see one. Me, Chanel, and Do' Re Mi have got the flavor, but these two have the voices, and together we can at least put on one show. But first, I know we better get a few things straight before we go blabbing before the committee.

All serious, I say to the twins, "We're gonna go in there and ask the board members to let us do this. How come the two of you don't want to sing by yourselves? What do you need us for?"

"Me and Angie aren't about drawing attention to ourselves. That's not how we were raised," Aqua says, moving her acrylic tips to her chest, then turning to look at her sister. It's crystal clear which of these two operates this choo-choo train.

"We sing in the church—that's one thing—but we're about being humble," Angie says, looking at me earnestly.

Then, like she's on the *True Confessions* talk show, Angie says, "I honestly don't think we are flashy enough to be in a group by ourselves."

I have to give it to them: There is more to these fabulous Walker twins than hot sauce, tips, and chedda waves. They seem serious. "So you think that the five of us together could do some serious damage?" I ask, smiling at Chanel and Do' Re Mi.

"I think we should try it. If it don't work out, at least we'll have had a little fun with the show, then split the money and keep on searching for the rainbow," Angie says, fingering her arts-and-craftsy earrings.

Do' Re Mi steps to the home run plate. "We'll have to agree on the costumes and stuff, because we are not gospel kinda girls."

"We know that. We can see!" Aqua claims. "You three have that New York style. We are not going to come into this and take over. We *want* to be in a group."

"Okeydokey, then. The committee will go for it, right, Chuchie?"

Chuchie nods her head yes.

"All right, then," I say. "It's time to get busy in the jiggy jungle—no diggity, no doubt."

Chapter 5

Chanel and her family, Pucci and Juanita, live in a cheetah-certified loft on Mercer Street in Soho. (Yes, Mom helped decorate it.) In one part of the loft, Juanita has built a dance-exercise studio completely surrounded by mirrors. She likes to look in the mirror when she's exercising, which she does a lot.

Today she is in the studio giving herself exotic dance lessons and listening to some music that sounds *très exotique*. Maybe Juanita thinks moving her middle will make her a riddle to Mr. Tycoon.

"Hi, Galleria," Juanita calls out to me when I peek into the loft. Juanita hasn't gained an ounce since her modeling days. She brags about it all the time. Today she has on a crop top, and a sarong (like you wear at the beach) wrapped around her waist. She is moving a leopard scarf in front of her face right below her eyes, like she thinks she's the Queen of mystery.

"You girls want to come in here?" she asks me without missing a beat.

"No, we're going into the den," I yell back, trying to keep a straight face. Juanita thinks it's cute that we are performing at the Kats show. She has been in a very good mood lately, thanks to Mr. Tycoon.

The way she is wiggling her hips is too much for me. I run into Chuchie's bedroom and start wiggling my hips with my hands over my head. "I know, *mami*," Chuchie says, giggling, then rolling her eyes to the ceiling.

We have been rehearsing for a week, and everybody is getting on everybody's nerves. We can't seem to agree on what music to play for the show, but now it's show time—or, I should say, a showdown. Aqua and Angie are already waiting in the den with the records they want to use for the show.

Me and Chuchie walk into the den prepared to battle. See, our music tastes are exactly the same. We both like Kahlua, and we both like my songs—simple! Right now, I'm ready to throw down for my songs, and I must figure out how to get my way.

Do' Re Mi is sitting there quietly, reading a book called *The Shoe Business Must Go On*. She's very into shoes lately—especially the kind that make her taller! And, of course, she's always into books. I guess that's why she's so smart. Well, I hope she's smart enough to be on my side now.

"Okay, y'all," I begin. "We gotta figure out what we're gonna sing at the bash."

"I love Prince," Chuchie says, starting the negotiations. "Can we do his song 'Raspberry Beret'?"

"No," I say without even thinking. I can't believe her! I mean, what is she thinking? And didn't I just get through saying our tastes were the same in music? Yaaa!!!

"Who gets to choose the music, anyway?" Do' Re Mi asks, getting right to the point.

"We all do, but can't we pick songs by girls?" I say, stumbling. This is not going well. I need a mochachino.

"Who do y'all like?" Chuchie asks Aqua, imitating the twins' accent.

Aquanette says, "I told you. Karma's Children, Jiggie, Ophelia—"

"Uh-uh. No gospel!" Do' Re Mi says, sucking her teeth.

"I brought some house records from my mom," I say. "They're tracks without lyrics, so it will be easy to put my music to them."

There. I've slipped it in. Let's see if anybody has any objections.

"What do you mean, *your* music?" Aqua counters.

Dag on! I think to myself, imitating her. Why can't she just accept that I'm the leader of this pack?

"The songs I write," I explain patiently, pulling out my Kitty Kat notebook. "Don't act like you haven't seen this. I'm writing in it all the time!"

"Oh, *those* songs," Angie says, snuffing me.

So it's like that. I realize I'd better be quiet, before I go off. I guess it's my own fault. What with all the excitement about formin' a group, I hadn't mentioned to them that we would be performing *my* songs, too.

On the other hand, what's wrong with singin' my songs? What do they think we're gonna sing: "Amazing Grace"? See, I'm 'bout to go off, so I'd better shut up for a change.

"What about that group, the Divas?" Angie says, trying to be the peacemaker. "Why can't we do one of their songs, like 'I'll Crush You Like a Broken Record' or 'I Will Defy'?"

It turns out that Angie and Aqua only like gospel singers. I say, "Good as we are, we aren't good enough singers to pull *that* off."

I knew I shouldn't have flapped my lips. I can see them looking at me like, what's she all mad about?

"Me and Chuchie like girl-group types of songs," I say, moving on to another point. "Do' Re Mi is partial to rap—plain and simple."

"Okay, what about 'Nothing But a Pound Cake'?" Aqua asks. This is her idea of compromise? That song is by Sista Fudge, who is a powerhouse singer. She *can* raise the roof off Jack in the Box.

"Aqua, can you just get it into your head that the rest of us can't carry a song like that? We don't have the vocal range!" I scream at her. "And can you pleez think about something else besides eating, okay?"

Oops, I went and restarted the Civil War. Aqua gives me a look that shoots right through me.

"Yeah, that's right. We're so used to singing together or with the choir, I forget y'all can't sing like us," she says, showing off, no doubt. "We definitely need to pick pop songs so y'all can stay in the middle notes."

After two hours of fighting, we finally pick two songs we can all agree on.

The singer we *all* like is Kahlua. We choose two of her songs: "Don't Lox Me out the Box," and "The Toyz Is Mine," which is a duet Kahlua does with Mo' Money Monique. It actually is perfect for five-part harmony because it has lots of choruses and refrains.

Of course, I still want to add some of my own songs to the mix. What is wrong with Aqua? I ought to clock her. And Angie, too. She is more sneaky. She'll smile in your face, then go along with her sister. First thing I'll do is drill right into Angie's chedda waves!

I can't deal with this drama today, not until I talk with Mom and figure out how to tell Aqua and Angie (without going off) that we are singing at least *one* of my songs. I know we are only doing this for a Halloween show, but it would make it so much more fun.

Forming the group (at least for the bash) has inspired me to write a song about it called "Wanna-be Stars in the Jiggy Jungle." I've been dying to let them hear it for days now.

Well, later for them. I know my songs are dope. They are probably jealous. They can sing, but they can't write songs. Angie and Aqua already told us that. They are gonna have to give it up.

"Okay, girls. Time to go home! I'm expecting company, and I don't want a bunch of kids hangin' round when he gets here," Juanita yells. Chuchie and me look at each other and stifle a giggle. We know who "he" is, all right. Juanita and Mr. Tycoon are doing the tango. Pretty soon, she's gonna be showin' off the rock—and is it ever gonna be a boulder! It'll probably topple her over.

"I have to go, anyway," Do' Re Mi says. "I've gotta go baby-sit my brothers and sisters while my mom takes one of the kids down to the foster care agency."

"Why, wuzup?" Juanita asks. "Is everything okay at home, baby?"

"Um . . . uh-huh," Dorinda says, pasting a

smile on her face. But I know, and so do Chuchie and Juanita, that things at Do' Re Mi's house are always in crisis. Kids comin', kids goin', all the time. I feel bad for her. It really makes me and Chuchie appreciate all we've got: two parents who love us (even though Chuchie's are divorced), and plenty of duckets for whatever we need (even if we do have to do a lot of cheesin' to get it).

I'm glad we got Do' Re Mi into our girl group. Once we perform, we're gonna get her into the Kats and Kittys for free. We already arranged to get her into Drinka Champagne's for nothing—Drinka calls it a "scholarship." Well, Do' is sure a scholar.

"Bye, Miss Simmons," I hear Angie and Aqua yell to Juanita.

Now that the others have gone, me and Chuchie have to go look at a few spaces. As the officers on the party committee, it's our job to find a club to hold the event.

We need to find a majordomo club, too, because a lot of Kats and Kittys will come to a party as laced as this one. Mrs. Bugge, the club president, will then work out an arrangement with the club owner after we choose a space.

That's the one thing I like about being an officer at the Kats and Kittys Klub: We get to feel large and in charge—even though we are "minors." (Yuk. I hate that word.)

"Let's check out the Cheetah-Rama," I say to Chanel, who is lost in her own *Telemundo* channel. I can tell there is something on Chanel's mind because she is real quiet, and Chuchie is not a quiet girlita, if you follow the bouncing ball.

Chanel leans on the refrigerator door, twirling one of her braids for a second, then takes a deep breath and blurts out, "Who's gonna be the lead singer of the group?"

"Me and you, *of course*," I answer, trying to be chill. "Look, Do' is the best dancer. No doubt. She can harmonize with us. Aqua and Angie are the background singers. That's cool, right?"

"*Está bien, mamacita*." She breaks out into a smile. I know she wants to sing lead on "The Toyz Is Mine." And that's fine by me, 'cause when we sing *my* songs—and we *are* gonna sing my songs—there's only gonna be one lead singer: and that's me.

Chapter 6

Seventh period, every Thursday, dance class is definitely the highlight of our week. Me, Chanel, and Do' Re Mi are a crew now. We meet during lunch and after school every day. Then we go over to Chanel's loft in Soho and practice our vocals with Aqua and Angie. (Things are still touchy between us, but I'm not touching it—for now.)

Today, I'm wearing a calfskin black blazer with a matching miniskirt and a cheetah-print turtleneck. Chanel has on leopard jeans and a red top. Do' Re Mi is wearing a black denim jumper. She has it zipped down a little so you can see her red tank top.

I want to surprise Do' Re Mi with a cheetah

backpack when we go to my mom's boutique on Saturday, so I've been really nice for a change. I've helped clean the kitchen every night and I've been reorganizing my room.

Last night, me and my mom watched a special on chimpanzees as we hand-sewed some new leopard pillow shams for the bedrooms. Dad says the best tailors in Italy still sew by hand, and he said he was proud of me. When we got ready for bed, I rubbed Mom's shoulders. She told me to stop tickling her. I'll get better at it. I'm sure Do' has a book I could read on massage.

In the locker room, Dorinda takes off her top. She always wears a white training bra, but she doesn't have much to train. She is flat-chested like Chanel. Ouch. I don't know if it bothers Do' Re Mi, so I don't have jokes about that. I wear a regular 34B bra already, and I've got the big hips to go with it.

Do' Re Mi hums to herself all the time, now that we are singers. She is so tiny, she easily could have been a ballerina. She has a perfect little body. She is really muscular.

"I took gymnastics all through junior high," Do' Re Mi tells us while she is changing. "I miss it."

"You have to have perfect balance for that, right?" Chuchie asks.

"No doubt," explains Do' Re Mi. "That horse is no joke. Once I came down hard on it. I was about six—and bam! I hit my thigh. I was crying. Mrs. Bosco—I mean my mother—had to come to school to take me home."

Mrs. Bosco. That is the name of her foster mother, I realize. Do' Re Mi never told us that before. I wonder if the kids in school ever made fun of her for having a foster mother instead of a real mom.

"Did you tell your mother about the show we're doing?" Chuchie asks her.

"Of course, silly. She says it's cool," Do' Re Mi explains, stuffing her clothes in a locker. "But she really wants me to be a teacher. I don't want to do that."

I wonder where Do' Re Mi's real mother is, but I'm not going to ask her that. I hope one day she will tell us.

"Where did you get your, um, last name from?" Dorinda asks me, hesitating. "It's so different."

"My dad is Eye-talian." I giggle. "He's from Bologna, Italy. There was a guy named

Garibaldi in Italy. He was a hero because he freed the country."

I change into the new leopard bodysuit I just got that I'm going to wear with black tights. "My dad says he saw his first opera when he was nine," I tell Do' Re Mi, because she is very into me talking about my family, anyway. "It had a Black opera diva from the United States, and that's when he knew he would come to the United States."

I wonder if my dad's dreams have come true. He says he wanted to marry a Black opera diva, but that Mom is the closest thing because she looks like one. When they joke around, she mouths opera for him, and he sits in the chair and watches her. I try not to laugh.

Me and Chanel like to stay in the back of the gymnasium, just in case we feel like doing different dance steps or making up new moves. Dorinda likes to stay in the front. She is the best dancer in the class, and Ms. Pidgenfeat smiles at her as she walks around to correct our movements.

"Everybody watch Dorinda," she yells whenever she wants us to get a dance step down. Do' Re Mi has all the moves down to jiggy perfection. I'm kinda jealous, but then I think about how much I like her. She is definitely crew forever.

Today we go back to Drinka Champagne's Conservatory for our vocal lessons. They were closed for a very long summer vacation because Drinka was on tour in Japan. She is a famous singer from the disco era, who founded the conservatory for divettes-in-training like me and Chanel. (After practicing with Aqua and Angie, I do realize how much practice *I* need.)

Drinka had an ultra-hit disco song back in the day called "Just Sippin' When I'm Not Tippin'." It was number one on the Billboard Dance Charts in 1972 for thirty-seven weeks. I know this because she has told us about the same number of times.

Drinka is finishing a class and standing by the receptionist. She is wearing silver spandex pants with a matching top, and a silver apple-jack hat that almost covers her face. Her pointy sequined slippers (yes, they're silver) curl up at the toes and make her look like Tinker Bell. "I think it looks like she's got tinfoil on her feet!" argues Do' Re Mi.

Everyone at the conservatory is excited about our singing at the Kats and Kittys Halloween Bash.

"Get paid, girls!" Miss Winnie, the receptionist, says, cheering us on. She is so nice. "You girls are gonna have to work hard together," she explains, giving Do' Re Mi her very own card stamped VOCAL 201. Do' Re Mi is supposed to start with Beginners Vocal 101, but because we're performing together, Miss Winnie lets her join our class.

For the first thirty minutes of class, we do scales. Wolfman Lupe plays the piano to guide our vocal warm-up. Doing scales means singing from the upper to the lower chambers in the voice to help loosen it up. It's kinda like stretching before dancing.

After warm-up, Drinka comes into the studio and teaches the vocal class. "Okay, pretty girls, show me what you can do," Drinka says, clapping. She tells us, "You have got to have a theme and a dream and a mind like a money machine."

We are lucky, no doubt, to be getting such primo vocal training for free. For the past two years, we've also gotten to take dance classes here, too. I mean we've learned all the global moves. Caribbean, Brazilian, and African are my favorite dance classes because we get to stomp around to the beat of live drummers. In salsa class, we dance to musicians playing conga drums.

After Drinka's, we have to hook up with Angie and Aqua at the subway station. I call them on my cell phone to make sure they're on the way. Angie and Aqua are coming from Ninety-sixth Street and Riverside Drive, where they live with their father. We meet them at the end of the platform at the Times Square station.

We have to take the N train to the Prince Street station to go to my mom's boutique. Aqua, Angie, and Do' (Do' Re Mi's shortened nickname) sit huddled together on one subway seat while me and Chuchie sit on a parallel one. I think the three of them—Angie, Aqua, and Do' Re Mi—feel more relaxed together, even though we are *all* a crew. I mean, Do' Re Mi loves to cook and sew, and so do Angie and Aqua. They all cook at home, too. They're huddled together peeping at a recipe for "Dumbo Gumbo" in *Sistarella* magazine. Like me, Chuchie is not interested in cooking. It takes her an hour to boil Minute rice. (She cooked it once. Yuk.)

The officers of the Kats and Kittys Klub were excited about our upcoming performance at the Halloween bash. "Why didn't you two think of this before, Galleria?" asked Ms. Bugge, when we told her our plans.

I told her, "Me and Chanel never wanted to perform by ourselves. That's not our idea of a show."

Now there are five of us. Five fab divettes. Hmmm . . . maybe that would be a good name for the group. . . .

I pull out my Kitty Kat notebook and start to dawdle and diddle. Five Fab Divettes. Nah. It sounds like a set of dining room chairs.

See, you have to have a catchy name for a group, and a theme that comes from the heart. That's what Drinka was tryin' to tell us.

Do' Re Mi looks at us and asks if everything is okeydokey. She is always looking out for her peeps. I like that about her.

"We're chillin'." I smile. "You like house music?"

"Some of it," Do' Re Mi says, shrugging. "Why?"

"We can borrow some of my mom's records to use as tracks for the show." Now that we have memorized the lyrics to both of Kahlua's songs (a small miracle), we can concentrate on my songs. And my songs need tracks. That's where my mom's house music comes in. All music, no words. Angie and Aqua still haven't given in on singing my songs, so I expect another battle on this. But I figure if I have Do' Re Mi on my side, that will make three against two.

"Sometimes my mom cranks up the house music in the store and dances. She says it's like going to church," I tell her.

"That's funny." Aqua laughs, hearing me. "She should come to our church. She'd have a good time, then. 'Cause we get down."

We are planning a trip to Aqua and Angie's church, but not until after the show, because we are all mad hectic. I pray that Aqua and Angie don't suggest we use gospel music tracks for the show. For now, it's too noisy to talk about it. That's the subway for you.

We are going down to my mom's store to see if she will make our costumes. Of course, I know my mom will make me sign an IOU—

which really means, pay now *and* pay later. Pay later in duckets, and pay now by cleaning my room. Not every day, mind you, but every hour.

I also want to give Do', Aqua, and Angie a surprise. The question is, will my mom cough up three more cheetah backpacks so we can look like a real crew? (Stay tuned, Kats and Kittys, to find out. . . .)

My mom's boutique is the brightest store on the block. You can see it all the way down West Broadway, which is a five-block-long strip of boutiques. A lot of famous divas come to my mother's store to shop.

We climb the five steps up to the big glass door entrance of Toto in New York. "If my mom offers you anything to eat, take it or she'll think there's something wrong with you," I whisper to Do' Re Mi.

Chanel presses the buzzer so we can get buzzed in. All the dope boutiques in New York have buzzers because a lot of shoplifters, or boosters, try to come in and "mop" stuff. That means shopping for free. Boosters don't usually come into my mother's store because they are more scared of her than of the police.

"Ooh, Toto in New York, that is so cute," Angie says, looking up at the lime green and hot pink sign flapping in the wind.

"Ooh, look at all the leopard clothes. They got clothes to fit us?" Aqua asks all excited when we get inside.

"You keep eating like you do and they will," I smirk as we plop down on the big leopard-print love seat and wait for my mom. We can't interrupt her because she is doing her leg lifts against the counter. A house music song, "You Think You're Fierce," is playing on the sound system.

"See, that's house music," I mumble to Aqua. Bet they've never met anyone like my mother in Texas. Aqua and Angie are watching my mother in awe. (Their mouths are open.)

Mom weighs 250 pounds. That's 120 pounds more than she did as a model—something "Madame" Simmons loves to make digs about—but she is as beautiful now as she was back then. And I'm not saying this because she is my mother. My mom was and is a real diva—not just "back in the day," but today.

"We can't walk down the streets without some man goospitating and whistling at her," I tell Do' Re Mi proudly. "One guy stopped us right and asked my mom, "Girl, is it your birthday, 'cause you sure got a lot of cakes back there?" She hit that bumbling Bozo over the head with her leopard pocketbook. "I'm sure he's still recovering, somewhere over the rainbow." I smirk at Do' Re Mi.

Get me through this show, I pray silently to Mom's Josephine Baker poster. (See, an old-school diva like Baker, who used to have a leopard for a pet, understands what I'm going through.)

"Where's Toto?" I ask.

"Toto, come here, cream puff. I said come here!" Mom screams. Poor Toto comes charging out of the dressing room, where he was sleeping on the cushion, and makes a beeline under the couch because he doesn't see me. His hair is matted on the side like mine is when I first get up in the morning.

"Galleria, look at Toto! He gets so scared when I yell at him—he looks like a dancing mop!" Mom screeches.

"Come here, Toto. I want you to meet my

friends," I coo, trying to comb out Toto's hair with my fingers. I like when his hair is perfect like cotton candy, but Mom likes the untamed look, so he only goes to the beauty parlor every two months. Toto is ignoring me and he starts walking on his little doggie booboo.

"Toto, that's enough. Stop dragging your furry butt on the floor. I just got it waxed!" Mom yells, then starts pinning some burgundy velvet fabric on a dress form.

"These your friends from Kats and Kittys?" she asks.

"Yup."

"Where are you two from?" Mom asks, looking at Aqua.

Turning to look at me, then back to my mom, Aqua asks, "You mean me?"

Chanel kicks me. I kick her back.

"Yes, you, darling. You see anyone else here I don't know? You can call me Dorothea, by the way," Mom says.

"Oh, I'm sorry, Ms. Dorothea," Aqua says. "I didn't know you were talking to us. Um, we're from Houston."

"Houston. They have the best shopping mall in the world." Mom swoons. "And I should know. I've been to every shopping mall from here to Hong Kong. Did Galleria tell you I named her after the mall there?"

"The Galleria? Is that right?"

"That is right," Mom says, all pleased with herself. I've heard this story a ca-zillion times. "I was in Houston modeling for a fashion shoot. I was so bored because I didn't know anyone there—well, anyone I wanted to see—so I went shopping at the Galleria. That's where I bought my first pair of Gucci shoes," she goes on. "I was pregnant and I wanted to remember the moment forever. Most beautiful shoes I've ever had. Burgundy-sequined pumps with little bows in front."

"Kinda like Dorothy's ruby slippers?" Do' Re Mi asks, perking up.

"*Exactly.*" I smirk. "Mom still has the shoes in a leopard keepsake box, along with my baby pictures and a personal ad that she answered before I was born."

Now why did I say that? I have *such* a big mouth.

"Personal ad, what's that?" Do' Re Mi asks.

"It's for meeting people," Chuchie snips.

"You mean, like, for dating?" Angie asks.

"Yes. Like, for dating," Chuchie says with her *boca grande*.

"'Lonely oyster on a half shell seeks rare Black pearl to feel complete,'" Mom explains with a giggle.

"Galleria's mom answered the personal ad out of *New York Magazine*, and that's how she met her dad. Get it?" Chuchie explains some more. I am gonna get her later.

Aqua and Angie look at each other like they have just met the Addams family, then "chedda waves" catches herself and goes to pet Toto. "Wait until he meets Porgy and Bess," Angie coos, trying to pat his head, but he looks at her and yawns.

"Oh, how cute," Chanel says. "What kind of dogs are they?"

"Oh, they're not dogs," Angie chimes in.

"They're our guinea pigs from home. We couldn't leave them behind," Aqua explains, waiting to see my mom's reaction. I move my feet from Chanel quickly because I know she is going to kick me, but Aqua notices. "What's the matter?" Aqua asks me.

"Oh, nothing," I lie. "I thought I saw a roach."

"A roach!" My mom huffs. "There better not be any roaches in here or I'll go to that exterminator's office and exterminate him!"

"I was just joking, Mom," I say, quickly realizing that I don't want to endanger some poor man's life and leave his wife a widow. Mom would do it. Trust me.

"There's nothing wrong with guinea pigs for pets," Mom says, coming to Aqua and Angie's defense.

Why is she doing that, I wonder?

"Josephine Baker had a pet leopard. That's her," Mom says, pointing to the poster of Josephine. "She was the most famous Black singer and dancer in the world."

"She danced in banana skirts," Do' Re Mi says excitedly. "I know all about her. She was so famous, they shut down Paris just for her funeral."

"That's right, darling," Mom says, approving of Do' Re Mi. "Say, what are you divettes going to wear for the show?" Mom asks.

My mom knows full well the Whodunnit and the Whodini: 1. Why we are there. 2. How cheesy I will get to have her help us. 3. That I am desperate.

What she doesn't know is, I know how to turn the tables.

"Mom, you gotta give us some ideas!" I whine, even though it kills me. Mom loves to give "advice."

"Leopard is always the cat's meow, darling. How about some leopard cat suits? Then you can go to Fright Night on Prince Street and get some leopard masks with the whiskers, like you used to wear for Halloween when you were little. Some little leopard velvet boots or something, and the five of you would look fierce."

"I love it!" says Do' enthusiastically.

"That sounds fabbie poo, darling," I say, imitating my mother, then add for good measure, "Mom, can I get a weave for the show?"

"Do you have weave money?" Mom asks, then continues with her investigation before I get a chance to respond. "What are you going to call the group?"

"We haven't decided yet." I yawn, then pull out my Kitty Kat notebook, where I have written down a few names. "We thought of names like The Party Girls, The Ladybug Crew, A Taste of Toffee—that was Aqua's idea. The Ruby Slippers."

"Oooh, I like that," my mom says, smiling, then she hesitates. "But that's not for you girls."

"Why not?" Do' Re Mi asks.

"Darlings, I've been in this jungle a lot longer than you. Why don't you just stick with what you are instead of looking all over the place for answers?"

Mom then turns and looks at me. "The spots worked for Josephine Baker. They've worked for me. They'll work for you. Don't turn your back on your heritage."

"Your mom is funny," Aqua whispers in my ear. I can't believe it, but somehow the twins are getting along better with my mom than I am!

"'Member what that boy Derek called you in the hallway once?" Do' Re Mi asks me.

"What on earth did that Red Snapper say that was so deep?" I ask her.

"He called you a Cheetah Girl," Do' Re Mi says, then squeaks, "maybe we could all be the Cheetah Girls."

"Do' Re Mi, you are so on the money," Chuchie says, all excited.

"Yeah, we could be the Cheetah Girls," Aqua chimes in.

Angie claps her hands in delight.

Mom had been right. I was trying to be something I wasn't. I guess I can live with the Cheetah Girls, even though it wasn't my idea. Actually, I kinda like it!

"I love it!" Chuchie screams. We hug each other and scream so loud, my mom threatens to gag us and tie us up with fabric.

I catch Mom's eyes, then point to the backpacks, then to my friends, and mouth the word, "*Posso?*" which, in Italian, means "Can I, please?"

Mom doesn't even put up a fight. She walks over to the cheetah backpacks and gives one each to Do', Aqua, and Angie, like it was her idea. "Now, would you please settle down so I can take your measurements for the costumes," Mom says with a smile and a sigh.

"Omigod!" Do' Re Mi gasps, and runs over to give Mom a hug. There is something special between those two already. I'm glad.

Do' Re Mi turns to Angie and Aqua and says, "Y'all are okay with wearing cheetah cat suits, right?"

"That's right," Aqua says with a smile. "Dag. It's just a costume, Dorinda. We do have

Halloween in Texas, you know!"

"Hey, we gotta have a costume for Toto, too!" I say, in a sudden burst of inspiration. "He can be, like, our mascot!" This gets howls of approval, and an okay from my mom. Awright!

When we leave, Toto runs to the glass door and stares at us with his begging, beady eyes. We all wave at him. "Bye, Toto!" "Bye, boo-boo." "See you at show time, doggie-poo!"

Chapter 7

I need to resolve this music thing with Aqua and Angie, today. We have to begin practicing the songs I've written, now that we have the other two down.

Today, Dad drives me down to Chanel's house for rehearsal. He is late getting to the factory, so he is lost in his own world. "How are rehearsals going?" he asks me.

"Don't ask," I groan.

Dad wants me to be a singer, too. I think secretly that my singing has kept him and Mom together. Whenever they fight, I always start singing, and it makes them laugh.

"*Ciao*, Dad," I say, blowing him a kiss as I get out.

I'm glad that my parents are not coming to the bash. It's for Kats and Kittys only, thank gooseness. Between school, rehearsals, dance classes, and vocal classes, I am about to explode like microwave popcorn.

We have two hours to rehearse our vocals before we have to do our dance moves with Drinka.

"Listen, can we just do this?" I say to Aqua and Angie. I am holding my breath because I don't want to fight with them anymore.

Do' Re Mi is going along with the program. She kinda likes my songs. But the "Huggy Bear Twins" (me and Chuchie's secret nickname for them) are hard to please.

"All right," Aqua moans.

"We'll just start with the first verse today," I say, "so that Chuchie and Do' Re Mi can join in. You two listen up and try to come in where you know the words."

We start to sing:

"Some people walk with a panther
or strike a buffalo stance
that makes you wanna dance.

Other people flip the script
on the day of the jackal
that'll make you cackle.

But peeps like me
got the Cheetah Girl groove
that makes your body move
like wanna-be stars in the jiggy jungle.

The jiggy jiggy jungle!
The jiggy jiggy jungle!

So don't make me bungle
my chance to rise for the prize
and show you who we are
in the jiggy jiggy jungle!
The jiggy jiggy jungle!"

Why are Aqua and Angie leaning so heavy on the chorus? You can't even hear the rest of us! I wonder if they are doing it on purpose. Sure, they are better singers, but they don't have to sing like they're at the Thunderdome.

"Aqua, Angie, maybe you should sing the chorus a little softer so we can hear the harmony more?" I suggest.

"Oh, okay," they both say.

Chanel doesn't say anything. For someone who can run her mouth like she's doing a TV commercial on *Telemundo*, I can't get a squeak out of her when I need her to represent me. Why do I always have to stick up for us? And why is Do' Re Mi singing so softly?

"Do' Re Mi—you need to sing louder after the first verse, I think, no?"

"'But peeps like me got the Cheetah Girl groove,'" Do' Re Mi sings—this time with more gusto. "Like that?"

"Yeah," Aqua answers.

I'm wondering if anyone will boo at us at Kats and Kittys. Could they be that cold?

After dance rehearsal, we are standing outside of Drinka's building. By now, I've had about all I can take. Not only did the singing rehearsal go badly, but the dancing rehearsal went even worse. Especially Chanel—she was so busy giggling she couldn't even get through the numbers!

"Why don't you pay attention to what you're doing!" I scream at her now, losing my cool completely. Angie, Aqua, and Do' Re Mi get real quiet.

"What happened?" Chanel yells. "What did I do?"

"Chanel, you better not mess this up. You have to try to pay attention to what we're all doing so we look like we're doing the same moves."

"I'm not the one messing it up. You are, with your big mouth!" she screams at me. Chanel never screams. Only I do. We argue right there on the street.

Angie, Aqua, and Do' Re Mi wait on the sidewalk while me and Chanel are fighting. "I hate when you act so stupid and you don't listen to me!" I tell Chanel.

"You don't know what you're talking about, you chocolate-covered cannoli!"

No, she did not go there. So what if I was half Italian? She is Black and Latin. I never make fun of her. Well, almost never. I run all the way to the corner and put my arm up to get a taxi back home. It is my last ten dollars till Monday, but I don't care. I just want to run far away.

Do' Re Mi runs after me. "Y'all need to stop! Hold up, Galleria."

"No. I'm going home. I need to chill for now. I'm sorry, Do' Re, okay? I'll see you all tomorrow."

Once I am inside of my safe cheetah palace, I grab a box of my mom's Godiva chocolates. She keeps it hidden in the back of the kitchen cabinet. I don't care if she gets mad at me. So what? Everyone else is.

I take the Godiva box and get as far as I can under my blanket. I cry myself to sleep, slobbering on my leopard velvet pillow while I'm chomping on the candy. How could Chanel call me that? I feel like dragging her by her fake braids right down the street. I didn't even know she knew what a cannoli was.

I miss Toto. He's out at the dog groomer's—finally. Oh, well. He's probably just as glad I'm not suffocating him to death right now. Here I am, just fourteen years old, and my life is finished, I think, as I doze off into a deep sleep.

Chapter 8

What's harder than hiding a spotted cheetah in the desert? Trying not to speak to your best friend when the two of you go to the same school! By the time I left homeroom to make a mad dash to my color theory class, I was seeing spots from trying to keep my eyes glued on my desk so I would never look up and make eye contact with Chanel.

As I walked down the hallway, I concentrated on the answers for my quiz on primary colors: Red and yellow make orange. Blue and red make purple.

Hmmph, I hiss to myself. Chanel No. 5 can get on the stage by herself and eat Meow Mix for all I care.

"Galleria, Galleria!" Chanel yells, puffing down the hallway. She finally catches up to me, even though I still try to ignore her. "I just wanna know. You still want me to do your hair today after school?"

I am so mad, I forgot all about that. My mom is finally gonna let me get a weave, and Chanel is supposed to put it in.

"*Ciao-ciao*, chinchilla, cheetah," I snarl, shooing her away with my hand. "Pretend I'm not here. It's a mirage."

Breathing really hard, Chanel chokes on her words. "I had a bad dream last night, Galleria, for real. Please talk to me. *Per favore*, pleez."

Cheez whiz, Chanel No. 5 has finally learned something in her Italian class. I open my mouth to begin reading her the riot act when all of sudden I hear the word "Okay" slip out of my mouth.

"I dreamed we were on the stage, and you were screaming at me to dance faster, and I was so scared that I was gonna fall because the heels were so high on my shoes," Chanel says without breathing. "I tried to dance, but I fell so hard, and somehow—this is the weird part—I fell right into the people off the stage.

So I started screaming, right, and you, Do' Re Mi, Aqua, and Angie kept on singing. You acted like you didn't hear me scream. Then I tried to run because the people started chasing me and I just wanted to get away."

By now Chanel is giving tears for fears—real drama. So we hug. This was supposed to be fun for us, and it is turning into a *Nightmare on Broome Street*.

"My mom gave me fifty dollars for my weave. You think I could get two strands of hair for that?" I ask.

Chanel blinks at me. She can't believe I'm letting her off the hook this easy. I've got to admit, it's not like me. But I can't be mad at her. She's been my best friend forever, and I was acting kinda bossy and mean.

"Three at least!" she says, giggling. Then she gets serious. "I'm sorry for what I said," she confesses. "You made me mad. I didn't like what you said in front of Aqua that time."

"What time?" I ask.

"When we were at the Pizza Pit and you said I would be giving out *piñatas* later."

"Oh, I'm sorry," I tell her. "I was just playin'."

I was showing off in front of Aqua and

Angie. Now I see that Chanel did the same thing in front of them.

By the time school was out, we were rollin' like usual. First, we had to pick up leopard paper masks with gold whiskers from the Fright Night shop on Prince Street. Then we had to take the subway to Harlem to pick up Do' Re Mi at the YMCA, since she works so close to "It's Unbeweavable!," where they sell hair by the pound.

Do' Re Mi works at the Junior Youth Entrepreneurship Leadership Program Store in the Harlem YMCA. The program is designed for teens who need jobs and it's supposed to teach them leadership skills. Do' Re Mi had to complete a twelve-week curriculum on Saturdays, attend workshops during the week, and work in the store. I don't know how she does it all. She is yawning till the break of dawn half the time.

Because we never miss an opportunity to harmonize, and I am determined to get Do' Re Mi's voice at least a tidbit stronger in the soprano department, we start singing on Lenox Avenue as soon as we pick her up.

"Let's take it from the last verse," Chanel

says to Do' Re Mi, taking charge for a change.

"To all the competition, what can we say?
You better bounce y'all 'cause every Cheetah has got its day.

You better bounce y'all
'cause the Cheetah Girls are 'bout to pounce, y'all
and get busy in the jiggy jungle
no diggity, no doubt.

Get busy in the jiggy jungle.
The jiggy jiggy jungle.
The jiggy jiggy jungle.
The jiggy jiggy jungle!"

We are stylin' again—and more important, we are crew again—now and forever!

"I've never seen you with hair so long, Miss Thing," my mom says, touching my new Rapunzel weave. "But I still prefer to take my girls off at night and scratch my head."

Mom is, of course, referring to her wig collection. Angie and Aqua get a giggle out of this. They both have gotten their hair done—on the press and curl tip—and I think they're amused by my mom's wild and woolly wigs.

"Is it me, or is it hot in here? I'd better open the door and get some air in here." Mom doesn't wait for us to answer: she just opens the glass door and puts down the stopper hinge to stop the door from closing on its own. We are so excited because we are getting our final fitting for our cat suit costumes for the show tonight.

"Let me see your nails," Mom asks Aqua, who is definitely growing into the supa-show-off of the two. "What is that? Dollar bills?"

"Uh-huh," Angie answers proudly, flossin' about the gold dollar-bill sign decals she has put on her red tips.

"You trying to stay on the money, huh?" my mom says, smirking. "Well, you gotta make some first."

Angie and Aqua only get twenty-five dollars a week allowance apiece from their dad, but he also pays for them to get their nails done twice a month. I wonder if Angie spends as much time on her homework as she does on her nails.

"Fabbie poo," Chanel exclaims as she slips into her cat suit. "This is so phat!"

"Chuchie, you are gonna be over the leopard limit tonight, girlita!" My mom giggles.

The cat suits are all that. Each one has a mock turtleneck collar and zips up the back. Do' Re Mi's has a tail, too, because we thought that would be cute. Do' Re Mi puts on her cat suit, then flosses.

"You know how to work it, Miss Thing," Mom snips. "Not too tight?" Mom asks Do' Re Mi, who is prancing around like she's the cat's meow.

Do Re Mi's cat suit looks really tight, but when Mom asks her again, she just shakes her head sideways, smiling, and answers, "Cheetah *Señorita, está bien!*"

Mom smiles, then holds out a plate of Godiva chocolates for us to munch. She is being so nice to us. I poke Aqua, who excitedly takes a piece of chocolate and smiles. "Thank you, Mrs. Garibaldi. I mean, Miss Dorothea!"

Mom has told them more than once, "Call me Miss Dorothea, but just don't call me Heavy D!"

Aqua and Angie are so used to being formal around grown-ups, sometimes you can tell they don't know how to act normal.

I thought again about Chanel calling me a "chocolate-covered cannoli." I wouldn't tell Mom or she would make Chanel eat a whole box of them.

Chapter 9

The beauty mark Do' Re Mi paints right above her upper lip looks less fake than mine. I decided to try painting one smack-dab in the middle of my cheek.

"She's a fake!" Do' Re Mi hums.

I rub off the cheesy dot of brown liquid liner and try it her way.

"Pa-dow! That's the dopiest dope one," Do' Re Mi says after I'm finished. She has dimples for days. I didn't think there was anyone cuter than Chuchie. I didn't think it was possible. But Do' is running a close second.

We have each painted on a beauty mark and put Glitterella sparkles around our eyes. Theme is everything, I keep repeating to myself. We are starting to be very meow-looking. (Even Aqua and Angie. It's amazing what a little makeup can do.)

"Harmony check!" yells Aqua.

"Welcome to the Glitterdome.
It's any place you call home.

Give me props, I'll give you cash,
then show you where my sparkles stashed.

Glitter, glitter. Don't be bitter!
Glitter, glitter. Don't be bitter!
Glitter, glitter. Don't be bitter!"

We were on point and almost finished "beating our faces," as Mom calls it. She says she thinks we may have a future. She came to one of the rehearsals at Chuchie's and watched.

"Dag on, Galleria. You should just give me this lipstick," Angie says, outlining her full smackers with my lipstick. Actually, we were splitting the one tube of S.N.A.P.S. lipstick in Flack between the five of us, but I was holding on to it.

"That's enough!" Chuchie yells. Flack is this metallic purple-blue color that may give mad effects under the Cheetah-Rama's strobe lights when we are onstage.

"It's not blue, Galleria. It looks more purple in the light,"Aqua says, holding up the tube.

"If you get hot sauce on it, it'll be red!" Chanel blurts out, then snatches Aqua's backpack. "Let me check your bag! You can't carry a bottle of hot sauce in your bag anymore. It could break and ruin everything. Just carry packets!" Do' Re Mi giggles.

"That's a Cheetah Girls rule!" I yell out. "Now, come on. We've got one hour to get to the club before show time."

"Do' Re Mi, you sure your cat suit isn't too tight?" Chanel asks, poking Do' Re Mi's butt and pulling her tail.

"No. I'm fine!" Do' Re Mi growls. "You think we'll be able to see onstage with these masks on?"

"We just ain't gonna move too close to the edge so we don't fall off!" says Angie.

Truth or dare be told, Angie and Aqua are lookin' more relaxed than the rest of us. They have more experience singing. And, besides, anyone who could get those church ladies to fall out in the aisles has serious skills. The only experience we had was talent shows and vocal lessons.

"Maybe we should just let Angie and Aqua sing for real, and we lip-synch into the mikes," I turn and say to Do' Re Mi and Chanel, 'cause I'm getting cold feet fast.

"Last dance. No chance," Do' Re Mi says, wiggling her matchstick butt.

We are gonna sing four songs—two of mine, and two of Kahlua's—"Don't Lox Me out the Box" and "The Toyz Is Mine." In the end, we decided to use tracks from all house music tapes to perform to, and sing the lyrics over them.

I can't believe this is happening. Not the performing part. I can believe that. Me and Chanel have been singing long enough into plastic hairbrushes to win the unofficial Wanna-be Stars in the Jiggy Jungle Award. I just can't believe we are actually going to make some money on the d.d.l. (the divette duckets license).

We walk over to the Cheetah-Rama in our outfits. "Cheetah Girls! Cheetah Girls are in the house!" Chuchie yells down the block. It's Halloween, so everyone is looking at us and smiling.

We are only five blocks away from the Cheetah-Rama, which is at the end of West Broadway near the Mad Hatter Lounge. My mom goes there for tea on Sundays. The Cheetah-Rama is the dopiest dope club. They have cheetah couches and curtains, and my mom has been here a few times to dance because they play house music on special occasions. She drags Dad along, or sometimes Juanita, but sometimes she'll come by herself because she has a lot of old school friends who are still single and who still like to hang out.

This isn't the first time I've been in a nightclub, because last year we had the Kats and Kittys Klub Christmas Egg Nogger at the Hound Club in Harlem. But this is the first time I've hung out at a club that my mom the diva has danced at. I feel like it's the jointski, and I'm glad that no grown-ups are allowed here tonight—except for the Kats and Kittys Klub's staff and treasury committee.

Me and Chuchie have only been to the Cheetah-Rama in the daytime. It is kinda dark inside now, and I step on Aqua's foot because I don't see the decline of the ramp inside the entrance. I stumble for a few steps, and Chanel grabs my arm.

"Oh, snapples, Chuchie, 'member that dream you had? Well, it's not a dream!"

I don't care if I fall on my face. We've agreed to make our entrance wearing our masks, but my eyes haven't adjusted to the darkness.

You can tell it's Halloween, all right. The Cheetah-Rama is definitely haunted, with hundreds of Kats and Kittys wearing some pretty scary costumes.

"Hi, Mrs. Bugge," Do' Re Mi yells out. Her costume is hee-larious. She is wearing a green Afro, baseball uniform, and sneakers.

"Who is she supposed to be?" I ask, poking Aqua, who is staring at her.

"Menace Robbins!" she snips back.

"Oh, that guy from the Houston Oilys basketball team?" I ask.

"It's the Oilers!" Aqua snips.

Okay, so I never watch basketball games. Apparently, sports are a very big thing down south, according to the twins.

This is definitely a live party. It is wall-to-wall thumpin'—the music, the crowd, the lights. The excitement in the air is thumping, too.

People turn to look at us. The Cheetah Girls have definitely made an entrance. It was worth almost falling on my face!

"Cheetah Girls come out at night, baby!" I scream, throwing my hands in the air like I just don't care. Every eye in the house is on us, including some I can't see.

"Bubbles, don't look now," Chanel whispers. She is in back of me, pulling the tail on Do' Re Mi's cat suit, causing Do' to squeal. I turn, and Chanel whispers, "Don't look. Don't look."

I look, anyway. There is someone grinning in a Batman mask. "Holy, cannoli!" I giggle to Chanel. "Batman has big feet." Batman starts walking toward me, but his cape isn't flapping in the wind.

"Hey, Cheetah Girl!"

I know that voice. Oh, no, it can't be. The Red Snapper turned into a Caped Crusader? Gotham City is in deep herring. "Derek?"

"That's me. *C'est moi!*"

"Since when did you become a member?"

"Since you are, *ma chérie.*"

"Oh, it's like that," I say, smirking. His family has the duckets. Why am I surprised that he joined? Copycat.

"Are you taking French in school?" Chanel asks him, poking fun at him.

"*Oui, oui, mademoiselle,*" Derek says, grabbing Chanel's hand to kiss it.

"We're glad to see ya, Mr. *Oui, Oui!*" Chanel says, choking, taking her hand back and wiping it on her cat suit.

Derek seems so different without his Johnny BeDown hookups.

"Where's Robin?" I ask, referring to his friend Mackerel, who also goes to Fashion Industries High with us.

"He's not a Kats and Kittys member. He thinks it's mad corny."

"Too bad. You coulda been the dynamic duo."

"I got a Batmobile outside. Wanna ride later?"

"I don't know."

"Well, if you decide to, just give me the Batsignal." Derek laughs, pointing a flashlight in my face.

"*Au revoir*, Batman." Chanel says, wiggling her fingers.

"*Ciao,* Cheetah," he says to me. "Remember—you could be my Catwoman."

He does have good comeback lines, even if he was super-nervy right out of the box. Maybe Chanel is right—maybe I do think he's kinda cute, even if that gold tooth of his makes me laugh. *Not!*

Mrs. Bugge is signaling us to go backstage. It's show time. We run backstage and pick up the cordless mikes on the floor waiting for us. Then we line up five in a row behind the curtain, just like we rehearsed. Me and Chuchie are in the center. Do' Re Mi is standing to my left, and Aqua and Angie are together, next to Chanel.

"May the Force be with you," I tell Chuchie. This is something mystical, from a Star Wars movie, I think, but my mom always says it. I say it over and over again to myself.

Chuchie squeezes my hand. "Your hands are freezing, Bubbles," she whispers.

I almost wish Mom was here, because I am so scared.

I'm definitely on my own now. With my crew. Not in Mom's shadow. Me and Chuchie have followed the Yellow Brick Road just like we said we would. We made that promise to each other when we were seven years old. We would follow the Yellow Brick Road until we were independent and on our own—and, yes, had money of our own in our cheetah purses. We are never gonna work at Mikki D's.

"We'll always be crew. No matter what happens," I whisper to Chuchie, winking at her. I really do love Chuchie, my ace *señorita*. My fairy godsister.

Do' Re Mi is sniffling. "Do' Re, you're not crying, are you?" Chuchie asks her.

"No!" she giggles. I swear she cries more than the Tin Man. (I'm not supposed to know this, but Chuchie told me.)

My heart is pounding through my ears. At least I know I have one. Deejay Doggie Dawgs is lowering the music. That means it is definitely show time. No turning back.

"Are y'all ready, girls?" Mrs. Bugge asks, sticking her head behind the curtain.

"Ready for Freddy!" Aqua quips. "Freddy Krueger, that is."

Aqua loves her horror movies—and her horror-scope. I can't help but laugh. Freddy is probably out there. And Aqua probably invited him.

"Kats and Kittys. It's show time, and we have a very special treat for you tonight," Mrs.

Bugge announces to the crowd. "It's Halloween. How many of you are scared out there?"

The crowd boos. She is so corny.

"Well, I'll tell you the truth. I'm scared of the girls that I'm about to introduce you to. You may know them as Galleria Garibaldi, Chanel Simmons, Dorinda Rogers, and those singing twins from Houston, Aquanette and Anginette Walker, but tonight they are THE CHEETAH GIRLS, so give them a hand!"

I want to remember this night, forever. Absolutely forever. That is all I keep repeating to myself as the curtain goes up.

The strobe lights blind me in the face if I look too far back into the crowd. Now it is all about the beat. On three, we begin to sing, as if we've done this a hundred times—and the truth is, we have, in rehearsals.

"Don't lox me out the box, baby,
because you'll never know what side I'm buttered on.
My taste is sweet.
I can feel the heat . . ."

The Kats and Kittys are live. They are clapping along to Kahlua's song, and we are really getting into it. Everything is going just as we planned. They won't stop clapping. We wait before we go into the next song, and I try not to look into the audience. There are too many people, and I will lose my concentration.

It's time to sing "Welcome to the Glitterdome." On this song, we are facing the curtain, then we are supposed to turn to sing from the side profile as the strobe lights flash on and off to imitate stars in the sky.

Even out of the corner of my eye I can see that Angie and Aqua are still seconds off from the dance cues. They don't turn as fast as the rest of us do! I do not let this distract me, but I pray that no one notices.

Oh, I could just die, I'm thinking, when it's Do' Re Mi's turn to take center stage and do her split. This is when I see people I know smiling at me. Kats and Kittys who live in Manhattan. They are all in the house!

I am smiling from ear to ear, then pouting on cue as the song goes along. My mike is going in and out, but I can hear a sound as distinct as the sweetest melody—it is the sound of Do' Re

Mi's cat suit splitting. A sound I will never forget! She is giggling, and so is everyone else. The people closest to the stage are pointing and giggling at her. They not only heard it, but they saw it happen, too!

Bless her little heart, as Aqua would say. Do' Re Mi keeps dancing, she doesn't stop, but she cannot do the somersault at the top of "Wanna-be Stars in the Jiggy Jungle" or everyone would see the split in her cat suit—and her leopard underpanties. "Go Cheetah Girls! Go Cheetah Girls!" the crowd is chanting.

By this point, me and Chuchie are laughing, but the show must go on. Everyone is clapping at us, and it doesn't matter that Do' Re Mi's cat suit is split, or that Aqua and Angie don't turn on the right cue. We did it! We did it!

The clapping doesn't stop. "Wanna-be Stars in the Jiggy Jungle" is the song the audience loves best. We can tell by how hard they clap at the end. We take our bows, and lift our masks off, and throw kisses, just like we planned.

When the curtain comes down, we scream. "Oh, my gooseness, lickety splits!" Chanel shouts, grabbing Do' Re Mi's booty as we scramble into the dressing room.

"That's what you get for showing off!"

When we get into the dressing room, Do' Re Mi chews out Aqua and Angie. "Aqua, Angie, you two gotta turn faster when we do that pivot step. What were y'all thinking about?" Do' Re Mi gets all bossy as she changes into her velvet leopard leggings. We stay in our costumes as planned and take our masks off. I'm sweating like crazy.

"We about to get paid, baby," Chuchie yells.

"We don't get our money till next week," I call out.

Chanel sighs. "I know. I'm just sayin'."

There is a knock on the door. "Go away. We're not ready to come out!" I shout.

Mrs. Bugge sticks her head in the doorway anyway. "There is someone who wants to see you girls, so hurry on out."

"It's probably Batman!" Chanel quips.

"No, it's the Joker." Do' Re Mi clowns, and spreads her lips.

"It's the Penguin!" I snap. "And he wants to dance with me." We all squeal and laugh.

"Seriously, though," I finally say, "we're gonna need more practice."

"Yeah," says Do' Re Mi. "And I'm gonna

need a bigger costume."

"Oh, snapples!" Chanel giggles.

"You should have told my mom," I say, trying to be nice to Do' Re Mi, because I know she must feel bad. "She would have made you a bigger one."

"I didn't want to say anything," Do' Re Mi says softly.

"Why not?" I ask.

"You don't understand," she says, blinking back tears. "You'll never know what it's like to have to take everything that people give you just because you're a foster child. Nobody ever made me anything before. I didn't think I deserved it, and I didn't want to screw it up. I'm sorry," she whispers.

"That's okay, baby. Next time, you better open up that little mouth of yours and speak up!" Angie says.

There will be a next time—that's for sure.

"We still coulda served seconds. They were loving us!" Aqua says, lapping up the victory. "Now everybody knows the Cheetah Girls are ready to pounce."

"*You* are, that's for sure," Chanel says, smirking.

Then I say what I cannot believe, but know to be true. "I want us to stay as a group, no matter what happens. Even if we don't make any money."

"Oh, I'm definitely buying a ranch back home," Angie says, snarling. "I don't know about y'all."

"You know what I'm saying."

"We know what you're saying," Do' Re Mi says sweetly.

I spread out my hands so we can form a call-of-the-wild circle. "Let's take a Cheetah Girls oath."

I make up the oath right on the spot.

"We're the Cheetah Girls and we number five.
What we do is more than live.
We'll stay together through the thin and thick.
Whoever tries to leave, gets hit with a chopstick!
Whatever makes us clever—forever!!!"

Then we do the Cheetah Girls hand signal. Stretching out our hands, we touch each other's fingertips, wiggling them against each other.

"None of us ain't ever gonna drop out of the

group, like Rosemary from The Spice Rack Girls, right?" Aqua jokes.

"*Riiight,*" Do' Re Mi says with a drawl.

"And none of us are gonna burn down our boyfriends' houses if we get famous, *riiiight?*" Chuchie yells out.

"*Riiiiight,*" we all chime in as we head out of our matchbox dressing room to get our groove on.

The music and screams are loud. Really loud. Mrs. Bugge is standing in the hallway with a tall man wearing a yellow tie and a red suit. I don't think it's a costume. But you never know.

"Girls, someone wants to meet you. He's a manager, and a business associate of Mr. Hare, the owner of the club. Mr. Johnson, I want you to meet the Cheetah Girls."

"How you doin'? I'm Aquanette and this is my sister, Anginette. Did you see us perform?"

I clear my throat so I can talk. "Hi, I'm Galleria, and this is Chanel and Dorinda," I say to Mr. Johnson. I wonder what he thought of our performance.

"Nice to meet you," Mr. Johnson says, shaking my hand. "Well, you girls are cute. I came down to pick up a check from Mr. Hare, and I thought I would stick around and check out your act."

Our act. That sounds pretty cool.

"I heard the name of the group—the Cheetah Girls, and it sounded cute. I was wrong, though," Mr. Johnson continues.

"What do you mean?" I ask him, feeling my cheeks turn red.

"You were splendiferous. Fantastic. Marvelistic. You know what I mean?" Mr. Johnson says.

He sure has a way with words. We all laugh and get excited. A manager! I wonder what that is.

"What do you do?" I ask him.

"Oh, I'm sorry. My name is Jackal Johnson, and I have a company called Jackal Management Group. I think you girls need a good manager like me to get you a record deal. You understand?"

"We understand," Do' Re Mi chimes in.

"Here is my card. I'll expect to hear from you soon. I think, with the right management and direction, the Cheetah Girls can really go places—and I'd like to take you there. We can set up a meeting for next week."

"We'll call you," Chanel says, holding my arm.

"Next week," I add.

When we head down to the party, it's like a dream. Just the way I've imagined it a thousand times. Now it's really happening!

"I have one thing to say," says Do' Re Mi, sashaying to the dance floor. "The Spice Rack Girls had better bounce, baby, 'cause the Cheetah Girls are 'bout to pounce!"

No diggity, no doubt!

"Wanna-be Stars in the Jiggy Jungle"

Some people walk with a panther
or strike a buffalo stance
that makes you wanna dance.

Other people flip the script
on the day of the jackal
that'll make you cackle.

But peeps like me
got the Cheetah Girl groove
that makes your body move
like wanna-be stars in the jiggy jungle.

The jiggy jiggy jungle!
The jiggy jiggy jungle!

So don't make me bungle
my chance to rise for the prize
and show you who we are
in the jiggy jiggy jungle!
The jiggy jiggy jungle!

Some people move like snakes in the grass
or gorillas in the mist
who wanna get dissed.

Some people dance with the wolves
or trot with the fox
right out of the box.

But peeps like me
got the Cheetah Girl groove
that makes your body move
like wanna-be stars in the jiggy jungle.

The jiggy jiggy jungle!
The jiggy jiggy jungle!

So don't make me bungle
my chance to rise for the prize
and show you who we are
in the jiggy jiggy jungle!
The jiggy jiggy jungle!

Some people lounge with the Lion King
or hunt like a hyena
because they're large and in charge.

Some people hop to it like a hare
because they wanna get snared
or bite like baboons and jump too soon.

But peeps like me
got the Cheetah Girl groove
that makes your body move
like wanna-be stars in the jiggy jungle.

The jiggy jiggy jungle.
The jiggy jiggy jungle.

So don't make me bungle
my chance to rise for the prize
and show you who we are
in the jiggy jiggy jungle!

The jiggy jiggy jungle.
The jiggy jiggy jungle.

Some people float like a butterfly
or sting like a bee
'cause they wanna be like posse.

Some people act tough like a tiger

to scare away the lynx
but all they do is double jinx.

But peeps like me
got the Cheetah Girl groove
that makes your body move
like wanna-be stars in the jiggy jungle.

The jiggy jiggy jungle.
The jiggy jiggy jungle.

So don't make me bungle
my chance to rise to the prize
and show you who we are
in the jiggy jiggy jungle.

The jiggy jiggy jungle!
The jiggy jiggy jungle!

The Cheetah Girls Glossary

bank: Money, loot.

boho: An artsy-fartsy black bohemian type.

bomb: Cool.

bozo: A boy who thinks he's all that, but he's really wack.

cheese for it: Manipulate.

cheez whiz: Gee whiz.

chomp-a-roni: Trying to catch a nibble on the sneak tip.

cuckoo for Cocoa Puffs: Going bonkers.

diva size: Dress size fourteen and up.

divette-in-training: A girl who can't afford Prada or Gucci—yet.

don't be bitter!: Go for yours!

duckets: Money, loot.
flossin': Showing off.
goospitating: Looking at someone cute like they're lunch.
growl power: The brains, heart, and courage that every true Cheetah Girl possesses.
jiggy jungle: A magical place inside of every big city where dreams really come true—and every cheetah has its day!
majordomo dope: Legitimate talent.
nosy posy: A person who is nosy and can't help it.
one up, two down: One-upmanship.
pastamuffin: A dog with wiggly hair.
peeps: People.
powder to the people!: Never leave home without your compact.
raggely: In need of beauty parlor assistance.
smirfs: Smirks.
wack-a-doodle-do: Very corny.
wanna-be: Not a real player—yet!

Shop in the Name of Love

For my fluffy,
smoochy, barky
boo-boo Cappuccino
I wuv you.

Chapter 1

Princess Pamela does *la dopa* braids, thanks to me. When I was ten years old, I taught her how to do all the *coolio* styles—frozen Shirley Temple curls, supa dupa *flipas* that don't flop, and even unbeweavable weaves. Of course, I was too young to go to beauty school, but sometimes, *tú sabes que tú sabes*—you know what you know—as my Abuela Florita says. *Abuela* means grandma in Spanish. And my *abuela* knows what she knows, *está bien?*

Doing hair and singing are what *I*—Chanel Coco Cristalle Duarte Rodriguez Domingo Simmons—know best. (You don't have to worry about remembering all my names, because everyone just calls me Chanel, Chuchie, or Miss

Cuchifrita—except for my Abuela Florita, who now calls me by my Confirmation name, Cristalle, because, she says, I'm a shining star—*una estrella*.)

Now that I'm part of the Cheetah Girls—a girl group that is destined to become *muy famoso*—one day I will have lots of *dinero* to open my own hair salons. Miss Cuchifrita's Curlz—yeah, there'll be two of them, right next door to both of my dad's restaurants, so that I get to see him more.

"Chanel, you musta wear the braids bigger, like thiz, from now on. Don't you think you look so boot-i-full?" Princess Pamela coos in her sugar-cane accent. I love the way she talks. She is from Transylvania, Romania, home of Count Dracula and a thousand vampire stories. Her native language is Romanian, which is one of the romance languages—like Spanish, my second language. Now me and Bubbles, my best friend since the goo-goo ga-ga days, say "boot-i-full," exactly the way Princess Pamela does.

My mom doesn't know that Princess Pamela braids my hair. She thinks that Bubbles does it. *Qué broma*—what a joke! Bubbles (aka Galleria Garibaldi) does not have a "green thumb" for hair. She knows how to write songs, and how to make things happen faster than Minute Rice—but I would look like "Baldi-locks" if she did my hair, *comprende*?

I think that once you find out who Princess Pamela is, though, you'll understand why a smart *señorita* such as myself must resort to "fib-eronis" (as Bubbles calls them) just to keep *poco paz*—a little peace—in my house.

"Oooh, they do look nice bigger like this," I coo back at Princess Pamela, looking in the mirror at my longer, fatter braids and shaking them.

I'm so glad I got my hair done today. I usually wait three months, or until I have collected "fuzz balls" on my braids—whichever comes first. But this time is different. We, the Cheetah Girls, have a very important *lonchando* meeting coming up, with Mr. Jackal Johnson of Johnson Management. He was at our first show: at the Kats and Kittys Halloween bash at the world-famous Cheetah-Rama nightclub. We turned the place upside down, if I do say so myself—and we even made four hundred dollars each after expenses, *muchas gracias*!

Anyway, Mr. Johnson came backstage after,

and said he wanted to be our manager—and take us to the top! *Está bien* with me, because the top is where I belong.

Now back to the real-life Spanish soap opera that is my *vida loca*—my crazy life—and why I have to make up stories about who does my hair.

Five long years ago, when I was nine years old, my dad left my mom for Princess Pamela. I still see him every once in a while, but I miss him a lot. So does Pucci, my younger brother.

Back then, when my dad first met Princess Pamela, she had a "winky dink" tarot shop around the corner from our loft in Soho on Mercer Street. It was so small, if you blinked or winked, you missed it, get it? Back then, her name was Pasha Pavlovia, or something like that, but we just called her "the psychic lady."

My dad's name is Dodo, but he is not a dodo. His nickname is short for Darius Diego Domingo Simmons. He was only four years old when he and his sister had to get out of their beds in Havana, Cuba, and escape when Fidel Castro took over. They were sent to relatives in Jamaica, but my dad says he misses his father every day. He misses the smell of the grass, too, and more than anything else, the water. There are no beaches like the ones in Havana, my dad says.

In that way, he and Princess Pamela have a lot in common. She had to leave Romania as a child when the Communists took over there, too. They both know what it's like to lose everything you have and never see your home again. They both have that sadness in their eyes sometimes.

Princess Pamela says when she saw my dad it was "love at first bite." He came into the shop for a reading and I guess he fell under her spell. Princess Pamela is a *bruja*—a witch—who can see the future. Mom hates her, but I think she is a good witch, not a bad one.

"Let me see how it looks with the headband!" I exclaim excitedly, and jump out of the beauty salon chair, hitting myself in the forehead with the red crystal bead curtains that divide the psychic salon from the beauty salon in the back.

"Ouch," I wince as I separate them to go to the front. See, thanks to my dad, Princess Pamela's Psychic Palace on Spring Street is now *muy grande* and beautiful. He built the whole place with his own two hands. He also helped Pamela install her Psychic Hotline, where she gives advice over the phone.

And thanks to her nimble fingers (and me), she now has a hair salon in the back. She even changed her name to Princess Pamela—because "it is a very good name for business—Pamela rhymes with stamina. It can unleash the secret energy into the universe."

Princess Pamela also loves music with flavor—*con sabor*—reggae music, rap, salsa. Sometimes I bring her cassettes, and we dance around if there aren't any customers. She likes Princess Erika, Nefertiti, and Queen Latifah the best. "Why not the Black people here should be like royalty? They can make their own royal family," she jokes, her accent as thick as ever.

My dad also built two other stores for Princess Pamela—Princess Pamela's Pampering Palace and Princess Pamela's Pound Cake Palace—both on 210th Street and Broadway. *The New York Times* rated her pound cake "the finger-lickin' best in New York City."

I am proud of her, and I think Princess Pamela is going to be Pamela *Trumpa* one day, and take a huge bite out of the Big Apple!

"Which headband do you think I should wear, the pink one or the green one?" I yell back to her, as I pull them out of my cheetah backpack. I just got these headbands from Oophelia's catalog—my favorite un-store in the entire universe.

Pink is my favorite color. Or sometimes red is. I like them both a lot. So does Princess Pamela—her whole place is covered in red velvet. Leopard, which is a "color" the Cheetah Girls use a lot, is my third favorite.

"*Ay, Dios mío*, what time is it?" I shriek. "I've got to get home!"

Bubbles, Dorinda Rogers, and Aquanette and Anginette Walker—the other members of the Cheetah Girls—are coming over to my house at seven o'clock so we can practice table manners for our *lonchando* meeting with Mr. Johnson. It may be the most important meeting I ever have. My mom is making dinner for us, and she doesn't like it if I'm not around to help—even though she won't let me get near the kitchen when she's working in there.

See, my mom is very *dramática*. She likes to have her way all the time—and know where I am *all the time,* which is right about now, so I'd better get home.

"I have to go!" I yell to Princess Pamela, who is on the phone fighting with someone.

"No! For that money, I can order flour from the King of Romania, you *strudelhead*!" she huffs into the phone. Then she wraps herself in her flowered shawl and comes toward me, with a little blue box in her hand. "Before you run off—this is for you, dahling," she says, smiling.

My heart is pounding. It is a present from Tiffany's!

"Chanel, this will bring you good luck with your meeting, so you will get many royalties," Princess Pamela says, kissing me on my cheeks and handing me my present. "You get my joke, no?"

"Joke?" I repeat, squinching up my nose.

"When you have a record, you get the royalties. You understand now?"

"Yeah," I giggle. "Besides, maybe I am going to be royalty for real, soon, because of my mom's new boyfriend, Mr. Tycoon, right?"

"Right, dahling. And how is he?"

"He's in Paris right now, and Mom's going crazy waiting for him to get back," I say, rolling my eyes. "You should see her—she's on my case all the time."

I don't want to get into my problems with my mom in front of Princess Pamela, so I keep my mouth shut and open the box. "*Ay, Dios mío!* Real diamonds!" I cry, and hug the princess. I hold up the diamonds to the light to admire them, and then I put my beautiful little diamond studs in my ears.

"Diamonds are a Cheetah Girl's best friend!" Princess Pamela sings, in such a funny voice that I can't stop laughing. "You think I could be a Cheetah Girl, too, and be in your group, Chanel?"

I just giggle at her, wishing I could stay longer. Princess Pamela is so dope—being with her is just like being with my crew. I wish it could be like that between me and my mom, instead of things always being so tense.

"*La revedere*—I gotta go!" I kiss her on the cheek, and hug her tight.

"*La revedere,*" she whispers back, saying goodbye in Romanian, and kisses me on the cheek.

When I get outside on Spring Street, it is really crowded. On the weekends, thousands of tourists and native New Yorkers come down to

Soho to shop. They will do the Road Runner over you, too, if you happen to be walking by one of the boutiques where there is a sale! One lady gets a little huffy, like Puff the Magic Dragon, when I don't walk fast enough in front of her—but that is like a breath of fresh air compared to the fire my mom is puffing down my back when I get home.

She is standing in the kitchen, with a spatula in her hand and an Yves Saint Bernard facial mask on her face. It covers her whole face except her eyes and mouth, and it is this putrid shade of yellow-green.

Cuatro yuks! She does the mask thing every Sunday afternoon. She thinks it keeps her looking young for her tycoon, and it must work, too, because he seems pretty gaga for her.

"Do you know what time it is? I'm not here to cook dinner for you and your friends, and to entertain them while you're out somewhere having fun, you understand me?"

"Lo siento, Mamí. I'm sorry. I know I'm late!" I exclaim.

"Why aren't you wearing a sweater?" Mom drills me.

"I'm not cold," I squeak.

"Wear a sweater anyway. And what is that on your head?" Mom waves the spatula at me, then uses it to stir the pot of Goya *frijoles* for our Dominican-style *arroz con pollo* dinner.

"It's a headband. Isn't it cute?" I exclaim.

"It looks like a bra strap!"

"It's not a bra strap. It's a headband, *Mamí*."

"Well, it *looks* like you're wearing a bra strap on your head, okay? And where did you get those?" Mom asks, pointing to my diamond stud earrings.

Uh-oh. Where is Bubbles when I need her? She'd be able to come up with something. She always does.

But I'm not that quick, and anyway, this is not the time to tell a real *mentira*—a lie that will come back to haunt me like *Tales from the Crypt*. So I decide to be honest. Why should I have to lie just because Princess Pamela gave me a present? After all, she is my dad's girlfriend, so she is *la familia* to me, I think, trying to get up my courage.

"Princess Pamela gave them to me as good luck for the meeting with Mr. Johnson. Aren't they boot-i-full?" I squeak, hoping to tap into Mom's weakness for "carats."

"She did *what*!?" she screams at the top of her lungs. Her facial mask cracks in a dozen places, and her eyes are popping big-time. Suddenly, she looks like The Mummy. Even through her tight lips, her voice is loud enough to send coyotes running for the hills.

"*When* did you see her? *Cuándo?*" Mom demands, standing with one hand on her hip and the other holding the spatula straight up in the air.

"I just stopped by there on my way home," I whine.

"Don't you *ever* take anything from that *bruja* again. Do you hear me? *Me sientes?*" she screeches, squinting her eyes. The Mummy is walking toward me. I think I'm going to faint.

"And if Bubbles did your hair, how come she didn't come back with you?" my mom asks me suspiciously. "That *bruja* Pamela does your hair, doesn't she? You think I'm stupid." She pulls on one of my braids. "You try and lie to me?"

I have not seen my mom this angry since my dad left and she threw his clothes out the window into the street, and the police came because she hit a lady on the head with one of his Oxford wing-tipped shoes.

"I'm sorry, *Mamí*," I cry, praying she will stop. "I won't do it again!"

"I know you won't, because I'm gonna hang you by your braids!" says The Mummy who is my mom.

I run to my room, grab the red princess phone by my bed and beep Bubbles, putting the 911 code after my phone number. Me and Bubbles have secret codes for everything. She will understand. I sure hope she gets the message, but I know she's probably already on her way here for our dinner together.

I listen to my mom clanging pots and pans in the kitchen, and I let out a big sigh. See, me and Mom fight a lot, especially now that I am a Cheetah Girl. It seems like everything I want, she's against. She does not want me to sing. She says I should get a real job—be a department store buyer or something—because if I keep chasing my dreams of being a singer, I will get my heart broken by living *la gran fantasía*—the grand fantasy. And most of all, she does not want me to see Princess Pamela.

I sit on the edge of the bed, waiting for Bubbles to call back, and I look into the sparkly eyes of my kissing-and-tongue-wagging Snuggly-Wiggly stuffed pooch. Abuela Florita gave him to me as a joke for Christmas, because I always wanted a real dog like Toto, who is Bubbles's "big brother." (Mom won't let me have a dog because she says she is allergic to them.)

Snuggy-Wiggly Pooch is sitting on my nightstand with his tongue hanging out, next to the *Book of Spells* that Princess Pamela gave me (my mom doesn't know about that either).

I sit on my frilly canopy bed and stare at all my dolls. I have twenty-seven collectible dolls. They are *muy preciosa*—very precious—and come from all over the world.

"Charo is from Venezuela and she never cries. Zingera is from Italy and she never lies. Coco is from France and she smells so sweet, *huit, huit, huit*," I repeat to myself, like I used to do when I was little. *Huit*, which sounds like wheat, means eight in French. It's a silly rhyme, but I like it. And right now, I just want to get my mind off my misery.

When I was little, I used to lock my bedroom door, use my hairbrush as a microphone, and sing into the mirror, thinking about all the people who would love me if they could only hear me sing. That's all I ever dreamed about—me and Bubbles singing together, and Abuela Florita sitting in the first row clapping and crying joyfully into her handkerchief.

I have always felt closer to Abuela than to my mother, because she understands me. She would never try to get in the way of my dreams the way my mom does. I know Mom's just trying to protect me from the heartbreak of failure, but why can't she believe in me the way Abuela Florita does?

I can hear Abuela's voice now, telling me what a great singer I am. She says, "*Querida Cristalle, tú eres las mäs bonita cantora en todo el mundo.*" I know it's not true, because Chutney Dallas is the best singer in the whole world, but it makes me want to sing just for her. Why, oh why, can't my mom see me the way Abuela does?

I let out a big yawn. Suddenly, even though Bubbles hasn't called back, even though it's not even dinnertime, I cannot keep my eyes open anymore.

Chanel is so sweet, *huit, huit, huit*. . . . I think, as I fall asleep, just like a real-life mummy. . . .

Chapter 2

The sound of the doorbell wakes me up out of my deep sleep. I'm still too scared to come out of my room. I can hear my mom talking with Aqua in the hallway. Aquanette Walker is one of the "Huggy Bear" twins (that's my and Bubbles's secret nickname for them) from Houston, Texas. We met them at the Kats and Kittys Klub barbecue last summer. They were singing, swatting mosquitoes, and eating hot dogs all at the same time. We *had* to have them in our group!

My little brother, Pucci, is running down the hall to the door. "Hi, Bubbles! I'm a Cuckoo Cougar! I'm a Cuckoo Cougar! You wanna see if you can outrun me?"

So Bubbles is here, too. I crack the door open and sneak out, to see if I can get her attention without my mom seeing me, and before Pokémon-*loco* Pucci drags Bubbles into his room to floss his Japanese "Pocket Monsters."

"I know you can run faster than me, Pucci. You are 'tha man,'" Bubbles says, hugging Pucci back.

"Are you singing, Bubbles?" Pucci whines, holding Bubbles by her waist. She is like his second big sister.

"We're all singing, Pucci—we're the Cheetah Girls—me and Dorinda and Aquanette and Anginette—and Chuchie, too," Bubbles says, pointing to our crew, who have all assembled in the hallway.

Pucci looks up at Bubbles with the longest face, and asks, "Why is it only for girls? Why can't there be Cheetah Boys, too?" Leave it to Pucci to whine on a dime.

"I wanna be a Cheetah Boy!" Pucci says, yelling even louder, then hitting Bubbles in the stomach. Pucci is getting out of control. When I see my dad, I'm gonna tell him.

"That's enough, Pucci!" Mom yells. I can tell she is still mad, by the tone of her voice. My crew can tell, too, and Bubbles looks at me like, "What's going on, *girlita*?"

"Hey, *Mamacitas,*" I yell at them in the hallway. I pop my eyes open real big when my mother turns her head, so my crew knows there is something going on. *Ayúdame!* Help me, my eyes are screaming.

"Go on, sit down at the table and I'll bring your dinner in." Mom sighs with her back turned. "I'm not eating now because I'm expecting a call from Paree."

She means Paris, of course. These days, Mom uses her new French accent "at the drop of a *croissant,*" as Bubbles says. I can tell Mom is still mad, but I also know she's not going to yell at me in front of everybody. So for now, at least, I'm safe.

As we file into the dining room area, I squeeze next to Bubbles. "What's going on?" she whispers in my ear.

"You got here just in time. I think my picture was about to end up on a milk carton!" I say, bumping into her.

We hightail it to the long dining room table, so we can eat dinner and practice the "soup-to-nuts situation." That's what we, the Cheetah Girls, call table manners.

My godfather—Galleria's dad, Mr. Garibaldi—is from Bologna, Italy, and he can cook like a chef. He says Europeans have better table manners than we do, so Bubbles knows everything. I have good table manners, too, because Abuela taught me. Dorinda, on the other hand, has table manners like a mischievous chimpanzee. That's why we are doing this dinner. She eats too fast and never looks up from her plate. One day, Aquanette, with her *boca grande*—her big mouth—blurted out to Dorinda, "Girl, the way you eat, you'd think you wuz digging for gold!"

Dorinda wasn't even embarrassed! She just giggled and said, "You gotta get it when you can." Do' Re Mi, as we call her, looks the youngest of all of us, and we all kind of treat her like our little sister. But in a lot of ways, she's lived through more than any of us.

Do' Re Mi's had kind of a hard life. She lives in a foster home uptown, with a lady named Mrs. Bosco and ten *other* foster kids. Dorinda says that sometimes they even steal food from each other's plates if Mrs. Bosco isn't looking.

So now that she is one of the Cheetah Girls, we're teaching Do' Re Mi how to "sip tea with a queen and eat pralines with a prince," as Bubbles says.

"*Mamacita*, the braids are *kicking*," Bubbles whispers to me, then touches my new headband and snaps it back into place.

"Ouch," I whimper, then giggle, adjusting my headband again.

"They got any leopard ones? How much was it?" Bubbles asks as we sit down at the table, on our best behavior.

"Eight duckets," I reply. "They came in green, and pink, and I think, black." Bubbles *loves* animal prints. She'd be happy if she could buy a headband that growled.

"You're gonna be broke and that ain't no joke," Do' Re Mi says, cutting her eyes at me. "How much money do you have left from what we earned at the Kats and Kittys show?"

"Not enough to buy an outfit for the *lonchando*," I say, cutting my eyes back. Compared to her, I've always had it easy—Mom and Dad always got me lots of things. Even now that they're not together, I can usually get what I want, up to a point. But see, I guess Princess

Pamela was right about me being "royalty," because nothing ever seems to be enough for me. I never met a store I didn't like, *está bien?* I never had a ducket that I didn't spend first chance I got. And now, my first "duckets in a bucket" for doing what I always dreamed of doing—singing with Bubbles onstage—are drizzling away *fast*.

"I didn't buy *anything*," Do' Re Mi grunts back at me. "I had to give all my money to Mrs. Bosco to help pay for her doctor bills."

"But we gotta look nice for the big meeting, don't we?" I moan. "We can't have you showin' up in old clothes from Goodwill!"

"Shoot, don't worry about it," Aqua huffs. "We ain't gotta impress nobody yet. Let's see what Mr. Jackal Johnson can do for *us* first."

"What do managers do, anyway?" Do' Re Mi asks.

"Nowadays, they just get you record deals and book you on tours," Bubbles explains to us. "You know, back in the day of groups like the Supremes and The Jackson Five, managers taught you everything, just like in charm school. How to talk, dress, sing, do interviews. That's what Mom says."

"Word. Well, maybe Mr. Jackal Johnson is just a jackal who'll make us cackle!" sighs Do' Re Mi, making a joke from one of the lines of Bubbles's song "Wanna-be Stars in the Jiggy Jungle."

After we stop giggling, I add, "Yes, but they are still talking about our show at the Klub."

"That's right. We are all that, and Mr. Jackal Johnson knows it." Aqua pulls out a nail file from her backpack to saw down her white frosted tips, which are covered with dollar-sign rhinestone decals. It's her trademark. She's "on the money"—get it?

"Aqua, you are not filing your nails at the table. That is so ticky-tacky!" screams Bubbles, then slaps her hand. "We're supposed to be learning table manners here—this is a big meeting and greeting, Miss 'press on.'"

"At least she ain't whipping out a Big Mac from her backpack," Do' Re Mi quips, making a joke about the twins because they always carry food or hot sauce with them.

"No Big Macs in my backpack, just got room for my dreams," Galleria says out loud, grooving to her own rhythm. Then she whips out her Kitty Kat notebook and starts writing furiously. "That's a song!"

"Shhh, my mom is m-a-a-d!" I whisper to her, then turn to Do' Re Mi. "To answer your question, I only have about thirty-seven duckets left!"

"That's all!?" the four of them say, ganging up on me.

"I knew you went and bought those Flipper shoes! You didn't fool me, Miss Fib-eroni!" says Bubbles, who is always supposed to be on my side but hasn't been lately.

"I don't care if you don't like them, I think they're *la dopa*!" I protest, talking about the sandals I bought the other day behind Bubbles's back. See, we were hanging out at the Manhattan Mall on 34th Street, and I saw them at the Click Your Heels shoe store. They are made out of vinyl, and have a see-through heel with plastic goldfish inside.

"I don't know why Auntie Juanita wants you to be a buyer, 'cuz you are a shopaholic waiting to happen," Bubbles quips. She calls my mom "Auntie" even though we aren't related. But we are just like sisters. Bubbles has a big mouth, but I'm used to that because she always used to back me up when my mouth wrote a check I couldn't cash. "Now what are you gonna do for a dress for our big *lonchando* with Mr. Johnson?"

"I don't know," I say, feeling like I want to burst out crying. "I've got these great diamond earrings Princess Pamela gave me, and those great shoes . . . but no dress. Bubbles, you still got some duckets left?"

Bubbles whips out her cheetah wallet to show us that she still has the money we earned from performing at the Kats and Kittys show stuffed inside. "I got all the duckets in this bucket, baby," she says, flossin'. "I'm not buying *nada*—and definitely no Prada!"

"Word, Galleria. Your wallet looks like it's having triplets," Do' Re Mi quips. She *would* be impressed.

"Maybe you could lend me some till our next gig?" I start to say, but Galleria cuts me off.

"No way, Miss Cuchifrito!" she says, putting the wallet back in her bag. "Duckets just fly through your fingers, *girlita*. I'd never see mine again. Maybe you ought to just borrow a dress from somebody—or make one, even!"

Just then, my mom comes into the dining room, so we all shut up about money. My mom puts the piping hot *panecitas* and butter on the table. These little rolls are my favorite. Do' Re Mi grabs one and starts spreading butter on the whole *panecita,* then does a chomp-aroni like Toto, and eats the whole thing!

"At least you're using a knife," I say, being *sarcástico,* then giggle. Everyone looks at me, because Do' and I are very close now. We talk on the phone a lot, and I even help her with her Spanish homework. So I guess I'm the one who's supposed to get this choo-choo train in motion.

"Do' Re Mi, watch this," I say, trying to be nice to her. "Break off a piece of the roll, then butter it and put the knife back across the plate like this."

"Word. I got it." Do' Re Mi giggles, then makes fun and starts spreading butter on the bread—oh so delicately, like a real phony baloney.

"You're on a roll, *churlita*!" I crack, then cover my mouth because I'm talking with food in it—and my mom has walked back in the dining room with the platter of *arroz con pollo*. She gives me a look that says, "I'm not finished with you yet." Aqua and Angie are giggling up a storm, like they think it's funny Do' Re Mi has to learn how to eat butter on a roll.

"Don't you two worry, we're gonna steam

roll over *your* choo-choo train, too," Bubbles warns them.

See, me, Bubbles, and Do' Re Mi have *tan coolio* style. We all go to Fashion Industries High School. The twins, who go to Performing Arts, dress, well, kinda corny, and act even cornier.

"Now, assuming Miss Cuchifrita here can make herself an outfit, all we have to do to get the Cheetah Girls on track is get you two some new do's—and outfits you can't wear at church!" Bubbles loves to tease the twins, who are unidentical but very much alike.

"Oh, and I got some virtual reality for you two," I add.

"Virtual reality?" Aqua says, taking her pink-flowered paper napkin off her lap and patting her juicy lips.

"I got the *Miss Wiggy Virtual Makeover* CD-ROM. It has one hundred fifty hairdos we can try, and one of them has just got to be fright, I mean, right for you!"

"We could do a sleepover here the night before our *lonchando*, right, Chuchie?" Bubbles asks. "That way we could take care of the do's right before the luncheon."

"I don't know about that," I say, croaking. "My mom's kinda down on me even *bein'* a Cheetah Girl. Maybe we better do it at your house." I roll my eyes at Bubbles, then toward the den next door, where my mom is talking on the phone to Mr. Tycoon in Paris.

I'm scared for my crew to leave, because then I will have to be alone with her. I take a deep breath, which is what Drinka Champagne, our vocal coach, tells us we have to do to help our singing voices stay strong.

After today's craziness with my *madre, lonchando* with Mr. Jackal Johnson will be a piece of cake. A piece of Princess Pamela's pound cake . . .

Later that night, I'm on the Internet chatting with my Cheetah Girls crew, when I hear my mom yelling over the phone to my dad. "I have a prediction for that *Princess Pamela,*" my mom says all *sarcástico* into the phone receiver. "If *she* doesn't stay away from *my* daughter, The Wicked Witch of the Yeast is gonna slice her up like that cheesy pound cake she sells!" my mom snarls, then hangs up the phone. Mom always has to have the last word. I hear her bare feet pounding down the hallway.

"*Ciao* for now!" I type furiously on the keyboard. That's the signal we use when a grown-up is coming. I run to my bed and open up my history book. All I need is for my mom to see what I'm talking about with my crew on the Internet, and she may figure out a way to stop that, too.

I know she's about to come in, and I'm dreading the screaming fight we're about to have. But to my total surprise, the knock on my door is so low I almost don't hear it.

"What!" I yell, pretending that maybe I think it's Pucci.

"Can I come in?" Mom asks, in a voice so soft and sweet I barely recognize her.

"Sure, *Mamí,*" I say more quietly.

When she walks into my room, she is smiling at me. Now I feel guilty for thinking bad thoughts about her. I've been assuming she was going to get on my case about every single thing in my life, and here she is, being sweet and nice.

"Hi, *Mamí,*" I say, trying to act normal.

"Hi. What are you up to? You and the Cheetah Girls have been talking in the chat room, right?"

She is still smiling! Weird.

"Yeah." I giggle, shutting the cover of my history book. No use pretending now. Besides, it doesn't seem to be necessary. She's obviously not mad—but why? *Qué pasa?*

"I've been wondering—what are you going to wear for the lunch meeting with Mr. Johnson, Chuchie?" Mom asks me, plopping down on my pink bedspread. She then crosses her legs, like she is practicing a pose for the Chirpy Cheapies Catalog. My mom used to be a model, you know. Right now, she has put her wavy hair up in a ponytail. She almost looks like she could be my big sister instead of my mother.

"Yo no sé," I answer. "I don't know. I really don't have anything good to wear."

"Well, why don't you go ahead and order that green leopard pantsuit from Oophelia's catalog," she says with a satisfied smirk.

"Well, I can't buy it, because I only have thirty-seven dollars left from the money I got from the show," I say, kinda nervous. Don't get the wrong idea—I didn't just buy shoes and headbands, okay? I also bought a new laser printer for my computer, so that we, the Cheetah Girls, can make flyers for our shows—if we have any more.

"I know you don't have any money left, but I'm glad you bought a printer. So the outfit is on me. A little present. Here," Mom says, holding out her credit card. "You can use my credit card and order that one outfit."

I sit there frozen, not even able to breathe. This is like, unbelievable! My mom offering to let *me*, the shopaholic deluxe, use her credit card? What is up here?

"You sure?" I ask nervously, not daring to take it, for fear I'll be struck by lightning or something like that.

"Yes, I'm sure. I've been thinkin' about it all day. You and I haven't been spending enough time together lately—what with me bein' with my new boyfriend, and you hangin' with the Cheetah Girls. I miss bein' close."

I smile. "Me too, *Mamí*."

"And I know how much this lunch meeting means to you and the girls. So I decided I want you to look your very best."

"Wow" is all I can say. I can feel the tears of gratitude welling in my eyes.

My mom looks up at the ceiling. "And it just bothers me that that *bruja* Pamela has been pushing her way into your heart, trying to buy your affection with diamond earrings and such. If anybody's going to buy you nice things, it's going to be me."

So *that's* it! "But, *Mamí*—"

"Now, you just tell her you can't accept them, and that she's to stop giving you expensive gifts. It puts a wedge between you and me, baby, and we don't want that."

"But—"

"Now, now," she says, stroking my braids. "I can afford to get you even nicer earrings, if that's what you want."

"I can't return them, *Mamí*," I say, holding my ground now that I know what she's after. So, all this niceness is just a trick, to try and turn me against Pamela! Well, it won't work. If people I like want to give me things, I should be allowed to accept them. "I can't and I won't!"

"All right," *Mamí* says, seeing she can't win on this one. "You can keep the earrings. But from now on, no more gifts from that *bruja*, you hear?"

"Yes, *Mamí*," I say, grabbing the compromise when I can get it. "Can I still buy the outfit?"

"Of course, baby," she says, smiling again,

although it looks more forced now than it did before. "I want you to look beautiful for your big meeting."

"But I thought you didn't even want me to *be* in the Cheetah Girls!" I point out. Then I want to kick myself for bringing it up. Why couldn't I just keep my *boca grande*—my big mouth—shut for once?

Incredibly, it doesn't seem to bother her. "I think it's just a phase you're going through, *mi hija,*" she says, still smiling. "But since you insist on this singing nonsense, you may as well go all the way with it." She pushes the card into my hands and squeezes them. "Buy yourself the outfit. And remember who bought it for you—*me*, not Pamela—*está bien?*"

"Sí, Mamí," I say, giving her a big hug and kiss. I'm still mad at her for not believing in me, but at least she's showing me she loves me.

"Now, you know the rules, Chanel. You only order that one outfit. You give me the card back as soon as you're done. And don't you ask 'that woman' for anything ever again. *Entiendes?* You hear?"

Now she is wiping imaginary dust off my

altar table right next to the window. My altar table is covered with a pretty white tablecloth. On top of it, there are candles and offerings to the patron saints—fruits, nuts, and little prayer notes.

"I didn't ask Pamela for anything," I whine, making the cross-my-heart-and-hope-to-die sign across my chest. "She just gave the earrings to me!"

"Well, *don't* accept anything else. And if your father asks you anything, don't tell him what I told you. *Entiendes?*" Mom asks me—again. Now I'm really getting annoyed.

"*Está bien.* I won't. I promise," I respond. Anything to make her stop being such a policeman. "And thank you sooooo much! Letting me charge a new outfit is the best present anybody ever got me!"

I give her another hug, and that seems to do the trick. She flashes me a big smile, kisses me on the forehead, and heads for the door.

When Mom finally leaves my room, a sudden feeling of total bliss comes over me. The credit card feels sleek and powerful in my hand, and I'm anxious to get my shopping groove on. Prada or *nada*, baby! Okay, so I am rolling more with the *nada* than the Prada—but that is all gonna change with one phone call!

As I flip through the catalog, looking at all the dozens of things I'm longing to own, I hum to myself, "Oooh, Oophelia's! I'm feeling ya!"

Chapter 3

I have never held Mom's credit card in my hot little hands before. Never. And now, the hologram on its face seems to wink at me, casting a witch's spell over me. I dial the 800 number and follow the computer instructions, punching in numbers here and there until I get to speak to a real-live person.

Meanwhile, I am thinking about poor Dorinda. She must feel so down about not being able to keep the duckets from our gig. It's so unfair that she had to give the money to her foster mom. My heart goes out to her. Surely, my mom wouldn't want us to lose out on making a deal with Mr. Johnson just because Do' Re Mi came dressed in rags!

I decide then and there to make one tiny little exception to Mom's rule. After all, she said I couldn't buy anything else—but that meant *for me,* didn't it? When the operator picks up, I order two of the green leopard outfits—one in my size, and one in Dorinda's. I give the credit card number to the lady on the phone, and as I do, my gaze wanders to the pages of the catalog. So many other great things, things I've always wanted, and will never have another chance to get . . .

What would it hurt to borrow just a little of Mom's credit to stock up on stuff? When we sign with Mr. Johnson, it will be no time till we're making big duckets from gigs, maybe even a record deal! I can pay my mom back before she even knows I've spent the money!

"Will that be all, ma'am?" the voice asks me.

"Uh . . . no," I hear myself say. "No . . . just one or two more things . . ."

Do' Re Mi looks so "money" in the new outfit I bought her. And on top of that, Bubbles's mom, who is my *madrina*—my godmother—since birth (and the best godmother in the whole world) made *her* a green leopard pantsuit to match ours for our meeting with Mr. Johnson!

Aqua is wearing a black-and-white-checked blazer with a red shirt and black skirt. Angie has on a denim suit with a hot pink turtleneck.

"At least they don't look like they're going to church," Bubbles giggles to me, sneaking a look in the mirror that covers one whole wall of the Hydrant Restaurant on Fifteenth Street, where we are meeting Mr. Johnson.

When we first tried to tell Angie and Aqua what to wear for the meeting, Aqua got all huffy and said, "*We* are saving *our* money to go home to Houston for Thanksgiving!" The twins are headed south for the holidays—in more ways than one!

"I feel so large and in charge, I'm loving it—and you all, too!" Bubbles says. "That was so nice of Auntie Juanita to let you buy Do' Re Mi a pantsuit, too, Chuchie!"

Okay, so I told Bubbles a little fib-eroni. I didn't want her to think that I did . . . well, what I actually did. I'll have to straighten her out soon, though, before she opens her *boca grande*—her big mouth—and spills the refried beans to my mom.

The table is covered with a bright red linen tablecloth, and six red linen napkins placed perfectly apart. Right in the middle of the round table is a big glass vase with lots of pink roses, my favorite *flores*.

"You nervous?" I ask Do' Re Mi, then I add giggling, "I feel like I'm at a seance and the table is gonna lift up any second!"

Mr. Johnson has gone to check our jackets. Yes, we have it like that. There is a waiter dressed in white, standing near our table. He smiles at me when I look in his direction.

"Somebody pinch me, pleez, so I can wake up!" I giggle, then look around at all the people who are having lunch at the Hydrant. I take the book of matches with the name of the restaurant out of the ashtray, and stick it in my cheetah backpack for a souvenir. All around us are grown-ups, and they are all dressed *adobo down*. The lady at the table next to us is sitting by herself.

"She must be waiting for *El Presidente,*" I whisper to Bubbles. The lady is wearing a big hat with a black peacock feather poking her almost in the eye! She looks at us and smiles. Then the peacock lady puts on lipstick without even looking in a mirror! "She definitely has the skills to pay the bills," Bubbles quips.

Do' Re Mi looks like she is getting nervous, too, because she is reading the menu like she is studying for a test at school. Then all of a sudden she whispers to me, "What should I order?"

"Just don't get spaghetti marinara," I whisper back.

"Do' Re Mi, try the *penne arrabiata*—that's the pasta cut on the slanty tip with red *pepperoncino.*"

"What's *that*?" Do' Re Mi quizzes Bubbles.

"Those crushed red pepper flakes that Angie loves to put on pizza. You can hang with that!" Bubbles blurts out.

"Here he comes," whispers Angie.

"Ladies, order to your heart's delight," Mr. Johnson commands us, as he sits down and puts the napkin in his lap. We all do the same thing. Do' Re Mi flaps the napkin really loud when she opens it, like it has wings, but we act like we don't notice. Mr. Johnson is wearing a yellow tie brighter than a Chiquita banana, and his two front teeth don't talk to each other. He has a *really* big gap.

"This place is majordomo dope," Bubbles exclaims, looking around once more.

"Yeah, and I've done some pretty majordomo deals here, as you would say," chuckles Mr. Johnson, looking at Bubbles. "So you're the writer of the group, huh?" he asks her.

"Yup," Bubbles says, smiling. Bubbles isn't afraid of anything. She just acts like herself. He obviously just looks to her as if she is the leader. Which *is* kinda true anyway. We wouldn't be a group, I think, if it wasn't for Bubbles. But I don't want Bubbles to be the *only* leader, because it was my idea too to *be* in a group, so that counts for something.

Today Bubbles is wearing her hair really straight and parted down the middle. I put her extensions in myself, so I know they won't come out even if Hurricane Gloria flies in from Miami!

"Pucci would love this place," I giggle, looking at the red brick walls. My mom says the Hydrant is a one-star bistro. I don't know what that means, but now that she has Mr. Tycoon for a boyfriend, she goes to places, she says, where they don't even have prices on the menu. I guess this one doesn't count, because it does.

"You know, this place used to be a firehouse," says Mr. Johnson. "Lotta action coming down that pole." Mr. Johnson is looking over in the direction of the big metal pole that goes all the way up the ceiling. "Back in the day, there were some pretty bad torch jobs in the city. Buildings burning down all the time. It kept firemen pretty busy, but things have gotten better, and they closed the firehouse down two years ago."

The waiters are sliding down the pole now, bringing food from the kitchen above. "Tourists love that," Mr. Johnson chuckles.

"I wonder if the waiters get scared," Aquanette asks, touching her pin curl, which is laid down and fried to the side of her face.

"Well, let's clear away the okeydokey and talk some bizness, here," Mr. Johnson chuckles. He definitely has more rhymes than Dr. Seuss. He looks at all five of us and says, "As your manager, I want you to know that I'm going to forego all production costs for a demo, and get you in the studio with some real heavy-hitting producers, arrangers, and engineers."

"Can we do some of my songs?" Bubbles asks, always looking out for *número una*.

"Not right away, Galleria. Now, I know your songs are smokin', 'cuz I heard you girls singing them the night I saw you perform at Cheetah-Rama, but let's start with the producers' songs." Mr. Johnson takes a sip of bubbly water from his glass, then licks his lips. "Pumpmaster Pooch has worked with some really big artists, so he knows how to turn a song into an instant hit," he says.

I hope the water doesn't make me burp, I think, as I sip some from my glass, too.

"Who has Pumpmaster Pooch worked with?" Do' Re Mi asks.

"Well, I don't want to say right now, because none of the songs have gotten picked up just yet. You girls have to understand. There is a one in a million chance for a record to turn gold, but if you go into the studio with producers who've got the Midas touch, you're likely to turn that song into gold."

"What happens to the songs after we finish them?" Angie asks.

"We—that means I—have to get your demo to the record companies. It takes a lot of wheeling and dealing, but don't worry about it, 'cuz it ain't no thing like a chicken wing."

We look at each other like we've just eaten some Green Eggs and Ham, or something.

Mr. Johnson catches on to our confusion. "What I mean is, I have a serious setup at Hyena Records. Me and the A&R guy—that's the artist development person, who goes out scouting the country for talent just like you—go way back. *And* I've been doing business with Mr. Hyena, the company president, for years. After he gets a taste of that growl power y'all got going on, he'll be chomping at the bit to sign some superlistic talent such as yourselves. Just let me handle it."

I sit there wondering how Mr. Johnson can talk so fast without even taking a breath. I wish Drinka could see him in action.

"Hyena Records. Who do they have on the label?" Do' Re Mi asks, all curious. When Mr. Johnson turns his head toward her, I motion quickly to Angie with my hand. She has a piece of green something stuck on a tooth in the front, and she is just smiling her head off.

"Now, they're not what they used to be back in the day," Mr. Johnson says, his pinky finger dangling to the wind as he sips his water. "But nothing is like it used to be in the music biz."

"Ooh, this is bubbly," Aqua says, her eyes popping open as she puts her glass down.

"Bubbles. That's me," Galleria says, starting to sway. "The Cheetah Girls are cutting a demo, so take a memo, all you wanna-be stars trying to get a whiff of what it feels like," Bubbles giggles. She is flossin' for Mr. Johnson.

"That's very good, Galleria." He chuckles. "You do that off the top of your head?"

All of this is going to Bubbles's head, I think. I wish I knew how to make up songs like her. Then Mr. Johnson would like me, too.

The waiter comes and takes our orders. After he leaves, Mr. Johnson whips a manila envelope out of his pocket and opens it. Inside are five pieces of paper.

"Listen, before our food gets here, I want each of you to give one of these to your parents. Have them look it over, then sign it. You can give it back to me the next time we meet, in the studio."

"What is it?" Do' Re Mi asks.

"It's no big deal—just a temporary agreement—a standard management contract, so we can get started right away on your demo. It's your time and my dime—so let's not waste it, Cheetah Girls!" Mr. Johnson quips.

He sure is making moves like a jackal. Just like his name. I guess I'll have my dad look it over. He is good with business. I wish I could give it to Princess Pamela, too. She is smart like that. But Mom would really go off on me if she found out I did that.

"Enough business for now," Mr. Johnson says with a big, gap-toothed smile. "Why don't you girls tell me all about yourselves?"

And we do . . . oh, do we ever!

Chapter 4

Things went really well today at our first business *lonchando*, I think to myself as I'm lying on my bed, clacking the heels of my black patent leather loafers together. I have the keyboard on the bed, and I'm yapping on the Internet with Bubbles, Angie, and Aqua. Dorinda is coming over so we can do our homework together. Meanwhile, I'm trying to get them to help me with this Princess Pamela situation, and end the frustration.

"I just don't think it's fair that you can't see Pamela, and I'm not being square," Bubbles says.

Angie has an idea: "Dag on, we got so many problems. We better have Cheetah Girls council meetings, so we can give each other advice, instead of rehearsing all the time and talking about being wanna-be stars!"

"It's a done wheel-a-deal," Bubbles types back, imitating Mr. Johnson. "Let's have Cheetah Girls council meetings once a week!"

My bedroom door is open, so I don't hear when my mom walks right in. "Chuchie," she says, almost scaring me.

"Oh, hi, *Mamí*," I say, hoping she isn't trying to peep my chat.

"You forgot to give me back my credit card," she says.

"Oh! Right!" I fall all over myself going to my dresser drawer, and take it out. Handing it to her, I say, "*Mamí*, that was so generous of you letting me get that outfit."

She smiles and gives me a kiss. "The meeting was good, huh?" she asks. Then she sits down on my bed.

"*Sí, Mamí*. Thanks so much."

She hands me back the management agreement form that Mr. Johnson wanted us to sign. "As long as you do your schoolwork and finish high school, *then* go to college, you can stay with this little group of yours. Just don't get any ideas that this is for real, okay?" she says, taking my comb and starting to comb her hair.

"Okay, *Mamí,*" I growl back.

My mom just won't get it into her head that I am very serious about being a Cheetah Girl, or that it means everything to me. I know I will do whatever my mom wants me to do, but on the other hand, I have to do what's right for me.

"You better let your father see that agreement, too, or he'll have a fit," Mom adds, while she looks in my mirror and combs out her hair.

That's how she gets when she talks about my dad. It makes me so sad that they fight all the time. I'll tell you one thing, though. She is not going to keep me away from Princess Pamela.

"Yes, *Mamí,*" I reply.

Deep in my heart, I know what I want. I want to be a Cheetah Girl and travel all over the world. Then I'm going to buy Abuela Florita a house away from Washington Heights and near the ocean so she can dream about the D.R.—the Dominican Republic, where she was born. I'm gonna live near her, so we can see each other more often.

Mom interrupts my *gran fantasía*. "So. You're going to the studio tomorrow, huh?" she asks.

"Yeah, I'm kinda nervous about making a demo tape," I explain.

"What's that?" she asks me, then looks at herself sideways in the mirror.

"It's a tape of songs that shows how we sing, so a record company will give us a deal. Maybe it's not a whole tape, but it's something."

"Mmm," Mom says, getting up off the bed. "You and your crazy dreams."

She leaves my room and goes back to the exercise studio. Lately, she has become an exotic dancing fanatic. She says it's great exercise, better than jogging. Her tummy is as flat as my chest, so it must be true. She's looking good, and she's got a boyfriend with *mucho dinero*, so why is she so worked up about Princess Pamela?

I ponder the situation. What am I gonna do? I love Princess Pamela, and she is so nice to me, but I know it makes my mom unhappy that I am close to her.

Our Cheetah Girls crew council is a good idea, for starters. Maybe I could ask Bubbles's mom, Dorothea, my *madrina*, who is super *simpática*, what I should do. But, then again, she and Mom are friends since their modeling days, so maybe I can't trust her with everything.

Then it hits me! I get *un buen* idea. I can call Princess Pamela's Psychic Hotline, disguise my voice, and ask *her* what to do!

I dial the 900-PRINCESS number and hold my breath. I can feel my heart pounding through my chest like a secret agent on a mission. "I like truffles, not R-r-u-ffles," I hum to myself, rolling my Rs. Everybody at Drinka's voice and dance studio is so jealous because they can't roll their Rs like I do.

That is my *cultura* for you, I smile to myself, as I take a piece of Godiva chocolate from the box Bubbles's mom gave each of us for Halloween. I've hidden the box from Pucci's little grubby hands.

A voice machine comes on, telling me the Princess is out, and to call back later. Great. There's never a psychic around when you really need one.

I get off the bed, and put a few oranges on my little altar table as an offering for Santa Prosperita. I don't know if she is a real saint, but she is *my* saint, and if you want something bad enough, you can get it, Princess Pamela says. She should know.

"I know it's not right to ask for anything

material, but *por favor*, I need just one little thing," I whisper to my Santa Prosperita. "Just one little Prada bag!"

See, the Kats and Kittys Klub is selling raffle tickets for community service. Each of the members has to sell as many raffle tickets as possible, and all the proceeds are going to the needy. The best part: the grand prize is two Prada bags! I have got to have them—at least one of them! The only problem is, I'm not too lucky at these kind of things. So I figure I'd better buy a *lot* of tickets.

Of course, that could be a problem, since my pile of duckets is now down to just fourteen. But hey—no *problemo*! I go to my math notebook and open it up to the last page. There, I have written the number and expiration date of my mom's credit card!

I know what you're thinking, but it's not true—I only wrote it down just in case I lost the card, or forgot the number or something! And I *meant* to cross it out when I gave the card back, but I haven't had the chance. And now . . .

Well, look. It's a worthy cause, *está bien?* All those poor needy people in the world—how could I not reach out to help them?

I'm sure my mom won't mind, especially since, if I win, I'll definitely give her one of the Prada bags. Besides, I'll pay her back for everything, once the Cheetah Girls hit it big—which we're sure to do, now that we're signing on with Mr. Johnson and making a demo tape! I mean, how long could it be before we're rolling in *dinero*?

I call up the Kats and Kittys Klub. Mrs. Goodge, the secretary, gets on the line. "Oh, hello, there, Chanel! What can I do for you?"

I tell her.

"A hundred tickets? Why, Chanel, that's very generous of your mother!"

"Yes it is, Mrs. Goodge," I say. "My mom is one of the most generous people there is, and she really cares about needy people, too!"

"How will she be paying? Cash or check?" Mrs. Goodge asks.

"Um, she gave me her credit card number to give you," I say.

"Oh. I see . . . well, I suppose that'll be all right," she says.

I give her the number.

"That's one hundred raffle tickets at two dollars each, for a total of two hundred dollars.

Thank you so much, Chanel—and be sure to thank your mother for us!"

"I'll do that, Mrs. Goodge," I say.

Yeah, right. Sure I will. That would not be a smart thing to do, now, would it? I hang up, feeling guilty but excited. I'm sure to win the Prada bags, with odds like these. A hundred tickets! How can I miss?

I flop back on the bed and flip through my Oophelia's catalog once again, even though I know every page by heart. How can I pass up these lime green suede boots? I wonder. . . .

My mom is gonna kill me. Well, at the rate the group is growing, the Cheetah Girls will probably be rich soon, so I can pay my mom back then, I tell myself. I pick up the phone and punch in a number, and I hear my own voice ordering the lime green suede boots from the Oophelia's catalog operator.

Then I spot something else I just have to have. Ooh, this rug is so cute. It has a big *mono*, monkey face on it. I love monkeys! Ooh, it has a matching blue stool with a *mono* on it, too! I guess it won't hurt if I order just one more thing. Mom won't mind, I tell myself. She knows my old daisy area rug has seen better days. It looks like someone has tiptoed through the tulips on it.

Mom *did* say not to use her credit card, but I don't think she will mind, since it's something for my room. At least that's what I tell myself. And if she does mind, too bad. I deserve a new rug, and the stool matches, so I just have to get that, too.

I am so good at making my voice sound grown-up, the operator never asks me anything. The stool is $156, and the rug is $38. Mono better do some tricks with a banana for this kinda money, I think, giggling to myself as I place the order. "Does it come in any other color?" I ask.

"No, just blue with the red monkey design," the operator replies.

The stool is real leather, not pleather, so I decide to go for it. But I have to have the cheetah picture frame, too, I suddenly realize. I *need* a new frame for my Confirmation picture sitting on the dresser. It is my favorite picture, not counting the one of me at my sixth-birthday party, standing with the piñata that I busted open all by myself. In it, I am making a face because I got a terrible stomachache after I ate everything that fell out of the piñata.

In the Confirmation picture, I'm wearing the holy red robe for the ceremony. This is the color that symbolizes the fire of the Holy Spirit. Abuela has her arm around me and she is smiling. My silver cross is draped across the picture frame, which is supposed to be silver, but it has changed colors and looks old. My mom picked it out. I wonder if she knew it was fake silver. Surely she'd want me to have a better one if she knew. A picture like this one deserves the best frame there is!

So I order it, along with everything else. I'm feeling dizzy from my little shopping spree—dizzy and happy, and a little bit scared. What if my mom finds out before I get enough money to pay her back?

Well, she won't, that's all, I tell myself. I'll just make sure she doesn't. I quickly shut my math notebook and put it away.

"Will that be all, ma'am?" the operator asks. Just as I'm about to say yes, I realize that I really need a new outfit to go to the recording studio, so I make the operator wait until I pick one out of the catalog. She adds it to the total, and when she reads me back a list of what I've bought, I almost chicken out, it's so much money.

But then, I think to myself, Why should I care if Mom gets mad? She's always mad at me anyway. No matter what I do, it's wrong—"Don't talk with that witch Pamela! Don't take the Cheetah Girls too seriously! Don't do this, don't do that . . ." Well, too bad for her. I'll do what I want.

"Yes, that will be fine," I tell the operator.

That's what you get, *Mamí*, for trying to control every move I make!

I have just hung up, when Pucci comes into my room without even knocking. "Get out, Pucci!" I yell at him. I hate when he does that. We aren't little anymore, you know? "What do I have to do to get rid of you?" I blurt out.

"Get me a dog. I want a dog!" Pucci giggles. "How come we can't have a dog?"

"You know *Mamí* isn't gonna let us have a dog, Pucci. Why are you bothering me?"

And then it hits me. Why *can't* Pucci have a dog? *I* want one, too. Nothing against Snuggly-Wiggly Pooch, but a real dog would be *la dopa*! Mom's always complaining how allergic she is, but there must be some kind of dog that doesn't shed. Why can't we get one of those? Yeah . . .

now, there's a great idea! Right away, I start to cook up how to get us a real-live dog.

Meanwhile, I don't feel like doing my ballet exercises, but I know I've got to, to help keep my body strong. Changing into my pink leotard, I groan to myself. All this shopping is exhausting, but hey—a Cheetah Girl's day is never done!

Chapter 5

These days, the Cheetah Girls are really living *la vida loca*—the crazy life. Rehearsals, school, homework, and, for me, fighting with my mom, and spending secret nights on the Psychic Hot Line with Princess Pamela, or shopping on the phone and ordering from Oophelia's catalog.

Thank goodness, history class is the last of the day. At four o'clock, we have to meet Mr. Johnson at Snare-a-Hare Recording Studios in Times Square. He has arranged for us to have a recording session with this Big Willy producer, Pumpmaster Pooch.

We did find out about Pumpmaster's "credits." He did the rap remix for the Sista Fudge single, "I'll Slice You Like a Pound Cake." That's something, huh? That song is one of Princess Pamela's favorites. It makes her giggle and makes me wiggle.

Speaking of Princess Pamela, I've been running up the phone bill calling her 900 number. I've been getting some pretty strange advice, too—she's been telling me to watch out for animals. I wonder what she means by that. . . .

Maybe I should forget about the dog I've been planning to get Pucci. Or maybe it's the Cheetahs I ought to stay away from. No, that can't be. Maybe Princess Pamela is off the mark this time. After all, she doesn't know who she's talking to. I've been disguising my voice, so maybe that's throwing off her predictions. Still, it's been bothering me, and I just can't figure it out.

I almost asked Princess Pamela about it yesterday, when I gave her the management agreement to pass on to my dad. But that would have been giving myself away, and I didn't want it getting back to my dad that I'd been running up the phone bill to get advice I could have gotten for free!

I also wanted to tell Princess Pamela about

all the money I've been spending, and get her advice on that, too—but I knew it would make Mom mad if she found out I'd been asking Princess Pamela for advice, let alone that I'd been using her credit card and running up her phone bill!

"How much did Mr. Johnson say it costs for an hour at the recording studio?" Do' Re Mi asks, bringing me back to reality. We are at our lockers after school, getting ready to go over to the studio for our recording session.

"The studio? It costs a lot, but we don't have to pay for it," I answer.

Me, Bubbles, and Do' Re Mi are looking *muy caliente* today—hot, hot, hot! We're all wearing matching red velvet jeans and crushed velvet leopard T-shirts from Oophelia's. Bubbles's mom paid for hers. I bought mine and Do' Re Mi's on my mom's credit card (surprise, surprise).

"Chuchie, you are lost in your own soap opera channel. What's the matter, *mamacita*, Snuggly-Wiggly Pooch ate your homework?" Bubbles chides me, putting her arm around my shoulders. "What's wrong? You're not giggling, and that's kinda like Toto not begging for food. Ya know what I mean, prom queen?"

I poke Bubbles in the side, because Derek Hambone and Mackerel Johnson are standing by their lockers across the hall. "Duckets in the bucket alert!" I whisper in Bubbles's ear.

Like the Road Runner, Bubbles makes a beeline to hit up the dynamic duo, and make them buy Kats and Kittys raffle tickets.

"Hit 'em up, Galleria!" Do' Re Mi says, egging Bubbles on.

Derek is this new "brotha from Detroit," as he calls himself, and the word is, he comes from a family that owns the biggest widget factory in the East—*mucho dinero, mamacita*!

"Derek, my Batman with a plan. Buy a raffle ticket for me and part with two dollars for a good cause. You, too, Mackerel. Come on, I'll let you two touch my vest—it's national velvet. Feel the pile!" Bubbles urges them.

"Awright," Derek says, reaching for the ticket, but then he looks at it, reads about the Prada prize, and says, "Cheetah Girl, you expect me to get jiggy in the jungle with a *Prada* bag? I'm not going out like that."

"Oh, come on, *schemo*, you ain't gonna win the raffle, anyway, just part with the two duckets!" Bubbles says, pouting. Derek is such a *pobrecito*—a real dummy. He doesn't even know Bubbles is calling him a dodo bird in Italian. I *know* Derek isn't going to win, because I *better* win. No one else deserves that Prada bag more than I do! "*Prada or nada*" is the motto I live and die by.

"Awright, I'm gonna let you hit me up this time, Cheetah Girl, Derek says, like he is a loan officer at Banco Popular, "but you owe me *big-time* for this one." Reaching into his baggy jeans, I wonder if Derek is ever gonna find the bottom of his deep, baggy pockets. I wonder how the "Red Snapper" is gonna get his money off the hook.

See, Derek likes Bubbles—and he's always snapping at her bait—that's why we nick-named him "Red Snapper"—and also because his best friend is Mackerel Johnson. Derek is the only one of his posse who is large enough to become a member of the Kats and Kittys Klub, though. It costs $650 a year.

Mackerel smiles at me while he's bouncing to some tune in his peanut-sized head. He is so hyper, he looks like a Chihuahua bobbing his head up and down.

Oh, snapples, that's what I could get Pucci! "My mom can't say *nada* about a Chihuahua—they are so little, who could be allergic to them?

Meanwhile, Bubbles is still closing the deal. "Thank you, *schemo*," she smirks to Derek and Mackerel, stuffing their duckets into her chubby Cheetah wallet.

"Shame on you, too, Cheetah Girl. Just be ready when it's time to collect, awright?" Derek says, winking. Then he walks away with Mackerel.

"You got one of them dog books from the library, right?" I say to Do' Re Mi. I'm on a bowwow mission now.

"Yeah, why?" Do' Re Mi replies.

"Look up the breed Chihuahua and see if they shed hair."

"Word. Wait, they ain't got any hair," Do' Re Mi counters. She is so smart. The most book-smart of all of us.

"Look it up anyway," I giggle. "I think Miss Cuchifrita just got lucky. See, if Chihuahuas don't shed, then I can buy Pucci one for his birthday!"

"If you buy Pucci a dog, *you're* gonna end up at the dog pound for sure," Bubbles quips to me.

"And where you gonna get that kinda money?"

"It's three o'clock, y'all!" Do' Re Mi says, setting off down the hallway in her size zero velvet jeans. "We better get over to the studio, and start gettin' down!"

"Oh, snapples, I forgot to get the agreement back from Princess Pamela," I sigh to Bubbles.

"What's she doing with it?" Bubbles asks me, like she's saying, "Don't play with fire."

"I gave it to her so she could give it to my dad," I said. "I didn't have time to go all the way uptown, baby, okay? My mom is watching me like a hawk when she isn't doing her exotic dancing!"

"Mr. Johnson won't mind if you don't have the agreement. Just tell him we'll bring it to him the next time," Bubbles says, grabbing my arm and pulling me along. "Come on, *señorita*. We've got some singin' to do!"

Recording studios have more gadgets on the control board than I've ever seen in my life. "They got so many buttons, how do they know which ones to push?" I exclaim to Do' Re Mi, who is *muy fascinado* with anything *electrónico* or *en la Web*.

"That's why he's making the duckets," Bubbles smirks to the engineer, who is sitting at the board with headphones on.

Bubbles's mom, Dorothea, has come with us to the studio, but the twins haven't arrived yet.

"This is Kew, the engineer," Mr. Johnson says, introducing us as the Cheetah Girls. No matter how many times I hear our group's name, it sounds like *la música* to my ears. I love it!

"Mr. Johnson, can I speak to you for a minute?" Dorothea says. The two grown-ups go into another room—so they can talk business, I'm sure. Dorothea is all about the "Benjamins" and she doesn't play. She looks *la dopa* today, too. She is wearing a big leopard hat, and leopard boots that make her look taller than "The Return of the Fifty-Foot Woman"—even though she is only six feet tall. I wish *I* was that tall.

At last, the huggy bear twins have arrived!

"You know the Cheetah Girls rule: don't be late or we'll gaspitate!" Bubbles says, warning the twins as they hurriedly throw their cheetah backpacks on an empty chair in the studio.

"Dag on, y'all, just when we think we know how to get somewhere, they change the subway line on us!" Aqua laments, fixing her pin curl in place. Aquanette and Anginette still haven't learned their way around the Big Apple yet.

"You're 'Westies' now like me, so you'd better get with the IRT program," Do' Re Mi grunts. She lives on 116th, on the Upper West Side, and last summer, the twins moved from sunny Houston to 96th Street and Riverside Drive.

Like mine, their parents are "dee-vorced" (as Angie says in her Southern drawl), and the twins live with their dad. He must be kinda cool, 'cuz he pays for them to go to the beauty parlor twice a month to get their hair *and* nails done. I think they should pay me instead because I would give them *la dopa* hairstyles instead of the "shellac attack" curls they like so much. Sometimes less is more!

Today, the twins are wearing makeup, so they look kinda cute. Aqua and Angie are *café sin leche* color, and they love that white frost lipstick on their big, juicy lips. They are screaming for a Miss Wiggy! virtual makeover.

Mr. Johnson and Dorothea come back into the room. His beeper goes off, and he looks at it nervously. "I got a situation I gotta take care of," he says. "That is Mr. Hyena—I told you about him—he is the Big Willy at Hyena Records. Mrs. Garibaldi, Kew will look after you. And Pooch will get with you girls when he gets through," Mr. Johnson adds chuckling, never too nervous to get a rhyme out.

Pumpmaster Pooch is in the other room on his cell phone. We can see him through the big glass partition. He waves at us with his five-carat fingers. I mean, he is wearing enough gold rings to start a gold mine. Kew is busy fiddling with the keyboard, so the five of us sit and watch the music videos on MTV, which are playing on one of the monitors over our heads.

"*Ay, Dios mío,* Krusher's latest music video!" I whisper.

Dorothea goes into the room with Pumpmaster Pooch, so we relax a little. I feel so nervous!

"Krusher's got it going on," Do' Re Mi says, looking up at the monitor and grooving to Krusher's new single, "My Way or the Highway."

"Look at Chanel getting all goo-goo-eyed!" Do' Re Mi says.

"I'm saving my first kiss for him," I giggle to my crew.

"You better hope it ain't the first 'dis!'" Do' Re Mi sighs.

"Oh, *cállate la boca, Mamacita*. Be quiet." I sigh, then hum aloud, "*Yo tengo un coco* on Crusher."

"What's that mean?" Do' Re Mi asks, smirking and squinting her eyes.

"Look it up!" I heckle. "I'm just playing with you, Dor-r-r-inda, *Mamí*," I say rolling my Rs like I'm on a choo-choo train. "You won't find it in *el diccionario*. It means I have a crush on Krusher."

"Coco is cuckoo for Krusher," Bubbles heckles, making a play on my middle name.

"Watch out, Chuchie, this may be your last dance, last chance," Bubbles says, pointing her finger excitedly at the monitor.

The Krusher music video has ended, and now there is a commercial for a Krusher contest. "Are you the lucky girl who will win an all-expenses-paid date with R&B's hottest singer, and spend two fun-filled days and nights with Krusher in sunny Miami? What are you waiting for? Call 900-KRUSHER right now!"

"*Ay, Dios mío*! I'm gonna enter," I squeal, jumping up and down.

"Okay, Cuckoo Coco, get over it, because here comes the man," whispers Do' Re Mi, secretly pointing to Pooch, who is on the move toward us.

"Ladies, ladies, I'm sorry to keep you waiting," Pumpmaster Pooch says, rushing into the engineer's booth. He has on dark sunglasses and a hat, and a black windbreaker. I can tell he thinks he's kinda *chulo*, kind of cute, too.

"Now, I got a song you are gonna love. I've picked out some material for you—the type of songs that will get you a record deal, so just trust me on this," he says, talking with his five-carat hands the whole time. "Okay, let's do this."

Pooch tells Kew what tracks to put on, then takes us to the recording booth. The five of us stand in front of the microphones and put headphones on our heads. "We're gonna practice it a bit, then take it from the top when we're ready," Pooch says.

"Where are the musicians?" Angie asks, like she's been in a recording studio before.

"We're just gonna lay down some lead vocals

over the tracks first so you can get the hang of the song, ya dig?" Pumpmaster says, looking at Bubbles mostly, and the twins. The twins have been singing in church choirs since they're nine, so they always seem like they know what they're doing. "Then we lay down the background vocals and arrangements later. That's my job. We ready, Cheetah Girls?" Pumpmaster Pooch says, flashing a grin.

"We're ready!" we say together. I am so excited—I cannot believe that we, the Cheetah Girls, are already in the studio, recording. Okay, it's just a song for a demo, but you know what I mean, jelly bean.

"'I Got a Thing for Thugs'?" Bubbles says, scrunching up her nose as we read the lyrics off the sheet music that Pooch has handed out to us. "That sounds radickio!"

"Bubbles, let's just listen to them, okay?" I say, trying to calm her down because I know we are lucky to be here in the studio and not paying for it.

But after we finish rehearsing the same song fifty thousand times, we are so tired I never want to hear that song again. Bubbles is right. The song is *la wacka*! Bubbles looks like she is about to explode. I guess she thought we would be doing one of *her* songs.

Mr. Johnson, who has returned, comes in and congratulates us. "Ladies, you did a wonderful job. Now the car service is gonna come and take all of you right to your door."

"That song was wack-a-doodle," Bubbles says, pouting, when we are finally in the car with Dorothea. "It just wasn't *us*."

"Maybe once we do some of their songs, they'll let us record some of yours," I explain to Bubbles. She is *caliente* mad.

"What did you think, Mom?" Bubbles says, putting her head on Dorothea's shoulder.

"There is something about that Mr. Johnson that I don't like," Dorothea says, then leans back into the car seat. "I told him that I have to have the agreement looked over by a lawyer first, and that made him kind of nervous. If anything isn't right with that agreement, I'm gonna be so shady to Mr. Jackal Johnson the sun is gonna go down on him!"

Yawning, I put my head on Dorothea's other shoulder, and sigh. "Bubbles, you're right—that song *was* wack-a-doodle!" We giggle, then get real quiet for the rest of the way home.

I can't wait to get home and call 900-KRUSH-ER. I'm gonna call a hundred times if I have to, because I'm going win that date with Krusher and make my dreams come true.

That's what me and Bubbles always said when we were little. We would follow the yellow brick road no matter where it led us. Well, Miami, here I come!

Chapter 6

It's time for me to head uptown to Drinka Champagne's Conservatory. All five of us are now taking vocal lessons and dance classes there. Aqua and Angie don't need it, because they go to Laguardia Performing Arts High School and they get *la dopa* training all week, but it helps us to sing better together as a group. We also practice songs that Bubbles wrote—"Wanna-be Stars in the Jiggy Jungle" and "Welcome to the Glitterdome"—just in case Mr. Johnson and Pumpmaster Pooch decide to let us record them for our demo. Hey, you never know!

If I don't leave now, I'm gonna be late. Class starts at eleven o'clock, and Drinka does not play. If you walk in one minute late, she will stop everything and read you like *La Prensa*, our local Spanish newspaper, right in front of *everybody*. Now I'm mad at myself because I wanted to get to class early today, so I could show Drinka and the Cheetah Girls how much work I'm doing on my breathing exercises.

I spritz on my favorite perfume—Fetch, by Yves Saint Bernard (Princess Pamela bought it for my thirteenth birthday last year). I also spritz some Breath-So-Fresh spray in my throat. It makes me feel better, even though Bubbles says buying that stuff its like throwing "duckets down the drain."

I'm the one with the sensitive vocal chords, so I have to try whatever I can. Bubbles has a throat like the Tin Man. She can eat a plate of *arroz con pollo* with a bottle of hot sauce, sing for three hours straight, then still be able to blab her mouth on the phone till the break of dawn!

I look at the clock again. Hmmm. Maybe I can get one more call in to 900-KRUSHER before I go. I pick up my red princess phone, and start sweating as soon as I hear Krusher cooing in the background of the taped recording. I *have* to win this contest. My *corazón* would be broken if some other girl gets a date in Miami with my *papí chulo*, my sugar daddy. No—I can't think like this, or I will faint for real.

I listen to the recorded message for the tenth time in a row. The instructions are simple: you have to tell, in your own words, why you think you should win the date with Krusher.

I have a *buen* idea! I'll *sing* to Krusher on the phone. One of the Cheetah Girls songs! I betcha none of the other *mamacitas* calling could do that. It'll be my ace to first base.

"Hi, it's Chanel Simmons *again*," I say, giggling into the phone. Then I get kinda nervous. "I think I should win the Krusher contest because I know all the words to every song you've ever done. Right now, I'm gonna sing you one of the songs from my own group, the Cheetah Girls. . . . "

My *gran fantasía* is fumbled, though, because all of a sudden, I hear my mother hang up the phone in the hallway and scream my name really loud. "CHANEL! Get out here! *Apúrate!*" I almost faint for real, and I get a knot in my stomach like when I know I'm in *trouble*.

"*Ay dios, por favor, ayúdame*—oh God, please

help me!" I say, doing the trinity sign across my chest, then kissing my Confirmation picture. I look really hard at Abuela's smiling face.

"Chanel, you better get out here!" Mom yells again.

Taking a deep breath, I walk out of my bedroom. My knees are shaking more than the Tin Man's in *The Wizard of Oz*.

If looks could kill, I would be dead, judging by the pained expression on my mother's face. Her dark brown eyes are breathing fire. She is wearing black leotards and tights, and she is sweating because she has been exercising.

"That was the credit card company on the phone. They were calling me because of the excessive charges made on *my* credit card. But I don't have to tell *you* who's been making them, do I?" Mom challenges me.

"No, *Mamí*," I whimper. I know I am *finito*. It is time for my last rites, and I wish Father Nuñez was here to read them.

"Why did you do it, when I told you not to?" Mom screams. "I give you an inch, and you take a mile. *Por qué*, Chanel? Why? *Por qué?*"

I start crying. I feel like such an idiot for thinking I could get away with charging all that stuff on my mom's credit card. "I don't know why I did it," I stutter. "I was just mad at you."

"*You* were mad at *me*?" she says, turning up the volume another notch. "Are you kidding me? I give you my credit card—I trust you—and you're mad at me?"

"You won't let me be close to Pamela," I complain, letting it all hang out. I figure at this point, *que sera, sera,* as they say in the old movie. What will be, will be. "She's not a *bruja,* like you always call her. She's nice. She's nicer to me than you!" I'm really crying now, and so is my mom. I don't know who is angrier at who.

"Oh, yeah? Maybe you'd like her for a mother instead of me?" she says, half sobbing. "I let you buy a new outfit, and this is how you repay me?"

"At least Pamela wouldn't complain about me being in the Cheetah Girls!" I say, really letting the hot sauce fly. "You don't want me to go after my dreams—you only want me to give up on them, like you did!" Years ago, Mom gave up on being a model when she got to "a certain age." I know what I'm saying is unfair and mean, but I'm so mad now that I just can't stop myself.

"I want you to get out of my face until I talk to your father about this, but don't think for one second you're gonna get away with it!" Mom screams. "You can forget about all your stupid Cheetah Girls, too. *Tu entiendes?* You understand?"

No way. She can't do that! The Cheetah Girls is all I care about besides Abuela and my dad and Princess Pamela and Pucci and *arroz con pollo* and Prada! The Cheetah Girls and my dreams to travel all over the world are my whole life! Without them, I have *nada*. *La odia mi mami!* I hate my mother.

"I have to go to Drin-ka-ka Conservatory," I say, so nervous I can't even get the words out. "I promised everyone I'd be there."

"All right. You can go to this one last class," she says. "But you come right back afterward and wait for me here. *Entiendes?*"

"Sí," I whimper, then grab my jacket and run out the door.

After vocal class, I am slobbering like a baby to my crew.

Bubbles is so mad at me, she won't even talk to me. "You have broken a sacred rule of the

Cheetah Girls, Chuchie, and I am so disgusted with you, I cannot even look at you," she yells in front of Angie, Aqua, and Do' Re Mi.

I do not know what sacred rule Bubbles is talking about, but I am sure she will tell me, and anyway, I'm too afraid to ask. Drinka, who runs the conservatory, has left us alone in the rehearsal space, because big mouth Bubbles has told her what happened. We are sitting on the hardwood floor in a circle.

"How come you didn't tell me what you were doing with that credit card, Chuchie? You were always so sneaky-deaky, even when we were little!" Bubbles blurts out. She won't stop.

"Is your mother really gonna make you leave the group?" Do' Re Mi asks me, looking worried and scared.

"I don't know. That's what she says!" I cry. I am so scared of going home. I want Bubbles to help me. She's always helped me when I get in trouble, ever since we were little.

"I have no idea why Aunt Juanita wants you to be a buyer. You would end up wearing all the clothes yourself! Like I said before, you're a shopaholic waiting to happen!" Bubbles yells at me.

"Dag, now you've *really* given your mother a good reason not to let you stay in the group," Angie clucks, looking down at her skirt, then pulling it past her knees.

"Yeah, and now she's gonna say that *we* are a bad influence on you. You better let her know we didn't have anything to do with this—and you can take back all those clothes you bought me. I don't want them!" Do' Re Mi yells at me. Her eyes are watering.

Dorinda is a big crybaby. I know because she calls me on the phone and tells me secrets that Bubbles doesn't even know about. Like the stuff about her first foster mother, who was really mean to her and gave Dorinda up, but kept her sister. That's how she got put in Mrs. Bosco's house when she was almost five years old.

"Chuchie, the Cheetah Girls are all we have," Bubbles says. "We are not like some other stupid group. We don't just sing. We are more than just some singing group, okay?" She waves her hand at me, rolls her eyes, and pulls out her cell phone. "Let me call my mom at her shop. Auntie Juanita will be there, too, Chuchie, and my mom will know what to do."

I cover my face with my hands. I just want this bad dream to go away. Everybody is real quiet while Bubbles talks to her mom on the phone.

"Keep Juanita there, Mom. *Please* help us. Think of something!" Bubbles pleads to my *madrina* on the phone.

She listens for a minute, then says to me, "Mom says get your compact out and powder your nose." I know that this is *madrina*'s way of saying "sit tight and get ready for Freddy, 'cuz anything could go down."

"Juanita is still in the store screaming, so Mom is gonna call me back," Bubbles explains to all of us. "She's gonna calm Juanita down and think of what to do. And you know my mom can think on her feet, even if she's wearing shoes with ten-inch heels that are too tight," she adds, flossing.

"I know that's right," quips Aqua.

Dorothea is no joke. She can wheel and deal and, hopefully, she will save me from being the subject of a missing person's report.

"You're gonna pay for this one, Chuchie. In full," Bubbles says, putting away the cell phone. "Your mom is *caliente* mad!"

Angie hands me a pack of tissues out of her backpack. I take one and hand it back to her. "No, keep the whole thing, 'cuz you're gonna need 'em by the time your mother gets through with you," Angie clucks, then unzips her backpack and takes out a sandwich. "I'm sorry, y'all, but I'm hungry. We didn't have time to eat breakfast."

"I hope you're burning a good-luck money candle, Chuchie, because you're going to need all the luck you can get," Bubbles says, rolling her eyes at me. "Even though those candles look like a bunch of green wax to me, I don't see any duckets dropping from the sky to save you right now!"

It's a good thing Bubbles's cell phone rings, because I want to crown her like a queen for being so mean to me. Bubbles pulls up the phone antenna and hops on her Miss Wiggy StarWac Phone like it is a Batphone or something. Then she says, "Hmm, hmm," all serious—at least ten times, and keeps us waiting in suspense like a soap opera. My godmother is obviously giving her the *super ataque,* the blow-by-blow report.

When Bubbles hangs up, she lets out a sigh.

"You are so lucky, Chuchie," she says, pulling one of my braids. Then she gives us a blow-by-blow of the soap opera that is filming at Toto in New York . . . Fun in Diva Sizes, *madrina*'s boutique in Soho.

"Chuchie, your mom came into the store screaming so loud that Toto ran into the dressing room and scared a poor customer who was getting undressed," Bubbles explains.

The twins laugh, but I don't. Neither do Bubbles nor Dorinda. "We have to go to the boutique right now. *All* of us," Galleria says.

We all look at each other and swallow hard. It's high noon. Time for the big showdown. Ready or not, here we come!

Chapter 7

Dorothea is yelling at a man outside the boutique when we get there. Toto in New York . . . Fun in Diva Sizes is a *muy famoso* boutique, and many famous divas shop there, including Jellybean Nyce, the Divas, Sista Fudge, Queen Latifah, and even Starbaby, the newscaster who wears so much gold you have to wear sunglasses when you watch her on television. Dorothea does not play hide-and-seek with all the riffraff that comes to Soho looking to pickpocket all the tourists.

"You see what the sign says? It says, 'Toto in New York . . . Fun In Diva Sizes,'" Dorothea says with her hands on her hips, drilling the man, whose clothes look rumpled and crumpled. "This is a clothing store, not a toothless-men-who-love-big-women dating service, so get outta here!"

The man grins at Dorothea, then smacks his lips like he hasn't eaten *lonchando*. Then he hobbles away with his bottle in his hand, babbling like a parrot.

"He doesn't have any teeth," I mumble to Bubbles.

Because the door of the store is wide open, Toto comes running out. He is probably still afraid because of all the commotion. He looks so cute and fierce in the little cheetah-print suit Bubbles made for him, and he's as fierce as a cheetah, too! He jumps on the back of the legs of the man who has never had a visit from a tooth fairy.

"Toto, come here! Don't go running after him like he has treats for you!" Bubbles yells, then grabs Toto and carries him back inside the store, rubbing his stomach. Toto likes to get attention from anybody.

"Hi, Toto," I say, giving him a rub, too. I love him so much. I guess I'll never get a dog of my own now, though. . . .

"Dag, it must be hard having a store in New York, because there are a lot of crazy people here," Angie says.

There are a lot of people in New York who are cuckoo, but maybe not as "loco as Coco," I think, feeling sorry for myself. I climb up the stairs and inside the store, like a prisoner going to the electric chair. There is my mom, sitting on a stool with her arms crossed in front of her, and her eyes shooting bullets at me.

Luckily, my *madrina* takes over the situation, as usual, as soon as I get inside. "Chanel, I'm going to lay out the situation for you like the latest design collection. Juanita doesn't want you to be in the group anymore. And in many ways I don't think you deserve to be," my *madrina* says.

Now both my mom *and* my *madrina*, who I love so much, are ganging up on me! I haven't eaten anything all day, and I feel really dizzy, but I don't say anything. I just stand there.

Dorothea, wearing a dalmatian-dotted caftan, has her hands on her hips and is looking at my mom but standing over me, which makes me feel smaller than Dorinda. I know I'm not going to be a Cheetah Girl anymore. I'm so sad, I burst into tears.

"Now, I don't think that making you leave the group is going to teach you anything,

Chanel, and I know how much this means to Galleria, so we've worked out a solution," Dorothea continues. "You are going to work part-time in my store and pay back every penny you charged up on Juanita's cards, even if it takes you till you're a very old Cheetah Girl!"

Gracias, Dios! I say to myself. Thank goodness! My prayers have been answered! I don't have to leave the Cheetah Girls after all!

"Thank you, Dorothea! Thank you, *Mamí*!" I gush, the tears streaming down my face. "I will pay back all the money, *te juro*—I swear! And thank you s-o-o-o much for letting me stay in the group!"

All the other girls let out a shout of sheer relief, and hug me tight. But a word from my *madrina* makes them quiet down.

"We're not finished with you yet, *señorita*," Dorothea says, looking at me and getting more serious. "You know, Chanel, we all love to shop. It's fun, but it is not something you do when you are unhappy, or mad at someone, or looking for *love*, or for approval from kids in school. Love you get from your family, your friends—your mom—not Oophelia's catalog. If you are shopping with money you don't have—whether you are a child or a grown-up—then you have a problem, and you've got to own up to it, and change your ways."

Even though I don't say anything, I nod my head so Dorothea and my mom know that I understand.

"Mom, I like that," Bubbles says all excitedly, then whips out her notebook.

"Like what, darling?" Dorothea says, not at all amused.

"What you said about shopping for love. I'm going to write a song about this!"

"That's nice, darling, just don't act like you're large and in charge with *my* credit card."

"Yes, Mom," Bubbles says meekly.

"Mrs. Simmons, I wanna give back the outfit Chanel bought me. Is that okay?" Do' Re Mi asks quietly.

"No, Dorinda, you keep that. Chanel is gonna pay for it, so you might as well wear it," Mom says.

Nobody is stupider than I am, I think to myself. Why couldn't I be smart like Bubbles, or Dorinda? "When do I start working?" I ask.

"There's no time like the present," Dorothea

quips, then looks at Bubbles and the rest of our crew.

"I got a Spanish quiz tomorrow, so I'd better study," Bubbles says, then picks up Toto and gives him a kiss on his nose. "Bye, Boo-boo—you be a good boy, and help Mom chase away all the bozos!"

"Knowing Toto, I'm surprised he didn't ask that man for a sip of wine from that bottle he was carrying!" Dorothea says, opening up the cash register.

Do' Re Mi picks up her backpack and puts it on her munchkin shoulders, saying, "Guess he's just tippin' when he's not sippin'!" She is making a joke on the Drinka Champagne's disco song from back in the day. I can see we're all feeling a lot better—most of all, me! Good old Dorothea—she is the best!

"It's gonna be all right," she tells my mom. "Don't write Miss Cuchifrita off yet. She isn't crazy, just lazy, but she'll learn that duckets don't drop from the sky. Trust me."

They both laugh. It's the first time I've seen Mom smile since we got here. But then, Dorothea could make anybody laugh. She is *tan coolio*.

"Come here, baby," my mom says. I do, and she throws her arms around me. I hug her tight. "You know I love you so much. I've just got to be able to trust you, that's all."

"You can, *Mamí,*" I tell her, meaning it with all my heart. "I'm gonna play it straight with you from now on." I hug her back, really tight. "And thanks for letting me stay in the Cheetah Girls."

"I know how much it means to you, baby," she tells me, as Dorothea and my crew look on, smiling. "After all, I've had dreams, too."

She and Dorothea smile at one another, and just for a second, I can imagine them when they were our age. Young, full of dreams, and chasing *la gran fantasía*.

"I love you, too, *Mamí,*" I whisper, smiling and crying at the same time. "And from now on, you can trust me one hundred percent!"

"That's my Miss Cuchifrita!" Dorothea says, smiling. And we all share a laugh together.

Chapter 8

Mr. Johnson called us with good news this morning. Not only has he booked us, the Cheetah Girls, for the Amateur Hour contest at the world-famous Apollo Theatre on 125th Street, but he has talked Hal Hyena, the president of Hyena Records, into coming to see us perform!

"He says he called in a favor—'cuz we got the flava!" Bubbles types to me on the computer screen.

The Phat Planet chat room on the Internet has become my hangout, because, as Pucci so loudly announces to everybody, "*Loco Coco* is grounded!" But Aqua's idea about forming the Cheetah Girls Council and having meetings sure comes in "handy dandy" for a grounded *señorita* like myself.

I only get to go out to go to school, to work at Dorothea's boutique, and take classes at Drinka's. So, of course, our meetings have to be on-line, but that's okay. They really help.

I am not sad anymore about what happened, because I've learned a good lesson. I'm only sorry that I caused everybody so much trouble. I like working at the store, of course, because I love Dorothea. And slowly but surely, I'm paying back the money I owe my mom. Of course, at the rate I'm going, it's gonna take me about a year, but like they say, I made my bed, now I've gotta lie down in it.

"Loco Coco is grounded, *Papí*!" I can hear Pucci on the phone with my dad in the kitchen, which is way down the hall from my bedroom.

I'm finally going to see my dad tonight, and I'm going to tell him everything. I know he must have heard the whole story by now, though, and I'm sure I'm going to get yelled at big-time.

"Do me a flava. Who's gonna come with me to see my dad?" I type on the screen.

"I want y'all to hear the lyrics I wrote for this

song," Bubbles types, ignoring my request. "Guess what the title is?"

"'You Think You Large 'Cuz You Charge'?" Do' Re Mi snaps.

"Cute, but no loot, Do' Re Mi! Anybody else want to take a crack at my new song attack?"

I have a title idea, so I type it in: "'Chanel Ain't So Swell'?"

"That was true when you broke one of our sacred commandments, but now it isn't, because you're working for the 'Benjamins.' Give up yet?"

"What's the sacred commandment, anyway?" Do' Re Mi types.

At least somebody had the nerve to ask.

"Um, let's see," Bubbles types in. I can just see her making up a snap on her feet. "'You can only do so much fibbing to your friends who've seen you in your spotted pj's before you're so far backed up in a corner, you come out boxing like a cuckoo kangaroo'? How's that?"

"Galleria, you're a mess!!!!" Angie types in. "But that is the truth you're preaching, because the Lord don't like lies."

"Or flies!" Do' Re Mi types in.

Oh, just what I need—for the gospel hour to begin. When Aqua and Angie get started, you never know when it's going to end.

Bubbles isn't having it, though. "Okay, back to name that tune? Y'all give up yet?"

"Yes!" we all type one by one.

"It's called, 'Shop in the Name of Love,'" Bubbles types.

Leave it to Bubbles. Nobody is better with words than she is.

"Come on, Bubbles, let's see the Cheetah-licious lyrics!"

"Not now, brown cows. I want Mr. Johnson to hear it first when we go to the studio again. Maybe he and Pumpmaster Pooch will let us record it for our demo tape!"

"What time do we have to be at the studio?" Do' Re Mi asks. "Mrs. Bosco has got to go down to the agency with Twinkie, another one of her foster kids, so I'm on baby-sitting duty."

"We have to be there by ten o'clock," Angie responds.

Basta. Enough. I need help here, and nobody's paying any attention. "Listen, I feel like a *holograma* because no one is answering me! I have to go my dad's store tonight—who's gonna come with me?" I type, hoping Bubbles will take the steak bait. She loves my dad's Shake-a-Steak sandwich.

"We'll go with you," Angie types.

"I'll come, too, but I gotta drop Toto off to Dr. Bowser, the doggie dentist, first," Bubbles types.

"Maybe if you didn't give him so much Double Dutch Rocco Choco ice cream he wouldn't have to go to the dentist," I type. I mean, Toto eats too many treats.

"I'm gonna let you slide the read ride this time, Chuchie, since you are seriously grounded, but we'll be there to back you up," says Bubbles.

"*Está bien!*" I type back. That's my crew for you. Always down for the 'do. And not just hairdos either.

We are really pouting on the way to my dad's store. It's a good thing we've still got Amateur Hour at the Apollo Theatre coming up, because our session at the studio did not go well at all. If the song Pumpmaster Pooch and Mr. Johnson had us singing the first time was *la wacka*, you had to hear the one he gave us the second time around.

"It was called 'Can I Get a Burp?'" Bubbles

moaned as soon as she read the title. "What are we now, cows? she asked. "I don't think these guys get our image, and I'm not going out like that. Did you hear how they responded to my 'Shop in the Name of Love' lyrics?"

"Word, I noticed it. When you showed him the song, he looked at you like you were a stray dog or something," Do' Re Mi says.

"Let's sing some of it together before we go in to Killer Tacos, yo?" Bubbles says, looking at us.

"We're always down for the singing swirl, Bubbles!" Do' Re Mi says, leading us on as we start to sing "Shop in the Name of Love."

"Honey may come from bees
but money don't grow on trees.
When you shop in the name of love
you gotta ask yourself
What are you dreamin' of?
What are you schemin' of?
What are you trippin' on, love?"

By the time we get to the refrain, we are on 96th Street and Broadway, two steps from my dad's store. Then we do the cute "call and response" refrain that comes at the end of the song. We're groovin' from all the people watching us sing.

"Polo or solo.
Say what?
I want Gucci or Pucci.
Say what?
It's Prada or nada.
Yeah—you got that?
Uh-huh, I got that.
Excuse me, Miss, does that dress come in red or blue?
Oh, no?
Well, that's alright 'cuz the cheetah print will always do!
The Cheetah Girls are large and in charge
but that don't mean that we charge up our cards!
The Cheetah Girls are large and in charge
but that don't mean we charge up our cards!"

We finish with a big dance flourish, and all of a sudden, people all around us on the street are applauding, whooping it up, and shouting for more!

"I don't care how many pound cake remixes

Pumpmaster Pooch did for Sista Fudge, nobody writes *más coolio* songs than my Bubbles," I exclaim.

"Yeah, but how are we gonna get in a studio and do the songs *we* love?" Do' Re Mi adds, hitching up her backpack.

"Yeah, 'cuz we sure don't have songs-we-love money for no studio time," Bubbles says sadly.

"Maybe I could ask Princess Pamela," I say excitedly.

"Sure, Chuchie, as if you aren't in enough trouble for two lifetimes!" Bubbles says, then pulls my braids. "Excuse me, does that dress come in red or blue?"

We are laughing, right up until we see my father standing by the door. He is obviously waiting just for us, and I can tell he is grasshopping mad.

"*Ay, Dios mío*, Chuchie, his eyes are breathing fire hotter than his Dodo Mojo Salsa Picante," Bubbles says, trying to make a joke. Nobody laughs, though. We all get real quiet.

"Hi, *Papí*," I say, squeaking. I have a little knot in my stomach, even though I want to hug him. I decide not to say one more word. I'm in enough *agua caliente*—hot water—as it is.

Then I see the anger go right out of his eyes. He takes a handkerchief out of his pocket and wipes his forehead. "You girls are late. I was getting worried. I don't like you walking around the city at night, *tú entiendes?"*

"Sí," I say softly.

He takes us inside, and we sit down in one of the red plastic booths. Both he and Princess Pamela have red chairs in their stores—hers are velvet, though. Dad looks right at me. His eyes look very sad. Then he reaches into his pocket, takes out my copy of Mr. Johnson's agreement, and lays it on the table.

"Now, listen," he says, lowering his voice. "I don't have an opinion one way or the other. But I just got off the phone with Pamela, and she says you girls shouldn't sign this agreement."

"Why doesn't she want us to sign?" I ask.

"You mean because she got a psychic feeling, or something?" Do' Re Mi asks.

"Yes, I guess that's what you could call it," he says, pulling on his salt-and-pepper goatee. "But if I know one thing about Pamela, her premonitions are not to be played with, *entiendes?"*

We all look at each other like we've just seen a monster.

"Pamela said, 'Tell the Cheetah Girls to stay away from the animals.' She said Chanel would understand," my dad explains, looking at me again.

"What animals?" I respond, acting all innocent, nervous that the spotlight is now on me. I realize she must have known it was me on the phone all those times. How embarrassing!

All of a sudden, *la lucha*—the light—goes on inside my head, and I see what Princess Pamela was trying to tell me over the phone. "Beware of predators who run in packs," I remember her saying to me. "They will prey on your good fortune. They will circle around you like vultures and steal what is yours."

It wasn't the Cheetah Girls she was trying to warn me about! "Oh, snapples—Mr. Jackal Johnson and Mr. Hyena!" I gasp. "Jackals and Hyenas. *Those* are the animals!"

"What should we do?" Angie asks, nibbling on one of her Pee Wee Press-On Nails, then tapping her hand on the table nervously. "I mean, it's only a premonition . . . and we've got this big gig comin' up at the Apollo. . . ."

"Let me see what my mom thinks," Bubbles says, acting large and in charge, and taking her cell phone out of her backpack. These days, we are depending on Dorothea *más y más*—more and more.

"My mom can't see the future, but she can smell an okeydokey from the OK corral a mile away!" Bubbles quips. Over the phone, she explains the situation to her mom.

When she hangs up, Bubbles has a satisfied smile on her face. She says, "Mom says she has a call in to Mrs. Eagle, her lawyer, to see what she thought about the agreement. She'll let us know as soon as she gets a peep."

"So," Dad says, turning to me like a secret agent. "Did you at least *win* that Prada bag?"

"Nope," I say, looking sheepish, because my dad obviously knows everything, thanks to the Mummy, aka my mom. "Can you believe Derek Hambone did—and he only bought one ticket!"

Shaking his head, Dad asks, "What about that date with Krusher?"

Ay, Dios! He really does know everything.

"Nope," I say, all sad, so at least my dad will feel sorry for me. "Can you believe some DJ from WLIB radio won? It's so unfair!"

All of a sudden, Dad lets out a roar of a

laugh, showing his big, big teeth. "That contest must've been rigged!"

"And you *know* Chuchie made more calls to that 900 number than the rest of us make in a year!" Do' Re Mi says.

We all laugh. Then me and my dad do something we haven't done in a long time. We hug each other real tight, and I start crying. "I love you, *Papí*."

"I know, *mía princesa*," he says, stroking my head as I lean against his shoulder. "I love you, too—but you really can't 'shop in the name of love.'"

I look at my dad in surprise.

"I heard you girls singing outside," Dad says, raising his thick eyebrows. "A deaf man could hear you down the block. I think Pamela is right, though—the Cheetah Girls are gonna make a lot of people happy—especially *my* Cheetah Girl!"

Chapter 9

I am humming to myself on the way out my front door, when I stub my toe really hard on a case of Pucci's Burpy's soda that is sitting in the hallway. "Pucci, could you put this box in the kitchen, *por favor*!" I yell out. "It's in the way! I just tripped right over it!"

"I don't care, just do it yourself!" Pucci says, running into his room. He has been mad at me all day because I got to see Dad and he didn't.

"You know, for all that money I spent on ballet lessons for you, you are *clumsy*," Mom yells at me from the kitchen. She is wearing a turban on her head with a big diamond broach in the middle, and is all dressed up to go meet Mr. Tycoon at the airport.

"Mom, how come Pucci gets to order Burpy's soda from the Internet?" I yell back at her.

"Your ordering days are over till you can buy it yourself, that's why!" she says.

"Mom, I'm going to the meeting at Mr. Johnson's," I say. Bubbles's mom has called the meeting, but she won't say why. Only that her lawyer called her back, and she wants to straighten things out with Mr. Johnson. I'm worried about it—I know Princess Pamela warned us about him, but he's the only manager we've got—and we've got our demo coming out, and the gig at the Apollo—if it doesn't work out with Mr. Johnson, what are we gonna do?

All Mom says is "Be back in time for dinner, Chanel. And tell Dorothea the Dolce & Gabbana sample sale starts at ten o'clock tomorrow."

"*Está bien*." Too bad I won't be going to the sample sale, I think to myself as I close the door. But these days, and until I pay off what I owe my mom, shopping and me are total strangers.

Everyone is quiet when I walk into Mr. Johnson's office, and they all turn to look at me.

They must be early, because I know I'm not late, I think. Nervously, I look at my Miss Wiggy! watch.

"Let's cut to the paper chase here, Mr. Johnson. This contract is not going to work," Dorothea says, looking up from her leopard brim and right into Mr. Johnson's eyes.

"Mrs. Garibaldi, I can assure you this contract is pretty standard," Mr. Johnson says, smoothing down his bright red tie. "We're only talking about production costs."

"According to my lawyer, at the royalty rate you have written in this clause, the only game the Cheetah Girls are gonna be able to afford for the next ten years is jumping jacks!" Dorothea snaps at Mr. Johnson, then leans over his desk.

Bubbles looks at me and puts her finger over her mouth. I can see that I have walked right into another soap opera.

"I am footing the cost of the demo tape, wheeling and dealing to make everything happen for the Cheetah Girls, so it's only fitting that *I'm* sitting on the throne and seeing my girls become stars," Mr. Johnson says, slamming his hands down on his desk.

"You're going to be seeing 'stars,' all right—right after I clunk you with my purse!" Dorothea says, her dark brown eyes getting squinty. "You are no longer going to manage *my* girls. And, if you ever come sniffing around them again, Mr. *Jackal*, or if you try to release any of those songs with their vocals on it, I'm gonna come back and be so shady the sun is gonna go down on you. Do you understand?" Dorothea says in that scary voice she gets when she is mad. Leave it to my *madrina* to throw her weight around and show who is the conductor on this choo-choo train.

"What about the girls' gig at the Apollo? I hooked it up so Mr. Hyena can be there. I mean, I'm digging your concern, Mrs. Garibaldi, but I think you're making a big mistake," Mr. Johnson says, swiveling in his fake leather chair. There are little beads of sweat on his forehead, like I get when I'm scared.

"The only mistake I'm making is that I don't hit you over the head with my pocketbook, you hungry scavenger!" Dorothea says, then motions for us to get up with her.

We all walk out of the office behind

Dorothea, and bigmouthed Bubbles says to Mr. Johnson, "See ya around like a doughnut!"

Why can't I think of the kinds of things that Bubbles says? I start smiling and looking at my crew, but Angie and Aqua look sad.

"It would have been nice to perform at the Apollo. What are we gonna do now?" Aqua says, popping her gum.

"Don't pop gum in public, darling, you're too pretty for that," Dorothea says, then puts her arm around Aqua.

"I'm sorry, Mrs.—I mean *Ms.* Dorothea. I was just kinda nervous in there," Aqua explains. She puts the pink blob of gum in a tissue and throws it in the garbage receptacle by the elevator.

"Now we don't have a demo tape. We don't have a show. We don't have nothing. What *are* we gonna do, Ms. Dorothea?" Angie says, crossing her arms and pouting like a Texas Tornado cheerleader.

"Maybe we missed our last chance, last dance. Was the contract really that bad, Ms. Dorothea?" Do' Re Mi asks, looking up at my *madrina,* who is more than a foot taller than her, especially with her high heels on. They are bright-red patent-leather pumps that look good enough to eat.

Eat? Suddenly, I realize that I'm hungry.

"Some Dominican-style *arroz con pollo* would be great right about now," I say to Bubbles.

"Darlings, I know this fabulous Moroccan restaurant we can go to around the corner. My treat!" Dorothea says, pulling out her compact. "Listen, Cheetah Girls, don't get so nervous you're ready to pounce at the first opportunity that comes along. We're gonna figure out something, okay? It takes more than one shifty jackal to chase us out of the jiggy jungle, am I right?"

Dorothea looks at us, extends her hands, and does the Cheetah Girls handshake with all five of us.

"You got that right, Momsy poo—we are gonna do what we gotta do!" Bubbles says, egging her on. "Even if we did miss the opportunity of a lifetime, and even if it takes us longer, we're still gonna get diggity, no doubt. It's just a matter of time."

"I hear that," Do' Re Mi says, then sighs. She's trying to keep her spirits up—we all are—but it's hard not to keep thinking about everything we've just lost.

Because we are so down in *la dumpa*, after our *lonchando*, Dorothea asks us to come to her store so she can give us a surprise. When we get to the store, my mom is there! I wonder what's going on.

"What are you doing here, Auntie Juanita?" Bubbles asks my mom. I'm thinking, I hope Mr. Tycoon's plane didn't get hijacked! Mom puts her sunglasses on her head, and holds up a newspaper. It's the latest issue of the *Uptown Express*. "Did you see this?" she says, handing Dorothea the newspaper.

"Hmmph, the hyenas are circling after all!" Dorothea says, showing it to us. "'Hyena Records Sings Its Last Note, And Its Founder Is Singing Like a Crow to the Feds!'" We all gather around the newspaper, as Dorothea reads us the article blow by blow.

"Seems that Mr. Johnson and Mr. Hyena were in cahoots all along," Dorothea explains.

"What's a cahoot?" Angie asks.

"That means they were the okeydokey duo,

get it?" Bubbles says. "They were flipping the flimflam together."

"Oh," Angie says, shaking her head. "They weren't doing right by us. I get it."

"Angie, they were crooks!" Do' Re Mi blurts out, then plops down on Dorothea's leopard love seat.

"Seems Mr. Johnson would steer artists to the record label," Dorothea says.

Before she can continue, Bubbles blurts out, "Signing them to these *radickio* deals, like the one he was trying to perpetrate on us!"

"That's right, darling," Dorothea says, reaching for one of the Godiva chocolates on the counter. "Then Mr. Hyena would cover the royalty tracks, so that the artists never knew how much they were making, and the two would skim the profits out of the company."

"So Princess Pamela was right after all!" I blurt out, then realize that I should buy some Krazy Glue and stick my lips together permanently.

My mom looks at me like she is already picking out the color of my coffin.

"Juanita, I'm gonna side with Chanel on this one," Dorothea says, putting her arm around my mom as she explains Princess Pamela's predictions to her. "She may not be your cup of tea, but she sure knows how to read tea leaves!" Dorothea says, doing the Cheetah Girls handshake with us.

Mom thinks for a minute, her face all serious. "I don't mind if you see her," she says to me all of sudden. "You just cannot take any presents from her, or call her Psychic Hot Line—I don't care if she invented the crystal ball!"

"I told you, *Mamí,* I won't take anything from her again," I say nervously.

"You know what mothers are?" Mom asks me.

"What?"

"Psychics who don't charge—you can get all the advice you need for *free*!" My mom smiles, slapping Dorothea a high five.

"Well, I'm glad you all are happy—but we still don't have a demo," Aqua says, reaching into the box of Godiva. She must be getting very comfortable around here, because she used to always ask Dorothea first.

"Help yourself, darling," Dorothea says.

"Oh, I'm sorry, Ms. Dorothea!" Aqua blurts out.

"That's all right, just enjoy yourself," Dorothea says, smiling.

"Chanel, are you sure those Chihuahuas don't shed hair?" Mom asks me.

"I'm very sure, because Do' Re Mi looked it up in a book!" I say.

"That's right, Mrs. Simmons, I did," Do' Re Mi says, helping me out.

"Maybe next weekend, we'll see if we find one for Pucci's birthday," Mom says.

I can't believe my ears. "Oh, *Mamí*," I say, and run over to hug her.

"Don't hug me yet. If he sheds one hair, he's going right back to the dog pound," Juanita quips.

"Why do you have to get a 'he'?" Do' Re Mi quips.

"Because Pucci hates girls—except for Bubbles," I volunteer with a giggle, then sit Toto in my lap. "He's not like you, Boo-boo, right?"

Ms. Dorothea motions for all of us to sit down. "Now, the reason why I wanted all of you to come back to the store . . ." She breaks out in a big smile. "I have a little surprise for you, Cheetah Girls." Dorothea brushes her wavy wiglet hairs out of her face. "Remember I told you Jellybean Nyce was in here shopping?"

"Really!" Angie says. "Omigod, we love her!"

"I know. And I told her about your predicament, and she is gonna hook us up with the producer who did *her* demo, Chili Dog Watkins."

"*Really*?" Bubbles blurts out.

"Really," Dorothea counters. "But I'm not finished. I, Dorothea Garibaldi, have secured the fabulous Cheetah Girls a spot on The Amateur Hour at the world-famous Apollo!"

"No way, Jose!" I say, my mouth hanging open. "How did you do that, *madrina*?"

"I did it the way *every* manager does—I sold you like the second coming of the Spice Rack Girls, that's how," Dorothea brags. "You'll never say I don't work overtime for *my* artists."

"Mom, are you saying what I think you're saying?" Bubbles asks, smiling and putting her arm around Dorothea.

"Darling, one can never be too sure what you're thinking, but I'll tell you what I'm saying," Dorothea says, looking at all of us. "It's time for the Cheetah Girls to have *real* management—and you're looking at her."

We scream with delight, while Mom just looks on from the counter, amused. "I hope you know what you're doing, Dottie, because these girls will wear you out!"

"Oh, I know what I'm doing. I'm taking the Cheetah Girls right to the top, where they belong."

Angie can't contain her Southern charm any longer, and screams out, "Come on Mr. Sandman, show me your hook, 'cuz I'm ready for Freddy!"

Angie, of course, is referring to the famous bozo with the hook who runs bad acts off the stage if they get booed by the audience. The Sandman kinda looks like a brown clown, but his antics are no joke, for sure.

"All I can say is, I hope Freddy is ready for us at the world-famous Apollo," Bubbles adds.

All I can say is, *la dopa!*

"Come on, Cheetah Girls," Bubbles shouts. "Let's give the world a taste of our latest, greatest hit!"

We break into "Shop in the Name of Love," and the whole place is rockin', customers and all. We look at each other and smile, nodding our heads. Me most of all, 'cuz I'm so glad this all happened. It was all worth it, all the grief, all the tears—just to come out of it with a song like this one.

Yeah—it's just a matter of time. Look out, world—the Cheetah Girls are comin'—and we are large and in charge!

Shop in the Name of Love

Polo or solo
Gucci or Pucci
Prada or Nada
is the way I wanna live

Ma don't make me wait
or I'll gaspitate
till I get my own credit card
and sashay right to the bargain yard!

That's right, y'all
Honey may come from bees
but money don't grow on trees.
You may think you're large
'cuz you charge
But you're looking good
and sleeping on a barge!

When you shop in the Name Of Love
you gotta ask yourself
What are you dreamin' of?

What are you schemin' of?
What are you trippin' on, love?

That's right, y'all!
The Cheetah Girls are large
and in charge
but that don't mean
we charge up our cards

The Cheetah Girls are large
and in charge
but that don't mean
we charge up our cards

Polo or solo
Gucci for Pucci
Prada or nada
is the way I wanna live

Say what?

Polo or solo
Gucci for Pucci
Prada or nada
is the way I wanna live

You got that?
Yeah. I got that.
Excuse, Miss,
does that dress come in red or blue?
Well, that's all right
'cuz the cheetah print
will always do!

The Cheetah Girls are large
and in charge
but that don't mean
we charge up our cards
You got that?
Yeah. I got that!

That's right, y'all
Honey may come from bees
but money don't grow on trees.
You may think you're large
'cuz you charge
But you're looking good
and sleeping on a barge

When you shop in the Name of Love
you gotta ask yourself

What are you dreamin' of?
What are you schemin' of?
What are you trippin' on, love?

The Cheetah Girls are large
large and in charge
but that don't mean
we charge up our cards
You got that?
Yeah. I got that!

The Cheetah Girls Glossary

Abuela: Grandmother.

Adobo down: Mad flava.

Arroz con pollo: Rice and chicken.

Benjamins: Bucks, dollars.

Bruja: A good or bad witch.

Caliente mad: Really angry.

Confirmation: Catholic religion ceremony at the age of thirteen.

Cuatro yuks!: When something or someone is four times yucky.

Do me a flava: Do me a favor.

Duckets: Money, loot.

Down for the 'do: Ready to support.

Está bien: Awright.

Fib-eronis: Teeny-weeny fibs.

Flipping the flimflam: Acting or doing something shady.

Floss: Show off.

Frijoles: Beans.

Gracias gooseness: Thank goodness.

La dopa!: Fabulous.

La gran fantasía: Living in Happyville.

La wacka: Something that is wack.

Lonchando: Lunching.

Madrina: Godmother.

Majordomo: Legitimate.

Mentira: A not-so-little lie.

Muy coolio: Very cool.

Pinata-whacking mad: When someone is madder than *caliente* mad.

Poco paz: A little peace.

Qué broma!: What a joke!

Querida: Dear. Precious one.

Radickkio: Ridiculous!

Ready for Freddy: Ready to do your thing, no matter what happens.

Schemo: Idiot

Tan coolio: So cool.

Tú sabes que tú sabes: You know what you know.

Weakness for carats: Someone who is a lifetime member of the diamonds-are-a-girl's-best-friend club.

Wheel-a-deala: Making moves, both good or bad.

Winky dink: Blink and you'll miss it.

Yo tengo un coco: I have a crush!

Who's 'Bout to Bounce?

For my mother,
Ruth Gregory,
wherever you are

Chapter 1

When you put the *C* to the *H* to the *A* to the *N* to the *E* to the *L*, you've got one supa-fast Cheetah *señorita*! I mean, Chanel "Chuchie" Simmons is all legs, even though she is only five feet two—which is just a little taller than me. All right, Chanel is *four* inches taller, but that's not the point.

Right about now, after jogging all the way from Soho, where Chanel lives, up to Harlem, where I live (which is more miles than the Road Runner does in one cartoon episode) the rest of us Cheetah Girls feel like wobbly cubs. We're desperate for a little shade and some soda!

Chanel, on the other hand, looks like *she's* ready to do pirouettes or something. Now I can see why she used to take ballet lessons. She's got "gamma ray legs"!

"Wait up, Cheetah *Señorita*, yo!" I yell to Chanel, just to help her remember that she's not out here all by herself—that she is running with her crew. *Our* crew, that is. The Cheetah Girls.

Besides Chanel "Chuchie" Simmons, that would be: Galleria "Bubbles" Garibaldi, who is the leader of our pack; Aquanette and Anginette Walker, aka the "Huggy Bear twins"; and, of course, lucky me—Dorinda "Do' Re Mi" Rogers.

See, not too long ago, the five of us started a girl group, called the Cheetah Girls. You could pinch me every time I say it, 'cuz I still can't believe we got it like that.

Before I met my crew, I only sang for fun—you know, goofing around at home to entertain everybody. Bubbles and Chanel are the dopest friends I've ever had, and I'm so grateful that they got me to sing outside my bedroom.

I met them on our first day at Fashion Industries High School, where we are all freshmen, and it's the best thing that ever happened to me. Before, I was just plain old Dorinda Rogers. Now, I'm Do' Re Mi, which is the nickname my crew gave me. Do' Re Mi—one of the Cheetah Girls!

Bubbles and Chanel say we're gonna take over the world with our global groove. I hope they're right. For now though, we're just happy that Galleria's mom, Ms. Dorothea, has hooked us up with the famous Apollo Theatre Amateur Hour Contest! It's next Saturday—only a week and a half till we're up there, performing on that stage where the Supremes once sang. That is so *dope*!

See, Ms. Dorothea is not only Bubbles's mom—she has now officially become our manager. Our first manager was Mr. Jackal Johnson. We met him at the Cheetah-Rama Club, where we performed for the first time. He tried to manage us on the "okeydokey" tip. That means he was a crook.

When Ms. Dorothea found out Mr. Johnson was trying to get his hands on our duckets (not that we have any yet), she nearly threw him out the window! She doesn't play, you know what I'm sayin'?

Of course, Ms. Dorothea isn't out here

running with us today, because she is very busy with her boutique—Toto in New York . . . Fun in Diva Sizes—she runs the store, designs the clothes, and everything.

Aquanette says, "Dorothea's probably eating Godiva chocolates and laughing at us."

Word. She should talk! In fact, Aqua and Angie *both* like to eat a lot. If they keep it up, they're gonna be bigger than Dorothea by the time they're her age! (Dorothea used to be a model, but now she is "large and in charge," if you know what I mean!)

"Come on, Do' Re *Poor* Mi, move that matchstick butt!" heckles Chanel, poking out her tongue and "bugging" her eyes. Chanel is on a jelly roll, and she won't quit.

See, I can run almost as fast as her, but I don't wanna leave the rest of my crew behind.

I'm not flossin'. I can dance, skateboard, jump double Dutch, *and* I was the top tumbler in my gymnastics class last year in junior high, so what you know about that, huh?

Jackie Chan's got nothing on me, either. If I wanted to, I could do karate moves—well, if I had a black belt I could. At this point, I'd settle for a polka-dot belt, 'cuz you gotta watch your back in the jiggy jungle, especially in the part where I live, way up on 116th Street.

We've been running for a kazillion miles, and right about now Bubbles is at the end of her rope-a-dope.

"Chuchie, would you quit runnin' ahead of us? If you don't stop flossin', I'm gonna pull out one of your fake braids!" she snarls at the Cheetah *señorita*.

I start giggling. See, sometimes I'm scared to snap on Chanel or Bubbles, because I'm afraid if I do, then they won't let me be their friend.

Me, I'm just the new kid on the block. It's okay for them to snap on each other, though, 'cuz they've been friends forever—ever since Bubbles stole Chanel's Gerber Baby apple sauce—so they fight like sisters all the time.

They don't *look* like sisters, though. Bubbles is very light-skinned, and she has a really nice, full shape. About the only running she likes to do is to the dinner table, or to a party. I wish I had a shape like hers, instead of mine, which looks like a boy's.

Chanel is more tan and flat-chested, like me, and really skinny, too. But because she's taller, it looks really cute on her. She's kinda like a

Mexican jumping bean. She'll eat Chub Chub candies all day on the run, and keep jumpin'.

Anyhow, the reason why we're out here panting like puppies is not to lose weight. It's because Dorothea is putting us through this whole "divettes-in-training camp" thing, so we can become a legit girl group, like the Supremes or the Spice Rack Girls. That means we have to do what she says:

- We have to run five miles, at least once a week, to build up our endurance and lung power. This way, we'll be able to sing in big stadiums, and travel on the road without getting sore throats all the time.

- We have to take vocal lessons and dance classes.

- We have to watch old videos. Once a month, we have "Seventies Appreciation Night," which means we all get together over at Bubbles's house, and watch old videos of groups and movies with peeps in *mad* funny outfits.

- We have to develop other skills so we don't end up on the "chitlin' circuit." That's where singers go who don't even have a bucket to put their duckets in. They end up performing for no pay—they just pass a hat around for tips!

- We have to do our homework in school, read magazines, and dress dope, like divettes with duckets.

Chanel's mother, Juanita, has volunteered to run with us, but she is in better shape than we are and she just runs way ahead by herself. Since she's a grown-up, we don't mind. Because she is running ahead of us, she won't see us making faces, whining, giggling, and snapping on the peeps as we pass them by. Right now, though, we're too tired to even snap on a squirrel.

Juanita looks kinda funny from the back when she's running, because the bottom of her feet come up fast, like hooves on a horse, and her ponytail keeps bouncing up and down. She's kinda tall and skinny for a lady her age. See, she used to be a model, just like Dorothea (but *she* exercises like the Road Runner). Every now and then she looks back to ask us, "You girls all right?"

Poor Bubbles's mouth is hanging open, and she looks kinda mad, but she never gives up on anything. She just starts snapping. She sweats so much, though—there are droplets dripping down the side of her face, making her hair stick together like gooey sideburns!

The twins are kinda slow, too, but they don't complain a lot about running. Their minds are on other things.

"Do you really think the Sandman comes with a hook and pulls you off the stage if the audience boos you?" Anginette whines, running alongside me.

The Sandman at the Apollo Theatre is supposed to be this guy dressed like a scarecrow, with a big hook or something, who chases Amateur Hour contestants off the stage if they're wack.

"You sure he ain't like Jason from *Friday the 13th*?" Aquanette asks, chuckling nervously. Aqua and Angie are *Scream* queens. They love to watch horror movies with people getting their eyes poked out.

"I don't know, Angie," I say, panting, "but if the audience even *looks* like they're gonna start booing, then I'm gonna bounce, *before* the Sandman tries to hook us!"

"Oh, no, that is too wack-a-doodle-do! And it's not gonna happen," Bubbles says, smiling again. "We're gonna be in there like swimwear."

Galleria always makes us feel better. That's why she's Cheetah number one. Anything goes wrong, and we all look to her, just naturally. She's not takin' any shorts.

We are running in Central Park now, and suddenly, a funny-looking guy with a silver thing on his head zooms by on his bicycle, and almost runs down Aquanette. "Dag on, he almost knocked me over," yells Aqua, looking back at him as he rides away.

The twins are not used to the ways of the Big Apple, or how fast everybody moves here. They say everybody moves a lot slower in Houston, which is where they grew up—in a big house with a porch and everything in the suburbs.

"Beam me up, Scottie, you wack-a-doodle helmet head!" Galleria yells back at the guy on the bike, then gasps for breath. She sticks up for us a lot, because she isn't afraid of anybody.

"Y'all, there are a lot of crazy people here," Anginette chimes in.

"Helmet Head probably woulda knocked her over if nobody was looking!" Bubbles says.

"I wonder if that was a strainer on his head," Chanel says, giggling.

"And what were those funny-looking antenna things sticking up?" I giggle back.

"Come on, you lazy *muchachas*!" Juanita yells back at us, waving for us to follow her.

I don't know how long we've been running, but I am so grateful when we finally reach the park exit at 110th Street.

"Thank *gooseness*," Galleria yelps, as we stop by the benches where Juanita is waiting for us impatiently, her hands on her hips. Bubbles bends over and is panting heavily, holding on to her knees. Her hair is so wild it's flopping all over the place like a mop.

This is where I get off, I think with a sad sigh. I wish I could invite my crew over to my house for some "Snapple and snaps." After all, I only live six blocks from here. But after seeing where *they* all live, I'm too embarrassed to let them see my home.

I live with my foster mother, Mrs. Bosco, her husband, Mr. Bosco, and about nine or ten foster brothers and sisters—depending on which day you ask me. We all share an apartment in the Cornwall Projects. We keep it clean, but still, it's real small and crowded. It needs some fixing up by the landlord, too—if you know what I'm sayin'.

It bothers me a lot to be a foster child but Mrs. Bosco is a pretty nice lady, even though she's not really my mom or anything—but now, I'm hanging with my new crew, and all of them have such nice houses, and real families. . . .

"Ms. Simmons, can't we at least *walk* to our house from here?" Angie asks, whining to Juanita.

Since I never invite anybody over, the next stop on this gravy train is the twins' house on 96th Street. Angie and Aqua live with their father in a nice apartment that faces Riverside Park. My apartment faces the stupid post office.

"Okay, lazy," Juanita huffs back.

"Well," I say, "bye, everybody."

Chanel puts her sweaty arms around me to kiss me good-bye.

"Ugh, Chanel!" I wince.

"Do' Re Mi, can't you see I love you!" she giggles back, kissing me on cheek and making silly noises. Then Chanel whispers in my ear, laying on the Spanish accent, "You know I was just playing *wichoo*. I know you can run as fast as me."

"Okay, *Señorita*, just get off me!" I giggle back. "Bye, Bubbles, and all you boo-boo heads!"

"Bye, Dorinda," Juanita says. Then she adds, "Don't stay up late, 'cuz *we're* going to bed *early*," giving me that look like "you better not be trying to hog the chat room on the Internet tonight."

See, Chanel's kinda grounded for life—until she pays back the money she charged on her mom's credit card last month. She's not supposed to be on the phone or the Internet, runnin' up more bills.

"See y'all tomorrow at school," I yell, then add, "not you two!" to Angie and Aqua. The twins don't go to Fashion Industries High, like me, Chanel, and Bubbles. They go to LaGuardia Performing Arts High School, which is even doper.

Maybe next year, me, Bubbles, and Chuchie can transfer to LaGuardia, so we can all be together. . . .

You know, you have to audition to get into LaGuardia. Chanel was too chicken to audition last year, coming out of junior high—even though Bubbles wanted to go to LaGuardia in the worst way. But Bubbles didn't want to audition without Chuchie, so they didn't go. That's why they both wound up at Fashion Industries, which is lucky for me!

But now, who knows? Sure, auditioning is kinda scary, but now that we're the Cheetah Girls, we've got each other, and we've had some experience performing—so I know we can do it.

Besides, Bubbles says if the Cheetah Girls really take off, and our lives get too hectic, we'll have to get private tutors anyway. Private tutors! Wouldn't that be the dopest?

That's Bubbles for you, always planning ahead to "destination: jiggy jungle." That's the place, she says, where dreams really do come true—*if* you go for *yours*.

Listening to Bubbles, we all feel like we really can do anything we set our minds to.

Chapter 2

I head uptown alone, on my way back to the apartment. Soon, my thoughts drift forward to next Saturday night.

What if the Sandman really does chase us off the stage? Or if somebody hits me on the head with a can of Burpy soda while I'm performing? Then I'll get a concussion . . . and I won't be able to take care of Mrs. Bosco and all my brothers and sisters. . . .

"Hey! Watch where you're goin', shorty!"

By the time I hear Can Man's warning, it's too late, 'cuz he's slammed his shopping cart filled with empty cans right into my back. I trip over a mound of rocks, and a thousand cans go flying everywhere.

"*You* watch where *you're* goin'!" I scream back at him. From my knees, I pick up a can and make like I'm gonna throw it at him.

Can Man is one of those people in New York who are out all day, collecting empty soda and beer cans, and returning them to places like the Piggly Wiggly supermarket around the corner for the deposit money.

In other words, he is a homeless man, but I think he is "sippin' more times than he is tippin'," because he screams a lot for no reason, and does wack things—like this.

"You better not take one of my cans, shorty!" Can Man yells. Now he is foaming at the mouth. His eyes are buggin', too.

I drop the can and run. I don't even listen to the people who ask me if they can help. No, they *can't* help me!

Why does everything happen to me? My real mother gave me away. My first foster mother, Mrs. Parkay, gave me up when I was little, for no reason. And now, Can Man runs into me with his stupid shopping cart!

My ankle really hurts, and I sit down on somebody's front stoop to massage it.

Sometimes I get scared that I'm just gonna

end up like a bag lady, and get married to Can Man or something. Who am I kidding? Maybe I'll never be anything! In fact, if it wasn't for my crew, I'd be just a wanna-be, I tell myself. Look at Bubbles and Chanel. You can tell they are born stars.

Me? Well, everybody says I can dance really good, and I guess I can sing okay. But I'm never gonna be famous. In fact, when I'm alone, and not with the group, I'm really scared of performing—and especially auditioning.

Now my legs *really* hurt from running all those miles, and I think Can Man might've broken my left ankle! I'm so mad, I wanna punch somebody. Let somebody—*anybody*—be stupid enough to get in my way now! Fuming like a fire engine, I hobble, step by step on my one good foot, to my apartment building.

"Hi, Dorinda! How come you limping?" asks Pookie, who is sitting in the courtyard. See, there are a lot of buildings in the Cornwall Projects, but only two of them have a courtyard, so all the kids hang out here.

Pookie is sitting with his mom, Ms. Keisha, and his sister, Walkie-talkie Tamela. We call her that because she never shuts up.

"Heh, Pookie," I respond, huffing and puffing. "Can Man hit me with his cart and knocked me over."

"You know he's crazy. You better stay out of his way, Dorinda, before he really hurts you," mumbles Ms. Keisha.

"I know, Ms. Keisha, but I didn't see him because he was behind me. Is Mrs. Bosco home?"

"Yep," she says, nodding her head at me. See, Ms. Keisha is nosy, and she knows that *we* know she's nosy. She sits outside all day, with a head full of pink hair rollers and even pinker bedroom slippers, talking about people's business like she's Miss Clucky on the gossip show.

Not that her motormouth doesn't come in "handy dandy," as Bubbles would say. See, if you're in trouble, and you wanna know if you're gonna get it when you get upstairs, you just ask Ms. Keisha. She knows if your mother is home—*and* if she's mad at you.

The courtyard isn't much of a playground for all the kids who live here, but it's better than hanging out in front with the "good-for-nothings," as Mrs. Bosco calls the knuckleheads who hang around all day and don't go to school or to work.

Some of the people who live here try to make it look nice, too. Once somebody tried to plant a tree right in the cement, but it was gone the next morning. So now there are no trees—just a few po' little brown shrubs that look like nubs. And there aren't any slides, swings, or jungle gym to play on, either—just some big old "X" marks scribbled with chalk on the ground, for playing jumping jacks.

I used to jump double Dutch rope out here all the time when I was little. I was the rope-a-dopest double Dutcher, too, even though Tawanna, who lives in Building C, thinks *she's* the bomb. She's such a big show-off, it just looks like she's got more moves than she *really* does.

It's getting dark out already. I know I've missed dinner, but Mrs. Bosco will still have something waiting for me. Hobbling on my good ankle, I open the door to the building, and get my keys out of my sweatpants. After dinner, I think, I'd better go see if Mrs. Gallstone down the hall is home. She's a nurse, and she'll know if my ankle is broken or not.

I hope little Arba is over her cold, too, I think, as I limp to the elevator. Arba is my new little sister. She's almost five years old—the same age I was when I came to live with Mrs. Bosco. She doesn't speak English very well, but we're teaching her.

Arba is Albanian by nationality, but her mother had her here, then died. Mrs. Bosco says a lot of people come to the Big Apple looking for the streets paved in gold, but instead they get "chewed up and spit out."

Most of the time, the caseworkers never say much about where foster kids come from, or what happened to them. They just drop them off, sometimes with bags of clothes and toys. Anyway, someone took Arba to the Child Welfare Department because she had no family, and they gave her to Mrs. Bosco to take care of until somebody adopts her—if anybody ever does.

You could say our house is kinda like the United Nations or something. My seven-year-old foster brother, Topwe, is African—real African, from Africa. He speaks English all funny, but it's his native language. They all talk like that over there!

Topwe gets the most attention, because he is

HIV-positive, which means he was infected with the AIDS virus. His mother was a crack addict, Mrs. Bosco told me, but I'm not supposed to say anything to Topwe or the other kids. I'm the only one, she says, who can keep a secret. It's true, too. I really can.

Like I said, the United Nations. There's Arba for one, and Topwe for another. Then there's my four-year-old brother, Corky, who is part Mexican and part Bajin. (Bajin is what you call people from Barbados, which is in the British West Indies.)

Corky is really cute, and he has the most beautiful greenish-gray eyes you've ever seen. His father is fighting with Child Welfare, trying to get him back. I hope he doesn't. I don't want Corky to leave.

I know kids are supposed to live with their families, but I feel like Corky's *my* family, too—I mean, he's been here practically his whole life! What's his father know about him, anyway?

See, sometimes the kids in our house go back to their real parents. Once in a blue moon, they even get adopted by new families, who are looking for a child to love. Nobody has ever tried to adopt *me*, though.

Sometimes I cry about that—nobody wanting me. See, most parents who adopt want little kids, and by the time I got to Mrs. Bosco's, I was already too old—almost five. So yeah, it hurts when one of my brothers or sisters gets adopted and I don't. But I feel glad to have a place to live anyway. It could be worse—I could be out on the street, like a lot of other people. Like Can Man . . .

Besides, we may not have much, but life is pretty good here. We all stick up for each other when the chips are down. And Mrs. Bosco loves us all—she just doesn't let herself show it very often. I guess it's because that way, it won't hurt so much when the caseworkers take one of her kids away.

Even in the lobby, I can tell that somebody upstairs is cooking fried chicken. I *love* fried chicken—with collard greens, potato salad, and corn bread. That's the bomb meal.

We call where we live the "Corn Bread Projects" since, when you walk down the hallway, you can smell all the different kinds of food people are cooking in their apartments.

That's actually better than the elevators, which sometimes smell like *eau de pee pee*.

When the elevator door closes now, I get a whiff of some nasty smell. I hold my breath the whole ride up.

Everybody says the Cornwall Projects are dangerous, but nobody bothers us around here. That's because my foster father, Mr. Bosco, is *really* big, and he wears a uniform to work—plus he has a nightstick he says is for "clubbing knuckleheads."

He is a security guard who works the night shift, so he sleeps during the day. Most of us kids don't see him much, but he is really nice. He laughs like a big grizzly bear. Both times I got skipped in school, he gave me five dollars and said, "I'll give you five dollars every time you get skipped again!"

Chapter 3

As soon as I open the front door of the apartment, Twinkie jumps out from the corner. That's the game we play every day.

"Hey, Twinkie!" I say to my favorite sister, who is nine years old. Her real name is Rita, but we call her Twinkie, because she has blond fuzzy hair, and fat, yummy cheeks.

"Don't call me Twinkie anymore!" she announces to me, shuffling the deck of Pokémon cards she has in her hands. Twinkie grabs my hand, and pulls me down the hallway to the kitchen. Everybody else has eaten already, but Mrs. Bosco always puts my food in the oven, covered in a piece of tinfoil. All the kids know they'd better not touch it, either.

"I have to whisper something in your ear," Twinkie says, pulling me down so she can reach.

"Okay," I say, hugging her real tight. Twinkie has lived with us for nineteen months, and we are really close—she will always be my sister forever, no matter what.

"You have to call me Butterfly now," Twinkie tells me, and her blue eyes get very big, like saucers.

"Okay, Cheetah Rita Butterfly!" I giggle, then tickle her stomach, which I know sends her into hysterics.

"Stop!" she screams. "You big Cheetah monkey!"

"What's a Cheetah monkey, Cheetah Rita Butterfly?" I ask, poking her stomach some more. "Tell me, tell me, or I'm not gonna stop!"

"I don't know, but *you* are!" she screams, and giggles even more hysterically.

"Okay, I'll call you Cheetah Rita Butterfly, if you promise that we are gonna be sisters forever. You're never gonna get away from me!"

"Okay, okay!" she screeches, and I stop tickling her. After a minute, she stops laughing. "We're not really sisters though, are we?"

Twinkie asks me with that cute little face.

"Yes, we are," I say.

"Then how come we have different last names?" Twinkie asks, suddenly all serious. She is so smart.

"That doesn't mean we're not sisters, Cheetah Rita."

"Okay, then, I promise," Twinkie says, teasing me, then she runs off, daring me to chase her. "I'm Cheetah Rita Butterfly! Watch me fly so high!"

Putting one of the Pokémon cards from the jungle deck over one eye, Twinkie turns, then squinches up her face and yells, "Dorinda!"

"What?" I turn to answer her back.

"You can call me Twinkie again!" She giggles up a storm as I chase her down the hallway into her room, yelling, "You little troublemaker!"

Twinkie shares her bedroom with Arba, who I already told you about, and my sister Kenya.

Kenya is six, and she is a "special needs child," because she is always getting into trouble at school, or fighting with the other kids. But I don't think she is "emotionally disturbed" like they say. She is just selfish, and doesn't like to share anything, or listen to anybody. Twinkie and Arba don't seem to like sharing a room with Kenya. Can't say I blame them.

I share a bedroom—a tiny one—with my two *other* sisters, Chantelle and "Monie the Meanie." Monie is the oldest out of all of us. She is seventeen, and has a major attitude problem. I'm so glad she has a boyfriend now—Hector—and she's over at his house a lot. She doesn't like to help clean or anything, and she likes to boss me around. I wish she would just go stay with Hector. It would make more room for me and Chantelle.

Chantelle is eleven, but tries to act like she's grown already, sitting around reading *Sistarella* magazine, and hogging my computer.

Mr. Hammer gave *me* the computer last year. He's our super, and he knows how to fix everything—and who throws out what. He told me that a tenant from one of the other buildings was gonna throw out her computer, and he got her to give it to me. I call Mr. Hammer "Inspector Gadget," 'cuz he's got the hookup, if you know what I'm saying.

The boys all share the biggest bedroom. That would be Topwe and Corky, along with Khalil (who has only lived here two months), Nestor (who we nicknamed Nestlé's Quik because he eats really fast), and "Shawn the Fawn" (we call him that because he's really shy, and always runs away from people). Four of the boys sleep in bunk beds to make more space.

Mr. and Mrs. Bosco's bedroom used to be the pantry—that's how small it is. But since Mrs. Bosco is up all day with us kids, and Mr. Bosco works all night, usually only one of them sleeps at a time—so I guess it doesn't seem as small to them as it does to us.

Every time one of us leaves for good, I always think the Boscos will switch bedrooms around. But they never do. They always go and get another foster child to fill the empty bed. That's the way they are. Lucky for all of us . . .

I have followed Twinkie into her bedroom. Arba is sitting there on the floor, drawing with crayons, and Kenya has her mouth poked out, staring at a page in her school notebook. She's always mad about something. I feel bad for her. But I know if I ignore her, then she will at least act nice for five minutes, trying to get my attention.

I pretend Kenya isn't even there. "There's Arba!" I exclaim, kissing her dirty face. Then I sit on the floor to take off my smelly sneakers and socks.

That gets Kenya. "Abba!" she yells, taking a crayon from Arba's hand. Kenya never pronounces anybody's name right. "Don't eat that!"

"She wasn't gonna eat it, Kenya," I say, forgetting that I'm trying to ignore her.

Kenya sticks out her tongue at me, happy to have gotten my attention.

"Abba-cadabra," chants Twinkie, suddenly taking off her shorts. "I'm smelly. I'm gonna take my bath first, okay?"

"I'm smelly, too." I giggle. "You feel better, Arba?"

"Bubba bath! Bubba bath!" she says, smiling.

Then I hear Mrs. Bosco coughing in the living room. "You take your bath first, Twinkie," I say. "I'll be right back."

Mrs. Bosco just got out of the hospital last week. She was real sick, and she still has to rest a lot. When I go in the living room, I see her lying on the plastic-covered couch, with a blanket pulled over her. The lights are off in here, so that's why I didn't see her when I first came in.

"Hi, Mrs. Bosco. What's the matter?" I ask

her. She doesn't really like to kiss or hug much, and she says I don't have to call her Mom. I guess that's good, because I called my last foster mother Mom, and she gave me away. Still, I sure wish I had *somebody* I could call Mom.

"My arthritis is acting up again." Mrs. Bosco moans.

"Lemme rub your arms," I tell her. She likes when I give her massages, and I think it helps her arthritis too.

"No, baby—or . . . what your friends call you now?"

"Do' Re Mi," I tell her with a giggle.

"That's right. You go and get your Do' Re Mi self some dinner. I'll be awright," Mrs. Bosco says, chuckling and waving her hand.

Then she gets serious. "Oh, Dorinda—Kenya's teacher called today, and said she's having trouble with that child. Seems she's stealing things from the other kids. Can you talk to her? She'll listen to you."

"Okay," I yell back.

"And when you get a chance, look at that letter from the electric company. I don't have my glasses on. Tell me what it says." Mrs. Bosco sighs, and lies down again.

Mrs. Bosco can't read or write. We're not supposed to know this, but I don't mind taking care of the bills for her, because if the social workers find out, she won't be able to have any more foster kids.

"Is something wrong with your leg?" Mrs. Bosco asks me as I hobble to the kitchen.

"Yeah, I think my ankle is broken," I whine.

"If it was broken, you wouldn't be able to walk on it, but you'd better let Mrs. Gallstone look at it. Oh, I almost forgot. What's the name of that lady where you take them classes?"

"You mean Drinka Champagne?"

"No, I remember her. You know, I was young once, too—'tippin' and sippin',' like her song says. No, I mean the other lady you talk about—at the YMCA."

"Oh, Ms. Darlene Truly?" I ask, squinching up my nose.

"What's that child's name?" is another "game" we play, because Mrs. Bosco can't write down the messages, so she tries to remember who called, and sometimes she forgets.

"Yeah, that's her. She said it's very important for you to call her if you ain't coming to class tomorrow, because she needs to talk to you—

and it's very important," Mrs. Bosco repeats herself. Then she adds, rubbing her forehead, "Lord, now I got a headache, too."

I want to tell Mrs. Bosco to take off her wig, and maybe that would help her headache, but Mrs. Bosco doesn't take off her wigs until she goes to bed at night. She is wearing this new one that we ordered from It's a Wig!, but it looks terrible. It's kinda like the color silver gets when it's rusted, even though the color was listed as "salt and pepper" in the catalog.

Why is Ms. Truly calling me? I wonder. I can feel a knot in my stomach. She's never called me at home before, and I don't like people bothering Mrs. Bosco. I must have done something wrong!

"I don't know what Ms. Truly wants," I say, "but I'll probably see her before class, since I'm working at the YMCA concession stand after school tomorrow."

I don't want Mrs. Bosco to worry about anything, or think I'm in trouble for some reason. She has enough to worry about.

"How'd you hurt your leg, Dorinda?"

"I fell," I say. "Can Man hit me with his cart.

Maybe it was my fault, anyway. I'm just gonna put ice on it and go to bed."

Luckily, Mrs. Gallstone said my ankle isn't broken. It's just strained. I hate going over to her apartment, because the kitty litter box really stinks. I made it a really quick visit, telling her I had to get back home and go to bed early.

It's only nine o'clock, but it's been a long, hard day. Once I lie down on my bed, I'm too tired to get up and put ice on my ankle after all. Chantelle is popping her gum so loud—but if I say anything, she'll get an attitude, so I just ignore her.

On a table in between her bed and mine is my Singer sewing machine. I'm trying to design a new costume for the Cheetah Girls, but I haven't figured out what to do on the bodice.

Oh, well. I'm too tired to work on it tonight. Instead, I turn my face to the wall. I'm even too beat to take off my shorts and take a shower!

As usual, whenever I'm lying awake in bed, things start bothering me.

What if I'm really not a good singer after all? If

the Cheetah Girls find out, then they are gonna kick me out of the group. They probably only let me stay in the group because they feel sorry for me, anyway.

"How come you wuz limping?" Chantelle asks me, popping her gum extra loud.

"Can Man hit me from behind with his shopping cart," I moan, hoping Chantelle will stop bothering me.

What does Ms. Truly want? I wonder. Please tell me, crystal ball. I wish I knew a psychic like Princess Pamela—she's Chanel's father's girlfriend, and she can read the future. But I'm not close enough to her to get her to read mine for free, and I don't have any money to pay her.

I get real quiet, thinking again. I'll bet Ms. Truly doesn't want me to take dance classes anymore, because there are other kids who need them more than I do. Or maybe the YMCA found out that I'm not really fourteen! That's it—they're gonna kick me out of the Junior Youth Entrepreneurship Program!

I know if I keep this up, I'll be awake all night. So I make myself go to sleep by thinking about my favorite dream. In my dream, I am dancing across the sky, and I see my real mother in the clouds, smiling at me. I can dance so high that she starts clapping.

Dozing off, I whisper to myself so that Chantelle doesn't hear me, "Dancing in the clouds, that's me—I'm not just another wanna-be. . . ."

Chapter 4

Two days a week after school, I work the concession stand at the YMCA on 135th Street as part of the Junior Youth Entrepreneurship Program, which teaches peeps like me skills to pay the bills—marketing, salesmanship, motivational training, and stuff like that.

It's almost six o'clock, and I'm kinda nervous because I haven't seen Ms. Truly walk by yet. She teaches a dance class here—earlier than the one I take—so I thought I would see her going to the cafeteria for a soda or something between classes. Sucking my teeth, I realize I must have missed her, because I was too busy folding these boring T-shirts!

Abiola Adams works the stand with me.

She's a freshman at Stuyvesant High School, and studies ballet at the American Ballet Theater School in Lincoln Center. In other words, she's smart *and* she's got mad moves.

I call her "Miss Nutcracker"—and she's really cool, 'cuz she's into flava like me. She has on this dope vest with red embroidery like paisley flowers, and baggy jeans. We are both wearing the same black Madd Monster stomp shoes.

"You know why nobody is buying these T-shirts?" I turn to Abiola with a mischievous smile on my face.

Abiola is sitting like a high priestess of price tags on a high chair, tagging baseball caps stamped with the YMCA moniker in big, ugly white letters. "Why?" she says, trying to stuff a yawn.

"'Cuz they're having a wack attack, that's why," I say with a frown. "See, if they would let me design the shirts, they'd be flying off the rack."

"Well then, why don't you ask them if you can? You could put, 'Cheetah Girl is in the house at the YMCA, yo!'" Abi says sarcastically.

"I'm not trying to floss. I'm serious, Abba-cadabra," I say, smiling, 'cuz I'm imitating my sister Twinkie. "This lettering could put a hurtin' on a blind man's eyesight. Who's gonna pay fifteen dollars for these T-shirts, anyway, when they can go to Chirpy Cheapies and get one for $5, with their *own* name stamped on it?"

"They don't charge extra for that?" Abiola asks me, like she's a news reporter or something.

"I don't know, but you know what I'm sayin'. I'm not playin'. Next semester, I get to take an embossing class, so I'll learn how to do some dope lettering. You watch."

"I will," Abiola says, shaking her head at me. What I like best about her is she can keep a secret. See, she's the only one here at the YMCA program who knows that I'm only twelve.

Sometimes I feel bad because I haven't even told my crew yet—but I don't want them treating me like a baby or something. I didn't mean to tell Abiola, but it just kinda slipped out one day.

See, she was telling me about the trick candles her mother put on her birthday cake. No matter how hard she blew, they wouldn't blow out. So I slipped, and told her how on my last birthday, Mrs. Bosco only put eleven candles on my cake instead of twelve. I thought it was so funny that she forgot how old I was.

See, when I was in elementary school and junior high, I hated how all the kids used to make fun of me, just because I was in the "SP" programs—that means Special Program for kids who are smart. But Abiola is real cool—she won't say anything, because I could lose my spot in the Junior Youth Program.

Okay, so you're supposed to be fourteen to be in the program. But on the other hand, it's for high school students—and that's what I am, right?

"Guess where I hear they're hiring?" Abiola says, all confidential like a secret agent.

"Where?" I ask, my eyes opening wide like flying saucers.

"At the Project Wise program at University Settlement, down on Eldridge Street on the Lower East Side," she whispers.

"Word?"

"Mmm-hmm. I hear they're paying the same as here—minimum wage, two nights a week. But in the summer, you can put in twenty-four hours a week, and they got all kinds of programs."

"Yeah?"

"Uh-huh. They got this dope dance program, I hear," Abiola says, nodding her head, then turning to see if anyone is looking. "You sit around and tell stories about your culture, then you interpret it into dance, and at the end of the year, you put on a big show called the Roots Celebration."

"Word? You think I could go down there?" I ask aloud.

"Try. They may not ask for your birth certificate or anything—just a letter from one of your teachers at school, so they won't know you're only twelve."

"Shhh," I smirk, putting my finger over my mouth.

"Nobody heard me," Abiola says, giggling, then putting some more of the ugly T-shirts in a stack on the concession stand.

"Look at the new leotard I got," I say, pulling my cheetah all-in-one out of my backpack to show to Abiola. "Mrs. Bosco bought it for me out of the money I gave her from the Cheetah Girls show at the Cheetah-Rama on Halloween.

Four hundred duckets! I couldn't believe it. But I didn't keep the loot, because I knew Mrs. Bosco needed the money for her hospital bills."

"She sick?"

"Uh-huh. She coughs all the time."

"Where'd she find a cheetah leotard like that?" Abiola asks, smiling. She thinks it's cute that I'm a Cheetah Girl now.

"I think at Daffy's, or Chirpy's," I say, then let out a sigh. "I wonder why Ms. Truly wants to see me."

"Don't know, but you'll find out soon enough, 'cuz it's time to go with the flow," Abiola says, then grabs her bag to leave. She goes upstairs to the computer room, to work on the youth program's newsletter, *Mad Flava*.

Sometimes Abiola acts like she's a newscaster or something, like Starbaby Belle on television—but she's learning mad skills. So I guess she's got a right to floss a little.

The butterflies in my stomach start flapping their wings again as I change into my leotard. Then they flap some more when I walk into the gymnasium where I take Ms. Truly's hip-hop dance class.

That's the only thing I really like about working here—taking free dance classes. And now I may even lose that? It's not fair!

Pouting, I think of something Mrs. Bosco always says. "You can get mad, till you get glad!" It makes me laugh. She used to always say it to Jimmy, one of my used-to-be foster brothers. He used to walk around with his mouth poked out so far, you'd think someone had stuffed them with platters. Then one day, his real mother decided she wanted him back, so they came and took him away from us. I haven't seen or heard from him since.

I wonder where Jimmy is now? I'm gonna ask my caseworker, Mrs. Tattle, when I see her. That's *if* I see her. Lately, the caseworkers have been coming and going, quittin' their jobs so fast it could make your head spin. Mrs. Bosco says, "For the little money they get paid, it's a miracle they show up at all."

"Dorinda! There you are. Why didn't you return my phone call?" Ms. Truly asks me sternly, as I take my place on the gym floor. She doesn't smile much, and it makes me kinda nervous.

"I thought you said to call you if I *wasn't* coming to class," I say, getting nervous again.

"No. I spoke to your mother, and I distinctly told her to have you call me *before* you came to class today," Ms. Truly insists.

"Oh, I'm sorry, Ms. Truly. Sometimes Mrs. Bosco, um, writes down the messages wrong because she's so busy," I say, trying to cover up for my foster mother. I wish Mrs. Bosco could read and write, but she never finished school.

"Well, that's all right, but don't leave without seeing me after class," Ms. Truly says.

I *hate* when grown-ups do that. Why don't they just blurt out whatever it is they want to say, and get it over with!

Usually, I stay near the front of the class, but today I'm so nervous that I go to the back, where Paprika is standing. Maybe *she* knows something, because she is one of Ms. Truly's "pets."

Ms. Truly always starts the class with warm-up *pliés*. So while we're doing them, going up and down, up and down, I turn to Paprika and whisper, "Did Ms. Truly talk to you about anything?"

"No, why?" Paprika asks, extending her arms out in second position.

"'Cuz she called my house and said she

wanted to see me after class today," I say nervously. I'm sweating already, and we haven't even started dancing yet.

"I don't know anything," Paprika says, giving me this serious look, like, "You must be in trouble, so get away from me!"

Bending my body over my feet, I feel like a croaked Cheetah.

Some hyena is coming in for the kill. I can *feel* it.

Usually, class is over much too soon, but today, I thought it would go on and on till the break of dawn! I guess that's good, though, since this will probably be the last class I take with Ms. Truly.

Sighing out loud, I pick up my towel and walk to the front of the gymnasium to wait for her. She's not even finished talking to the other students, before I start apologizing again for not calling her back.

"That's all right, Dorinda," Ms. Truly says sternly, "it's just that you won't have much time to practice."

"Practice?" I say, squinching up my nose because now I'm really confused. "Practice for what?"

Who's 'Bout to Bounce?

"Come inside my office for a second," Ms. Truly says, taking me by my arm and leading me outside the gym to her office.

I can feel my heart pounding right through my cheetah leotard. I think it's gonna pop out of my chest like in *Alien* and start doing pirouettes or something!

Ms. Truly's perfume is strong. I know this smell. It's Fetch by Ruff Lauren, the perfume Bubbles likes.

"Sit down," Ms. Truly says, then closes the door.

I flop down in the chair like I have spaghetti legs. I must *really* be in trouble, 'cuz Ms. Truly is being super-nice to me. That's not like her.

Suddenly, a lightbulb goes off in my dim head. Ms. Truly probably wants to hook me up with an audition at *another* school or something, so she can get *rid* of me! I am getting so upset, I have to fight back the tears.

Ms. Truly pulls out a folder, looks at a piece of paper, then mutters, "There's still time. Can you stay after class tonight?"

"Yes." I croak like a frog, because the word got stuck somewhere down my throat. I wish Bubbles were here. She'd stand up and fight for me. So what you know about that, Ms. Truly? What a phony-baloney. Always acting like she likes me, but she doesn't!

"Okay," Ms. Truly says. Then she sighs, like she's Judge Fudge on television and she's gonna read me the verdict for a death penalty or something. "A friend of mine just got hired as the choreographer for the upcoming Mo' Money Monique tour, 'The Toyz Is Mine.' It's a one-year tour around the world, and they're looking for backup dancers, with hip-hop and some jazz training." She gives me a look. "I think you should audition for it."

All of a sudden, I feel like the scarecrow in *The Wizard of Oz* when he got cut down off his post. I just wanna flop to the floor in relief. *Ms. Truly thinks I can audition for Mo' Money Monique!*

"The only thing is, the audition is tomorrow morning. But if you stay after class tonight, we can practice for about half an hour. That way you'll go in there with full confidence, and be able to work your magic," Ms. Truly says, all smiley-faced.

I am so stunned, I must be acting like a zombie, because Ms. Truly looks at me and says,

"Dorinda, are you with me?"

"Yes, Ms. Truly. I'll, um, stay after class and go to the audition," I say, stuttering with excitement.

"Here, take the name of my friend, and the address where you have to go for the audition." Ms. Truly hands me a piece of paper.

"Dorka Por-i-," I read, but I'm having trouble pronouncing the lady's last name.

Ms. Truly helps me. "Por-i-skova," she says with a smile.

"Poriskova," I say, this time pronouncing it correctly. "What kind of name is that?"

"It's Czech."

"Oh," I say.

"The Czech Republic is a country in eastern Europe," Ms. Truly says.

"I know that," I tell her. I do, too. Geography is one of my best subjects in school. "It's near Albania, where my new sister Arba is from."

"I'm impressed!" Ms. Truly beams at me. "Anyway, you're gonna like Dorka. She's a fierce choreographer, and she's got 'mad moves,' as you would say. We studied at Joffrey Ballet together, back in the day."

"I didn't know you took ballet, Ms. Truly!" I

say, getting more excited. "My best friend, Chanel, used to take ballet. It's really hard, right?"

"Sure is," she agrees. "I wouldn't trade anything now for hip-hop, though. It gives you the cultural freedom to express yourself—and that's more important than any perfect *plee-ay*," she says, stretching out the word.

"I always had this secret fantasy about being a ballerina," I confide in Ms. Truly. "I wish I could have taken classes when I was little."

"Well, that's what daydreams are for," Ms. Truly says, chuckling like she knows. "You've got a feel for hip-hop though, Dorinda, and if you stick with it, you'll probably be able to write your own ticket."

I'm not sure what kind of ticket Ms. Truly is talking about, and I'm afraid to tell her how much I like being a Cheetah Girl. I don't want her to think I'm not grateful for the chance to audition for the Mo' Money Monique tour.

As if reading my mind, Ms. Truly says, "You're thinking about that group of yours, aren't you? I see you girls together all the time. It must be very exciting for you."

"Yes, Ms. Truly," I admit.

She sighs, gives me a sad smile. "I tried to be a singer once," she says. "But it just wasn't happening. I couldn't play the games you have to play to get a record deal."

She gives me a big smile now. "You'll have more control over your career as a dancer, Dorinda. The worst that could happen is, you'll end up a teacher, like me—and that's not so bad, is it?"

"No, Ms. Truly. You're the *best* teacher. You're dope," I say, hoping I haven't hurt her feelings.

"And you're the best dancer, Dorinda. It's a joy to teach you," Ms. Truly says, then comes around the desk to put her arms around me. Her hug makes me feel like a grilled shrimp, because she is so tall. *Everybody* is taller than me.

"I just hope one day you'll know what a great dancer you are," she says.

I can barely believe it's true—that Ms. Truly thinks I'm such a great dancer. But what about the Cheetah Girls? How can I leave them and my family, and go off around the world for a whole year?

All of a sudden, I feel like a total crybaby. I'm so exhausted from being nervous, I just let the tears come, one by one.

Ms. Truly holds me, and whispers, "Just give it all you've got tomorrow at the audition. God will take care of the rest." She lifts my chin in her hand and gives me a wink. "And make sure to wear this leotard," she adds. "It's *fierce*."

Chapter 5

I smile all the way home, thinking about Ms. Truly and my audition. That is, until I have to hold the stupid ice pack on my ankle for a whole hour so that the swelling will go down. I shouldn't have taken class, I tell myself.

But how was I to know it wasn't going to be my last class? How was I supposed to know there was a big audition in my future? What do I have, a crystal ball?

I ask God to please make the swelling go down tomorrow for my big audition. I also wonder if God could get Chantelle to stop popping her gum like a moo-moo.

Since I'm too nervous to go to sleep, I hobble quietly into the kitchen to call Bubbles's and

Chanel's pagers. When one of us wants to talk in the chat room on the Internet, but it's too late to talk on the phone, we page each other. Whoever gets the page first is supposed to call Angie and Aqua, then all five of us assemble in the chat room. I wish I had a telephone in my room, but then Monie would probably hog it anyway, talking to her knucklehead boyfriend.

When I was little, she used to wake me up when I was sleeping, because she said I snored. That was before I got my tonsils out, but I don't think I really snored. She just hated me because, even then, I was Mrs. Bosco's favorite.

As I log on to the Internet, it hits me—*I can't tell my crew about the audition!* That really makes me feel like a Wonder Bread heel. What was I thinking, agreeing to audition as a backup dancer, when I'm already a part of a superhot group?

Well, it's too late now. I already said I'd go. Besides, it won't be the first secret I've kept from my crew. They still don't know how I live, really. Or how old I am.

Besides, I'm not gonna get this gig anyway. I don't care how good a dancer Ms. Truly thinks I am. I mean, we're talking about Mo' Money

Monique, you know what I'm saying? I bet Ms. Truly is sending a lot of girls to audition for the Dorky lady. I'll probably run into Paprika there.

As it turns out, I don't have to worry about telling my crew anything, because Bubbles needs to blab tonight. So I'm safe—for now.

"What makes you think your mom has hired some Bobo Baboso private detective?" Chanel types on the screen. That makes me laugh, 'cuz Chanel is making a snap on this television show on the Spanish channel, about a bumbling detective, Bobo Baboso, who fumbles cases.

"I'm telling you, my mom's hired a private detective, Miss Cuchifrita, so don't get 'chuchie' with me!" Bubbles types in.

"Why would she need to hire a private detective, Bubbles, can you tell us that?" Chuchie asks.

"NO! If I knew the answer to that, I wouldn't be asking all of you!" Bubbles is mad—she's reading Chanel.

"Why don't you just ask your mom what's going on—maybe she'll tell you," I type on the screen.

Then I feel sad, because I wish I could take my own advice and just be *honest*. Now that would *really* be dope.

My fingernails look like stub-a-nubs. I've bitten them off because I'm *mad* nervous. I'm so glad Bubbles isn't here, because she would be readin' me, but I couldn't help myself!

I feel *really* guilty that I didn't tell my crew last night about the audition, but I don't want them to think I'm not mad serious about being a Cheetah Girl. On the other hand, sometimes you gotta flex, you know what I'm saying?

Not that I'm flexing now. There are so many tall girls at the Mo' Money Monique audition that I feel like a grilled shrimp, as usual. I think maybe Ms. Truly made a mistake, because most of the girls here look older than me. *None* of them looks my age. My *real* age, you know what I'm saying?

I've got to chill. Maybe they'll never get to my number. After all, just by looking at these dancers' "penguin feet," I can tell they've got *mad* moves. They'll just send the rest of us home long before they get to my piddly place.

Who's 'Bout to Bounce?

I have never seen so many people waiting in line before. Not one, but *two* lines. Not even at the MC Rabbit concert last summer. Both lines are trailing like an out-of-control choo-choo train, all the way down the endless hallway outside of Rehearsal Studio A, where the audition is.

I'm so far back in line, I can't even hear what music they're playing inside the studio. I can only feel the vibration from the bass, thumping through the wall. They're probably using one of Mo' Money Monique's tracks. I really like her songs, so that's cool.

Right now, she has two of the dopiest dope hits out: "Don't Dis Me Like I'm a Doll" and "This Time It's Personal." They play them a kazillion times a day on the radio. I like the second one better, because it has more of the rap flava that I savor.

I wonder if I'm in the right line. . . . One line is for even numbers, and the other is for odd numbers. I'm number 357. Since I don't have any nails left to bite, I start yanking and twirling the curls on the side of my face. I'd better ask somebody if I'm on the right line, I think—just to make sure.

"What number are you?" I nervously ask the girl in front of me, who is wearing a red crop top and a baseball cap turned backward. I don't think she heard me, because she doesn't answer me, so I ask her again.

"Three hundred and *fifty-five*," she turns and snarls at me, giving me a nasty look, like, "I heard you the first time, shorty."

That's awright, Miss Pigeon. At least I'm not wearing wack contact lenses that make me look like the girl in *The Exorcist*!

"Girls, keep the aisles clear, please," yells a *really really* tall guy wearing a black leotard and tights. He is the one who wrote my name down and gave me a number, like we're in the bakery or something. All I can see of him now is the top of his really bald head, until he comes closer a few minutes later, with his clipboard in his hand like he's a high school principal.

"Everyone is going to get seen," says the exasperated giant, "and crowding the front, or hanging out in the middle of the hallway, isn't going to help the lines move any faster!"

All of a sudden, he adjusts his headset, then barks into it, "They're coming out? Okay, copy that. I'll send the next group in." Then he prances away like a gazelle. You can always tell a dancer, because they don't run like normal people. Except for me, 'cuz I don't floss like that.

Another hour goes by, which means I've been waiting in line for *two* hours now, and my throat is so dry it feels like it's gonna start croaking up frogs any minute.

I shoulda brought a Snapple and an apple, I chuckle to myself. But it's no joke, how sore my ankle is getting from standing around here so long. What if I can't dance because my ankle stiffens up or something?

The girl in front of me must be getting nervous too, because all of a sudden, she starts acting nice. "I need to stretch my legs," she says, sucking her teeth, then takes off her cap and pulls out a mirror to fix her hair. "I'm gonna be mad late for class. Do you think I should wear the cap, or keep it off?"

"I think you should keep it off—and maybe put your hair up, or something," I advise Miss Pigeon. She's dark brown, like Aqua and Angie, and her long blond extensions are so thick and straight, it looks like somebody played pin the donkey on her head. I think she should take off her big gold earrings, too, but I'm not gonna tell her that.

"You know how many dancers they're gonna pick?" Miss Pigeon asks me, pulling down her red crop top.

"No, but it must be a lot, 'cuz they're seeing a lot of dancers," I say, trying to act like I know something.

"No, I don't think Mo' Money Monique likes a lot of dancers onstage with her. It wrecks her flow. I bet you they're gonna pick about five—at the most," Miss Pigeon says, looking at me with those scary green *Exorcist* eyes.

"Where do you, um, go to school?" I ask, trying to be nice back. She must be a senior, I'm guessing.

"LaGuardia," she says nonchalantly. Folding her arms in front of her, she leans on the wall, like she is *really* bored.

I get so excited, I almost tell her that part of my crew goes to LaGuardia too. Then I realize—*What if she knows Aqua and Angie*? Then she'll tell them she met me at an audition for backup dancers!

Probably everybody at LaGuardia knows Aqua and Angie because they're twins—who can sing. I get so scared thinking about what I almost just did, I don't even hear Miss Pigeon asking me a question.

"I'm sorry, what'choo say?"

"Where do *you* go to school?"

For a second, I think about lying, but then I'll be frying, so I decide to tell the truth. "Fashion Industries."

"Oh," she says, like I don't have skills.

I am so grateful when the not-so-jolly giant calls our numbers, so I don't have to talk anymore to Miss Pigeon. My own thoughts come flooding back at me—mainly, "How could you go on an audition without telling your crew?"

"Okay, you girls can go inside now," Mr. Giant with the clipboard says, pointing to five girls, including me and Miss Pigeon. This is it—time to do or die.

When I get inside, I nervously look around and see one, two, *five* people sitting at a long table with a pitcher of water on it and some paper cups. I'd audition with that pitcher on my head, just to get a sip of what's inside!

I don't see Mo' Money Monique anywhere. At least I won't make a fool of myself in front of her.

A tall lady with a long ponytail and a bump on her nose motions for us to stand in a single line in front of her. She is really pretty, and I can tell that she used to be a ballerina, just by the way she is standing.

"Hell-o, lade-eez, I'm Dorka Poriskova, the choreographer. First I want you to introduce yourselves one by one, then I'll give you the combee-nay-shuns for the dance sequence to follow."

"I'm Dorinda Rogers," I say, speaking up loudly when it's my turn. Dorka has a really heavy accent, and I want to make sure she understands me.

"A-h-h," says Dorka with a smile. "We have the same name."

"I said *Dorinda Rogers,*" I repeat, louder, 'cuz she obviously didn't understand me the first time.

"I know what you *said,* Dor-een-da," Dorka says, stretching my name out.

Omigosh! Now I've made her mad at me! Why did I have to open my big fat trap—my *boca grande,* as Chanel would say. I'm finished even before I get started!

"Each of our names means 'God's gift,'"

Dorka explains patiently. "Yours is the Spanish, um, var-ee-ay-shun, and mine is Czech."

"Oh," I say with a smile, but I'm so embarrassed, I want to shrivel right down to the size of a pebble and roll away! I act like I'm so smart, but I didn't even know what my own name meant!

"That's okay—you are too young to know ever-r-r-ything," Dorka says, smiling.

"Word, that's true, because nobody ever told me what my name means before," I say with a relieved laugh. In fact, everyone in the room laughs at my joke. Whew! Now I hope I can dance. Please, feet, don't fail me now.

While Dorka calls out the other girls' names, I start to think again about my name: Dorinda. God's gift. I wonder who named me that. Was it my real mother? If I was God's gift to her, then how come she gave me up?

I asked Mrs. Bosco once about her. Mrs. Bosco told me my "birth mother" was on a trip around the world. She must've gone around the world more than once, if you know what I'm saying, because that was seven years ago, and I'm *still* living at Mrs. Bosco's.

Flexing my ankle so it doesn't stiffen up on me now, I decide to go to the library after the audition and read some name books. I'm so nervous, I don't even hear what the other girls say about themselves, but like a zombie, I snap out of it when Dorka begins to give us the combinations to follow.

"Let's start in fifth position, right foot front. Move your foot to the side on *two*, then back on *three*, and close in first position on *four*," Dorka instructs us.

It's basically hip-hop style with jazz movements. I've got this covered on the easy-breezy tip.

But wait a minute . . . did she say back on two or three?

"Are you ready, girls?"

"Yes!" we answer in unison, and I quickly figure out that she had to have said "on three." The whole combination wouldn't make sense otherwise.

They're playing the MC Rabbit song "Can I Get a Nibble?"—which is straight-up hip-hop. I'm groovin' so hard, I don't even feel nervous anymore—until we're finished a few minutes later, and Dorka says, "Thank you, girls. If you've been chosen, you will receive a phone call. You were gr-e-a-t."

As I'm leaving, I say thank you to Dorka, since she knows Ms. Truly.

She smiles at me and says, "Good-bye, Dor-i-n-d-a!" That makes me feel like, well, "God's gift," if you know what I'm sayin'. She's so nice!

Chapter 6

As we are led back out by the giant in tights, I'm feeling dope about how the audition went. I worked it, Dorka liked me, and they all laughed at my joke. They won't forget my name, either.

Then, just like that, I feel like a wanna-be. I wonder why that is . . . Galleria and Chanel aren't like that at all—they never think of themselves that way. Even Aqua and Angie aren't exactly shy. A lot of times, I feel like I don't really belong with them at all. Like, with all my skills, I still don't feel like I got it like that.

Sometimes, I dream how they'll find out I'm twelve, and they'll think I'm wack, and a liar, and a fake, and they'll kick me out of the Cheetah Girls, and not be my crew anymore. . . .

As I come back out into the hallway, I can't believe there is still a long line of girls waiting to audition. They'll be here till the break of dawn.

Who am I kidding? There is no way I'll get picked for the Mo' Money Monique tour—no matter how dope I think my moves were. I'm only twelve. Look at how gorgeous these girls all are! Why did I even come here?

And then, I answer my own question. "I came here to prove to myself I could do it," I say. "And I did. I'm not a wanna-be—I'm a really good dancer, just like Ms. Truly said. Even though I have no chance at this job, I was great in there. And I'm as good a dancer as any of those other girls. *Better.*"

I take a deep breath and exhale, smiling. All of a sudden, it doesn't matter anymore whether I get the job as a backup dancer, because right now, I feel like dancing till the break of dawn.

"Float like a butterfly and sting like a bee, all the way to the library," I hum to myself as I step outside onto Lafayette Street.

Maybe Ms. Truly is right. Maybe I should give up singing, which I'm just okay at, and stick to dancing. I do like singing though, even if I'm not that good. And I am getting better at it, thanks to Drinka Champagne's lessons.

Sitting down at a library desk, I settle down with the fattest name book I can find—*Boo-Boos to Babies Name Book*. Word. They have so many names in it from all around the world—and most of them I've never seen before.

Starting with the "A's," I decide to look up Arba's name, but I don't see it listed. Then I think, What about Topwe's name? I look it up . . . Here it is: "In southern Rhodesia, the topwe is a vegetable." I'd better not tell Twinkie, I think, 'cuz then she'll tease Topwe, and call him "Hedda Lettuce" or something. She is smart like that.

Then I see my name. Ms. Dorka is right. "Dorinda" means "God's gift." Ooh, look—the English variation of the name is "Dorothea." That's Bubbles's mom's name! Wait till I tell Bubbles that I have the same name as her mom!

Suddenly I get a pang in my chest. I *can't* tell Bubbles, because then she'll ask me how I met Dorka! It hits me full force that I'll never be able to tell my crew anything about my big audition! I'll never be able to say how Ms. Truly praised my dancing, or how I was brave enough to show up, and how I came through when it counted most. They'll never hear about Dorka.

It's a good thing I haven't got a chance at this job, I think with a laugh, 'cuz what would I tell them then? "Hey, y'all, I'm going on a 'round the world tour with Mo' Money Monique. See you later, cheetah-gators!"

I laugh at the thought of it. "Fat chance," I say, thinking of the hundreds of girls trying out for the job.

Hmmm . . . but there *is* a job I *can* possibly get, I think, remembering what Abiola told me.

Walking out of the library, I decide not to go home just yet. If I could get up the courage to go on the audition, then I can go downtown to see if I can get a job in the University Settlement's after-school program.

Being a Cheetah Girl is dope, but since our first gig, we haven't made any money at it, and the Apollo Amateur Night, while it's good exposure for us, doesn't pay either. Meanwhile, I need to start making *serious* loot.

Sure, we make a lot of our own outfits, but there are some things a Cheetah Girl just has to go out and buy. That's no problem for the rest of my crew. But as for me, my job at the YMCA concession stand doesn't pay enough, and I hate asking Mrs. Bosco for *anything*, because I know she can't afford it.

On the subway, I wonder again why my name is Dorinda. Did my real mom name me after someone? Why do I have a Spanish name? Nah, I can't be Spanish!

One thing is for sure—the receptionist at the University Settlement is *definitely* Spanish. "May I help you?" she asks, pushing her long, wavy black hair behind her ear.

"Um, I'm a freshman at Fashion Industries High School, and I want to apply for the after-school work program," I say, feeling large and in charge now that I've been to a big audition for a job that pays a zillion times what this one does.

The pretty *señorita* hands me an application form and says, "You'll have to fill this form out, then someone will be right with you."

Word. I knew this would be on the easy-breezy tip. I'm in there like swimwear! Smiling from ear to ear, I sit down on the marble bench across from the receptionist to fill out my form.

"Excuse me, miss," the receptionist says to me.

I jump right up and go back to her window so she doesn't have to talk loud. Drinka says it's very bad for your vocal cords.

"You're going to need three pieces of identification. Do you have your birth certificate with you?" she asks me.

"No, I . . . didn't know I was supposed to bring it," I mutter, my face falling flat as a pancake.

"That's okay. You can fill out the form and leave it here, then come back with your ID when you have it," she says nicely. "You can see a job placement counselor any time from nine to five, Monday through Friday."

Where's the trapdoor in the floor when you need it? How am I gonna get out of this one?

"You know, I have to go home now anyway, because I have to baby-sit," I fib, but I'm so embarrassed because I know the receptionist *knows* I'm fibbing. She's probably wondering where my bib is!

Not batting an eyelash, the receptionist says,

"Sure, just come back another time, and bring your birth certificate, social security card, and a letter from one of your teachers. We just need proof that you're fourteen years old and attending school. You understand."

She knows I'm not fourteen! I walk out the door with my Cheetah tail between my legs. I walk past a big hole in the middle of Eldridge Street, where they're doing construction work. I wish I could just fall into that hole and disappear, and save everybody the trouble of having to put up with me!

Chapter 7

Mornings are always madness in my house, because all the kids try to get their breakfast at the same time, and "make some noise," like they're at a concert or something. Kenya is banging her spoon on the table. Topwe is playing his mouth like a boom box, and Twinkie is jumping up and down, trying to reach the knob on the cupboard over the sink.

"Twinkie, sit down, baby. I'm gonna get your cereal," Mrs. Bosco says, yawning and opening the cupboard. "Which box you want?"

"Oatmeal," Twinkie announces. In our house, there are no brand names with cute pictures of leprechauns or elves—just "no name," Piggly Wiggly supermarket stuff, with big black letters that say Corn Flakes, Rice, Beans and on and on till you could yawn.

"I want toast! I want toast!" Kenya yells, then thumps her elbow down on the counter.

"Kenya! *Can ya* please hush up!" Twinkie says, exasperated, causing all the kids to burst into a chorus of giggles.

"What's so funny?" Mrs. Bosco says, turning around to look at us, and pushing her bifocal glasses farther up her nose.

"Kenya, *can ya*, please hush up. Get it?" I volunteer.

"Oh." Mrs. Bosco chuckles, pouring the milk into Twinkie's cereal. "I'm sorry, Kenya, but you gonna have to have cereal today—so *can ya* please eat it before my nerves leave town?"

That's good for another round of hysterical giggles. Mrs. Bosco just smiles, and wipes her hands on a dish towel. "And y'all better hurry up, because we ain't got all day to get to school."

Kenya sticks her lip out as far as she can, then gets up from the table and storms out of the kitchen.

"I'll go get some bread. I'll be right back," I moan, then tell Kenya to come back to the table. I don't have time to fight with her today, even though she can be such a pain.

She doesn't say anything, but she does act like she feels a little guilty, so I can see that the little talk I had with her before bed last night must have made a difference. I explained to her how lucky we are to live here, and how sick Mrs. Bosco is, and how stealing kids' stuff at school isn't going to make her *any* friends.

I guess Mrs. Bosco was right, asking me to talk to her. The littler kids all listen to me—kinda like I was their mother or something. I don't think Mrs. Bosco would have wanted me to say anything about her being sick, but I said it anyway, and I'm not sorry. She needs us all to help her, not to get in her way. And whatever it takes to keep Kenya behaving, I'm going to do it.

As I'm slipping on my windbreaker hood, the phone on the kitchen wall rings. Mrs. Bosco answers it, then says, "Hold on a minute," before passing me the receiver.

"Who is it?" I ask, afraid.

"It sounded like she said 'Dokie Po' something," Mrs. Bosco says. She wrinkles her forehead with a puzzled frown, causing Topwe to burst out laughing.

"Oh, I know who it is," I say, because I don't want to embarrass Mrs. Bosco.

"Hello?" I say nervously into the receiver.

"Dor-e-e-nda?" asks a strange voice with a heavy accent.

"Yes," I answer cautiously, because I still don't know who it is.

"It's Dorka Poriskova, the choreographer. Dor-e-e-nda, I have good news for you."

Suddenly, I feel like someone could blow me over with a peacock feather or something. "Yes?" I ask in a squeaky voice.

"We want you for the Mo' Money Monique tour. Rehearsal starts on Sunday morning at ten o'clock. Can you make it?"

"I—I have to ask my mom," I stammer. What I really want to do is scream for joy!

"Okay, but let us know today, because we haven't much time to prepare before the tour begins," Dorka says excitedly.

I am so numb when I put down the receiver, for a second I don't hear Kenya's piercing voice yelling at me to get her some toast.

I'm in such a daze, I just turn to Mrs. Bosco

and say, "They want me to tour with Mo' Money Monique as a backup dancer. . . . "

"Is that right?" Mrs. Bosco says, surprised, then wipes Topwe's crumb-infested mouth with a napkin. "Ain't that somethin', now!"

Stuffing my hands in my pockets, I stand motionless for a minute. How could they have picked *me*, out of all those dope dancers? There must be some kind of mistake, I tell myself, and they'll realize it as soon as they see me again. . . .

I start to feel a wave of panic creeping over me. I don't have time right now to even *think* about this. About leaving my family . . . my *crew* . . .

"You awright, baby? That's good news, right?" Ms. Bosco asks—'cuz she can see I'm not happy. She spills the orange juice in Topwe's cup, because she's so busy looking at me.

"Yeah," I say, my throat getting tight, like it does whenever I get nervous. "But I don't know if I wanna go."

What I *wanna* do is go back to bed and hide under the covers! I can't go to school and tell my crew *more* fib-eronis. So what *am* I gonna tell them?

I'd better bounce, I tell myself, so I can get to

school early and see Mrs. LaPuma, the freshman guidance counselor. I met with her when I first registered, and she was really nice. She told me if I ever had a problem, or needed career guidance, to come to her. Well, I guess I sure need it now!

I know I'm supposed to be happy, but all I feel is scared and confused, like that time my polka-dot dress came apart in school in sixth grade. It was the first dress I ever made, and I stayed up all night sewing it—by hand, since I didn't have a sewing machine yet.

I was so excited to wear it to school, but the seams started popping open by first period! I waited until everybody left the classroom before I got up and ran home. Everybody was laughing at me in the hallway.

I didn't go to school the next day, either. I was too embarrassed. Mrs. Bosco had to walk me to school herself the day after that, or I wouldn't have gone back even then!

"Can I help you?" asks the girl sitting at the front desk outside Mrs. LaPuma's office.

"Do you think Mrs. LaPuma could see me for a few minutes?" I ask her really nicely.

The girl's gold chains clank as she goes in to

ask Mrs. LaPuma, then they clank again as she walks back to her desk. "Mrs. LaPuma has a few minutes," she says. "Go on in."

I go inside, sit down by Mrs. LaPuma's desk, and tell her the whole drama.

"Well, Dorinda," she says when I am finished, "I think it would be good for you to go on the Mo'—what is her name?" Mrs. LaPuma asks, arching her high eyebrows even higher. I wonder how she draws them so perfect, 'cuz they both look exactly the same—like two smiley faces turned upside down and smiling at me.

"Mo' Money Monique. She's a *really* big singer right now," I explain, trying to impress Mrs. LaPuma so she won't think *M* to the *M* to the *M* sang at The Winky Dinky Lizard or something. "She has two songs on the chart right—"

"Yes, my daughter listens to rap music," Mrs. LaPuma says, cutting me off. She takes a sip of her iced coffee through a straw, leaving behind a red lipstick stain.

"Dorinda, I know how attached you feel to your friends, and your foster family. But this is a great opportunity for you. You deserve to try new experiences, dear, even at your young age.

Besides, if I may say so, it seems like you have your hands full at home. I know you may think you're not ready, but getting a break from your everyday life might be the best thing you ever did."

Mrs. LaPuma folds her hands on the desk, and looks at me for an answer. I sit there frozen, not knowing what to say. Why is Mrs. LaPuma trying to make it sound like I should run away from home?

"I'm not unhappy at home, Mrs. LaPuma," I try to explain, and I can feel my cheeks getting red because I'm getting upset. I don't want Mrs. LaPuma to tell Mrs. Tattle, my caseworker, that I was complaining or anything. See, I know that my teachers send reports about me to my caseworkers, since I'm legally a ward of the state.

"I'm not saying you are unhappy at Mrs. Bosco's, Dorinda," Mrs. LaPuma says sternly.

If there is one thing I hate, it's when grownups get that tone of voice like they know everything—and they don't!

"But what I *am* saying is, I don't think you realize what kind of daily strain you're under," Mrs. LaPuma goes on. "Being in a whole new environment, especially a creative one, may open up a whole world of new possibilities for you."

"I'm not trying to be funny, Mrs. LaPuma, but what strain am I under, washing dishes every night? It makes me feel good to help Mrs. Bosco. She's my *mother*. And the Cheetah Girls help me with *lots* of stuff."

"Dorinda, don't get so defensive," Mrs. LaPuma says, frowning. "The Cheetah Girls are wonderful, I'm sure—but you have to think about your *own* future. Being part of a major artist's tour, traveling around the world at your tender age . . ."

She sighs and leans forward, giving me a searching look. "I know that you're exceptionally bright, because I've looked at your junior high school records, but if it is your calling to be a dancer, then—"

At that moment, the girl with the musical jewelry comes in and interrupts us. "Mrs. LaPuma, may I speak to you a moment?" she asks, giving the guidance counselor a look.

"Excuse me for a moment, Dorinda," Mrs. LaPuma says, agitated. "Yes, what is it, Chloe?"

She follows the secretary into the outer office, and is gone for half a minute or so.

When she comes back in, she says hurriedly, "Dorinda, there's an emergency I have to attend to. We're a little short-staffed right, now so there is never a moment's peace around here. Good luck with your decision, and come back and see me if I can be of any further assistance."

"Oh, okay, bye, Mrs. LaPuma, thanks a lot," I say, getting up quickly in case she needs the chair. Emergency—yeah, right. I'll bet. The coffee machine is probably broken or something. Oh, well. I already got her point of view, and I know she's right—but I still feel really really bad.

Like it or not, it's show time. Time to see Bubbles and Chuchie before homeroom period. The three of us meet every morning, by the girls' lockers on the first floor. I hesitate now. How am I gonna tell them I got this job? They're gonna yell at me for not telling them sooner, and then—then, they're gonna talk me into *turning it down*! They're going to *hate* me!

Without even thinking, I walk over to the pay phone on the wall and deposit some change. I dial Ms. "Dokie Po," as my foster mother called her.

"Hi, Ms. Dorka, it's Dorinda Rogers. Yes. I just wanted to let you know that I'll be at rehearsal on Sunday. Yes. Ten o'clock. Thank you so much! Bye!"

Hanging up the phone, I feel instantly relieved. For better or worse, I've made my decision. There's no way for my crew to talk me out of it now.

I know Mrs. LaPuma is right. It'd be better for everybody if I just go away somewhere. Better for Mrs. Bosco. Better for the Cheetah Girls . . .

I mean, they don't need me, I tell myself. After all, Chuchie and Bubbles have each other, and Angie and Aqua have each other. Who do *I* have?

Besides, if this tour leads to more jobs, Mrs. Bosco can make room for some other foster child who needs a home. That's probably what Mrs. LaPuma was trying to say, but she was trying to be nice about it.

As I walk toward the lockers, I can see Chanel standing with her back turned, talking with Bubbles. Actually, I see Chanel's cheetah backpack first, and suddenly I feel the butterflies fluttering in my stomach again. They are the dopest friends I've ever had. How can I leave them?

When Chanel turns around, I see she has red scratches on her nose. I wonder if she and her mother have been fighting or something. I know Ms. Simmons is still upset with Chanel for charging up her credit card.

"Where'd you get the scratches, Cheetah *Señorita*?" I ask Chanel, trying to act normal.

"Kahlua's stupid dog Spawn did it," Chanel sighs, then starts twirling one of her braids, like she does whenever she gets nervous.

Kahlua is one of Chanel's neighbors. Chanel doesn't like her, because she says she's stuck-up, but since Kahlua has a dog and Chanel doesn't, she visits her anyway. Chanel loves dogs.

I ask, "What happened? Spawn caught you drinking out of her bowl?"

"It's a *he*, Do' Re Mi," Chanel smirks. "And where have you been?"

"Wh-what do you mean?" I stutter. Suddenly, I can feel my cheeks turning red for the second time today.

"I called you *twice* last night, and spoke to Mrs. Bosco for a long time," Chanel says, looking at me like I was a sneaky Cheetah.

"Word. She didn't tell me," I say, getting *really* nervous. I wonder what they talked about. And why didn't Mrs. Bosco tell me? Maybe she didn't *forget* to tell me. Maybe she didn't tell me for a reason!

"I talked to her, too," Bubbles says nonchalantly.

"You called, too?" I ask, squinching up my nose like I do when I'm confused. Sometimes the dynamic duo act like they are detectives or something.

"No, silly willy, we just did a three-way conference call," Bubbles says, flossing about her phone hookup.

Right now, I can feel something is happening on the sneaky-deaky tip, but I'm feeling too guilty to ask them what it is. These two are definitely up to *something*. If I'm lying, I'm frying!

"We have a surprise for you," Chanel says, then Bubbles pokes her.

"You're always blabbing your *boca grande*, Chuchie!"

"What kind of surprise?" I ask. I get the feeling

I'm being played like one of the contestants on "It's a Wacky World" who finds out they've won the wack booby prize.

"We'll tell you after school," Bubbles says, winking like a secret agent. Then she pulls out her furry Kitty Kat notebook, the one that she writes songs in, and scribbles something.

"Why don't you tell me at lunch?" I ask, trying to peep the situation.

That's when Bubbles and Chuchie give each other a look, and I *know* something is jumping off!

"Bubbles is gonna help me study for my Italian test. You know I'm not good at it, and I'm gonna fail if I don't study! So we can't meet you today at lunch, okay, *Señorita*?" Chuchie gives me a hug. "Don't be upset. We'll see you at three o'clock."

"I'm not trying to hear that, Chanel," I say—with an attitude, 'cuz now I am getting a little upset. "I know you two. You're up to something."

"You never answered our question," Bubbles says, butting in. "Where *were* you last night? How come you got home so late?"

"I, um, went to the library to study and I

couldn't take the books out 'cuz I owe too many," I say, trying to act on the easy-breezy tip.

"Yeah, right. What were you studying?" Chanel asks me, trying to act like Bobo Baboso again.

"Shoe design books and, um, I was reading this book about names and stuff," I volunteer.

"Names?" Bubbles asks, curious.

"Yeah," I say, exasperated, "*Boo-Boos to Babies Name Book*."

Chuchie and Bubbles fall over each other giggling, then Bubbles stops laughing on a dime, and asks, all serious, "Do' Re Mi, is there something *you're* not telling us?"

All of a sudden, I feel like a frozen Popsicle got stuck to my tongue. They're just playing with me, 'cuz they already *know* about the Mo' Money Monique tour! Or even worse—they know I'm only twelve! Mrs. Bosco must have slipped and told them!

When Chuchie pats my tummy and bursts out laughing, I suddenly realize what they *really* mean. They *are* playing with me.

"I'm not picking out baby names, silly!" I blurt out. If they only knew that I'm twelve, and haven't even gotten my stupid period yet like they have, maybe they would stop laughing at me!

"Okay, Do' Re Mi, but a little fishy told me that you were playing 'hooky' with Red Snapper or Mackerel," Bubbles says, cackling just like a jackal!

Red Snapper and Mackerel are these two bozos who go to school with us, and seem to like Cheetahs, if you know what I'm saying. Their names are Derek Hambone and Mackerel Johnson, and they are ga-ga for Bubbles and Chanel.

They don't pay too much attention to me, which is good, 'cuz I'm not interested in them either. But that doesn't stop Bubbles and Chanel from teasing me about it.

"Yeah, well those fish had better keep swimming upstream, if you know what I mean," I say, playing back with Bubbles.

"Now *that's* the flava that I savor," Bubbles says, winking at me.

The three of us do the Cheetah Girls handshake. Then Bubbles and Chanel run off, screaming, "See ya at three, Do' Re Mi!"

I wave after them, my secret still a secret. But for how much longer?

Chapter 8

It's "five after three" and I'm trying not to "see what I see." My foster mother is standing right outside my school, right next to troublemaker Teqwila Johnson and her posse! What is Mrs. Bosco doing here, anyway? Something *must* be wrong.

I'm 'bout to bounce, but Mrs. Bosco sees me before I can make my move. "Hi, Mrs. Bosco," I say with a smile, trying to act normal.

I always call her Mrs. Bosco, even when we're in public, so kids don't make fun of how she looks. The first time she came to my school, I was in the first grade, and kids teased me the whole year, saying, "That's not *really* your mother! She's ugly!"

"What you are doing here?" I ask my foster mother nicely. Mrs. Bosco doesn't really like huggy, kissy stuff, especially in public, but I would really like to smooth the wrinkles down on her hot pink dress, which is shaped just like a tent.

"I just wanted to surprise you," Mrs. Bosco says, grinning from ear to ear.

Suddenly I feel sick to my stomach. I remember the day when I was almost five years old, and Mrs. Parkay was *really* nice to me for the first time. That was the very day the caseworker, Mrs. Domino, came to take me away.

"You're going to live with really nice people," she had said, as she held my hand and we crossed the street together. *Is that what Mrs. Bosco is gonna tell me now*? That I'm going to live somewhere else, with "*really* nice people"?

Well, I'm going away on tour with Mo' Money Monique, anyway, I remind myself. And I'll be gone a whole year. So it doesn't really matter whether she wants me or not. So there!

All of a sudden, I start to notice all the things about my foster mother that really bother me.

Like her false teeth, which she takes out at night, and puts in a glass of water on her dressing room table. And her thick mustache! Why can't she wax it off like most ladies do? And her really thick bifocal glasses!

And why didn't she wear the dope brown dress I made for her, with the big, oversized patch pockets in the front? Why couldn't she wear it to school if she really loves me?

I decide that I can't let Bubbles and Chanel see her—not looking like this. "I'm not gonna wait for Galleria and Chanel today, so we can leave now," I say to Mrs. Bosco, praying we can make it to the subway station before the dynamic duo come breaking out of school, which will happen any minute now.

"No, baby. I wanna see—I mean, meet your friends. You never bring them over to the house," Mrs. Bosco says, still smiling.

"I heard that!" Teqwila Johnson says loudly, letting out a big laugh like the stupid hyena she is. She whispers something to her friend Sheila Grand, whose last name fits her, because she's always acting like she's large and in charge.

Both of them are in my Draping 101 class,

and they never even talk to me. Now they must be making fun of me! I throw a cutting glance in their direction, but they pretend they're not looking at me.

All the people from my school are standing on the sidewalk, trying to act like they've got it going on. Fashion Industries is like that. We style and floss a lot.

All of a sudden I feel sad, like a wave washing over me. Suddenly, it doesn't matter that Mrs. Bosco isn't nice-looking, or that she dresses all frumpy. She's *real*—she never styles or flosses about anything. I don't wanna leave Mrs. Bosco, or Twinkie, or Arba.

And I don't wanna leave my crew, either. They're the dopest friends I've ever had in my whole life!

Just as I'm thinking all this, I hear, "Hi, Mrs. Bosco!" coming from my left side. It's Chanel, hiking up the waist on her pink plaid baggy jeans.

Wait a minute! How did she know this was my foster mother?

"Hi, Chanel. How you doin'?" Mrs. Bosco asks Chanel, like they've known each other their whole lives or something.

"Good. I just took a quiz in Italian class. I hope I pass it." Chanel giggles.

"Is that right?" Mrs. Bosco asks, acting all interested.

"Galleria made me switch from Spanish to Italian—but it's a lot harder," Chanel tells her.

"Y'all are matching," I say, pointing to Chanel's pants and Mrs. Bosco's dress.

"I know," Chanel says, smiling at Mrs. Bosco, then she even gives her a hug!

I can't believe it when Bubbles walks up and does the exact same thing to Mrs. Bosco! What's up with this situation?

Now *everybody* is looking at us. See, where there is Chanel and Bubbles, there is *mad* attention. Everybody is kinda jealous of them, because they're so pretty, and have the dopest style. Everybody knows we're in a group together, too, but I don't think anybody is jealous of me.

So what if they are, anyway? I don't care about that. All I wanna know is, what is this big surprise Chanel and Bubbles were flossin' about earlier? And how do they know Mrs. Bosco?

Picking up on my confusion, Chanel pipes

right in. "Do' Re Mi, *mamacita,* you are not gonna believe what we hooked up for you."

"That's the truth, Ruth," I say, squinting my eyes. This better be a good one.

"Princess Pamela has given the Cheetah Girls an all-day Pampering Pass at her Pampering Palace! Facials, pedicures, manicures, seaweed body wraps—the works, *mamacita*! We'll be so hooked up for the show at the Apollo, we'll win just because we look and feel so good, *está bien?"*

"Word!" I say in total surprise. So *this* is the big surprise the dynamic duo have been concocting! Mrs. Bosco was probably in on it, too—that's probably how she got hooked up with Bubbles and Chuchie. Now I feel stupid for being so worried.

"Can my mom come, too?" I ask my crew, calling her "mom" in front of everybody. I mean, Mrs. Bosco is always being nice to me, and here I've been acting like a spoiled brat, thinking about everything that's wrong with her. *She* deserves to go to Princess Pamela's—not me.

But my foster mom is not having it. "No, baby, I got too much to do around the house to be sitting up in some beauty parlor, like you girls. The only show I got to get ready for is the one I watch on TV," she says, chuckling. Then she suddenly starts coughing again. She doubles over, one hand over her mouth, the other on her chest.

It sounds like she's getting sick again. Please, I ask God, don't let her have to go back to the hospital! If she got sick again before I left on tour, I wouldn't go. I'd stay here and take care of her, I say, still praying.

And I guess my prayer is answered, 'cuz Mrs. Bosco stops coughing as fast as she started. She takes a deep breath. "Whoo," she says. "That's over. I feel better now. Uh, what were you tellin' me again?"

"Mrs. Bosco, I wuz sayin' that it's Princess Pamela's Pampering Palace—not just any beauty parlor, *está bien?*" Chanel says, giggling.

"Who is this Princess Pamela? She some kind of royalty?" Mrs. Bosco asks, amused.

"She's a gypsy," Bubbles chimes in.

"She's a psychic," Chanel continues.

"Well, she's a gypsy psychic gettin' paid," Bubbles adds. "I mean, she's got businesses all over the Big Apple. Princess Pamela's got growl power, and she doesn't even know it!"

"*And*, to top it all off, she's my father's girlfriend," Chanel flosses. She really loves Princess Pamela.

"What is growl power?" Mrs. Bosco asks, 'cuz now she is really finding my friends funny.

"That's when you really got it goin' on, and you got the brains, courage, heart—and businesses—to prove it," Bubbles says. She loves to explain our whole vibe to anybody who asks—and everybody who doesn't.

"We'll get you to Princess Pamela's one day, Mrs. Bosco, you wait and see," Chanel says, laughing. "'Cuz you haven't lived until you've had a Fango Dango Mud Mask, *está bien?*"

"The passes are for a full day treatment, plus a free touch-up the week after. So if we go with the flow this Saturday right after Drinka's, we can get our touch-ups next Saturday afternoon, right before our show at the Apollo. We'll be lookin' so phat, we're bound to make people sit up and take notice," Bubbles finishes, flossing for Mrs. Bosco's sake.

That makes me a little uncomfortable. I mean, getting to perform one song in the Apollo Amateur Hour isn't exactly a show, if you know what I'm saying—not like doin' a whole world tour with Mo' Money Monique.

I give Mrs. Bosco a quick look. Did I warn her not to say anything about the tour to my friends? I can't remember! I've got to get her out of here, quick, before she starts blabbing about it. I know I'm going to have to tell my crew eventually, but not yet—not now! I'm not ready to face their reaction. No way!

"Why you calling yourself fat, baby?" Mrs. Bosco says to Bubbles, misunderstanding. "You so pretty, and there ain't nothing wrong with a little meat and potatoes."

We all start laughing so hard, *everybody* is looking at us—including Derek Hambone and Mackerel Johnson.

"Mrs. Bosco, *phat* doesn't mean fat—it means *dope*," Chanel tries to explain, confusing my foster mother even more. This sends us all into fits of giggles again.

"It means, like, fabulous," Bubbles adds, sounding like her mom, Dorothea—my namesake.

Now the Mackerel and the Red Snapper have worked their way over to us, and are standing behind Bubbles, listening to our conversation!

I'm trying to get Bubbles's or Chanel's attention, but they aren't looking at me.

"Oh, I understand, baby. You girls are so smart, with all your words. Dorinda is always telling me some new words y'all made up," Mrs. Bosco says, fixing her bifocal glasses again.

"Hey, Cheetah Girls, what's the word for the day?" Derek busts in, trying to cash in his two cents.

"Cute but no loot, Red Snapper," Bubbles says, but nicer than she usually talks to Derek-probably because my foster mother is standing right there.

"Come on with it, Kitty Kat, and show me where the money's at!" Derek says, slapping his boy Mackerel a high five, like he's saying something.

"See ya, *schemo*, we gotta bounce," Bubbles says, then motions for Chanel to walk with her.

Mackerel and the Red Snapper follow them for a while, then give up and walk away. I'm so relieved that I didn't have to introduce them to Mrs. Bosco.

Not that I'm ashamed of her—I'm not. But

still, I don't want everybody at school to know my business. My private life is private, you know what I'm sayin'? Why should they even know I have a foster family, not a real one? I mean, not even my crew knows everything about me, right?

Bubbles and Chanel are off to Toto in New York. I'm alone with my foster mother now, and she's being really quiet. Unusually quiet. I wonder what's up with her. "Are you okay?" I ask, scared. "You're not getting sick again, are you?"

"No, baby, I'll be all right. Doctor says all's I need is rest."

"Rest? You never rest," I say, worried.

"Don't worry 'bout me," she says. "I'll be all right. Long's I have my nap every afternoon . . . "

"But how will you do that when I'm on tour?" I ask. "Who's gonna look after Kenya and all them?"

"Monie will have to help out. She's been spending too much time with that Hector anyway. Don't you worry, baby, like I said. You go off on your tour and don't even think about us."

Yeah, right. "Here. Let me hold that bag."

"Awright, child." Mrs. Bosco hands me the Piggy Wiggly shopping bag, but it's really heavy.

"What's in here?" I ask.

"Q-Tips," Mrs. Bosco says, chuckling at her little joke. See, she uses Q-Tips dipped in peroxide to clean Corky's ears, 'cuz she says he must be hard of hearing. She always yells at him, "Why else do I have to tell you to pick up your socks and pants fifty times and you *still* don't do it?"

We're almost to the subway entrance now, and I start thinking again about why Mrs. Bosco is being so quiet. And how my friends all acted like they knew her, when I know I made sure they never got to come to my house.

Something is definitely going on, I can feel it. And if it isn't about Mrs. Bosco's health, then what is it?

As if she can hear my thoughts, Mrs. Bosco stops at the bottom of the subway steps and turns to face me. "How would you feel about me and Mr. Bosco adopting you?" she asks all of a sudden.

We've never talked about this before. Never. When I first got to her house, she told me that my birth mother might come back to get me at any time, so I shouldn't get too attached to her or Mr. Bosco—but that she would always be my second mom.

I wonder why she's asking me this now? "I don't know how I feel about it," I say. This is making me really nervous. "What about my, um, *real* mother?" I ask her, but I'm looking down at my shoes. I can feel my whole body shaking.

"Well, I'm just asking you a question. If I could adopt you, would you want me to?" Mrs. Bosco repeats, coughing into a tissue. She always loses her breath when we have to go up or down subway stairs.

"But what about the money you get from foster care for taking care of me?" I ask nervously. I don't want Mrs. Bosco to have to stop getting her foster care checks, just to adopt me. I know she loves me anyway. I wouldn't want to cost her that money.

"Don't worry about that," Mrs. Bosco says. Then she puts her arm around my shoulder and leans in toward me. She always used to do this when I was little, and I know exactly what she is going to say.

"I know when you grow up, we gonna go live in a big ole fancy house together, with a whole lot of bedrooms—'cuz you always had the smartest head on your shoulders."

Now I *do* smooth down the crease that's riding up in the front of dress, and she lets me, too. "Yeah," I say.

"Yeah, what," Mrs. Bosco asks.

"Yes! Yes, I want to be adopted!"

"Awright, baby," she says with a sweet smile. "I'll see what I can do, but I can't promise you anything—'cuz you know how trifling those people can be."

"Those people" are what my foster mother calls everyone who works at the Department of Child Welfare, Division of Foster Care Services, which is a big, dingy office in downtown Manhattan. I go once a year for psychological testing, and to visit my social worker, Mrs. Carter. She is in charge of all the caseworkers who make visits in the field.

"Do you really want me to go on tour with Mo' Money Monique?" I ask my foster mother.

"If that's what you want to do, that's fine with me, Dorinda. You always was dancing around the house, even when you wuz little. I know you got your new friends, and you don't wanna leave them—but you got to do what's right for you. You know I always say, ain't nuthin' wrong with Mo' Money!"

Mrs. Bosco puts her arm through mine, and leads me onto the subway platform. "But if you're not ready to go off around the world and be a working girl, don't worry 'bout that, either," she says. "After all, we got plenty of time to go live in that big ole mansion somewhere."

Suddenly, I feel like crying. It's almost too good to be true. Me—adopted after all these years, with Mr. and Mrs. Bosco as my real parents. And going on tour with Mo' Money Monique!

I guess Monie the meanie will have to finally help out for a change. And I guess the Cheetah Girls will have to carry on without me.

I wonder if I'll still be around for the Apollo Amateur Night. I mean, the tour probably won't leave town that soon, right? Maybe I can get away with not telling my crew about the tour until after we perform at the Apollo. That way, I can still be a Cheetah Girl for just a little longer.

I like this new plan of mine. Sure, it means I have to keep my secret for a whole 'nother week. But it's worth the stress. I mean, what if I go to rehearsal tomorrow, and it turns out there was a big mistake, and I didn't really get the job after all? You know what I'm sayin'? Or what if I mess up so bad at the rehearsal that they fire me? I'd be so embarrassed if I'd already told my crew about my big new job!

Besides, I figure, the longer I don't tell them, the better. 'Cuz once I do, the Cheetah Girls are really gonna pounce. They'll probably never even speak to me again!

Chapter 9

When you're standing on the corner of 210th Street and Broadway, you'd think that Princess Pamela owns the whole block or something. Both of her businesses Princess Pamela's Pampering Palace, and Princess Pamela's Poundcake Palace—take up several doorways on each side.

The Pampering Palace is really the bomb. It's got a glittery ruby red sign outside, with stars, balls, and moon shapes hanging in the window.

"The stars, moon, and planets are supposed to symbolize another galaxy—'cuz that's where you are when you step inside the Palace," Chanel explains to us proudly.

When you walk in the Palace, you feel like

you're taking a magic carpet ride, because everything is covered in red velvet, and the floor is covered with red carpet! When I look up at the ceiling, there are all these chandeliers that look like crystal drops falling from the sky! It's the dopiest dope place I've ever been—besides Bubbles's mom's store, Toto in New York.

"Close your mouth!" Bubbles instructs Angie, who is as awestruck as I am by the Princess's Palace. It's a diggable planet look, all right.

"Ah, my boot-i-full Chanel and her friends!" Princess Pamela says, rushing to greet us with open arms. She goes over to Chanel and starts crushing her to death. I wish my foster mother would hug me like that. Maybe once she really adopts me, she will. . . .

When you put the *P* to the *P*, Princess Pamela looks just like a gypsy psychic lady is supposed to. She is really pretty, and she has dark, curly hair streaked with white in the front. Her eyebrows are dark and thick, and she has a red, red mouth. She probably doesn't eat bologna and cheese sandwiches like I do, because she has to keep her lipstick looking so dope.

Who's 'Bout to Bounce?

"Is that rayon crushed velvet?" I ask Princess Pamela, goggling at all the yards it must have taken to make her dress, which is sweeping to the floor like Cinderella's gown.

"Yes, dahling. You like?" Princess Pamela asks me, her big brown eyes twinkling. "I know where you can get an *excellent* price on velvet. Let me know if you want to go, dahling."

"Awright, 'cuz I'd be hooked up if I had a dress like that," I tell her.

"You, dahling, are so boot-i-full, like my little Chanel, that you could wear nothing but a leaf, and e-v-e-r-y-o-n-e would be *green* with Gucci Envy!" she says, pinching my cheeks. Usually I hate when grown-ups do that, but she's so cool, I don't mind.

You can tell Chanel is proud of Princess Pamela by the way she beams with pride at the Princess's jokes.

The receptionist, who has a hairstyle that looks more like a "boo-boo" than a bouffant, tells us in this heavy British accent to "go back and change into your robes and slippers in the dressing room, and someone will be with you in a jiffy." Then she starts sneezing into a tissue, and her eyes are watering like she's crying.

"Is the English lady sick?" I ask Princess Pamela. I don't know the lady's name, but I don't want to call her a receptionist, in case she turns out to be royalty, or something.

"No, she has allergies, dahling, and she's not from England. She's from Idaho," Princess Pamela whispers, putting her arm around me.

"Then why does she talk like that—with an accent?" I ask, puzzled.

"When you're from a place named after a potato, you have to do something to make yourself interesting, no?" Princess Pamela says, smiling mischievously. Now I see why Chanel loves her. Princess Pamela's got mad flava.

"Okay, Mademoiselle Do' Re Mi, what will it be?" Bubbles asks, whipping out the beauty menu like she's a French waiter. "Le lavender mousse conditioning body scrub, or le peppermint pedicure?"

"Gee, Bubbles, I never really thought about it," I quip. "But now that you mention it, I would like a cherry sundae back rub!"

"You're a mess, Dorinda!" Aqua heckles me. Then she turns to Galleria and asks, "You think they got anything for athlete's foot? All these dance classes are giving me fungus right in between my toes. See right there." Aqua holds up her foot so Bubbles can get a good view.

"If I were you, I wouldn't be worried about fungus 'till I took care of those *Boomerang* toes, Aqua," Bubbles says, holding her nose closed like something stinks. "I mean, you got any hot dogs to go with those corn fritters?"

"That's all right, I'm not mad at you," Aqua says. "But I sure hope they got something for them."

Seriously studying the beauty menu, Bubbles exclaims, "Aqua, look, it says here that a tea tree oil bath is such a powerful antiseptic, it will even get rid of the cock-a-roaches between your toes!"

"Lemme see that menu, 'cuz I know it does not say that," Angie says, coming to the defense of her twin sister.

Angie is the more "chill" of the two, but sometimes the Walker twins are so much alike I can't tell them apart—especially now that they are wearing matching red velvet robes and slippers.

I wish I had a twin sister like that. A *real* sister, anyway. Someone who'd stick up for me. When I turn around from putting my robe on, I catch Bubbles, Chanel, and the twins whispering together.

"Don't be making fun of me!" I say, wincing. "So what if the robe *is* really big on me!"

My crew looks at me all serious, and Aqua says, "What makes you think we wuz talking about you anyway, Dorinda?"

"'Cuz I know you four. You'll read me through the floor," I say. Aqua never calls me by my nickname, Do' Re Mi, but I like the way she says Dorinda, because it sounds cute with her southern drawl.

"Well, we have a special treat for you, Miss Dorinda," Bubbles says.

All of a sudden, an attendant appears, in a white uniform and white shoes, with a white towel draped around her arm. She looks like a nurse in a cuckoo hospital, and I'm beginning to feel like a cuckoo patient.

"Could you come with me, *mademoiselle*?" she says, looking at me.

Princess Pamela's place is like the United Nations, I think to myself. Kinda like my house. But I think the French nurse's accent is real, and I'm not sure I wanna go anywhere with her.

"Not having it," I moan, looking right at Bubbles, who is probably the ringleader behind this whole situation.

"Come on, Dorinda, we're going with you, too," Aqua volunteers. They all escort me to a room with red velvet walls, and a long, pod-shaped tub that looks really weird.

"What's this for?" I ask the French nurse lady.

"It is for *ze cell-yoo-lete* treatment, *mademoiselle,*" she explains to me.

"*Mademoiselle* doesn't want any treatment," I say, looking at Angie and Aqua, and not even trying to pronounce whatever that word was she said.

"Dorinda, that's the whole idea. This is so you won't get any cellulite," Aqua pipes in.

"How am I gonna get something that I don't even know what it is?" I exclaim, sucking my teeth. How did Aqua know what it is, anyway? She's such a show-off.

"Cellulite is that lumpy cottage-cheese-looking stuff that girls get on the back of their thighs," Aqua says, pointing to her butt.

If I didn't know any better, I'd swear Aqua and Angie are making this stuff up as they go along. "Where's Bubbles and Chanel?"

"They're in the, um, other—" Angie hems and haws.

"Super cellulite treatment room," Aqua joins in.

"Please try, *mademoiselle,*" the attendant begs me.

"Okay, but *mademoiselle* doesn't like this one bit," I moan, giving in to what I have a feeling is somebody's idea of a Cheetah Girl joke.

"You have to stop talking now, *mademoiselle,*" the French lady whispers in my ear. "For all of the impurities to leave your body, it requires absolute silence."

She wraps this Saran Wrap stuff around me—so, so tight that I swear *I'll* be leaving my body soon. Then she seals me in the pod, and turns on a dial. Just what I need. Some science project experiment gone wrong!

I lie there, wrapped in plastic like a sandwich in the fridge. Suddenly, I feel real sleepy, like my body is being deprived of oxygen or something. As I doze off, I swear to myself, if I grow up and have cellulite after this, I'm gonna sue—guess who!

When I wake up, I'm the only one in the room

with the French nurse lady, who peers up her nose at me over her little glasses. When I get some more duckets, I'm gonna buy Mrs. Bosco nice little glasses like that.

Yawning, I wonder how long I've been in this "invasion of the body snatcher" pod, but I'm definitely ready to bust out.

"C'est bien, mademoiselle?"

"No, *mademoiselle* is not all right." I moan. At least that gets her hopping like a hare, and soon, I'm out of the Baggie. I'm so happy to be back in a robe, just chilling.

But before I know it, the nurse has covered my face with a gucky banana-cream facial mask, and my eyes are covered with cucumber slices! I'm beginning to feel like an appetizer, if you know what I'm saying!

"Now what?"

As I try to recline in the chair and relax, I wonder—why am I always in a room by myself? I thought this was supposed to be fun. You know, the Cheetah Girls sitting around in some big bubble bath all day, talking and giggling.

Why do ladies do all this stuff, anyway? It's *boring*. I don't know how long I'm leaning back in the reclining chair, looking like a moonpie, before I finally hear the voice of the mischievous one.

"Do' Re Mi, can't you see how boot-i-full you look?" says Galleria. The nurse removes the cucumber slices, and I see Bubbles, Chanel, Aqua, and Angie standing over me, giggling.

"Was I sleeping again?" I ask them. I'm so annoyed, I don't think I'm ever gonna get a facial, or even wash my hair, ever again.

"Like Sleeping Beauty," Chanel says.

"It's time to bounce," Bubbles says, standing by while the French lady helps me off the table and hands me a glass filled with bubbles.

"This will help replenish your epee-dermis," advises the French lady.

"What's an epee-dermis?" Angie asks.

"It's the top layer of your chocolate skin, missy," Bubbles explains.

"Ooh, epidermis," Angie says, sucking her teeth. "We don't just sit around and sing all day at school, Galleria. Sometimes we have classes, and study things like *biology*."

"Let's all go over Dorinda's house, and eat popcorn, and watch *Scream*," Aqua says, interrupting her sister—and looking straight at *moi*.

"Are you crazy? The only 'scream' you two are gonna see at my house is all my brothers and sisters doing it for real," I say, rolling my eyes.

"Well, we already called your—um, Mrs. Bosco, and she says it's okay if we come over," Angie volunteers.

"No way," I say, looking at all four of them like I'm gonna pounce. "We're not going over my house."

"*Sí, sí,* Do' Re Mi," quips Chanel. "We're there, baby!"

"Word, I don't know what y'all have been drinking, but I'm not having it, okay?" I say, changing back into my clothes—*finally*!

Chapter 10

When we finally get outside on Broadway, Bubbles announces that we're taking a taxi, because we're late.

"Late for what?" I ask.

"Um . . . you know that show we watch on television?" Aqua chimes in. "Aqua—what's the name of that show we watch on Saturdays?"

"Dag on, don't *poke* me," Angie whines, rubbing her arm. "I can't remember."

"Taxi!" Bubbles yells loudly. She runs to the curb, and waves her hand in the air.

In the Big Apple, the yellow taxis fly by faster than Can Man with his shopping cart. I've been practically run over by them more than once. But Bubbles knows what she's doing. She stands on the edge of the curb, waving and tilting way forward. Then she quickly leans back whenever a car zips by. A real native New Yorker.

"Let's take a 'gypsy' cab!" Chanel giggles, making a joke on Princess Pamela, but Aqua and Angie don't get it.

"What's a gypsy cab?" asks Aqua, squinching up her nose. We all heckle. We love to tease Aqua and Angie because they're kinda, well, Southern. They've only been in New York since last summer, and they don't know the ways of the Big Apple.

Chanel explains the gypsy snap to her, and then Bubbles explains what a gypsy cab *really* is: "The seats are always dirty in the back, and they always have some smelly pine freshener stinking up the whole car. You only take 'em when you're desperate, or when your hairdo is gonna flop from the sopping rain."

"Oh," Aqua says, nodding her head, then laughs, "How you know 'Freddy' or 'Jason' ain't driving the cab, though?"

"'Cuz they wouldn't pick *you* up!" I throw in. "They'd be too scared of you, the way you two scream!"

We all start screaming—"Aaahhh!"—imitating Aqua and Angie last Halloween, when they screamed so loud, all the kids were scared of *them*.

"We're in!" Bubbles says, motioning us to hop in a yellow taxi. Since we're heading downtown from 210th Street, the first stop is gonna be my house on 116th Street. Then the taxi can keep going downtown and drop off the twins at 96th Street before taking Bubbles and Chuchie home.

When the taxi pulls up in front of the Cornwall Projects, though, Bubbles, Chanel, Aqua, *and* Angie jump out, and hightail it to the entrance of Building A, where I live.

"Come on, y'all, I already told you—you can't come to my house," I whine, slamming the taxi door. How'd they know which building I lived in, anyway?

"Oh yes we can, *Señorita*, 'cuz Mrs. Bosco invited us. *Está bien?"* Chanel says, leaping along like a ballerina.

Suddenly I realize the danger I'm in. Never mind that my house is small and crowded. What if my foster mother slips, and says something about the Mo' Money Monique tour?

Mrs. Bosco probably thinks I've already told my crew about it.

Panicking, I run as fast as I can to warn her, but Chanel is hanging on to my jacket for some reason. I pull at it, trying to get free. I can't have my secret come out. Not yet!

"Do' Re Mi, we don't care if you don't live in a palace. Leave that to Princess Pamela!" Chanel says. Then she gives me a *really* tight hug, while ringing my bell with her free hand.

"Chanel! Let go of me!" I giggle. "Why are you ringing my doorbell when I have keys?"

Mrs. Bosco opens the door, and me and Chanel fall on top of her. Except, I'm not so sure it's my foster mother. It doesn't really *look* like her. She looks . . . *better*, if you know what I'm saying.

"Hi, baby, we've been waiting for you."

I would know that voice in a tunnel. It's my foster mother, all right—and if I still had any doubts, she starts coughing into a tissue.

But look at the pretty flowered dress she's wearing. And I like her new wig—it's nothing fancy, just a nice soft brown, with curls.

And she's wearing *makeup*! My foster mother *never* wears makeup.

Now I know why she looks so different. She doesn't have a mustache anymore!

"Mrs. Bosco, you look *really* nice," I say.

Bubbles starts heckling. "You should have seen what we had to go through to wax her mustache!"

This sends everyone into a fit of giggles. "We told her we had a surprise for her, *está bien?*" exclaims Chanel. "Then we blindfolded her, and Bubbles put the wax on her upper lip—then pulled it off while me, Angie, and Aqua held her down!"

"When did you do all that?" I ask, surprised.

"While you wuz getting cell-yoo-leeted!" Angie says, beside herself with laughter.

Then I look around at the crowd of people in the living room. I hadn't noticed them all at first—and they start yelling, "Surprise!"

I mean, all of my brothers and sisters—including Monie the Meanie—Dorothea and her husband, Mr. Garibaldi, Ms. Simmons, and even some people I don't know! Everyone is standing around like they're at a party. Even Mrs. Gallstone from down the hall is here.

I *really* don't get whazzup with this situation. I mean, it's not my birthday. And then it hits me. Oh, no! *They already know my secret!*

If I wasn't so young, I think I would have a heart attack. My heart is beating so fast, I'm still not sure I won't be the first twelve-year-old to have one—and get written up in the *Guinness Book of World Records*. I'm not lying.

Mrs. Bosco must have told everybody that I'm going on the Mo' Money Monique tour! That's what this party is all about! I could just scream. How could she do this without asking me? I'd like to read her right now!

But instead of saying what I want to say, I hear myself blurting out, "Look at all the pretty flowers."

Then my eyes feast on the long banquet table that Mrs. Bosco always borrows from Mrs. Gallstone when we have a party. It's filled with all my *favorite* foods—fried chicken, potato salad, collard greens, rice and beans, black-eyed peas, corn bread, and one, two, *seven* sweet potato pies! Too bad I'm not the least bit hungry.

But wait a minute. If everybody knows I'm going on tour, how come they're not all upset? They're being so nice, even though I'm leaving them.

I feel so sad. Look at all the trouble they went

to for me! And I was about to yell at them! I flop down in a kitchen chair, like a scarecrow stuffed with straw. I don't deserve all of this. I feel so stupid—like Chanel did when she got caught using her mother's credit card.

"You and my mom did all this?" I ask, looking at Bubbles, Chanel, Aqua, and Angie.

"Yep. The body snatcher contraption was Princess Pamela's idea. We got you *good*," Aqua says proudly. "And me and Angie helped Mrs. Bosco cook all this dee-licious food just for you."

"Oh, no, honey—it's for us, too," Angie counters, "'cuz you know I'm hungry after all that tea tree oil!"

"Ah, ah, ah, don't forget about my Italian pastries," Mr. Garibaldi adds, waving his hand.

"Yeah, that's right. Dad made Chuchie's favorite—chocolate-covered cannolis!" Bubbles says, beside herself.

I heave a huge sigh. All this beautiful food. Too bad I'm not the least bit hungry. In fact, I feel sick about everything.

I look around the room, and I see people I don't even know. Who is this tall man with a mustache? Who is the tall woman with the

African fabric draped around her, and a turban that almost touches the ceiling?

The man catches my look. "Dorinda, I've heard so much about you from my daughters, and I'm quite honored to be here. I'm Mr. Walker," he says, extending his hand to me.

"Oh," I say smiling. It's Aqua and Angie's father. He looks like a successful businessman, all right.

"And this is my girlfriend, Alaba."

She looks like a model from some African tribe or something. I wonder what her name means? I'll have to look it up in the *Boo-Boo* name book. Aqua is behind her, making a face.

Galleria isn't finished talking. She puts a hand on my shoulder, and points the other one at my foster mom. "I want you to know that, even though we helped put it together, throwing the adoption party was always Mrs. Bosco's idea."

Adoption party? Did Bubbles say adoption party?

Now I need *my* ears poked with a Q-Tip dipped in peroxide, 'cuz I must be hard of hearing, like Corky. "Did you say, 'my adoption party'?"

"Mrs. Bosco has adopted you, silly willy Do' Re Mi!" Bubbles blurts out.

So *that's* why Mrs. Bosco was asking me all that stuff by the subway the other day. And that's how they all knew each other—they were planning this whole party together, complete with the visit to Princess Pamela's to get me out of the way!

I burst into a round of tears that would make the Tin Man in *The Wizard of Oz* squeak. Mrs. Bosco has *already* adopted me! I have a *real mom*!

"Dorinda, look at you, you're going to ruin all the effects of that delicious banana cream pie facial mask!" Dorothea says. Coming over to hug me, she pulls a leopard-print tissue out of her pocketbook. I notice that she's crying, too. "You don't know how happy I am for you," she says.

"Thank you, Ms. Dorothea," I say through my tears. I look across the room at my crew, who are all beaming at me. They all love me, I can see that. Look at the trouble they went to for my sake. How can I keep on lying to them?

I can't.

"I'm so sorry to be leaving all of you," I say.

"Huh?" Ms. Dorothea says. "What's this about leaving?"

"It won't be forever," I say. "Just for a year. As soon as the tour is over, I'll be back, and we'll be better than ever, I promise."

"Tour? What tour?" Galleria asks, looking at me, puzzled.

That *really* makes me start bawling like a crawling baby.

"Dorinda is a crybaby! Dorinda is a crybaby!" Kenya says, sucking her teeth.

"Kenya, *can ya* please hush up for a second," Mrs. Bosco says, putting her finger to her mouth.

"What tour?" my crew says in unison.

I just blurt out my whole confession, all at once. I tell them about the trail of lies I told to cover up my big audition, and about the rehearsal tomorrow.

Suddenly I feel everybody's eyes staring at me. Behind Alaba, I see Angie and Aqua looking stunned. And Chanel looks like she just got hit on the head with a brick.

They all turn to Galleria, waiting to see how she's gonna react. I look at her, too. She's our leader. Whatever she says, goes. If she says I'm out, then that's it. I lower my eyes, waiting for the verdict.

"Don't let us stop you from making 'Mo' Money,' Do' Re Mi. If you want to go on tour, you *go*," Bubbles says proudly. She looks at the rest of our crew as if she's answering for all of them. "We're proud of you for getting such a big gig. And don't worry—we'll always take you back as a Cheetah Girl, even if you come back when you're a hundred! Ain't that right, girls?"

"Right!" they all shout, gathering around me.

That gets me crying again, and I feel *really* bad, because now I don't know what to do about anything! I love my family and my crew so much—how can I bear to leave them?

"Are you happy about it?" Bubbles says, kneeling down next to me and holding my hand.

"I don't know. I don't wanna leave y'all now," I mumble.

"No, I mean about being adopted. You said you always dreamed about being adopted, and now it's happening. Dorinda, it's your dream come true."

Before I can answer Galleria, Ms. Dorothea suddenly bursts into tears! She runs out of the living room, her peacock boa dropping feathers behind her.

"Mom, what's wrong?" Bubbles turns around to look, but all she sees is the flurry of feathers falling to the floor, like snowflakes.

Dorothea locks herself in the bathroom, and she won't come out. After what seems like—well, forever, me and my crew and Ms. Simmons put our ears to the bathroom door.

"Ms. Dorothea is still crying," Angie whispers.

I feel terrible. "Do you think it's something I said?"

"No, Dorinda, I think Dorothea has always been a little dramatic," Ms. Simmons says.

She should talk. That "off-Broadway performance," as Bubbles called it, that Ms. Simmons pulled when Chanel got caught charging on her card would have sent the Wicked Witch of the West flying away on her broomstick!

"Ms. Dorothea, can I come in?" I yell through the keyhole.

"Only if you come in by yourself," Dorothea says, sniffling, then bawling again.

Bubbles looks at me like, "Whazzup with that?" But she has to understand that she can't always take care of everything.

"I'll handle this," I whisper, then knock softly on the door.

"Dorinda, I'm so glad we can talk by ourselves," Dorothea says, sniffling and laughing after she's closed the door behind us. "Sorry we have to meet like this," she says, balancing herself on the edge of the bathtub.

I feel embarrassed because the paint has chipped off, but Mr. Hammer, the super, keeps saying he's going to repaint it soon. I wish my apartment was dope like hers, with cheetah stuff everywhere.

"You know, Dorinda," she says, sniffling into her tissue, "from the first time I met you, I felt close to you."

"I know, Ms. Dorothea. I feel close to you, too," I reply.

"Now I know why," she says, pausing, then pulling down her leopard skirt over her knees. "I, um, I, um, always wanted to be adopted, too." Then she starts bawling again.

"You were a foster child?" I ask, amazed. "Bubbles never told me that."

"Bubbles doesn't know," Ms. Dorothea says, smiling at her daughter's nickname. "I never told her."

"Oh," I say, then we both hug. I would never have known Ms. Dorothea was a foster child. She is so beautiful and everything.

"I've hired a private detective to help find my mother, but I'm not having much luck," she says, sobbing some more.

So that's why she hired a detective! I think, remembering Bubbles and Chuchie's conversation in the chat room that night. "Oh, I'm sorry, Ms. Dorothea," I say, comforting her. "Don't give up, you'll find her."

"Maybe, maybe not," Dorothea says, then pauses. "Do you know what happened to your birth mother?"

"No. Um, Mrs. Bosco says she went on a trip around the world or something, but I don't know." I'm whispering, because I don't want anyone to hear me through the door. "I never told anybody that. Not even them."

Pointing outside the door, Ms. Dorothea smiles. "Well, let's just keep this our little secret, okay?"

"Okay. I won't say anything."

"I'm not ready to tell Galleria about my childhood. I never told her, because I've always wanted her to have a perfect life. But watching you just now, telling the truth, I felt so proud, like you were *my* daughter. One of these days, I'm gonna tell Galleria the truth—she deserves to hear it."

"Yes, she does," I agree.

"And you, Dorinda—now you have two mothers, whether you like it or not, okay? Mrs. Bosco—and me."

"Yes, Ms. Dorothea," I say. Now I'm crying harder than ever, and she holds me for what seems like hours. Then I remember about our names.

"Did you know that Dorothea and Dorinda are both variations of the same name—meaning 'God's gift'?"

"No, I didn't know that," Dorothea says, wiping her eyes with what's left of her tissue. Then she starts laughing uncontrollably. "God's gift—wait till Ms. Juanita hears that one!"

We're still laughing when I open the bathroom door, but Dorothea wants to stay in there for a while longer, so I go out by myself. Of course, Bubbles, the rest of my crew, and Ms. Juanita are still standing outside the door—being nosy posy, no doubt.

"What were y'all laughing about?" Bubbles says.

"I told her that my name and her name both mean 'God's gift.'"

"Really?" Bubbles exclaims.

"No wonder she's so conceited!" Juanita says, huffing.

"I wonder what *your* name means!" I heckle, then the six of us huddle outside the bathroom door, hugging and giggling together.

"We should leave her alone in the bathroom for a while," I say, pushing everyone toward the living room.

"That's for sure, 'cuz she wouldn't be caught dead crying and then not fixing her makeup!" Juanita chimes in.

Bubbles gives us a look behind Juanita's back, then blurts out, "Neither would *you*, Auntie Juanita!"

Chapter 11

Yesterday I may have been adopted, but today, nothing has changed in my house. Mrs. Bosco is washing dishes. Topwe is fighting with Kenya over the last slice of sweet potato pie, and Monie the Meanie is still here, talking on the phone with her boyfriend Hector. "Shut up!" she screams at the other kids. "Can't you see I'm talking?"

I don't pay much attention, though. I've got bigger things on my mind. Today is do-or-die day. I'm going to my first rehearsal for the Mo' Money Monique tour. Not only are the butterflies fluttering in my stomach, but I actually feel *nauseous*. That must be from the three slices of sweet potato pie I ate last night—I think two must be my limit.

I'm too sick to eat anything, but luckily my ankle feels a whole lot better. Drinking a glass of orange juice, I wonder who helped Mrs. Bosco with all the papers she must have signed for my adoption? If there is one thing I know about the Child Welfare Department, there are more forms to fill out than at the CIA, ABC, or FBI, if you know what I'm sayin'. And normally, I'm the one who helps her fill out forms.

After the kids finish breakfast, I help Mrs. Bosco clear away the plates, then get ready to leave.

"Dorinda, baby, I gotta tell you something," Mrs. Bosco says, walking over to a kitchen chair and sitting down real slow. Pulling out some papers from the knickknack ledge, she coughs, then says slowly, "When I got these papers and signed them, I didn't have my glasses on, so I guess I didn't realize what they were saying."

Mrs. Bosco pauses for a long time, which makes me feel uncomfortable, so I say something to fill up the empty space. "Yeah?"

"Well, Dorinda, I guess the adoption didn't go through," Mrs. Bosco says, letting out a sad sigh. "I found out on Friday, but I didn't want to say anything to your friends, since they were so excited setting up the party and everything,"

I sit there, too stunned to move. "So, I'm not legally adopted or anything?" I ask—but I already know the answer.

"I guess not, baby—but I'm gonna keep trying, you hear," she says, looking at me so sad. "You know how trifling those people downtown can be. They can't do nuttin' right but mess up kids' lives. That's the only thing they seem to do good."

"It doesn't matter," I say, although of course it does. I guess Mrs. Bosco will straighten it out with "those people" eventually. One of these days, I really will get adopted. Still, after all the celebration, it feels pretty empty to know it isn't really true.

I get a sudden urge to ask Mrs. Bosco where my real mother is. Or if it's true she's really around the world on a trip—but I think I already know the answer to that. Besides, looking at how sad Mrs. Bosco is, I don't think it's a good time to talk about it now.

"I don't mind being a foster child," I say, "as long as *you* are my foster mother."

She lets out another sigh. "You always were the smartest child I ever had. Nuttin' you can't do if you put your mind to it. That's what I always said."

At least I can be sure of one thing—if Mrs. Bosco went to all that trouble to adopt me, then no matter what happens, at least I don't have to worry about her giving me away, right?

I decide this is as good a time as any to ask her for the one thing I *really* want. "Can I call you Mom now, instead of Mrs. Bosco?"

"Yes, baby. I guess after all these years we've been together, you can call me anything you want!" Mrs. Bosco beams at me, then pulls out a tissue to cough.

I know it would be pushing too much if I started hugging her, so I don't. And I don't wanna start crying again like a crybaby, as Kenya says, so I tie my jacket around my waist and get up to go. "See ya later, Mom."

"See ya, baby," my foster mom says.

It's a good thing I'm early for rehearsal, because my stomach starts acting up again, and this gives me a chance to sit on the studio floor and calm down.

Pigeon girl from the audition was right. So far, there seem to be exactly five dancers. There are two guys and three girls, including me. They are all definitely older than I am, but they are all kinda small, like me—okay, they're taller, but not *that* much taller.

I smile at the dancer with long black hair down to her waist. She is so pretty. I don't remember seeing her at the audition. She musta been near the front or something.

She smiles back and introduces herself. "Hi, I'm Ling Oh."

"Hi, I'm Dorinda," I say, because I'm not sure if she just told me her first name, or her first and last name—so I wanna be on the safe side. Now I feel sorta self-conscious, because all the dancers are wearing black leotards, and I'm wearing my cheetah all-in-one. It makes me feel like a spotted mistake in the jiggy jungle!

Rubbing my ankle, I hear cackling in the hallway, and a whole group of people comes in, bringing in the noise.

Omigod, I can't believe my eyes. It really is Mo' Money Monique herself!

She is *really* pretty. Her hair is really straight, and her skin is a pretty tan color, and she isn't even wearing any makeup. I read in *Sistarella* magazine that she is sixteen now, but she still lives with her mom in Atlanta.

Mo' Money Monique adjusts her black leotard, and stands next to Dorka, the choreographer.

"Hi, Ms. Dorka," I say, because I can't pronounce her last name, and I don't want to embarrass myself by trying.

"Hello, Dor-een-da. I'm so glad to see you."

Mo' Money Monique comes over and introduces herself to us. We introduce ourselves back, and then she says to me, "I love your leotard, It's dope."

Word, she's *really* nice!

Dorka then takes over, and tells us that we are going to be practicing the moves without music first, just to get the combinations down.

The moves in hip-hop dancing are all about attitude. You have to move quick, sharp, *and* give attitude, as opposed to being graceful, like with jazz. For me, that's what makes it so dope.

Suddenly, it hits me that I'm doing what I've always dreamed of doing—dancing in real life, instead of in the clouds—and yet, I don't feel happy at all. I don't even feel nervous anymore. I just feel, well, *sad*.

At the end of rehearsal, the not-so-jolly giant from the audition, who it turns out is also the principal dancer, tells us to fill out a form.

That's when it hits me. I don't want to fill out any form. I don't want to be a backup dancer. I wanna be like Mo' Money Monique—the star. And if I can't be with my crew, then I don't want to be here, 'cuz I really am a Cheetah Girl.

Now my legs are shaking, as I go over to Dorka to break the news. "I can't do this, Ms. Dorka," I say, even though I'm so nervous, my throat feels like it's shaking.

"You can't do what?" she responds.

"I, um, can't go on the tour—because I'm already in a group," I say, proud of myself that I'm acting like a Cheetah instead of a scaredy cat.

"What kind of group, Dor-een-da?" Dorka asks, genuinely interested in what I have to say.

"We're the Cheetah Girls. It's five of us, and we sing and dance, and we're gonna travel all over the world one day too."

Now Dorka seems amused. "I remember when I left my country to come to America. I got accepted to ballet school here, and I was so scared that I told my mother, 'I don't want to go.' Do-reen-da, I hope you're not doing the same thing, are you?" She gives me a searching look.

"No. I'm not scared anymore. I'm just sad," I reply. "Sad that I could let myself forget so quickly how happy I was that the Cheetah Girls wanted *me* in their group."

"Okay, Dor-een-da. It's up to you. We would like you to tour with us, but remember, there are hundreds of girls who would be very happy to be in your place."

"I know, Ms. Dorka, and I'm sorry, but right now, I'm not one of those girls. I'm a Cheetah Girl."

"Good-bye then—Cheetah Girl," Ms. Dorka says, smiling. "God's gift is a good name for you. You are very brave, and also very talented. And so young, too . . . only twelve years old."

I gasp. How did she know? Of course—Mrs. Bosco must've told her.

"We would have gotten a tutor for you and everything," Dorka says. "Of course, it will be less expensive to hire someone older than you—but you are very special. I'm sure you and your Cheetah Girls will be touring the world someday, just as you say."

"Thanks, Ms. Dorka," I say. "Bye, now. Bye, everyone."

"Good-bye, Dorinda!" they all say, waving to me as I walk out the door, and close it behind me forever.

When I walk outside onto Lafayette Street, I practically run all the way to Chanel's house, which is only a few blocks away. I am so mad at myself for missing rehearsal with my crew! I should have made up my mind yesterday, but I guess I really wanted to know if I got the job for the Mo' Money Monique tour—*for real*, if you know what I'm sayin'.

"Well, looky, looky," says Aqua, when I walk into the exercise studio in Chanel's loft, where my crew have just finished rehearsing.

"We didn't think you were coming," Bubbles says, her eyes twinkling. Her hair looks nice. She's put it up with one of those cheetah squingee hair things.

"I didn't think I was, either, but I missed y'all too much—so I'm not going on that tour," I blurt out. "I'd rather be 'po' up from the floor up,' and a broke Cheetah Girl, than some back-up dancer."

All four of them jump up and down, and start yelling and screaming.

"Chanel, what's going on in there?" Juanita yells from the kitchen.

"Nada, Mamí!" Chanel yells back. "We're just happy!"

"We knew you'd be back," Bubbles says, poking out her mouth at me. "Now, listen. We only got a week left before we perform at the Apollo Amateur Hour contest. But we're gonna sing 'Wanna-be Stars in the Jiggy Jungle,' okay? I mean, we rocked the house at the Kats and Kittys Klub Halloween bash with that number, remember?"

"Yeah, that was a dope night," I say. Then I realize something. "Hey, how come you didn't write a song about *me*?"

Bubbles gives me that cheetah-licious look of hers, and says, "Who said I didn't? I just didn't finish it yet."

"What's it called?" I ask, excited.

"Guess."

"Do' Re Mi, Can't You See?"

All four of them heckle me, and Aqua says,

"We'd be po' for sho' if you wuz writing the songs!"

Bubbles stops laughing long enough to say, "The song's called, 'Who's 'Bout to Bounce, Baby?'"'

"Word. That's dope."

Juanita walks into the studio, huffing. She's wearing her running sweats and shoes, and she's got a towel around her neck. "Let's hit the road, girls. Running your mouth isn't the same thing as running, *está bien?*"

"What? You mean we're running *again*?" Angie moans.

"That's right," Juanita says sharply. "Any complaints?"

"Dag on," Angie says. "We sure do run a lot."

"Yeah, well, I'm ready for Freddy today, baby," Bubbles says, giving me a little squeeze of affection.

Without any further delay, we hightail it down to the East River and start running uptown. One week until show time, I tell myself as we go. That is really, really dope.

Bubbles is right. We are "ready for Freddy." We're gonna rock the Apollo, so what you know about that, huh?

I look around at my crew—Chanel up front as usual, the rest of us lagging behind—and I realize something. In spite of everything that's gone down, they still don't know the *whole* truth about me.

Telling them I'm really twelve years old right now might push my crew right over the edge. I mean, they put up with me lying to them about the Mo' Money Monique tour, but I'd better not rock the boat again—at least not for a while.

While I'm at it, I decide I'm not going to tell my crew that I'm not legally adopted, either. If I do, then I'll have to tell them what happened, and I don't wanna embarrass my mom.

"My mom . . ." I like the way that sounds. Besides, I know they want me to be happy, so I wanna pretend that I'm adopted for a while longer. Who knows? Maybe by the time I decide to tell them, Mrs. Bosco will have adopted me for real.

Anyway, the deal is, I can be a good friend to my crew, and still keep one or two little secrets to myself, you know what I'm sayin'?

By the time we get to 23rd Street, I notice something very strange. I've been so busy thinking about stuff that I suddenly realize I'm running by myself. Even Angie, Aqua, and Bubbles are running faster than me!

I can't believe that—*Bubbles*, running faster than *me*! She should eat sweet potato pie *every* day! Trying to catch up, I yell, "Hey, Bubbles, wait up!"

She pays me no mind, and yells back, without looking, "Yo, God's gift to the world—*catch up if you can*!" That sends them all into Cheetah heckles.

Yeah, I'm back, all right. Back where I belong. I'm not a wanna-be—not when I'm with my crew. That's what the world needs now and they're gonna get some at the Apollo Theatre, on Saturday night!

Wanna-be Stars in the Jiggy Jungle

Some people walk with a panther
or strike a buffalo stance
that makes you wanna dance.

Other people flip the script
on the day of the jackal
that'll make you cackle.

But peeps like me
got the Cheetah Girl groove
that makes your body move
like wanna-be stars in the jiggy jungle.

The jiggy jiggy jungle!
The jiggy jiggy jungle!

So don't make me bungle
my chance to rise for the prize
and show you who we are
in the jiggy jiggy jungle!
The jiggy jiggy jungle!

Some people move like snakes in the grass
or gorillas in the mist
who wanna get dissed.

Some people dance with the wolves
or trot with the fox
right out of the box.

But peeps like me
got the Cheetah Girl groove
that makes your body move
like wanna-be stars in the jiggy jungle.

The jiggy jiggy jungle!
The jiggy jiggy jungle!

So don't make me bungle
my chance to rise for the prize
and show you who we are
in the jiggy jiggy jungle!
The jiggy jiggy jungle!

Some people lounge with the Lion King
or hunt like a hyena
because they're large and in charge.

Some people hop to it like a hare
because they wanna get snared
or bite like baboons and jump too soon.

But peeps like me
got the Cheetah Girl groove
that makes your body move
like wanna-be stars in the jiggy jungle.

The jiggy jiggy jungle.
The jiggy jiggy jungle.

So don't make me bungle
my chance to rise for the prize
and show you who we are
in the jiggy jiggy jungle!

The jiggy jiggy jungle.
The jiggy jiggy jungle.

Some people float like a butterfly
or sting like a bee
'cuz they wanna be like posse.

Some people act tough like a tiger
to scare away the lynx
but all they do is double jinx.

But peeps like me
got the Cheetah Girl groove
that makes your body move
like wanna-be stars in the jiggy jungle.

The jiggy jiggy jungle.
The jiggy jiggy jungle.

So don't make me bungle
my chance to rise to the prize
and show you who we are
in the jiggy jiggy jungle.

The jiggy jiggy jungle!
The jiggy jiggy jungle!

The Cheetah Girls Glossary

At the end of her rope-a-dope: To run out of moves. When you wanna give up.
Boo-boo: A mistake. A cuddly dog like Toto.
Boomerang toes: Feet that have corns, bunions, or critter-looking toenails.
Bouffant: A puffed-up hairdo.
Bounce: To leave. To jet. To go away and come back another day.
Cellulite: Lumpy fat that looks like cottage cheese and makes grown-up ladies go to beauty parlors and throw duckets out the bucket trying to get rid of it.
Chitlin' circuit: Wack clubs that don't pay singers well.
Diggable planet: A cool place.
Dopiest dope: The coolest of them all.
Easy-breezy tip: When something doesn't take a lot of effort. When you're not sweatin' it.
Knuckleheads: Bozos who don't have jobs and hang out all day doing nothing.

Large and in charge: Successful.
Mad moves: To dance really well.
My face is cracked: I'm embarrassed.
Not having it: When you don't like something.
Penguin feet: Dancer's feet that are slightly pointed outward.
Pigeons: Girls with fake eyeballs and tick-tacky weaves.
Rope-a-dope: When you're doing something *really* well—like double-Dutch jump rope, freestyle moves.
She's on a jelly roll: When someone is jammin' with snaps, knowledge, or moves.
Something is jumping off: When something is about to happen.
Stub-a-nubs: Fingernails that have been chomp-a-roni'd to the max.
Whazzup: A popular salutation for greeting members of your crew.
Word: Right. I hear that. Is that right? I know that's right.

Hey, Ho, Hollywood!

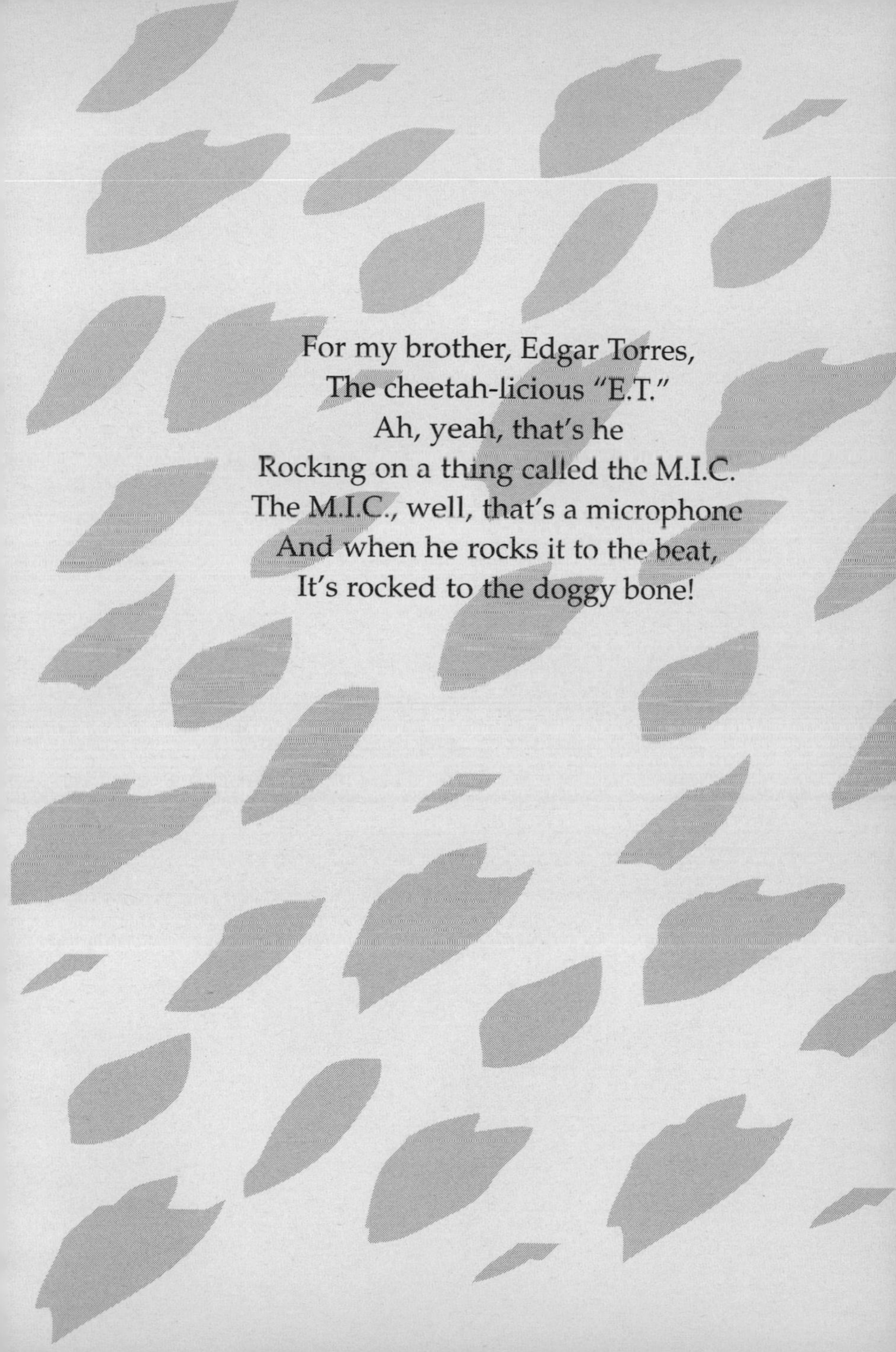

For my brother, Edgar Torres,
The cheetah-licious "E.T."
Ah, yeah, that's he
Rocking on a thing called the M.I.C.
The M.I.C., well, that's a microphone
And when he rocks it to the beat,
It's rocked to the doggy bone!

Chapter 1

The plastic slipcover on the couch makes a real loud *crunch* sound when Galleria sits down. Me and Angie are used to the funny noise so we pay it no mind, but Galleria looks kinda embarrassed like she farted an "Alien egg," or something strange like that. Me and Angie just look at each other and smile because we're probably thinking the same thing. That's how it is when you're twins—you can read each other's mind, finish each other's sentences, *and* know when each other is "lying, crying, or testifying," even when you're not in the same room.

My sister Angie and I are as much alike as any identical twins you're ever gonna meet.

When we stand together looking in the mirror, it's almost like we're two of those alien clones in horror movies (which we *love*).

I remember way back in sixth grade we fooled *both* our homeroom teachers by switching places on April Fools' Day. We didn't get into trouble, but we did get called to the principal's office. Still, "the Fabulous Walker Twins" pulled the best April Fools' Day joke that school ever saw! We go to high school in New York City nowadays, but we have not been forgotten. I guess you can't blame them for never putting identical twins in the same class again after that!

Now that we have turned thirteen (our birthday is September 9, which makes us practical-minded Virgos), Angie and I don't always dress alike anymore—which makes it easier to tell us apart. But even when we do put on the same outfit, you can tell I'm Aquanette. I'm the one who's always running my mouth. Anginette is more the quiet type. But as Big Momma says, "She doesn't miss a trick."

Big Momma is our maternal grandmother, and she loves to brag about us—even to ladies in the supermarket! "I can't tell which one of them is smarter or cuter sometimes," she'll say. Or, "You know they've been singing like angels since they were cooing in the cradle."

That's not exactly true. I think we started singing when we were about three years old. Anyway, Big Momma says, "Singing is a gift from the Lord." Well, nobody else in our family can even hold a note, so it must be true.

And I *guess* we're kinda cute: Angie and I are both brown-skinned, with nice "juicy" lips and big brown eyes. Still, we're not *real* pretty, like the rest of the Cheetah Girls—that would be Galleria "Bubbles" Garibaldi, Chanel "Chuchie" Simmons, and Dorinda "Do' Re Mi" Rogers. That's right—Angie and I have only just moved to New York, and here we are, already in a singing group!

Angie and I met Galleria and Chanel at the Kats and Kittys Klub Fourth of July Bash last summer. It was right after we moved to New York from Houston, leaving Ma, Big Momma, and all our cousins behind. We woulda been real lost if it hadn't been for our fellow Kats and Kittys.

In case you've never heard of it, the Kats and Kittys Klub is this national organization for young, up-and-coming African Americans. They do lots of things for the community, and we used to go all the time back home. So we were real happy to join the metropolitan chapter in New York City, and that they were havin' a Fourth of July bar-b-que. It was our first chance to meet kids our own age in the Big Apple.

So there we were, singing up a storm by the barbecue grill, when Chanel and Galleria started looking at us *real* funny. I guess we were kinda showing off. They were the prettiest girls we had seen in New York, even though Galleria wasn't very friendly to us at first. Luckily, Chanel was, and now we're all *real* good friends and singing together.

We can't wait till Ma meets Galleria and the rest of the Cheetah Girls—which may not be anytime soon. See, she and Daddy are getting a dee-vorce, and Ma remained in Houston, while Daddy moved up here to New York.

Of course, Daddy sent for us to come live with him, so he could keep an eye on us. He feels that Ma can't properly supervise us. See, she's a regional district sales manager for Avon, and travels quite a bit for her job. Daddy used to be her boss, but you knew that wasn't gonna last long, because he can be *real* hard on people.

Even though he's *real* hard on us, too—making us do our vocal exercises and clean our rooms *every* night—we know he loves us. And we are real glad he let us invite our friends over here tonight.

That's right—he told us we could invite the Cheetah Girls over! This is the first time we've had company in New York. And the only reason Daddy said okay is because his new girlfriend came over, too.

Her name is High Priestess Abala Shaballa Bogo Hexagone, and believe it or not, she really is some kind of priestess from some far-away place we never even heard of (even though we don't really know what a High Priestess is for sure). Angie and I don't like her much, but Daddy sure does. She's real tall and pretty, so I guess I can understand why.

Anyway, she came over today with her . . . well . . . friends, if that's what you want to call them. If you ask me, they are some of the strangest people you'd ever want to meet. And tonight, they're cookin' up some kind of spooky ritual for the Cheetah Girls!

I told my friends all about this at our last Cheetah Girls council meeting. But they thought I was just joking! Well, I wasn't, and they're about to find that out!

See, as a singing group, we've only performed together once—at the Cheetah-Rama club last Halloween night. It was a lot of fun! I think the Kats and Kittys liked us, and we got paid, too! We even got a manager out of it—but Mr. Jackal Johnson turned out to be a crook.

Still, even though we haven't performed much, we've got the biggest night of our lives coming up. Tomorrow night, the Cheetah Girls are performing at the world-famous Apollo Thee-ay-ter! Angie and I have never been there before, but we've seen it on television, so we know it's *real* big, with a lot of seats and bright lights and everything.

Don't get me wrong. We're just performing in the Apollo Theatre Amateur Hour contest—but we're still real nervous about it. Most of all, we're *real* scared about the Apollo Sandman. He is this kooky guy in a clown outfit who pulls you off the stage if people start booing at you!

So High Priestess Abala invited her friends over here to conduct this ritual to give the Cheetah Girls more "Growl Power." That's what she said. It sounds okay, till you get a good look at what they're doing back there in the kitchen. They're all standing around this table preparing stuff and jabbering something or other. And believe me, they are a weird collection of folks. I'll tell you, I don't know who I'm more scared of—the Sandman, or High Priestess Abala and her friends.

While they're all back there makin' their "witches' brew," Galleria is putting on a show in our living room. (Chanel and Dorinda are on their way over, too. They're just late.)

"Well, Miss *Aquanette* and *Anginette* Walker, that's downright plummy that you *finally* invited me to your house. Well, you Southern belles are just so swell!" Galleria says, fluttering her pretty eyelashes, and mocking Angie and me.

She loves to do that, and we think it's kinda funny, how she can find a way to rhyme almost anything. We know she's just playing with us, though, because we have a lot of fun together. There is nobody back home in Houston like Galleria Garibaldi. As Big Momma would say,

"They threw away the mold after they made her."

Next year, we hope Galleria and the rest of the Cheetah Girls are gonna transfer to *our* high school. See, they're freshmen at Fashion Industries High, but Angie and I go to LaGuardia High School of Performing Arts. It's very prestigious and all, so we're *real* lucky to be going there. We had to come to New York just for an audition, then go back home, all the way to Houston, and wait to see if we got accepted!

Angie and I just can't wait till the kids in our school see the Cheetah Girls singing together. They're gonna be so jealous—especially JuJu Beans Gonzalez, who's in our vocal and drama classes, and thinks she's the next Mo' Money Monique, just because she can rap and wiggle her shimmyshaker.

Angie and I don't dance *that* good, but still, we've got the shimmyshakers to do it, if we try real hard. That's all I'm saying. And we sing better than JuJu Beans does, even when we have colds (Angie and I always get sick together, too).

JuJu treats me and Angie like corn bread

bakers, or something "country" like that, just because she has never been to Houston. Houston is beautiful—even Galleria's mom, Ms. Dorothea, says so.

Anyway, we've got all year to convince our teachers to let us perform together as the Cheetah Girls for LaGuardia's big June talent showcase. We've been praying on it, and God always gives us an answer (even though most of the time it's not near as quick as we'd like!).

Galleria is acting like company. She sips her lemonade all dainty, then places the glass on its coaster on the coffee table—like it's Aladdin's lamp or something, and she's afraid all the wishes are gonna fly out of it!

Then she sits back on the couch with her legs tight together and her hands on her knees—just like some of the New York ladies sit in church (like they don't belong in the house of the Lord, or they don't know how they're supposed to sit in the pew).

"Dag on, Galleria, you don't have to be so proper. You can just be yourself," I heckle her, then throw Angie another glance. After all, we have seen the real Miss Galleria, and believe us, she does *just* as she pleases.

Now Galleria's eyes are moving around the living room like a pair of Ping-Pong balls. "Those drapes look like they belong in the Taj Mahal," she says, like she's amusing herself at a porch party down South, or something fancy like that.

The drapes *are* kinda nice, though. They're ivory chiffon, with a scarf valance that has fringes, just like the panels.

Daddy decorated the living room himself, right down to the plastic slipcovers—and he's real proud of it. The big glass coffee table has a brass lion base, and the only thing we're allowed to keep on top of the glass is a big white leather-bound Holy Bible. Then there's a big white shag rug shaped like a bear, lying in the center of the floor. The head has real ivory-looking fang teeth—we checked his mouth with a flashlight!

Daddy keeps his new snow globe collection in a big white wooden case with glass partitions. The snow globes are on the top shelves, and the bottom shelves are lined with his *precious* collection of LP albums—not CDs, but real records of people like Marvin Gaye, the Supremes, the Temptations. Daddy says he's invested too much in his record collection to start buying CDs now. When we were little, if we ever messed with Daddy's records, or broke one, he would get *real* mad at us.

"Holy cannoli, we got records like this too—but Momsy keeps them in storage, where they're just collecting dust!" Galleria says, laughing. "We could play Frisbee with one of these!"

She pretends to toss the vinyl record at me, but she knows better, because she's *real* careful putting it back into its jacket. Even *she* can tell Daddy is real particular about things. That's why he keeps the sofa and sectionals covered in plastic—"because the fabric is a very delicate imported ivory silk," he says. So nobody ends up sittin' on the couch but company.

Even Daddy, when he sits in the living room, sits in the big brown leather reclining chair—so he can watch the big television, which is behind a set of wooden panels. The couch just sits there, showin' off, "no use to nobody," as Big Momma used to say. But this is Daddy's house now, and he decorates it like he pleases.

One thing is for sure—our house in New York (we call it a house even though it's just a two-bedroom duplex apartment) is decorated *real* different from the way Ma decorated our house in Houston. Daddy likes everything to be white, ivory, or brown, which are *his* favorite colors. Ma liked peach, and green, and blue colors.

Before I start making myself jittery again—about tonight *and* tomorrow night—the door-bell rings. Thank God, it's finally Chanel and Dorinda. After quick kisses and hugs, Chanel becomes fascinated with our house too.

"Ooh, *qué bonita*! My abuela Florita would love these," she coos, pointing to Daddy's prized collection of snow globes. (That's her grandma she's talkin' about. That's how they say it in Spanish.)

"Abuela just loves the snow here. She'll go outside on her stoop and sit there all day, waiting for snowflakes to hit her on the nose!" Chanel takes the castle snow globe and shakes it up and down, to see the snow fall.

"Daddy just started collecting those. It's really kinda strange," I explain, my voice trailing off as I start to think how much Daddy has changed since he moved up here to New York.

"Aqua, what's wrong with collecting snow globes?" Dorinda asks.

Galleria has finally jumped up from the couch, now that Chanel and Dorinda are here. "Your *daddy's* probably fascinated by the snow we have here in 'New Yawk,'" she says with a laugh. "Wait till he experiences his first snowstorm—he'll be throwing those things out the window!

"My dad used to love the snow," she goes on. "When I was little, he would get more upset than I did if it didn't snow before Christmas. Then we had that majordomo snowstorm a few years ago, and it completely covered my Dad's van. He sat at the window for three days, cursing in Italian till he could shovel his van out!"

"It's not just the snow globes, *Galleria*," I say, exasperated. "That was only the beginning. Then he bought a blender—"

"What's wrong with a blender?" Chanel asks.

"Now everything he eats comes outta that thing!" I say, exasperated.

Chanel bursts out laughing, which makes Galleria and even Dorinda smirk.

"I wish *I* had a blender," Dorinda says,

narrowing her eyes at me, which almost makes her look like a real cheetah. "Where I live, I've got to chop up all the vegetables by hand." Dorinda lives in an apartment with about ten foster brothers and sisters. Bless her heart. I wouldn't trade with her for nothing in the world. Lucky for her, her foster mother just adopted her—so at least she knows she can keep on living where she is, instead of going to another foster home.

Galleria is still riffing about Daddy's blender. "Oh, snapples, he blended apples, and now Aqua thinks he's gonna turn into Freddy!" Galleria snaps, doing the Cheetah Girl handshake with Chanel.

"What Aqua means, is—" Angie says, coming to my defense, "he used to love to cook, you know? Cajun crawfish—"

"—Steaks smothered in onions and gravy," I chime in, so they understand that our Daddy used to like to *eat*. "Now he's blending strange vegetables and fruits, and he sits there and drinks it, like it's supposed to be dee-licious."

"And he expects *us* to drink those dees-gusting shakes too!" Angie cuts in.

"I mean, celery and turnip shakes—please, where's Mikki D's?" I say, rolling my eyes. My friends start laughing again, because they know *we* love to eat, too.

"Snow globes, a stupid blender, and now *this*," I say, pointing to the kitchen, where Daddy is standing with his new girlfriend and those other strange ladies she brought with her.

"What's her name again?" Chanel asks, pulling on one of her braids.

"High Priestess Abala Shaballa Bogo Hexagone,"I tell her. "She says she is a Hexagone High Priestess, and her ancestors reigned in Ancient Hexagonia." I roll my eyes like I can't believe it myself.

"Is a Hexagone High Priestess supposed to be like Nefertiti or someone like that?" Dorinda asks, narrowing her eyes again. She knows about all kinds of stuff, because she reads a whole lot of books.

"I don't think so, 'cuz this 'High Priestess' has definitely got a broomstick parked around the corner! Right, Angie?"

"I think High Priestess is just a fancy name for *witch*!" Angie answers.

"*Parate*, Aqua," Chanel says, bursting into giggles. "Help, you're killing me—maybe she's a good witch, *mija*?"

"Well, I don't know, but I'm glad y'all are here, because the show is about to begin! Right before Galleria came, they went to the Piggly Wiggly Supermarket to buy ingredients—'for the ritual!' they said!"

Finally, Galleria and Chanel aren't laughing anymore. Now they're sitting on the edge of their seats, like they're about to see a horror movie. And, believe me, I think we are!

Chapter 2

Suddenly, we hear a loud, grinding noise coming from the kitchen.

"You hear that?" I ask, my eyes popping open.

"*Sí,*" Chanel responds.

"That's the blender going—see?" Angie says, her eyes getting wide.

"You know, you and Angie do the same things with your eyes," Chanel says to me, bugging her eyes wide and imitating us.

"I'll bet you they're blending the witches' brew for us to drink!" I whisper.

"That's it—I'm outtie like Snouty," Dorinda says, crossing her arms and looking at Chanel.

"What's that you said, Dorinda?" I ask

politely. Sometimes, when Galleria, Dorinda, and Chanel talk, Angie and I don't understand them. I mean, everybody in New York talks so fast—but our friends just have their *own* way of talking.

Angie says we shouldn't ask when we don't understand what they say, because it makes us look stupid. But as Big Momma always says, "If you don't ask, you gonna miss a whole lot of conversation!"

"It means, Aqua, that I'd rather go get a soda and some chips at the Piggy Wiggly Supermarket than sit here and wait to get hit over the head with a broomstick!" Dorinda grunts, then sits up straight on the couch and folds her arms across her little chest.

Oh, *I* get what she means. She's talking about the snout on the plastic pig outside of Piggly Wiggly. That Dorinda is so cute. She sure can eat, for someone so little. She must have had three slices of our sweet potato pie at her surprise adoption party. (We made it from scratch, too. Not like those store-bought winky-dinky pies and cakes that people serve their families here. Shame on them!)

"Do' Re Mi, why you trying to flounce, when

we know you wuz 'bout to bounce?" Galleria says in her singing voice. "That's why I'm writing my new song about you. You're always trying to bounce!"

Dorinda just sits with her arms folded, looking *real* sheepish, but Galleria lets her off the hook. See, Galleria wrote a new song about Dorinda, because she almost left the group when she got offered a job as a backup dancer for the Mo' Money Monique tour. Do' Re Mi turned the job down in the end, 'cuz she wanted to stay with all of us. But I guess Galleria and Chanel are still sore about it, since they were the ones who made Dorinda a Cheetah Girl in the first place.

"It's time to 'winter squash' this situation, if you know what I'm saying," Galleria says, laughing. "Let's go in the kitchen and blend us a High Priestess Abala shake!" She jumps up, like she's gonna march into the kitchen herself. We all start giggling.

"Dorinda's 'bout to bounce!" Chanel sings, and we all sing a call-and-response verse:

"Who's trying to flounce?"

"Dorinda! Dorinda!"

When we finish singing, I ask, kinda

nervous, "Do you all understand *why* we're waiting for Abala and her friends?" I'm not quite sure how to get through to them.

"No, why?" Chanel asks, sipping her lemonade. One of her braids accidentally dips in the glass, and she starts to giggle nervously. "Oops, *Lo siento*. I didn't see the glass coming!"

"Y'all better listen to what I'm sayin', Chanel," I continue, "and all the rest of you, too! The High Priestess Abala Shaballa says she wants to put a 'Vampire Spell' on us—so we'll captivate the audience at the Apollo Theatre tomorrow night."

The living room gets *real* quiet. It's so quiet, if you listen real close, you can probably hear the fake confetti snowflakes swirling around in Daddy's snow globes in the showcase.

"A 'Vampire Spell'?" Dorinda repeats, narrowing her eyes like a cheetah cub ready to pounce on its prey. "How do you spell, 'I'm outtie like Snouty'?"

She jumps up, but Galleria pushes her down. "Aqua, how could you have us come over here? This is not just some guy jumping out of his coffin and chasing us with his fake rubber arm, like at the haunted house in Madison 'Scare' Garden. This is *for real*!"

"Dag on!" I say. "I told you all during the Cheetah Girl council meeting this was *serious*." Looking at my hands in my lap, I try to figure out what to say to get the Cheetah Girls to help me and Angie. *God, give me the words.*

"What do you expect us to do? Stay here by ourselves, and let these people turn us into frogs instead of Cheetah Girls?"

"Aqua is right," Angie says, speaking up for me. "Then what are y'all gonna do without us? Aqua and I can't exactly go on stage hopping around and croaking, can we?" Angie folds her arms, like that's supposed to really make them help us, but all they do is start laughing.

I'm thinking this whole thing is a lost cause, but when they finish their latest round of giggles, Galleria quips, "Okay, we'll stay. But after this, you owe us, so don't snow us, Aqua." She turns, and looks at Chanel and Dorinda for backup.

"Dag on, all right, we owe y'all, Galleria," I say, giving in. "We're crew now, like you said, right?"

"Yeah," Galleria says, looking at me like, *what's your point?*

"Well then, we have to help each other out no matter what, right?" I continue.

"Yeah, but like I said before, after this you owe us, so don't snow us." When Galleria gets that tone in her voice, we know that's the final word—like she's Reverend Butter at church!

Angie cuts us a quick look, to tell us that Daddy is coming this way. We just sit *real* tight and wait for the fright show to begin.

"Hello, ladies," Daddy greets my friends. Right behind him are High Priestess Abala Shaballa and her coven of witches pretending to be normal ladies.

Abala is real dark—darker than *us*—and it makes her teeth look real white. She is real pretty, though, and she wears African fabric draped around her body and head.

Her friends, on the other hand, are real strange-looking. They trail into the living room, with their long gowns sweeping the floor, and their arms full of all kinds of what look to be witchcraft things. One of them is this dwarf lady, carrying the little folding table Daddy uses when he eats in front of the television.

"Good evening, ladies," High Priestess Abala Shaballa Bogo Hexagone says in a booming voice. "All blessings to Great Hexagone, and the bounty she has prepared for us this evening." Abala Shaballa stretches out her arms to us.

I give Daddy a look, like, I hope you know what you're doing. But what I'm really thinking is, How could you do this to us?

"The Piggly Wiggly Supermarket here is *divine,*" says the dwarf lady, in a squeaky voice that sounds like the Tin Man in a rainstorm! "Ah, I see your friends have arrived. I'm Rasputina Twia."

"I'm Hecate Sukoji," says a woman with long black hair and no eyebrows. I wonder, did she shave off her eyebrows, or was she born that way?

"I'm Bast Bojo," says the third lady. She has a bald head, and is looking at us with beady eyes that are so dark and slanty, she looks like a spooky black cat!

"Let us begin," High Priestess Abala Shaballa says.

Rasputina puts down the folding table. On top of it, High Priestess Abala and her three friends put a goose, some tomatoes, beets, Tabasco sauce—

Now, wait a minute! I know Daddy is not

gonna let us use *that*. He always says hot sauce is bad for our vocal cords! But he's just smiling proudly, looking on.

I know—she probably already put a spell on Daddy! *And now we're next*!

Bast pulls some strange-looking fruits out of her pockets. "These are kumquats," she says, as if reading our minds. Then she pulls out a head of lettuce and a teddy bear from the basket she's carrying. Well, at least our pet guinea pigs Porgy and Bess will have something to eat for later—the lettuce, that is.

"You got that at Piggly Wiggly?" I ask in disbelief, looking at the raggedy teddy bear. *What on earth are they gonna do with a teddy bear, anyway*?

"Yes. Apparently it was left over from last Christmas," Rasputina says, all proud of herself.

High Priestess Abala kisses the garlic necklace around her neck. Then she pours some Tabasco sauce into the witches' brew in the blender, shakes it a little, and pours it out into five big glasses!

"Now, let us stand in a circle and drink up, Cheetah Girls, so that tomorrow night, when you're out for blood on the stage, you'll be able to hold your ground!" The High Priestess gives us a big, scary smile.

"What's in this, um, brew?" Dorinda asks, kinda nervous. Good for her. At least she has the nerve to speak up! Daddy must be in a trance or something!

"Raw steak, beets, tomatoes . . . I added pimientos, Tabasco, and, um . . . other things, to prepare you for battle!" High Priestess Abala smiles again, revealing her big, white teeth.

Sniffing at my glass, I think, I'll bet she put blood in it, too!

"Drink up," Abala commands, watching me closely. I drink the dag on thing—which to my surprise, actually tastes kinda good.

"Excellent! And now the rest of you! Come, drink up, girls!" Abala commands.

After we all drink the brew, we hold hands. "We must finish the ritual by paying homage to the sylphs of the east, the salamanders of the south, the bats of the west, and the gnomes of the north," Abala says, her voice sounding stranger and stranger.

At the end of the ritual, Abala gives each of us a shoe box. "You must not open these," she tells us. "Just put them in your closets, and close the door."

"What's in here?" Galleria asks, trying to hide a smirk.

"Parts from stuffed animals—teddy bear eyes and noses, poodle tails, rabbit whiskers . . ."

The High Priestess looks Galleria right in the eye, and Bubbles seems to shrink. "After midnight, the teddy bear, poodle, and rabbit will merge with you, and give you the strength of a true Cheetah Girl!"

"Oh," says Galleria, still smirking. "Well, I guess I'd better let my dog Toto know we'll be having company later—I wouldn't want 'Mr. Teddy Poodly' to get his nose bitten off when he comes out to play."

We all start laughing. High Priestess Abala just looks at us, amused. I wonder what's going through her mind. I don't like all this one bit, I'll tell you that!

Angie and I are gonna do some real praying tonight—and I'm gonna Scotch-tape our shoe boxes so tight, even the Mummy himself wouldn't be able to get out of them!

That High Priestess may have Daddy under a spell, but she doesn't fool me. Tonight, I'm gonna ask *God* to please help us win the Apollo Theatre Amateur Hour Contest—and not to let High Priestess Abala Shaballa turn Daddy into a salamander!

Chapter 3

Mr. Garibaldi wanted to drive us Cheetah Girls to the Apollo Theatre tonight, but Daddy insisted that *he* drive us. It made us feel *real* important to have everybody fussing over us, like we're a big singing group already, with cheetah-licious ways.

Daddy has two cars—a white Cadillac with a convertible top, and a white Bronco—and, can you believe this? He has to *pay* to keep them in a garage near our house!

He's always fussin' about that. Back home we had three cars—including the blue Katmobile, which is now Ma's—*and* our own four-car garage in the back of the house. And we didn't have to pay a dime extra for all that parking space! I'll tell you, New York City sure is strange—and expensive. I'm surprised they don't charge for breathing air here!

Anyway, Daddy *insisted* that Mr. Garibaldi and Ms. Dorothea drive with us to the Apollo. (Chanel's mom is out on a big date with her boyfriend, Mr. Tycoon, so she can't come see us tonight. She's tryin' to get Mr. Tycoon to marry her, but he's playin' hard to get, so *she's* taking belly dancing lessons to "get" *him*!)

Ms. Dorothea doesn't like us to call her Mrs. Garibaldi, because she isn't a "prim and proper" kind of person. If you met her, you would understand where Galleria gets all her personality. I mean, Galleria is tame compared to her mother—Ms. Dorothea even eats Godiva chocolates for breakfast, and hits people over the head with her Cheetah pocketbook when they're acting up. We just love her! By putting up the two extra seats in the back of Daddy's Bronco, we're all able to fit. Since Dorinda and Chanel are the smallest, they sit on the two little seats way in the back. Galleria sits next to her mom and dad.

We're *so* glad High Priestess Abala Shaballa couldn't come with us tonight to the Apollo

Theatre, even though she says she is "with us in the spirit." Well, I keep looking out the car window to make sure I don't see her in the *flesh,* flying by on her broomstick with her flock of kooky friends! (So far, the coast is clear.) I'm sorry, but Angie and I decided last night that we don't trust "High Priestess Hocus Pocus," as Galleria calls her.

"Angie, would you look at all these people?" I say, as we drive across 125th Street. It seems like there are millions of people in New York, and they are *all* walking around up here in Harlem. I mean, the sidewalks are so crowded, it looks like they're having a fair or something!

"*Mira,* look at their outfits. Some of them look like they're dressed for church!" Chanel exclaims.

"What church is *she* going to in a yellow satin cape?" Dorinda chides Chanel, pointing to a lady whose earrings are so big, they look like plates hanging from her ears. Girls in New York just *love* their jewelry.

"Well, you never know—this is the Big Apple," Angie chimes in.

"I know. I've never seen so many neon signs before in my life!" I say.

Dorinda points to a hair-supply place with a giant neon sign that says RAPUNZEL. "Word, that's the hair place Abiola at the YMCA told me about!"

Dorinda has a *real* after-school job—through the youth entrepreneurship program at the YMCA—even though it doesn't pay that much. "That's where we should buy hair, so we don't look like wefties!" she adds, chuckling. Wefties are girls with weaves that are so tick-tacky the tracks are showing, as Galleria says.

"*Mamacitas,* they've got some hefty wefties up here," Chanel says, looking at more girls walking by in their fancy outfits. "They must be going to some kinda club around here."

"Yeah—a club for vampires!" exclaims Galleria, as we pass the Black Magic movie-theater complex. "Ooo, look, Aqua and Angie, they're having a Fang-oria Festival there!"

From what I can see, the Black Magic looks big enough to fit all the people in New York *and* Houston. "Let's go see Freddy before we get ready!" I say excitedly.

"Hmmph—then Freddy will have to deal with me, because no ghoul is gonna stop this show!" Ms. Dorothea quips, then yawns into her leopard-gloved hand.

"Gee, Momsy poo, I think the Sandman has already sprinkled you with some poppy dust or something," Galleria giggles.

"I'm fading *pronto*, too," says Mr. Garibaldi, who is also yawning. "I get up every day at five o'clock, you know."

"Before the rooster can say cock-a-doodle-do!" Galleria chides her father.

Ms. Dorothea is getting up early too these days. She's working *real* hard now that she is our manager, and she still runs her fancy boutique—Toto in New York . . . Fun in Diva Sizes—which is the most beautiful store I've ever seen.

"Ooh, they got *Blacula* there! We've never seen that one!" Angie says to me, getting real excited. We just love horror movies—especially the old ones, because they show more gory stuff up close, like eyeballs hanging out of the eye sockets, or brains popping out of the skull.

The only thing I love more than singing is looking at dead bodies, and figuring out how they died, and wondering if they'll tell any secrets. I guess that's because our Granddaddy

Walker is a mortician and owns Rest in Peace, the biggest funeral parlor in Houston.

Over the last forty years, Granddaddy Walker has buried half of the dead people in Houston. That's what Big Momma says.

When our singing career is over, I'm going to become a forensic scientist, like that guy on the old TV show—you know, the one who solves crimes by examining the victims. Angie wants to be a neurosurgeon, so she can operate on people's brains and stuff.

I'm so scared, I wish we could see a horror movie right now. When Daddy gets out of the car to find out where he should park, we all start cackling about last night's strange events.

"Did any of y'all dance with a teddy bear or a poodle last night?" I ask. Then I wonder, What on earth did Abala mean by giving us stuffed teddy bear heads in a shoe box? How was that supposed to help us win this competition?

"I couldn't believe Aqua got up in the morning and checked our shoe boxes in the closet, just to make sure they were still taped," Angie says, acting all grown.

"Angie, don't act like *you* didn't look at your box, too," I shoot back.

"Can you believe Abala says Galleria was probably Egyptian royalty in her past life?" Dorinda remarks, still in disbelief about last night.

"Well, she's definitely not psychic, or she would know that we don't like her!" I say, huffing and puffing. Angie and I are squeezed into the front seat, and we're trying not to breathe, so we don't bust out of our Cheetah Girls costumes.

"I'm gonna ask Princess Pamela about her, *para seguro*," Chanel says. "Just to be safe. You can count on that, *está bien?*"

Like I said before, Princess Pamela is Chanel's father's girlfriend. Chuchie's parents have been divorced for a while, and she just loves Pamela. The Princess owns a whole lot of businesses—she does hair and nails, bakes the best pound-cake in New York, and tells people's fortunes. Princess Pamela is a psychic. She may not be a High Priestess like Abala, but I like Pamela a lot better. *She* can tell *my* fortune any time.

"I think my jumpsuit is tighter than it was the last time," I say.

"Those sweet potato pies you made for Dorinda's surprise adoption party were dope-a-licious, but did you have to eat five of them all by yourself, Miz Aquanette?" Galleria asks, laying on that syrupy Southern accent again.

"No, I guess not, Miz Galleria," I sigh back, playing along with her. "And I guess it didn't help that I ate all of your father's chocolate cannolis at the same time!"

"Aah, *mama mia,* I wondered who ate them all!" Mr. Garibaldi says, waving his hand.

I take another deep breath. I'm scared I'm gonna pop out of my costume right on stage, and the Sandman is gonna tear the rest of my costume with his big ol' hook!

Now I feel like poor Dorinda did when she tore her costume onstage at the Cheetah-Rama. You should have seen her face when she ripped her jumpsuit. That's right—there we were, in the middle of a song—and Dorinda did a lickety-split, right there on stage!

"Don't worry, Aqua. You won't be a witch without a stitch," says Galleria, leaning from the back of the car and whispering in my ear. "And it's just a matter of time before we pull the curtain on the High Priestess of Hocus Pocus. The Wizard of Oz she ain't, or I'll faint!"

"What does she do when she isn't concocting Vampire Spells?" Dorinda asks.

"Daddy says she teaches this, well . . . witchcraft stuff to people. And she has a store called Enchantrixx up here somewhere."

Then I see Daddy on his way back to the car. "Shh, he's coming," I whisper, then announce loudly as he opens the door, "Well! Here we are at the world-famous Apollo Theatre."

Mentioning the Apollo reminds me of why we're here tonight, and how much is at stake. It makes me start feeling nervous, and when I get nervous, my stomach starts churning like it's mashing potatoes or something.

"Y'all feeling scared like I am?" I ask, this time turning around so I can look at Galleria.

"Sí, mamacita," admits Chanel.

"I guess that's natural, right?" Dorinda asks Ms. Dorothea. Ever since the adoption party, the two of them seem like two peas in a pod—which we're all *real* happy about.

Dorinda needs all the love she can get. She's been a foster child all her life—till now, that is. The day her foster mother, Mrs. Bosco, adopted her was the best day of Dorinda's whole life. It sure made Ms. Dorothea cry a lot, though. I wonder what that was all about. She seemed *so* sad about something.

"Darling, when the day comes that you're not afraid as you walk on that stage—cancel the show immediately!" Dorothea says, reaching for the door handle to get out.

But Mr. Garibaldi quickly says, "*Cara*, no, let me get the door for you!"

Mr. Garibaldi is such a gentleman. Galleria says he's very "old school," because he grew up in Italy and not here in the States.

That's probably true. When we were at Ms. Dorothea's store, Galleria showed us the personals ad from *New York* magazine that Ms. Dorothea answered to meet Mr. Garibaldi. We almost died right there on the spot! He called himself a "lonely oyster on the half shell" in the ad. I can't imagine him like that. He seems like the happiest man we've ever seen. We wish Daddy was more like that—just a lot of fun, that's all I'm saying.

After Mr. Garibaldi helps all of us out of the car, we take a look up at the sign for the Apollo Theatre. "Look at all the lights up there!" I exclaim.

"They should have *our* name up there in bright lights, taking up the whole marquee!" Galleria says, giggling.

"Darling, one day they *will*," Ms. Dorothea says, then flings her fur boa around her neck, which hits Mr. Garibaldi in the face.

"Don't knock me out with your love, *cara*!" he quips, then puts the boa back on her shoulder.

We are giggling up a storm, because we are just so happy to be here. People are looking at us as we walk in, and Ms. Dorothea tells the usher that we're The Cheetah Girls and we're here to *perform*.

"Go right in, ladies," the usher says, smiling at us. He looks so nice in his uniform. He's wearing a red jacket, black pants and white gloves—and his teeth are almost as bright as the neon lights in the sign!

As we're walking by all the people waiting to buy popcorn and stuff at the concession stand, these two tall, skinny guys with baseball caps and real baggy pants start calling to us. "You're grrrr-eat! Yo, check it, D, there's Tony the Tiger with his girlfriends!" They stand there stuffing popcorn in their mouths, and heckling up a storm. They are so loud that everybody turns and looks at us.

"Well if it isn't the baggy, bumbling Bozo brothers, trying to get full at the concession stand!" Galleria hisses back.

"Shhh, darling, never let them see you sweat," Ms. Dorothea tells her. "Besides, those children look like they could use a home-cooked meal."

It's still so hard for me and Angie to believe how rude people in New York can be. I mean, we have *some* "bozos" in Houston, but not like this. People will just walk up to you anywhere and get in your face, for no reason!

"Dag on, I hope everybody ain't like him, or this is gonna turn into a 'Nightmare on 125th Street,'" I turn and say to Galleria. (One of my favorite horror movies is *Nightmare on Elm Street*, 'cuz that scar-faced Freddy Krueger always finds a way to get in your dreams and scare you to death!)

"Not to worry, Aqua. There is always one sour bozo in a bunch of grapes!" Galleria mutters.

"Let's find our dressing room," quips Ms. Dorothea, acting now like our manager—which is what she *has* been, ever since she helped us get rid of that no-good Mr. Jackal Johnson.

"Darling, I'll see you later," Mr. Garibaldi says, kissing Ms. Dorothea on the cheek. Then he says good-bye to us, so he can find some seats up front for himself and Daddy.

"Try to sit in the first row, Daddy!" Galleria yells back to him, as we walk toward the back.

Ms. Dorothea speaks to another usher in a red jacket who points straight ahead of us. "Right that way, ladies."

"Look at all the people!" Chanel says excitedly. Lots of them are already filing into the theater and finding their seats.

"It *is* as big as it looks on TV!" I whisper to Angie.

"You think it'll get filled up?" Dorinda asks, kinda nervous.

"*Sí, sí, Do' Re Mi,*" says Chanel, giggling. "As soon as they find out *we're* here, *está bien?*"

At the base of the stairs, there is a woman with a walkie-talkie and earphones. Before Ms. Dorothea says anything to her, the woman tells us in a brisk voice to "go up the stairs."

Dag on! She could be a little friendlier, I think to myself, as we all climb up a real tiny staircase. It seems like the longest time before we get to the stairwell landing for dressing room "B."

When we open the stairwell door, there are a lot of people crowded in the hallway! *Are we supposed to share a dressing room with all these people*? I wonder.

"Excuse me, darlings," Ms. Dorothea says firmly, pushing her way through the throng of people.

"You'd think we were at the mall or something, and they were giving things away!" Angie exclaims.

As we pour into the dressing room, just to plop down our things, Ms. Dorothea quips, "They said the dressing room would be small, but this looks like a *prison cell*!"

"I guess it's a good thing we already have our costumes on," I say nervously, looking around at the other people. They are in costumes too, but not like ours. One man looks just like The Cat In the Hat or something, his hat is so high up on his head. He has striped kneesocks, too, and shorts, and big cartoon-looking glasses!

Galleria whispers, "If all we've got to deal

with is The Cat In the Hat, then we've got it made, like green eggs and ham!"

I sure hope so, I think nervously—because between my too tight costume, this too tight dressing room, and High Priestess Abala's too spooky Vampire Spell, this whole thing is turning into a New York frightmare!

Chapter 4

"I bet Dressing Room 'A' is for the stars," Dorinda says, looking kinda sad, then puts her cheetah backpack down on the floor.

"What *stars*, darling?" Ms. Dorothea says. "In my humble opinion, you girls are the most cheetah-licious thing the Apollo Theatre has ever seen—or will ever see!"

We may not exactly believe her, but at least her words make us feel less nervous. Now we have to push through the people again, and climb all the way back down those steep little stairs until we get backstage. *Then* we have to wait backstage for our number to be called.

"I'm exhausted already!" I moan to Dorinda, who is scratching herself through her costume.

Oh, no, not again. She can't be busting out of her costume, after Ms. Dorothea took all that time to fix it!

As if reading my mind, Dorinda squints her eyes and says, "Don't worry, Aqua, my costume is not gonna rip again. I must have got bitten by mosquitoes or *something* last night. Our screens at the house have holes in them."

"Maybe it was the little teddy bear vampire from your shoe box!" Galleria says, her eyes lighting up.

"Lemme see," Chanel says to Do' Re Mi, who rolls up the left leg on her cheetah jumpsuit. "*Ay, Dios!* Look how red they are. *Mamacita,* it sure looks like mosquito bites to me."

"Maybe you got bitten by those mosquitoes carrying the killer virus!" Galleria says, concerned.

"Maybe it was one of those six-foot bloodsucking mosquitoes like in the movie me and Aqua saw," my twin blurts out.

"I'm not trying to hear this," Dorinda says, getting upset.

"Don't worry, Dorinda. I know how to stop the itching," I say.

"How, brown cow?" Bubbles asks, giggling.

"Darling, that's not funny," Ms. Dorothea says suddenly.

"What, Mom? I'm just riffing off a *nursery* rhyme!" Galleria protests.

"Even so, darling, sometimes you have to give your 'riff' the 'sniff test' before you 'flap your lips'—if you 'get my drift,'" Ms. Dorothea says, looking at Galleria like she's not the only one with rhyme power.

Galleria gets real sheepish. Ms. Dorothea is real nice, but she doesn't play.

"That's all right, Ms. Dorothea, I know Galleria didn't mean anything bad. She's just being, well, herself," I offer as an explanation.

"Well, she can stir that saying with some jam, and make *flimflam*," Ms. Dorothea says, closing her cheetah purse with a loud snap.

We all get quiet, but I don't want Galleria to feel bad, so I say, "I can go upstairs and get the deodorant out of my backpack."

"For what, *mamacita*? You trying to say we smell now?" Chanel asks me.

"No, Chanel! It's an old Southern remedy. If you rub deodorant on a mosquito bite, it stops the itching!"

"Word?" Dorinda asks hopefully.

"Well then, go get it, Aqua, 'cuz we don't want Dorinda wiggling around like Mr. Teddy Poodly onstage," Galleria says, making a joke about the stuffed teddy bear head and poodle tail in the shoe boxes Abala gave us.

"Dag on, I hope that thing doesn't try on any of my clothes while I'm gone!" I retort. That gets everyone laughing, which is good, because we don't want to get a bad case of nerves before we perform.

"I'll go with you, Aqua," Ms. Dorothea says. "You girls stay here, so nobody takes our spot." She looks annoyed. "Of course, at the rate they're going, we'll be here until the Cock-a-doodle Donut truck pulls up to make a morning delivery!"

When we get back upstairs, I can't believe that those bozo boys we met when we came in are hanging out near our dressing room. They're putting on yellow satin jackets, with the words "Stak Chedda" written on the back in blue letters. That must be the name of their group, I figure.

I grab the deodorant for Dorinda and we head back downstairs. "I bet they're probably rappers," I say to Ms. Dorothea, once we're safely out of hearing range.

"Like I said, darling, that is still no excuse for bad manners!" Dorothea quips.

When we get backstage and rejoin the others, I give Do' Re Mi the deodorant for her legs, and she starts working on herself.

"Guess who's performing!" I moan. "Those bozos we met outsi—"

Galleria jabs me before I can finish, so I turn around. Can you believe it? Those rude boys are coming our way!

"Whazzup, ladies?" the one with the Popeye eye sockets says to us, chuckling under his breath.

"Are you performing too?" Dorinda asks. Galleria is propping her up while Angie puts the deodorant on the mosquito bites on her leg.

"Yeah. We're rappers—'Stak Chedda.' I'm Stak Jackson and this is my brother Chedda Jackson," Popeye says to us.

"Who are you lovely ladies?" Chedda asks. His head is bigger than his brother's, but the rest of his body still looks like he could use a home-cooked meal—just like Ms. Dorothea said.

"We're the Cheetah Girls," Galleria answers for us, then gives them a smirk, like, "don't try it."

"See? I knew y'all were related to Tony the Tiger!" Popeye riffs. "Those costumes you're wearing are fierce, though."

"They're not costumes—it's our survival gear for becoming stars in the jiggy jungle—not wanna-be's like you." Galleria sniffs, then adds, "And you two must be related to Dr. Jekyll and Mr. Hyde?"

"Oooops," Chedda says, then slaps his baseball cap at the crown.

"I mean the rappers, not the loony doctors," Galleria assures them. "But maybe . . ."

"We could have it like that. You never know, with how we flow," Popeye says, then slaps his brother a high five.

"It's show time at the Apollo!" booms the announcer's voice from the front of the stage. Then we hear loud applause.

"It's crowded out there, right?" says one of the girls in back of us, really loudly.

"Quiet, please, and keep your places, so you can be called on," says an attendant with a walkie-talkie.

When the girls in back of us keep yapping, Ms. Dorothea gives them a look, then says, "Shhh!" Then she huddles the five of us together in a circle. "It's time to do your Cheetah Girls prayer."

Even though the area backstage is small and crowded with all the contestants, we try to ignore everybody and do our Cheetah Girls prayer. We have plenty of time, because we're the fourth contestants—even though I wish we were the last, because I'm starting to feel real nervous. The hamburger I ate for dinner is churning around in my stomach.

Ms. Dorothea instructs us to join hands, bow our heads, and close our eyes. Galleria starts the prayer; then we join in, keeping our voices low, so the other people around us don't start looking at us.

"Dear Head Cheetah in Charge, please give us the growl power to perform our cheetah-licious best, and make you proud of all the gifts you've bestowed on us . . ." We end the prayer by doing the Cheetah Girl handshake together and chanting, "Whatever makes us clever—forever!"

The other people backstage cheer us on

quietly. But they don't have to worry—there is so much noise coming from the stage and the audience, you can't even hear us back here.

"Bacon, Once Over Lightly—please stand here by the curtain. You go on first," the attendant barks sharply. She is talking to four girls who look a lot older than us—maybe about nineteen—and are wearing brown leather jumpers and kneesocks.

"I hope they're crispy," whispers Galleria, who is standing between me and Chanel.

"Their earrings sure look like plates—big enough to hold a few strips," I whisper back.

"Ladies and gentleman," booms the announcer, "we've got four sisters from Buttercup, Tennessee. Let's give a hand to Bacon, Once Over Lightly!"

Sisters. They must not be sisters for real, 'cuz they don't look very much alike. Maybe that's just a stage act or something. We hold our breath, waiting for the girls to start singing.

First we hear the track for the Sista Fudge song, "I'll Slice You Like a Poundcake," booming on the sound system. They'd better be real good singers to mess with that song, I think, shaking my head.

Pulling down my jumpsuit, Galleria slaps my hand and mouths, "Stop it!" but I don't even care, 'cuz I can't believe my ears. These poor girls are more like Spam than bacon—they sound like the noise from an electric can opener!

All of a sudden, the noise from the audience is even louder than their singing.

"Omigod—are they booing them?" Angie asks, bobbing her head around to see if maybe she can sneak a peek through the curtain. But we can't see a thing. The attendant is standing right near the heavy curtain, and it's not budging.

Suddenly I start sweating. There is no air back here. It's hot, and I'm nervous. Those girls are getting booed out there! Are *we* gonna get booed too? I can't believe how blasé the attendant is acting! She must be used to all this.

"I think they're awright. They didn't have to boo them like that," Dorinda says, folding her arms. Her lower lip is kinda trembling, and I can tell she feels sorry for Bacon, Once Over Lightly. Ms. Dorothea puts her arms around Dorinda's little shoulders and gives her a squeeze.

All of a sudden, we hear this funny music, and the audience laughing real loud. We just look at each other, like, "Where's Freddy?"

"That means the Sandman went onstage," Ms. Dorothea tells us.

That really did sound like *clown* music or something. I have to catch my breath and say a prayer to God. *Please give us the strength to perform after all this. And please don't let the Sandman take us!*

Then I get the strangest thought: What if High Priestess Abala Shaballa *did* put a spell on us? What if we go out there and start croaking like bullfrogs?

No! That's so silly! We had rehearsal today, and we sound just as good as we always do. And at least we're singing original material, I remind myself. Galleria writes songs—she's *real* talented like that, even if we did fight in the beginning 'cuz she likes to have everything her way.

She wrote the song we're singing tonight, "Wanna-be Stars in the Jiggy Jungle." When we performed it for the first time at the Cheetah-Rama, everybody *loved* it!

They'll probably love us tonight, too. That's right, I tell myself. Angie and I look at each other, and I know she's thinking the same thing.

Two more acts go on—the Coconuts and a boy named Wesley Washington, who tries to sing falsetto like Jiggie Jim from the Moonpies, one of my favorite singers. (He just gives me goose bumps, his voice is so high and beautiful.) This boy sounds like he has been inhaling helium or something. He is definitely singing too high for his range.

"I think we're the only ones singing an original song," I whisper in Galleria's ear.

She pokes me in the stomach and says, "No diggity, no doubt!"

Now it's our turn. The walkie-talkie attendant motions for us to hurry up and stand by her.

I whisper to Chanel, "Ain't you scared? We don't know what's waiting for us beyond that curtain!"

"Fame!" giggles Chanel, grabbing my hand.

"Ladies and gentleman, our next contestants are five young ladies from right here in the Big Apple, and they got a whole lot of attitude!"

How come he didn't say two of us are from Houston? I feel kinda mad, but I just smile when he says, "Give it up for the Cheetah

Girls!" What counts is, he got the name of our group right.

We run out onto the stage, and everybody starts clapping. I guess they like our costumes, 'cuz who wouldn't? We stand side by side, and hold our cordless microphones in place, waiting for the track to begin. We smile at each other, and our eyes are screaming, "Omigod, look at all these people!"

Then the music comes on, and we start to sing:

"Some people walk with a panther
or strike a buffalo stance
that makes you wanna dance.

Other people flip the script
on the day of the jackal
that'll make you cackle . . ."

People start clapping to the beat. They like us! We even get our turns down, 'cuz Angie and I have been working real hard to improve our dance steps. I just wanna scream when Dorinda does her split—and gets right back up without splitting her pants. *Go, Dorinda!*

By the time we take our bows, to a huge round of applause, I feel almost like crying. *This* is why we love to sing—Angie and I have dreamed about moments like this all our lives!

"You were *fabulous*!" Ms. Dorothea screams when we get backstage. "I didn't hear one jackal cackle!"

"That's 'cuz he's in prison, eating his own tough hide right about now," Galleria humphs.

We all laugh at her joke. We know she's talking about Mr. Jackal Johnson—our brush with a real-live jackal. Mr. Johnson wanted to be our manager, but he didn't have good intentions. Lucky for us, Ms. Dorothea got wind of it before he had some Cheetah Girls for lunch. Like I told you, she doesn't play.

"I just *know* we're gonna win!" Chanel says, dancing around in the back while we wait for the rest of the performers to go on.

Pushing up the sleeves on their satin baseball jackets, those two annoying boys, Stak Chedda, posture like *they're* ready for Freddy, then walk out onstage like they think they're all that and a bag of fries.

"I know *you* ain't gonna win!" I say under

my breath, sucking my teeth behind their backs. We all start giggling, then huddle against the end of the curtain so we can hear them when the rap track drops.

"I *know* they got weak rhymes," Angie says, egging us on as they start to do their thing.

"Well, I'm the S to the T to the A to the K
Stak's my name and you know I got game.
When I'm on the mike, I make it sound so right
I rip the night till it gets way light
I think I'm gonna do it right now
So let's get to it—and if you wanna
Bust a rhyme, go ahead and do it!"

Even though the audience is doing a call and response with these cheesy rappers, we aren't worried about the competition, because their rap is, well, kinda like the alphabet—it starts with A, ends with Z, and gets real corny by the time they get to M.

Stak Chedda does get a lot of applause, but we're still not sweating it. "Get ready for Freddy, *girlitas*!" Galleria says. We do the Cheetah Girls handshake again, and wait for our cue to come out.

"Okay, ladies and gentlemen. It's that time again—time to pick the winner of this month's world-famous Apollo Amateur Hour contest. Come on out! Come on out!"

There's a drumroll, and we are all waved back onstage by the attendant. The lights are so bright, and there are so many people, it's kinda scary.

The announcer calls the name of each group in turn, and they step up to the center of the stage, so the audience can decide who should win the contest. Whoever gets the most applause wins.

"Lord, we need that prize money!" I say, grabbing Galleria's hand. "Just for once, I'd like to pay for my own tips."

Of course, I'm exaggerating, because we did spend some of the prize money we earned from the Cheetah-Rama show. But Daddy usually pays for us to get our hair and nails done twice a month. Maybe if we earned our own money, he wouldn't complain so much about having to pay the garage bill every month for two cars.

I'm getting so jittery I grab Angie's hand real tight. We both look at the front row, to see if we can spot Daddy. We were too nervous to look while we were performing.

Omigod, there he is! Angie and I give him a real big grin. Mr. Garibaldi is waving at us so hard, you'd think he was at the Santa Maria Parade in Houston.

I can't believe how many people are in this theater! I try not to look too far into the crowd, because the lights are so bright they almost blind me.

When the announcer calls our name to come up to the center of the stage, I really do think I'm gonna faint. We step forward, and I can see the little beads of sweat on the announcer's shiny forehead. He's wearing a red bow tie and a white shirt. His hair is slicked down, and his teeth are whiter than the neon sign outside.

I look around, trying to catch a glimpse of the Sandman. Where does he hide at, anyway?

"Okay, ladies and gentlemen. *You* decide. What did you think of the Cheetah Girls!" he bellows into the microphone.

The audience is clapping—louder than they did for Wesley Washington; Bacon, Once Over Lightly; or any of the other performers!

I'm so excited, I can't believe this is happening! We stand together at the back of the stage, and I can feel how excited all of us are by the sparkle in our eyes.

Now there is only one group left—and we know we got them beat by a bag of bacon bits!

"Okay, ladies and gentlemen—what did you think of the rapping duo, Stak Chedda!"

Of course, Popeye and his brother step forward like they own the place, but we know they ain't the cat's meow, as Big Momma would say.

All of a sudden I can't believe my ears. We look at one another in sudden shock when the audience claps louder for these bozos than they did for us!

The announcer's voice echoes like something right out of a horror movie—"And the winner of tonight's Amateur Hour contest at the world-famous *Apollo* Theatre is—STAK CHEDDA!"

"That's what I'm talking about!" Popeye yells into the mike, holding up his hands like he's Lavender Holy, the boxer, and he's just won a title bout.

I can feel the hot tears streaming down my face. *Why did tonight have to turn into Nightmare on 125th Street? Why?*

Chapter 5

Dorinda is crying, and she's not even trying to hide it. Bless her heart. She's probably kicking herself and thinking, Why didn't I take that job as a backup dancer for the Mo' Money Monique tour?

I can't blame her. For me and Angie, singing is our life. We *have* to sing—but Dorinda can *dance*. Maybe she doesn't even *want* to sing, but she's doing it for us, because *we* want her to.

Galleria looks so mad her mouth is poking out. I can't even look at Daddy right now. I feel so ashamed.

"Stak Chedda. They wuz more like Burnt Toast. This competition is rigged, yo!" Dorinda blurts out through her tears when we get backstage.

Ms. Dorothea doesn't say anything. She just holds Galleria, and then we all start crying.

"I can't believe we didn't win, Mommy," Galleria moans, tears streaming down her cheeks. She doesn't seem like herself at all—more like a little girl.

The attendant is now directing traffic, and sending everyone back up to the dressing rooms to get their belongings. "If you don't have anything in the dressing rooms, just move toward the rear exit. Do not try to exit in front!"

"Can we just stay here a minute?" Ms. Dorothea asks the attendant very nicely.

"Yes, go ahead, but you're gonna have to move shortly," she says briskly. She must have seen a million people like us, crying like babies just because they lost.

I don't know what we're gonna do now. We just can't seem to get a break! Angie and I wanted to sing gospel in the first place, but we got into pop and R&B music, because everybody kept telling us that was the only way to break into this business. Dag on, it seems like *rappers* are the only ones who are getting breaks now!

Mr. Garibaldi is waiting outside for us. "Your father went to get the car," he tells me and Angie, then turns to Galleria with his arms outstretched.

"Daddy! *Ci sono scemi.* I hate those people! Take me home!" Galleria is crying so hard, I can't believe it.

Angie is holding me now, because she is crying too. Chanel is holding Dorinda. People are standing around, looking at us. "Y'all were so cute!" this girl says to us as she walks out of the theater.

"Don't say nothing, Aisha. Can't you see they're crying? Leave them alone," her mother says, grabbing the girl's arm.

I look away from them. I don't care if we never come back here again!

Daddy pulls up outside the theater in the Bronco. Why couldn't he pull up down the block where no one could see us? Doesn't he understand how embarrassed we are? I don't want people looking at us, then laughing behind our backs.

I wish we hadn't worn our costumes here.

Then we could have changed back into our street clothes, and no one would have noticed us—the losers. "The Cheetah Girls."

I can't even look Daddy in the face when we get into the car. I try to sit in the back, but Chanel pushes me up front. She and Dorinda are *real* quiet now, slumped down in the back seat. They don't say a word.

"Those boys weren't that good. I don't see what all the fuss was about. You girls shoulda won," Daddy says, to no one in particular.

"Well, we didn't," I say, then sigh.

This is the worst day of my life. Worse than when Daddy first moved out of the house, and Ma stayed in bed crying for a week. Worse than when Grandma Winnie died from cancer. Worse than when I fell from the swing, and got seven stitches in my knee.

If you ask me, it doesn't really look like the Cheetah Girls are meant to be. I mean, we knew it would be hard, but not *this* hard. Every time we turn around, something is going wrong! "We can't get a break to save our lives," as Big Momma would say.

"Anybody want to go to Kickin' Chicken?" Daddy asks.

"No, thank you," we all say, one by one. I don't feel hungry at all. I just want to go home and get in bed, and pray to God to help us find some answers.

"You're cryin' all over your costume," Ms. Dorothea says to Galleria, reaching for a tissue out of her purse.

"I don't care about this stupid costume anymore!" Galleria blurts out between sobs.

We all get real quiet until Daddy stops in front of Dorinda's house at 116th Street. I feel bad that Dorinda has to live here, with all these people living on top of one another like cockroaches and always getting into each other's business.

Dorinda turns to ask Ms. Dorothea one more thing before she closes the car door. "How come they didn't like us?"

"They *did,*" Ms. Dorothea tells her. "But one day, they're gonna *love* you. You'll see. The world is cruel like that sometimes."

Ms. Dorothea gets out of the car, and gives Dorinda a big hug, and she doesn't let go for a long time. Ms. Dorothea looks like a big cheetah, and Dorinda looks like a little cub who is happy to be loved.

I hope Galleria doesn't feel jealous. She can be that way. Now she's acting like she doesn't even see them hug, and she doesn't even look up to say good-bye to Dorinda.

"Come here, *cara*," Mr. Garibaldi says to Galleria, then holds a tissue to Galleria's nose. She blows into it so hard it sounds like a fire engine siren.

Galleria is such a Daddy's girl—just like me and Angie—but her dad is a lot nicer than ours. I can't imagine Mr. Garibaldi getting as mean as Daddy gets sometimes. Now I feel more tears welling up—and these tears have nothing to do with the Cheetah Girls.

"Can I have one, Mr. Garibaldi?" I ask him, reaching for a tissue.

"Call me Franco," Mr. Garibaldi says, smiling at me with tears in his eyes as he hands me a tissue.

That is so sweet. He feels bad, just 'cuz his baby feels bad. He's always calling Galleria *cara*. I think that means *baby* in Italian. She's so lucky she gets to speak another language and all. That's one reason why she and Chanel seem so mysterious to us.

It gets real quiet again when it's just us and

Daddy in the car. He doesn't know how to say a lot of things to us. That's just how he is, 'cuz he has a lot of things on his mind—even though he does seem happier now that he has that girlfriend of his. He sure is crazy about her. Too bad we don't like her at all! Angie and I hold hands all the way home.

When we get home, Daddy lets us go right upstairs to bed, without saying anything. Good. I'm too tired now to even try to talk.

"I'm real proud of you girls," Daddy calls after us as we climb the stairs to our bedroom.

"Good night, Daddy," I say.

Daddy goes over to the stereo and puts on an LP. He loves this time of night. He likes to sit by himself, and smoke his pipe, and drink brandy while he watches television or listens to some music. He likes to listen to the legends like Miles Davis, Lionel Hampton, and Coltrane late at night, 'cuz, he says, that's when you can really hear "the jazz men trying to touch you with their music."

"Good night, Daddy," Angie says, and we continue on upstairs.

Angie is real quiet as we change into our pajamas. She doesn't even make any jokes about the shoe boxes in the closet. I wish Mr. Teddy Poodly could come out of his shoe box and dance with us right now. Anything would be better than this misery.

I go to my shoe box and look at it, then decide to take the Scotch tape off it. If Mr. Teddy Poodly wants to come out and dance, let him—he just better not bother Porgy and Bess, our pet guinea pigs.

After I throw the Scotch tape in the wastebasket, Angie and I kneel down by our beds. Tonight, it's Angie's turn to lead our prayer.

"God, please help us see why you didn't let us win the contest tonight," she says. "If you don't want us to be singers anymore, please let us know. Just show us the signs. We'll do real good in school so that we can go to college, like we said. If you don't want us to quit singing, then please give us strength to do better, so we can stay in New York and not let Ma down.

"Please look over her in Houston, and Big Momma, and Granddaddy Walker, too, because his blood pressure is acting up, and he didn't sound too good on the phone. Oh, and please tell us if High Priestess Abala Shaballa is a witch—and if she is, if she is a *good* witch. Just give us the signs. We'll understand. Amen."

After we say our prayers, Angie and I curl up in our beds. We reach out to each other, and hold hands across the space between—just like we did when we were little, and would get afraid of a lightning storm.

"I wish Ma was here," I whisper to Angie.

"Me, too."

"I wish Grandma Winnie was here," I add, crying.

"Me, too."

And that's the last thing either of us says before going to sleep.

The next morning, when I wake up, I feel bad already. That's when I realize that what happened last night wasn't just a bad dream—it was a waking nightmare! If somebody came to me right now with an Aladdin's lamp or something like that, I would wish that last night never happened, even if it meant that Freddy would have to visit me in my dreams.

How could God let all our dreams get shattered just like that?

On Sunday mornings we are usually so happy to get up, because we go to church and we go to Hallelujah Tabernacle, and they let me and Angie do two-part harmony songs on "teen Sundays." Also, during convocation season, we get to sing in the choir sometimes.

Right now, my hair looks a mess. I was so upset last night, I forgot to put the stocking cap on my head to keep my wrap smooth. I hate when I do that!

"Angie, those are my shoes!" I yell, as she tries to sneak her feet into my black pumps instead of hers. She can be such a copycat sometimes—trying to act like she doesn't know her things from mine. She's always trying to switch stuff—especially when she loses a button, or scuffs her shoes bad.

I know Angie is real upset, because she doesn't even pretend like she *didn't* know she was putting on my shoes. She just sits on the edge of the bed and waits for me to put on my clothes.

I reach for the navy blue dress with the gold buckle, because that's what we decided we would wear. When we go to church, we *always* dress alike, and we can't wear pants. "Do you think Daddy is gonna let us be Cheetah Girls anymore?" Angie asks, real quiet.

"I don't know, Angie, but I bet you he's gonna call Ma and tell her we lost." I open the bottom drawer of the white chest of drawers to get out a pair of navy blue panty hose. I feel so bad, my head hurts when I talk. I hold up the panty hose and run my fingers through them.

"Dag on, Angie, these have a run in them!" Sucking my teeth, I throw the panty hose in the white wicker wastebasket under the nightstand. "It's a good thing I checked before I wasted my time putting them on. I told you not to put tights *back* in the drawer if you put a run in them!"

"I musta not noticed!" Angie exclaims, getting real defensive. Then I give her that look we have between us, and Angie cracks a little smile. She knows I know when she's lying. I don't know why she even bothers sometimes.

"Don't forget," I mutter. "It's your turn to clean Porgy and Bess's cage."

I can smell the bacon frying downstairs. High Priestess Abala came over this morning, and she's cooking breakfast for us. She's going to *church* with us, too, believe it or not! I think that's pretty strange, considering all her weird rituals and stuff. To tell you the truth, I wish she wasn't here, because I don't feel like being nice to anybody this morning.

"What if we had been on that stage by ourselves, Angie?" I ask, as walk out the bedroom door to go downstairs and eat breakfast. "We woulda frozen solid like a pair of icicles!"

Angie just nods at me. I know that means we're both thinking the same thing—what will we do if we aren't the Cheetah Girls anymore?

The spiral staircase in our duplex is *real* steep, so we always come downstairs slow and careful. (I'm afraid of heights. So is Angie.)

"Omigod!" Angie gasps when we get to the bottom landing. "I *know* the Evil One is in our house now." `

"What's the matter, Angie?" I ask, trying not to bump into her from behind.

"What *is* that thing?" Angie asks.

I take a few steps forward, so I can see what it is she's talking about. Then I let out a loud, surprised scream. This ugly thing—some kind of huge, horrible mask—is hanging on the wall in front of us. It gave me such a fright it almost scared me to death—right into Granddaddy Walker's funeral parlor back home!

"Good morning, ladies," High Priestess Abala Shaballa says, walking from the kitchen into the living room. Angie and I get our manners back *real* fast, because we know that Abala musta had something to do with this strange thing hanging on the wall. It's just as weird as she is.

"Good morning, Abala," I say politely, making myself be nice to her, even though I don't want to. I hope Daddy didn't tell her that we lost the Apollo Amateur Hour contest. How *could* we lose that? I *still* can't believe those boys won! "The devil is a liar," just like Big Momma says.

"Do you know what this is?" High Priestess Abala Shaballa asks, pointing to the thing on the wall.

"No, I—we—don't," I say, looking at Angie for some support. Now that Abala is Daddy's girlfriend, it just seems like we never know anything anymore.

It's not like before. At least, in the old days, Daddy, Angie, and I got to learn things together. Now it seems like everything new he knows, he learned from her.

"It's a Bogo Mogo Hexagone Warrior Mask," Abala says proudly.

No wonder it's strange, I think. It's something named after *her*.

"You see the markings here," Abala continues, pointing to the bright red marks across the cheeks of the big mask, which looks like the head of a space alien.

"Yes, I see them," I respond, trying to act interested, even though I know there is something deep-down weird about this thing.

"When the markings change colors, it means it's time for Hexagone to reign once again, and the world will become a magical place. With Bogo Mogo here, you will have someone to watch over you all the time now."

Oh, *great*. Now we not only have Daddy, we have this thing's beady eyes watching us, too. I try not to look scared.

"You *do* believe in magic, don't you, Aquanette?"

"Yes, High Priestess Abala," I say. I don't tell her what I really think—that she needs some more magic lessons, because Mr. Teddy Poodly didn't come out of his shoe box to help us win the contest. So why should this mask do anything—except maybe scare me in the middle of the night when I come downstairs to get a snack?

"Well, let's go eat. I've fixed a divine feast for the two of you," High Priestess Abala says, outstretching her arms the way she does, like a peach tree with big ol' branches. (Grandma Winnie had one in her backyard, with the biggest, juicy peaches we ever ate . . . then it just withered up and died when Grandma did.)

"Good morning, Daddy," I say as we join him in the kitchen. I'm still not able to look him in the eye. I wonder if he told High Priestess Abala that we lost the contest. Dag on, how *could* we?

Angie and I sit down at the dining room table real quiet, and High Priestess Abala serves us some ham, eggs, biscuits, and fried apples. Then, for herself and Daddy, she pours some green stuff from the blender into two glasses.

I can't believe that's all Daddy is eating for breakfast! He used to eat a whole plate of bacon and tin of biscuits, with a whole pot of coffee! Daddy looks into Abala's eyes all goo-goo-eyed, and they clink their glasses of green goo together. Yuck!

"To you, my divine Priestess—because I've never felt younger," Daddy says, then gulps down his shake.

I just hope he doesn't start looking younger, or I'm gonna call Granddaddy Walker to come up here and make sure Abala's not slipping embalming fluid in Daddy's blender! (Granddaddy Walker says that's why dead people look so good sometimes even better than they did in real life!)

Thank God, the phone rings before these two lovebirds fly over the cuckoo's nest together. Daddy answers, then hands the phone to me. "It's your friend," he says.

"Hello?" I say, taking the receiver.

"Aqua, you're not gonna believe this," Galleria says, without even saying hello. I can't believe how much better she sounds!

"What?" I reply.

"Mom just had her hair done at Churl, It's You! and Pepto B., her hairdresser, told her that *he's* hooking up Kahlua Alexander's braids later!"

"Really?" I answer, but I still don't understand why Galleria is so excited.

"So guess who he's gonna hook *us* up with?"

"No! *Kahlua?"* I gasp. You *know* I'm surprised, but now I'm getting excited, too.

"That's right, dee-light. We have hatched a plan. Mom says for you and Angie to be ready by six o'clock, 'cuz 'Operation Kahlua' is in full effect."

"Okay," I respond, even though I'm still not sure what she's talking about.

"And Aqua—don't wear the same clothes you and Angie wear to church, okay?"

"I know that, Galleria."

"Wear the cheetah jumpers and the ballet flats, okay?"

"Okay, Galleria. Bye!"

When I hang up the phone, I'm smiling from ear to ear. Angie, of course, knows something is up.

"Galleria is picking us up at six o'clock," I say, smiling at Daddy. "We should thank God we have Galleria, because I've never seen anyone rise from the dead faster than her!"

Now Abala is looking at me like she approves, but I don't want to give her the wrong idea. "That's just an expression Granddaddy Walker uses," I explain. "She didn't *really* rise from the dead."

"Your granddaddy is wise, because there are more ways than one to levitate your fate," Abala says, sipping on her witches' brew. "There is nothing for you to worry about, my dears. Bogo Mogo magic is working for you. If not today, then surely tomorrow."

Well, I sure hope Mr. Bogo Mogo can do his wonders from the bottom of a garbage can, 'cuz that's where he's ending up.

Chapter 6

It's so nice of Galleria's folks to offer to pick us up and take us to Pepto B.'s salon, Churl, It's You! Otherwise, Daddy would have probably insisted that *he* drive us. He thinks seven o'clock is kinda late for us to be out without a chaperone! Dag on, even Chanel can come home unescorted up until nine o'clock on school nights, and her mother is kinda strict. Our Daddy takes the cobbler, though.

I shoulda known something was up, though, when Galleria rings the bell at six o'clock. We're not due at the salon till seven thirty, and it only takes ten minutes to get there.

"Toodles to the poodles! You *fab-yoo-luss*

Walker twins, *we've* got a surprise for you!" Galleria says in her funny Southern accent.

She is definitely feeling better because she's acting like herself. And when Galleria acts like herself, the whole world is a brighter place. Even the cheetahs in the jungle are probably smiling right now.

Angie and I have been feeling better too, because Reverend Butter's sermon at church today did us a world of good. We crowd the front doorway of our building, waiting for Ms. Dorothea, Chanel, and Mr. Garibaldi to come in.

"You're so lucky you don't live in an elevator building," Dorinda comments, coming in and kissing us hello.

That's the truth. I would be scared to have to go up in an elevator every time I wanna get to my apartment. Like I told you, Angie and I are afraid of heights. That's why Daddy got a ground floor apartment in a town house.

It's quiet on our block, and we got a nice view of Riverside Park, so at least it feels a little like back home. I don't know if I could take all that noise over where Dorinda lives.

It's good to hear a pigeon chirping every now and again.

Ms. Dorothea is taking some garment bags and stuff from the van, and Chanel is helping her carry them inside. Chanel works part time at Toto in New York . . . Fun in Diva Sizes, 'cuz she has to pay her mother back all the money she charged on her credit card.

See, I think Chanel lost her mind after we did that first show at the Cheetah-Rama. She started shoppin' till we wuz *all* droppin'! I guess Chanel thought everything was gonna come real easy. But it's not—you gotta work *real* hard just to hold onto your dream. By the time she came to her senses, Chanel owed her mother a whole lot of money! Lucky for her, Ms. Dorothea offered her the job at her store.

"What's that?" Angie asks, pointing to the garment bags.

"You didn't think we were gonna let you wear just plain ol' anything to meet the biggest singer in the world, did you?" Galleria asks, batting her eyelashes.

"Now, I was gonna surprise you girls with your new outfits after you won the Apollo Amateur contest. But that was their loss. And anyway, now we have bigger prey to pounce on," Ms. Dorothea says, all optimistic and funny like she is. Opening the garment bag, she pulls out matching fake-fur cheetah miniskirts and vests.

"Oooh!" Angie exclaims, putting her hands on her cheeks, like she does after she opens her Christmas presents.

"We're gonna go in there looking like a *real* group," says Galleria, all proud. Then she pulls a tube of lipstick out of her cheetah backpack. "Look at the new shade of S.N.A.P.S. lipstick we got. It's called Video."

"Oooh—it's got silver sparkles!" I say, grabbing the tube. I never saw silver lipstick like this before. "So what are we gonna do at the hair salon—act like we're getting our hair done?" Knowing Galleria and Ms. Dorothea, there has to be some plan.

Galleria, Chanel, and Dorinda look at each other like I just ate a whole peach cobbler pie without offering them a slice.

"No, silly, we're gonna go in there and *sing* while Kahlua's getting her hair done," Galleria pipes up.

"Ohhhhh," Angie and I say in unison.

"That's right. That's a good plan. Then what?"

"Then Miss Kahlua Alexander will be so inclined to wave her magic wand—and have her fairy godmother help us . . . I don't know, get a record deal . . . or at least a Happy Meal!"Galleria says, waving her hand like it's a wand.

"We know that's right," I chuckle. Kahlua Alexander is the *biggest* singer, and she can do just about anything with all her "magic powers."

"Operation Kahlua will be in full effect," Galleria says, smiling. Then she whispers to me, "Ask your Dad if it's okay for us to practice here."

"Right here?" I ask, smiling. That's Galleria—when she has a plan, there is no telling *what* she'll do to make it happen!

"Come on. We can sing two songs—'Wannabe Stars,' because we know it so well, and the new song, 'More Pounce to the Ounce.'"

I hesitate a little, because I don't know if we're ready to sing Galleria's new song yet.

"Come on, Angie. We're ready. We've been practicing it for two long weeks!" Galleria begs me, reading my thoughts.

"I'll ask Daddy!" Angie says all excited, running toward the den, where Daddy is sitting with High Priestess Abala Shaballa.

Dag on, she's over here a lot now. Doesn't she have some new spells to practice at home?

Daddy and his High Priestess come into the living room with Angie tagging behind them. "Greetings, sacred ones," Abala greets our guests.

She gives Ms. Dorothea a little bow. Those two met at Dorinda's adoption party, and I don't think Ms. Dorothea likes the High Priestess too much. High Priestess is even taller than Ms. Dorothea, if you can believe that—even with Dorothea's new hairdo, which is higher than a skyscraper! Abala is so tall she looks like a weeping willow tree, ready to sway if the wind blows in her direction!

Abala turns to Galleria, Dorinda, and Chanel. "Tell me, sacred ones," she says. "Did the Vampire Spell work?"

Abala does look real pretty today—kinda like a . . . well, a High Priestess I guess. She does have real pretty eyes too. I guess I can see why Daddy likes her so much.

"No," I volunteer sourly. Daddy *musta* told

her by now that we lost the contest. Why is she asking us if the spell worked?

"Then either you didn't follow my directions, or High Priestess Hexagone has bigger plans for you," High Priestess Abala Shaballa says solemnly.

Galleria mumbles under her breath, "Whatever makes you clever."

Finally, Daddy senses the situation is a little tense, because he pipes up, "Listen, girls, I know you have to get ready. My home is yours, and do whatever you need to do to get ready. We'll be in the kitchen if you need anything. Come on, Abala," he says, touching her arm gently.

That makes me feel real proud. Daddy still believes in us! He never says much, but I guess that's just his way.

"Aah, che bella!" Mr. Garibaldi says, looking at Daddy's snow globe collection. "May I touch?"

"Go ahead," I say with a smile, looking at Galleria, who is rolling her eyes to the ceiling. I think her Daddy still loves the snow.

"Just don't start collecting them, Daddy," Galleria giggles.

* * *

After we practice for one hour, we climb into the van. I guess, you could say, we are ready for Freddy—and definitely for Kahlua Alexander!

"I can't *believe* how high Pepto teased my wig this time!" Ms. Dorothea says, looking in the mirror on the dashboard. "It looks like a torpedo ready for takeoff!"

We just chuckle and look at each other. I mean, Ms. Dorothea's hair does look a little like a skyscraper, but if anyone has the personality to carry it off, she does.

"Honey, he is so lucky I didn't pull a diva fit! But then he let the glass slipper drop—that Miss Kahlua is in town, to make a movie called *Platinum Pussycats*, with Bertha Kitten. He *also* let it slip that he is giving Kahlua a new 'do, because Bertha, or 'Miss Kitten' to you, said 'those braids have to go.' So I just started pouncing instead of pouting."

"But how did you angle an intro?" Dorinda asks.

Angie and I look at each other, like, "there they go again, saying things we don't understand!"

"Pepto was complaining about how his

mother just couldn't find the right dress for her thirtieth wedding anniversary," Ms. Dorothea explains. "So, naturally, I volunteered to make the dress of Ms. Butworthy's dreams—*for free!* Darling, Pepto and I have played this cat-and-mouse game for *years*, and believe me, his mother is no Happy Meal. She's such a pain, she's probably banned from every diva-size department in the country."

"Ohhhh, so that's what the B stands for," Dorinda says, smiling.

"Mr. B. speaks way too fast to get his whole last name out!" Ms. Dorothea says smiling. "You'll see."

As we pull up in front of the Churl, It's You! hair salon on 57th Street, Ms. Dorothea takes a deep breath, and announces, "Okay, girls, it's time to give them more 'pounce for the ounce!'"

"Ooh, look at how *la dopa* this place is!" Chanel exclaims as we approach Churl, It's You! "I'm gonna bring Princess Pamela here!"

The pink lights in the Churl, It's You! sign are so bright they sparkle like stars. In the window, there are floating brown mannequin heads with pink, blue, yellow, green, and purple wigs!

"Ooh, Angie—look at the heads!" I say, ogling the window display. "Look at the beautiful sign! We don't have anything like this in Houston."

"A blue Afro?" Angie says, smiling. Blue is our favorite color, but neither of us would have the nerve to wear a wig like that on our head. Galleria and Chanel would, of course. I wish we were more like them. They have so much style—but I have to admit, we *all* look fierce in our matching Cheetah Girl outfits.

Of course, Chanel runs to the door first, and we have to hurry to catch up to her. "Wait up, yo!" Dorinda snaps.

"Chuchie, we have to make an entrance *together*," Galleria says, taking the lead.

When Galleria opens the big glass door, musical chimes go off, and a recording starts playing: "Churl, It's You! Work the blue! Think pink like I do! Get sheen with green! We love—guess who!"

"Ooh, that is so dope!" laughs Dorinda.

"*Ay, Dios mío*, the whole place is pink. *Qué bonita!*" exclaims Chanel, looking around the salon like she's in a candy store. Pink is one of her favorite colors, and her whole bedroom is pink. She even has a pink cheetah bedspread!

"Wait till Kahlua sees your braids," I say to Chanel proudly, because she *looks* like Kahlua, with her braids and pretty eyes and all—she's just a lighter complexion.

"Welcome to Churl, It's You!" says a nice lady wearing a pink dress with an apron over it. Even her *shoes* are pink—and so is her *hair*!

"Hi, darling," Ms. Dorothea says, extending her hand to the pink lady. "We have an appointment with Pepto B."

"Yes, of course. So nice to see you again, Mrs. Garibaldi. Right this way. You must be the Cheetah Girls," she says, looking at us.

"Yes, ma'am," Angie says, giving the lady a big smile.

We look around the salon in wonder as we walk to the back. There are two huge cases with pink cotton candy, pink soda, and bags of pink popcorn! The hair dryer helmets are pink, and so are the chairs—even the sink where you get your hair washed!

"Oooh, look at the pink jukebox," I exclaim. The salon we go to doesn't have a jukebox. It's *boring* compared to this. "We have to ask Daddy to let us come here and get our hair done!" I whisper to Angie.

"It's even doper than Princess Pamela's!" Angie whispers back. "But don't tell Chanel I said so."

"I can't believe we're gonna meet Kahlua!" I say. We grab each other's hand and give a quick, tight squeeze, and I know Angie's thinking the same thing.

All of a sudden, a brown-skinned man with a short, pink Afro comes running over to us. He kisses Ms. Dorothea on both cheeks. I've never seen anyone do that before, except in the movies. He must be French or something. Then he turns real quick, and says to us, "Pepto B., that's me!"

We are just tickled—well, pink, I guess! As we introduce ourselves to Pepto B., I suddenly don't feel so nervous anymore.

Pepto B. grabs Ms. Dorothea's arm and whispers loudly, "Churl, your timing is *purrfect*. I just finished putting in Kahlua's weave. Wait till you see it. Churl, it took two hours to get those braids outta her hair! You woulda thought they were stuck on with Krazy

Glue! But you know those *Hollywood* hairdressers—you need a magician to fix your hair after they get through with you!"

Pepto B. and Ms. Dorothea dissolve into fits of giggles. Angie and I are just staring at them.

"Close your mouth, Aqua and Angie!" hisses Galleria. She says we watch people with our mouths open sometimes. I guess we do, but she has to understand—we're not used to all the ways of the Big Apple, the way she and Chanel are!

After the two grown-ups finish "cutting up," as Big Momma calls it, Pepto B. puts his hand on his chest and says, "Churl, you're killing me. Can you believe Bertha Kitten is coming out of her hermetically sealed coffin to do a movie? *Churrrl*, believe it!"

Then he turns to us, and says the words we've been waiting to hear—"And now, if you all are ready, it's time to meet the one and only . . . Kahlua!"

Chapter 7

When we get to the back of the salon, Kahlua is seated in the beauty parlor chair, reading a magazine. Standing next to her by the counter is a lady in a light-blue sweatsuit. That must be her mother, I figure. I heard she's managing Kahlua now, and that they even started a production company called "Kahlua's Korporation."

All of a sudden, I feel *real* nervous again. My stomach starts getting queasy, while my brain is screaming: *"It's really her! "*

Kahlua looks up at us, all curious, and says, "Hi!"

Oooo, she's even prettier in person than in her music videos! Staring at Kahlua, I wonder how she keeps her skin so smooth like that. It's the prettiest chocolate shade I've ever seen. She must be about a shade lighter than me and Angie. No, maybe two shades lighter, because she's got a lotta makeup on.

"Close your mouth, Angie!" Galleria whispers behind me, and pokes me in the butt.

Then Kahlua's mother introduces herself to Ms. Dorothea. "Hi, I'm Aretha Alexander. And who are all these cute girls?" she asks, smiling like a curious cat.

"We're the Cheetah Girls!" Galleria bursts out, giggling.

"Do you sing?" Kahlua asks, smiling now from ear to ear.

"Yes, churl, they do," Pepto B. offers, butting in. "And you should let them sing while I finish. I could sure use some entertainment, after fixing this tragedy that was up in yo' hair!"

We all giggle—even Kahlua—and she has the cutest dimples when she smiles, just like Dorinda's.

"Pepto, you are so *wrong*—but you are *right*," Kahlua says, all bubbly. "After putting up with *you* for four hours, I could use some entertainment!"

"Oh, don't let me take this comb and use it like a forklift on your head, churl!" Pepto B. warns, putting his hands on his hips.

After we all finish giggling, Ms. Dorothea clears her throat and says, "I guess it's time for growl power, girls!"

"'Growl Power!' Oooo, that is so cute!" Kahlua exclaims.

Ms. Dorothea takes our cheetah backpacks and puts them in the corner. Then the five of us huddle together, right there in the middle of the beauty salon, and sing *a capella* (that means without our instrumental track) the song we have practiced fifty million times, "Wanna-be Stars in the Jiggy Jungle."

I wish Ma could see us now—singing in the beauty parlor again, just like we used to when we were three years old, sitting in the double stroller next to her while she got her hair done.

Everybody claps when we're done—even the customers under the hair dryers!

"You wrote that song yourselves?" Kahlua's mother asks, and you can tell she is real impressed.

"*She* did," I say excitedly, pointing to Galleria.

Galleria looks like she's blushing, and I can tell Chanel feels a little bit jealous. Those two fight like sisters—more than Angie and I do—and we *are* sisters!

I think Chanel wants to be the leader of our group, and that's why she's jealous. I guess she's gonna have to learn how to write songs, instead of charging up clothes on her mother's credit card!

"Do y'all have another song?" Kahlua asks excitedly.

"Churl, I hear they got more songs than my jukebox!" Pepto B. says as he teases Kahlua's hair.

Ms. Dorothea looks at us, and motions for us to sing again. "We haven't performed this song before," Galleria says, then looks at us. "I, um, just finished writing it a few weeks ago."

"Go, ahead, we love it!" Ms. Alexander says, egging us on.

On the count of three, we then sing "More Pounce to the Ounce." I can feel my hands sweating, because singing a capella is a lot harder than singing with tracks—especially when you have five-part harmonies. See, you have to make sure everybody sings on the same level, and my and Angie's voices tend to be a little stronger than theirs are.

"Snakes in the grass have no class
but Cheetah Girls have all the swirls.
To all the competition, what can we say?
You had your day, so you'd better bounce, y'all,
While you still got some flounce, y'all,
'Cuz Cheetah Girls got more pounce to the ounce y'all!!"

After we finish the song, I look over at Angie. She leaned a little too hard on the chorus, I think—but I'll tell her that later. I think we still sounded good, though, because Kahlua and her mother are grinning from ear to ear.

"I love y'all!" Kahlua exclaims. "You got a record deal?"

We shake our heads "no."

I just wanna scream, *Get us a deal, please!*

"Momma, let's talk to Mr. Hitz about them," Kahlua says to her mother. Mrs. Alexander nods her head in agreement. "He's the president of the label I'm on—Def Duck Records," Kahlua explains.

"That would be groovy like a movie!" Galleria says, jumping up and down, she's so excited. Then she kisses Kahlua on the cheek, and gives her a big hug.

"You have so much energy—doesn't she, Momma?" Kahlua asks, her slanty eyes getting wide. "She reminds me of Backstabba a little, don't you think so?"

People have always thought Galleria looks a lot like Backstabba, the lead singer of Karma's Children. That band comes from our hometown—and Angie and I have decided we're not going back until we become as big as them!

"How did y'all become the Cheetah Girls?" Kahlua asks.

We tell Kahlua all about the jiggy jungle, growl power, and our Cheetah Girls rules and council meetings. She just loves it—especially when Galleria tells her about the dream she's had since she's a little girl:

"We wanna go to Africa and start a Cheetah conservancy. When we get rich, we're gonna get lots and lots of acres of land, so all the cheetahs in the jungle can live there and just chill, without worrying about anything. Then we'll travel all over the world, singing to peeps on two legs *and* four!"

"You are *too much,*" Kahlua says, crossing her legs and waving her hand at Galleria. Kahlua has nice nails. I bet you they're tips, though—like mine.

I'm looking at the chip on my nail when I hear Galleria blurt out, "We performed at the Apollo Amateur Hour Contest Saturday night—and we lost!"

How could she say something so dumb? I wonder. Why is she telling Kahlua that?

But Kahlua's reaction is the last thing I expected. "Honey, that's nothing. *I* lost it, too!" she says. "You know, the record company doesn't let me talk about it in interviews, but Momma will tell you—I cried like a baby for two weeks after I lost!"

Kahlua is beside herself laughing now. "You know how many famous recording artists have performed at the Apollo Amateur Hour Contest and lost?"

"How many?" Dorinda asks, her eyes wide with wonder.

"Let's see—Toyz II Boyz, The Moonpies, even Karma's Children lost!" Kahlua says, nodding her head like she knows things we don't.

"*What!?*" I say, all surprised. "I didn't know that!"

"No—no one is gonna tell you about their failures, but you have to stick to your dreams in this business, girls—'cuz people will trample on them like elephants!"

Kahlua sips her soda, then looks at Galleria's lips real close. "What color lipstick is that you're wearing?"

"Video. It's dope, right?" Galleria says, beaming.

"Oooo, I haven't seen this one yet! Can I try it?"

"Wait, I'll get it." Galleria runs to get her cheetah backpack, to show Kahlua the new shade of S.N.A.P.S. lipstick we're all wearing.

"Y'all look so cute in those outfits," Kahlua says, putting on the lipstick. Then she and Galleria start "ooohing" and "aaahing" up a storm.

"Tell us about your cheetah-licious movie," Galleria says, egging Kahlua on, now that they're like two peas in a pod.

"It's *such* hard work, you can't believe it! I

have to get up at five o'clock in the morning tomorrow to start shooting," Kahlua says. Then she starts playacting a yawn, and leans on Pepto B.'s shoulders for a hug.

"How are they going to get that 'Mummy' Bertha Kitten to the set on time?" Pepto B. quips. "Churl, she better be *grateful* she got this gig, 'cuz the only thing *she's* been doing for the last thirty years is her nails! She gives you any trouble, we'll sic these Cheetah Girls on her!"

We all hug each other good-bye, then do the Cheetah Girls handshake with Kahlua, Pepto B., and Mrs. Alexander—which they all just *love*. Ms. Dorothea gives Mrs. Alexander her business card, and they hug good-bye.

"We'll let you know what happens," Mrs. Alexander says, "but you don't have to worry, Dorothea. Your Cheetah Girls have 'more pounce for the ounce,' just like they said. The other girl groups won't stand a chance, once the Cheetahs show up."

Mr. Garibaldi is waiting for us outside in his van. "How did it go? *Bene?*" he asks Galleria as we get in the car. But he already knows the answer, from our big grins. "I knew it. That's why I made you girls a fresh batch of chocolate cannolis—Aqua's favorite," he says, handing us a big box of Italian pastries.

We all look at Galleria and burst out laughing. I munch on my dee-licious treats, which I shouldn't be eating, because Daddy doesn't like us to eat anything two hours before we practice—and I *know* we have to practice tonight before we go to bed. He let us off the hook last night—but lightning doesn't strike twice in the same place!

I give Angie a look, and she knows what I'm trying to say—*Don't tell Daddy we ate these!* The one thing I love about Angie is, she sure can keep a secret.

"Darlings, isn't this place something?" Ms. Dorothea says to me and Angie. She points to a beautiful skyscraper with a tiny, brightly lit tower topped by a steeple.

"It sure is," I respond, ogling the tower like it's a secret place in a castle or something. "You know, Ms. Dorothea, I thought for sure it was all over for us when we lost that contest."

"I know," Ms. Dorothea says with a sigh. "You take one wrong turn on the road to your dreams, and all of a sudden, you're in hyena territory. Then you stumble upon a right turn, and there it is right before your eyes—"

"—that magical, cheetah-licious place called the jiggy jungle," Galleria pipes in. Then, chuckling, she adds, "Your one-way ticket to *get-paid paradise*!"

Chapter 8

Biology class is my favorite class at school, besides vocal, but I have no interest today in cutting open a frog—and that's not like me at all. I know we shouldn't expect anything to come from our meeting with Kahlua, but dag on! We can't think about anything else!

We pray to God every night to please give us one itty-bitty sign—*anything*—even a shoe falling from the sky and hitting us over the head would be good enough!

It seems like *years* since "Operation Kahlua," and now we're down in the bottom of the crab barrel again, just moping around, trying not to get bit by the other crabs.

Look at this poor little frog, I think. He is just

lying there dead, on his back, waiting to be cut open. "I wonder if you can tell if someone tried to choke it and murder it or something. You know—'frog autopsy,'" I chuckle to Paula Pitts. She's my biology classmate, and we record all our experiments together.

"The eyeballs *are* kinda big—it does look like something scared it a little before it—you know—croaked," Paula says, all sad. "I don't know what you find so interesting about looking inside of bodies, Aqua. I think it's creepy."

Paula is a drama major, and she wants to be an actress, so she can be a little dramatic at times. "I hardly call opening a frog cadaver *The Night of the Living Dead*," I quip back. "Miss Paula, you are acting like the Pitts again."

I always tease her. She gets so squeamish, and she just doesn't like biology class or science projects the way I do. She likes to slink around, "like she's the cat's meow on Catfish Row," as Big Momma would say. Opening her big brown eyes wide, Paula asks, "You heard anything from Kahlua yet?"

She just loves to talk about show business. *Everybody* at school knows about our meeting with Kahlua—including JuJu Beans Gonzalez, who really cuts her eyes at us now.

I can't blame her for being so jealous of us. Angie and I are kinda popular at LaGuardia, I guess, because we're twins and come from Houston—even though there are kids at our school from all over the country.

The kids here nicknamed us SWV—Sisters With Voices—because, I guess, we do sing up a storm, if I say so myself. We're getting real good training here at LaGuardia, too—singing pop and classical music, which is good for our range. When we were younger, we kinda had our hearts set on singing gospel, but like I said, it just seems like pop and R&B music get more attention in the business.

That's why we got together with the Cheetah Girls. We thought about it real hard, and talked to Ma, and Big Momma, and everybody else about it before we made up our minds. Now we just don't know if we made the right decision.

Letting out a big sigh, I turn to Paula and moan, "This whole thing is like a big roller coaster ride. When you're on top, it's the greatest feeling in the world. But when you get ready to roll to the bottom, you'd better strap yourself in and start screaming your head off again, because it feels so *scary*."

"Yeah, you gotta kiss a lot of frogs in show business before you get anywhere," Paula agrees with a sigh. "That's how I feel in drama class sometimes, too. I give until it hurts, and it never feels like enough." Now she's fiddling around with the knob on the microscope, and her face is pained, like she's getting ready for her monologue. She is so *dramatic*.

"Ooh, look at his little lungs," I exclaim, finally getting excited by Freddy the frog's insides.

Then I feel a wave of pity come over me. "Freddy, I hope your little dreams came true before you left this earth," I mutter. "I hope all of our dreams come true. . . ."

After school, Angie always waits for me outside, and I can tell by her long face that she's still feeling down at the bottom of the crab barrel. "I wish we could go to Pappadeux's and get some Cajun crawfish right about now," I moan.

She nods her head like she could put a bib on

and chow down, too. They've got everything in New York except Pappadeux's—and *I'm sorry*, but nobody makes crawfish like they do. You get a big ol' pot of Cajun crawfish, with pieces of corn on the cob, and small red potatoes, and all this spicy juice. Then you just crack the itty-bitty shells in your hands, and suck out those tasty "chil'rens," as Big Momma calls them. Those were some of the best times we ever had as a family, going there on Friday nights for dinner. Everybody would come—Uncle Skeeter, Big Momma, Grandma Winnie, Ma, and all our cousins, too.

"I don't understand why we have to go to Drinka Champagne's Conservatory today," Angie says sheepishly. "What's the use of practicing if we're not performing anywhere?

"I know that's right, but you know what Galleria says. We should be practicing more, just in case we get to perform somewhere, for somebody, *somehow*."

My voice trails off, because I see the newspaper in Angie's hand, and I realize we haven't read our horoscope today.

"What's it say?" I ask, as we cross the street to catch the subway.

I hope it's not real crowded today, I think, as we wait to ride the IRT down to Drinka's. Dag on, there are so many people on the sidewalks and subway platforms in New York, you feel like you're gonna get trampled or something!

"Dag on, don't you know what page it's on by now?" I say, getting annoyed at Angie, who is still fumbling with the newspaper as we get on the crowded train. But why I'm really upset is because this man with a big ol' briefcase keeps knocking into me like I'm a rag doll.

"Here it is," Angie says, all serious, like she's getting ready to give a sermon in church. Sometimes she is so *slow*! "Let's see. 'Get ready for a big unexpected trip. You're gonna be flying the friendly skies real soon. Pack your party clothes!'"

"Oh, great, that just means we gotta go home to Houston for Thanksgiving, and do something *real* exciting, like work in Big Momma's garden. We know that," I say, curling my upper lip. (Angie and I both do that sometimes when we get mad.)

Angie gets quiet and closes the newspaper. She doesn't have to tell me. I know she feels disappointed, too.

We normally don't go to Drinka Champagne's Conservatory on school nights. But they have a new choreographer, and she can only work with us tonight, because she's working on Sista Fudge's new music video all weekend. Sista Fudge is one of our favorite singers, because she can "scream and testify"—back home, that's what we say when a singer can really *wail*, and has vocal "chops."

But we're not here studying singing. We're here to get our *moves* down. See, Galleria is always fussing at us to get the dance steps right. It's very important when you put on a show to have real good choreography—to give people something to watch. That's just as important when you perform as how you sing.

Since Angie and I are the background singers, we don't have to dance as much as Dorinda, Chanel, and Galleria, but we all have to do the same dance steps.

"Hi, Miss Winnie," I say, smiling to the receptionist at Drinka's as we enter the building. I like Miss Winnie, because she's real nice, and she has the same name as our grandma who passed.

The rest of the Cheetah Girls have already

changed into their leotards, and are waiting in Studio A for us. They are huddled together in one corner, while the rest of the class is on the other side.

After we do our Cheetah Girls handshake, which just tickles me to death, Galleria hugs us. "Smooches for the pooches!" she says. Every day she has a new saying, and we never know *what* to expect.

Galleria and Chanel are wearing such cute leotards! Angie and I look so plain, in our white shirts and black jeans. It'll be so nice when we can all dress alike all the time, like a real girl group. Yeah, right . . . like that'll ever happen.

"How's Porgy and Bess?" Chanel asks. She thinks it's cute that we have guinea pigs, because she isn't allowed to have any pets. She *loves* animals, too.

"They iz fine," Angie says, playing back.

"What do you feed them?" Dorinda asks.

"They love lettuce," I answer.

"Yeah, I bet—sprinkled with hot sauce!" Galleria blurts out, then looks at the door, because our dance teacher has arrived.

"Hi, I'm Raven Richards," says the teacher, who is real tall and skinny. She is wearing a red leotard and skirt, with a big black belt in the middle. None of us are tall like that. It must be real nice, having those long legs!

"Okay, let's get some combinations down," Raven says, moving her hips. "The movement in the hips is to a one-two, one-two-three combo. Okay, girls?"

Raven looks at me and adds, "Slink, don't bounce."

Raven? She looks more like Wes Craven! I say to myself, because she makes me so mad, embarrassing me like that in front of everybody. It's bad enough that Galleria is always on us about dancing, and Daddy is always on us about practicing more . . .

Dag on, I suddenly realize—she's right. I *am* bouncing!

After class, I feel real tired and sick. "Forget about buffalo wings—I could eat a whole buffalo right about now," I moan.

"That's funny. I thought you were on a seafood diet, Aqua," Galleria quips, pushing me with her backpack.

"Seafood?" I say, squinching up my nose. I just wanna go home and get into bed. I don't care if Kahlua never calls.

"Yeah, you *see* food, and you *eat* it!"

Galleria always makes me laugh. She is *real* funny.

"Don't be down, Aqua and Angie," she says then, holding my arm. "Operation Kahlua is in full effect. We just keep doing our thing, so that we're ready for Freddy. You know what I'm sayin'?"

"Yes, Galleria. We know what you're saying!" I answer, feeling a little better—at least good enough to get on the subway again and go home.

Chapter 9

Daddy is grinning from ear to ear when we get home. His job interview this morning must have gone well. See, he wants to leave his job as senior vice president of marketing at Avon. He and Ma decided that, since he used to be her boss, it wasn't a good idea that they work at the same company anymore.

"Daddy, how did the job interview go?" I ask. Angie and I sit down at the kitchen counter, and wait for Daddy to give us our dinner.

"I took the job," he says smiling. "Now I'm a SWAT man."

"That's real good, Daddy," I exclaim, then kiss him on the cheek. SWAT is the biggest bug repellent company in the country, he told us. They make all kinds of sprays for crawling insects, flying insects, lazy insects—you name it, they got a spray for it.

"Here's the campaign I'm gonna be working on," he says, pushing a black folder toward us. On the folder it has the company's slogan, *Flee, Flea, you hear me?*

Now Daddy is grinning and looking at us. I guess he wants us to say something funny about the slogan or something.

"What?" I ask, looking at him.

"That's not the best news I had all day," he says, still smiling like a Cheshire Cat who ate an insect.

"No?" Angie asks sheepishly.

"No. The best news I got just arrived in a phone call," he says, still smiling.

Daddy sure knows how to drag things out. When we were little, it used to take us two hours just to open our Christmas presents, because he would have to hand them to us first, then wait till *he* said to open them!

"Well, girls, maybe you should call your friend Galleria and find out for yourselves. She just called."

"Daddy, how could you wait so long to tell us?" I whine playfully. He always gets us real good with his tricks.

Angie and I jump up and down and hug each other, then I dial the phone, and she listens at the receiver.

When Galleria picks up the phone, she is yelling so loud, I can hardly understand her.

"Stop screaming, Galleria!"

Trying to catch her breath, Galleria says between gasps, "They're gonna give us a showcase in Los Angeles!!!"

"Hush your mouth!" I exclaim—the same thing Big Momma always says when she gets excited. "For real?"

"Wheel-a-deal for *real*!" Galleria retorts. "Kahlua and her moms told the Def Duck Records peeps that we were 'off the hook, snook,' and they said, 'Well, come on with it!'"

I'm not exactly sure what Galleria means, so I have to ask again, "Does that mean we got a record deal?"

"No, Aqua—just try and go with my flow. It *means* they'll fly us to Los Angeles, and arrange a showcase for us. They'll make sure all the right peeps are in the house to get a read on our

Cheetah Girl groove. There are no guarantees, but at least we get a free trip to Hey, ho, Hollywood!"

"Omigod, I think I'm gonna faint!" I scream into the phone receiver. Angie grabs it from me, to talk to Galleria herself. I stand in the middle of the kitchen with my hand on my forehead. Then I just hug Daddy, and start crying tears of gratitude. I can't believe I ever doubted what God had in store for us! Now, the rest is up to us.

"How'd you find out?" Angie asks Galleria, then yells to me and Daddy, "They called Ms. Dorothea at her store, and asked her if *we* would be *interested*. Can you believe that?"

"*Please*, I'll pack my bags and fly the plane right now myself!" I yell, so Galleria can hear me—and trying to sound like I'm not scared of airplanes, which I *am*.

Daddy gives me a look, like "We'll see how you feel when you get up in the air." That's all right—I'll take a whole box of Cloud Nine pills if I have to, to keep from getting sick on the plane. Hallelujah, thank you, Jesus, we are going to Hollywood!

Chapter 10

After we finish talking with Galleria, we go over the whole story again with Ms. Dorothea. Then, of course, we call Chanel, and after that, Dorinda. But we're only just crankin' up. We call Big Momma to share the news. And finally, we reach our Ma, who is in Seattle on business.

She is surprised to hear from us, because unless it's an emergency, we usually only talk on Sunday after church.

"But this *is* an emergency, Ma," I tell her, "because if I wake up tomorrow and find out this is all a dream, I'm gonna need mouth-to-mouth resuscitation!"

"Hush your mouth, Aqua," Ma says.

"You're gonna let us go, right?" I ask Ma nervously. She gets mad if we do things without asking her permission, even if we are living with Daddy. She says she's "still the boss of this house," no matter what Daddy thinks.

"You just make sure you do your homework while you're there, so you don't fall behind in school," Ma warns us. "But you go and have a good time. It's a shame the two of you haven't really been anywhere before this."

I feel like the whole world is right outside our front door, waiting for us. "That's all right, Ma—if things work out, we're going to be going *everywhere*—and we'll send plane tickets for you to come see us perform!"

"Well, for now, I think you'd better just get off the phone and go to bed, it's past your bedtime," Ma says sternly.

"Yes, ma'am, we're going right now. You wanna speak to Daddy?" I ask, hoping our good news will help them not be mad at each other—for at least a little while. As it is, I have to bite my tongue half the time, not to blurt and tell Ma about High Priestess Abala Shaballa.

"No, Aquanette, I don't have the time. I have

to finish some reports before I go to bed. I'm real proud of you, though. *Real* proud."

I don't even look at Daddy when I get off the phone, because I feel so bad Ma didn't want to talk to him.

"Good night, Daddy," I say, kissing him on the cheek.

"Good night, Daddy," Angie says, then kisses him on the other cheek. When I pass that scary-looking Bogo Mogo Warrior Mask on the way upstairs, I stick my tongue out at it, then poke Angie in the stomach, and we both start giggling.

"That's enough, y'all," Daddy says, leaning over his record collection in the living room. Daddy doesn't like us playing around before we go to bed—he wouldn't care if God came to the door and said it was okay. He likes peace and quiet when he's getting ready to play his music.

Angie and I spend another hour yakking in whispers about this most incredible day. When we're finally lying in bed, trying to get some sleep, I suddenly hear a noise in the bedroom closet!

"Angie, you hear that?" I whisper, sitting upright in my bed. "Lawd, you think that thing got out of the shoe boxes or something?"

We hear more scratching noises in the closet, and we both sit real quiet. "I don't care if it did, 'cuz I ain't going in there to find out!" Angie says, then hides under her covers.

It figures. That scaredy cat. Well, I ain't getting out of the bed either. They'll have to *drag* me out the bed before I get up and go look in that closet.

All of a sudden, I have the strangest thought. "Angie! You don't think that Teddy Bear Poodle thing brought us good luck, do you?"

"Maybe," Angie says, real quiet. "But I don't care—I'm just going to Hollywoooooood!" she says, imitating Galleria.

"Not without me, you ain't!" I retort, and hide farther under the covers, till my feet are hanging out the bed. Feeling the cool air on my toes, I get a creepy feeling, and scrunch them back under the covers real quick. I'm not taking any chances—I mean, what if that thing in the closet is *hungry*?

Please God—make it stop raining! If it keeps

raining this hard much longer, Mighty Mouth Airlines will cancel our flight for sure!

Daddy keeps coming up to our room, to give us the latest weather report—like he's Sonny Shinbone, the weatherman on television. Daddy used to travel all over the country with his job at Avon, so I guess he *could* be a weatherman, but right now, he is "getting on our last good nerve," as Big Momma would say. I wish he would just stay downstairs with the "sacred one," so we can pack our suitcases in peace.

"'Furious Flo' is heading north," he says, hovering over us in our bedroom. Furious Flo is this terrible tropical storm that started a few days ago in Florida, and is wreaking havoc all over the place.

She must be mighty mad, because she's making people lose their homes and everything, with all the water she's sending their way. Thank God, Big Momma called and says everything is okay in Houston. Daddy is pacing back and forth, wearing out our rug. He's making us more nervous than we already are!

"What if you don't have enough material to

perform?" Daddy asks, smoking his pipe. He must be *real* nervous, too, because he usually only smokes his pipe late at night, when he's listening to his music or watching television. I hope he doesn't drop any ashes on our white carpet. He's always fussing at *us* to be careful about staining the carpet, because it costs a lot of money to get it cleaned professionally.

"Daddy, we're not the only singers performing in the New Talent Showcase," I explain to him. "The record company does this all the time. They have scouts all over the country looking for new artists. Then they fly them to Los Angeles, and put them in a showcase in front of industry people. There'll probably be a lot of other singers there. We'll be lucky if we get to perform three songs."

"That's right," Angie adds. "They told us to have three songs to perform."

"Okay, okay, I'm just trying to understand how all this works," Daddy says, puffing on his pipe quietly—which means he's thinking about *something*. "You think maybe that magic spell Abala prepared for you girls had something to do with this stroke of luck?"

"Daddy!" I yell. "This is no stroke of luck! If

it wasn't for Galleria and Ms. Dorothea, we'd be packing to go to Big Momma's, and playing 'Tiptoe Through the Tulips' in her garden—*again*!"

Daddy gives me that stern look, like, "Don't get too grown for your britches."

"I'm just asking a question," he says. "Maybe the spell worked just a little late, that's all I'm saying."

Angie and I get real quiet.

"What's the name of the place where you're performing?" Daddy asks for the *hundredth* time!

"The Tinkerbell Lounge," I say quietly. "It's in West Hollywood, and we wrote down all the information on the paper on the kitchen table—*and* we gave it to Ma, too."

I carefully fold the leopard miniskirt and vest that Ms. Dorothea made for us, and put it in the suitcase. I'm just waiting for Daddy to say something else.

"You know, maybe you should bring the navy blue dresses you wore to church last Sunday."

I don't want to fight with him anymore. "Yes, Daddy," I mumble, then go to the closet to get the dresses he wants us to wear.

Thank God, Daddy walks out of our bedroom then, to go downstairs. Angie and I stop packing, and just plop down on our beds.

I'm so nervous, I'm sweating like a tree trunk. Angie and I look at each other, and I know we're thinking the same thing. Giggling, she jumps up and takes the navy blue dresses and sticks them back in the closet!

"No, silly willy," I exclaim, imitating Callerla, "stick those things in the *back* of the closet, so he doesn't see them if he comes snooping around our room while we're gone!"

"Yeah, that's if we get to go," Angie sighs, going over to the window to look at the rain.

"Well, let's pack our bathing suits just in case. Maybe they'll have a swimming pool or something."

Angie runs to the closet and gets out our bathing suits.

"Did you see anything strange in the back of the closet?" I ask her, kinda joking. But inside, I'm kinda serious. What if Daddy is right about Abala's magic spell? What if Mr. Teddy Poodly is running around in there?

That's when I remember something *real*

strange. "Remember, Angie, I took the Scotch tape off that shoe box?"

"Yeah," she says, smiling at me. "Maybe that's what High Priestess Abala Shaballa meant, when she said the Vampire Spell didn't work 'cuz we must not have followed her instructions."

"I don't get it," Angie says, shrugging her shoulders.

"I put Scotch tape on the shoe box in the first place. She didn't tell us to do that. Maybe that's why the spell didn't work! Maybe Mr. Teddy Poodly could only do his thing when he was able to get out of the box!"

"Well, there has to be *some* reason why those boys won, because they sure weren't *that* good. Not as good as we are," Angie says, sitting on the bed and crossing her legs Indian style.

"Yeah. I know that's right. When did I take the Scotch tape off my shoe box?"

"I don't know. After we came home from the Apollo, I guess," Angie says.

"That's right. It *does* seem kinda strange that this happened—"

"Well, nothing *has* happened, Aquanette. I mean, we don't know what's gonna happen when we get out there. They didn't say they're gonna give us a record deal or anything."

I can tell Angie is getting exasperated. And I know what's wrong, too. She is being stubborn because she wants to stay mad at High Priestess Abala Shaballa.

Neither one of us is happy about Daddy getting a girlfriend so quick. Dag on, he and Ma just broke up! Okay, it's been a year, but that's *nothing*. And why did he have to pick *her*?

"I'm just saying, Angie, that maybe we're wrong about Abala," I say, giving my sister that look.

Angie just drags the suitcase off the bed. "We going, or what?"

"Let's ask Daddy and find out," I say, trailing behind her down the stairs. "Daddy! Can you help us with the luggage, please?"

High Priestess Abala Shaballa comes to the bottom of the stairwell. "Your father is on the phone with the airline, checking to make sure your flight isn't canceled," she says, looking like she feels bad for us if we don't get to go.

When we put the luggage by the front door, she turns and winks at us, "I see the Vampire

Spell worked, no?" Her eyes get real squinty, like a mouse's! I never noticed that before.

"Let's go, before the airline changes their mind," Daddy says chuckling, then hustles us out the door and into the Bronco.

The traffic is so bad going to the airport, I don't think we're ever going to get there! I'm really sweating now. "Angie, are you hot?"

"Yeah," Angie says, then sighs. "It's the traffic in New York. It makes me *nervous*, too. I didn't even know they made so many cars!"

"I don't know. It gets pretty crowded in Houston around rush hour," Daddy says, not looking up from the wheel.

Finally, we arrive at the airport, and by now, I'm dying of thirst.

"Did you pack some water, Angie?"

"Yes, Ma!" she says all huffy.

"Daddy, don't forget to feed Porgy and Bess," I mumble. All of a sudden, I'm feeling real jumpy. "They're real particular about their food—they only like fresh lettuce, and they don't like their water too cold."

"Yes, Aquanette, I'll take them for walks too," Daddy says, rolling one of our suitcases through the airport terminal.

"There's Ms. Dorothea!" I say, waving my arm so she can see us. She has on a cheetah coat and big cheetah hat, and is standing with Mr. Garibaldi.

Then she moves aside a little, and I see that they're not alone. "Oh, there's Galleria, too!" Galleria looks so small next to her mother. She is wearing a cheetah coat and hat, too.

"Don't they look like a cheetah and a cub together?" I joke to Angie.

"They sure do!"

"My, she is tall," High Priestess Abala Shaballa comments about Ms. Dorothea.

I wanna say to her High-Mightyness, "Yeah, well, at least she don't put hexes on people like you do!" But I keep my mouth shut, because I'm not so mad at her anymore.

People are looking at us, probably because of all the fabric Abala has wrapped on her body and head. They probably think she's African royalty or something like that.

"There's Chanel and Dorinda," Angie says, pointing to where they're standing by the window. When Chanel and Dorinda see us, they come running over with Galleria and Ms. Dorothea.

"*Pooches gracias* for showing up!" Chanel giggles, then we all hug each other, screaming and carrying on.

Everybody is looking at us now. Daddy gives us a look, like, "calm down."

"Let me check at the reservation desk and make sure the flight is on time," he says, holding the High Priestess's arm.

"You didn't pack any crawfish in there, did you?" Galleria asks, teasing us.

"No, because Porgy and Bess ate 'em!" I chuckle back.

"I miss Toto already," Galleria whines.

"How come you didn't bring him?" I ask.

"We're going to Los Angeles for a singers' showcase, not a poodle convention, darling," Ms. Dorothea quips, but I can tell she feels guilty about leaving him behind. Galleria told us her mother gets hysterical if Toto chokes on a dog biscuit or anything.

"Dad is gonna take care of him," Galleria says, then turns to Mr. Garibaldi, "right, Dad?'

"*Sì, cara, sì!* " Mr. Garibaldi chuckles. He has on one of those real funny hats that looks like a raccoon, or something furry like that.

I look away, to see that Daddy is walking toward us wearing the longest face.

"Oh, no," I moan.

"The flight is canceled," Daddy announces.

I just want to fall on the floor and pull a temper tantrum. Dag on, we can't take any more disappointments!

"But they've put the six of you on standby, in case they can get you on a later flight," Daddy says, delivering the bad news like Granddaddy Walker does when he's telling a family he can't make a corpse at the funeral parlor look real good.

"Whatever makes them clever," Galleria says, disappointed. "I guess their mouth ain't mighty enough for Furious Flo."

"Well, we ain't going home," I announce adamantly. "I don't care if we have to stay in the airport all night."

"I know that's right," Angie pipes in.

"Don't worry, darlings," Ms. Dorothea says, putting her arms around us. "It's just another wrong turn on the road, and we've landed in hyena territory once again—but when the hyenas have eaten their fill, they'll leave us alone, and then we'll be on our merry way.

All's we gotta do is click our heels and *pray.*"

Chanel starts clicking her heels together. They are real cute vinyl sandals, and have goldfish in the heels that you can see—but they do make her feet look kinda wet.

"I don't know how you could wear those goldfish on your feet in this weather, Chuchie," Galleria says, rolling her eyes. "Oh, I get it, maybe you'll be able to swim upstream if the water gets too high!"

Chanel is too crestfallen to care what Galleria says. "I hope we have somewhere to swim to," she mumbles.

We all drag our luggage to the check-in storage room. Galleria and Ms. Dorothea's cheetah luggage is so pretty. Ours looks kinda ugly next to theirs. It's just plain ol' blue vinyl. When Angie and I get some money, we're gonna buy ourselves pretty luggage too. I wonder if we are ever gonna get some money of our own. Not soon enough, that's for sure!

After we eat some hamburgers and french fries at Pig in the Poke Restaurant, we get real sleepy, and head to the waiting area, where we sit on the ugly vinyl chairs. "How come they don't have real velvet chairs or something?" Chanel moans.

I put my coat on the floor so I can lie down. "Sweet dreams," Chanel coos. She seems so sad.

I can't take the noise anymore. People are walking around like they're in a hurry, but I know they're going nowhere. All this is making me *real* sleepy.

I don't know how long we've been sleeping, but I hear a loud noise, and I think it's in my dreams, but then I realize it's an announcer's voice on the loudspeaker. "Mrs. Gari-bolda, please come to the reservation desk. Mrs. Gari-bolda, please come to the reservation desk."

"Mom, wake up!" Galleria says, shaking her mother. Ms. Dorothea jumps up, like one of the creatures from *Night of the Living Dead.*

"Wait here!" she orders.

"What time is it?" Chanel says, rubbing her eyes open.

"It's ten o'clock. We've been waiting for four hours," Galleria answers. Then, humming aloud, she sings, "Rain or shine, all is mine. . . ."

We look at each other real quiet. It feels like we're waiting to see if we won the $64,000 prize on the game show *My Dime, Your Time!*

Running toward us, Ms. Dorothea announces, "Come on, Cheetah Girls! It's time to head for Hollywood!"

We all jump out of our chairs and let out a cheer. Then we gather our stuff, and say good-bye to Daddy and Abala. The High Priestess kisses me on the forehead, and says, "Look for the Raven when she opens her wings."

"I will, Abala," I say. Yeah, right. Whatever.

Galleria is trying not to smirk, and as we're running through the terminal to keep up with Ms. Dorothea, she spreads her arms out and coos, "Caw! Caw! I'm the raven! Nevermore! Nevermore!"

Everybody is looking at us as we give our tickets to the attendant, giggling up a storm.

"Oh, and by the way, darling, tell that dreary announcer of yours it's Mrs. *Garibaldi*!" Ms. Dorothea tells the attendant.

"Ooh, this is dope!" Dorinda says, looking at the red velvet seats we pass in the first-class section. She has never been on a plane before.

"This is where all the rich people sit," I whisper in Dorinda's ear. The flight attendants are giving out newspapers and bubbly-looking drinks in plastic cups to the first-class passengers.

"Momsy poo, can we sit in first class?" Galleria asks, giggling.

"Do you have first-class money? You can sit there, darling poo, when *you're* paying."

We go back farther, and get to a section where there are more seats—and they're a *lot* smaller.

"Hold your breath, girls, and tuck it in," Galleria giggles as she sits down.

"Do' Re Mi, *mamacita*, you take the window seat," Chanel says to Dorinda. Bless her heart, she won't be able to see much out the window, even though the rain has stopped. It's so dark out now. But it was still nice of Chuchie to give her the seat. After we settle in, a pilot's voice comes over the loudspeaker and welcomes us aboard.

"*Hola, hola*, everybody, the Cheetah Girls are in the house!" Chanel coos. The lady in the row across from me and Angie looks at us in curiosity. How'd she get her hair teased so high in this weather? I wonder.

"She looks like she's ready for takeoff!" Galleria whispers to me. She is seated in the row behind me.

A screen gets pulled down by the flight attendant, and a movie explains all about safety, and what to do if something happens.

I start getting *real* scared, and my hands are sweating. But I have plenty of time to calm down. We sit and wait in the plane for *two hours*!

Finally, the captain announces that we are "ready for takeoff." Everyone in the plane starts clapping.

"We're ready for Freddy, yo!" Dorinda says, and lets out a hoot. She is so excited. For someone who's never been on a plane before, she seems so much calmer than we do.

I reach down to get my Cloud Nine pills out of my carry-on bag, and put them in the flap in front of my seat. Just in case I get sick, I don't want to be barfing up a storm and embarrassing myself in front of my friends.

Galleria starts singing: "Snakes in the grass have no class/But cheetah girls have all the swirls."

We join in, singing together, and people start clapping all around us, cheering us on.

When the plane finally starts ascending into the air, though, we get real quiet. I think we're all pretty scared.

When we finally reach cruising altitude, I let out a sigh of relief. "We're going to Hollywood!" I yell.

"Hey, we never did get to see the Sandman at the Apollo, did we?" Galleria turns and asks me, then chuckles. "I was kinda disappointed."

"Don't be, Miss Galleria," I say, laying on my Southern accent and fluttering my eyelashes, "If we turn 'stinkeroon like loony toons' at the Tinkerbell Lounge, neither Freddy nor the Sandman is gonna be able to help us—'cuz *Captain Hook* is gonna yank us off the stage himself!!!"

But I just know that ain't gonna happen. We all know it. Maybe it's High Priestess Abala Shaballa's spell, or maybe it's God's Way, just that we know we're due—whatever. It really doesn't matter. What matters is that we're the Cheetah Girls, and we've got growl power. It's only a matter of time till the whole world knows it.

So hey, ho, Hollywooood, the Cheetah Girls are looking gooood!

More Pounce to the Ounce

We wuz walking down the street
eating Nestlé's Crunch
when a big babboon
tried to get a munch.
Please don't ask for bite
'cuz that's my lunch
Times are hard and
you should know the deal
So please stop breathing
on my Happy Meal.
Here's the wrapper
take the crumbs
Next time you try to sneak a chomp
you won't get none!!!
Snakes in the grass have no class
but cheetah girls have all the swirls.
Big baboons don't make us swoon
'cuz Cheetah Girls can reach the moon

To all the competition, what can we say?
You'd better bounce, y'all

'cuz every Cheetah has its day
You'd betta bounce, y'all
While you still got some flounce, y'all
'cuz Cheetah Girls are gonna pounce, y'all
and we got more pounce to the ounce *y'all*

More Pounce to the Ounce
We don't eat lunch
More Pounce to the Ounce
Come on with the brunch!

The Cheetah Girls Glossary

Angling for an intro: When you're cheesing for the purpose of an introduction to someone.

At the bottom of the crab barrel: When you're down in the dumps.

Churl: A word made up by combining "girl" and "child" together.

Corpse: The body of a dead person. A cadaver.

Crispy: Supertasty "flow" or food.

Diva size: Size fourteen and up.

Flounce: Show off.

Groovy like a movie: Dope. Cool.

Heffa: A girl who thinks she's all that and a bag of "juju beans."

Hex: A witchcraft spell.

Hush your mouth!: An affectionate response that's really asking, "Is that right?"

Monologue: A dramatic sketch performed by

an actor—or a "drama queen" kind of person.

Off the hook: Dope. Cool

Outtie like Snouty: When a situation gets a little cuckoo and you need a time-out break.

Passed: When someone dies.

Pouncing: A very important Cheetah Girl skill for taking control of a situation and making things happen.

Ready for Freddy: Ready for anything. Ready to do your thing.

She takes the cobbler: When someone is really too much. Can also be used like, "He gave me a C in math. That really takes the cobbler!"

Stinkeroon like loony toons: When you're having an off day with your "flow."

Wefties: Weaves that are so tick tacky the tracks are showing!

Wreckin' my flow: When something is interfering with your ability to talk, sing, think, or whatever it is you're trying to do.

abc
Kids

She was waiting for him in the dining room, dressed in a demure looking little gown of sprigged muslin in various shades of rose and pale pink. "You look like a concoction sugar candy," he said, causing her to turn suddenly and e him. She clutched a glass of wine in both hands. "Of rse, the neckline is rather . . . concealing, but the way fill out the bodice almost makes up for that deficiency. way, since I'll soon see what lies beneath the layers of hing, it doesn't really matter, does it?"

'You delight in tormenting me with your crude taunts, 't you, Lucero?" Her tone of voice indicated it was a orical question. "I used to shiver and blush and stammer n you made remarks like that."

e stalked closer. "Oh, I can still make you blush, as ly as your girlishly sweet dress. Did you choose it to make me feel I was robbing the cradle again—taking that insipid little virgin who bored me so four years ago?" Two could play at rhetorical questions, he indicated with a smile. "As you've already made quite clear to me, you aren't that fainting miss any longer." His eyes swept to the glass in her hand. "For courage? Surely the *patrona* of Gran Sangre doesn't need it." He took the heavy crystal glass and raised it to his lips, turning the rim to drink from the exact spot where her lips had touched. "You may not faint, but I promise to make you shiver . . . in satisfaction."

Bride of Fortune

SHIRL HENKE

St. Martin's Paperbacks

BRIDE OF FORTUNE

ISBN: 0-312-95857-9

Printed in the United States of America

St. Martin's Paperbacks edition/May 1996

10 9 8 7 6 5 4 3 2 1

"One does what one can." A few do more.
For James Ashley Houck, one of the few.

Chapter 1

Spring 1866

Mercedes Sebastían de Alvarado stood on tiptoe to peer out from behind the grillwork on the *sala* window of the great adobe palace which had become her home over the past four years. Forty-foot-high willow trees shaded the courtyard where a group of excited servants crowded around her husband, Don Lucero Alvarado.

"I must face him, not cower like a ninny behind the draperies," she scolded herself. Turning to the floor-length cheval mirror brought all the way from France, she smoothed her hair and noted the sudden pallor of her face. Good. At least he could not carp at her for being sunburned as Don Anselmo had done. *But I won't cringe before him. Never again*! She swept from the *sala* into the entry hall to await him.

Mercedes watched him approach the portico. He was still surrounded by servants.

At least Innocencia is not among them, thank the Blessed Virgin.

Lucero's mistress, who, in her lover's absence, had been assigned to work for Angelina in the kitchens, had been sent to help out at a neighboring hacienda during a fiesta. Mercedes could still see the two of them laughing drunkenly as they walked arm in arm across the courtyard to Innocencia's quarters the very night she had arrived from Mexico City to celebrate her betrothal to Lucero. How that had humiliated her! And yet, how much worse had she been humiliated after the marriage was consummated?

She stiffened her spine, using the anger of past hurts to block out the fear. Standing in the shadows of the great hall, she studied him from afar. He looked even more dangerous than when she had first met him. Noting the narrow white scar on his left cheek, she supposed the years of war had hardened and seasoned him. His complexion, always swarthy, was sun bronzed an even darker shade now with tiny lines crinkling at the sides of his eyes when he laughed. His smile still blazed whitely. Her *dueña* used to say it was sensual enough to charm Lilith. Odd that he was enjoying the servants' adulation so much. In the past he seldom bothered with them, but then this was his homecoming after God knew what horrors of war.

Her eyes measured his profile, which was just as she remembered, as perfectly chiseled as dozens of generations of Castillian breeding could make it, with a high forehead, boldly slashing black eyebrows, a straight prominent blade of a nose and a wide, elegant mouth. The dark shadow of a heavy beard was well evident across his square strong jawline. Night-black hair curled wildly at his nape and one lock fell wickedly over his brow. He was as lithe and graceful as a stalking mountain lion, there had never been an ounce of fat on his body. His hands were strong and slender with long tapered fingers, the hands of a gentleman, yet for all of that, she remembered how cruel his touch could be and shuddered.

Now he was dressed like a brigand in dusty trail gear and armed like a one-man arsenal. A pistol was slung low on one hip, a long knife strapped to his other thigh and twin bandoleers crisscrossed his broad chest. He reached the open front door and peered inside, cocking his head slightly to one side. Those hypnotic black wolf's eyes with their eerie silver irises fastened on her.

Mercedes could feel the old familiar pull of fascination and revulsion. She had always feared his overpowering male vitality. *No more! I'm not a green virgin any longer.* She walked steadily into the light and met his gaze. "Welcome home, husband."

His eyes swept from the halo of darkly burnished golden hair across her small heart-shaped face and down to rake her dainty figure with appreciative boldness. She was barely over five feet tall with fragile fine bones, but even clad in a loose *camisa* and full *paisana's* skirts the unmistakably feminine curves of hip and breast were evident to his practiced eye. When she greeted him in a cool musical voice, his eyes raised to study her solemn face. And a very beautiful face it was with wide-set amber eyes and slim dark eyebrows. Her small pointed chin jutted out stubbornly, her cheeks were flushed and that tiny nose was well elevated, as if she had just smelled something noisome. In spite of her words of welcome, her soft pink lips did not smile for him.

"Aren't you happy to see me, Mercedes?" His voice held a taunting dare as he took another lazy stride nearer, stalking her.

She shrugged. "Let us just say I am surprised."

He grinned. "You thought I'd been killed by the Juaristas."

"I would not be guilty of praying for the event, but I had hopes." Her voice was dry.

He threw back his head and laughed aloud. "The kitten has grown claws in my absence, I see."

"And a right long absence it's been," she said with asperity. "I'm not a kitten any longer."

"I can see that," he replied, once more letting his eyes rake the soft curves of her body until he could see the telltale stain of pink move up her chest and neck to heat her cheeks. "You've filled out quite nicely . . . claws and all."

She tried to ignore the hunger in his fathomless night eyes. As they stood facing each other in the thickening darkness, the silver irises glowed satanically. His whole body seemed tense, poised to pounce on her as if she were a wounded fawn. And yet, rather than the paralyzing fear of the past, she felt some strange new emotion, beyond the anger that blazed deep within her soul.

What is it about him? Or is it me? Refusing to analyze

it, she moistened her lips and changed the subject. "She is waiting for you."

"No doubt. I'm all she has left to hate now that my father is dead," he replied bitterly.

"She'll soon join Don Anselmo. The hope of your return is all that has kept her alive."

He scoffed. "To be more precise, her hope is that I'll breed an heir for Gran Sangre." His eyes studied her intently for a reaction.

Unflinching, she replied brusquely, "Greet your mother. Baltazar will have your quarters prepared by the time you've seen her. You and I will speak of our duty to Gran Sangre at dinner." She turned away from him, desperately needing time alone to sort out her emotions and regain her composure.

His footfalls followed close on hers as they walked down the long tile hallway. She refused to give him the satisfaction of speeding up to place more distance between them. Then a large shaggy shape came bounding toward them from the opposite end of the hall.

"Bufón, no!" she commanded ineffectually as the huge mottled sheepdog careened around her. *Mother of God, don't leap on him! Lucero will gut you with that fearful knife!* Only a half-grown pup when her husband had left, Bufón had seemed to sense her dislike and fear of the *patrón*. He had growled and bared his fangs more than once. Then Lucero had only laughed and kicked him aside. Now . . . she shuddered to think about it.

Mercedes tried to seize the dog's well-worn leather collar but he eluded her and jumped up on the tall man with a loud whoof. Before she could intercede, Lucero began to scratch the dog's great head, chuckling and turning his face away from the fulsome slurps which were the huge beast's way of welcoming most visitors to Gran Sangre. She stood frozen in shock, watching as the long fluffy tail wagged furiously. "Bufón likes you," she said inanely.

"I'd say he has rather changed his mind about me," he replied, struggling to contain eighty pounds of wriggling dog. "You are a fine fellow but a nuisance." He ruffled the dog's fur and thumped him affectionately, then commanded, "Down."

At his firm tone of voice, Bufón amazingly obeyed, lowering his forelegs to stand before Lucero, tail still madly thumping from side to side. At once, Mercedes reached out and grabbed his collar. "I'll put him out."

He gave a husky laugh and his eyes met hers. "Just so you don't put him in your bedroom tonight." He watched her slender throat work as she swallowed nervously, but she returned his gaze boldly. "As I said, we can discuss sleeping arrangements at dinner." His mocking laughter followed her down the hallway as she half led, half dragged the affectionate beast to the kitchen.

"Until dinner then, my wife. I trust it won't be too late. I'm *very* hungry."

The words, delivered in his low silky voice, caused a shiver of fear—or was it excitement?—to dance down her spine. She did not look back as she heard him climb the wide low steps to Doña Sofia's quarters in the east wing.

He paused in front of the door, wondering what his greeting would be from the hateful old woman inside, a cold, unnatural mother who had always despised her only son. *Just one way to find out.* He knocked and a frail voice, thin and brittle with age, bid him enter.

The room stank of death. Heavy wine velvet drapes were drawn across the windows and a thick dark carpet in the same hue covered the floor. An ornate jeweled gold crucifix hung on one wall. Statues, candles and religious paintings filled every available space. The bed, with its high narrow mattress, was hung with an ivory silk canopy. Mosquito netting cast a gauzy haze across the figure lying propped up by pillows behind its protection.

Doña Sofia was only fifty-two, but she looked at least twenty years older, thin and wasted, her flesh leached away by the consumption that was slowly draining the life from her. Her complexion was the color of the fat tallow candles flickering by her bedside. The skin across her high Castillian cheekbones was stretched tight. Her dark brown eyes were set deeply as if giving animation to a death mask, but they were clouded with cataracts. In odd contrast, her hair remained inky black with only one streak of silver running through it, woven into the tight coil of braids atop her small head.

"So, you've returned to take his place." Her eyes squinted at him shrewdly as he approached her bed and pulled aside the sheer curtain.

"I could never take Don Anselmo's place, Mamacita." She stiffened at the mocking endearment, just as he knew she would.

"You could far outstrip your father in debauchery by now, I'd warrant, after the years of war, living with the kind of riffraff who are paid to fight that foreigner's battles."

His eyebrows rose in surprise. "Would you rather see that Indian peasant Juarez rule Mexico than the Emperor Maximilian?"

"Do not be absurd. You know I despise that godless despoiler of Holy Mother Church." Her bony fingers fiercely clutched a rosary of lapis lazuli and diamonds.

"We have no other choice but Juarez or Maximilian."

She sighed wearily. "I no longer care for politics. God and his saints will preserve the holy faith. Your duty no longer lies in fighting for the emperor."

"I know my duty to the House of Alvarado," he said with stiff formality.

She tried to give a snort of disgust but her lungs were so weak that it came out a wheezing of breath. "Neither you nor your sire have ever given evidence of knowing your duty before this."

"Must the sins of the father always be visited upon the sons?" he asked bitterly.

"You've sins enough of your own to answer for and well you know it," she snapped. "Leaving your bride's bed to cavort with harlots, then riding away a scant few weeks after your marriage."

"Well, I've answered Father Salvador's summons now," he replied tersely.

"It took your father's death to bring you to heel. Even

he was displeased when you left without planting your seed in Mercedes' belly."

The image of shimmering dark gold hair and luminous amber eyes flashed into his mind. A slumberous expression came over his face, but it did not soften the harsh beauty of his features. "She's matured into a very beautiful woman. Providing an heir for Gran Sangre won't exactly be an onerous task."

"She may think otherwise. The girl has nurtured some foolish notions in your absence. You should never have left her alone all these years."

His expression became wary. "What do you mean?"

"You will see soon enough. But I don't fear your failure to bend her to your will—you were ever your father's son," she said with bitter irony.

His body stiffened in outrage, but he bowed formally to her. A long-buried anger resurrected, churning his guts. "I'll do my duty."

"A pleasing promise to your father could he hear it. Hateful news to your wife when she does," Sofia said smugly.

A chill settled over him as he studied her in silence. She seemed amused by some secret jest. Without replying to her cryptic remark, he turned and strode through the heavy oak door, slamming it as he departed.

The room was once more as dark and quiet as a sepulcher, the silence broken only by the soft clacking of beads as Doña Sofia resumed her rote prayers.

He stormed down the hallway headed in the direction of the master suite when a slight figure with a halo of white hair materialized from a side door and stood directly in his way. The snowy brilliance of his shoulder-length hair contrasted with the heavy black cassock he wore.

"Father Salvador. I should've expected you to be hovering somewhere nearby, like a vulture circling, waiting for the death throes. Have you given her last rites yet, or are you saving that for a special treat?"

Ice-blue eyes set narrowly in a deceptively frail-looking face fixed on him with fierce intensity. "I might have known your years away from home would change nothing. You are as unfeeling and irreverent as ever, Lucero Alvarado."

"God, I certainly hope so," he replied with a grim laugh.

"Your father has passed to his just reward. Now your mother will soon ascend to hers." Father Salvador's expression left no doubt of his certainty that Lucero's parents would not end up in the same place. "The least you could do is show a shred of compassion for her while she still lives."

"Why? She never showed any for me, not even when I was a small child."

"I remember that small child. He stole communion wine from the sacristy and came to my classroom reeling drunk."

"I'd forgotten that," he replied in amusement. "I threw up all over my catechism."

"And my cassock." The priest's voice held no levity.

"Only because you grabbed me by the neck and caned me."

"You also stole coins from the poor box."

"Just as the emperor steals from his subjects."

Father Salvador stiffened in outrage. "You fought for the emperor!"

"So I did. After all, the Juaristas don't pay as well," he replied lightly, enjoying baiting the priest.

Realizing the game Lucero played, Father Salvador bit back his ascerbic reply. "You are the *patrón* of Gran Sangre. Your irresponsible behavior should be in the past. You have a duty to perform, *Don* Lucero." He stressed the title.

"So I've been reminded once or twice. But that matter is for me and my wife to settle."

"And best you do so quickly. Doña Mercedes has far exceeded her station. She is merely a woman, the weaker vessel meant to rear children and oversee the great house, not the *patrón* to ride out with coarse vaqueros, hobnob with common merchants in Hermosillo—even defy the army."

His eyebrows rose. "Meek little Mercedes? My little mouse?" He chuckled wryly. "She has certainly changed, but then since my father's death, I imagine a great deal has fallen on her shoulders."

"Long before your father's death. I do not entirely blame her, although her behavior has been most unseemly," the priest added righteously. "Even when he was alive and well, Don Anselmo attended to matters of running Gran Sangre most indifferently. He was always off pursuing carnal pleasures."

"There is much to be said for carnal pleasures, Father Salvador. And surely they make confessions ever so much more interesting, don't they?" There was a silky insult lurking beneath the words.

The priest stiffened. It was apparent he wished Lucero a small boy once more so that he might give him another good caning. He swallowed his bile and crossed himself, offering up a small prayer for patience. "Gran Sangre is doomed if the Alvarados must depend on you to preserve their heritage."

"Perhaps I may just surprise you all."

As he sat soaking in a tub of steamy water, his eyes drifted closed while he remembered his long journey to Sonora. Riding northeast from Tamaulipas he had seen so much senseless destruction of a land once rich and beautiful that it made his stomach turn. The thick adobe walls of pueblo churches were scorched black and desolate, lesser buildings reduced to utter rubble. Dry ocotillo grew in clumps up and down streets where once small gardens had been lovingly tended.

Wherever the Emperor Maximilian's armies rode, they exacted a terrible vengeance on the populace who overwhelmingly supported President Benito Juarez and his republic. Imperial forces burned out rebel villages and poisoned the water supplies so no one could inhabit an area. After they departed, the peons returned, grimly struggling to reclaim a meager existence amid ruins.

The most brutal of all Maximilian's soldiers were the *contre-guerrillas*, small bands composed mainly of foreign mercenaries along with a smattering of Mexican imperialists. He was all too familiar with the way the *contre-guerrillas* did their work. He had ridden with them until the summons arrived and his days as a soldier had come to an end.

As he had ridden toward Gran Sangre, he had wondered what he would find at journey's end. The vast hacienda was a feudal kingdom carved out of the splendid isolation of southern Sonora, four million acres of prime grazing and timberlands. Five generations of Alvarados had been the *patróns* of noble blood for which it was named. That noble blood of royal Spain flowed in their veins . . . in his veins.

The Alvarado hacienda was a land that had first belonged to deer and wolves, panthers and jaguars. It was wild and mountainous, grooved with lush valley meadows that gave way to slopes studded with deep stands of walnuts, sycamores and pine. Fierce Mayo Indians roamed the interior, raiding the outlying herds of cattle and more especially the blooded horses raised by the wealthy *hacendados*. But nothing the Indians could do equaled the destructive fury of the civil war.

Twilight had approached when the great house finally lay spread before him, gilded by the last rays from the setting sun. It stood, still intact, an immense adobe structure two stories high, hundreds of feet across with a large courtyard in the center. A silvery arc of water from the fountain sparkled in the dying light. Elaborate wrought-iron grillwork covered large, high windows, softening the fortresslike effect of the thick outer walls.

He had guided his great pewter stallion Peltre down the twisting rocky trail to the valley floor where a tough-looking old half-caste Indian herded three milk cows toward a long, low stable on the west side of the big house.

Hearing the approach of a horse, the man had raised his head and peered from beneath the wide floppy brim of his straw sombrero. His normally impassive face became awestruck. "Don Lucero, is it truly you?" He quickly removed the hat in a gesture that was oddly awkward yet courtly.

"Hilario? The years have not dulled your eyesight, old man. How is it my father's finest horsebreaker is reduced to herding milk cows?"

Hilario's gray head bowed and he shrugged with disgust at the cattle, using his hat to swat them along the path to the stables. "Since the imperials came and took the best horses in the stable, I have been afoot. We have hidden the few that remain. Both sides need horses to ride and cattle to eat. These old bags of bones are of no use to them else we'd do without milk, too. I am very sorry for the *patrón*'s death," he said, making the sign of the cross. "It is good you have returned home, Don Lucero."

"It has been a hard time since my father died, then?"

"Yes."

Before he could question the old man further, a squeal of delight echoed across the grassy pasture. A young girl, fourteen or fifteen years of age, stared at him for a moment, then turned and raced for the house, calling for the *patrona*.

A smile etched his wide, beautifully chiseled lips. "It seems my wife awaits me. He had nodded to Hilario and urged Peltre into a trot toward the front gate. Servants emerged from various outbuildings along his route, crowding around the big stallion, their bronzed faces mirroring their excitement at the return of the hacienda's only heir.

He greeted several by name. A tall, buxom woman of middle years with iron gray hair plaited in two thick braids that hung down her back inspected him from the stone steps of the smokehouse. She stood clutching a ham in her large capable hands. Her shrewd dark eyes measured the dusty young *patrón* as he smiled

"Angelina. You never change. Will you cook a feast tonight for the prodigal's arrival?"

"But of course, Don Lucero. I will roast this fine ham in your honor. Your lady will be most surprised to see you returned without any word."

"There is little chance to write during a war and even less likelihood that letters will be delivered." He shrugged and turned away from her intent gaze, noting that most of the servants were old and infirm men with a number of women and young children scattered among them.

The war had reached with greedy hands this far into the northern wilderness to pluck the youths in their prime. How many had he seen die, cannon fodder before modern French weapons? Or impressed into the imperial army and killed in guerrilla skirmishes by their own kind. Yet as he had ridden closer to the front steps of the Alvarado ancestral home, the tragedies of war had fled his mind. The great sprawling hacienda was his!

Shaking his head to clear away the dreamy reverie, he shifted in the tub and surveyed the master suite in which he was now ensconced. The massive darkly stained oak furniture had been brought over from Spain in the eighteenth century. Nicks and scratches marred it and a fresh coating of dust covered the intricately carved surfaces. The heavy dark blue draperies were liberally coated as well, the silk frayed and dull with age. The Tabriz carpets had once cost a grandee's ransom, but now they were stained and threadbare. The room reeked of age and neglect.

Had Mercedes closed it up as a gesture of defiance? Thinking of her, his eyes strayed to the big wide canopied bed in the center of the room. For five generations the heirs of Gran Sangre had been conceived upon it. And he would do his duty as Alvarado men had done theirs for decades before him, Father Salvador be damned. His reverie grew troubled thinking of the confrontation to come with Mercedes. What had that old crone and her priest meant when they said Mercedes had "nurtured some foolish notions," and "far exceeded her station"? She obviously had changed over the past four years. No more the meek, terrified virgin—certainly not pallid and plain either. He wondered about how she had acquired her golden complexion and speculated about how far the sun-kissed color extended downward over her seductively soft curves. His body responded to the erotic reverie and he felt his phallus grow rock hard beneath the hot water.

There had been many women over the years, all sorts from coarse camp followers greedy for his money to highborn ladies titillated by the thrill of lying with a dangerous mercenary. Some had been beauties, some ordinary, and in straits, a few downright ugly. In the past, all cats were gray in the dark. *But Mercedes is different.*

Or was she? Did Doña Sofia mean to imply that the young *patrona* had been unfaithful to her marriage vows? No, surely not. That would be too bitter an irony. But then life was filled with ironies. He leaned back in the tub and considered how he would handle her at dinner.

While her husband soaked, Mercedes considered how she would handle him at dinner. A good thing there was so much to do, else her nerves would have snapped worrying about the matter. The kitchen was always shorthanded these days, and with Innocencia gone, it fell to the *patrona* to help Angelina. While the old woman ground fresh cornmeal for tortillas and chopped chilies, Mercedes basted the fragrant ham, then washed and sliced fresh peaches from the orchard. She would use the last smidgen of Armagnac to marinate the fruit as a dessert in honor of Lucero's homecoming.

Such an honor! How desperately she wished he had stayed away, playing at being a soldier. She had heard the stories about what the *contre guerrillas* did. Butchers and brigands every bit as savage as the republican rabble, perhaps even worse. Lucero was perfectly suited for such a life. Or death.

Do I honestly wish my own husband dead? God forgive me. She squeezed her eyes closed and his beautiful, implacable face flashed in her mind. Shaking her head, she blinked and resumed slicing peaches with the smooth economy of movement that indicated long hours of practice with the paring knife.

Once such menial tasks would have been beneath a daughter of the House of Sebastián. She had been educated in an exclusive convent in Mexico City which only the most aristocratic *gachupíns*, those who were born in Spain, attended. She had come to Gran Sangre as a seventeen-year-old bride with a dowry of half a million pesos to preside over one of the wealthiest haciendas in the country, no matter that it was situated in the wilds of Sonora.

The war had not touched it then, had not touched the Alvarado family until old Don Anselmo's only son rode off to fight for Mexico's foreign emperor, leaving behind his bride of scarcely three weeks. Then she had thanked God and all his holy angels for the war which lured Lucero away. But that was before the French army reached Hermosillo and sent its patrols to impress soldiers from the surrounding haciendas. As time passed the fighting raged on and their situation became desperate.

With a muffled oath she shoved a lock of hair back from her temple and used her forearm to rub away the perspiration beading her forehead. She would need a bath. There was only dried lavender to scent the water and perfume her hair. Once she had used one of the most expensive French bath oils. Now she had learned to improvise. Hah! She had even learned to make soap!

Her guardian in Mexico City had commissioned an extensive trousseau, most of which was still in good condition. The gowns, designed for a slender girl, had grown a bit tight across the bust in the past few years, but she had always been expert at plying a needle, although the nuns who taught her delicate embroidery did not expect that a lady of her consequence would ever be reduced to altering her own clothing. The emerald silk would do. It was the most sophisticated gown she owned, even if it did reveal a bit more of her breasts than she would have preferred. Perhaps the pale blue muslin with the high neck would be safer. Then she reconsidered. No, better to look mature and in charge of her own life, not like a girl fresh from the schoolroom.

How could she best broach the topic? With charm? Or briskly like a forthright business proposition? "I'm discussing my marriage, not how many sacks of seed to order for next year's crops," she gritted out, scolding herself. Damn Lucero for coming back into her life!

Charm was a double-edged sword. If she tried any flirtation, it would only remind him that, unlike the merchants, soldiers and vaqueros she bargained with, he had the right to use her body in any way he wished. A small shiver of fear rippled through her.

"You have sliced enough peaches. I will finish mixing the compote," Angelina said, taking the knife from her. "Your bathwater is warm and Lazaro is filling the tub in your room. Go prepare yourself for your husband. I will handle things here."

"I doubt either the dinner or my company will please him, no matter how much I prepare," Mercedes said bitterly.

Sympathy flashed in Angelina's liquid chocolate eyes as she looked down at her slender mistress. Life had dealt harshly with Doña Mercedes but the young *patrona* was as tough as rawhide. Only Don Lucero could bring that haunted look back to her face. "You have both changed over the years. Perhaps it will be better between you now," she said gently.

"*Lo del agua al agua*," Mercedes replied with resignation. "There are some things that can never change, Angelina." Then her chin lifted stubbornly. "When she has finished with the table setting, have Lupe lay out the emerald silk gown for me."

Sophisticated and businesslike, that's the way she would handle the situation. If only Lucero would agree to her request. *What will I do if he refuses*?

Chapter 2

He walked into the large dining hall and surveyed the table setting bathed in the golden haze of soft candlelight. Two places were set, his at the head of the table, hers at his right hand rather than at the opposite end of the massive oak slab, which measured twenty feet in length. Sensible. At least they would not have to yell at one another to carry on a conversation.

He walked around the room, studying the big window that ran the length of the interior wall, affording a splendid view of the courtyard fountain and gardens. Thick timber beams of dark-stained oak ran across the high-arched ceiling. A heavy chandelier of wrought iron hung suspended from the center beam, but its candles had not been lit. In fact, they were burned so low, it was doubtful they would have lasted through the meal. Closer examination revealed that the fresh candles in the silver candlesticks on the table were homemade of tallow, not the expensive imported spermaceti normally used in the great hall. The table linens, freshly pressed and sparkling white, were frayed gently with age and the gold flatware with the Alvarado crest was suspiciously absent. In its place an old set of sterling had been laid out.

Mercedes stood in the doorway, watching Lucero make his silent inspection. How frightfully intimate the two place settings looked. Perhaps she should have instructed Lupe to seat her at the opposite end of the table. *No. That's cowardly*, she scolded herself.

She studied her husband intently. He looked entirely too resplendent for the shabby setting, dressed in an elegant black wool suit with silver trim down the pant legs that molded so scandalously to his long hard thighs. The short, fitted suit coat stretched smoothly across his shoulders, their breadth accentuated by the silver-gray sash at his narrow waist. Silver gray to match the color of those wolf's eyes, which she feared would stare through her. He moved with unconscious grace, as arrogant and self-possessed as he had always been.

Yet there *was* a difference in him. Something that she could not put a name to, a subtle nuance bred no doubt by their years apart, as they grew and matured in opposite directions. Yes, that must be it. Or was she just wishing it because the idea fell in with the proposal she planned to make?

He ran his fingers through that thick inky hair, brushing one recalcitrant lock back from his forehead. It was a gesture she remembered from their first meeting. Then he turned smoothly to face her.

Black eyes locked with startled golden ones. "How long were you planning to stare at me before you found courage to announce yourself, darling?" A white smile slashed his dark face as he advanced on her, slowly, like a puma stalking its prey. He raked her from head to toe and back with his eyes, feeling the breath drawn in a sudden rush from his body. God above, she was lovely. Her hair was piled high on her head in shimmering golden curls, held in place with tortoiseshell combs. Slender emerald pendants sparkled at her earlobes, swaying as she tilted her head. A matching emerald stone hung suspended on a thin golden chain at her cleavage. His throat went dry as the jewel cast its rich reflection on her soft flesh. The deep green silk gown billowed softly from her incredibly tiny waist and clung like a lover's caress to the subtle curves of her breasts, which mounded enticingly above the deep vee of the bodice. He could see the golden kiss of sun extended as low as the neckline. How he ached to pull away the thin silk and see how much of her skin had been touched by the sun.

"Green becomes you." His voice sounded hoarse in the quiet room. "It's not an easy color for most women."

"I am not most women," she replied flatly, refusing to

stand frozen or to back down. Instead she stepped forward to meet him. "And I want for no courage to approach you. I merely chose to observe you while you were unaware of my presence."

He chuckled low as he took her hand and placed a light salute on her fingers. "And what makes you think I *was* unaware? I've survived years of war by learning to sense an enemy's presence behind my back, in my sleep, anywhere. Besides, your perfume gave you away."

"And am I an enemy, Lucero?" She met his bold, cynical gaze levelly as he released her hand.

"Are you? I don't know. Before I left, I gave you good reason to dislike being my wife . . . but perhaps I'll change your mind now."

She felt the faint brushing of his fingertips as they grazed her bare shoulder where her gown dipped low. He did not trespass to the swell of her breast but skimmed along her collarbone instead. She'd forgotten how tall he was. Her head reached only to his shoulder. He filled her vision and she had to tilt her face up to his at such close quarters. His masculine scent teased her nostrils, clean and pungent, shaving soap combined with expensive tobacco.

"You never used to use cigarettes," she said, then wanted to bite her tongue for the unthinking comment, which was somehow more intimate than she intended. His breath was warm on her cheeks as he laughed, a low, wicked chuckle that was at the same time husky and silky.

"One of many new vices I acquired during my years as a soldier. You will find me greatly changed, I fear."

She had to move away from him. "Bufón has already noted your . . . transformation. He used to hate you." As she spoke, she glided past him, heading for the bellpull.

"We were both pups then," he replied lightly. In a couple of swift strides he stood behind her and stayed her hand just as she reached up to summon Angelina. "Now if I can only win you over as easily as I did him."

Mercedes willed herself not to flinch, but a tremor began somewhere deep inside of her, radiating outward to her arms and legs. She withdrew her wrist from his grasp, noting how slender and pale it appeared encircled by his strong dark hand. "You sound as if you plan to court me. Such will not be an easy task, Lucero. I'm not a house pet to greet the master with tail wagging." She spoke sharply, feeling a sudden surge of anger at her reaction to him.

He chuckled. "No house pet indeed, but my lawful wife. As to the tail wagging . . . I'm sure that will require more than a scratch behind the ear."

"Your insolence is one thing that has not changed," she said tartly.

"Your meekness, or rather the lack of it, certainly has."

"You left behind a green girl with no experience of the world." She reached up and gave a defiant yank to the bellpull. "The war has honed my survival skills as well as your own."

He chuckled again. "You've learned to survive quite handily, I warrant."

"Let me enlighten you about the war here in the north. The French may hold Hermosillo but they can't hold the countryside outside the city. We're at the mercy of the Juarista guerrillas—and the *contre-guerrillas*, too," she added bitterly.

"I know all too well what imperial mercenaries have done in the south. I feared Gran Sangre might not remain standing when I returned, but it has."

"No thanks to you—or your father. Come, let us drink the last bottle of good French wine from the cellars while I explain what has befallen our once great estate."

As if on cue, Angelina entered the dining room, bearing a bottle of claret and two fine crystal goblets. Silently she placed the tray on the serving board, then withdrew at Mercedes' nod of thanks.

"Allow me?" He picked up the bottle and inspected it. "My father had excellent taste," he said as he poured the rich ruby liquid into the goblets and handed one to her.

"Your father had no money with which to indulge his excellent taste these past years, but that didn't stop him from living as profligately as ever." The mellow flavor was acrid on her tongue as memories of past years rolled over her.

He raised his glass in a salute, studying her over the rim with those hungry black eyes. "The wine cellar is not all that is depleted, I gather. Hilario told me about the livestock. What happened to the gold table service?"

"Sold to pay taxes. I received a good price in Hermosillo last spring."

"I see you still have the emeralds. What of the rest of the Alvarado family jewels?"

"I've managed to hold onto the heirloom pieces but some of the larger diamonds had to go, mostly to pay off your father's gambling debts in Hermosillo. There was also the matter of buying medicines and a bull to replace the one butchered by a band of Juaristas." She took another sip of wine for courage.

He shrugged. "Papa was always impractical, even in the best of times."

"These are not the best of times."

He drained his glass and poured a refill. "I'm aware of that, believe me."

There was a grimness in his voice which she did not wish to examine. Instead she accused, "You're just like him."

"I'm nothing like him," he replied harshly. The silver irises of his eyes contracted, turning the black centers to small glowing pinpoints. "At least," he added carefully, "I'm no longer like he was. War has a way of forcing a man to examine his life . . . if he's fortunate to live long enough."

"And you obviously were fortunate."

"Fortune is my middle name," he replied wryly, saluting her with his glass.

"Shall I have Angelina serve dinner before you drink the last of the wine?"

"By all means," he replied with a small flourish.

Angelina responded to her summons, carrying in a heavy silver platter heaped with thickly sliced ham, surrounded by fresh vegetables. Lupe assisted her, bringing bowls of condiments and a basket of steaming hot tortillas. While the servants arranged the food on the serving board, he took Mercedes' arm and escorted her to her seat.

"Allow me?" He pulled out the heavy chair and leaned over her as she slipped gracefully into it. "Your skin smells sweet with lavender."

The whisper softness of his voice was matched by the warmth of his breath brushing her bare shoulder. "I grow it in the herb garden and dry it myself. It's the only perfume left I can afford." *I sound too shrewish. Too nervous.*

"Perhaps the fortunes of war will turn in our favor soon." He moved around the corner of the table and took his seat before motioning for Angelina to serve them.

"I very much doubt the war will end anytime soon," she said, breaking apart a tortilla.

"Now that I'm home to assume control of the hacienda, I'll talk to the French commander in Hermosillo about increasing patrols in outlying areas."

"Don't. All that will do is provoke reprisals from the banditti in the mountains when the French ride off. And imperial soldiers always do ride off, Lucero."

"Is that a complaint I hear in your voice, my darling wife? You have my word I'll not leave you again for a very long while."

"You know it would delight me if you did precisely that," she replied when the servants had left them alone in the big room.

"Perhaps that would please you, but it would not please my mother. Nor Father Salvador. They both reminded me of my duty. Need I remind you of yours?" He studied her intently.

The bite of sweet spicy ham tasted like ashes in her mouth but she forced herself to swallow it. "No one need ever remind me of duty, Lucero. I've devoted my life to Gran Sangre, working alongside the peons, bartering with merchants, negotiating with petty bureaucrats—I even held a French colonel at gunpoint once last year."

His eyebrows rose in surprise. "You used to be terrified of guns."

"Circumstances forced me to learn how to use your father's LeFaucheaux double barrel. It takes no great skill to aim a shotgun."

He leaned back in his chair and studied her with renewed interest. "But it does take nerve. You possess the courage to fire a shotgun, but do you possess the courage to let me touch you without pulling away?"

He slowly reached out and took her hand in his, drawing her closer. She did not resist.

"Your hands are small and delicate—the hands of a lady." He could see the marks where blisters had formed calluses in spite of her obvious efforts to soften the work-worn skin. Her nails were neatly buffed but far shorter than a lady of her station would normally wear them. The only adornment on her fingers was her heavy gold wedding band with its matching pearl and diamond betrothal ring.

Mercedes felt her pulse race as he examined her hand, holding it in both of his far larger ones, turning it this way and that. She knew the condition of her skin was deplorable, sunburned, dried out, callused. "I told you I had to work alongside the peons. There is scarcely a man younger than sixty or a boy older than twelve left on the hacienda. Those the French haven't impressed have run off to join the accursed Juaristas in the mountains."

A smile lit his eyes and he replied in a silky voice, "I'm neither an old man, nor a green boy, Mercedes."

"Nor am I a servant to tend crops and do chores, but I must."

"I wish I could promise you a whole retinue of new house servants, but I cannot."

Could he feel the blood beating in her wrist? "I don't expect miracles, Lucero," she replied, struggling to maintain her calm facade without jerking her hand away from him.

"But you would love it if I were to vanish in a puff of smoke."

"As I said, I don't expect miracles," she replied tartly as he finally released her hand.

He threw back his head and laughed. "No, I'll not leave after riding a thousand miles to answer my family's summons." His expression lost all traces of levity and grew thoughtful. "My father knew he'd failed in his duty. I don't intend to fail in mine."

This is your opportunity. Take it. "We must discuss that duty, Lucero. In your absence I've had a good deal of time to consider our marriage." She took a small sip of wine to fortify herself, then met his eyes. He had leaned back in his chair again, studying her with renewed interest.

"What about our marriage?" he prompted.

"For all practical purposes we have none."

"To some extent that's true," he conceded. "I've been away, performing my duty to emperor and country. Now I've returned to . . . perform for you." He could see the pulse at the base of her throat accelerate. A blush stained her cheeks beneath the golden touch of sun on her skin.

"We're strangers to each other. You can't just ride back into my life after all these years and expect me to welcome you to my bed. I don't know you. I never did know you."

"Ah, but I did know you—in the biblical sense of the word, at least." Her blush deepened under his onslaught.

"For a scant three weeks." Her voice was laced with scorn. "After that, you weren't the least bit interested in doing your duty anymore. I was merely a tiresome encumbrance keeping you from your harlot."

"I pledge to remedy my inattention to you now, my darling," he said, trying to see beyond her anger. Was this vulnerability—hurt, perhaps? Dismissing the thought, he added lightly, "Now that you mention her, how is Innocencia?"

Mercedes sat rigidly straight in her chair, her chin held high, exuding the pride of her illustrious Spanish father, combined with the stubbornness of her English mother. "She'll return from the Vargas hacienda tomorrow, overjoyed to have you back."

"Which you obviously are not," he said dryly, waiting to see where this twist in the conversation was leading.

"She desires you in her bed. I do not, which should be apparent to any man not possessing absolute arrogance—or the wits of a flea."

"I've often been accused of arrogance, never of stupidity, Mercedes. Your desires—or my own, for that matter—aren't the issue. You are my wife, not Innocencia. It's your duty to submit to me and provide Gran Sangre with a legal heir." He shoved back his chair and stood, staring down at her, watching the pulse in her throat beat furiously. His fingers caressed her hair, taking one shiny golden curl and lifting it free of the combs, letting the light catch it as he rubbed it slowly back and forth against her heated cheek. "I won't find making an heir such an onerous task. I don't think you will either."

She moistened her lips with the wine but could not swallow any. If only he were not so close, she could think, could speak. *Damn him! I've faced armed brigands and not felt this defenseless.*

But none of her previous adversaries were her husband. None had the legal and moral power over her that he could command. Unless she convinced him otherwise. *Be calm, reasonable.* "I've been raised to do my duty, just as my mother did hers."

"Perhaps that's the trouble—the English don't view life's responsibilities in the same way Mexicans do."

Her eyes blazed with golden fire. "My mother gave up her home and country to wed my father and follow him back to Spain, then to Mexico. She placed her duty to family above all else." Mercedes took a swift calming breath, feeling his scrutiny, knowing she must speak now or it would be too late. "Both her example and that taught me by the holy sisters at Saint Theresa's have inculcated a sense of duty in me, Lucero. I've been an excellent steward in your absence. Even before your father fell ill it was left to me to run Gran Sangre, to see that bills were paid, protection secured from the army, crops planted and livestock tended. I've not only been in charge of the household but of the entire hacienda, all four million acres of it."

"A formidable task for a lone female, even one with your rather startling temerity." He released the fat shining curl, which bounced softly onto her bare shoulder. He could feel his whole body growing rigid with desire.

She, too, stood up, then walked to the sideboard where a crystal decanter of *aguardiente* sat. Pouring the potent locally distilled brandy into two tiny goblets, she handed him one, willing her hands to remain steady no matter how she trembled inside. "You're going to be even more startled by my temerity, I fear." She raised her glass to salute him, then waited until he followed suit and took a drink. "Our marriage was a mistake, but a marriage before God it remains and cannot be undone, no matter how much either of us might wish it."

"But I don't wish it undone, Mercedes." Her name fell off his tongue sibilantly, whisper soft.

"Then you well and truly have changed. Before you went away you wanted nothing more than to be rid of your 'pallid scrawny little virgin'—I believe those were the words you used to describe me to Don Anselmo after our betrothal dinner."

He winced. "I'm sorry you overheard that conversation. I had no idea, but it's over and done with now. You aren't pallid or scrawny anymore and you certainly aren't a virgin." He let his eyes linger hungrily at the deep cleft between her breasts where the emerald pendant nestled.

"But I am a stranger to you and you to me," she countered. "You can force yourself on me—claim your legal rights just as you did on our wedding night, but you won't find me so docile and accommodating now as I was then, I warn you."

"After I claim my rights, what will you do, Mercedes? Slash my throat while I sleep—bash my brains in with one of Angelina's iron skillets? Or perhaps something more subtle like slipping bits of torvache in my wine to drive me mad?" He held out his brandy glass for a refill, a dare dancing in his black eyes.

"I would appeal to your conscience, if I believed you had one," she said sourly, pouring him another generous slug of *aguardiente*. Perhaps she could get him too drunk to perform and win herself one night's reprieve—or drink herself into oblivion so he would leave her in disgust.

Divining her intent, he took one sip, then set his glass aside and reached for the decanter before she could pour herself another drink. "Is overindulging in spirits one of *your* new vices acquired in my absence?"

"Rather, one more appropriate for your unexpected return," she muttered beneath her breath, emptying her glass with a delicate shudder. She set it down on the sideboard and turned to face him. "I want time, Lucero. Time for us to become acquainted, time for me to get used to the idea of having a husband."

"You never expected me to return, did you?"

His bald accusation startled her, but why lie? He seemed to have developed an unsettling knack of seeing through her. "Frankly, no. The war has claimed many casualties. I know life with the *contre-guerrilla* bands is far more dangerous than with the regular army. Even if you weren't killed, I never thought you cared enough about Gran Sangre to come back for it even in the unlikely event Father Salvador's last letter reached you."

"And you, Mercedes? Do you care so much about Gran Sangre?"

"It's my home now and its people are my family. I've had neither since my parents died. Being a diplomat, my father was required to travel from country to country throughout my childhood, taking my mother and me with him. The convent my guardian placed me in was merely temporary until a marriage could be arranged. I had thought to spend the rest of my life caring for this place."

"So this is the 'foolish notion' my mother spoke of. Have you told her of your feelings about our marriage?"

"Speak of such an intimate matter with Doña Sofia?" She looked at him as if he'd lost his wits. "No. For her my folly lies in striving to hold this place together on my own. Women aren't supposed to do more than embroider and pray—and bear children, of course," she added angrily.

"And you want none of that. No husband? No children? A desolate choice for a beautiful young woman . . . being alone."

"Being alone doesn't mean one is always lonely, but you've returned to your birthright. All I ask is that you give me—give us—time . . . before . . ."

He watched her falter, choking on the final words.

Although the audacity of such a request stunned him, he could not help but admire the courage of the woman who had been left to struggle and survive, holding together a crumbling land grant in the midst of a war. "Before I invade your bed and force my husbandly attentions on you?" he finished for her. "Father Salvador would give you a stern lecture for such an impudent suggestion."

"He has already given me too many to count. One more shall scarcely matter."

"Very well, I'll grant you a stay of execution for tonight, Mercedes. Truthfully, I'm exhausted. Maybe I'm even feeling a bit benevolent," he added with a wicked smile.

The look she gave him indicated how much she believed that notion. Suddenly she was exhausted herself, all the fight gone out of her after wresting such a small victory from him. Fighting her own tightly strung nerves during the hours since he had ridden back into her life had left her utterly spent.

"I'll wish you a good night's rest, then." She wanted nothing more than to run down the hall and bar her bedroom door against him, but steeled herself to deliberately walk past him.

He let her pass, watching in silent amusement as she turned to leave. At the last second an impulse overtook him as her lavender fragrance teased his nostrils. He swept out one arm, pulling her against his chest. His other hand lifted her chin to meet his lips as they descended to claim hers. A soft mewling protest formed deep in her throat but was swiftly muffled by his hot and seeking mouth.

She felt his tongue brush deftly along the seam of her lips, slipping inside when she gasped in surprise, then retreating. Just as quickly as he had seized her, he released her and leaned back against the heavy sideboard with casual arrogance, his arms crossed over his chest. Those dark wolf's eyes studied her reaction, sensing her confusion.

"Sweet dreams, Mercedes," he whispered, watching her eyes darken from amber gold to the color of hot molasses. Her fingers curled up and bit into her palms. He knew she itched to slap his face but feared he might renege on his reprieve if she provoked him.

"Good night, Lucero," she said coldly, turning her back on him and walking slowly from the room, regal as a queen dismissing a courtier.

The walk down the hall to her quarters had never seemed so long. She could sense his eyes on her, dark and fathomless as a starless desert night. Granting her this night was only a whim. She had been a fool to try reasoning with him. Lucero had always been a gamester. This was merely another of his cat and mouse ploys, something to amuse himself with until he tired of seeing her jump this way and that in the futile hope of staving off his attentions in bed.

Perhaps it would have been better to let him come. The sooner he did his duty and planted his seed, the sooner he would tire of her and seek out other women. Innocencia's coarse earthy beauty flashed into her mind, the dark sensuous serving wench entwined in a passionate embrace with Lucero, digging her blunt strong fingers into his curly hair and pulling him down to her in a devouring kiss. Mercedes had caught them in this very hallway a week after her marriage. They had been so wrapped up in each other, they never even noticed her. She had run crying to her *dueña*. The dour old widow had explained that most men were at heart base, immoral creatures and that she should consider it a blessing if Don Lucero spent his amorous attentions elsewhere.

Mercedes' youthful pride had been shattered, but in light of how much she detested the methodical disinterest with which he had despoiled her of her innocence, she should have been happy that he did not desire her. Conjugal duty was painful and degrading, yet when she thought of the avaricious hunger in Innocencia's eyes, Mercedes could not help but wonder if her own untutored young body was missing something.

Lucero had frightened and fascinated her as a girl, then he had left her. Now all the fears and humiliations of girlhood were behind her. She had built a rich satisfying life in spite of the hardships she had endured. He should not have returned to spoil everything. If only he would accept what she had tried to explain, realize that she was a different person now.

And do what? Court her as if he were a youthful swain? That was absurd. He would never understand who she was or what she felt. Why did she want him to?

He desires you now. Yes, she could see that in those night-dark eyes. She had learned to recognize male hunger over the past years, even learned how to manipulate it to her own advantage. It had been that or give over Gran Sangre to soldiers, merchants, whatever men threatened to despoil it. Sensing that hunger in him had soothed her wounded pride, she assured herself, nothing more. Surely nothing more, for he was a ruthless war-hardened soldier. He was danger personified. Yes, he desired her. Did she desire him in return?

Trembling, she closed the door to her room and leaned against it in the darkness. After gathering her wits, she walked over to where a fat tallow candle sat on her dressing table. She struck a match and lit it, then sank down on the velvet cushioned chair in front of the mirror to stare into the haunted golden eyes of a stranger.

Next door in the master suite, the *patrón* of Gran Sangre dismissed Baltazar for the night, after the servant laid out a maroon brocade robe. He quickly shed his formal clothes and slipped it on, then rolled a cigarette and lit it. The tart sweet smoke seared his lungs like a lover's scouring nails, the pleasure familiar and reassuring amid so much that was changed.

Mercedes had certainly undergone a striking metamorphosis. He could still picture her standing before him in the big dining hall, so small and delicate for all her sweetly filled-out curves, announcing to him that she was a different woman. He took another pull on the tobacco and laughed aloud at the irony of the whole situation. His eyes shifted from the starlit Sonoran skies outside his bedroom window to the door separating his suite from hers.

"Yes, you're not the woman Lucero Alvarado married, beautiful Mercedes, but that's only fair, since I'm not Lucero Alvarado."

He flicked the cigarette out into the darkness of the courtyard, tossed his robe onto the floor and sank naked into the soft feather mattress, where he lay staring at the ceiling as his mind moved back through time.

Chapter 3

What a bizarre twist of fate had brought him to this Sonoran stronghold. He grinned into the darkness, whispering, "The fortunes of war."

He was Lottie Fortune's boy Nicholas, the illegitimate son of a New Orleans whore. Hell, Fortune was just a stage name the would-be actress made up, but Nicholas chose to keep it rather than use her real one. His mother had sent him to live with her pappy Hezakiah Benson when he was seven. The brutal fire-and-brimstone-breathing old Bible thumper had made his life a misery on that hardscrabble west Texas farm. He had run away to war, thinking it would be glamorous.

Glamour! His expression grew grim as he thought of all the vile sinkholes he had fought in since becoming a mercenary at the age of fifteen. There had been so many he'd lost count: the Crimea, the Austro-Italian border, North Africa . . . but none could compare to Mexico for utter savagery. He had sailed into Vera Cruz back in January of 1862 with the French invaders, full of absurd notions about getting rich on Hapsburg gold and retiring to live in luxury in a tropical paradise. One look at the bleak pestilent harbor, its beaches blackened by carrion-eating vultures, had immediately disabused him of that pipe dream. But then the French columns had moved inland. Orange, lemon and fig trees grew in the lush green highlands where poplars towered over sparkling streams and brilliantly colored birds sang.

The wealthy *hacendados* welcomed their imperialist saviors into homes that were virtual palaces, furnished with every luxury and staffed by hordes of Indian servants. As they drew near to Puebla, the small villages were picturesque and lovely with ornate churches and riotous banks of purple bougainvillea growing in the central plazas. The cantinas had decent whiskey for soldiers to slake their thirst and voluptuous sloe-eyed women to appease their lust.

Then came Puebla and the Cinco de Mayo. The republican victory against crack French troops had been an omen of things to come, even though the imperialist forces eventually carried the day, marching the next year all the way to Mexico City. But every inch of twisting mountain and jungle terrain, so lushly beautiful, was ever so deceptively treacherous. Without warning, Juarista guerrillas swarmed from behind rocks and trees. With guns and machetes they attacked the invaders in swift deadly forays, then melted away as quickly as they had come.

The money had been good at first. It still was when the imperial treasury was moved to shake loose some of its hoard of silver, but this far in the hinterlands pay periods were as irregular as the soldiers. Most of the troops lived off the land, which was well and good when they chanced upon a wealthy *hacendado* with a corral full of blooded horses and a cellar full of *aguardiente* which they could liberate at point of bayonet. After all, it was at the request of just such pro-monarchist conservatives that the invaders had come to establish Maximilian on his throne. But in recent months the army had encountered only republicans, small farmers and villagers with little to give. Some *contre-guerrillas* looted the churches. Even though he was not religious, Nick had refused to do that. He had a small cache of money hidden away in Tampico as a hedge against the future. He bided his time, waiting to see what would develop.

Nicholas Fortune had a bizarre love-hate relationship with Mexico. It was the most marvelous country he had ever seen and Nick had seen many around the globe by the time he had reached his twenty-ninth birthday. Yet for all its exotic tropical lushness and stark desert beauty, Mexico had been bitterly rent by war. The scars were everywhere, especially inside the people who had been born, lived and died between pronouncements, revolutions and occupations. People like Don Lucero Alvarado.

He drifted off to sleep, remembering the day they first met. It was in what had once been a sleepy village in the state of Nuevo Leon.

Fall 1865

"Why the hell do they keep coming back? Damn, they're out of ammunition—half of them don't even have machetes." Nick had watched as two of his men rifled the bodies of the dead Juarista officers. He scoffed. Officers, hell, just like *he* was an officer. They were guerrillas and he was a *contre-guerrilla*. But he had been paid in gold to lead this band of cutthroats. The rebels had little beyond the few bits of gold in their teeth, and that Lanfranc and Schmidt were quickly chiseling out.

His question had been rhetorical, one he'd asked himself many times in recent months, but the stoop-shouldered older man standing next to him answered it anyway. "They'll fight till the last man jack of 'em is dead, Capt'n."

Captain. What a joke the "commission" was. He had been "promoted" by Colonel Ortiz back in Monterrey last week. The colonel was having such an excellent time with the beauteous wife of the *alcalde* that he decided to send Fortune and a small band out on the reconnaissance mission he himself had been assigned to lead.

Sean O'Malley sent a thick brown stream of tobacco juice flying across the sandy reddish soil, then continued, "Men with a cause, sure 'n they're the most dangerous kind. Buckos like you 'n me, we fight fer our pay. Makes us no niver mind what country, what king, but this is their home, where their fathers lived for centuries, where their wives and children live. They may be poor but Juarez is one of their own and they chose him, not the likes of some fancy-britches Austrian archduke."

Nick grinned at Sean. "You may be a mercenary, but beneath whatever uniform you wear still beats the heart of an Irish patriot. And don't tell me if the emperor was English instead of Austrian that you'd be standing here beside me."

O'Malley shrugged his brawny shoulders. "I lost me home and the girl I loved back in thirty-seven. Nothing there but a price on me head and lobsterbacks in every village pub, but I understand why it is a man fights this kind of war even when he's outnumbered and outgunned."

Nick sighed and inhaled his cigarette. "Yeah, well, I don't. All I know is I liked it better when I could fight soldiers with rifles, not boys and old men with machetes."

"Time to get out, boyo?" O'Malley cocked one shaggy gray brow at Fortune and studied his superior officer with shrewd blue eyes.

"And go where? Do what? Fighting is all I know. I have no home—never had. That's why I joined the Legion back in forty-nine."

"Sure and it may have slipped your mind, Capt'n, but yer not in the Legion anymore," O'Malley said with a glint of humor as he inspected Fortune's well-worn buckskins. Few of the imperial irregulars made any attempt to impose military discipline or wear uniforms.

"The side benefits are better with the *contre-guerrillas*," Nick replied grimly. "All the gold we can loot—or dig out of dead men's teeth." He dropped the cigarette into the dust and ground it beneath his boot heel.

"Heard we'll be getting a few new men from General Marquez's old command. Sparkly white uniforms 'n all that," the older man said as their sentries signaled the approach of friendly forces.

"At least if they're dressed in uniforms that match each other's, we'll know they aren't rebels," Nick replied as his eyes scanned the narrow opening at the mouth of the canyon for riders.

His men had just finished a fierce hand-to-hand fight with a band of Juaristas they had stumbled upon in this brushy area. Stunted pines and desert elderberry bushes grew densely across the jagged landscape. In the distance the Sierra Madres glowed like coals of fire as the sun set against them. It had been a long, bloody day and it was not over yet. The rough low-lying terrain would make them sitting ducks for enemy snipers.

Fortune was about to give orders to mount up when a shot whizzed past his ear. He dropped instantly to the ground as he barked out the command to take cover, rolling himself into a patch of mescabean, returning fire all the while. Years of fighting experience had taught him every tactical trick in the book and a few that weren't. Some of the Juaristas had taken a lesson from the same school. He knew the rebels had his reinforcements pinned down at the opposite end of the road and were using the advantage of height, firing from the steep, tree-covered sides of the canyon. His only chance was to get his men out of the slaughter pit.

"O'Malley, Schmidt! Here!" He signaled them to follow him, running for the copse of paloverde where their horses were tethered.

The three seasoned veterans reached their mounts as the rebels fired sporadically, unwilling to waste precious ammunition on chancy shots. Leaning low on his big gelding, Fortune yelled out orders in English, which all of his motley multinational band understood but few of the Mexican enemy did.

"Grab a mount and scatter into the trees. Make for the opening of the canyon. Try to link up with the imperials after dark!"

What followed was a repeat of dozens of earlier skirmishes. They split up in twos and threes, riding and firing, fending off machete wielding rebels until darkness fell. Once fighting became impossible after sundown, the Juaristas would evaporate. Nick would round up the remnants of his men in the morning and try to track their attackers, who were probably from a small village nearby.

He sent O'Malley, who had managed to stay with him, in search of stragglers while he looked for the men from Marquez's command. Fortune had heard stories about the Tiger of Tacubaya, Leonardo Marquez, a Mexican national who had deserted the republican government of Juarez and joined Maximilian's imperial forces. Marquez had earned his nickname with a reputation steeped in blood. At Tacubaya he had ordered the wholesale massacre of the town, including women and children. He took no prisoners, unless for his own amusement, flinging them from mountaintops and using them for bayonet practice, but his favorite sport was burying them up to their necks in sand, then stampeding horses over them.

Nick was not looking forward to riding with men who had participated in the general's idea of a good time. But, hell, all of them had done things in this war that they were not proud of, and stories were distorted and exaggerated in the retelling. He was scarcely the man to cast the first stone, he thought wryly.

Suddenly he felt a prickling begin at the back of his neck and move lower, centering between his shoulder blades. Nick knew someone was drawing a bead on him from the shadows. How the hell had he let someone slip up behind him? *Getting careless can get you dead*, he thought as he slid from his gelding and rolled toward the black chasm of the arroyo at the side of the trail.

Silence. Whoever it was had not wasted a bullet. He slid his knife from the sheath strapped to his thigh and hunkered soundlessly in the darkness, waiting. Then he heard a faint rustling noise over to his right, the soft shifting sound of sand trickling down the steep embankment. A grim smile slashed his face as he circled around to the left.

Nick's adversary was crouched with his back against the trunk of a tree, peering toward the lip of the arroyo where he had vanished. Although his hat brim hid his face in shadows, the uniform of an imperial guardsman was plainly visible. Fortune drew his .44 caliber Remington and cocked it. "That flashy gold braid may impress the ladies in Monterrey but out here it'll only get you shot," he said in French.

The imperial officer whirled in his direction, his French Chassepot breechloader raised. "You speak French. Identify yourself at once," he replied in Spanish.

"Captain Nicholas Fortune, General Ortiz's *contre-guerrilla* forces," he replied in Spanish, for it seemed the soldier was not fluent in the language of his allies. There was something naggingly familiar about him. When the other man did not lower his rifle, Nick added in a low purr, "I wouldn't think of shooting that thing. Even if I miss, these woods are full of my men and you'll make a beautiful target in that parade ground costume."

"A thousand apologies," the imperial officer replied, lowering the breechloader and standing up. "You took me by surprise. That hasn't happened in a long time. Your voice . . ." He cocked his head quizzically to one side and the brilliance of the moonlight fell full on his face.

The face of Nicholas Fortune.

Nick, too, moved into the light now and the stranger hissed in amazement. "Who in the name of all that's holy *are* you?"

"I just told you," Nick replied, sheathing his knife and holstering the sidearm. "Better question is, who the hell are you?"

"Captain Lucero Alvarado, late of the Imperial Guards, now assigned to General Marquez's command," Nick's mirror image replied, clicking his heels smartly. "I was assigned to make contact with you but I had no idea . . ."

The two men walked slowly around each other. They were of an identical build, lean and tall, although Fortune had perhaps an inch in height over Alvarado. They stared into each other's dark eyes, trying to gauge the color.

"Amazing. Absolutely incredible," Lucero breathed.

"We'd best skip the mutual admiration for now. These woods could be crawling with Juaristas," Nick said dryly, motioning his companion toward the road. "Where are the rest of your men? You know how many survived the ambush?"

"We split up when they opened fire. There were six of us. Now, who knows?" he said, shrugging.

They searched for the horses. Nick's chestnut gelding was grazing peacefully a dozen yards down the trail. Lucero whistled and a superb gray stallion with the unmistakable bloodlines of the Andalusian trotted obediently up to him.

"I raised him from a colt," Lucero said, noting the way Nick's eyes studied the arched neck and clean lines of the horse. "His name is Peltre."

As he swung up on his gelding, Nick repeated in Spanish, "Peltre." The name was perfect, for the stallion was indeed the rich silvery shade of pewter. "When we rode into the canyon, we passed a cave, about two miles from here. It's a good place to spend the rest of the night. We'll look for O'Malley in the morning."

Fortune awakened with that old familiar itch that meant he was being watched. He lay on a hard rock surface that was faintly damp. The cave. At once last night's incredible events flashed into his mind. Without opening his eyes, he slid his hand beneath his blanket to feel the .32 caliber Sharps pepperbox hidden in his coat pocket for reassurance. Then he blinked.

"So you're finally awake. It's past sunrise," Lucero said. He sat against the opposite wall, staring at Nick with hooded dark eyes.

"I've been in the saddle for three days, chasing those raiders we tangled with yesterday. I took my turn as sentry during the night," he said, throwing off his blanket and sitting up. Alvarado's eyes followed his movements intently and Fortune was certain the man had been watching him in his sleep for some time. He felt uncomfortable about that yet could not keep his own eyes from returning the perusal.

"We have the eyes of a wolf, black with silver irises. The only other person I've ever known with them is my father," Lucero said, "Don Anselmo Mateo Maria Alvarado. . . . And your father?"

"You're one up on me. I haven't got the least notion who my father was," Nick replied in a flat voice. He stood up and walked to the mouth of the cave, studying the road that wound across the canyon below them, looking for riders.

He rolled a cigarette and lit it, inhaling deeply as Alvarado asked, "Did your mother have eyes like ours?"

Fortune laughed but it was a metallic sound. "No, she had blue eyes. Is there some point in this line of questioning?" he inquired curtly, knowing what Alvarado was leading up to but not liking it.

"Your mother . . . who was she?"

"Single-minded bastard, aren't you," Nick said with false geniality.

Lucero grinned with typical Hispanic grace and replied lightly, "I'm not the one who's a bastard—not literally, at least."

Nick's eyes narrowed at the insult, but then he realized he'd set himself up for it and shrugged. "I've shot men for calling me a bastard."

"My dear mother believes my father and I are far worse," Alvarado said.

Fortune grinned. "Really?"

Lucero threw back his head and laughed in earnest, exactly the same way Nicholas Fortune had always laughed when something suddenly struck him as funny. The two men laughed together briefly, then the humor died as they studied each other again. The bright morning light revealed their amazing resemblance even more clearly.

"You're slightly taller, and there is that scar on your cheek," Alvarado said appraisingly, noting the thin white line that ran just below Nick's left cheekbone, a tiny flaw marring the perfection of his features.

"A saber graze taken in Sebastopol. Women tell me it adds to my charm. I have more all over my body, some not nearly so neat, depending on who the surgeon was at the time."

"You can't be much older than me."

"Twenty-nine."

"And you've been a soldier all your life?" Lucero was fascinated.

"I learned to fight at an early age. A survival skill in the New Orleans slums."

"Tell me about your mother."

"Not much to tell. She was a whore. Worked in some of the best fancy houses in the city—that is until she began to lose her looks and took to the bottle a little too regularly."

"My father had a cousin in New Orleans. I understand he used to visit him occasionally before I was born." Alvarado looked at Fortune speculatively. "She was very beautiful, your mother?"

"Like I said, until the life and the liquor caught up with her," Nick replied cynically, turning his back on Lucero. *My brother.*

"Aren't you interested in our father? He is still alive, you know."

"Why should I care? He obviously never knew I was alive and wouldn't have given a damn if he did. I'm just a scarlet poppy's bastard to a rich don like him."

"He has only one heir. Perhaps a spare wouldn't be amiss, who knows?" Alvarado said cavalierly.

"I don't want to see him any more than he'd want to see me."

"He looks exactly like you—even the harsh expression around his mouth," Lucero taunted silkily.

Nick swore a particularly obscene oath and ground out his cigarette. "I don't give a damn if they stamped us out of the same bloody mold and then broke it! You're the heir, rich boy. Leave it at that."

His angry outburst was interrupted by the sound of hoofbeats. At once both men dropped to the ground and reached for their weapons, peering down the cliff. Sean O'Malley rode out of the trees leading their horses, calling out for his captain. The expression on his face when he saw Lucero Alvarado standing beside Nicholas Fortune was so goggle-eyed it was comical. Every man in Nick's band was equally as amazed, as were the two other men from Alvarado's unit when they located them.

The men burned with curiosity over the next few days, but it was apparent their captain was not going to discuss the appearance of his seeming twin. Sensing Nick's reticence, Luce, as his comrades quickly dubbed him, did not speak of their relationship either, except when the two of them were alone.

In spite of himself, Nick was curious about the life of luxury his brother had led and Luce was most obliging in describing Gran Sangre in all its splendor, as well as his family, the servants, even the blooded livestock. It was a world out of a Dumas novel to Nick, who found himself drinking in the stories like a starveling.

In turn, Luce was fascinated by the mercenary's life his half brother had led since he was a boy, a life that he had only discovered over the past few years. Alvarado was a natural-born soldier, uncomplaining about long hard rides, sleeping on cold ground, and eating short rations on horseback. He was eager to learn from his brother all the tricks of the killing trade. And Luce was an excellent pupil.

In one particularly vicious hand-to-hand fight, he had dispatched a brute of a man with a knife trick that Nick had taught him. As they were cleaning up after the skirmish, Luce had murmured to Nick, kneeling alongside him at the stream's edge, "You're a good teacher, brother. In fact, you've taught me more in a few brief months than I learned in years with tutors who didn't give a damn about me. That particular lesson just saved my life."

Then he chuckled. "The grammar of the knife is far more entertaining than Father Salvador's Latin lessons."

Entertaining. Yes, that was what all this amounted to for Don Lucero Alvarado. Entertainment! He especially enjoyed masquerading as a Juarista to ferret out sympathizers in the various towns and hamlets they passed through.

They had been sent by Colonel Ortiz on just such a mission one rainy afternoon in October. "Serving with Marquez was the first time I really felt alive, you know?" he said as the two of them rode into a small village in Tamaulipas suspected of supporting the rebels. "Two years with the imperial army was little more than a continuation of my old life. I was posted in the capital with the empress's entourage. Lots of balls, dress uniforms, rules. God and all his saints, the damned rules."

"And Marquez, he was different?" Nick asked casually, wondering about the rumors he'd heard about *El Tigre*.

Luce laughed as he took a long pull on his cigarette. "The man is truly a tiger. Cunning, deadly. He takes what he wants and makes his own rules. And he rewards his men generously. When we sacked San Dimas there was a wool merchant's daughter . . ." His eyes glowed ferally as he remembered her wildness and the pleasure he had taming her. "We drank the bishop's whole wine cellar dry—and a very large cellar it was, too. I rode off with enough silver to weigh down even a mount as strong as Peltre. My companions and I spent it all in Vera Cruz."

He shrugged carelessly in a way Nick understood. Men in their line of work quickly adopted an easy-come-easy-go attitude toward money, spending it profligately on the fleshly pleasures it could buy, for who knew if one would live to drink another bottle of whiskey or caress another woman's soft body?

They dismounted in front of a small adobe cantina and walked inside the smoky room, which was crowded with armed men who eyed the damp muddy strangers suspiciously. A sultry looking barmaid approached Fortune, hips swaying seductively. Leaning forward to reveal the bounty spilling from her low-cut *camisa*, she smiled.

"What do two such pretty men want—pulque? Or perhaps something stronger . . .?" She wet her carmined lips suggestively. "I have fine *aguardiente* for only thirty centavos."

"Bring us pulque. Do we look like rich men?" Luce said dismissively, his eyes scanning the room surreptitiously. She left in a huff to fill their order, angry at his curt manner. Then he leaned over to Nick and said, "The two by the window are carrying new Yankee rifles."

"Springfields, .58 caliber." Fortune's eyes narrowed. Shipments of American arms were finding their way across the border to Juarez's forces at Matamoros, then being sent south to arm Escobedo and Diaz's armies. The *contre-guerrillas* had been assigned to intercept just such a shipment. "Keep them entertained here while I see what there is to see around the plaza."

"The *puta* favors you. I'll do the searching," Luce replied as she returned, her eyes riveted hungrily on Nick.

After buying several rounds of drinks, Nick had become the hero of the day. The men swapped stories of how they had routed the cowardly traitors who served the Austrian emperor. After a couple of hours had passed everyone was exceedingly drunk and Lupita was growing insistent in her advances to Nick.

Although taking care to hide the fact he was the only

sober man left in the place, he was beginning to grow concerned that Luce had not returned. Had he been caught snooping? Surely there would have been an alarm raised. An outbreak of gunfire would bring his men riding in, weapons blazing. He would prefer to seize or, if necessary, destroy the shipment of rifles before the fighting broke out.

Finally he excused himself to answer the call of nature and staggered out the back door, leaving Lupita sulking at the bar. A few quick steps down the street away from the noise of the cantina, he heard the sounds of a scuffle coming from a small adobe building. Drawing his Remington, he quickly kicked open the door and stepped inside. Luce was straddling a slender dark-haired girl whose torn clothing and wide terror-filled eyes clearly indicated she had not encouraged his advances. He held her wrists pinioned above her head with one hand while his other was poised at his belt buckle. Her skirts were already rucked up, revealing slender pale thighs which he had pried apart with his legs.

Alvarado looked up at Fortune, a grimace of lust hazing his vision. "The guns are there." He gestured to the back of the room where several crates were stacked. A man's body slumped in front of them, his throat cut. "Her father was guarding them. She brought him his dinner. He can't eat and my appetite runs in a different direction tonight," he muttered, running his hand over her mound and feeling her quiver.

"The cantina has women eager for your company. Use them when this is over," Nick said tersely. "This isn't the time or place for sport. Besides, this waif is far too skinny for your taste."

With a disgusted oath Alvarado got to his feet and started to yank the girl up with him, but she twisted away with ferretlike speed and darted toward the back of the room, now screaming at the top of her lungs.

"No need to give the signal. Let's just hope we can hold them until our men get here," Nick said, seizing two of the rifles from the crates.

"At least we're well armed," Luce countered, doing the same.

Both men flattened themselves against the thick adobe walls as a hail of bullets flew through the window and door. They returned fire, taking turns reloading until O'Malley's familiar yell sounded from the plaza. Fortune's men poured into it from every direction. Schmidt and Lanfranc rode up the narrow backstreet, cutting down all resistance while O'Malley gave commands from the roof of the cantina, using the height to oversee what had quickly turned into a rout. Men and horses slipped and slid in the yellow-brown mud. The big Irishman picked off two Juaristas who were attempting to reach the corral, then yelled for Nick and Luce.

Within ten minutes it was over. The rain had stopped, as if it had surrendered like the village. The unarmed people filed into the square. Most were frightened, their eyes huge as they stared at the hard-looking band of imperial mercenaries who spoke in a polyglot of Spanish, French, English and German. Women clutched crying babies while children hid in the folds of their skirts. Men, some stoic, others unable to mask their blazing hatred, walked into the plaza with hands raised, prodded by the rifle barrels of the victors.

"Do we shoot them, *mein herr*?" Schmidt asked, his small blue eyes moving across the lines of prisoners.

"I doubt there were two dozen able-bodied men in the whole village and most of them are lying dead in the mud," Fortune said, surveying the carnage. In fact, lots of the bodies in the muck were far from able-bodied and some not even male. "Bust up what rifles we can't carry with us and we move out."

"They're our prisoners," Lanfranc protested in rapid French. "They were hiding a shipment of weapons for Escobedo's army. You know the decree—"

Luce's bark of laughter interrupted the fat little Frenchman's tirade. "Our commander here doesn't approve of the emperor's Black Decree. Thinks it breaks all the rules of civilized warfare."

"There is no such thing as civilized war," Nick snapped, "but butchering prisoners wholesale only creates more resistance."

Maximilian had promulgated a decree giving official sanction to what had already been a common practice, the execution of all men caught bearing arms against the empire. The so-called Black Decree stated there was no legitimate republican government, hence no republican army, only bandits. Considering how Marquez and other *contre-guerrillas* operated, Fortune thought it an irony that several of Juarez's regular army generals had been executed as brigands. Such mindless brutality only increased the ferocity with which the enemy fought.

"The young ones we should kill—see the hate in their eyes?" Schmidt said, his own eyes gleaming.

Fortune kicked over a corpse lying in his path as he walked into the plaza. A boy who couldn't have been more than twelve years old. "Is this young enough for you?" he snarled.

He combed his fingers through his hair and glared at the armed group surrounding him. He'd spent half his life with men of this ilk, men like his half brother, who grew to love the killing more with every battle. Nicholas Fortune felt like a stranger among them. "O'Malley, are the rifles taken care of?"

"That they are, Capt'n."

"Then mount up. Schmidt, you and Lopez stampede their horses after we cull the ones worth taking with us."

Reluctantly his orders were obeyed. They rode out of the silent village just as the rain resumed in a steady, sullen downpour.

Stupid. The whole stinking mess was senseless, leading nowhere. For every boy with a machete they shot, two more rode down from the mountains to take his place. Lord God above, he was sick unto death of the slaughtering. The coppery smell of blood filled his nostrils and for the first time since he was sixteen, he felt sick with loathing it. Nick had to get out.

If only Luce's careless words about their father were true, he might have a place to belong, but that was absurd. He'd met enough haughty *hacendados* to know how one would feel about a man like him, no matter how much he resembled the old son of a bitch. Besides, he had his pride. In all his life, Nicholas Fortune had never begged and he was too old to start now.

He looked across the fire at his brother, who was dallying with one of the camp followers, a coarse wench with a lusty laugh and great masses of curly black hair. The image of Luce straddling the terrified girl back in that village flashed into his mind. His brother liked women to fight him before he took them. Riding with Marquez had given him a taste for rape as well as plunder and killing. He thrived on danger, volunteering every time a point had to be taken under withering fire or a Juarista town had to be infiltrated before they hit it.

Last week he had gone into Tampico, which was currently occupied by the rebels, and set a charge of dynamite in the customs house. When it ignited too soon, he was caught in the mob. Nick rode in with Peltre and the two of them made good their escape in a hail of bullets.

Luce had the devil's own luck. In fact some of the men, especially the Mexicans, had started calling him *El Diablo*. The Devil. An ironic conceit considering his name Lucero meant "light." Everywhere he went, Luce brought darkness.

"So deep in thought, *hermano*," Luce said in halting English. Since joining his brother he had begun to pick up the language although he detested it even more than French. His mewling pale little wife was half English, but Nick was Americano. A very clever Americano whose uncanny likeness to himself fascinated him almost as much as the incredible life Nick had led. Indeed, his brother had become a hero of sorts to the spoiled young *criollo*. "What troubles you?" he asked, already knowing the answer.

Nick tossed his cigarette into the fire. "I thought you were busy with Esmeralda."

"She's just a *puta*."

"So was my mother." Nick's eyes bored into Luce's.

The tense exchange was broken when a rider came galloping into camp. Expecting dispatches from Colonel Ortiz, Nick stood up and signaled the man to him.

"You are *el capitán*?" the grizzled older man inquired in broken English.

Fortune identified himself in Spanish, asking for the orders from Monterrey. He was handed a small satchel by the rider, who then cleared his throat and held up another envelope.

"I have a letter of great importance, entrusted to me by the colonel himself. He received it all the way from Sonora, from a great *hacendado*. It is for Don Lucero Alvarado. I was told he rides with you."

By this time a crowd had gathered, including Luce, who stepped forward, hand extended. He read the crumpled, water-stained missive with a look of peculiar resignation on his face, then stalked off.

Nick perused the news from the capital and other areas, all the while wondering about the message for Luce. Finally, his brother ambled into camp and sat down beside him.

"Cigarette?" he asked, rolling one with deft fingers.

"When you have that cagey look on your face, I've learned to smell trouble," Nick replied, taking the tobacco. "You walked away a couple of hours ago looking like the sky had fallen on you. What's happened?" He lit up and inhaled the pungent smoke, then choked on it when Luce replied.

"Our father is dead. I've been summoned home. What would you say if I offered to trade places with you? I'll take charge of the men and you go to Gran Sangre as Don Lucero."

"Why the hell would you do that?" Nick asked incredulously.

Luce shrugged carelessly. "Why the hell not? I don't want to settle down, but I think you do." He studied Nick with hooded speculative eyes. "You've saved my life more than once and you've for sure taken a damn sight more interest in me than anyone else ever did." Then his mood shifted abruptly, as if he were uncomfortable, revealing too much. He grinned sharkishly. "Hell, just call it life's payback to you, big brother."

SPRING 1866

Nick coughed again, then rolled over on the wide soft mattress and awakened in the master bedroom at Gran Sangre. His dream had seemed as real as the hard wooden chest sitting beside his bed. He rolled up and reached over to it, picking up the makings for a cigarette. But he was no longer dreaming. He had done it, really done it, traded places with his half brother and come to Gran Sangre to claim the birthright his illegitimacy had denied him as Anselmo Alvarado's firstborn son.

Chapter 4

Wiping the sweat from his brow, Nick sat up on the edge of the bed and stared out the window. He was Don Anselmo's heir now, even if he was a nameless bastard the *hacendado* had never known existed. He felt nothing for the man who had sired him. At least that was what he had believed, but Luce told him he was only fooling himself.

Maybe he was. During his years growing up he had been shuffled from whorehouse to tawdry whorehouse as his mother's looks and price declined. Lottie had never talked about his old man. Hell, he had thought she didn't know who his father was. Nick assumed he was just another down-and-out farmer or tradesman like the average run of her customers. Around the time he had turned six or seven she had occasionally looked at him strangely—never with affection, for she did not consider him anything but a burden. Perhaps that was when he first began to resemble Don Anselmo. A few years later she had packed him off to Hezakiah Benson, who assured him that he was the spawn of Satan.

Life had been hellishly hard, but he had been so busy just surviving he had little chance to ruminate on his paternity. The very idea that he was the son of a noble house would have seemed laughable before he met Luce. Once their bargain had been struck, his brother had made him intimately acquainted with every detail of their ancestry, which went back all the way to fifteenth century Andalusia in Spain.

"What a joke on the old son of a bitch," he murmured to himself, looking around the big room filled with fine furniture and paintings. "Luce has turned into a hired killer who loves pulque and *putas*. And I end up with Gran Sangre and Mercedes."

Mercedes. He could picture her sleeping behind that heavy oak door, her dark gold hair spread like spilled doubloons across the white pillowcase. Just thinking about her made his body grow rigid with lust and ache. She was a fine lady with high morals and great pride, the sort of woman he had never dreamed of possessing.

There had been rich women from good families who had thrown themselves at him in the past. Hell, by the time he was seventeen he had learned that his looks were exceptional. All sorts of women fancied him and the aura of danger that his profession lent him only intensified the fascination. But he had always understood that such casual liaisons were mere diversions for bored rich ladies, who would not acknowledge that they even knew him if they passed on the street. He had grown to prefer the company of whores who were at least open and honest about their relationship with him.

But now he had a wife. *Your brother's wife*. "No, dammit, she's *mine* now," he growled into the silence. She had grown into a woman of spirit and, doubtless, had reason to despise Luce's touch. From the way his brother had described their brief time together, Nick could understand her unwillingness to share his bed. Yet when they had first laid eyes on each other, Nick had sensed a magnetic pull. She had responded to him, he was certain of it, and Nicholas Fortune was no novice at such matters. He wanted to win her over slowly, to woo and seduce her so she would come to him eagerly, desiring his touch. But he knew the role he was playing all too well. He knew Lucero Alvarado all too well. Patience was not one of his virtues, least of all where women were concerned.

Nick smiled grimly and inhaled the cigarette smoke. Luce liked his women with fire, but he also liked them cheap and lusty. And no woman, regardless of her station, would dare refuse his advances without risking his wrath. Nick had ridden with him for over six months and seen his casual brutality toward women, which was not unusual among soldiers. He had done some pretty ugly things himself, but never rape. However, on several occasions he'd come close to blows with Luce to keep him from taking an unwilling woman.

Luce had laughed and given in, humoring his "big brother" because it amused him to do so. But here at Gran Sangre, Nick knew that everyone expected the *patrón* to claim his husbandly rights. Not to do so would be completely out of character for Don Lucero. Mercedes herself knew she had made an impossible request. Luce would never let his own wife defy him. If he acceded to her wishes, people might become suspicious. But if he acted as Lucero, would he forever forfeit the chance for happiness with his beautiful wife?

The soft hum of insects and the melodic call of a night bird gave him no answer. He would have to make a decision soon. Muttering a curse, he ground out his cigarette and stretched out on the big lonely bed.

Nick slept late the next morning, a luxury his hard life on the trail as a *contre-guerrilla* had not afforded him. When he walked into the dining room, Baltazar bowed officiously. Seeing the food had been taken from the sideboard and Mercedes was not in the room, he asked, "Has my wife broken her fast yet?"

"Doña Mercedes always arises at six, sir. She rides, then eats her breakfast in the courtyard. She is working on accounts this morning. Shall I summon her?"

"No, don't disturb her now."

"Shall I tell Angelina to prepare your breakfast, *Patrón*?"

"Yes, and be certain the steak is seared and bloody," he reminded the old steward, knowing Luce's penchant for exceedingly rare meat, a taste he himself had acquired by force of necessity.

"But of course, *Patrón*," Baltazar replied, then vanished into the kitchen.

There had been so much to learn—and unlearn—while Luce had been coaching him. He was ambidextrous, a trait passed on from his mother and a handy skill for a professional soldier, but Luce was right-handed, so he had practiced doing everything with only his right hand. He loved French food in mellow cream sauces, but his Mexican half brother detested all things foreign and preferred the burning hot tang of chilies. Since Luce, too, had taken up smoking, there at least was one thing he had decided not to change. They were both skilled horsemen and when he had admired Luce's splendid Andalusian his brother had carelessly gifted him with Peltre, saying it would be remarked upon if he did not ride home on the big gray.

He was contemplating what to do first that day when the kitchen door opened behind him and a voluptuous woman with waist-length black hair and bold striking features emerged carrying a tray laden with a silver coffee service. The smoldering look in her dark eyes and the provocative sway of her hips as she set down her load would have indicated that they had been lovers even if he did not recognize the woman Luce had described in such detail.

"Cenci," he said coolly, appraising her with the hard, off-handed expression he had learned from watching Luce.

"Have you missed me, darling?" She wet her plump rosy lips and let her eyes undress him, moving down the length of his body from the open-collared white lawn shirt to his polished riding boots, then back up to his face. "They have marked you," she said in a husky voice, touching the scar on his cheek.

"A rebel saber grazed me."

"Every day seemed like a year waiting for you to return," she whispered, lowering her hand and letting it rest against his heart, feeling it beat through the thin fabric of his shirt.

He threw back his head and laughed. "I'll just bet you repined all alone in your bed from the day I left."

She moved closer to him, letting her breasts brush back and forth against his chest until her nipples stood out in dark, nubby points beneath the thin cotton of her low-cut *camisa*. "I have spent little time in bed," she said petulantly. "Your pale little stick of a wife has worked me like a peon. Look."

She held up her hands for his inspection. They were red

and work-roughened but so were his wife's. There the resemblance ended, for Innocencia's were large and heavy-boned as was her whole build. She was supple and curvaceous to the point of lushness, but in a few years her body would go to fat unlike the aristocratic slenderness of Mercedes' elegantly boned limbs. How could Luce have preferred this coarse slut to a beauty such as his wife?

Luce had cautioned him about his old mistress, saying if anyone could detect the masquerade, it would be her, for he had taken her as his lover when he was only eighteen years old. She knew every nuance of his body, how he made love, even how he tossed in his sleep. His brother had spent a great deal more time describing Innocencia than he had Mercedes, but seeing her now, Nick was not inclined to resume the old relationship.

Her busy hands quickly glided up his chest and around his neck as she fused her body against his from breasts to thighs, rotating her pelvis in blatant invitation. Her fingers dug into his scalp and she pulled his head to hers for a fierce kiss. Her mouth was wide and mobile as she opened it and plunged her tongue against the barricade of his lips, then withdrew with a pout.

"You no longer find me desirable after all your fancy French women in the capital? I can do anything they can—and more, my stallion—much, much more! Touch these and tell me you do not remember."

She seized his hands and placed them around her heavy breasts, cupping them as the large dark nipples protruded against her *camisa*. She arched her hips against his and whispered obscenities in his ear, moaning low.

He thrust her away none too gently as Luce would have done with a woman who no longer held his interest. "I'll decide when—and if—I want you, Cenci. And this isn't the time or the place."

"Surely you aren't afraid of what the high-and-mighty *patrona* will say? When she came here as a trembling bride, you ignored her. You took me on the floor of your father's library!"

"That was a long time ago. I've come home to perform my duty. To give Gran Sangre an heir—a legitimate heir."

"Ha! She is probably barren. You will soon tire of her and come back to me . . ." She slipped his restraining hands from her arms and quickly lifted her arms to his shoulders, wriggling her body against his. "Remember how it was, my great stallion?"

Mercedes stood transfixed in the doorway, having overheard only the last fragments of their conversation. She watched that brazen slut undulate her ample charms against Lucero's body and heard his cruel words. *I've come home to perform my duty.* A killing rage seized her and a red haze glazed her vision as she stepped into the room, her hands curled into claws ready to rip his mistress from her faithless husband's embrace. But before she could reach them Lucero seized Innocencia's wrists and pushed her away from him with a low oath.

"I told you no, dammit! I'm no longer the boy who found you irresistible."

Neither of them saw Mercedes enter the room. Innocencia stomped her foot and hissed at him, "You will be sorry for this. I am the one who taught you everything about making love."

"But I am the *patrona* of Gran Sangre and you are still a scullery maid," Mercedes said in a sharp voice.

Nicholas turned in surprise and observed the flushed cheeks and unholy glow in his wife's eyes as she advanced on them. *The little cat is jealous*. A strange surge of elation filled him as he raised one eyebrow mockingly and watched the rapid rise and fall of her breasts. She was dressed in a simple blue linen gown with a high collar of white lace at her throat. The cut was demure but the way it softly molded to her gentle curves had quite the opposite effect. He grinned rakishly at her, letting her know that he was aware of her jealousy.

Lucero's mistress smothered a gasp of outrage and stepped forward. "You cannot let her punish me, Don Lucero. You are the *patrón*."

"So I am, Cenci," he said evenly, his eyes never leaving the *patrona* as he placed a restraining hand on Innocencia's arm. "Return to your work. I'm certain Angelina has much to keep you busy."

She gave him a look of wounded outrage, then whirled around, sending her full red skirts flying, revealing well-turned ankles as she huffed off.

"I only hope she won't poison me when she serves my breakfast," he said dryly.

Mercedes watched him as he crossed the room to stand in front of her. She could feel the male heat emanating from him and fought the urge to back up a step. Instead, she met his sardonic gaze with a boldness she did not feel. "There was a time when you would've sent me away. You've changed, Lucero."

He shrugged carelessly, reaching up to touch a stray curl that rested on her breast. "Perhaps. But you *are* the *patrona* and she's only a servant."

"But she is your mistress."

He heard the icy accusation in her voice and knew his instinct about Lucero's story was right. His brother had hurt Mercedes by flaunting his affair with a household servant in front of his bride. "She *was* my mistress. My tastes have grown a bit more sophisticated over the years. Now I prefer blondes." He was rewarded by the deepening flush that stained her cheeks. No woman was immune to flattery.

The tension thickened between them as they stood with eyes locked. Her fists were clenched tightly at her sides, partially concealed in the folds of her gown. His fingers continued to play idly with her hair. Their breaths mingled, warm and swift.

"Here is your breakfast, *Patrón*. I fixed—oh, a thousand pardons." Angelina stood in the doorway holding a heavy serving tray heaped with steaming food.

Nicholas turned to her with a grin. "That's all right, Angelina. I'm starved for one of your famous steaks."

"I fear you'll find the meat tough and stringy. We had to butcher an old steer yesterday. It was all Hilario could run down." Mercedes knew her voice was breathy and that she spoke too fast, but she injected a note of justifiable anger into her words.

"Alas, it is true, *Patrón*. I have done the best I could with the steak. We have fine fresh peppers and tomatoes and Montezuma's spoons crisply baked to scoop up the salsa accompanying the meat." She held up the basket filled with fresh tortillas.

Nicholas looked from the old cook, who was now busily placing dishes on the table, back to Mercedes. "Hilario told me about the livestock, but surely on a hacienda as vast as Gran Sangre there must be remnants of our herds."

"I've already explained that the army appropriates what they will and the Juaristas steal what is left. There are pockets of cattle and horses scattered hither and yon, but precious few men to gather and tend them."

Nicholas rubbed his jaw consideringly. "I know you've already eaten, but join me for coffee while we discuss what to do about the livestock and the shortage of men." He pulled out a chair for her and his expression dared her to back down.

Warily she took a seat and Angelina poured them each a steaming cup of thick black coffee, then excused herself to return to the kitchen. When he picked up his cup and inhaled the fragrance, Mercedes said, "Coffee is getting scarcer every month. I'm told the fighting in the south has destroyed the current crop and disrupted shipping. It costs dearly and we can't afford to buy more when this runs out. I've ordered Angelina to cut it with chicory to make it last."

He took a sip. "You should see the gray muck soldiers drink. This tastes wonderful."

She studied him over the rim of her cup. "The war has changed you in many ways."

He flashed her a smile. "Only wait and you'll see many more . . . for the better, I hope."

What had possessed her to give him such an opening? The situation was growing altogether too intimate. She shifted the conversation back to the problems of running Gran Sangre.

"Hilario has only a dozen or so riders who are able-bodied enough to work the stock. We had over a hundred before you left."

"I might be able to recruit some men in Hermosillo. There are always mercenaries down on their luck, looking for a way to make a few pesos."

"We have no pesos to pay them with," she reminded him, "unless we sell more of the Alvarado heirlooms."

"To save Gran Sangre we may have to do that in time—but not just yet. I have accumulated a little gold over the past years. It's not much, but it's a start."

"I can imagine how you managed to 'accumulate' your gold," she said waspishly.

"No, my dear wife, I don't think you could possibly imagine at all . . . or that you'd want to," he added grimly.

She studied the haunted look in his eyes thoughtfully. Then when the silence became awkward, she said, "I have seen rough-looking young men idling about the plaza and markets when I was in Hermosillo. Perhaps they would be willing to work for you. I think you should ride to the city today."

His mood lightened abruptly and he chuckled. "Ah, yes, you'd like that—for me to take off on a two-day ride to Hermosillo, leaving you to your solitary bed. Who knows, fortune might even smile on you. I might fall off my horse and break my neck along the way. The grave of a horseman is always open."

She wrinkled her nose at the old cliché. "Don't be melodramatic. If all of Benito Juarez's rabble couldn't kill you, I doubt a ride to Hermosillo will do you in."

He took her hand and placed a tingling kiss on the back of it. "Ah, such tender wifely concern."

Nicholas did not ride to the capital that day. Instead he had Hilario take him out to inventory what livestock was left scattered over the hacienda, leaving word for Mercedes that he expected to be gone for the better part of a week. He had found a legitimate excuse to grant her request for a reprieve.

The ride was long and grueling as they traveled through mountainous high desert, searching out well-hidden water sources, which would attract horses and cattle yet be unknown to the armies that preyed upon them. Fortune was used to spending days in the saddle with the blazing sun beating mercilessly on his back and nights sleeping on cold rocky earth with the howling of wolves to lull him to sleep. Hilario kept up with him, making no complaints, showing no signs of tiring in spite of being twice his age.

The old vaquero had been born and bred in the wild Sonoran backcountry where the air was so clear and thin the wind could peel the skin right off a man's flesh. Temperatures rose to ninety by noon and fell to twenty by nightfall. He was one of the intrepid *hombres del norte* who used livestock worm medicine to treat their cuts and abrasions and inserted red-hot wires into the cavities of their rotting teeth to kill the nerves.

During the first day the old man was respectful and reticent, observing the proprieties of his class—he was a mere horse handler in the company of the *patrón*. That night Nicholas opened a bottle of mescal after the two of them had shared camp chores preparing their simple meal of frijoles and coffee.

Taking a long pull from the bottle of potent liquor, Fortune passed it to the old man. "It'll keep us warm through the night."

Hilario's wizened face reflected surprise for an instant. Then he reached for the bottle. His shrewd dark eyes glowed like coals as he studied his boss. "The war has changed you."

"So my wife says," Nicholas replied with a faint smile.

"In the old days you would not have kept up with me," the tough wiry old vaquero rejoined, taking a cautious sip and handing the bottle back to the *patrón*.

Without hesitation, Fortune took another swig and passed the mescal back. "In the old days I could not have kept up with you."

"Yes, you were a boy then, and I was a full-grown man. So we all grow older and perhaps wiser . . . if the fates are kind. And if they are not, who knows why?"

Nicholas cocked one black eyebrow. "You speak of fate the way a soldier does."

Hilario accepted the mescal again and took a far more generous pull this time. "I have learned to accept what life has to offer. I do not think God and his saints have any more interest in cowhands than they do in soldiers. We leave the praying to the peons."

He began rolling a cigarette and Nicholas did the same. They smoked and drank in companionable silence for a while.

"I will tell you a story of the peons at Pueblo San Isidor."

Fortune looked at the old man whose eyes crinkled with mirth now. "That's on old Don Esteban's land, isn't it?"

"Yes, but really it is a joke that could be told of any farmers. I do not know if it is true." He shrugged guilelessly, then launched into his tale. "Just before planting time, the peons came to the village priest and asked permission to take the statue of their patron saint out into the fields to guarantee a good planting. He agreed and they did so. The corn sprouted and the tender young shoots grew thickly, but then a terrible drought fell upon the land and the corn plants began to shrivel. Again they approached the priest, this time asking to take the statue of the Holy Virgin into the fields to pray for rain. Again he agreed and they did so. The rains began, but instead of the gentle drizzle they had prayed for, a terrible storm gathered and the heavens opened up. When it was finally over, every stalk of corn had been beaten to the earth and lay in the mud, dead and rotting.

"The villagers approached the priest for the third time, this time asking for the statue of Jesus. 'God help me!' the priest cried out. 'Surely you don't want to pray for more rain?' 'No,' their head man said, 'we want to take Him to the fields to show Him what sort of a mother he has!'"

As Fortune threw back his head and laughed, Hilario took a final swig draining the spider from the bottle of mescal. "As I said, *Patrón*, it is only a harmless story."

Still chuckling, Nicholas replied, "Somehow I don't think Father Salvador would find it at all amusing."

"Pah! That one. He would have us doing such penance that we would have more calluses on our knees than we do on our hands."

"He's certainly kept my mother busy at her beads as long as I can remember," Nicholas said, recalling the childhood memories of Doña Sofia that Luce had shared with him. Although Lottie Fortune had certainly not been devout, there were similarities in the way he and his brother had missed having a mother's love.

"He came here as her confessor when she arrived to wed your father. His first loyalty has always been to your mother."

"I would expect he'd support her against my father."

"And your father against your wife, as well, but it is not my place to speak of what goes on inside the great house. The mescal has loosed my tongue."

Nick's lethargic demeanor changed. He sat up and studied the old man. "Don Anselmo and Father Salvador always hated one another. Why would the old priest take his side in anything?"

Hilario grew uncomfortable. It was foolish of him to bring up the plight of the young *patrona*, for he knew Don Lucero and his lady did not get on any better than Don Anselmo and Doña Sofia had. "Your lady had to make difficult choices after you went to war, *Patrón*. You know how your father enjoyed life in Hermosillo. He was not much interested in being *patrón* of Gran Sangre."

"He preferred the high life in the city, cards, drinking, horse races, cockfights, women, yes. Mercedes told me she was forced to take over running the estate even before he fell ill. I wasn't certain whether to believe her or not."

"Believe her, Don Lucero. She has worked harder than anyone on the place."

"And even though he refused to do the work, he begrudged letting a woman usurp his place when he was away?" He could read the truth on the old man's face. "It must've been hell for her. And that rigid old priest would've thought it unnatural for a mere female to accomplish what she did."

"He scolded her for riding with me and my men. We are a godless lot, you know," Hilario said with a roguish grin, then sobered. "But she always stood by us, even when it cost her a fearful penance. She held Gran Sangre together for the day of your return, *Patrón*. Now that you are here, things will be better."

"I hope so, Hilario, I hope so." *If the little spitfire will give up the power she's grown so fond of wielding without a fight.* "Do you think we'll be able to get any of the drifters in Hermosillo to ride for us?"

"You told me you can pay in gold. There is an old saying. No matter how high the chickens roost, they always come down for corn. Times are hard and men who do not want to be soldiers still need to eat. You will find your riders."

"I only hope we find enough horses and cattle to make them worth the hiring," Nicholas groused, poking at the fire.

"Do not fear. Once we are far enough away from where the soldiers can patrol in comfort, we will find horses and cattle aplenty."

Hilario was as good as his word. The next afternoon they crested a ridge and looked down on a wide stretch of open grassland dotted with fine fat longhorns. By the third day out they had located a band of horses led by one of his father's prize Andalusian stallions. It was apparent that there was indeed much left to salvage on Gran Sangre land now that he was there to lead the work. They headed back to the great house on the fourth day, filled with plans for gathering the herds and wintering them in the box canyons of the western mountains where they would be safe from marauders, imperial or republican.

Late that afternoon they rode up to the corrals at the ranch, dust-covered, bone weary and elated. Hilario handed his horse over to one of the boys in the stable and then headed to his *jacal*. Not wanting to trust the youth with Peltre, Nicholas led the lathered stallion into his stall for a rubdown.

The low-ceilinged quarters were hot and close. Earthy aromas of man and horse blended together as he worked on the big gray. Midway through the task, he peeled off his shirt and tossed it onto the stall railing along with his weapons.

After a ride to the fields to check on the crops, Mercedes, too, was hot and tired as she dismounted in front of the stable. The old dun mare she had managed to salvage from confiscation was no prize but she treasured the horse. She patted the mare and stepped inside to see that the boy took care of her. The sudden dimness of the interior caused her to blink. Dust motes swam before her eyes and she heard sounds coming from the rear of the long building, the soft whickering of a horse and a man's low silky voice, crooning to it. Lucero's voice!

He's back! Her heart accelerated as she shooed the mare quietly into a stall and padded soundlessly through the soft straw toward them. As her eyes adjusted to the light, she could make out her husband's figure. He had his back turned to her as he gathered up his things, laying his gun belt over one bare shoulder and slinging a damp shirt carelessly over the other. Should she slip into a stall and avoid a confrontation? She looked a fright, dusty and disheveled. No. After all, it was hardly as if she wanted to attract him. She stood in the aisle as he turned and walked around the stall door, then stopped directly in front of her, startled at her sudden appearance.

"I thought I heard someone," he said as his eyes swept from her tangled mane of tawny hair down the length of the threadbare brown riding habit. The color would not have favored most women, but Mercedes was not most women. Her sun-gilded skin and amber eyes took on a rich luster when she wore the warm chocolate shade. In spite of being old and much mended, the habit was molded to her soft curves. She had unbuttoned the collar low enough to reveal the slight swell of her breasts.

She could feel his wolf eyes scorching her breasts and fought not to fumble with the buttons of her jacket to cover herself. Instead she faced him pugnaciously. "We didn't expect you back until tomorrow. There's little for dinner, but I'll have Angelina kill a chicken. Lazaro will draw water for your tub."

His body was soaked with sweat and caked with yellow dust. He grinned. "Do you find me offensive?" he asked, adjusting the weight of the holster at his shoulder and stepping closer to her.

"In more ways than you could imagine," she snapped, angry at her reaction to his nearness. She could smell the scent of his perspiration, male and pungent yet not an unpleasant blend with the scent of leather and horse. Beads of sweat formed tiny rivulets, some catching in the pelt of hair on his chest, others running lower to seep into the waistband of his tight black trousers. When they were first married, he had shared her bed, but she had never before seen him naked for he always came to take her in darkness, then departed quickly when the deed was done. His body looked as hard and sleek as it had felt when he lay atop her, pumping his seed into her unreceptive womb.

Her eyes seemed to have a will of their own, unable to get enough of studying the muscles beneath his sun-bronzed skin, which was marked with numerous scars, some small nicks, others large and jagged. She stared at one awful slash that ran from his chest around his side. His words finally broke into her trance.

"A saber scar, compliments of one of General Escobedo's soldiers," he said dryly, amused by her untutored fascination with his body, yet also concerned she might wonder how he had acquired so many scars since she had seen him last. Most of the wounds, including the saber slash, were old. He hoped she could not tell that. "It's been an . . . active four years."

Mercedes blinked, then met his mocking eyes. "Yes, I can see it has, but it would be inappropriate for the *patrón* to stride into the *sala* half-dressed and armed like a brigand.

Would you please replace the shirt and leave your guns here for one of the servants to fetch?"

"You asked that rather prettily for such a tart-tongued wench. Miss me, darling Mercedes?" He reached up and took hold of the unbuttoned lapel of her jacket, pulling her closer to him. "I'm not the only one who's inappropriately undressed." He sniffed her damp skin, which smelled of lavender blended with her delicate female musk. "And in need of a bath as well. Shall we ask Lazaro to fill a large tub for both of us to share?"

She tried to jerk back. Genuine alarm filled her eyes. "Certainly not!" Her hands pressed against the springy hair on his chest. He towered over her, satiny muscles bunched in his arms as he drew her closer until she could feel his silver belt buckle press against her rib cage and the cartridges on his gun belt cut into the tender flesh of her shoulder. The scabbard holding that awful knife jabbed into her hip when she tried to twist away.

He laughed and drew her closer, tangling his hand in the mass of hair trailing down her back. "God, you are a beauty," he growled low, looking as if he might devour her.

Mercedes could feel the bulge growing in his tight breeches as he held her between his thighs and rocked his hips against hers, lowering his mouth toward hers as his hand immobilized her head. This was what she had feared from the moment he returned to Gran Sangre, or so she tried to tell herself. She did not want him forcing her to submit to him, his body punishing hers. And yet . . . she felt her heart pounding in her chest as his warm breath fanned her cheek. She tried to remain cool and passive, to be the limp rag doll he had scornfully accused her of being four years ago.

But now everything felt different. She could not remain passive. A part of her tensed, eager for him to kiss her. But he surprised her by releasing her instead. She stumbled back, dazed.

Nicholas had never done anything more difficult in his life than let her go. He ached with wanting her and had come within an inch of branding her with a harsh punishing kiss. *That's the way Luce would do it. I'm not Luce, dammit*!

"Tonight," he whispered softly.

A threat or a promise? She was not certain which he intended—or how she felt about it either way.

Chapter 5

Nicholas watched her step away from him, her breath still coming in short jagged gasps. Those luscious breasts rose and fell quickly, then subsided as she forced herself to regain her calm. He grinned at her with Luce's arrogant nonchalance and raised his hands in mock surrender. Glancing down at the blatantly visible proof of how badly he wanted her, he said, "You see how it is between us, love."

"I see you're the same rutting stallion who couldn't leave a female between the age of fourteen and forty untouched," she snapped, then wanted to bite her tongue. Enraging him was stupid and would only guarantee that he made his retribution all the more swift and ugly.

But he surprised her with a rich low chuckle and slid the gun belt from his shoulder, tossing it on the top rail of Peltre's stall. Then he reached down to his long hard thigh and unfastened the leather tie of his knife scabbard. He laid it next to the gun belt.

Turning back to her he shrugged. "Now, you see? I'm completely defenseless before you."

"You have never been defenseless since the day of your birth!"

"That's not true at all, Mercedes. When I—" He stopped short, aghast at what he had been about to blurt out. God above, what was the matter with him! The woman made him lose all judgment. Pretty soon he would give away the whole charade and end up a landless bastard with his gun for hire again. *Keep your wits about you. Play Luce, dammit!*

She saw the flash of anguish pass over his face, but before

she could even wonder what had triggered it, he was grinning in that old hateful, lascivious way. He shrugged his damp, crumpled shirt over his broad shoulders. She found herself licking her lips and swallowing nervously as she watched the play of bronzed muscles beneath the sheer white linen. "I'll see to dinner and your bath," she said with all the dignity she could muster, turning around before he said anything more humiliating.

He called after her retreating figure, "Don't forget your own bath, Mercedes. We wouldn't want to dirty the bed linens with sweat."

Her back stiffened slightly, but she did not break stride. If he was the rutting stallion she accused him of being, then she was an elegant little mare—*his* elegant little mare. Tonight would be good, he vowed as he called the stable boy over and instructed him to feed Peltre and then bring his weapons to the house.

By the time he reached the top of the stairs from the entry hall, he was whistling to himself, but then he saw the narrow black figure of the priest bearing down the hall toward him. Damn, what did Sofia's confessor want with him? He thought of Hilario's sacrilegious jokes and smiled to himself as he greeted the older man. "Father Salvador, you wish to see me?"

"I'm glad you have returned. A matter of some urgency has arisen. A rider from Hermosillo brought this for the *patrón* this afternoon." He handed an envelope with the seal broken to Nicholas.

Frowning at the open seal, Fortune flipped the letter over. It was addressed to Don Anselmo. As he reached inside, the priest hastily explained, "Because it was sent to your father and you were not at home, I felt it my duty to see if I could resolve the matter."

"The rider—did he wait?" Fortune asked as he unfolded the small sheet of plain, inexpensive paper.

"No. He was paid by the Ursuline Sisters only to deliver this on his way to Durango," the priest replied nervously, watching the *patrón* scan the small cribbed handwriting.

Most Noble Sir,

As you know, we have cared for the infant you sent to us four and a half years ago, along with her mother, Rita Hererra, who worked in the kitchens of the convent. I regret to inform you that Senorita Hererra has been stricken with cholera and passed on to the blessed mercy of our Lord this past week.

We would be most happy to continue looking after Rosario, who is a bright and beautiful little girl, but the epidemic which swept away her mother has also claimed many of my sisters in Christ, leaving our convent desperately understaffed during this turbulent time. I fear for her safety if she remains with us. Therefore, I regretfully request that you reclaim your son's child and see to her upbringing elsewhere.

Understanding the delicate nature of the situation, may I be so bold as to suggest you seek assistance from the Convent of the Holy Cross in Guaymas, which has been as yet untouched by the war. A small monetary gift accompanying the child, as you sent to us with her mother, would be greatly appreciated by Mother Superior Mary Agnes. If I do not receive word from you by the end of the month, I shall be forced to return Rosario to Gran Sangre.

The closing of the letter with its formal title and signature blurred before his eyes. He crumpled it, balling it up tightly as his mind raced. *A child.* His own flesh and blood, his niece, and Luce had never even mentioned her or her mother! Of course, knowing how Luce felt about women, he probably did not deem a cast-off serving wench and her illegitimate brat worthy of remembering. Luce was his father's son all right.

At the time the baby and her mother were being packed off to Hermosillo, arrangements for the betrothal between Mercedes Sebastián and Lucero Alvarado were being finalized. Don Anselmo had decided to get rid of the embarrassment of his son's bastard, but why would he bother when he let Luce cavort with Innocencia so openly, in front of his bride? Grimly Nicholas realized the old man simply had not been able to control Luce, else he would never have allowed his only son and heir to ride off to war before performing his conjugal duty.

Father Salvador coughed delicately, breaking into his ruminations. "Er, what are you going to do, *Patrón*? Your lady mother would be greatly upset if this child were to arrive in such a public manner."

"The child is her own granddaughter," Fortune said coldly.

"The child is the get of a sinful young woman you flaunted in front of God and your family," Father Salvador said in confusion. "When she confessed her fall to me, you wanted no more part of her than did your father. Surely that has not changed. I will go to Hermosillo and take her to—"

"No!" Nicholas interrupted furiously, then clamped a rein on his temper and continued calmly, "You will do nothing. I was planning to ride into the city myself on business. I will see to my daughter."

The look of incredulity on the priest's face indicated how out of character such a statement was for a man like Lucero Alvarado. Did he suspect that Nicholas was an impostor? He had known Luce since his half brother was a boy, although Luce had made it clear that he had always heartily detested the priest and stayed as far away from him as possible. Don Anselmo had even brought in tutors for his son so his wife's confessor did not have to soil his holy soul by teaching a son of Satan like Luce.

No, the sour old priest disliked him, but that only aided Nicholas' masquerade for Father Salvador expected the *patrón* to behave scandalously. He gave the priest an insolent grin and sauntered past him as if he had not a care on earth.

While he prepared for dinner, however, Nicholas felt anything but carefree. What would he do about the complication of females in his life? If he brought Rosario home, not only would it infuriate Doña Sofia, it would also humiliate Mercedes. She had already inadvertently betrayed how shamed and inadequate her husband's affair with Innocencia had made her feel. Bringing the physical proof of his philandering to raise as his own child would no doubt build a wall between them he could never breach.

And he did want to breach the defenses of this proud and lonely woman who had become his wife. *His* wife. When had he begun thinking of her as his instead of Luce's? *From the moment you laid eyes on her and smelled her lavender scent and knew he was mistaken about her passion, that's when.*

Damn. What could he do about Rosario? Follow Father Salvador and the Mother Superior's suggestion and salve his conscience by sending her to Durango with a sack full of coins? That was certainly an easier way to handle matters than claiming her as his own at this late date. Yet the idea sat sour on his gut, eating at him like a canker. He knew all too well what it felt like to be shipped off, to live with people who wanted you no more than had those who already deserted you.

"She's my blood. I can't leave her with strangers," he muttered grimly, wondering how disastrously his decision would affect Mercedes. Bringing home a bastard child would be uncharacteristic enough for the *patrón*. He dared not defer to her wishes and avoid his duty to provide a legitimate male heir. Anyway, the sparks between them this afternoon had been undeniable. The lady may have thought she wanted to sleep alone, but he knew women. And he knew damn well she was mistaken. If he had the time to woo her slowly he could convince her of the truth, but that was not an option.

Cursing the rotten timing, he slipped on his jacket and inspected the elegantly clad stranger in the mirror. Luce's suit of charcoal gray wool fit him with the grace only bestowed by custom tailoring on a man of superb proportions. A white silk shirt and snowy ruffled stock accented his sun-darkened face. He studied that face, feature by feature, as if discovering it for the first time.

My father's face. Hispanic, haughty and hawkish. Yet did it hold the indolent decadence that he detected in Don Anselmo's portrait, hanging in the *sala*? He hoped not, although he had certainly never taken any pride in his mother's heritage. He had seen firsthand the stock from which she had sprung. Perhaps there was some distant ancestor on the Alvarado side who had character and integrity.

Sliding a sapphire signet ring on his finger, he grinned sardonically at the reflection in the mirror. Here he was wearing another man's clothes and jewelry, living under false pretenses in his house and planning to seduce his wife tonight—and he dared to think about integrity! He had done many things to survive over the years, things of which he was not proud. Perhaps rescuing Rosario would erase a few of the sins weighing on his soul, not the least of which would be his enjoyment of the beauteous Mercedes.

She was waiting for him in the dining room, dressed in a demure-looking little gown of sprigged muslin in various shades of rose and pale pink. "You look like a concoction of sugar candy," he said, causing her to turn suddenly and face him. She clutched a glass of wine in both hands. "Of course, the neckline is rather . . . concealing, but the way you fill out the bodice almost makes up for that deficiency. Anyway, since I'll soon see what lies beneath the layers of clothing, it doesn't really matter, does it?"

"You delight in tormenting me with your crude sexual taunts, don't you, Lucero?" Her tone of voice indicated it was a rhetorical question. "I used to shiver and blush and stammer when you made remarks like that."

He stalked closer. "Oh, I can still make you blush, as pinkly as your girlishly sweet dress. Did you choose it to make me feel I was robbing the cradle again—taking that insipid little virgin who bored me so four years ago?" Two could play at rhetorical questions, he indicated with a smile. "As you've already made quite clear to me, you aren't that fainting miss any longer." His eyes swept to the glass in her hand. "For courage? Surely the *patrona* of Gran Sangre doesn't need it." He took the heavy crystal glass and raised it to his lips, turning the rim to drink from the exact spot where her lips had touched. "You may not faint, but I promise to make you shiver . . . in satisfaction."

His low, sibilant words sent a frisson of white heat coursing through her like a bolt of lightning. He was standing beside her now and she could feel his warm breath on her cheek as he bent down and pressed his mouth to the curve of her throat. *Blessed Virgin*! She had thought his words had scalded her. What did the fiery burn of those beautiful lips do?

She would not flinch away like the insipid little virgin he named her. But neither could she stand as unresponsively still as she wished to do. The strange, mesmerizing combination of his sexual hunger and his tenderness made her ache to melt against him.

He could feel her sway imperceptibly toward him. Sitting through a formal dinner at the large oak table would only allow her more time to think of what lay ahead and resurrect all sorts of long-buried fears. The way she studied the wine bottle on the sideboard indicated her need for its false courage. Best he strike now. She was showing some promise of giving in to the naturally passionate instincts he sensed.

Suddenly her husband's arm swept around her. He picked her up and pressed her against his chest in one fluid motion that left her so breathless with surprise all she could do was let out a small gasp. "Lucero—"

"To hell with dinner. We'll eat later. I've plans for us that will work up sufficient appetites for Angelina to roast us two fat chickens!"

Just then the old cook stepped through the heavy doorway to the kitchen, carrying a steaming tray which she almost dropped in amazement. Her meaty reddened hands tightened on the handles as she set it on the sideboard, then watched the *patrón* carry his wife from the room. Her expression was impassive but for the sadness in her dark eyes.

Nicholas half expected Mercedes to struggle or scream out in protest as he carried her across the foyer to the wide curving stairs.

Instead, her voice was low and rigid with controlled fury. She hissed in his ear, "Do your worst. I cannot stop you. Father Salvador would only remind me that it's my duty to submit to my husband."

The bitterness in her voice almost made him relent. She sounded so desolate. Again he cursed his brother for treating her so shamefully, then vowed to show her how different things could be between a man and his woman.

And she is my woman, my wife. Or, she would be after tonight. When he reached the door to his bedchamber, Baltazar stood inside it, a set of clean towels on his arm. Like Angelina and the rest of the old house servants, he had learned to school his emotions, revealing nothing to his master. Yet there remained a silent reproach in his eyes. He held the door ajar for the *patrón*, then stepped outside it so Don Lucero could enter with his wife in his arms.

Mercedes could not bear to look at the dignified old servant who had always been so kind to her. She stared over her husband's shoulder as he turned to step through the door with her. That was when she saw Innocencia. The other woman stood at the top of the staircase staring at them. Her whole body was rigid with rage and her face was contorted with hate. The venom in her black eyes was a palpable thing.

Just as quickly as her rival's face flashed before her, it vanished as she was carried into the softly lit bedroom, his room. In her four years on Gran Sangre she had never set foot inside it, although she knew his mistress often had.

It should be Innocencia, not me, in his arms. All too soon it would be again, she was certain.

Unaware of Innocencia's presence outside, Nicholas strode toward the bed as Baltazar quietly closed the door behind them. He could feel a renewed stiffness in her body as he neared the big canopied bed, but he attributed it to the proximity of the bed and all it must symbolize to her. Slowly he set her on her feet beside it, still holding her closely against his body.

"This is your bed," she said coldly. "You've never brought me here before because you always have other visitors in the night after you've finished with me."

After you've finished with me. The words spoke volumes to him. "Ah, wife, but I don't plan to finish with you until first cock," he whispered with a chuckle at the pun. First cock was a Mexican idiom for the rising sun.

Fury sluiced over her in fresh waves. At least before he had strode through his door under the cover of darkness and done the hateful act quickly, then left her alone while he cavorted with his harlot. "What cruel new game do you play, Lucero?"

"Not cruel at all, but a very delightful game, I promise," he whispered, ignoring her frosty facade and her anger. He stood back and studied her with the deliberation of an artist examining a potential model for a nude painting.

Her heart came leaping into her throat when she divined his intent. "Surely you don't . . . you can't expect me to . . ."

He let his hand graze her jaw, then brush down the curve of her breast. "Yes, I can . . . and yes, you will."

"The candles—at least douse the candles." She broke out of her horrified trance and tried to step around him and seize the silver snuffer lying on the table beside the freshly turned back bed.

Nicholas reached out and wrapped his hand around her wrist, holding it firmly but gently, preventing her from achieving her goal. "We would only fumble around and get tangled in our finery if we attempted to undress in the dark."

Such reasonableness. Such sadistic pleasure. No doubt Innocencia loved to undress for him! Mercedes looked at his restraining hand, so large and dark, enveloping her slender golden arm. Then she forced herself to look up into his face. His eyes were hooded but she could see the eerie silver lights that sparked in their black depths. His features were taut with hunger. Male predatory hunger. She could not escape, but she determined at least to salvage a shred of her pride.

"You must allow me the courtesy of summoning my maid to help me undress. A gentleman—"

"I'm afraid you'll find me no longer a gentleman—if I ever was one. War does bring out a man's true colors," he added wryly. *Mine and Luce's*. He placed his hands on her shoulders and turned her around. "I'll be your maid, for tonight, beloved."

She allowed him to handle her. What choice was there? To fight and claw, kick and scream? Humiliate herself by letting his mistress and all the other servants hear how he forced her? No, but neither would she cringe and shiver. No, damn him, she would not shiver—in fear or pleasure. Least of all pleasure!

Yet the gentle urgency of his touch, the way he breathed low and raggedly, had a peculiar effect on her. She felt wanted, cherished as his hands deftly unlooped the long row of tiny buttons down her back and then slid the frothy pink dress from her shoulders. His lips were warm and firm as they trailed soft, moist kisses over the skin he bared, inch by inch until the gown and its petticoats fell to the rug, pooling around her ankles. Then he turned her until she faced him and he cupped her breasts in his hands.

Mercedes knew she was far less well-endowed than Innocencia. Was he making invidious comparisons? Her face flamed in embarrassment when she felt her body betray her, reacting with a strange new volition to his caresses. Her breasts seemed to swell and grow taut, and her nipples burned as his fingers circled them through the silk and lace of her camisole, teasing them to pucker and stand in hard little points. Sweet Mother of God, what was happening to her? She wanted to ask him where he had learned such devilish tricks, but perhaps he had always known them, just never showed her before. And how she wished he would not do it now!

Nicholas felt her response and smiled inwardly as he pulled her to him and lowered his head to kiss her throat, pulling the pins from the heavy mass of her perfumed hair and running it across his face so he could inhale the fragrance and feel the silky softness. Slowly he slipped her camisole straps from her shoulders and then tugged the lacy undergarment down until her breasts were free. They were perfect pearl-white globes that stood up proudly with their palest pink nipples at rigid attention. His mouth went dry just thinking of feasting on them. He lowered his head and suckled greedily, one hand splayed across her back, holding her to him while the other tore the front lacing loose and tossed the frilly thing to the floor.

Mercedes stood still as the room spun around her and her knees turned to jelly. His hands and his mouth were everywhere, leaving her naked, exposed and wanting him to continue. She clenched her fists at her sides to keep from burying them in his dark shaggy hair and pulling him closer to her for more of the sweet torture. No! Any overt sign, any move on her part to show she wanted this would only lead to shame when he left her. And he would leave her for Innocencia. She felt her nails bite into her palms and was grateful for the distraction of the pain.

She did not fight him as he untied the tapes of her lacy pantalets and slid his hand inside. But neither did she touch him of her own volition. Her arms remained stiffly at her sides. He cupped her soft buttocks and kneaded them gently, pressing her hips against his lower body, willing her response, knowing she felt the heat building between them. Her breasts gave that away. So would her soft moist nether lips, he was certain.

Go slow, give her time to become accustomed, his mind hammered out, but his body craved nothing so much as to throw her on the bed and plunge inside of her sweetness. Instead, he gently took her into his arms and laid her on the bed. Then he began to undress himself, forcing his hands not to tear the buttons from his shirt or rip the carefully tied stock off his neck. All the while he looked at her, lying bathed in the pale golden light, willing her to return his gaze, to watch him as he had watched her.

She could feel his eyes scorching every inch of her half-naked flesh. The rustling sound of his clothing sliding off made her burn to look at his body. But she dared not. Yet even with her eyelids lowered discreetly, she could envision him as he had been that afternoon, with the clever patterns of black hair that covered his wide chest and narrowed in a vee over his hard flat belly. The dull thud when he tossed his boots away was quickly followed by the sharp snap of his trousers being yanked down and kicked off.

When she sensed him standing completely naked beside the bed, staring down at her, Mercedes could no longer continue the pretext. Her eyes flew open and locked with his. Hungry black wolf's eyes glowed silver in the dim light. A feral grimace distorted his perfectly chiseled features, giving them a satanic cast. She had never seen him naked before, had never in her wildest imaginings thought she wished to, but she did now.

Her eyes, like the rest of her body, seemed to have a will of their own as they swept down the hard dark planes of his face to his shoulders and that hairy powerful chest, then lower to where the sun had not touched his skin, to where his male organ pulsed like a great living spear, ready to impale her and put his seed in her womb. He had caused her such pain and degradation in the past, yet in spite of that, she recognized that he was beautiful, a splendid male animal.

With his eyes still gazing into hers, he lowered one knee into the soft mattress and slowly sank down beside her. She remained rigidly still, her hands lying at her hips, small fists balled up tightly. Taking a deep breath to steady himself, he reached down and removed her slippers. Her feet were small with delicate bones. He caressed her instep and watched her toes curl in reflex. Smiling he slid his hands up her shapely calves and thighs to pull down her garters and then peel the sheer silk stockings from one sleek leg, then the other. Taking a slender ankle in his hand, he raised her leg and trailed kisses along her calf up her inner thigh until he felt her quiver. *More progress.*

"Raise your hips," he commanded hoarsely as his hands grasped her pantalets and began to pull them down.

She would be as stark naked as he! Fighting down the panic that flared up again, she did as he demanded. Even the lace of her undergarment felt erotic as it scratched her skin sliding down. Then he threw the frilly thing away and replaced it with the heat of his hands. Long fingers teased and pressed, glided and stroked until she was desperate to remain passive beneath his ministrations. She was certain she could bear no more without writhing in delirium. Through clenched teeth she bit off the words, "Get on with it and be damned!"

Nicholas felt a stab of fury at her sudden outburst. Every fiber of his body screamed at him to do precisely that. But he knew her fears made her lash out. He rolled down and covered her with his big body.

Heat enveloped her as he pressed her into the mattress. In the past he had never undressed her, only pulled up her nightrail to plunge into her, but at least this contact was more familiar. She dug her nails into the mattress and waited for the dry rasping pain to begin. It did not. Instead he rolled to one side of her and kissed her cheek and ear, then buried his face in her hair to breathe in her fragrance. Murmuring low love words, he teased the inside of her earlobe with his tongue. His scorching hot mouth placed light brushing kisses across her face, on her eyelids, nose, then her lips.

He felt her resistance as his tongue rimmed her mouth and pressed against the tightly closed seam of her lips. Continuing the seduction of the kiss, he cradled her head in one arm and used the other hand to graze over her breasts, then glide lower to the pale concave silk of her belly. God, she was so soft and smooth, so perfectly formed, fitted just for him as he held her molded against his side with his thigh lying possessively across hers. When he inched lower, grazing the silky curls at her mound and caressing the damp folds of her sex, she gasped. At once his tongue plunged into her opened mouth and pillaged it as his hand stroked her until the creamy moisture told him that she was ready for him.

In spite of her vow, she was trembling. The raw jolt of sensation when he touched her there would not have been such a surprise if she had ever felt the least flicker of it in their previous encounters. But she never had. The heat pooling deep in her belly and the ache of her breasts were completely new, too. What was he doing to her? *Soon I'll be begging him to take me*! She whimpered in protest and tried to writhe away, but he held her fast.

Nicholas had to have her now or he would spill his seed uselessly, so desperate was he to feel that final caress of her soft, beautiful little body. When she cried out, he lost the last vestige of his control. He had not had a woman in the past several months. Perhaps it had been a mistake to pass up the invitation of the camp followers, but none of them had appealed to him any more than Innocencia did. What man would want a coarse slovenly slut when he could have a beautiful woman like Mercedes? His brother was a fool, but Nicholas was grateful as he moved over Mercedes and parted her thighs.

She felt the hard tip of his phallus probe at the opening and braced herself for the hurt, but it did not come. Always in the past she had been dry and sore, but in the past he had never done such things to her as he did tonight. Was this how a man cavorted with harlots like Innocencia? The chilling thought served to erase the slick gliding pleasure as his staff plunged deep.

Nicholas felt her stiffen and panic when he started to enter her but there was no way he could stop now. He knew she was ready, her petals wet and creamy. His throbbing shaft slid all the way to the hilt and he froze, afraid to move lest it all be over far too quickly. She was so tight and hot all he could think of was to pump away to glorious oblivion. That was what his brother would have done had always done before. He was sure of it. But he would not. He could feel her tense, lying perfectly still except for the pounding of her heart next to his. Making low crooning sounds, he tilted her face up to his and kissed her again. Then slowly, an inch at a time he raised his hips, fighting for control, until he could set a careful, even rhythm.

He longed to have her wrap her arms around his shoulders and arch up to meet his thrusts, but this was all too new to her, she who had never been loved before, only hurt and humiliated. "I'll make this as good for you as I can . . . for as long as I can last, love," he murmured against her mouth.

The words alarmed her. Her fingers dug into the mattress as he moved over her, sliding in and out, relentlessly, for what seemed an incredibly long time in spite of the fact that it was infinitely less uncomfortable than it had ever been before. In fact, the slick hot friction was beginning to feel altogether too pleasant. She could not succumb to his wiles. He had returned home to play a new sort of game for God only knew what reasons. The only thing she knew for certain was that Innocencia would be waiting when Lucero finished with her.

That thought was enough to keep her rigidly immobile as he labored above her. She could feel droplets of his perspiration fall onto her face and shoulders as his sweat-slicked body pressed into hers. Then he gave a strangled cry, an oath that sounded almost like an endearment. His whole body stiffened and shuddered. This was familiar to her. Soon it would all be over. His shaft swelled and throbbed deep inside her and he collapsed on top of her, panting for breath.

Mercedes expected him to roll quickly away and leave the bed. He always had in the past, but that was in *her* bed. Would he expect her to get up and crawl away naked to her room? She waited. He did not move, only supported his weight on his forearms and cradled her.

Finally he pulled out of her, but instead of releasing his hold on her he further surprised her by holding her close to his side with one arm while he reached down for the sheet at the foot of the rumpled bed. The soft linen settled over their bodies as he lay back down, fitting her against him. Obviously he did not intend for her to leave just yet.

Nicholas could not remember when he had ever felt so sated. She was restless and unsatisfied as yet, he knew, but there was no remedy for that tonight. Her body would be tender now and it would take time to teach it to accept the pleasure, to give in to her own release. With that pleasant thought tantalizing him, he drifted off to sleep.

Mercedes felt his even breathing and knew he slept. She wanted desperately to leave his bed, to be alone, to think and assimilate all that had happened between them in the brief time since he returned home. The candles had burned very low and one by one now they sputtered out, leaving the room in the silvery darkness of a moonlit Sonoran night. His arm still held her fast. Dare she remove it and slip from the bed?

Cautiously she raised up and folded back the sheet. He stirred in his sleep. She froze. Then he relaxed again and murmured something in what sounded like English. But of course that could not be, for Lucero despised the language and understood very little of it. He had been forced to learn a smattering of French but spoke it haltingly and only when social occasions had made it imperative.

Perhaps during his years in the war he had learned English, too. His experience had certainly changed him dramatically. She could not resist studying him as he slept. With those hypnotic fathomless eyes closed, she could drink her fill of his male beauty with no fear of taunting reprisal. And she realized suddenly that she wanted to look upon him, even touch him, but touching might awaken him and that would be humiliating.

She would be content just to study him with her eyes. His face was younger-looking in repose, the hard, dangerous aura gone. There was something subtly different about his features. Maybe the scar? But surely it could not change much. She inventoried his high sculpted brow with those dramatic eyebrows and thick black eyelashes, that perfect long blade of a nose, the high cheekbones and the mouth. Just thinking of what he had done to her with that mouth made her whole body burn.

She had to get away. Some intuition made her realize that if she did not and he awakened to take her again, she might do something very foolish. Very foolish indeed.

Chapter 6

Nicholas awakened to the sounds of a cock crowing and blinked his eyes, then rolled over in the wide bed and sat up. The delicate essence of lavender still clung to the rumpled sheets, mixed with the scent of sex. But Mercedes was gone. He felt a stab of loss which took him by surprise. Sleeping through the night with a woman after making love was not something he customarily did. In fact, he had never done it. Yet he had wanted to sleep with the woman everyone called his wife.

"She *is* my wife," he said, then realized how that sounded. Was he trying to convince himself that she belonged to him? She belonged to his brother, who had bequeathed her to him with no more thought than he had given when handing over Peltre. Lucero had not valued Mercedes, but Nicholas did, most probably too much for his own good.

Fortune had agreed to the charade to gain Gran Sangre and respectability. He had wanted the land, and if he were honest, he wanted the recognition that he belonged to it, that he could be the *patrón*. Mercedes had only been incidental to his plans when he had set out to assume Luce's identity. The "pallid plain little virgin" his brother described had not interested him any more than did the coarse and lusty Innocencia.

But that was before he saw the *patrona* of Gran Sangre and realized just how wrong his brother had been. No surprise there, he thought ruefully, knowing Luce's taste in women. That Mercedes was a beauty with wit and spirit was a surprise, but his attraction to her was a double-edged sword. He could make himself vulnerable to a woman who had good reason to hate the man she believed him to be.

"Tread cautiously, old son," he admonished himself grimly as he threw off the sheet and stood up. The worst mistake he could make was to let her see how much power she had over him. Luce would not have cared enough about her to want her in his bed for more than perfunctory breeding. It would be extremely out of character if he stormed into her room and berated her for slipping away in the night. He had taken enough of a chance by seducing her so patiently last night. Of course, bringing a bastard daughter home to Gran Sangre was taking an even greater chance. Nicholas knew he was a fool to do either one. And he knew he could do nothing else.

He rang for Baltazar and prepared to face the morning. As he bathed and shaved, he mulled over whether he should tell Mercedes about Rosario now or simply bring the child back from Hermosillo with a governess as a *fait accompli*. The arrogance and lack of consideration for his wife's feelings in the latter course was more in keeping with Luce's character. As he dressed, he still could not decide on a course of action.

A soft knock on his bedroom door interrupted his ruminations. He bid the caller enter, assuming it was Baltazar.

Father Salvador glided into the room. His pale blue eyes glittered as he stared at Nicholas. "Your mother requests you attend her at once."

Nicholas arched one brow. "Before mass? The matter must be of great moment," he replied sardonically. Although she was too ill to take her meals with the family, Doña Sofia faithfully attended mass every morning in her quarters.

"I assure you that it is most urgent." There was a warning note in the old man's voice, but he said no more, only turned and left the room.

When Nicholas knocked on her door, a maid opened it at once. Doña Sofia sat up in bed, fully dressed, her hair done up with tortoiseshell combs. She looked pale as death but her expression was set in a grimace of determination as she dismissed Lupe, then waited until the two of them were alone. He said nothing, waiting for her to make the first move.

"It has come to my attention that you have a responsibility to attend in Hermosillo. I admonish you to do your duty at once." Her voice cracked like brittle paper rustling in the wind.

"I should've known Father Salvador's meddling would go beyond merely reading a letter that was not addressed to him."

"He did not make the decision to burden me with the matter lightly, but he knows how little you care for your moral responsibilities. The child requires a dowry for the convent in Durango. Do you have the money to pay it?" In spite of her labored breathing, there was surprising forcefulness in her voice.

"I don't intend to pay it," he said curtly.

"I thought as much." She smirked disdainfully. "I will direct Father Salvador to send an offering in your stead."

"No. You will not." His eyes glittered in challenge. "I don't intend to send anything because I don't intend to have my daughter growing up in an orphanage and being forced to take the veil."

"You should have thought of that before you took her mother to your bed!"

"I am thinking of it *now*! Rosario is mine and I'm bringing her home to Gran Sangre to raise."

Doña Sofia's eyes nearly popped from their sunken sockets as she recoiled against the pillows. She struggled with her breath, then hissed, "You cannot be serious!"

"Ah, but I am."

"You were willing enough to allow your father to make sensible arrangements when your whore was with child."

"Her mother was alive then. Now she has no one."

"She *is* no one, the bastard of a peon serving wench."

"Her blood is half Alvarado."

She did not sense the hard edge in his voice, nor take note of his rigidly controlled stance as she berated him. "You're doing this deliberately, ignoring your duty to breed a legitimate heir—further alienating your wife by shaming her in this manner."

"Your concern for my wife's sensibilities touches me deeply," he said with a sarcastic sneer. "I'll deal with Mercedes."

"The same way you've dealt with the rest of your responsibilities on Gran Sangre? The same way your father did before you?" Her mouth was thin and pursed with loathing for the both of them. She had never been able to look upon the son without seeing his sire . . . and hating them both for it.

"I've returned precisely to assume my responsibilities to Gran Sangre and to my wife. It would be best for you and your meddling priest to stay out of our affairs." He turned and stalked out of the room, slamming the door behind him.

The decision whether or not to tell Mercedes about the child had been taken from him. Perhaps it was better to prepare her for the shock. Bringing Luce's child here would be a blow to her pride just as it was to his mother's. The sensible thing would be to send Rosario to Durango, but dammit, he could not do it. She was Alvarado and had just as much claim to Gran Sangre as he did, which he realized bitterly was nothing in the eyes of the law.

Bastard. God how he hated the word he had been branded with all of his life. Lottie Fortune's bastard. As long as he was *patrón* of Gran Sangre, he would see that Rosario did not grow up scorned, impoverished or alone. He had never been any good at family. Hell, he had never had the chance, until now. If only taking this chance with the child did not destroy his chance with the woman.

Mercedes reined in her mare and looked over the valley where the vast adobe house lay shaded by stands of willows, wondering if her husband had arisen yet. He had certainly been soundly asleep when she slipped from his bed last night. After hours of restless tossing, she had given up any attempt to sleep. Before first light she was at the stable, saddling her own mount. She had to escape, if only for a few hours.

Last night replayed itself in her mind over and over. She could still feel his hands and lips on her, his body filling hers. Perhaps he had already planted his seed inside her. That would mean he could quit her bed in a short while and return to carousing with *putas*. The thought caused such pain that it frightened her. She had hated her marital duties, been degraded by the way he used her before he left for the war. But last night everything had changed. He had made her feel things she had never known existed, experience urges she had never needed to have appeased.

He had made her desire him.

In his absence, she had gloried in her hard-won independence and self-reliance. Now that he was back, he could overrule her decisions about the hacienda, but if she grew to crave his touch, to want his love, what a deadly weapon it would be in his hands. Her plight would be even worse. He could mock and taunt her, wield frightening power over her. Thinking about it made her chest tighten with pain. And yet that was the old Lucero who had thought her unattractive and boring.

Last night he had certainly acted differently. He had desired her and had taken the time to seduce her. Perhaps the way a man might a bride on her wedding night? Of course, she had no way to be certain exactly how a wedding night should go, but hers—Mercedes gave herself a mental shake.

"I'm spinning girlish dreams just as I did when first I saw his portrait."

Her guardian had brought a miniature of Lucero to her at the convent school when he explained the marriage alliance he had made for his charge. Seeing how splendid looking he was, she had spun foolish fantasies about love and devotion. Her hopes had turned to ashes when she met him. Was she being given a second chance now?

How would she act when she had to face him? What would she say after the intimacies they had shared last night? One thing Mercedes had learned over the past years as *patrona* was to face her problems head-on. With a flicker of renewed hope she kicked her mare into a trot and headed home to confront her husband.

When she entered the dining room he was waiting for her, seated at the table, sipping from a cup of steaming black coffee. She felt the heat stealing into her cheeks when he rose.

"Good day. I trust you enjoyed your ride . . . this morning." She was beautiful when she blushed that way and the flames leaped in those big golden eyes. He could not resist the chance to tease, arrogantly daring her to approach as he held out a chair for her.

"Good morning." She held her voice steady and met his eyes, ignoring the wicked innuendo. "I ride every morning. One time is much like another," she added with feigned indifference, accepting the proffered seat and reaching for the coffee urn.

"You left me in the night. Were you afraid to awaken by my side, beloved?" He brushed her jaw with his fingertips.

She did not flinch as once she would have, but neither did she deign to meet those mesmerizing eyes again. "I'm used to sleeping alone, Lucero. I always have."

"So you told me. A pity. I'll remedy that lonely deficiency when I return from Hermosillo in a few days."

A small frisson of disappointment that he was leaving her so soon surprised her. "Then you're going to hire more men?"

His expression clouded. "Yes, that and I have another matter to attend. Yesterday I received a letter from Hermosillo about a woman with whom I was involved before our betrothal." He could see the wariness in her eyes as her chin lifted proudly.

"You've had many 'involvements,'" she stressed the word scornfully, "both before and after our marriage, Lucero."

"But only one child by such a liaison." No use trying to sugar the medicine for her. He could see her stiffen in outrage but gave her no chance to lash out at him. "Rosario has been raised under the care of the sisters at the Ursuline Convent where her mother was employed as a cook."

"You sent her away when she became pregnant," she said with accusation in her voice.

"My father arranged it," he conceded with a shrug. "But the mother has died and Rosario is alone—a four-and-a-half-year-old child."

"What will you do with her?" she asked in an icy voice. How many other children had he gotten on serving wenches and other gullible women? She doubted he counted—or cared. His next words stunned her.

"I'm bringing her home with me. To be raised as my daughter. Of course, I'll hire a nurse to care for her. I'll see that they're given private quarters in the guest house out beyond the creek as soon as it can be made habitable."

Mercedes could not believe what she was hearing. "You actually plan to acknowledge her this way?"

An angry expression hardened his features. "My mother has already advised me of the impropriety of my intentions. Rosario is a small child with no one to care for her."

"I wouldn't have thought you would even note her name, much less care what becomes of one orphaned girl child," she said. Oddly, her mood softened as she studied him.

"Perhaps I've seen too many orphans in this hellish war," he replied obliquely. "Or . . . I've made too many. Whatever the cause, I'm leaving for Hermosillo this morning. It should take a week to hire the riders we need and to engage a suitable nurse. Until then." He sketched a bow and raised her hand for a brief salute, then turned to go.

She bit her lip and cried out, "Lucero, wait. Let me come with you."

He turned in amazement as she stood up and walked toward him. "Why in God's name would you wish to do that? It's two days' hard ride and as you've already pointed out to me, we have precious little money to waste on divertissements such as new gowns—if such were even available with the Juaristas waylaying every trade caravan to and from the city."

"I don't want divertissements. I want to bring Rosario back myself."

He looked at her as if she had taken leave of her senses. "You can't be serious."

"Yes, I'm serious. You're right. We have little coin to waste on nonessentials and a nurse for Rosario is unnecessary. I can care for her. I was often given charge of the younger girls at the convent school. I know how to care for a child."

"Rosario isn't *criolla*. Her mother was a serving girl with Indian blood."

"And her father is an Alvarado," she countered.

"Why do you want to do this?" He could not fathom her motive. She was too proud for tears or pleas, but as the daughter of a *gachupín*, she should have been appalled and furious at this insult.

"Let's just say I'm pleased to see you develop some shred of conscience in your tarnished soul and I want to encourage it," she replied primly, embarrassed by his scrutiny. "Do you think me so selfish as to condemn an innocent child for your sins?"

"My mother did."

She had learned over the years of his absence just how thoroughly his mother had detested her son, even as a little boy. "Doña Sofia and I frequently do not see eye to eye," she said gravely.

He measured her with a steady gaze for a pregnant moment, then said, "We leave within the hour. Can you be packed to travel in that short a time?"

"If I leave my ball gowns at home," she replied dryly.

"Leave not only your ball gowns. The countryside is dangerous, swarming with guerrillas and *contre-guerrillas*. We don't want to attract any attention."

"I told you, I've overcome my aversion to guns. I know how to use a shotgun."

"You'd better pray none of the local banditti get that close. If they learn you're a lady, it would be twice as hard to drive them away. Pin your hair up under your hat and wear those *paisana* clothes you had on the day I rode home."

"Might I bring along one change of respectable clothing for Hermosillo?"

"Only remember we travel light."

"I've learned to be immanently practical over the past years."

Her tone was accusatory but he chose to ignore it. Perhaps in time they could make a real marriage of this charade. No more had the thought sprung unbidden into his mind, than he quashed it. Who was Nick Fortune to know anything about marriages—felicitous or otherwise?

"I'll be at the stables seeing to the horses, what precious few we have available."

True to her word, Mercedes brought one small valise which Nicholas strapped behind her saddle. She was dressed in a loose *camisa* and full cotton skirt, clothes normally worn by lower-class females. A gray rebozo or long muffler was draped over her head and shoulders and secured in a loose knot at her waist, thickening her figure. Her face was disguised by a battered old straw hat beneath which she had pinned up all her golden hair.

The small group set out in barely over an hour. Nicholas instructed Hilario to ride point, staying well ahead and to the side of the other riders. Five vaqueros, two older than the wizened horse breaker and three beardless youths, accompanied them. All were heavily armed. Their mounts would once have been culled out and sold off in better days at Gran Sangre, but now the fat old mares and spiritless geldings were all that were readily available. If they had taken time to bring in some of the better stock, it would only have attracted the attention of bandits. Even the *patrón* left Peltre behind and rode a thick-legged bay with an uneven gait.

The way was grueling and monotonous, crossing vast arid stretches of trail and climbing over jagged outcroppings of rock on a trail that was more a thing of imagination than substance. The Sierra Madres loomed in the east as the little band plodded through thick yellow dust and crumbling gravel. They forded a few shallow streams, muddy and desultory in the scorching heat, but sufficient to quench the thirst of the riders and their mounts. Greasewood and mesquite grew in bleak greenish-gray clumps amid the rocks, along with wind twisted pines whose gnarled limbs reached heavenward as if in supplication for mercy.

Sonora was harsh and unforgiving yet starkly beautiful at the same time. Towering spiky cacti stood tall as cathedral spires. All around them the big blue bowl of sky reflected dazzling white light and the high thin air was perfumed with the fragrance of acacia.

Mercedes kept up with the steady pace, enduring blistering heat and searing wind uncomplainingly. She watched Lucero's eyes repeatedly scan the horizon for the silhouettes of riders. Whenever they approached a narrowing of the trail or were hemmed in by the topography, he called a halt while Hilario circled to be certain there was no possibility of ambush. Her husband's wary demeanor cast a chill of apprehension over the older men and even the young boys responded with alacrity to his low, terse orders. *No wonder he survived those years as a* contre-guerrilla.

After the sun reached its zenith and began to move toward the distant Pacific, they discussed the best site for their overnight camp.

Tonio had made the journey to Hermosillo many times. The old vaquero with leathery skin and watchful eyes said, "There is a fork in the trail a mile or two ahead. The higher way will remain difficult for the horses, but it is less traveled. I know a hidden pool of the hot muddy waters just off of it near the base of that mountain." His callused hand with broken blackened nails pointed to a rise several miles in the distance.

"Good. We'll use that route," Nicholas said. His eyes were fixed on the trail stretching ahead of them. "I'd prefer going to high ground for the night."

"Do you anticipate danger?" Mercedes asked her husband.

"There's always danger. That's why Hilario's riding point for us."

"What about when we camp for the night?" He turned to her with a slumberous look in his eyes and she blushed, stammering furiously, "I . . . I meant, will Hilario have to stay out there on lookout all night?"

A mocking smile spread across his face. "Hilario will need to be near the fire when the sun goes down. Nights in the desert are cold when you sleep out in the open. I'll post guards. Every man will take his turn."

"I've slept on the ground every time I traveled to Hermosillo. I know how cold it gets." She could still feel her cheeks tingling with embarrassment, hoping none of the men had overheard their exchange.

"This time you'll be warmer. Two people in the same bedroll generate more body heat." He kneed his horse and rode ahead to talk with Mateo and Tonio.

Mercedes was left to fret about their sleeping arrangements. Would her husband take her again as he had last night—right here in the open? Surely not with all the vaqueros sharing the same camp. She had asked to go with him to Hermosillo on impulse. His desire to acknowledge Rosario had not only surprised but touched her as well. Had she made a rash mistake in coming with him? He was an enigma to her, a dangerous stranger she had never understood. Since his return his behavior had grown even more unsettling. What if—the sharp report of a rifle shot broke into her reverie. Mercedes looked ahead to where the trail forked as old Tonio had described.

"I would not be so foolish, *Patrón*," a mocking voice said in harsh American-accented Spanish.

A tall, gauntly thin man with cold gray eyes emerged from behind a stand of weeping juniper at the side of the road. His unshaven face was deeply grooved with the squint lines of a man who had spent a lifetime in the desert. He held an expensive-looking American-made rifle aimed squarely at Nicholas' chest. Four more men showed themselves, arranged on either side of the narrow draw, all hard-faced and armed with Henry repeaters and Sharps breechloaders. These grizzled foreigners were not likely working for the republican cause. They had the look of pro-imperial mercenaries about them, but might as easily be banditti eager to kill anyone for a fresh horse and supplies regardless of politics.

The leader's eyes settled speculatively on Mercedes, who wisely tilted her head down letting the wide brim of her battered hat obscure her face. *He'll try to take her*, Nicholas thought with an oath, simultaneously wondering how he could get her out of the line of fire.

Raising his hands and smiling, he said, "I am Don Lucero Alvarado, once a rich man, but you can see how the war and those accursed republican scum have reduced my lot, traveling with nothing but a group of my peons. We fight for the same side, do we not?"

As they spoke, he edged closer to the man with gray eyes, trying to count all of the gunman's followers. Five of them. Even numbers, except that the *contre-guerrillas* were deadly professionals who could make short work of his men.

"I reckon you could say we're on the emperor's side," the leader replied as several of his men guffawed. "If you're loyal to old Maximilian, then you'd be willing to share your woman with us." He gestured to Mercedes with a leer.

"Yeah, we been without a woman fer weeks," one of his companions said in English with a thick Southern drawl. He wore the tattered remnants of a Confederate uniform, probably a deserter from one army already.

"Get off those horses and let's have a look at her," their leader commanded. Nicholas motioned to his men to comply. They could move more easily and shoot better from the ground—if only they knew how to hit anything! Old Tonio and Mateo both knew guns and would be levelheaded in a pinch, but the three boys were about as likely to panic as to follow his orders. He scanned the rocks and spiky cactus along the trail for possible cover as the *contre-guerrillas* converged on them with rifles leveled.

"Just so there's no misunderstanding, why don't you men drop those guns," the leader said with a genial smile that did not reach his wintry eyes.

As his prisoners complied, the boys with sullen alacrity and the older men with stoic slowness, Nicholas placed one hand on the gun belt at his waist, watching the way the gray-eyed man studied Mercedes. Even in the loose shabby garments it was obvious that she was young and comely.

One of the men jabbed his rifle in Nicholas' back just as his chief seized the hat from Mercedes' head and yanked her rebozo free. Her hair spilled down her shoulders like a golden curtain as the pins holding it up were ripped loose.

The outlaw sucked in his breath and spat an obscenity, grinning at her with pure evil. "A peon wench, eh? You looked too fine in spite of your disguise. You'll look even better with your clothes off."

All his men gawked, transfixed at the beautiful golden-haired woman in their midst. The leader reached out to pull the drawstring on her *camisa.*

"I'll kill you if you touch her," Fortune said in the cold, deadly voice of a stranger.

Mercedes' eyes flew to her husband in shock. He issued the threat in English. The outlaw's hand froze in midair without touching her coarse cotton blouse. He turned those chilly eyes toward Lucero.

"Well, *Patrón*, it looks to me as if you can't do a whole hell of a lot to stop me." He eyed the rifle his man had jammed into his enemy's back, then turned his attention to the woman once more.

Before he could untie the drawstring, Nicholas yelled, "Now, Hilario!" and spun, drawing his Remington and knocking the rifle away from his back at the same time. He seized the barrel as it discharged in the air, then fired a slug into the center of the man's chest. From the hill behind them a series of shots rang out. Two of the outlaws crumpled as the scene erupted in chaos. In blindingly fast continuous motion Fortune rolled to the ground, firing and yelling orders for his men, who leaped to retake the weapons they had dropped while the *contre-guerrillas* fled to cover.

The gray-eyed man attempted to grab Mercedes and use her as a shield but she raised her knee and jammed it into his crotch while her hands clawed at his face. He doubled over, pulling her down with him onto the dusty earth. Nicholas feared risking a shot. Holstering his pistol, he leaped forward, yanking her attacker to his feet with his right hand, while unsheathing his wickedly gleaming knife with his left.

She struggled to her feet, searching frantically for a weapon as her husband yelled for her to take cover. She saw old Mateo sprawled in the dust clutching the ancient rifle he had been unable to fire. She scrambled over to him. By the time she freed it from his lifeless hands and crouched down to take aim, the shooting had stopped. Two of their men were dead as were all of the bandits, except for the gray-eyed man who was locked in a desperate struggle with her husband.

Fortune crouched with the knife in front of him, its gleaming tip already red with blood he had drawn from his foe. The outlaw, too, had pulled a knife and the two antagonists circled each other like two wolves, feinting and slashing, thrusting and parrying with the cunning and calm of seasoned veterans of numerous deadly contests. The three remaining Gran Sangre men stood at one side of the road. Hilario came sliding down the embankment, then stopped twenty feet away with his rifle raised. He could have shot the outlaw, but something he sensed in his *patrón* stopped him for the moment.

Mercedes, too, watched the lethal ballet being played out before her eyes. She had never imagined her husband could be this utterly ruthless. He had left her four years before, a spoiled, arrogant young aristocrat. Lucero had been capable of cruelty, the petty, careless sort of an indulged only son of wealth, but this was completely different. This Lucero was a killer, ice-cold and taunting.

"You're pretty fair with that knife, for a *gringo*," Fortune said as the blade missed his throat by a fraction of an inch, allowing him the opening to inflict a long diagonal slash across the outlaw's chest.

Both men were bleeding profusely from superficial cuts, sweating in spite of the cool evening air. The sun dipped below the horizon, pooling sinister purple shadows around the combatants. Sweat slicked their arms and chests, mixed with blood, soaking through the ragged tatters of what remained of their slashed shirts, now reduced to little more than rags. Several times Hilario raised his rifle, only to lower it again. The bandit chief lunged and they went down with the outlaw on top. They rolled across the rough ground, each man with a death grip on the other's knife hand.

Mercedes muffled a cry of terror as Lucero's grip slipped and the outlaw's knife plunged toward his throat, but at the last second the blade missed its target, grinding harmlessly into the dirt beside her husband's face. Suddenly the gray-eyed man's body went rigid, convulsed and then collapsed on top of Lucero. She bit down on her fist to keep from screaming.

Nicholas shoved the outlaw's dead body from his and climbed to his hands and knees, panting for breath. "I said I'd kill you if you touched her," he rasped out, again in English.

His knife was imbedded in his foe's heart. A long gash gutted the corpse, moving from his belly up beneath the rib cage to reach its deadly destination. Fortune pulled the blade from the spread-eagled body whose sightless gray eyes stared unseeing at the darkening sky. Wiping the knife on the dead man's pants, he calmly replaced it in the sheath on his thigh. Then his eyes quickly swept the scene of carnage, counting the dead *contre-guerrillas* to be certain they were all accounted for.

Mercedes watched his calm methodical actions in horrified fascination. When he finally looked at her, she could not meet his gaze and quickly glanced away.

Hilario also stared with great interest, his own eyes fixed on the knife strapped to the *patrón's* thigh. Don Lucero had handled the weapon superbly. The skill might have been perfected during his time with the *contre-guerrillas*, but it seemed most peculiar to the shrewd old vaquero that in acquiring such deadly dexterity with the blade the *patrón* had also learned to use it with his left hand.

Nicholas's eyes remained riveted on Mercedes as he pulled the tattered remnants of his shirt together. Most of it had been sliced from his body. He was covered with gore. Dust and blood were caked into a slimy yellow-brown paste that only a bath could cleanse. She had looked at him with such shock and revulsion that it rocked him. *This is who I really am*, he thought grimly, then remembered the casual brutality with which his brother killed men. Luce loved the stink of death. Nick had always hated it.

"Are you unharmed?" he asked her dispassionately.

She looked up and faced him then, swallowing the bile that rose in her throat. There was concern for her beneath his guarded expression and something else—a fleeting trace of pain? "I . . . I'm fine," she said, realizing how inane that sounded. "You gave the command to shoot—how did you know that Hilario was up there?"

"I saw a gleam from the setting sun strike his rifle barrel and I gambled." He shrugged. "It was that or let him tear your clothes off while I stood by. You're my wife, Mercedes. I protect what's mine."

"And you always keep your promises," she added softly, remembering his threat to the outlaw. And that he had made it in flawless, American-accented English.

"Always." His voice was flat.

Neither could say how much time passed as they continued the silent exchange. Finally, Mercedes broke the spell.

"You're hurt. I'll get bandages to stop the bleeding."

He shook his head. "Not now. We have to move out of here. The shooting could draw other unwanted attention to us. I've had a lot worse injuries that these few scratches."

"Few scratches? You're blood soaked."

"Most of it's his," he replied with that familiar cheeky arrogance, grinning at her. Then he turned to Tonio. "Have Tomás and Gregorio load Mateo's and Jose's bodies on their horses. We'll bury them in the foothills when we camp."

Hilario approached Nicholas who said to him, "We all owe you our lives, old man. I thank you most especially for my lady."

The vaquero nodded shyly in the *patrona's* direction. "I am pleased that you are safe, Doña Mercedes." Then he turned back to the *patrón*. "You fought with great skill, Don Lucero."

His fathomless dark eyes met Fortune's for an instant, then swept down to the knife on his left thigh. Neither man said anything more as they mounted up and rode toward the trail to the mineral pools.

By the time they reached the water hole, it was full dark. Nicholas chose a shelter naturally fortified by several steep rocky embankments. Everyone was subdued as the men made camp. The dead bodies strapped to the horses were mute testimony to how near they had all come to dying that afternoon.

Mercedes fished through her saddlebags for the small sack with emergency medical supplies she always carried when traveling. When she looked around for Lucero, he was nowhere near the campfire. She followed the low gurgling sound of the mineral pool and found him sitting on a rock at water's edge. Bright moonlight reflected on his bare upper body as he bathed the dried blood from his skin.

"Here, let me do that," she said, approaching him and taking the compress which he had applied to a particularly nasty slash on his left shoulder.

He looked up at her, startled for an instant before the familiar mocking arrogance spread across his features. "After this afternoon, I thought you'd want to keep your distance."

"I said your wounds should be tended." Her hands were steady as she wrung out the cloth and reapplied it, feeling the heat of his body and the flexing of sleek satiny muscles beneath the skin.

"Always the dutiful wife, my darling," he whispered. His whole body was on fire for her but he dared not touch her, his lady with her hair unbound, flowing over her shoulders like a glowing silvery curtain in the moonlight. He wanted to tangle his fists in that hair and crush her against him, to inhale her sweet feminine heat and plunge deep inside the velvet depths of her body, right here, right now. *In the mud.*

He looked down at his blood-caked filthy pants and boots, knowing what he was, what she was, and how unworthy he was of a woman like her. He had tried to tell himself that he deserved her more than his brother did, that Luce cared nothing for her and had treated her abominably. *But I'm no better than him. I'm a killer, too.*

She could sense the leashed tension in him. Stark lines of anguish were etched on his face. Moonlight shadowed the boldly handsome planes and angles, making his expression difficult to read. His hand began to tremble. "Are you in pain?" Why had she asked that?

He gave a shaky laugh. "Not the sort you imagine," he replied grimly, taking the cloth from her. "The cuts are shallow. This water has healing properties in it. I'll be fine." He started to stand up.

"I have salve and a clean shirt," she volunteered quickly, too quickly.

He studied her, puzzled, then reached out and touched her cheek with his fingertips. "You were very brave today."

"I was frightened to death."

"You handled yourself very well."

"So did you." Her eyes dropped to the knife, then back to his face. She finished opening the ointment vial as the thought struck her. "You fought left-handed."

Nicholas knew Hilario had noticed. He had hoped she would not, but should have realized she would. He shrugged. "Once, a couple of years ago, I took a fall from a horse and my right arm was broken. I had to learn to use my left." A glib answer. Also a reasonable one, he hoped.

The war had changed them all so much, she thought. He had lived through so many campaigns in faraway places, journeyed all the way to Mexico City, even been presented at court. When his letters to Don Anselmo described that, she had been jealous, but now it seemed so long ago. Mercedes was not exactly certain why these things were important to her. "Is that also when you learned to speak English?"

"I found I possess a great many talents I never suspected I had."

Mercedes studied him in the moonlight. Her throat was dry. She swallowed and wet her lips, wondering how to respond. She had witnessed him kill with such cool barbarity that it shocked her, yet still this enigmatic man, so changed by the war, drew her. She finished applying the ointment and handed him the shirt. He stood and slipped it on, then pulled her up to his side.

Wordlessly they walked back toward the flickering campfire.

Chapter 7

As they rode through the broad fertile valley of the Sonora River toward Hermosillo, Mercedes stared at Lucero from behind, watching the way he rode with the effortless grace of all Hidalgo horsemen. He sat the horse arrogantly, every inch the haughty aristocrat she had married over four years ago. Yet he was different. Her thoughts drifted to the way she awakened this morning, enfolded in his arms beneath the warmth of their heavy woolen blankets. She had seen the hardened brutal killer yesterday, a man of war whose touch she should have dreaded. But last night he had made no attempt to claim his rights.

Instead, he had quietly made up their bedroll in front of the fire, directly across from Hilario and the other men. When she slipped fully clothed beneath the scratchy covers, he did the same, protectively enfolding her against his chest. Then he slept. She had felt oddly pleased by the simple act, in no way embarrassed or demeaned in front of their servants. And she had awakened with a sense of security and warmth that extended far beyond the physical protection offered by his hard male body.

What was this man she had sworn to hold at bay doing to her? Already he had given her, in one brief night, a glimpse of passion, of the mysterious and sensual hunger between men and women. That was threat enough to her untutored young body. This new aura of protectiveness and security drew her into yet another level of emotional involvement. What power to wound he could have over her! If she allowed it. But she had sworn never to give in and must now summon the resolve to keep her vow, lest she end up a bitter husk of a woman like her mother-in-law.

Riders crested the hill, a long caravan of heavily laden pack mules accompanied by fat merchants and hard-eyed gunmen, bound for the port city of Guaymas to the south. After that they encountered more travelers as they neared their destination. Hermosillo was a large and beautiful old city situated in the lush Sonora River valley. The spires of its magnificent cathedral gleamed in the distance, their bells pealing out the call to worshippers. A series of fountains surrounded by long low benches were shaded by fragrant orange and lemon trees, offering a refuge from the sticky noontime heat. Here and there tall cottonwoods rustled softly in the breeze, casting majestic shadows across the rows of adobe buildings that lined the long narrow cobblestone streets.

The city was tense, occupied by a French garrison whose commander had forced the allegiance of the populace at bayonet point. Merchants and tradesmen were threatened with imprisonment and the confiscation of their property if they did not accept the authority of imperial officers and collect the emperor's taxes from their unhappy countrymen. Shops and market stalls were open, but few buyers examined merchandise or haggled over prices. Hard-eyed pistoleros lounged in the shadows, watching all the strangers who entered the city. Their eyes were speculative and cold, their hands resting casually on the gun belts strapped to their hips. The bright blue and white uniforms of French soldiers were everywhere in evidence. The lilting cadence of their language rang out from cantinas and public buildings. When laughter was heard, it was from French voices. Others on the streets were sullen and silent.

"I do not think you will have any trouble hiring vaqueros, *Patrón*," Hilario said to Nicholas as they rode past one particularly large cantina.

"There are many mercenaries available, but they're not the kind of men I'd prefer to hire." He shrugged.

"Most would not work with livestock," Hilario agreed.

"But I could make inquiries for men who know the difference between longhorns and burros."

"I'll pay fifty pesos a month. See who you can find. I'll meet you at the Snake and Cactus Cantina this evening. I need to get my wife and daughter settled first."

Hilario nodded, signaling Tonio and the two boys to go with him.

After asking directions to the Ursuline Convent, Nicholas and Mercedes rode down a twisting side street. Rough wooden doors guarded the squat ugly building. A cross atop the small chapel was the only thing visible above its high and forbidding walls. Nicholas dismounted and rapped on the door. Finally the small hole cut in its center creaked open and an austere face peered out, blinking in the bright afternoon sunlight.

"What do you want?" the nun asked timidly.

"I am Don Lucero Alvarado. I must speak with Mother Superior on a matter of some urgency."

The little nun blinked again, then opened the door for them and stood to one side with an expression of prim dislike on her small bony features. He helped Mercedes from her horse and they entered the courtyard of the convent.

"Follow me," the nun said officiously, then turned and began to walk stiffly down the dusty path that ran in a diagonal line toward the church. The courtyard was enclosed on all four sides by long low adobe rooms built along the walls of the convent. A narrow porch with a thatched roof fronted the rooms, affording meager shade from the sullen heat.

Mercedes saw the effects of the epidemic which had claimed Rosario's mother. Most of the rooms stood vacant, their doors ajar. What had once been a classroom had been turned into a makeshift hospital, the wooden benches shoved aside. Pallets lay in rows on the floor, most now ominously empty, but two patients still suffered the ghastly dehydration of the final stages of cholera, moaning in feverish pain.

Was this where Rosario's mother had died, Mercedes wondered? Did her husband think about his dead lover as they walked quickly past the infirmary? Were his feelings for her the reason he was willing to claim his child? The thought that she was jealous of a dead woman niggled uneasily at the periphery of her consciousness but she squashed it, turning her thoughts to Rosario.

There were no children in sight. Where was the little girl? How would the child feel about going on a long journey with two complete strangers? Mercedes could not imagine Lucero as a father.

Two more sisters dressed in frayed gray habits conversed in somber tones by the well in the center of the courtyard, their voices obscured by the creak of the crank and rope as they labored to pull the bucket up from below. The door keeper and her charges passed the well and headed to a room just off the left side of the church.

A sharp rap on the open door by the little nun brought a response in the deep, well-modulated voice of an older woman. "What is it, Sister Agnes?"

"Don Lucero has come about Rosario," was the terse reply.

"Show him in." The tall elderly woman stood up, her spare figure unbent by age as she studied the man and woman with shrewd brown eyes set in a long face with blunt mismatched features. Her bulbous nose, deep-set eyes and pronounced jawline gave her a look of intense tenacity. "I am Mother Superior Catherine, Don Lucero. I had not expected Rosario's father to come in person," she added, tilting her head in Mercedes' direction, waiting for him to introduce his companion.

Nicholas felt her cool assessment and read between the lines. She had sent the letter to his father, expecting Father Salvador or some servant would arrive with a small sack of coins, the child's entrée to another orphanage. "I realize you did not know, but my father, Don Anselmo, is dead these past months. I was summoned home from the war to take over my responsibilities at Gran Sangre."

At the mention of the old don's passing, the nun made the sign of the cross. "No, I did not. I will, of course, see that novenas are said for his soul." Her tone of voice indicated that he was in considerable need of them.

"Our family will be most grateful, Mother Superior. May I present my wife, Doña Mercedes Sebastián de Alvarado."

The nun's thin gray eyebrows raised a tiny fraction but her angular horse face remained otherwise expressionless. "It is my pleasure to welcome you to our humble convent, my lady." She indicated the crude wooden stools. "Please be seated. I can offer little in the way of refreshment, I fear, but perhaps a bit of cool water?"

Thinking of the nuns laboring at the well, Nicholas replied, "We thank you but we have already quenched our thirst on the way to your convent. Could we see my daughter now?"

"I do not think that wise, my lord. Rosario is still frightened by the death of her mother and will have a long journey to Guaymas with Sister Agnes. Introducing two strangers would only serve to upset her more. You may leave whatever you can spare to help her on her way."

"You misunderstand, Mother Superior. I've come to take her home—to Gran Sangre with me," Nicholas said, struggling to remain patient. The look of patent disbelief that washed across her features made it difficult.

The old nun turned to Mercedes. "And this is your wish as well, my lady?"

"Very much. I asked to accompany my husband here to bring her home," Mercedes replied.

"This is most remarkable considering the circumstances," Mother Superior replied dryly, looking at Mercedes with curiosity.

"No child is responsible for the circumstances of its birth," Mercedes said, acutely aware of the child's father sitting so close beside her. "May we please see her now?"

"Very well. You will find her still grieving for her mother, but she is bright and quick for her age. Perhaps she will accept you," the nun said, rising.

They followed her outside and down the porch, passing several doors until they came to a long low building with high, small windows and thick walls. It was cool inside and very quiet. Three girls sat in one corner with Sister Agnes, who was instructing them in saying the rosary. Once the spartan dormitory had housed twenty children, but most of the children had been placed elsewhere with the loss of nuns to care for them, the Mother Superior explained as they stepped into the dim interior. She summoned Rosario. The smallest of the trio stood up, curtsied to Sister Agnes, then walked obediently down the long aisle between the empty pallets.

Rosario was a bit tall for being a little past four years, a legacy from the tall Alvarado men, as was the curl in her thick raven hair. She moved carefully between the blankets, holding up the frayed edge of her coarse gray cotton skirt with one small hand. Huaraches flopped on her small feet, the leather straps tightened to hold the oversized shoes on. She kept her head down as she stopped in front of Mother Superior.

Mercedes' heart went out to the thin little waif who stood obediently before them as the old nun said, "This is Rosario Herrera. Rosario, make your curtsy to Don Lucero Alvarado and Doña Mercedes, his wife." She elaborated no further, leaving up to the *criollo* how he chose to acknowledge his child.

Nicholas stood awkwardly, feeling totally at sea as the girl complied. How did he talk to a little girl who was supposed to be his own? "Hello, Rosario," he said quietly.

Mercedes, sensing his uncertainty, knelt and placed one hand on the child's thin shoulder, smiling at her as she said, "We've ridden a great distance to meet you. We would like you to come live with us at our hacienda."

Rosario's small elfin face appeared from behind the curtain of curls when she raised her head. Her nose and mouth were delicate and pretty, her cheekbones finely chiseled. The only evidence of her mother's Indian blood seemed to be her dark complexion. She gazed at Mercedes with eyes that were large and solemn, black with silver irises. There was no doubt she was an Alvarado. She began to raise her right hand to her mouth, then quickly glanced at Mother Superior and dropped it into the folds of the shapeless gray shift she wore.

"I am your papa, Rosario," Nicholas said softly, as he knelt beside Mercedes, unsure of what a child this young would understand. Had her brief life been as hellish as his own at that age?

"Mama said I have no papa. She is dead now. Sister Agnes told me I was going to live at another convent, to become a nun."

"There is no need for that," Nicholas replied gruffly, then added, "I'm sorry your mother has died, but I truly am your father. Now it's my turn to take care of you. You won't have to become a nun or live in a convent."

The child looked warily from the tall man to the pretty lady. Being raised in a world of women, she was uncertain of what to make of his declaration. "You're pretty as an angel," she said to Mercedes. "They all have golden hair, you know."

"No, I did not," Mercedes answered gravely. "I think a few angels might have shiny black hair with curls like yours." She touched one coarse springy lock, thinking how like Lucero's it was, then stroked the child's cheek and opened her arms. Quite naturally, Rosario melted into Mercedes' embrace.

"Is he truly my papa?" she whispered shyly in Mercedes' ear.

"Yes, he is," Mercedes assured the child.

"None of the other children had papas. I was the only one who had a mama . . . until . . ."

Mercedes held Rosario pressed to her breast letting her sob, stroking her hair softly.

Feeling a suspicious tightness in his chest, Nicholas stood up and faced the old nun. "Would you have a place for my wife to sleep tonight? We cannot begin our journey to Gran Sangre until tomorrow and the inns and cantinas in town are unsuitable for a lady. Anyway I think it would be easier on Rosario if she spent the night with my wife, here in familiar surroundings."

"She is welcome to share our humble accommodations while we remain. Within a fortnight the convent will be closed. I can only wish you Godspeed in your journey."

Mercedes stood up, struggling to hold the leggy child, who was heavy for her.

"Here, let me carry her to your quarters," he volunteered, reaching for the little girl, who weighed nothing to a man his size. Rosario went unprotesting into his arms. As the child's thin arms clamped around his neck, that nagging tightness in his chest returned along with a suspicious dampness in his eyes. He felt a kinship with Rosario that he could never have shared with his father or his brother.

As dusk settled on the narrow street, the noises coming from inside the Snake and Cactus grew more raucous. The cantina was large with high ceilings and a second-story balcony around three sides of the floor. Upstairs were the quarters of the *putas*, who plied their ancient trade while the sounds of revelry echoed up from the card tables and bar below.

Fortune edged between two drunken workers from the silver mines outside the city and signaled the bartender to pour him a glass of foaming warm beer. Sipping it, he surveyed the smoky room with slitted eyes, noting the brightly uniformed French soldiers scattered in small clusters dallying with the women and playing cards. Sighing with relief, he recognized none of them.

Hilario sat in the farthest corner at a scarred pine table. He nodded unsmiling at his *patrón*.

Nicholas sat down beside him, casually polishing off the beer with a grimace of distaste. While serving in Sinaloa, he had acquired a liking for it served cold, chilled with ice from the caves outside Mazatlán. "Any luck?"

"Yes. There are many young men from poor families who do not wish to be the emperor's cannon fodder . . . or to join Juarez. At least not while they have hungry children or infirm parents to feed."

"Have any of the French officers noticed you making inquiries?" Nicholas's eyes swept the crowded room. The French were mostly drunk, boisterously pursuing fleshly pleasures, oblivious to the undercurrents of dislike from the locals.

"I have gone places they do not know of, *Patrón*," Hilario said with a feral grin that revealed his blackened teeth. "Tonight around a dozen riders will meet us at moonrise outside the Santa Cruz Mines. I think they will like your offer."

"If you approve their skills, we'll have enough men to begin our search for the remaining cattle and horses. I think we can winter them in those box canyons we found at the source of the Yaqui River."

They exchanged ideas for a breeding program to improve the stock on the ranch. Hilario did not inquire about his *patrón's* daughter and his boss did not volunteer anything.

As the hour grew late, they finished their drinks and sauntered from the saloon, preparing to ride to the silver mines for their rendezvous. Across the big, dimly lit room a pair of colorless eyes watched them go but made no move to follow. The observer sat in a secluded alcove on the upper balcony overlooking the cantina.

Even had he not been sequestered, Bart McQueen was a man people seldom noticed. Chameleonlike he blended into any crowd. Thinning sandy hair framed a face that was neither handsome nor ugly, merely innocuous. Like his visage, his body was neither large nor small, simply of a compact medium build. He habitually wore light neutral colors of clothing, purchased from a modest St. Louis haberdashery. His one vice was the ornately scrolled heavy gold watch he always carried well-concealed in the inside pocket of his oversized suit jacket. Equally well-concealed was the rare .31 caliber lever-action Volcanic pistol slung beneath his left arm. On the infrequent occasions he drew the gun, no one remained alive to remark on the unusual weapon.

Turning his attention from Nicholas Fortune, McQueen nodded at the man standing in the doorway, deferentially waiting for instructions. "My contact confirms the rumors, Porfirio. Juarez's wife left New York and every red carpet in Washington has been rolled out for her. The Johnson Administration has continued Lincoln's friendship with your little Indian and his lady. She'll address both houses of the American Congress and will no doubt receive a standing ovation."

The other man scoffed. "Women and politicians. What do they mean? It is guns and soldiers that matter."

McQueen rubbed the bridge of his nose with two fingers, then sighed patiently. ''Only if used skillfully. Grant's already sent Phil Sheridan with over fifty thousand men—and guns. They're deployed along the Rio Grande. Our friends in Paris can't be too thrilled with that news.''

''It will make Napoleon very nervous,'' the other man conceded thoughtfully.

''I daresay,'' McQueen replied dryly, then shifted topics. ''The tall *criollo* who just left here. Who is he?''

Porfirio Escondidas made it his business to know everyone who came to Hermosillo. ''Don Lucero Alvarado is the heir to one of the largest haciendas in Sonora. He was summoned home from the war when his father died. The word is he looks for vaqueros.''

McQueen smiled. ''Able-bodied men are scarce these days.''

''They are available for a price,'' Porfirio replied cynically.

''Everything is available for a price,'' McQueen replied without inflection. ''You know where to deliver my news,'' he said by way of dismissal.

After Escondidas had departed, the Americano sat staring across his steepled fingers. *It's been a long time since Havana,* Don Lucero. *What dangerous new game are you playing this time, I wonder . . . and how could it be useful to me?*

Doña Sofia leaned forward in her chair, careful not to set off another spasm of coughing by moving too fast. Lupe hovered beside her, plumping pillows and wringing her hands. The old woman would have reprimanded her sharply for fussing if she had not caught sight of the riders approaching the main gate. Lucero and Mercedes had returned with his bastard. It was his responsibility to provide for the product of his sordid liaison, but to bring the child under Gran Sangre's roof was unthinkable. So was his wife's acceptance of the insane idea. Better she give the House of Alvarado a male heir, but perhaps she preferred raising another's child to submitting to Lucero's lust.

The old woman could understand that. Even under the

best of circumstances a woman's duty was difficult, but she herself had done what was expected of her and given Anselmo his son. Mercedes could do no less. "It is that strange English blood that taints her," Sofia murmured to herself, ignoring the serving girl as if she were no more than a stick of furniture.

She watched as the *patrón* and his wife rode up to the big courtyard door. He was actually carrying the sleeping waif in his arms!

"What remarkable tenderness he seems to exhibit for the child. Misplaced, but perhaps it augurs well for the kind of a father he will be for his legitimate heirs," Father Salvador said as he walked up behind Doña Sofia.

The old woman's eyes narrowed as she took in the scene below her window, wishing her vision were not clouded by age and illness. "This is a scandal. The shame he brings down on our house!"

The priest sighed. "Has it not always been so? But he has brought a dozen new vaqueros back with him to work the land. One day he may rebuild Gran Sangre into the great hacienda it was in the past. I would not have thought it likely that such a wastrel could learn diligence, but war is obviously a more rigorous teacher than ever I was."

Pensively, the priest watched the young *patrón* place the sleeping child in his wife's arms, then dismount and hand both their horses' reins to a vaquero. He took his daughter from Mercedes and together they walked into the house side by side. "God has plans we often cannot understand, my lady. This child may be the means by which He brings together your son and his wife as befits a marriage blessed by Holy Church."

"I will pray on that, Father," she murmured softly, dismissing him and bidding the serving girl to leave her as well. She stared sightlessly out the window, waiting for the echo of footfalls down the hall, knowing they would not dare to come near her quarters.

An act of God indeed! Her lips thinned disdainfully. Lucero had always detested children, as had Anselmo, who made it quite clear to her the day of his son's birth that she need not bother him with the infant until he was old enough to introduce to the pleasures of the flesh. And Anselmo had kept his word. Upon Lucero's fourteenth birthday he had taken the boy all the way to Durango to one of the city's most expensive bordellos for his initiation into manhood.

How she had despised the pair of them as she lay isolated in her invalid's bed while they cavorted with whores. But now Lucero had returned, apparently a changed man who loved Gran Sangre and took responsibility for his wife, even his illegitimate child. Could it be . . .? No, for surely Mercedes and Father Salvador would know. Or would they? Over the many years of her illness, Doña Sofia had come to believe that people saw what they expected to see or what they chose to see. . . .

A wintry smile spread across her face, emphasizing the deep hollows of her eye sockets and the desiccated skin across her cheekbones. It was a ghastly smile, serenely malevolent. "What a splendid irony . . . I shall have to share it with him . . . before I die."

"We'll have to decide where you will sleep, little one. How do you like your new home so far?" Nicholas asked as Rosario gaped at the lavish surroundings in the *sala*. He set the yawning child down and looked at her with a smile.

"The house is daunting for a little girl the first time she sees it," Mercedes said. "I ought to know, for it quite frightened me the first time I saw it."

"Did you live in a convent, too?" Rosario asked, holding onto the lady's skirts.

"Yes, I did," she answered, glancing over at Lucero, who said nothing during their exchange. Did he remember how in awe of Gran Sangre she had been as a bride?

As the two adults' eyes met and held, Rosario's eyes grew round as saucers. She blinked and looked around the *sala*. The walls were whitewashed to a snowy brilliance and massive oak beams arched across a ceiling that seemed high as the sky. Beautifully carved furniture glowed, hand-rubbed with lemon oil. Ignoring the two adults, she slipped over to look at a figurine of a beautiful lady. She started to reach out to touch it, but drew back at the last second. Then the glittering candlesticks sitting on the credenza caught her eye. There was more silver in this great room than in the whole Ursuline chapel! And paintings, pretty paintings hung on the walls, not of religious subjects but of finely dressed lords and ladies.

"I can really live here?" Her voice was a high-pitched squeak of disbelief as she turned back to Nicholas and Mercedes.

"Really and truly," the man who claimed he was her papa replied.

Then a loud woof sounded down the hall and Bufón came bounding toward them. Mercedes intercepted her pet, throwing her arms around him before he accidentally knocked the child down. "This is Bufón," she said, dodging great slurping licks to her face. "He likes little girls very much. Would you like to pet him?"

Rosario had instinctively moved behind Nicholas for protection, watching the behemoth who wrestled playfully with the lady. "He won't hurt you," Nicholas assured her, kneeling himself to give one floppy ear a tug.

When both adults petted the shaggy dog he quieted and sat down, cocking his head inquisitively in Rosario's direction. She mimicked his action, then giggled. "He is funny." Timidly she reached out one small tan hand and Bufón licked it. She jerked back in surprise but then quickly repeated the movement, this time letting his tongue thoroughly bathe her fingers. Step-by-step she inched closer until she could bury both small sets of fingers in the dog's thick fur.

"I think Bufón has made a new friend," Nicholas said with amusement.

"That makes two in the past few days," Mercedes replied, studying the way he was patting her pet with a thoughtful expression on his face.

Before Nicholas could reply, a smiling Angelina appeared in the doorway. "I have some fresh-baked bread sweetened with sugar and cinnamon just waiting for you," the cook said as she walked into the room. She looked down at the child. Her eyes swept from the little girl's delicately chiseled features and distinctive eyes to the *patrón's* face and back. She nodded, extending a large work-roughened hand to Rosario. "I am Angelina, the cook."

This time Rosario could not help placing her thumb in her mouth again. After leaving the convent, she had done so for reassurance numerous times. Neither Sister Agnes nor Mother Superior was there to forbid it. The beautiful lady and her papa did not seem to care. She clutched Bufón tightly with one arm. Too many strangers were offering her kindness. She was uncertain of how to respond.

"This is Rosario," Nicholas supplied for the child who stared curiously. "But I fear you've made a mistake, Angelina." He sighed. "Little girls must not like sweets."

"Oh, yes!" Rosario pleaded, her thumb suddenly forgotten as she stood up. "I am hungry and I love cinnamon bread." She looked beseechingly up at the tall man with the smiling face.

He picked her up and handed her into Angelina's open arms, knowing she had raised six daughters and would deal well with the little girl. Rosario went to the cook without protest, laying her head on the big woman's shoulder.

As they disappeared down the hall with Bufón padding patiently beside them, Mercedes said, "Your daughter does have a way about her when she holds onto you for dear life."

"Echoing my very thoughts again. We're becoming surprisingly attuned, my love," he murmured.

She looked up at him with frank surprise on her face. "I suppose we have dealt well together on this trip. You have a natural way with children, although I would never have imagined it likely."

Nicholas chuckled. "Or me either, but I think I like being a father." He moved closer. "Now we must work on making you a mother, eh?"

Mercedes could feel his breath warm against her cheek, but he did not touch her. She knew if she looked up he would have that mocking smile on his face again. Edging casually away, she ignored his comment. "I'll have Lupe prepare the room at the end of the hall for Rosario."

"That's the nursery, for the heir you will give me." He knew she had chosen the room because it was adjacent to her own bedroom.

"It's not in use now," she countered evenly, not wishing to be drawn into his obvious opening.

"Neither will your bedroom be in use, for you'll sleep with me from now on." He watched her body stiffen.

"Would you allow me no privacy? A lady is always granted her own quarters. That's how this house was designed."

"This house was designed for the most infelicitous marriages of my forebears. I don't choose to live as they did," he added with a touch of bitterness.

"You always have up until now," she snapped as visions of him and Innocencia flashed before her eyes. "It would seem to me this has been a most traditionally infelicitous marriage."

"Perhaps we've been given a second chance," he replied in a silky voice, determined not to allow her to sleep in her own bed any longer. Lying beside her without being able to make love to her when they camped along the trail had not been nearly as difficult as he had imagined. On the return journey they had slept with Rosario between them. For the first time in his life, Nicholas Fortune felt protective of the two females who were now in his charge. It was a totally new and unsettling experience for him.

She read the shuttered look on his face, and knew he would come for her that night and carry her back to his room if she resisted his plans. There was nothing she could do to stop him. *If she wished to stop him.* That shocking thought came unbidden. She looked away, murmuring, "I shall see to Rosario's room, then order you a bath lest those cuts fester."

He grinned at her. "I'll expect you to come tend them when I'm finished bathing," he replied, a dare in his eyes.

"You were the one who assured me they were shallow and you've had far worse. Merely keep them clean and there'll be no harm done."

His softly mocking laughter followed her up the stairs as she called for Lupe to assist her with the nursery bedding.

Chapter 8

Mercedes sat in front of the large oval mirror in her bedroom, brushing her hair, a ritual she had performed for herself in recent years since servants had become scarce and were so overburdened with other duties. She had grown to love the solitude and relaxation of the leisurely rhythm, a blessed respite after the long days of hard work. But tonight she could not relax, knowing that her husband would come through the door adjoining their bedrooms at any time.

Lucero had left her after dinner and retired to his study for *aguardiente* and cigarettes. She had gone to Rosario to be certain the child was not frightened in her new surroundings. Lupe had tucked the girl into her new bed and seemed genuinely fond of her quiet little charge. Once Rosario was sleeping soundly, Mercedes had nothing to do but prepare for the night ahead. A good stiff drink of old Anselmo's *aguardiente* might give her courage, but to reach it she would have to go to the study where Lucero was ensconced.

"I will never come to him," Mercedes vowed, pulling the brush through her hair with faster, harder strokes.

She stared at the stranger's face in the mirror, hardly knowing herself anymore. Over the past four years a quiet, pampered schoolgirl had grown into a secure, strong woman, a woman who knew her worth and valued her freedom. The specter of Lucero's return had always hovered over her, but she had come to terms with it, feeling certain she could maintain her identity after they reached some accord regarding their cold and mutually unwanted marriage. He had made it clear before he left that she held not the slightest interest for him. She had expected to submit to him briefly in bed and do her duty by providing an Alvarado heir. Then he would move on, living a separate life, letting her raise his child and run Gran Sangre in peace.

But he had turned the tables on her, changed all the rules. This new Lucero looked on her with smoldering eyes, desiring her body yet demanding more—much more than she knew how to give. Most certainly more than she wished to give.

Nicholas opened the door between their rooms silently and leaned casually against the frame, a crystal snifter of brandy in one hand, watching his wife at her nighttime toilette. He could tell she was deep in thought, no doubt troubling thought about him. In time she would come to him, he arrogantly reassured himself. He would win her if he was patient enough to overcome the lifetime of ladylike reticence inculcated into her by convent schools and reinforced by his brother's cavalier cruelty.

But God, could he be so patient? Play the game so skillfully? His throat went dry and his pulse hammered as he watched her. She sat on the bench, her back arched provocatively, her firm young breasts moving ever so slightly from side to side with each stroke of the brush. She wore a soft robe of rich green wool that clung lovingly to every lush curve of her body. He would bet anything she wore a high-necked, long-sleeved nightrail beneath it. Just thinking of removing it to reveal the pale silky beauty of her skin made him go rigidly hard. The candlelight cast shimmering reflections across her mantle of deep golden hair as it cascaded down her back and around her shoulders.

"Here, allow me," he said as he stalked into the room with predatory grace and set his glass on her dressing table.

Mercedes gave a small gasp of surprise, pulling the brush from her hair and clutching its ivory handle tightly with both hands as she twisted around on the bench to face him. "Must you always sneak up on me like a thief?"

His forehead creased in a fleeting frown at her words. "Sorry. A habit from the war, I suppose." He pried the brush from her nerveless fingers. Taking her shoulders firmly in his hands, he turned her back toward the mirror, then stood behind her so they faced one another in the glass. Her eyes were huge and luminous, a dark magical shade of gold that matched her hair. What was she thinking? He saw the faint blush of color on her cheekbones, the rapid pulse that beat at the base of her throat. And he knew.

A slow smile curved his lips as he let the brush massage her scalp, then pull down the length of her hair, which crackled and glowed in splendor. "You have fire, Mercedes," he murmured. "See the sparks that fly from your hair?"

"The cool night air causes such sparks," she replied in what she hoped was a frosty tone which came out altogether too breathy to suit her.

"Then I'll have to warm you," he said, smiling.

She stiffened angrily at the arrogant smirk on his face. He was so self-assured, so certain of his power over her. And he had every right to take such liberties with her, damn him. If only this were the old Lucero, who was not interested in her or in playing this strange, sensuous new game. Her eyes could no longer meet his in the mirror, yet they could not stop from staring at the picture the two of them made as she sat, pale and small while he towered over her.

He wore the same snowy white lawn shirt he had worn to dinner earlier that evening, but now he had shed his stock and unfastened the studs, leaving the front open halfway to his waist, revealing an unsettling amount of black curly chest hair. She could see evidence of the healing cuts from that vicious knife fight and shuddered remembering it. His shirtsleeves were rolled up almost to his elbows, exposing slim forearms that flexed sinuously as he plied the brush.

His hands were deft, long-fingered and elegant. How well she remembered those hands on her body that first time after he returned home. Patient hands. Cunning hands. And lips. Quickly she looked down, away from his dark, disturbing image in the mirror. He was barefoot, clad only in shirt and pants. No wonder she had not heard him enter!

When she made no reply to his provocative comment about warming her, he laid down the brush and took her hair in his hands, running his fingers through it. "It spills over my hands, like golden silk,'' he whispered hypnotically resting one hand lightly on her shoulder. As he began easing the robe down to reveal a prim white batiste nightrail, a sultry smile spread across his face. ''I thought you'd choose something virginal, but we both know that's a lie, don't we, wife?''

Mercedes stood up and faced him, untying the sash of her robe with clumsy fingers. She jerked the robe off and flung it across the bench. ''Do with me as you will, Lucero, and be done with it.''

''Such a brave little martyr. Then why, if you loathe my touch so . . .'' His fingers grazed the frilly white lace on the front of her gown, brushing the tips of her breasts, clearly outlined through the sheer fabric.

She drew back angrily but not before the sudden frisson of pleasure traveled through her breasts and pooled deep within her belly. Her nipples contracted, standing out in rigid points, tingling, aching. She knew he could see what she felt. He knew what she would feel before he even touched her. Tears of vexation and humiliation gathered behind her eyelids, but she willed them to abate, just as she forced her arms to remain at her sides, fighting the overpowering urge to clasp them around herself, covering her treacherous body.

''Give in, Mercedes. You know your body craves what I can give you.'' His hands ran up and down her arms, stroking them. Then he raised one hand and traced the outline of her collarbone from one side to the other, watching the way her breathing suspended, then resumed unevenly. ''So determined to show no fear, give no quarter.''

''I no longer fear you, Lucero.''

''You'll do your duty, is that it? Duty but nothing more?'' He continued tracing gentle patterns on her arms and chest, feeling his fingertips glide over the sheer soft cotton and the heat of her flesh beneath it. Then he moved up to brush the delicate column of her throat where the erratic pulse beat furiously in spite of her pose of calm.

''What more would you have of me—that I follow you about, panting like a bitch in heat? Like one of your whores?''

"Forget my whores! They have nothing to do with us," he said tightly, beginning to lose patience.

"Considering the evidence of your past liaisons lies sleeping in the next room, that's rather difficult to do," she blurted out angrily.

His eyes narrowed to slits. "I thought you were fond of the child."

"I . . . I am, very much. I didn't mean to involve her in our quarrel. She's only an innocent victim but I don't understand you anymore—if I ever did. I can't be like Inocencia or the others."

"You could never be like the others, like any other. You're my wife," he said, pulling her against him with one arm. He seized her hair, taking a great fistful and tugging it back, forcing her to look up into his face as he swooped down for a fierce possessive kiss.

When his hot seeking mouth covered hers and his tongue probed for entry, she did not resist him but opened for his possession. He plundered her lips and teeth, twining his tongue with hers. Her hands rested, palms flat against his chest, neither pushing him away nor embracing him. She willed herself to remain passive, to let his maelstrom of passion pass her by, but it was impossible. Feeling his heat, smelling the keen sharp scent of his arousal, her senses were swamped. She heard his voice, low and raspy, whispering love words in her ear as he plied her with caresses, trailing kisses down her throat. How could she withstand the onslaught?

Slowly, Nicholas raised his head and looked down at her. The rigid evidence of his desire pressed intimately against her belly. His breathing was labored and he trembled with wanting her. Yet she stood stock-still in his embrace, forcing herself to remain impassive, utterly motionless.

"Deny yourself and be damned—if you can do it," he muttered savagely, sweeping her into his arms and carrying her into his room. He kicked the door closed and strode to the bed where he tossed her like a small rag doll. Then he stripped off his shirt and peeled down his trousers, which had grown miserably tight and uncomfortable.

He grinned wickedly at her. "You see the effect you have on me? Men, unfortunately, have no way to hide our desires." He kicked the pants aside and climbed on the bed beside her on all fours. Reaching down for the hem of her nightrail, he yanked it up, bunching it around her hips, then groaned at the way her slim thighs clenched together involuntarily.

This was how Luce had taken her. He knew it in his bones. She wanted him to use her the same way his brother had, to plunge in and finish quickly, leaving her emotions untouched. But he was not his brother, and he would not settle for that. A slow feral smile spread across his face. He stopped abruptly, releasing her gown and letting his fingers graze the bones of her pelvis, then caress the hollow of her belly.

His finger ringed a circle around her navel until she knew her muscles were quivering. Mercedes felt his palm cup the curve of her hip, then glide down her thigh. When he insinuated his hand between her legs at her knees and teased his way upward, she could remain still no longer. The aching that had begun so deep inside of her when he brushed her hair and spoke in that low mesmerizing voice, now flared into a sharp pain. Her back arched and her legs separated slightly as her heels dug into the soft mattress. She could not look at him.

Nicholas grazed the golden curls at the juncture of her thighs as she writhed beneath his touch. "You do want me . . . don't you, wife?"

She burrowed the back of her head into the pillows and refused to answer his taunt. He would know soon enough. She could feel that strange telltale wetness between her legs that had slicked his way the last time he took her. The response, so new to her, had pleased him, and she did not wish to please him.

"Stubborn woman," he murmured as he began to unfasten the nightrail's ribbon tie at her throat. Once it was open he reached for her hands and undid the buttons at her wrists. "Sit up and slide the gown over your head," he commanded.

She lay immobile, refusing to strip herself naked while

he watched her as if she were some dancing girl in a cheap bordello.

"Do it, Mercedes." There was steel in his voice now.

His hand moved to her mound and he began massaging it ever so gently. The maddening pain throbbed in her now, drawing her under, into a vortex that frightened her. She could feel those harsh black eyes on her, boring into her as she lay exposed to him, at his mercy. It was intolerable, unbearable. To still his touch, she sat up abruptly and yanked the gown over her head, throwing it to the foot of the bed, then flopped back down, breaking the delicate buildup of sensation when he withdrew his hand.

Her hair flew around them like a golden explosion, releasing a fresh burst of her lavender perfume combined with the very essence of feminine arousal, musky and warm. He cupped one breast and laved the other, taking the pale pink bud between his teeth and biting softly, then suckling. She arched against him the tiniest bit. He called it a victory.

But he could not hold off much longer. His staff lay rigidly across her thigh, rubbing back and forth, the tip pearly with his leaking seed. Nicholas rolled on top of her and positioned himself to enter, feeling the velvety wetness of her, knowing her body at least wanted what her mind rejected. He ran the head of his phallus up and down over her petals. Her thighs opened wide and he plunged home in a white-hot surge of ecstasy.

His entry was slick and smooth yet startlingly swift. His big body pinioned hers in that most primitively male way, and she could feel the stretching tightness as he filled her, then stilled, letting her body adjust. And traitorously it did, sheathing him tautly. She felt the wonder of the joining which took two people and made their flesh one. A great mystery. One she feared to understand.

Then he began to move, very slowly, stroking her until she had to bite her lip to keep from crying out for him to hurry. For if he did not, the gliding pleasure of the caress would drive her over the brink into some unknown abyss. She dug her fingers into the covers and tried to think of anything but Lucero, sweating and straining above her, sealing his possession of her, perhaps giving her a child.

A child, yes. That was the one thing good they could do together. He could give her another baby like Rosario to love and raise. She thought of names, blocking out what he was doing to her body, to her.

Nicholas could sense the restive response she could not totally hide, but his own body clamored for release. Knowing she was not yet ready to surrender, he gave in to the glorious surcease of climax, pumping into her in earnest now, long, hard, swift strokes until a universe of stars burst inside of him. He arched his back and with a ragged triumphant growl spilled his seed high in her womb, then collapsed on top of her.

His flesh was slick with perspiration. The scent of male sex hung pungently in the cool night air. She found the smells were not unpleasant, but they were disturbing as was the feeling of emptiness when he withdrew and rolled from her. Still breathing heavily, he flung one arm across his eyes and lay flat on his back. Shivering with the sudden chill, she looked over at the man lying beside her. She could see the angry red lines, now freshly smeared with blood where he had reopened several of his wounds in his exertions. Her own body bore a few faint traces of his blood as well, but she was certain he felt no pain. Only a primitive animalistic satisfaction that had always eluded her. Yet there was still that persistent ache low in her belly, tightening her muscles and clawing at her even more fiercely than it had the first time he finished with her.

Damn him, she ached! Mercedes tried to slip from his bed, but he caught her wrist just as her feet touched the floor.

"This is where you sleep from now on," he said, pulling on her wrist until she was forced to return to the bed. "Is it so distasteful to stay with me?"

"I'm cold. I was only getting my nightrail." *Liar.*

He chuckled. "You don't need nightrails to keep warm." He slid to her side of the bed, yanked the covers down and climbed beneath them, then patted the mattress, inviting her to join him.

"I'll keep you warm," he said simply.

Silently she slipped beneath the cool white linen and was enveloped by his heat. He pulled the covers up and fitted her into the curve of his body. Mercedes felt cocooned, yet restless, hungering for something she feared to acknowledge.

Dawn came stealing softly into the big room, its soft golden fingers pulling away the last dim shadows of night. Nicholas blinked and gazed out the window, awakening at once as years of sleeping outdoors on campaigns had conditioned him to do. He lay quietly, feeling Mercedes' soft warm body so close beside his. Strands of gold hair spilled across his face and chest and the delicate essence of lavender filled his nostrils. Her heart beat in sync with his own. If only their minds were of such accord. For now, her body was weakening. In time he would teach her how to accept and enjoy the pleasure he could give her. He asked for nothing more, indeed did not even consider that he could give anything more of himself.

Love was not a word in Nicholas Fortune's vocabulary. But what about his feelings for Rosario? For the children he and this woman would have together? Could he love them? Strange that he should feel such an immediate kinship with Luce's daughter, he who had never had any contact with other children, who grew up alone in a harsh world of uncaring adults. When he had come here, the prospect of providing heirs for Gran Sangre had been a daunting consideration that he had not wanted to dwell upon. But after his response to Rosario and hers to him, he felt reassured.

Maybe there is some shred of honest humanity in me after all, he thought in surprise. Very carefully he placed the long golden glory of Mercedes' hair on the pillow and slid his arm from around her shoulders. One milky breast peeped from beneath the covers; its pale pink nipple stiffened when the cool morning air touched it. The temptation to remain in bed and take her again was great, but he reminded himself of his responsibilities. The *patrón* of Gran Sangre had to ride out with his new men. As it was, Hilario and the other men were probably saddled up and ready to go.

Sighing, he slipped from the bed, then covered up Mercedes' lovely nakedness once more. His riding gear had been laid out last night. On silent bare feet he walked across the frayed carpet and picked up the heavy broadcloth pants and pulled them on. Just as he was buttoning the fly, he sensed her eyes on him and turned.

The loss of his body heat had drawn her from sleep. Something was amiss, she thought as the room came slowly into focus. She could hear faint rustling noises and rolled over, only then realizing that her husband was no longer in bed. How quickly she had grown accustomed to sleeping with his lean, hard body curving protectively around hers. She looked across the room at his back, scarred and bronzed, the muscles moving with fluid, peculiarly male beauty as he tugged on a pair of tight pants and fitted his sex carefully inside the fly. Heat colored her cheeks as she remembered how that now flaccid staff had pulsed with life, huge and rigid within her body.

Then he looked up and their eyes met. Instinctively she pulled the covers up to her chin, then felt foolish. He had seen all there was to see the last two times he had made love to her.

Made love. The thought struck her oddly. Never had she felt Lucero made love to her during their first few weeks as husband and wife. Not wanting to consider the disturbing implications of her own thoughts, she blurted out the first thing she could think to say. "Where are you going? It's barely daylight."

He raked her tousled hair and flushed face with hungry eyes, lifting one black eyebrow sardonically. "You tempt me to stay, my love, but Hilario awaits. We're going to begin rounding up whatever cattle and horses we can find running loose within a day's ride. I have several excellent hiding places where we can winter the best of them down on the Yaqui. After we clean out the immediate vicinity, we'll have to start ranging farther out, two, three days' ride, until we cover every quadrant of the range," he explained.

She watched him don a blue cotton shirt, covering up that hard hairy chest with all its mysterious and sensual scars. A disturbing heat began to build deep in her belly. She struggled to concentrate on his words. "What time will you return tonight?"

"Not until dark, I expect. Have Angelina leave a plate for me on the kitchen hearth."

"I'll be working with Juan Morales today."

"The old gardener? What the devil for—we can't spare men for growing flowers."

"Of course not," she replied indignantly. "He and a dozen or so of the older servants are helping me with vegetable gardens. We've planted our own fields of corn as well as beans, chilies, tomatoes, yams—just about everything that can be dried or preserved for winter. Your father thought it demeaning that I muck in the mud with the peons, but we can't afford to buy staple foodstuffs even if they were readily available, which they aren't."

"If my father disapproved, I can imagine what my mother had to say," he replied dryly, walking over to the bed and unclenching one of her hands from the cover. He held it, examining the calluses, then kissed them. His eyes met hers. "Don't work too hard while I'm away, Mercedes."

At the tender gesture a shiver of warmth coursed through her. He replaced her hand on the cover, then walked over to where his weapons lay on the large dressing table beside the window. Strapping the knife to his thigh, he slung the gun belt over his shoulder, then picked up his Henry rifle and left the room as she sat bemused by their homey exchange of plans for the day.

Mercedes spent the cool early morning hours out in the fields, weeding alongside the peons. Finally she leaned on her hoe and looked out at the green rows of young corn struggling to grow in the dry, hard soil. Wiping the perspiration from her brow, she grew pensive.

"The crops need water, Doña Mercedes," Juan said as he, too, stopped his labors.

"I've been thinking about that. A branch of the Yaqui River flows past the fields to the east, on the higher ground.

If we could divert part of that, it would flow down to where most of the cleared fields are planted. I've read about such irrigation in books."

Juan's expression remained respectfully impassive. "It has always been said that the Indians to the south in the great valleys of Mexico irrigated fields so vast the eye could not span them. They even built pipes of clay to carry the water for hundreds of leagues."

"The aqueducts, yes," she murmured, looking at the wizened little Indian in baggy white *calzones* and *camisa*. Fathomless black eyes were set deeply in a flat face that seemed somehow ancient yet ageless, the way she often thought of Mexico itself. Had he sprung from such illustrious ancestors as the fabled Aztecs? At times this harsh and beautiful land remained alien to her even though she had spent almost all of her life in it. She was a *gachupín*, born in Spain, in some ways still an outsider. But she loved the land, *her* land, with a passion born of hard labor and the struggle to survive the turbulent times in which they lived.

"Do you think we can dig so far, Doña?"

Mercedes stared out at the parched earth. "We'll have to, Juan. This afternoon we'll walk the banks of the tributary and decide the best place to start."

By the time she returned to the house, the sun was high overhead. Rosario had most probably already eaten breakfast and been sent to play around the kitchen. She had given the child to Angelina and Lupe's charge, but both women had many chores. Perhaps it would be better to bring Rosario with her to the fields, but it was hot and dusty with scant shade close by.

A smile touched her lips as she thought of Father Salvador, who did little around the household after morning mass but pray and read religious tracts. She would have to discuss Rosario's tutoring with Lucero. The stern old priest had always intensely disliked her husband. Lucero might not want him teaching his daughter. Yet there was no one else unless she did it herself, a task she would ordinarily have relished if not for the heavy burden of responsibility she bore for running Gran Sangre.

Perhaps Lucero would really be able to make a difference now that he was home. She was not certain she wanted to give over her hard-won position of command to a man who came from a long line of wastrels. Yet he seemed to have been honed by war into a disciplined and mature man. Remembering his examination of her work-roughened hands earlier that morning, she felt her heart skip a beat.

After stopping outside the kitchen to wash the worst of the dust from her feet in a bucket of water kept just for that purpose, she started toward the kitchen. Suddenly a loud screech and a string of oaths rent the warm air, followed by furious barking. The hubbub was coming from the courtyard on the opposite side of the kitchen. Cutting through the big room, Mercedes saw Angelina in the doorway to the courtyard, yelling at someone.

"Stop this at once, Innocencia," the old cook commanded.

"Look what the child and her cur have done! All my morning's work ruined! My hands are red as a fishwife's and for what? You rotten little bastard!"

Mercedes flew past Angelina and crossed the flagstone patio in a trice. Rosario was huddled in the mud beside an overturned tub filled with white table linens, her eyes huge with fright, small hiccuping sobs rending her thin little chest. The big dog sat protectively by her side. Reaching down to the child, the *patrona* took her in her arms and glared at the murderous look in the slattern's black eyes. "Don't you ever speak that word aloud again in this house, or I will banish you forever!"

"You cannot banish me. Only Don Lucero may dismiss a servant and you know he will never let me go." She smirked insolently at her mistress, then turned her wrath back at Rosario. "Look at the mess. She is the one who should go," she said, pointing at the quivering child. "Her and that hound from hell you keep!"

"I did not mean to be bad," Rosario choked out. "Please, neither did Bufón!"

"It's all right," Mercedes said, stroking a lock of inky hair from Rosario's forehead. "Tell me what happened."

"We . . . we were playing with Bufón's yarn ball, the big

blue one," the child began, pointing to the soggy blue wool toy that lay atop the spilled linens, its dye leaching a pale grayish stain onto a once snowy white tablecloth. "I threw the ball to him but . . ." Tears clogged her voice and she began to sob harder. "It landed in the laundry tub. I ran to pull it out . . ."

"But that big rascal beat you to it and overturned the tub in his eagerness to reclaim his prize," Mercedes supplied for her.

"There is no real harm done," Angelina said cheerfully, hefting the tub onto the high wooden bench as if the vat weighed nothing. "We will bleach out the dye with lemon juice in no time." She turned to Innocencia. "You fetch the jug of lemon juice, then begin refilling the tub with clean water from the well. I will wring out the linens."

Innocencia stamped her foot. "We'll be all afternoon redoing this wash—it was never my job to begin with. I am no washerwoman," she said, daring the *patrona* to do anything about her defiance.

Bufón growled low in his throat and shook his head, spraying mud on the hem of her brightly colored skirts. Innocencia began another shrieking diatribe and jumped away, only to slip in the mud and fall on her amply padded backside. She struggled to scoot backward in the ooze, her earlier rage now transformed into fright.

Mercedes smothered a chuckle as she set Rosario down and commanded Bufón to be still, then turned her attention to the cowering tart. "You're right—you're not a washerwoman—or a cook or a maid. You're a harlot . . . an unemployed harlot, and if you say one more word to me or ever again threaten the *patrón's* daughter, you won't even have a roof over your head!"

Innocencia's dusky complexion blanched. For the first time she really looked at the little girl, seeing the finely chiseled Alvarado features and signature black and silver eyes set in the swarthier face of an Indian mother. Realization of what she had done slammed into her. "I . . . I did not know she was the *patrón's* daughter. I only thought—"

"You thought she was one of the serving girls' children

and could be bullied as you always try to bully people," Mercedes cut in angrily. "Now get up and get to work. If I hear you speak one cross word to Angelina, I'll personally rip every hair out of your head, then let Bufón use you for his play ball. Is that clear?"

Nodding sullenly, Innocencia slipped and scrambled to her feet, then trudged over to the well and began to draw up water. Mercedes heard a soft giggle of laughter and looked down at Rosario, who was watching her nemesis wade like a duck through the muck.

"She looks like the brown milk cow Mother Superior had at the convent."

A grin spread across Mercedes' lips. "Yes, she rather does, doesn't she?"

While she and Lupe washed the mud from Rosario and then tackled Bufón—always a formidable task—Mercedes considered how her husband might feel about her threats to his old mistress. True, he had not bedded her since returning home. At least she had seen no evidence that he had done it. But she had usurped his authority in a manner that could displease him. Then thinking of the *puta's* cruel words to his daughter she reassured herself that he would never allow anyone, even his mistress, to abuse the child. Still, as the day wore on, she fretted about what Innocencia might do.

Nicholas came in from the range at twilight, covered with dust, sweat-soaked and saddle sore. All his thoughts centered on a bath—a long, lovely soak in a big tub of warm clean water. He walked into the arched entry hall and headed toward the kitchen, expecting Angelina to be busy cleaning up from dinner. There was probably a feast set out for him if he knew the old cook, but at this point, he was too tired to even be hungry. All he wanted was that bath.

Before he got halfway down the hall, Lupe emerged from one of the side doors and curtsied shyly for the *patrón*. She was a small young woman with a round face and merry brown eyes. "We were expecting you late, Don Lucero. Your dinner—"

"That's all right, Lupe. Dinner can wait. Please have

Lazaro fetch bathwater to the bathing room and then have Baltazar bring me my razor, soap and some fresh towels along with a change of clothes."

She nodded in acquiescence and he began to stroll across the courtyard, feeling too dirty and foul-smelling to remain indoors and go in search of Mercedes and Rosario. He ambled by the fountain and loitered in the shadows of a fig tree while Lazaro filled the tub with fresh water. Then he went into the long narrow room reserved for bathing, stripped off his clothes and slipped into the large tub. It was specially made of copper with a porcelain interior, large enough for two.

In the unadorned adobe room with simple plank floors and tiny windows, the tub was rather out of place. His father had ordered it from Spain with plans to build an elaborate bathing room on the second floor of the family's private quarters but after the war started, Don Anselmo quickly lost interest. Besides, it was more discreet for him to philander with serving wenches here at the opposite end of the courtyard rather than to do so near the angry disapproval emanating from Doña Sofia's room just across the hall.

Nicholas sank beneath the heavenly water and laid his head back on the rim of the tub, remembering all Lucero had told him about his family, their family. Much of it was not pleasant, although the picture of decadent wealth he painted seemed to overshadow any problems to a boy raised in a series of succeedingly more sleazy brothels.

Luce had hated his cold mother but doted upon his wild carousing father. Although Nicholas empathized with what it meant to miss a mother's love, he hated Don Anselmo even more than his brother hated Doña Sofia. Don Anselmo had planted his seed and carelessly walked away from the foolish young mistress he had kept for a passing amusement.

Suddenly his troubling reverie was interrupted by the low purring voice of Innocencia. "I see the war has scarred that perfect stallion's body. I only pray one vital part of you has not been wounded."

She licked her carmined lips provocatively and swished into the room, carrying an armful of towels. Having overheard his directions to Lupe, she had quickly decided this was her perfect opportunity to appeal to Lucero before his bitch of a wife further poisoned his opinion of his old mistress. Blessed Virgin, if only she had noticed that the brat was his child before acting so foolishly!

He watched her deposit the towels beside the tub, then pose seductively at the edge. She leaned forward to give him a better view of her heavy breasts which hung almost out of a low-cut blouse. He smiled wearily at her posturing. "That part of me is no longer your concern, Cenci."

She pouted. "I do not believe you will say so in a few weeks when you tire of that shrew you married. Let me see how she has been taking care of you," she said as she reached beneath the water and seized hold of his staff with quick clever fingers.

He clenched his teeth and cursed as her unexpected ministrations had the natural effect on his body.

"I am good for you, no?" By now she had pulled free the drawstring at the neckline of her *camisa* and one large pendulous breast with its dark brown nipple spilled free.

"You are no good for me," he whispered, reaching down to disengage her hand from his private parts. When he pried her fingers loose and raised her hand from beneath the water, she tangled her other hand in his hair and leaned herself forward over the tub in an attempt to push her bare breast against his mouth.

"Baltazar said you wanted—" Mercedes' breath caught in her throat as she saw the steamy tableau when she opened the door. Throwing his clean clothes and toilet articles on the floor, she said in an icy voice, "Now I can see very clearly what you want."

Chapter 9

Mercedes turned and walked out of the room, refusing to give in to her impulse to run into the night. She kept her back rigidly straight and blinked back the tears stinging her eyes, trying not to think of the humiliation. *Again. Just like it was when I first saw them.* She forced herself to stop. Focusing on the anger was easier. And she was very, very angry.

Lucero had ever been a gamester and this whole new seduction ritual was only a bedroom game to amuse him. Bitterly she wondered if he had described to Innocencia his wife's maidenly modesty, her awkwardness, her coldness. A grim smile twisted her lips. She hoped he had thought her cold. How they would be laughing at her if he suspected she was weakening and beginning to desire him. She had come much too close to revealing those feelings. Never again would she risk making a fool of herself.

She walked across the courtyard and entered the family's side of the house, heading to Don Anselmo's study where she knew he had kept his guns.

Nicholas shoved Innocencia away with a vile oath and climbed out of the tub. "Get out of my sight before I snap your filthy little neck. I've told you it's finished between us, Cenci, and I meant it."

The water that had splashed on her blouse had turned the sheer fabric translucent. She pulled it tightly over her nipples so they stood out, dark and large. Her mouth formed a pout as she watched him dry off with swift angry movements. "Surely the *patrón* will not run after his skinny little convent girl? After all she cannot refuse you her bed, even if she is so frigid and foolish as to try."

He looked at his brother's mistress with utter contempt. What could Luce have seen in the slattern? He had allowed her to grow exceedingly bold for one of her low station. "What is between me and my lady is of no concern to you, Cenci," he said in a silken tone that was all the more deadly for its seeming civility. "I am the *patrón* and she is my wife. You are only a servant—a servant in grave danger of banishment from Gran Sangre if you ever do anything like this again. Do I make myself clear?" His eyes bored into her, sharp as French bayonets.

Innocencia stepped back, her expression fearful. "Yes, yes, *Patrón*. I don't wish to be sent away." She let her eyes tear and her voice quiver as she added, "I have nowhere to go, no family, no one." She did have family in Guyamas, but they were desperately poor fishermen. The thought of cleaning fish for a living was infinitely worse than any household chores.

She did not understand what was happening. Before Lucero had left, everything had been so wonderful. The sloe-eyed beauty studied him from beneath thick black lashes as he jerked on his clothes, turning his back on her. She had the urge to reach out and caress the scars on his body but intuitively knew to do so when he was this angry would be a dangerous blunder. Her expression hardened as she slipped silently from the room, vowing to have the *patrón* back in her bed and to have revenge against the pale little *gachupín* who had robbed her of his attentions.

Nicholas walked across the courtyard, pausing beneath the fig trees by the fountain to collect his thoughts. Luce would never run after his wife or offer explanations for his infidelities. Just when he was beginning to make headway with her, she had been given more reason to mistrust him. Shit, he wasn't even guilty of anything! He damn well could tell her that. And she damn well would listen. But it would be totally out of character to rush after her immediately. Cenci had set the whole artful little scene up to connive her way back into his affections and it had hurt Mercedes.

A drink would give him time to calm his nerves and give his wife time to cool down. If he knew Mercedes—and he was beginning to know her pretty well—she was spitting mad about now, fashioning her hurt into anger. He grinned in the darkness. Ah, what fun they would have making up tonight.

Nicholas stopped by the kitchen and found Angelina scrubbing pots and pans. "I smell something heavenly. After the day I've put in, I could eat a wolf!" he said.

"No wolf, *Patrón*, but roasted lamb. We were able to hide a few of the sheep and their spring lambs when the last soldiers came. I have saved this finest delicacy for you. Your favorite, the *macho*." Her wide face was split with a prideful smile as she set before him the fatty intestines from the lamb, looped and tied in a ball, then roasted until the whole mass was brown and crispy. Alongside a fresh stack of steaming hot tortillas and the platter with the *macho* on it, she set down a bowl of chilies and tomatoes.

Nicholas swallowed, remembering the first time he had watched Mexican soldiers devour a *macho*. It was a taste he had never acquired, but then in North Africa he had not much liked goat's eyes boiled in cream either. However, he had known better than to offend his host by not indulging. Luce loved this greasy treat, so Nicholas would eat it. *A good thing I am starving*, he thought ruefully to himself as he took a seat at the table, wishing he had followed his first impulse and gone directly to the study for a drink. The fortification would not have been unwelcome.

Manfully he dug in, trying not to think about what he was eating, taking large spoonfuls of the hot vegetables to kill the fatty taste. "You are still the finest cook in Sonora."

"And you are very hungry, *Patrón*," she replied, beaming at the compliment. "Did you gather many horses and cattle?"

"We found more than we had hoped, but the vaqueros we've hired are young and inexperienced. We drove a dozen head of sturdy longhorns into a box canyon off the Yaqui but one of our best stallions and his herd eluded us. There were seven foals and two colts with them, fine and strong. Enough to begin rebuilding."

"I am very glad, *Patrón*. This war is a terrible thing. The *patrona* has worked so hard to hold Gran Sangre for you. It's good that she has not sacrificed in vain."

He looked up at the shrewd old cook. There was subtle censure behind her earnest words. "I know about war, Angelina. It's changed me—taught me to value things I never appreciated before."

"Like your wife, *Patrón*?" she dared to ask.

"Yes, like my wife," he echoed. "One day she'll be the lady of a grand hacienda again."

She measured him with her warm dark eyes. "Yes, I do believe the war has changed many things," she replied obliquely.

Upstairs, Mercedes paced back and forth in her room clutching the pistol she had taken from Anselmo's gun case. Her eyes kept returning to the door leading to Lucero's room, which she had bolted as she had the hall door. He would not dare come to her tonight. Yet what would she do if he did? All the servants would overhear them. Well, let them. It was scarcely as if there were a soul on Gran Sangre who did not know about Lucero and Innocencia.

"I will shoot him if he dares set foot in this room," she murmured aloud. The words echoed false on the cool night air.

She stared out the window at the starry night, so tranquil and lovely, trying to draw strength from the peaceful scene. Only calm and rational thought, free of emotion, would serve her now. *You can't revert to being the shocked and hurt little convent girl you were the last time he and Innocencia laughed at you*, she scolded herself. Steeling her nerve, she lay the pistol down on the bedside table and massaged her temples with her fingertips.

At first she had half expected that he would come storming after her, demanding that she accept what she had seen. But he had not even cared enough to pursue her. Why was she surprised? Before retiring to her room, she had gone over the bookkeeping accounts and had discussed the plans for the irrigation project with Juan. Then she had come upstairs to read Rosario a fairy tale and tuck her in bed. And still he did not return to his room.

Obviously he was with Innocencia in the servants' quarters across the courtyard. At least she should be grateful that he did not bring the *puta* upstairs into the bed he had shared with her. An unholy light shone in her eyes, darkening them to polished bronze as she thought of Lucero and that woman right next door to her. "If he dares bring her up here, I'll burn the mattress with them on it!" she gritted out, then realized how shrewishly jealous she sounded.

Jealous? She was not jealous. Let him go to loose women like Innocencia, but do it discreetly. It was just a matter of her pride. After all, as the *patrona* who had governed Gran Sangre these past four years, she was due proper respect. The words echoed hollowly in her mind and she knew they were a lie. Mercedes again massaged her temples as a fierce headache began to build. She was so confused. "I don't want him yet I hate the idea that any other woman has him either." A fine dilemma. How could she possibly be jealous of him with that whore? Especially after the way Innocencia had treated Rosario that very morning?

Her turbulent ruminations were interrupted when his footfalls sounded down the hall. She held her breath and picked up the gun as he walked into his room and began to undress. He did not try the door at once. Good. He was going to be civilized about it. That whore had probably tired him out in the bathhouse. *I wish they'd both drowned*! She stood alone in the darkness, waiting for the light to go out on the opposite side of the door, unable to even *consider* getting into bed before he was asleep.

Then the doorknob turned with a sharp rattle, followed by a muffled oath when the bolt barred his way. He pounded on it twice, sharp raps that sent jarring shivers down her spine.

"Go back to your mistress, Lucero," she said clearly.

He hit the door again with considerable force. "Open this door or you'll regret it, Mercedes."

"Don't threaten me, Lucero."

A loud crash reverberated through the house, followed by a sharp crack as the sash splintered, tearing the bolt from its moorings and sending the door flying inward. Lucero stood in the opening with the light at his back, a tall, dark, menacing silhouette. His face was cast in shadows. Only his eyes glowed in the moonlight. Fathomless wolf's eyes with silver irises.

He ignored the old Walker Colt she held in both hands, leveled at him. "Don't ever bar a door to me again. Not in my own house, or anywhere else," he said in a soft, sudden rush. His voice was harsh, angry. He stepped into the room but she did not lower the weapon.

"You've made your point, Lucero. Now get out or I'll use this," she said quietly.

He advanced another two steps, smirking arrogantly. "Go ahead. Shoot." She hesitated, just as he knew she would. The pistol wavered the tiniest bit in her white-knuckled grip. "It isn't so easy to shoot a man up close in cold blood, is it?"

Now he was near enough that she could feel his heat surrounding her. Sweet Virgin, he had been drinking! She could smell the brandy fumes. "You obviously prefer Innocencia's skills," she argued, still holding the gun on him. "Heaven knows she's had enough practice and I've had none. Go back to her and welcome. You don't want me."

"Like hell I don't," he ground out, stepping directly in front of her, the barrel of the Colt pressed tight against his heart. "Cenci set this up just to drive a wedge between us and you're falling right into the trap." He grabbed her wrist and the gun dropped to the floor with a soft thud. She allowed him to pull her against him. "I told you, you couldn't shoot me, love." His voice was a soft purr now.

"You smell like a distillery," she said, turning her face away. "Did it take courage from an *aguardiente* bottle to confront me?"

"You're going to listen to me, dammit! I did not encourage Cenci. She came into the bathing room while I was asleep in the tub."

It had not occurred to her that he would deny what her

own eyes had seen. "Don't insult my intelligence, Lucero," she said contemptuously.

"Then use it. Think about what you saw—or *thought* you saw. She unfastened her blouse and leaned over the tub." He snarled a filthy oath that made Mercedes flinch as he added, "She had a hold on my cock when I woke up! A man is at a distinct disadvantage under those circumstances."

"Then you must've spent most of your adult life at the mercy of women," she snapped back, her cheeks red with mortification. If her *dueña* had lived to hear this, she would have been prostrate!

His angry scowl suddenly turned to an arrogant grin. "Your jealousy is showing, my little shrew. Only you have no reason for it. I don't want Cenci anymore. I want you." He put his arms around her and lowered his head to kiss her.

"You think it's just that easy. That I'll give in and let you have your way with me after you've consorted with that—that *puta*? Just because I couldn't shoot you?" She twisted away from his mouth.

"You're jealous of her, aren't you?"

"I despise her. She called Rosario a bastard this morning! If not for Bufón she would've struck your daughter." Mercedes was quivering with fury now.

He went very still, loosing his hold on her. "What do you mean? Explain what happened."

Mercedes bit her lip. Should she waste her breath? Did he care enough for his daughter to understand her anger with Innocencia? One look at the implacable expression on his face led her to outline the ugly scene in the courtyard and the exchange with his mistress. "I threatened to banish her. She reminded me that only you could do that," she concluded bitterly.

"So that's why she lay in wait for me tonight. She was afraid I'd send her packing," he said more to himself than to her.

Mercedes did not believe his story about the scene at the tub, but realized he would protect Rosario. "What will you do with her?"

"She won't ever again do or say anything that would hurt my daughter. I'll handle her." He tangled his hands in Mercedes' hair and forced her to look up into his face again. "Now . . . where were we, hmm?"

"I'm just supposed to accept that. You'll *handle* her, as I'm supposed to accept your dalliance with her? No, Lucero. Not anymore." She pushed suddenly and twisted out of his arms, her fury over his arrogance once more ignited.

"Yes, you will accept my word. I'm your husband and I've made you a damn sight more promises tonight than any good little wife has a right to expect." Damn, he knew Luce would never countenance her stubborn jealousy! He had already given in far too much. He reached out for her again and caught the edge of her robe, pulling it open and tearing the seam at the sleeve.

In pure reflex she slapped him, still shaking with rage and hurt and all the conflicting emotions that roiled inside her. The instant she felt her hand connect with his beard-roughened cheek, Mercedes knew she had committed a terrible blunder. His face was a satanic mask now, smiling, his voice a soft, deadly growl.

"That wasn't well done, for a dutiful wife, not well done at all." He advanced on her, his arm closing around her waist like a vise as he slammed her against him and held her, crushing the breath from her. Rage boiled inside him. Damn her, she was putting him in an impossible situation. "You know you're wrong, don't you, Mercedes?"

Mercedes looked up into his eyes, those blazing pitiless eyes. She pressed her palms against the wall of his chest. "I'm not wrong, I'm merely weaker. You will do what you wish. I can't stop you from raping me."

"Technically a husband cannot rape his wife," he said in a flat voice. *But you are not her husband*, an inner voice reminded him. He sighed, looking into her haunted eyes, dulled by resignation, then he released her. She stumbled back a step, surprised by his sudden move. "I've never resorted to rape, not even in the war where I saw my fill of it. I find I've no taste for it. No taste at all, Mercedes."

He turned and walked from the room, closing the bedroom door as best he could, leaving her standing alone in the darkness.

Over the next two weeks Nicholas and Mercedes slept apart, avoiding each other as much as possible. Every day he arose at dawn and rode out with his vaqueros, returning at dusk, sweat-soaked and exhausted. He fell into dreamless slumber, only to awaken with the first light and repeat the cycle like a man driven. Six days after he had broken down her door, he left with Hilario and the vaqueros to drive the fine horses they had finally captured to a safe hiding place in the maze of canyons around the Yaqui River valley. He told Angelina when he would return; he did not tell his wife.

Mercedes, too, kept herself continuously busy. Considering the way she had spent these past years, it was no novelty to her. But there was an obsessive quality to the way she worked. She was brittle, short of temper and unsmiling, not at all her normal self. The only exception to her taciturn behavior was in the way she treated Rosario, for Mercedes had come to adore the *patrón's* daughter. The household servants could sense the palpable tension between Don Lucero and his lady. They knew the *patrona* and her husband were feuding and did not sleep together. Smiling, they said once the proud *patrón* brought her back to his bed, all would be well with both of them.

After a long day supervising the digging of the irrigation ditches, Mercedes came back to the house, covered with mud, disheartened and bone weary. The work was going far too slowly and the crops desperately needed water. She soaked the mud from her body and washed her hair, then headed to the kitchen for a light supper at Angelina's hearth, shared with Rosario, a ritual that they had begun since the child had come to Gran Sangre. Rosario's wheedling voice carried across the courtyard as she approached.

"But why not? Please, Angelina, read me the end of the story. The lady has been so tired these past nights I dare not ask her, but I do so want to know how the prince finds his princess after the wicked queen banishes him."

"I'm sure they live happily ever after," Angelina replied as she stirred the pot of beans steaming on the stove. "Anyway, I do not know how to read," she added patiently. "People of our class have no time for education. That is for fine ladies like the *patrona*."

"Will I learn to read? Mother Superior said if I wanted to become a nun I might learn . . . but I really don't think I want to be a nun. I only want to read."

I only want to read. Mercedes read such a wealth of wistful sadness in those soft words. Rosario wanted more than an education. She wanted to feel she was worthy and that she belonged. No one had ever spent enough time with her, especially needful since her mother had died. She had been thrust into a strange new home with so much to assimilate. The child deserved much better than she had received from life.

Vowing that she would not neglect attending to Rosario's education another day, Mercedes entered the kitchen and walked over to the little girl who sat on the hearth with Bufón at her side. He stood up and barked a greeting, interrupting Angelina's awkward attempts to sidestep the child's direct questions, for the old cook had no real idea about the *patrón's* plans for his illegitimate daughter of mixed blood.

Mercedes thumped the big dog, dodging his slurping kisses, as Rosario giggled. Then she hugged the little girl. "What have you been reading—let me see?" She examined the book. "I don't remember this one," she said with a frown of confusion.

"That's because my papa gave it to me. He read half the story before he left to catch horses. See, here's the place." She flipped through the book and found the page, recognizing the line drawings at the top of the chapter.

Mercedes was taken aback. "Your papa has been reading to you?" At once she felt color flood her face as Angelina's eyes averted from her in compassion. *Everyone knows we're not sleeping together, barely even talking.*

"Oh, yes. He said he would finish it when he returned, but I can't wait," Rosario replied, unaware of the byplay between the lady and the cook.

Given his long hours in the saddle, Mercedes wondered when Lucero had found time. Rosario's chatter quickly answered that question.

"When you were getting cleaned up after you worked so late in the fields, he came to my room and read to me before you tucked me in bed. I guess I got so sleepy by then I didn't tell you," she added uncertainly.

Mercedes swallowed the lump in her throat. "I've been neglecting you since we've been working on those accursed ditches," she said, taking Rosario in her arms.

"Don't feel sad. It's all right," the child consoled her. "Papa was there and now that he has to be away, you're here." She touched Mercedes' lavender-scented hair, still damp from her bath. "You smell sweet. Different from Papa. His hair would be wet, too, but it didn't smell sweet. I like the way it smelled, though. Do you?"

Angelina's spoon clinked into the bean pot, then was quickly retrieved as the cook busied herself, hiding the sly smile she could not contain by turning her back on the red-faced *patrona*.

Ignoring the child's question and the cook's reaction, Mercedes said to Rosario, "From now on I promise never again to forego reading to you." *And tomorrow I'll tell Father Salvador to begin your formal education,* she vowed to herself.

Facing the stern old priest was a lot more difficult than making the promise to herself the night before. Mercedes had been raised to be devout by her parents and later by the kindly example of the Carmelite nuns who had taught her, yet she had felt intimidated by her mother-in-law's confessor from the first time she was introduced to him by Doña Sofia.

Mercedes had gone weekly to confession and mass and always observed fasts and holy days, but Father Salvador's icy blue eyes seemed to pierce her very soul, even through the grille of the confessional. When she had assumed the duties that should have belonged to the *patrón*, she had elicited the censure of Doña Sofia's priest.

At first Father Salvador had advised and cautioned sternly.

When she had ridden out with the vaqueros and worked beside the peons, he had been outraged. Then Colonel Rodriguez and his Imperial Lancers had ridden up to the great house, arrogantly assuming in the *patrón's* absence that his woman would give over anything the soldiers wished. The colonel had cornered her in the wine cellar the second night of his "visit," intent on raping her. She had faced him down with that old Walker Colt which she had been unable to use on Lucero.

After she had seen the French patrol on their way with her weapon cocked and aimed at Rodriguez's chest, Father Salvador had given her a fearful penance. Considering how killingly angry she had been and how greatly the sin of murder would have weighed on her conscience, Mercedes had accepted his pronouncements. But the course of their relationship thereafter had been tense and fraught with mutual mistrust. He did not understand a woman driven to assume a man's role. It was unnatural, against the will of God. But Mercedes had been unable to give up her new identity. So they had reached a stalemate.

At least since Lucero's return, the priest could no longer accuse her of usurping his role, and the animosity between Father Salvador and her husband was so intense her sins had paled by comparison. With that thought to fortify her, she knocked on the door of his study and entered when he called out for her to do so.

Father Salvador looked up from his breviary, his pale eyes fixed on her intently. "Good morning, Doña Mercedes. What may I do for you? Is there something special you wish to confess?"

"No, Father, I haven't come to make confession."

"Well, what then? You've missed the mass I celebrated in Doña Sofia's room an hour ago. It would be of comfort to her if you would join her more often."

Mercedes grimaced inwardly. The very last thing her mother-in-law wished was for her to be present each morning. She barely tolerated her son's wife on Sundays. "I've come about Rosario, Father."

"Rosario? You mean the child your husband brought here?" His pale face reddened.

"His daughter, yes."

"But not yours," he put in, studying her keenly.

"She is my husband's child, an innocent, beautiful little girl, and I'm concerned for her future."

"Ah," he interjected, walking around the desk to place a consoling hand on her shoulder.

It felt stiffly unnatural to Mercedes.

"It would be best if you had children of your own. In time the Lord in his mercy may provide. Perhaps if you prayed to Our Lady—"

Now it was her face with the heightened color. "No—that is, of course I want more children, but that has nothing to do with caring for Rosario."

"I realize your husband's responsibility toward the girl, but it would have been far wiser if he had provided for her elsewhere than at Gran Sangre. Flaunting his infidelities has been a painful reminder to his mother of his and his father's shortcomings. I would think you, too—"

"Rosario is a little girl—not a *painful reminder* of anything," she retorted angrily. "She is Doña Sofia's first grandchild."

He shook his head, for once not at all the sternly self-assured naysayer, but an uncertain old man. "Yes, yes, I've thought of that . . . prayed on it a great deal. She understands the Alvarado family's responsibility for the little girl . . . but the child's mother was a mixed blood."

"That makes Rosario none the less Lucero's daughter." There was cold accusation in her voice.

He sighed. "No, it does not. I have tried to gain Doña Sofia's acceptance of that fact, but her son was never an easy child himself, always a trial to her as was his father. She finds it difficult to accept the idea of an illegitimate child living in the family quarters of the great house. She is old, used to the traditional ways."

"And what about you, Father? Are you too old to change as well?" she asked, shifting the focus to him, for she sensed his guilt and confusion. *Let Sofia be damned for the hypocrite she is.*

His chilly blue eyes softened the tiniest bit. "I am an old man who has spent his life attempting to guide the spiritual welfare of the Obregón and Alvarado families, two of the noblest houses in Mexico. Now it is nearing time for me to turn my attention to the younger generation. In my grief for your mother-in-law, I have not been as diligent a counselor for you as I should have been."

"I'm not the one who needs your counsel now, Father," Mercedes said, surprised by the old priest's startling revelation. "It's Rosario."

He looked puzzled. "Surely she has received Holy Baptism with the Ursulines."

"Yes, of course," she replied, dismissing the mistaken idea and blurting out her request. "I want you to teach Rosario to read and write. I know you didn't teach Lucero, but we can't afford private tutors now."

He considered, then walked toward the small window facing out to the mountains where Lucero had ridden. "Have you discussed this with your husband?"

"No, but he was reading to her the same as I—I know he will wish it, too."

"I do not mean to sound callous, but it was a mistake, his bringing the child to Gran Sangre. The *hacendados* will never accept her. If she is educated, raised as a *criolla*, what will happen to her when she is of marriageable age? Her expectations may be beyond what our society permits." The old man's concern seemed genuine.

Mercedes could not argue with his logic for she knew what he said was true, but still she heard the voice of a lonely little girl saying, *I only want to read.* "As she grows up, we'll deal with the situation. Lucero has chosen to bring her into our home and asked her to address him as Papa. She will be raised with all the advantages of the Alvarado name."

"But she will not have them," he gently chided.

"I have heard there are ways legitimacy can be arranged," she said hopefully.

"For natural sons in the absence of legal heirs, perhaps, but for a girl, it would not be easy even in ordinary times, and these are not ordinary times in which we live, Doña Mercedes."

Her eyes grew haunted, thinking of Lucero's oblique references to the horrors of his wartime experiences. Quashing that thought, she asked doggedly, "Will you teach her, Father?"

His shoulders sagged wearily. "Bring Rosario to me after she has broken her fast and we will begin. I only pray she will prove a more tractable pupil than her father."

With a small smile of triumph, Mercedes went in search of Lucero's daughter.

For the next several days after Mercedes went out to the fields in the morning, Lupe took Rosario to Father Salvador for her lessons. Then just before the noon hour, Mercedes would return to the house to share luncheon, and take Rosario back to the riverside where her men toiled on the irrigation project. Bufón, the child's ever constant companion, watched her zealously.

"When will my papa be back? He told Angelina it would be yesterday, but he isn't here," Rosario said plaintively early one afternoon at the riverside.

Wiping the rivulets of perspiration from her eyes, Mercedes replied, "I'm not certain. When the vaqueros have to ride out so far, it sometimes takes longer than they can predict. Remember, Gran Sangre has over four million acres of land."

The little girl's eyes widened as she tried to imagine four million of anything, an impossible feat for a child not yet five years old. Then abruptly switching back to her own earlier query, she said, "I miss him. Do you miss him, too?"

Mercedes was unprepared for the question and quickly glanced about to see if anyone else had overheard it, knowing how the servants gossiped about the marital problems of their *patrón* and *patrona*. No one was within earshot as she replied equivocally, "I've been wondering when he'll return."

In fact she had been losing considerable sleep over Lucero's homecoming, knowing he would by now expect her to come to his bed again. After all, they did have their duty to the vaunted Alvarado name. Gran Sangre must have an heir. And since his return from the war, her husband was amazingly attentive to his responsibilities.

She had heard the servants comment on the long grueling hours he put in on horseback and had seen firsthand how dust-covered and bone weary he was, had even seen the rope burns on his hands and bruises on his body from working with half-wild cattle left to roam free until they were rounded up and driven into safe hiding. If his plan succeeded, the hacienda would actually have preserved a good number of cattle and even some superb saddle mounts.

If only her own project were going half so well. Bleakly she surveyed the irrigation ditch through the withering heat. They had dug the main channel only thirty yards after all these days of backbreaking labor. The soil was hard and dry, but the men were strong and willing to dig. They would have moved three times the distance but for the dense chaparral and prickly pear cactus that grew across the only low-lying area between the river and the arable soil they had cultivated for crops. The sharp spines and dense root systems had to be hacked away with machetes, leaving the workers cut and scratched. The scent of their blood brought the torment of flies and there was the ever present danger of infection in the hot climate.

The crops will all die before we reach them with water, she thought despairingly, looking up at the cloudless blinding azure of the noon sky. Then she felt the vibration of the horses' hooves before she spotted the dust cloud stirred up by the group of riders coming toward them.

"Don Lucero!" several of the men called out, recognizing the magnificent stallion her husband rode. Rosario joined the servants, who dropped their tools or paused from eating the last bites of their midday meal, to go greet the *patrón*. His wife alone held back, standing beneath the shade of the willow near the river, watching the joyous reunion.

Lucero picked up his daughter and spun her around to squeals of delight as Bufón whoofed loudly in welcome. She watched him wrestle affectionately with the big dog, wondering again what had wrought the mutual change in disposition between man and animal. Rosario clapped her hands and giggled at their antics, then joined in.

What a good father he's proving to be, she thought, amazed. Who would have imagined that Lucero Alvarado would ever even look at his children, especially a by-blow he need never acknowledge. He had even gone to his daughter's room at night and read to her. Mercedes found it too much to reconcile with the dangerously angry man who had broken down her door in a drunken fit.

Then her husband whispered something in Rosario's ear. The child and Bufón remained behind as he walked past the riders watering their horses at the river's edge. He approached her. His hair was matted with sweat and his clothes plastered to his skin. Several fresh cuts and bruises on his hands attested to long and difficult hours working stock. He had shed the bandoleros crisscrossing his chest and opened his shirt, revealing sun-bronzed skin furred with black hair. He studied her through eyes narrowed against the sun's glare, his flat crowned hat pushed rakishly back on his head after playing with Rosario and Bufón. His expression revealed nothing.

"Hello, Mercedes." He waited expectantly, knowing everyone surreptitiously watched them, waiting to see what she would do.

Her throat collapsed and her mouth was drier than the clouds of dust kicked up by the horses' hooves. He looked hard and dangerous. She could still conjure up the image of him standing in her doorway after smashing it in. "You're late. Rosario and Angelina hoped you'd return yesterday," she finally managed to blurt out.

A sardonic smile creased his face. "And you, of course, hoped I never would."

"Don't expect me to deny it," she replied acerbically.

He laughed and stepped closer, his arm snaking out with amazing speed to clasp her about the waist and pull her to him. "For the benefit of our audience," he murmured low as his lips came down on hers.

Chapter 10

Mercedes stiffened at the sudden assault as his mouth took hers savagely. She could taste the salty tang of male sweat as his tongue plunged inside her lips and thrust across her teeth, brushing her tongue. Then abruptly he withdrew, raising his head and looking down at her with hooded eyes. She would have fallen if he had not been holding her up. His musky scent was tinged with tobacco and leather. The male smell permeated her senses as she held onto his biceps, bemused and breathless. The look of predatory hunger on his face was no longer masked. She could feel it arc between them like a lightning strike.

He took a lock of her hair in his fingers, brushing it from where it lay plastered by perspiration to her forehead. "You've been working too hard. Your nose is sunburned."

Mercedes suddenly realized how dreadful she must look in an old muslin *camisa* and faded blue skirts, her leather peasants sandals caked with river mud, her hair ratty. "Your mother continually reminds me of my failure to maintain a proper degree of ladylike pallor."

"I didn't intend that as a chastisement." He released her, yet stood close, waiting to see if she would back away.

She did not. "Your father said mucking about in the dirt with peons was beneath an Alvarado."

"As I'm certain you noted, my father could be something of a pompous ass as well as a lazy son of a bitch."

She smiled in surprise. "I never expected you to say a word against your boyhood idol."

His teeth gleamed whitely in a rakish grin. "Boys do grow up sooner or later . . . just as girls do."

The sexual overtones of his words and his demeanor were unmistakable. Why did he not just go to Innocencia and have done with it? *He wants you*, an inner voice taunted. Ignoring it, she changed the subject. "You got the black stallion and his herd?"

"All safely penned up for the winter. No one, not even the Juaristas, will find them."

"I only wish my project were as successful," she said, looking out to where the peons hacked at the unyielding wall of spiky cacti and gnarled chaparral. "We've been digging for over a week and we aren't halfway there yet."

"You need a more effective way to clear the brush."

She looked at him crossly. "A well-directed lightning strike would be very helpful but I don't think you're in any position to arrange it."

He threw back his head and that rich deep laugh again rumbled. "No, but my vaqueros might be able to do the next best thing."

As Lucero walked across to the cluster of horsemen and issued instructions, Mercedes called Rosario to her. Bufón bounded beside the child. The three of them watched while he mounted Peltre and the others rounded up their horses from the riverbank. Then the men set to work with reatas, roping the big squat clumps of prickly pear. The ropes bit into the cactus, impervious to its lethal spines. Wrapping the reatas around their saddle horns, they spurred their horses, pulling up giant clumps of earth along with the plants.

"Oh, look! Papa and his men are making the ditch so much faster," Rosario said, ignoring the dust clouds billowing around them.

Bufón ran out to the horsemen, chasing the great bundles of brushy roots as they bounced along the ground, barking excitedly at the wonderful new game. Mercedes and Rosario laughed at his antics as he veered off course, darting after jackrabbits, lizards and small rodents displaced by the uprooted vegetation.

Within a few hours the riders had cleared a channel over fifty yards long. Juan directed the course of their labors and his men followed behind with their shovels, deepening the ditch easily through the loosened earth. The vaqueros accomplished more by late that afternoon than the peons had in a week of backbreaking work afoot. They would clear a path to the fields within another day.

Everyone returned to the house that evening, coughing from the dust, too exhausted to talk except for Rosario, who rode in her father's arms, chattering excitedly about her lessons.

"Father Salvador is cross sometimes, but he is ever so smart. Already I've memorized the alphabet. He says soon I shall be writing my letters." Nicholas cocked an eyebrow in surprise, looking across at Mercedes, who rode beside him.

"I convinced him that your daughter would make a good pupil . . . unlike her father," she said, daring him to object, yet certain that he wanted this for Rosario as much as she did.

"I'm astounded the old . . . er, that is, the good father would take to teaching a child." *Especially Luce's child.*

Rosario piped up, "He does say I'm his cross to bear in old age—but he says you were awful wicked when you were a little boy, Papa."

Mercedes hid a smile.

When they reached the house, Mercedes took Rosario from Lucero and looked up at him. "Our crops would've died for certain without the irrigation. Thank you."

He nodded. "What is a husband for?" His eyes locked with hers, his meaning clear as the promise for that night. Then he rode toward the stables.

Nicholas expended more energy grooming Peltre then he normally would have, especially considering the hellishly hard week he had just put in on the range. He needed the time to think and to cool down himself before he did something foolish. Mercedes had haunted his dreams nightly while he slept on the cold hard earth and had filled his head daily as he chased horses. The visions of her lithe golden body incited him to lust, just as her repressed desire and jealousy incited him to anger. And he had been angry that awful night. Killingly angry. He had come within an inch of doing what his brother would have—raping her without a thought of the ultimate repercussion for their relationship.

Never before in his life had a woman stirred his emotions so intensely. Since Lottie had shipped him off to Texas he had made it a point to remain aloof from any personal entanglements. Women were a commodity to a professional soldier, pleasure and divertissement to be bought like whiskey and tobacco, used and discarded the same as he tossed away empty bottles and cigarette butts. Innocencia was that kind of a woman. Mercedes was not.

He, Nicholas Fortune, had a wife and a child through the good offices—however unintentional—of his brother. The child he was finding amazingly delightful to deal with, but not the woman. She was a lady like none he had ever met before. He could still see her standing sweaty and sunburned when he rode up. Even wearing drab loose fitting *paisana's* clothing, no one could mistake her for anything else but the *patrona*. Every patrician feature, every movement right down to the regal tilt of her head bespoke generations of breeding. And pride.

Mercedes was proud and Luce had shamed her. That was what complicated their relationship now. She could not trust him. But even deeper lay the question that ate at him as he curried Peltre with long smooth strokes. Could a loner like Nicholas Fortune ever trust a woman like Mercedes Alvarado? "I have to control this obsession with her, dammit! She's my wife and she *will* come to me. I don't have to beg crumbs from the *patrona's* table!"

Finally he finished with the stallion and turned him over to the elderly stableman, then went to the bathing room to scrub off a week's worth of ground-in grime. As he dressed for dinner, all he could think of was how much he wanted to make love to his wife. An intimate dinner in the large dining room with only the two of them would fray his already taut nerves past the snapping point.

When he walked downstairs, Lupe greeted him shyly. "Doña Mercedes asks that you come to the kitchen." Surprised by the unusual request, he nodded and headed toward

Angelina's fragrant domain as the smell of spicy rabbit stew filled the air. No *machos* tonight, glory be to God! He walked into the room and found Mercedes and Rosario sitting at the long trestle table by the courtyard window.

"Papa, are you going to eat with us? We missed you while you were gone."

"I decided to eat informally while we were all working late outdoors. It's been easier. If you wish, I can have Lupe set the dining room table," Mercedes said.

She was fresh from her own bath, her hair piled up on top of her head in damp ringlets, her skin glowing rose gold from days in the sun. She wore a simple peach-colored muslin gown trimmed with white embroidery. He forgot all about food. "This will be fine for tonight," he said, pulling up a heavy pine chair, crudely bound together with rawhide strapping

They ate the hearty fare, exchanging bits of conversation about the stock roundup and the growth of crops, speculating on what the weather might be over the rest of the summer season, with occasional interjections from Rosario. It would have seemed to a casual observer that this was a happy family, comfortably ensconced in a familiar routine. But the promise of the night to follow created a subtle tension between Nicholas and Mercedes that belied the mundane words they spoke.

Outside in the shadows of the stable, two men held another sort of conversation.

"I say he has changed. Porfirio is right. We should do as the *gringo* asks," the young vaquero argued.

The older man inhaled his cigarette, his eyes glowing in the darkness that surrounded his weathered features. "Oh, Don Lucero has changed, all right," he said with a wry laugh. "You did not know him as a boy or you would recognize just how much he has changed."

"I know *criollo* haughtiness," the youth replied. "There was a day when he would never have ridden with us, sweaty and rope-burned as we are. Now he has slept beside us, shared our humble food and taken his pull at the jug of pulque when it was passed around the campfire. He has become a man of the people. The war made him see things differently. He left the army because he could no longer support the usurpers."

"Don Lucero did not spend much time in the army," the older man corrected his youthful companion. "He ended up a *contre-guerrilla*, the worst of the lot, cutthroats in imperial pay." He spat in disgust, remembering the last time he had seen their handiwork in a nearby village.

"I don't understand. You said you liked the man he has become since he's returned to Gran Sangre," Gregorio said in bewilderment.

"That does not mean I would trust him enough to approach him openly. Not yet. We need time to see if this man is as he seems to be."

"We have no time to waste. I know Don Lucero will help us."

"If he *is* Don Lucero . . ." Hilario replied emphatically. "If not, perhaps we can trust him more. Or perhaps even less."

When Mercedes realized her husband stood in the doorway to her room, she set her hairbrush down on the dressing table and turned to him. His hand grazed the smooth new wood of the door sash and he glanced at it, then quirked one eyebrow at her.

Mercedes recalled the knowing smirk of the carpenter who had come to refit the broken door. "I had it repaired," was all she said.

"But you didn't relock it. Perhaps we're making some progress." His voice was smooth as he glided into her bedroom.

"I've tucked Rosario in. She enjoyed the story you read her very much," she evaded, nervously moistening her lips.

"Soon she'll be reading herself. But this isn't the time for discussing fairy tales." He emanated a dark current of sexual heat that touched her before he so much as laid a hand on her.

"No, I suppose not. Our marriage could scarcely be

described in fairy-tale terms unless you wish to make an analogy to *Beauty and the Beast*," she replied tartly.

"Ah, but which of us is which?" He chuckled as he reached for her hand, pulling her up. "Time for bed, Mercedes."

Then to her utter amazement and chagrin, he turned and walked arrogantly back through the door, as if expecting her to follow like some obedient pet! "I suppose you expect me properly chastised enough to heel," she said, fighting the urge to fly at his broad back and shred the elegant brocade robe from his shoulders.

Nicholas had deliberately left her, determined to win the contest of wills. He turned to face her, standing beside the big four poster bed. "I will not drag you nightly into this bed you've sworn to occupy with me, Mercedes. You must know I desire you by now. I've explained all I intend to about Cenci. She doesn't interest me in the least and I'll not waste any further breath on her."

"Or on me, it would appear," she replied, disgusted by his male ego.

He grinned rakishly. "Oh, I intend to expend a great deal of breath—hot labored breath—on you. And it won't be a waste at all. Come here." His voice was hoarse and low, rasping out the command.

Obediently she crossed the threshold and removed her robe.

Over the next few months they fell into a pattern, working in cooperation through the days, putting in long arduous hours: he handling the stock, she in charge of the crops which grew lushly rich because of the irrigation ditches. They both played with Rosario, although Mercedes did so at the noon break, Nicholas in the evenings. The child was incredibly bright, finishing her first primer within six weeks. At every meal the *patrón* and *patrona* spoke of everyday matters pertaining to the hacienda, the weather, politics, much as any ordinary couple might.

But when night fell and they retired to the master bedroom, they were transformed. Nicholas became the passionate aggressor, claiming a husband's rights to her body while Mercedes remained coolly resistant—on the surface. She acquiesced to her marital duties but was painfully determined to suppress any spark of answering fire which would give him an emotional hold on her. He stalked her, sometimes seducing her with incredible gentleness, taking hours to caress and tease her body, which occasionally betrayed evidence of how difficult it was becoming for her to lie passive beneath his touch. Other times, in frustration, he took her quickly with no preliminaries, then rolled over and fell asleep while she lay beside him, staring into the darkness with the deep persistent ache in her belly still unassuaged. As for the ache in her soul . . . that she never dared consider at all.

She spent every night in his bed for he would permit it no other way. Part of her cried out at the humiliating invasion of her privacy, of the breach of civilized tradition for husbands and wives of their class—separate bedrooms. Yet there was an insidious sense of warmth and familiarity that grew with the passage of time as he held her against his long hard body every night. She slept with his heartbeat steady and strong in her ear.

A small voice deep inside her reminded her that if he was with her, he was not with Innocencia. After the one incriminating incident in the bathhouse, Mercedes never saw Lucero pay the slightest attention to his former mistress. Perhaps he had merely tired of her after encountering far more exotic and sophisticated women during the war. Or perhaps he really desired only his wife. Had he not repeatedly said so in his mockingly arrogant manner? Could that mocking arrogance be *his* shield? She felt an increasing tension building inside her as time passed and she sensed that only Lucero could assuage her restless spirit . . . if she gave in to his touch. Could she ever learn to trust her husband?

One bright autumn morning sunlight poured in the narrow slit between the heavy velvet draperies of Doña Sofia's room. The old woman had rallied a bit with the coming of cooler weather. She had been sitting up in a chair for brief intervals after mass. Now she leaned forward and peered through the opening in the draperies. The window overlooked the well at one end of the courtyard. Mercedes was passing by the shelter of the fig trees when Lucero emerged from the thick foliage to intercept her.

The old woman's rheumy eyes narrowed avidly as she watched him pull Mercedes against his chest for a swift scorching kiss. His hands tangled in her gold hair, bending her head backward while his mouth ravaged hers. He was hard and dark as an Aztec god in contrast to her English paleness. His hands caressed her with such practiced familiarity that it drew a stuffy gasp of outrage from Dona Sofia

From her vantage point it seemed to the old woman that Mercedes participated in the sinuous blending of their bodies. Then he released her abruptly and she disappeared behind the fig trees, leaving him standing beside the well with an arrogant grin on his handsome face. The devil's face. His father's face. But was it her son's face?

"From the look of things, he'll soon enough have her breeding if she isn't already carrying his child," she muttered to herself, leaning back in her chair, weakened by the exertion of sitting forward. How Anselmo would hate it, she thought with relish.

"You will roar up from hell, old man, when your bastard's bastard lays claim to Gran Sangre!" Her laugh was dry as parchment in the quiet darkness.

A sudden shortness of breath seized her then and she began to cough, quickly bringing Lazaro running into the room. The servant scooped up the frail old woman and deposited her against the mound of pillows at the head of her bed. She weighed no more than a child these days. Then he rang for help as the old *patrona* struggled to breathe.

Father Salvador was summoned at once and the physician from a nearby village was sent for. When she began to spit up fresh blood by early evening, Father Salvador administered the last rites as Nicholas and Mercedes looked on in silence. The old woman was unaware of their presence.

The doctor arrived late in the evening but could do little to alleviate her shortness of breath. He did agree to allow Angelina, who was an excellent herbalist, to distill a drink of aromatic royal salvia and walnut bark. Patiently she and Mercedes took turns spooning the broth down Doña Sofia's throat. By midnight she was sleeping peacefully.

Mercedes stepped from the sickroom into the hall, thinking only of a hot soak and a good night's sleep when she saw Father Salvador standing by the stairs. He approached her, his expression grave.

"There is something of urgency, Doña. I beg a private word with you."

She nodded, then followed him down the hall where he ushered her into his small office. The walls were filled with religious books. A stark wooden *prie deux* stood against the fourth wall with a heavy crucifix hung in front of it. Statues of various saints looked on with solemn eyes as he offered her a seat.

He paced across the bare wood floor, then turned to face her. "While I have attended Doña Sofia these past months of her illness, she has spoken little or nothing of her son's return."

A tiny smile twitched at the corner of Mercedes' mouth in spite of her fatigue. "I'm surprised she hasn't made confession to you of uncharitable thoughts about him."

He fixed her with an intent blue gaze. "I could never, of course, violate the sanctity of the confessional," he replied sternly, then sank onto the hard-backed chair behind his desk with a sigh. "I will say that I am troubled over the state of her soul."

"You mean because she hates her son?"

His head jerked up abruptly. "How did you—surely she has never spoken such aloud!"

"Not in so many words, no. Nor has my husband been any more forthcoming on the subject. But I've seen them together—and even more, I've lived with her these past four years while he was away. She blames him for his father's sins."

"He has quite enough of his own to answer for," Father Salvador replied testily.

"Yes, he does, but that doesn't excuse her treatment of him. I think she disliked him even as a boy," Mercedes said thoughtfully, recalling oblique comments Lucero had made in past months.

"There was much to dislike," he said quickly, then leaned his elbows on the desk and rubbed the bridge of his nose, deep in thought.

When he resumed speaking, his voice was distant and soft, recalling painful memories of long ago. "He was a difficult child, willful and spoiled, as most *criollos* seem born to be. But incredibly bright, quick of mind. That very inventive mind was what continually got him into trouble, but I should have seen the potential in him as I do in his daughter now. Alas, I did not and for that I will have to answer one day." He looked up for a moment, staring at nothing at all, then resumed, "He was impious and defiant, willing to take the most severe caning rather than recant any wicked words or actions. He would steal, lie bald-faced. When he wished he could charm the birds from the trees."

Her smile was brittle. "Traits no doubt inherited from Don Anselmo."

"Yes," he replied. "Lucero adored his father's debauched way of life and attempted to emulate it."

"As Don Anselmo's only son and mirror image, it was only natural he'd turn to his father, no matter how poor an example he was. Perhaps Lucero was only looking for someone to love him," she added softly.

Father Salvador seemed to age visibly before her eyes. "Yes, I have been forced, here of late, to consider that and to examine my own culpability in not seeing how the son came to be set on the father's course. However, it is not my guilt, but rather his mother's that concerns me now. She and Lucero should be reconciled before she dies."

Mercedes looked startled. "Is that why you wanted to speak to me?"

"Who else? You are his wife. He would take the suggestion more readily from you than me. We have not dealt well together since the first time I caught him beating one of the peons' sheepdogs with a leather harness. There always was a streak of cruelty in Lucero."

Remembering how Bufón had grown to love her husband

now, she quickly interjected, "But he's changed. He has a natural way with animals."

He smiled thinly. "There, you see? You are the only one who can approach him. Perhaps if he goes to his mother as she lies dying, the two of them can reach some sort of accord. It is not only for her that this is important, but for him as well."

She could feel his eyes piercing her, willing her to agree. "I will try, Father, but I can promise nothing."

"Surely you're not serious," Nicholas said with the jaundiced lift of one eyebrow. They stood facing each other in his study the following evening. He busied himself pouring predinner glasses of Madeira, then handed her one and said, "Ah, but ever devout Christian that you are, you must be serious. So, I'm to be reconciled with my beloved *mamacita* on her deathbed, eh? It will serve nothing, Mercedes," he stated flatly. "She's despised me from the day I was born and she may take her hate with her to her grave and welcome." Bitterness laced the words as another cold unnatural mother's face flashed before his eyes.

"Father Sal—"

"And that old bastard with his hickory cane may hastily join her," he interrupted, then gulped down the last of his Madeira.

"I think he regrets how he treated you. Rosario has made him see his mistakes. He wants to atone, Lucero."

At the mention of the child's name, Nicholas's expression softened. "Rosario does seem to get on well with the old goat. She read to me from her primer yesterday. Her progress is amazing."

"We owe it to Father Salvador," she countered.

Before he could say anything, Baltazar walked hurriedly into the room. His normally reserved, cool face was now set in lines of agitation. "*Patrón*, there are soldiers coming."

"Imperial or Juarista?" Nicholas asked, heading quickly to the cabinet where he kept his weapons.

"I do not know. I have sent for Gregorio as you instructed me to do in such an emergency."

"Good. My men know what to do," Fortune replied, levering open the breech of his Henry and checking its load. Snapping it shut, he turned to Mercedes. "Get Rosario and take her to the kitchen. Stay with Angelina, behind the stone hearth. Whatever you do, stay out of sight."

"I know how to fire a gun, Lucero. I've faced soldiers on my own before. I had to," she retorted, angry at his clipped dismissal.

"Well, you no longer have to—do as I say. Think of the child if not yourself," he snarled impatiently.

The reminder of Rosario stilled her angry retort. She nodded but did take the shotgun with her.

Fortune had arranged a contingency plan with his men in the event that marauders of either side menaced Gran Sangre. The massive square adobe building had four-foot-thick walls. Although the windows facing the inner courtyard were large and low, those to the outside were high and narrow, good rifle ports. Like most of the great haciendas in the north, it had been constructed as a natural fortress.

By the time he reached the courtyard, all the men were in position atop the roof and in the gateways. When he was in Hermosillo hiring new vaqueros, he was also able to procure some contraband weapons with which to arm them. The new Sharps breechloading carbines were secured from an enterprising group of *contre-guerrillas* who had stolen the American weapons enroute to General Escobedo's army in Chihuahua.

He quickly crossed the courtyard to where Hilario and his young companion, Gregorio, were waiting by the main gateway facing the road. Although only eighteen, the boy had a levelheaded assurance about him that struck a chord of recognition in Fortune, who had been a seasoned veteran of several campaigns by that age. He had not asked Gregorio Sanchez for which side he had ridden; he did not care. His only concern was that Sanchez was loyal to Gran Sangre now. And Hilario, whom he knew to be a lifelong Alvarado retainer, had vouched for the youth.

Gregorio was peering out at the trail where a plume of dust rose as the column of soldiers approached, his expression intent as he plied the spyglass. "They are Juaristas, *Patrón*. Around twenty of them, traveling fast." He handed the glass to Fortune.

Nicholas studied the column, recognizing the insignia of the Republic of Mexico that the officer was wearing. "They're not well armed. I doubt they'll want to make a fight of it. I wonder what the devil they're up to?"

"Perhaps the French chase them?" Hilario speculated.

Nicholas shrugged. "Not very likely. Wrong direction. They're headed toward Sinaloa, but there's only one way to find out." He watched as the lieutenant signaled his men to halt down by the bank of the river, where it snaked nearest the house. He noted they were careful not to trample Mercedes' fields. Most of the corn and other crops had been harvested now, but should she see any damage inflicted, she would probably open up with that shotgun, he thought with grim humor.

The lieutenant was a small, thin man with almost delicate features offset by a heavy straight mustache. He rode up to the front gate, flanked by two of his men. After assessing the three armed men with a practiced eye, hc dismounted. "Good day," he said, smiling broadly. "I am Lieutenant Bolivar Montoya, Army of the Republic of Mexico."

"Don Lucero Alvarado, *patrón* of Gran Sangre, a hacienda lately fallen on evil times," Nicholas replied.

"Who among us in these times has not found them evil, Don Lucero? My men and I mean you no harm. We are on our way to join with General Diaz in the south. Our horses are drinking from the river but my men could use fresh water from your well, if that is possible?"

Montoya was the soul of courtesy, if that was all indeed he "could use." Fortune observed the man's uniform, scarcely up to French standards of spit and polish but a real uniform nonetheless. He had the bearing of a career soldier and his men were uniformed, albeit poorly. They were not banditti, but that did not mean they would be adverse to appropriating any loose livestock, food or other materials for the republic. "Your men are welcome to water but you will understand my reluctance to admit twenty armed men to the interior of my courtyard, Lieutenant Montoya?"

The mustache lifted in a genial smile. "But of course, I understand." He shrugged. "It will scarcely be the first time we have drunk muddy water with our horses and been grateful for it."

"There's no need," Fortune said. "My men will draw buckets and bring them outside the compound for your soldiers to fill their canteens. We have little in provisions left but if you need cornmeal or beans, we could let you have some."

"You are most gracious, Don Lucero. We could most certainly use extra rations," the lieutenant replied as Nicholas indicated the officer should follow him into the courtyard and have a seat.

After giving terse instructions to Gregorio to have the houseboys haul water and fetch some sacks of corn and beans, he said to his guest, "Angelina will bring us some coffee, although I must apologize that it is cut with chicory."

"It does not matter, for we have tasted no coffee in weeks. Few of the *hacendados* have been so hospitable," he said dryly. "Are you a supporter of President Juarez then?"

Nicholas shrugged, then grinned frankly. "I support the side that wins."

Lieutenant Montoya laughed, then his narrow face grew earnest and his black eyes glowed with conviction. "If that is so, I strongly advise you to stand behind the republic. I've just come from El Paso del Norte where I met Don Benito. A very great man."

"So I've heard," Nicholas replied thoughtfully, as they sipped the coffee Angelina brought from the kitchen. Over the years he had heard stories of Juarez from friend and foe alike. The more time he spent in Mexico, the more he had acquired a grudging respect for the integrity and stubbornness of the little Indian from Oaxaca. Juarez was a country lawyer with an utter lack of self-aggrandizement. When he had arrived in Mexico City to assume his legal role as president of the republic, Juarez had worn a plain wool suit and ridden in a small black carriage without fanfare. It was a startling contrast to the extravagant pomp and lavishly gilded lifestyle of the emperor and his court, and that contrast was not at all favorable to the puppets the French had placed on the throne. Montoya's next words immediately caught Fortune's attention.

"The president has just held a secret meeting on the border with the North American General Sheridan. The Yankee brought assurances from Washington that now the Southern rebellion has been crushed, the Union will turn its attention to the French invaders on Mexican soil."

"Noble sentiments," Fortune replied, "but what is he doing to back them up?"

Montoya's eyes lit up. "Much! The whole arsenal in Baton Rouge has been emptied out. The guns and ammunition are already being distributed among General Escobedo's army in Chihuahua. Within a year we will sweep from the north while General Diaz comes out of Oaxaca in the south. The French—if they are so foolish as to remain—will be caught in a great pincer along with Maximilian's so-called Imperial Mexican army."

Nicholas rubbed his jaw in consideration. "I've heard rumors in Hermosillo that General Bazaine has received orders from Napoleon to begin a withdrawal. At first I didn't believe it." He shrugged.

"Believe it," Montoya replied earnestly. "With the United States government supporting us now that their war is over, Juarez cannot lose."

Mercedes stormed out of the kitchen no sooner than Lieutenant Montoya's troops had ridden away, saying, "I can't believe you gave our food—*my* cornmeal—to those republican rabble!"

"Best to keep our options open, beloved."

She looked at his thoughtful expression. "You actually think they'll win?" she asked incredulously.

"I'd say the chances are becoming better than ever. While you've been isolated here in Sonora, struggling to hold the hacienda together, I've ridden from Guerrero to Coahuila and back. I've seen the way the imperials take a state or a town, then can't hold it against the constant guerrilla assaults. These people never give up, Mercedes. They fight with their machetes, hell, with their bare hands if they have to. You of all people should understand that kind of stubbornness."

She could feel his eyes on her and knew he was also alluding to their own nightly warfare. Fidgeting with her apron pocket, she replied, "You seem to admire them, even after all the times they've wounded you."

He reached for her hand and raised it to his lips in a mocking salute. "My cross to bear—I seem to most admire the adversaries who wound me deepest."

She knew again that he did not speak only of the war.

Chapter II

"The day after we rode southeast into Chihuahua, a French patrol arrived at Gran Sangre. Gregorio Sanchez reported to me that Don Lucero directed them west, saying we had headed toward Guaymas. I think you can use him," Lieutenant Montoya said to the man seated on the opposite side of the crude wooden table.

"Ah, but can we trust him?" His slight figure was clad, as always, in a serviceable black suit and plain white shirt, which contrasted sharply with his swarthy bronze complexion. His face was *Indio*, with a square stubborn jaw, blunt-featured, homely. There were those who likened it to that of his North American counterpart Abraham Lincoln. President Benito Juarez's expression was impassive as he inhaled his Cuban cigar, a small indulgence he had begun while exiled in New Orleans many years past. His eyes, large liquid black pools, were his most dramatic feature. Right now he fixed them intently on Lieutenant Bolivar Montoya.

"I believe he is sympathetic to our cause. Why else would he misdirect the French?" the lieutenant asked.

"Why indeed?" Juarez echoed. "He may simply have decided to support what he thinks will be the winning side." He tapped his pencil thoughtfully on the scarred pine table strewn with papers and documents. The men were seated in a small shanty on the outskirts of El Paso del Norte. The humble cabin had been the presidential headquarters for the past year, the last in a succession of rude outposts as the republic's government in exile retreated from the capital, moving ever northward from San Luis Potosí to Durango to central Chihuahua and finally to this isolated border hideaway.

But now the little man of law's stubborn determination was at last being rewarded. The course of the war had finally begun to turn. The relentless tenacity of republican guerrilla tactics had worn down and utterly frustrated General Bazaine's French regulars. Even the barbaric retaliations against the Mexican population by General Marquez had served only to stiffen resistance to the imperial cause. Now at last the president had two armies in the field under Diaz and Escobedo, troops actually equipped with enough guns and ammunition to face the imperials head-on. Soon he would be moving south again as the perimeter of Maximilian's empire continued to shrink.

"We need a man in Sonora, Mr. President," Montoya said earnestly. "The *hacendados* there are solidly in the imperial camp and far too wealthy and powerful to ignore. A man like Alvarado, as *patrón* of Gran Sangre, would be a decided asset spying for us."

"But if his only motivation is expediency, it might not be worth the risk of revealing Gregorio Sanchez and the others to him. The *patrón* still has the power of life and death over every person on his estate," Juarez reminded gently. "I will consider the matter," he said, dismissing the young officer with thanks.

"But Nicholas Fortune isn't the *patrón* of Gran Sangre." Bart McQueen spoke as soon as Montoya had closed the door. He had been sitting in the corner, obscure and unnoticed. In his line of work, McQueen preferred it that way.

"Tell me everything you know about Fortune." Juarez took another puff on his cigar and leaned back from the table as the methodical American crossed the room and took Montoya's chair.

"Nicholas Fortune, born sometime around 1836 in New Orleans, mother a stage actress turned prostitute, father . . ." He shrugged. "Most probably Don Anselmo Alvarado, who was keeping Lottie Fortune in high style around that time."

"But the don made no attempt to recognize the boy," the president interjected.

"None. Probably didn't even know of the boy's existence and, doubtless, would not have cared. In any case, by the time Lottie was pregnant, he'd lost interest in her and moved on to the arranged marriage with Sofia Obregón. The boy spent his early years on the New Orleans streets, then a brief period in Texas before joining the Legion."

Matter-of-factly and with amazing thoroughness, McQueen described Nicholas Fortune's life up until the time the spymaster had encountered him in Havana four years earlier. "Nick was working for the cane planters. Hired to suppress a local rebellion among the workers. He was supposed to lead a team of professional soldiers against a bunch of unarmed field hands, but he walked away from it."

"So, the man has a conscience?" Juarez inquired skeptically.

McQueen's smile was thin. "It's possible, but frankly, I doubt it. The sugar interests in New York who had hired him underwent some severe financial setbacks. They couldn't pay him. He drifted into Saint Augustine, then hired on with his old employers, the French, to invade Mexico. Apparently he and old Don Anselmo's son stumbled across one another by accident."

As McQueen described the circumstances under which Nicholas Fortune and Lucero Alvarado had exchanged places, Juarez was again amazed at the *Norteamericano's* incredible skills as an intelligence agent. He had been dispatched by President Lincoln to act in strictest secrecy as liaison to the government of the Mexican Republic. Over the past two years Juarez had found him to be completely dependable and utterly ruthless in pursuing the goals of his superiors in Washington. As a man of single-minded devotion to his own republic, the president of Mexico was just as happy he and Bart McQueen were on the same side.

"Essentially we have Fortune just where we want him," McQueen concluded. "If he wants to continue masquerading as his half brother, he'll have to cooperate with us."

"To be my eyes and ears in Sonora," Juarez supplied.

"Especially with that coterie of *hacendados* surrounding

our old friend Don Encarnación Vargas. I hear he's holding a large ball next month, to honor the visit of Prince Salm-Salm and his American wife who will be touring the northern states as special emissaries of the emperor."

"Does anything go on in the capital to which you are not privy, Mr. McQueen?" Juarez asked with a slight smile on his austere features.

"Very little, Mr. President. I have good sources—although yours are higher placed. Have you heard from Miguel Lopez lately?"

Juarez grimaced in distaste. "I dislike dealing with traitors such as Lopez. He would sell his own wife and children if it were politically advantageous. I suppose that's why I dislike using a man like Nicholas Fortune. He's spent his life for hire with no allegiances to any cause but his own."

"But that very allegiance to himself will work for us. After a life of rootless wandering, he wants desperately to be *patrón* of Gran Sangre. The only way he can is if he helps us." McQueen shrugged cynically. "And, who knows, our doubts notwithstanding, perhaps Fortune has developed a conscience."

Nicholas leaned up and propped his head on his hand, looking down into Mercedes' face. His other hand brushed lightly across her breasts, causing the nipples to harden and distend. He had just finished making love to her for a protracted period of time, holding off his own climax, driving slowly and deeply into her body until at last he had been forced to give in to the shuddering ecstasy.

She could no longer be cool and unresponsive to him. At first she had been physically frightened of him, remembering her husband's roughness. Then she had grown wary of an even more frightening threat when she had found her body beginning to betray her. The natural hungers she had been unaware of and then suppressed were tearing at her now. Yet to give in to them was to give in to him and she was still afraid to trust him. Lucero had scarred her deeply in the first weeks of their marriage.

"Don't you ever feel as if you're missing something?"

he asked softly, watching the bowstring tautness of her body, lying so still and silent beside him. "I know you ache . . . here"—he skimmed over her breasts again, before moving lower—"and here." His palm flattened on the concave hollow of her belly. Then his fingers brushed the soft dark-gold curls at her mound. "Most of all, here."

He massaged her pubic bone in a slow rotating circle, wanting to see if she could remain still. When her hips arched infinitesimally, he smiled.

Mercedes ground her teeth in frustration as tears stung her eyelids. Sweet Virgin, how she did ache! What was he doing to her? What did her body want—no, crave? Yet she knew that if she surrendered to his sensual torture she would lose her self-respect, her hard-won independence, perhaps her very soul.

"What we do is to create children. There's nothing more to it," she replied with a tight finality, wishing desperately for him to pull the covers over her burning nakedness, roll over and go to sleep. But he did not. Instead his soft silky laughter, oddly sad, caressed her cheek.

"Spoken like a good little girl raised in a convent. But there is more, so very much more, Mercedes. Pleasure beyond imagining, even by that facile busy mind of yours. But only if you allow yourself to experience it. Do you dare?"

"I thought you wanted to do your duty for Gran Sangre, to get an heir on me. Do it and let me be gone from your bed." She hated the ragged plea in her voice underlying the command.

"Ah, so you admit it at last . . . a part of your fears, at least."

"I know my duty. I have no fears about having children."

"But you do fear I'll introduce you to passion—a passion I can fuel and assuage until you're breeding. Then I might leave you. Isn't that it, beloved?"

"You will leave me once I'm great with child. You'll have to seek your amusements elsewhere when I can no longer . . ." Her voice trailed away in embarrassed misery as she realized what she had just blurted out. She could feel his smile.

"Being great with child doesn't impede a woman from making love. Believe me I saw enough soldiers' wives during the course of the war to know that for a fact," he replied dryly.

"You don't like shapeless, ugly women, Lucero," she accused. The more she said, the worse she sounded, like a jealous shrew, perfectly pitiful!

"What makes you think I'd find a woman carrying my child to be unattractive?" The question caught him by surprise. He had never looked at the *soldaderas'* swollen bellies with anything but pity for their harsh life. *Enciente* rich ladies did not even appear in public. Certainly he would never have felt inclined to dally with one even if the opportunity had presented itself.

In fact, his own bastardy and harsh childhood had made him exceedingly careful in the matter of birth control. He wanted no innocent children of his left behind to grow up despised and abused as he had been. But the idea of Mercedes—his wife—filled with his baby was suddenly immensely appealing. He was shocked at his reaction to the prospect.

For the first time Mercedes looked up into his eyes, sensing an undercurrent of uncertainty that emanated from him. "You obviously found Rosario's mother of less interest after she was breeding," she snapped.

"Let me rephrase my question," he said, again cursing Luce for this tangle. "What makes you think I'll find *you* unattractive when you're pregnant?"

"Perhaps I'm barren and we'll never know. Lord knows you've labored diligently enough with no result for the past months."

"Would it bother you, not being able to bear my children?"

"It would mean an annulment. Freedom from you. Perhaps it would be worth it," she replied, striving for a light tone of voice, not succeeding. Nicholas knew that she loved children, had been raised to believe that the main function of her life was to give a husband heirs. Rosario was a great joy to her. He knew how she would feel the pain of barrenness.

"Liar," he whispered. "Anyway, I wouldn't give you up even if you were barren, which I very much doubt. A few months is far too short a time to prove your fertility. I have every confidence I'll be watching that little belly grow round within the year. Now as to laboring diligently, perhaps I ought to persevere . . . just to set your mind at rest about your infertility as quickly as possible."

He lowered his mouth to take hers, ravaging it hungrily as he murmured against her lips, "You're my wife and I never give up what's mine."

Mercedes stood watching Lucero with his vaqueros in the dim light of dawn. He rode Peltre with the inbred grace of a *criollo*. Every move of his lean, elegant body was arrogant, powerful, completely self-assured as he issued crisp orders for the day's work. Even from the distance of the upstairs window, she could see that errant curl slip over his forehead when he removed his hat. She remembered what that lock of hair felt like when it brushed her skin as he kissed his way over her body. Just thinking of last night sent a hot, hard stab of pain deep in her belly.

Biting her lip in vexation, she turned from the window. Each night her struggle to lie passively beneath him grew increasingly more difficult. She wanted to know what she was missing, what made her ache, what drove him to that final apex of shuddering, explosive violence that ended their congress each time he took her. It must be pleasure so intense as to almost shatter the soul. Might it be the same for a woman as for a man? Surely not . . . yet why did some women tease their men and follow them adoringly with their eyes? She had seen such behavior between married couples on the hacienda, even between men and women of her class in Hermosillo.

The memories of her parents were hazy, yet she seemed to recall her mother's trilling laughter issuing from behind their bedroom wall. But that was different. Her father and other men were not like Lucero Alvarado. He would use her, then discard her. Had he not done it once already?

Mercedes had tried every trick she could think of to keep herself from responding to his caresses, recalling his harsh words at their betrothal, his casual cruelty on their wedding night, even the lethal and bloody way he had dispatched that bandit with whom he had fought on the Hermosillo road. When all thoughts of him, especially those since his return, proved too dangerous, she resorted to mentally inventorying grain supplies, even counting chickens and sheep.

But nothing worked. She was so tense there were nights she feared she would shatter when he touched her. His possessive hungry words last night still haunted her. Had he meant them? *I wouldn't give you up even if you were barren. . . . I never give up what's mine.*

"He's so different now than he was before. He confuses me," she murmured, rubbing her temple against the headache beginning to build. She bent over the basin of water on the oak table in her dressing room and splashed her face. There was simply too much work to be done for her to waste time indulging in self-pity. What would be, would be. A part of her prayed that she would conceive quickly so that he would leave her. Yet another part, not so deeply repressed as she would like, wondered if he would keep his word and continue lying with her after she began to increase. Did she hope he was telling the truth? That was insane, for all too soon she knew her resistance to his seductive lovemaking was going to crumble, leaving her defenseless.

As Mercedes performed her morning toilette, Nicholas rode to the east pastures where several small herds of beef still remained scattered in the foothills. His thoughts, too, were centered on the troubling relationship he and Mercedes shared. Then suddenly his reverie was interrupted by one of his vaqueros, calling out to him from the ridge directly ahead. He kneed Peltre into a canter.

"What is it, Gomez?"

The hard-eyed rider flipped the cigarette he had just finished smoking carelessly into the grass, then replied, "The men here caught a pair of trespassers. Peons from San

Ramos. They've butchered a steer with the Gran Sangre brand on it." His narrow dark face took on an expectant expression. "Do you want me to exact the usual punishment?" He reached for the whip coiled like a black serpent on the back of his saddle.

Fortune's stomach knotted but he gave no outward sign of his agitation. He knew the rules in this feudal country where any peon caught poaching livestock from a *hacendado* was subject to a severe lashing. And that was only the milder punishment. Maiming with a knife, even outright hanging of the miscreant was not unusual.

"I'll deal with them," Fortune said calmly, passing Gomez with a curt nod of dismissal.

Caesar Ortega stood frozen in horror as the arrogant-looking don rode up. Even though he was dressed in simple work clothes, any man in Mexico would have recognized him as an aristocrat, the finely chiseled features, the lean elegance of his body, the way he sat his mount as if born to command.

Caesar wished he had not come with Antonio, but his brother had been so convincing. Who on Gran Sangre would miss one steer when the *patrón* had thousands? The plaintive cries of his hungry children had added great validity to Antonio's argument.

Now who would feed their families when they were crippled or dead? "Mercy, *Patrón*, I beg of you." Antonio was crying as he fell to his knees in front of the big gray stallion. Caesar remained mute, studying the haughty *criollo*. It would have gone better if he had taken Sylviana and the children and gone into the hills with the guerrillas. At least that way he could have died fighting like a man. But he would not beg like Antonio.

Nicholas looked at the two men, the younger one groveling while his companion stood ramrod stiff, utterly silent. They were dressed in dusty white cotton pants and loose overblouses, frayed and filthy with age. Even the baggy clothes could not disguise the stark thinness of the peons. Their faces were seamed with deep lines, etched not by the passage of years but rather by the harshness of eking out an existence tilling the soil in this unforgiving land.

With no horsemen to clear irrigation ditches, the peons in the small villages had to rely wholly on rain for their crops. And this was an arid land. There had been little rain during the growing season, less last year, according to his wife, who had been forced to become a proficient farmer. The two men were ravaged by hunger. In the past fifteen years as a soldier he had ridden through hundreds of villages like the one they no doubt came from. Whether it was the Crimea or North Africa, or Mexico, hunger always wore the same face.

Ignoring the hysterical man, Fortune turned to his older, stoic companion. "What have you to say for yourself?" he asked in a level voice.

Caesar gestured to the animal, lying with its throat cut in the narrow ravine where they had by luck cornered it. The blood on his machete was ample proof of their guilt. "We killed it, yes. Our children have eaten nothing but cornmeal and water mixed with ashes from the fireplace for weeks. The drought has withered this year's crops. We were desperate. And you had so many cattle. We had nothing." His statement was eloquent in its simplicity.

"You're both young enough. Why haven't you gone to fight for Juarez?" Fortune asked and was rewarded by the startled look that quickly flashed in the older man's eyes.

"I thought of it, yes, but a dead soldier cannot feed his children. I have four. My brother Antonio has three. His wife is expecting again."

"They breed like animals," Gomez said with a sneer.

Antonio, who finally realized that his brother had elicited a calm response from the don, fell silent, then got up from his knees and stood beside Caesar. "We will take our punishment," he said quietly.

"And we'll be happy to give it," one of Gomez's companions said with an ugly laugh.

Nicholas looked from their smirking expectant faces, avid with the promise of violence, to the two haggard wretches standing before him. *This is how Juarez recruits. We do it for him.*

When had he begun to think of himself as a part of this land, a *criollo*, a *hacendado*? The same time he had begun to think of Mercedes as *his* wife? With an oath of frustration, he said, "Take the damn cow back to your village—but if I ever see you on my land again, I'll personally stake you over a clump of tuna cactus and let you bleed to death while the buzzards pick out your entrails!"

Giving a curt sign of dismissal to his astonished men, he wheeled Peltre around and headed back to the road. As he happened to glance over toward Hilario, he saw the gleam of a secret smile in his eyes. Then it vanished, leaving Nicholas to wonder if he had merely imagined it.

The gossip about the *patrón's* bizarre behavior filtered across the hacienda. Don Lucero, who had fought four years for the emperor, now fed republican soldiers and misdirected French patrols. He had even freed two peons whom he could have had summarily whipped to death if he had so chosen. The war did strange things to men, they murmured. Usually they returned meaner, embittered, cynical. But the high-living, haughty young don had returned sober and industrious, working beside his people to rebuild what the old don had squandered. He was truly worthy of his lady, whom they all adored.

All but Innocencia, who bided her time in sullen silence, waiting and watching the mysterious transformation of her former lover. As the months had passed and he remained faithful to his pale little wife, she gave up all hope of ever luring him back to her bed. He was well and truly lost to her and so was the life of ease to which she had dreamed of returning.

"Lazy girl, quit your mooning and scrub the pots on the hearth," Angelina chided her assistant.

Innocencia had been staring out the window at the well where Lucero stood in the blazing noonday heat. She watched as he dumped a bucket of cool water over his sweat-soaked, dust-caked body while his skinny blond woman, also sweating and dressed like a peon, joined him with that brat daughter of his. Innocencia's eyes narrowed in hate as the three of them laughed and bantered while they cooled off from their labors.

Angelina's voice grew more strident, forcing the serving girl to obey her commands. She walked to the hearth and seized the heavy iron cauldron, setting to work resentfully under the stern eye of her taskmistress. All the while, something niggled at the periphery of her consciousness, something about Lucero . . . but what?

Late that afternoon Lazaro interrupted the *patrón*, who was working on the hacienda accounts with Mercedes. Entering the study, he faced them uncertainly, saying, "A party of men has arrived, Don Lucero, and they have women and children with them."

Nicholas rose from behind his father's massive oak desk, a look of curiosity on his face. "I take it they are not soldiers then."

"No, *Patrón*. But I do not recognize them. They are *gringos*."

He made a small grimace of distaste that gave Nicholas an inward chuckle. *What would you say if you knew I was one, too*? "What the devil are a group of Americans doing riding through Sonora with women and children in tow?" he murmured aloud to himself. "I'll see to them, Lazaro."

"We should, of course, offer hospitality," Mercedes said as she rounded the desk, brushing the wrinkles self-consciously from her plain cotton skirt. Lord, with her hair plaited down her back, dressed in *paisana's* clothes, she was scarcely fit to greet foreign visitors, no matter how road weary they might be.

Nicholas watched her fuss with a few damp tendrils of hair. "As always, you look superb. Let's go greet these uninvited guests. They may be nothing more than a pack of *contre-guerrillas* with their whores in tow, in which case they won't be joining us for dinner."

"But if they're American—"

"Lots of the men I fought with were drifters from across the border, especially disaffected Southerners whose cause was lost when the Confederacy began to go down to defeat."

"I've heard of Maximilian's Imperial Commissioner of Immigration, Matthew Maury. They say he's bringing thousands of his fellow Confederates to relocate in Mexico. Maybe they're some of those people."

"Maybe." His tone was skeptical as they walked down the hallway and into the foyer where the group stood waiting, looking dusty and weary but not at all like the hardened mercenaries he had fought beside for so many years.

The men ranged in age widely, some in their middle years, a few younger. Their women had two small girls and a slightly older boy with them. Several of the men wore faded Confederate uniforms with gold epaulets on the shoulders. The rest were dressed in quality clothing, but well-worn and frayed. The women, in dark linen riding habits, carried themselves with the demure dignity of respectable society belles fallen on hard times, standing wilted and silent behind their menfolk.

"Colonel Grayham Fletcher, at your service, sir," the leader of the group said in a soft west Texas drawl. Fletcher offered his hand to Nicholas. He was a big man with reddish hair and a long narrow face that indicated Scots and English antecedents. His smile was genial as he studied Nicholas with bright blue eyes that crinkled at the corners. The Texas sun had blasted his buttermilk pale complexion to a freckled ruddy tan.

"Welcome to Gran Sangre, Colonel. I'm Don Lucero Alvarado and this is my wife, Doña Mercedes," Nicholas said in English, the faint traces of his New Orleans origins still identifiable.

Fletcher made a courtly bow to Mercedes, then asked Nicholas, "You a Southerner?" He studied the dark-skinned Hispanic-looking man with obvious puzzlement.

Nicholas smiled. "No, but I've fought here in Mexico beside many Southerners. They taught me to speak English."

"Well, that's good, cuz most o' us cain't speak a speck o' Spanish," another tall, cadaverously thin man with a decided border state twang interjected, identifying himself as Matt McClosky.

"We're on our way to meet with General Jubal Early. He

was our commander in the late war," Fletcher said, "but I'm afraid we've lost our way. We were to rendezvous with another larger party of immigrants, but somehow we've missed them."

"I'm afraid that was my fault." A man of medium build with colorless eyes and hair materialized from the cluster of people. "I'm Emory Jones, and I was supposedly the guide, but I'm afraid I misread the signs along the trail from El Paso and we ended up here."

The bland-looking man was oddly familiar to Fortune, although he could not have said why. Emory Jones was unremarkable in every way. Even his Southern accent was less pronounced than that of his compatriots. Yet there was something . . .

"Emory here's a Reb from Saint Louie," McClosky explained with a guffaw. "Ain't many o' them in that damned Yankee stronghold."

"My mother's family were Virginians, resettled in southern Missouri," Jones said smoothly as Mercedes and the sad-eyed and tired-looking women quietly became acquainted. Upon hearing her precise British English, they were delighted. The *patrona* ushered them and their children into the *sala*, then went to fetch refreshments and have bedrooms made up. Hospitality was a sacred tradition among the Mexican *criollos*. If her larder was depleted, it did not matter. She would make do.

When Mercedes returned, the men had followed Lucero into his study for a liquid libation stronger than the cool lemonade the women were enjoying. Angelina served them as Rosario stood shyly in the doorway, clutching her doll Patricia against her chest, watching the *gringo* children with curious eyes.

"Rosario, come meet our guests." Mercedes was proud of the way Lucero's daughter made her curtsy when she was introduced. Lucinda Mayfield's daughter Clarissa looked longingly at the doll Mercedes had bought Rosario while they were in Hermosillo. "Perhaps you could share Patricia with Clarissa and Beatrice for a little while?"

The three little girls went off to the courtyard to play,

the language barrier seemingly unimportant in their newly discovered friendship.

"My Bea really misses her toys," Marian Fletcher said sadly. Her gray eyes grew flinty cold as she continued, "The Yankees burned us out. We lost everything, even her dolls. It took all we could scrape together to get a stake to relocate in Mexico."

The other women chorused the same wistful sadness tempered by an underlying current of bitterness and uncertainty.

"Is . . . is all of Mexico as barren as Sonora, Doña Mercedes?" Lucinda asked timidly. She was a thin, birdlike brunette whose once luminous peaches and cream complexion had turned the wan color of parchment, now stretched tight across her delicate cheekbones.

"No, much of my country is lushly tropical with rich fertile valleys. Many crops grow yearround," Mercedes replied, understanding. "When I first came to Sonora as a bride, I, too, found the land forbidding, but there is a kind of stark wild beauty to it that one gets used to. If not for the war, this hacienda would flourish. As it is, we're irrigating nearly a hundred acres for food crops and my husband has rounded up several thousand head of beef as well as fine-blooded horses."

"We were told we'd be given land—large tracts of it. Like this," Marian said hopefully. "How do you keep up such a lovely home in this isolated area?"

The women discussed various mundane domestic topics. It was obvious to Mercedes that Lucinda and Marian had come from considerable wealth while Callie McClosky mentioned that she was from a small Tennessee farm. All were daughters and wives of the vanquished soldiers who had lost their land, if not their pride, in the American war. Now they dreamed of starting a new life but were intimidated by the alien land. She did what she could to reassure them but tempered it with explanations about the ongoing war in Mexico. War was a subject about which they were all too familiar.

While the women discussed their fears and hopes, the men cut directly to the heart of their immediate problem, namely getting from Sonora down to Durango where they were to meet the main train of Confederate immigrants bound for the capital. Nicholas got out his map and showed Emory Jones and the others the easiest route. After that matter was settled, the conversation turned to plans for the future.

"I heerd the Valley o' Mexico is rich as sin, filled with songbirds and lots o' Injuns to work fer us," McClosky said to Nicholas.

"Yes. Commissioner Maury assured us each family will receive a thousand acres of prime land," Fletcher added.

"Much of Mexico is rich, but the war has changed the old way of life here, too," Fortune began cautiously. "I doubt anyone, even the emperor, can guarantee you that much free land, much less enough Indians to work it."

"You sayin' your government lied to us?" McClosky asked, his voice growing angry.

"Mexico hasn't really had a government in nearly a decade," Nicholas replied. "Warring factions of liberals and conservatives have taken turns seizing the reins of power. That's what brought the French in to set Maximilian on the throne. But I've heard it said that one can do anything with bayonets—but sit on them.' "

Emory Jones swirled the *aguardiente* around in his glass, then sipped it as he peered over the rim, fixing his host with those odd colorless eyes. "Those sound rather like Juarista sentiments to me, Don Lucero."

Nicholas shrugged. "The French emperor Napoleon the Third's son, Prince Plon-Plon, said it. As for me, I've lost interest in politics."

"But you said you served with the imperials," Fletcher said, unable to understand a man who would give up on his cause.

"Let's just say I want the war to end . . . any which way. I haven't even got enough men to care for my horses, much less round up the cattle this spring."

"I hear they're all off fighting for Juarez," Jones said mildly.

''I heerd 'bout thet Injun who claims to be president o' Mexico,'' McClosky scoffed.

''The idea of a savage, president of anything,'' Fletcher said dismissively.

''Oh, I wouldn't underestimate this Indian,'' Fortune replied. ''He's held onto his tattered constitution since 1857. Now he's enlisted your Yankee enemies to help him. He just might win.''

An uncomfortable silence settled on the room as Fortune and Jones exchanged glances. There was a knowing assessment in the guest's eyes as he raised his glass. ''To the Emperor Maximilian the First.''

Everyone followed his toast, including the *patrón*, who sensed a subtle mockery in the gesture. And that nagging familiarity. Who was Emory Jones?

Chapter 12

While their guests rested and refreshed themselves before dinner, Nicholas walked down to the stables to check with Hilario about the condition of their animals. The immigrants' horses were used up by the long arduous trek. They had six pack mules which had fared somewhat better. If the newcomers had been smart they would have bought more mules and fewer horses for traveling through desert country, but then if they were smart, they would have remained in Texas and not pursued Matthew Maury's pipe dream. Bad enough the men believed Maximilian's vague idealized promises. Bringing women and children to face an uncertain future in the middle of another civil war was nothing short of criminal stupidity to his way of thinking.

"Hilario, how do their horses look?" he asked as his eyes adjusted to the dim light inside the stable.

The old vaquero shrugged, setting aside the rubbing cloth he was using on Fletcher's big bay, without doubt the best of the lot. "They have been ridden hard and fed poorly. They need several days of rest and grain if they are to survive the trip to the Valley of Mexico. Mules would stand the trip much better than horses."

Fortune grinned cynically. "I don't think Mrs. Fletcher would exactly fancy being seen riding a mule. Anyway, we don't have the stock to spare."

"You could trade them mules for horses. This fine fellow"—Hilario patted Fletcher's bay—"would be fat and sleek with a few weeks of proper care."

Fortune studied the crafty look in the old man's eyes. "You don't much care for them, do you?"

"Do you believe they will receive vast tracts of land from the emperor?" Hilario answered with a question of his own.

Nicholas muttered an oath. "No. They'll be damn lucky to get as far as Durango without having their throats cut."

"That doesn't say much for my skills as a guide." Emory Jones materialized out of the shadows behind Fortune.

As Nicholas turned, he noticed that Hilario did not seem at all surprised by Jones' appearance. He quirked an eyebrow. "You have strayed rather far off the beaten track." Again that niggling sense of familiarity made the hair on his nape prickle in unease.

"You're thinking we've met before," Jones said, as if reading his host's thoughts. "We haven't, strictly speaking, but . . . I know who you are."

The last words dropped like stones in the quiet stable. Hilario turned around and resumed rubbing down the bay as if he knew what the conversation would be.

Fortune studied the smaller man, who was so nondescript he could blend in almost anywhere. Schooling his expression to utter neutrality, Nicholas said, "You seem to have the advantage, Mr. Jones . . . if that is your name. Perhaps we'd best discuss this out back by the corrals." There was a deadly undertone lurking beneath the silky invitation as he gestured for Emory Jones to precede him out the rear door of the stable.

"As you wish." The mysterious Americano walked casually past Fortune. When they reached the large open area, he turned calmly and said, "Hilario already knows you're not Lucero Alvarado."

Nicholas regarded him with fathomless black eyes. "Really. Then who the hell am I?"

"Nicholas Fortune, an American mercenary originally from New Orleans, where old Don Anselmo Alvarado was known to while away some pleasurable hours in his youth, you being the by-product of one such indiscretion." All traces of his soft Southern accent had evaporated completely.

Fortune leaned against the corral rail, then asked lazily, "Who the hell are *you*?"

"A fellow American." There was a hard edge beneath

the casual words. "My name's Bart McQueen. And I am from Saint Louis."

"But you're not a Confederate."

"I work for the United States Department of War. This immigrant party provided me with an ideal cover to reach you in person."

"How did you know who I was?"

"I make it my business to keep track of men in your business," McQueen replied briskly. He went on, "As you're no doubt aware, our government is determined to see the French out of Mexico."

"I've heard rumors in Hermosillo that the Americans were dispatching an army to the border, but that doesn't have anything to do with me. I've never been employed by *our* government," Nicholas replied sardonically.

McQueen's smile was ironic. "You will be now. Our army's already on the Rio Grande. President Juarez will be leaving El Paso in a few months. He'll start to travel south following Escobedo's army. There have already been several attempts to assassinate him. He's the only thing holding the Mexican resistance together. Without Juarez, the republic is dead. And that would be a disaster for the United States government."

"I don't give a damn about the United States government. As *patrón* of Gran Sangre it makes no difference to me whether Maximilian or Juarez sits in that palace."

"You'll remain *patrón* of Gran Sangre only as long as you do what I say, Fortune." There was an aura of utter ruthlessness behind the clipped words.

"I'm the law here. You could meet with an unfortunate accident out in the desert. It happens every day in Sonora. Bandits, *contre-guerrillas* . . ." Nicholas shrugged.

"President Johnson would only send someone else to take my place." There was not the slightest inflection in McQueen's voice. "Anyway, you might find me rather difficult to kill." He nodded toward the far end of the corral where young Gregorio Sanchez stood well out of earshot, silently watching them.

"How many of my men are in your pay, McQueen?" Fortune's face was stony.

"None. They're loyal Juaristas."

"Well, I've already told you, I'm not."

"Then why did you help Lieutenant Montoya escape that patrol? Or turn loose those two peons with the butchered steer? For a man with your sanguinary reputation, you've developed a rather soft heart here of late. Perhaps the influence of your beautiful lady, Doña Mercedes?"

Nicholas' expression shifted from anger to cynical amusement. "Then you really mistake the case. My wife is a loyal daughter of the Church. She despises the godless republicans almost as much as her mother-in-law."

"Your wife. You've grown to think of her that way, haven't you? What would such a devout lady do if she learned the man who shares her bed isn't her husband at all but his bastard half brother?"

Nicholas reacted with pure gut instinct. He seized McQueen's shirt collar in his fists, lifting the smaller man up and slamming him against the corral post. "The only reason you don't have your throat cut right now is because I'm unarmed, but I have been known to kill men with my bare hands."

McQueen did not blink. "Think you can snap my neck before I can pull this trigger?" he asked as casually as if he were discussing the weather.

Fortune could feel the barrel of a small gun pressing against his left side, alarmingly near his heart. Slowly he lowered McQueen, then shoved him away.

"I know your kind. You won't shoot me because you need me—but you'd be wise to leave Mercedes out of this."

McQueen stepped back and replaced the Volcanic pistol inside his jacket, showing no emotion whatsoever. "Agreed. I believe I've made my point."

"You've made your damn point, McQueen. I'll hear you out." Fortune folded his arms across his chest, waiting.

"The *hacendados* in Sonora and Chihuahua are mostly in the imperial camp," McQueen began.

"I'd hardly call it loyalty," Nicholas said dryly. "They'll side with anyone who acknowledges their feudal privileges."

"True, but there's a small faction of fanatics who know the French are going to pull out of Mexico, leaving them to the mercy of the republic. They can never buy a man like Juarez."

"So they want him dead," Fortune said grimly. It made sense. With Juarez gone, they could set up someone they could control in the ensuing power vacuum, perhaps even break the northern states away from the rest of the republic.

"That's where you come in. As one of the largest landholders in the state, you could infiltrate their inner circle and give us vital information about their plans, especially any attempts on the president's life."

"And just how do I do this? I was a soldier, McQueen, not a damned spy."

"You were a mercenary," McQueen corrected in that same uninflected tone.

"I picked my assignments," Fortune replied.

McQueen allowed himself to exhibit a fleeting trace of amusement now. "Yes, you did on rare occasions show a surprising flash of scruples. In Havana, for instance." He could see Fortune make the connection, then went on, "You're going to receive an invitation to the ball Don Encarnación Vargas is giving next month in honor of a Prussian prince from Maximilian's court."

"Vargas is in on the assassination plot?" Nicholas was moderately surprised. He knew old Don Encarnación had been a friend of his wastrel father, but little more about him. He would have expected the don to be too provincial and self-absorbed for this sort of dangerous intrigue.

"Encarnación Vargas is their leader, but the old man has someone else behind him—someone who's canny enough to recognize Juarez as the linchpin of republican success."

"And you want me to find out who this is," Nicholas replied.

Getting down to business as nonchalantly as if they were negotiating a livestock deal, McQueen said, "The Vargas conspirators will be discussing what their spies have gleaned about Juarez's movements. Then they'll decide when to make another assassination attempt. Isolated in the mountains outside of El Paso, the president could be protected, but on the road south headed to the capital it's going to be considerably more difficult."

"You think Vargas will confide his plans to me?" Fortune asked dubiously.

"No, probably not, but as Don Lucero you'll gain entry to places none of my other operatives could. Keep your eyes and ears open. We need to know when and where they'll strike. You'll be instructed about how to pass along whatever you learn to appropriate authority. Porfirio Escondidas is my agent in Sonora. If something should happen to him, Gregorio and old Hilario know how to contact local Juaristas."

Nicholas' eyebrows raised. "I knew that Hilario had figured out I wasn't Luce, but I wouldn't have taken him for a Juarista."

"Appearances can be deceiving," McQueen replied mildly. "I believe you'll make an excellent agent, Don Lucero."

Nicholas' eyes narrowed, their silver irises glowing like lightning. "By the way, Mr. Jones. I don't much like being blackmailed. Once this assassination plot is foiled, I'm done with you. I won't work for you or your government."

"Just work for Juarez. I don't think you'll find it unrewarding. He's going to win this war."

"Then that means you and your government will butt out of Mexico," Fortune replied, turning to stride across the yard toward the opposite end of the corral.

"You play the role of *hacendado* well for a *gringo*," McQueen said to himself. He retraced his steps back to the house, being careful that no one observed him reentering the courtyard.

But someone did. Innocencia picked at the bits of straw caught in her tangled mane of hair and brushed the wrinkles from her rucked-up skirts. After a pleasant tumble in the loft with one of the new vaqueros, she had fallen asleep when he had left, only to be awakened by voices speaking in English. One of them was Don Lucero's. She had quickly climbed to the open bay of the loft, where she could make out what the men were saying.

Innocencia's grasp of the language was tenuous at best, but she had lived a few years with an aunt and uncle in the busy seaport of Guaymas, which North American and English argonauts used as a stopping-off point in their rush to the California gold fields. She was quick and clever enough to understand the gist of the conversation.

No wonder her old lover had not welcomed her back into his bed! This man was a penniless bastard, a *gringo*, who had taken Lucero's place and fooled them all, and he was working for the Juaristas!

Watching to see that both Hilario and Gregorio had gone to their quarters first, she made her way out of the stable and back to the kitchen, all the while considering how she could best use this damning information.

With a myriad of things preying on his mind, the last thing Nicholas wanted was to run into Father Salvador. He had been avoiding the old man's request through Mercedes to make peace with Doña Sofia. As the priest walked down the long hallway with his ice-blue eyes fixed on his target, Fortune laughed wryly to himself. He was reacting like a schoolboy caught in some infraction. *Just as if I really was Lucero Alvarado.*

"Good morning, Father. I trust you enjoyed your visit with our guests last night, instructing them regarding their duty to become members of the Church." Few of the Confederate immigrants were of the Roman faith. In spite of a widespread outcry from the Church and other conservative elements in Mexico, the emperor had not reinstated the laws making conversion a condition of citizenship. The priest had attempted to cajole Fletcher's group into realizing that they would find no other religious solace in their adopted home and should seek instruction when they arrived at their destination. They had been polite for the most part, except for the McCloskys, but Nicholas was certain that spiritual matters were low on the immigrants' list of priorities.

Father Salvador made a dismissive gesture. "I did not

come to discuss the North Americans. Your wife has spoken with you regarding your mother?"

"My mother's health has improved remarkably since you gave her the last rites. She's not ready to depart this mortal coil."

"No, she is not. There are matters that weigh heavily on her soul—and yours—that the two of you must confront before it is too late."

"Her soul is your concern," Nicholas replied coldly. "As to my soul, you yourself pronounced it beyond salvation when I was a boy."

"With God, nothing is beyond redemption, and I have never ceased praying for you, my son. As to what I said in anger . . . I, too, have much to answer for."

Startled, Nicholas looked at the old priest's face, now grown pale and weathered by age. Deep seams around his mouth and across his forehead made his expression infinitely weary. The crystal blue eyes that Luce had described so accurately had lost their accusatory glare. Was there actually a shred of compassion, even regret in them? He sighed, weary himself. "She doesn't want to see me."

"I know. But she must before she can die."

"Is that an enticement to get me to visit her?" he asked with a sardonic lift of one eyebrow.

"Do it, I beg of you," was all the priest replied.

"Rosario really likes you," Nicholas said, surprising himself. "I'll do it for her granddaughter's sake."

The priest smiled faintly. "Do it for your own sake."

The room was not as dark and cloying as usual when Lupe opened the door for him. Nicholas dismissed her and looked over to where the old woman sat up in an enormous chair, propped up in a sea of fluffy pillows facing the window. Doña Sofia's skin was whiter than the linens surrounding her.

"I see you've renewed your interest in this world rather than abandoning it for the next."

She did not turn her head but continued staring out into

the courtyard. "Come closer. I am not strong enough to bite you."

He chuckled mirthlessly. "Your bite was never physical, *Mamacita*." Then, reminding himself of why he was here, he said, "We need to put all that behind us. Be kinder to each other."

Her answering laughter was dry as kindling. Once she recovered her breath she said, "Lucero Alvarado did not know the meaning of the word *kindness*."

"Maybe that was because no one ever taught me."

"Perhaps no one did." She looked up into his face now, studying it with narrowed, watery eyes that seemed startlingly alert, perceptive. "Your resemblance is truly amazing. The scar helps, I think."

A surge of apprehension rippled down his spine. "My father remained unmarked. I was not so fortunate," he said, shrugging casually.

"Oh, you resemble your sire, right enough," she rasped bitterly, "but you are not Lucero."

His blood chilled to ice. "Have you taken feverish again, Mother? I'll summon Lupe."

"My mind is clear. Summon no one, for I do not think you will wish them to hear what I have to say."

"And that is?" he prompted, taking a seat on a hard wooden chair beside her.

"I have watched you since your return, watched how everyone accepted you, listened as they rejoiced in what a fine and dutiful *patrón* you had become. Even Mercedes has been pleased with how hard you work, toiling as she does to reclaim the hacienda from ruin." Her dry chuckle eerily broke the silence. "That was your biggest mistake. Lucero, like your father, cared nothing for responsibility. He would not have brought his bastard here and ensconced her in our family home, or forsaken his whores in favor of his wife, a wife whom you allow to demean herself laboring beside peons. You are far too soft."

"The war gave me a new outlook on life. It can do that for some men—make them appreciate what they've left behind, make them want to return and rebuild."

She shook her head. "Lucero is not such a man, is he?" Her gaze riveted on him, unblinking.

Nicholas sighed. "No. You're taking quite a chance confronting me, you know? What if I simply smothered you with one of these pillows? No one would question your death."

"But you will not, will you? That is part of the reason I know you are not my son. For you see, he would kill me or anyone else who got in his way."

Nicholas cocked his head, studying her. "True. Ruthlessness he inherited from you, perhaps?"

She scoffed. "Certainly not from your weakling father. Anselmo was too indolent to be ruthless, too mired in his own debauched pleasures."

"But you admit I am my father's son." He was puzzled, waiting to see what she would do, all the while turning over in his mind ways to counter her accusations. "What are you going to do?"

"Why nothing, nothing at all," she replied serenely.

"I don't understand."

"Think of it, bastard son of Anselmo Alvarado!"

In spite of himself, he flinched at her insult, but remained silent, impassive.

"Your father despoiled a magnificent hacienda and dishonored his marriage vows, but he always took great pride in the Alvarado name, in our pure undiluted bloodlines. The very thought of a child born nameless, the son of one of his lightskirts, inheriting Gran Sangre, getting more illegitimate heirs on Lucero's wife, passing on the Alvarado heritage through them—this will make him writhe in hell such as no other punishment on this or the other side of eternity could ever do." Her voice was cool and calm, as considered as if she were explaining household duties to a servant.

Nicholas Fortune thought he had seen all the faces of hate after growing up destitute and surviving the carnage of war on three continents. But he had been wrong. This was a more terrible visage than any he could ever have imagined. Twisted. Malevolent. Ice-cold. Without a word he stood up, but before he could quit the room, her voice called out after him.

"Did you kill Lucero?"

"No. I regret to inform you I didn't perform that service for you."

After the door slammed, she closed her eyes wearily. The silence in the room was broken only by her raspy uneven breathing. This unexpected interview had taken a great deal out of her. She would pay, in the next world as well as this one, but then, had she not always been the one to do so? She looked down at the rosary lying unused in her lap.

Suddenly the sun's rays caught the diamond beads, which blazed like fire, accusing her of sacrilege. She picked them up but could not pray. Father Salvador would have to do that for her from now on.

Nicholas sat staring at the brandy bottle, which he had nearly emptied that night after everyone else retired. Tomorrow Bart McQueen and Fletcher's band of immigrants would be leaving. Yet the troublesome and expensive hospitality, even the federal agent's blackmail, did not trouble him half so much as the ugly scene with that old woman this morning.

What a nest of vipers his brother had grown up in! He raised his glass in salute, then tossed down the contents. No wonder Luce had turned out the way he was. With parents like Anselmo and Sofia, what child stood a chance!

Of course his own haphazard upbringing shunted between Lottie and her father hadn't exactly made him into a paragon. Fortune had always blamed his bitter and violent life on them. Perhaps his Alvarado blood was more significant than he could ever have imagined. By comparison to Doña Sofia, Lottie Fortune no longer seemed so bad. Pitiable and weak, yes, but his mother could never have been capable of the awful vengeance old Sofia believed she was wreaking on the House of Alvarado. Using him and her daughter-in-law. *Mercedes.*

"Admit it," he muttered to himself with a slurred oath. "It isn't what she did to Luce that's really eating you—it's what you're doing to Mercedes."

If Hilario and Bart McQueen knew his secret and Doña Sofia had guessed it, how long would it be before his wife—no, his *brother's* wife—guessed it, too? How would she feel, having given herself to a man who was not her husband? A nameless bastard with blood on his hands? What if there were a child? She might already be carrying his seed. No matter if it bore the Alvarado name, it would still be as much a bastard as he was.

And Mercedes, by lying with her husband's brother, had committed incest in the eyes of her church. Nicholas had been raised outside the Roman faith but when he lived in Italy and Mexico, he had picked up enough of Canon Law to understand the ramifications of his deception. Luce had even explained it to him when he instructed his brother about how to handle Father Salvador and any religious observances he might be forced to attend.

Fortune had long ago abandoned hope for his own soul, but he was becoming increasingly concerned about anything that could hurt Mercedes. She was sincerely everything Sofia was not, a true Christian who practiced her faith devoutly. Damn! It had all seemed so easy, this exchange agreed upon by two hardened men. Now they had drawn innocents into their web of deception. Mercedes. Rosario. Perhaps an unborn child.

But Nicholas would not give them up. Certainly their lives would be far worse if his brother had returned instead of him. Even that twisted old woman had admitted as much. He was ensnared in the web he himself had helped to spin. There was no answer.

Mercedes lay in the big bed alone. The hour was late and still Lucero had not come upstairs to his room. She had long ago abandoned waiting in her own quarters for him to claim her. He had made it clear that he would do so every night. The humiliation had been worse when he strode through her door and arrogantly commanded her to follow him.

If nothing else, she had been certain that he desired her body. Until tonight. Was he with Innocencia or one of the other servant girls? She had observed the way women looked at him, devouring his dark dangerous virility, seducing him with slumberous eyes and often in even less subtle ways. Sweet merciful heavens, she sounded jealous—after all the anguished nights of praying he would stop making love to her before she succumbed to his skillful touch!

Her troubling reverie was suddenly interrupted by the sound of footfalls coming down the hallway. Lucero's steps, yet they sounded erratic—almost as if he were . . . drunk! Brandy fumes preceded him as he opened the door and walked into the moonlit room, weaving slightly, then stumbling against the heavy oak wardrobe. With a muffled oath he began to strip off his clothes, throwing them carelessly hither and yon, not at all his usual tidy way, but more like she would have expected the old Lucero to respond.

Accustomed to the darkness, her eyes watched the play of his muscles as he shed shirt and pants. He was a splendid male animal whose hard, hairy torso and long sinuous limbs were made even more virile and appealing by the mysterious scars that marred what would otherwise have been unreal perfection. It was dangerous to dwell on such thoughts, but she could not seem to tear her eyes from him as he climbed into bed beside her.

She tensed expectantly as he lay down, wondering if he would reach for her. Instead of drawing her possessively into his embrace, he simply lay spread-eagle across the wide bed and fell fast asleep. Soft male snoring quickly fell into a steady low rhythm.

Never since his return had she known Lucero to get drunk, although he had when they were first wed. Somehow she sensed that this was different. Could it be related to her husband's morning visit with his mother, about which Father Salvador had told her? There had been no time during the busy day to talk with him in private with a house full of guests.

Mercedes feared Lucero and his mother would never make peace. As a child who had enjoyed a loving relationship with both parents and mourned their loss, Mercedes had always felt the bitterness between Lucero and Doña Sofia was tragic and inexplicable and that it must have begun when he was very young. Perhaps at the moment of conception.

She leaned up on her elbow and tentatively reached one hand out, her fingers itching to brush the errant lock of dark hair from his brow. He muttered in his sleep, something low that she could not understand, then tossed his head restlessly, as if having a bad dream.

"Shh, don't let her trouble you. You need not pay for your father's sins." She smiled sadly, realizing he had enough sins of his own for which to atone.

The Fletcher party left just after daybreak, enroute to Durango. The small caravan, now riding rested and well-fed mounts, vanished in the distance. Mercedes watched Lucero pensively stare after them. "Do you think they'll make it?"

"To Durango? I suppose so," he replied absently. His head pounded so badly from the excess of brandy last night that he scarcely heard her question. He had been wondering how he would implement Bart McQueen's orders, glad to have the unnerving man gone from Gran Sangre. Then he continued, "If you mean will they survive resettlement in the valley and become assimilated as Mexicans, no. They're Americans. Hell, they don't even speak enough Spanish to communicate."

"What about the emperor's new immigration plan? You don't believe it will succeed anywhere, do you?"

"Not with people like those," he snapped irritably.

"You act as if you've known many Americans."

"More than a fair share fought with the *contre-guerrillas*," he replied guardedly. "You don't want to know about the war, Mercedes." *You don't want to know about me.*

She could see he was not feeling well but hesitated to bring up his solitary drinking binge last night or the possible cause for it. Worry about the survival of Fletcher's party was the least of his concerns. She was certain of that much.

He stalked off toward the stables, leaving her standing alone in the courtyard, perplexed.

"Why should I care what's troubling him?" she murmured to herself. *He is your husband*, the voice of duty reminded her.

The only way to find the answer lay in asking her husband's mother, something she was loath to do.

Chapter 13

Mercedes went through her morning chores, still preoccupied with Lucero's troubling behavior. As noon drew near, she grew eager for Rosario to finish her lessons and join her in the kitchen as was their routine. The child had been blossoming, overcoming her shyness and growing into a bubbly curious five-year-old girl.

When she entered the kitchen, Angelina set down her heavy stirring ladle with a worried expression on her face. "My lady, Rosario is late. Did Father Salvador keep her because she did not recite her lessons properly?"

"She isn't here?" Mercedes chewed her lip. "I'll go see, but she's been doing so well, I doubt it. He seems quite pleased with her progress."

The priest had dismissed Rosario at the usual time and knew nothing of where she might be found. Now he, too, was concerned and they instituted a search of the house. Mercedes, remembering the little girl's love of the flower beds, found her a short while later huddled in between the high rows of hollyhocks by the trellises. The child was sobbing forlornly.

"Tell me what's happened," she said after sending Lupe to call off the search. Mercedes stroked the small dark head and held her close.

Rosario hiccuped, then dug two small tan fists into her eyes. "I'm s-sorry. I did not mean to make her angry."

"Who, sweet one?" Mercedes asked, thinking that if Innocencia had again spoken harshly to Rosario, she would personally flog the nasty whore.

"She . . . she *is* my papa's mother, isn't she?"

The question took Mercedes completely by surprise. "You mean Doña Sofia?" A sudden ugly suspicion began to form. At the child's woebegone nod, she asked, "Did you go into her quarters?"

"I only wanted to see her . . . to ask her if . . . if . . ."

Mercedes hugged Rosario. "Ask her what?"

"If she was my grandmother. My mother is dead but I have my papa now and I have you. He said we were a family . . . but I overheard Lupe and Angelina talking about his mother who is so sick she never leaves her room. I thought she might be lonely so I brought my new primer. I wanted to read to her, to cheer her up. I only wanted her to like me."

Mercedes' chest tightened painfully as she imagined the scene unfolding—a small waif in search of her long-lost grandmother, wanting to show her she was worthy, to belong. And Sofia, enraged at the temerity of a bastard with no right to the vaunted Alvarado name daring to approach her.

Mercedes held Rosario tightly and rocked her back and forth, crooning as the child sobbed, offering assurances that Grandmother Sofia was too ill to know what she had said and it was not Rosario's fault that the old woman had been angry.

Everything the twisted old woman touched withered with her hate. Lucero had come away from his last conversation with her so upset he tried to drown himself in liquor. Now even this innocent child had been hurt. "Come, let us get you some lunch. Angelina has made sopapilla. I think there is some fresh honey to go with it. Would you like that?"

Rosario nodded sadly.

In a few minutes Mercedes had climbed the stairs and approached the door to her mother-in-law's room. Without even knocking she opened it and stepped inside, too angry for any pretense at amenities. "I wish to speak with you, Doña Sofia," she said, striding across the room to where the old woman sat in her high-backed chair, facing the window.

Something in her daughter-in-law's tone of voice alerted the old *patrona* even before Sofia saw the blazing anger pinkening her cheeks and darkening Mercedes' amber eyes. Surely that fool had not confessed to her—but no, of course not. If so the chit would have come to her with incredulous tears, not mantled in righteous indignation. It must have been that damnable child. "What has so beset you that you barge in rudely unannounced?" she asked, taking the offensive.

"I am most *beset*, yes," Mercedes replied, pacing agitatedly by the window, trying to marshal her scattered thoughts. "Rosario isn't even five years old. I regret that she disturbed you, but she only wanted to meet you—"

"She is not even your child," Sofia scoffed.

"She is my husband's daughter—your granddaughter."

"I do not acknowledge his indiscretions any more than I did those of his father. You would be well advised to heed my example. Provide Lucero with legitimate heirs as is your duty. And pray you do not prove barren, else he would be forced to seek an annulment."

Her words fell like chips of ice, dispassionate, yet threatening in a veiled sort of way. Mercedes stood in front of the chair, her head held proudly as she looked down at the cold shell of a woman. "If there is one thing I know, it is that my husband will never put me aside, barren or not." He had sworn it to her in the heat of passion. Was it really true?

Intuiting Mercedes' underlying uncertainties, Sofia replied, "Do not be so certain. Barren wives are easily dealt with in a noble house such as Alvarado. If God does not bless your union with fertility, then it is a sign that there was no true marriage."

Beneath the sanctimonious platitudes, Mercedes sensed the viciousness, brutal as a slap. "I know my husband better than you know your son. I've seen him with his child. If we have no children, he will make Rosario his heir." *Let her choke on that*!

Sofia's small black eyes studied the haughty Sebastián woman with malice. "You are a fool if you believe that. Admittedly he has grown bizarrely fond of the child, but he will never let her inherit Gran Sangre. The ranch has become his passion. Do not deny that you have seen it. I myself have watched him ride out every morning. He is rebuilding this place to be as glorious as it was in the days of old Don Bartólome. He will wish a son of his loins—a legal heir recognized by *criollo* society—to become the next *patrón* of Gran Sangre."

"He cares nothing for *criollo* society," Mercedes retorted. "If he did, he would not have broken so many of their sacred rules of propriety—bringing Rosario into the household, giving poached beef to starving farmers instead of having them whipped—even aiding Juarista soldiers!"

"Bah! None of that matters," Sofia said dismissively. "Perhaps it was the war that changed him thus. Once he was a wastrel. Now he knows what is important. Only do your duty to the House of Alvarado. That is what women of our class are born to do."

"I am more than a brood mare to Lucero," Mercedes said stubbornly, fighting to remain calm.

"If you wish to remain *patrona* of this hacienda, you had best pray you are precisely that. Forget about that insignificant bastard child." Her admonitions were clipped with finality. The discussion was over.

"I would be tempted to hate you, Doña Sofia . . . if I did not pity you so much," Mercedes said as the old woman turned her head away and closed her eyes.

That afternoon the bitter exchange with her mother-in-law replayed itself over and over in Mercedes' mind as she rode out to inspect the irrigated crops, which were growing lushly in the late seasonal heat. While Rosario was taking her afternoon nap, Mercedes had enticed Bufón to lope along with her, feeling a need for some silent, unquestioning company on her solitary excursion.

Would her husband put her aside in order to give Gran Sangre a male heir? The man she had married would always abide by the rules of *criollo* society, but the man who now made such fierce demanding love to her each night, who slept holding her close to him, who swore he would never let her go—would *he*?

Sofia had been right in saying that he was obsessed with

his birthright. He loved this land, labored for it, gave his sweat and his blood to rebuild it . . . with a passion the indolent Lucero of old would never have imagined. But the Lucero of old would never have acknowledged Rosario or done any of the other things he had done since riding back into her life.

Mercedes rubbed her aching head, trying to ignore the troubling specter that her confrontation with Sofia had raised. The old woman said the war had changed him from a wastrel into the man he was now. Mercedes admitted to herself that it was true. But more than that, he was also a man whose touch no longer made her flinch in revulsion but rather ignited an answering response in her, a response she was terrified to acknowledge.

"What if—" She froze, pressing her fingertips to her lips and shaking her head in denial. No, it was absurd, ridiculous. She was upset by the way Lucero made her feel, that was all. Kicking her horse into a trot, she rode determinedly away from the river, where the peons were diligently hoeing between the tall rows of corn. The dog loped contentedly at her side.

An overpowering need to be alone seized her. Before long she was clear of the cultivated area, heading down a steep arroyo. Catclaw and mesquite grew, dusty gray in the afternoon heat as her horse wended its way aimlessly. The deep gully, carved by the force of seasonal rains, wound tortuously near the back of the great house. If she wished, she could return and wash up for dinner by taking the shortcut, but Mercedes felt unwilling to face Lucero just yet. He would be heading home from the south range any time now, intent on soaking his saddle-weary body in a big tub of warm water. She could still remember how his muscular frame had looked, glistening with water that fateful time she had interrupted him and Innocencia in the bathing room. *Innocencia.* Another troubling question—why did Lucero ignore his old mistress?

Suddenly, Bufón's loud bark echoed a warning from up ahead where he had disappeared around the curve in the gully. Forgetting her troubling reverie, Mercedes called out his name. The snarling of a puma blended with the low growling of the dog. Her horse reared up, frightened by the cat's scream. She fought to bring the mare under control, then urged it forward, reaching for the shotgun on her saddle. Just as she seized the stock of the gun, the horse bucked and twisted, pitching her from the saddle. She tumbled to the ground and rolled. The weapon clattered out of her reach.

Dazed and aching, Mercedes scrambled to her knees, then froze. Bufón stood between her and the large puma, who edged nearer, snarling low in his throat, ready to attack. Behind her lay the open mouth of a small cave, the cat's lair. The dog had stumbled on him as he emerged and tried to warn her away! If she spooked the cat it could well leap in any direction, even past the dog and directly at her. She had to inch her way over to the shotgun.

Taking a deep breath for courage, she stood up and took a step toward the gun. The cat caught the movement and leaped with blurring speed. Bufón blocked the beast's desperate move with his massive body but the cat's claws bit deep as he raked across the dog's back with a feral scream.

"Bufón!" Mercedes cried, taking two quick strides to reclaim the shotgun. She tried to aim the weapon, but a blast from the LeFaucheaux would surely kill both animals. Dog and cat thrashed through the brush, rolling and twisting, growling and snarling, but never breaking apart long enough for a clean shot. Several times Mercedes sighted the weapon, only to give up with a sob of frustration. Bufón was covered with blood now, his growling low and desperate. Her pet was going to die for certain if she did not do something.

Just as she raised the shotgun again, a man's hand seized the barrel, shoving it down. "You'll kill the dog," her husband said to her, slipping his knife from its sheath.

"Lucero, don't—" Mercedes bit back a cry of pure terror, reaching out to him, but he pushed her back. "Get the hell out of here!" He sprinted toward the embattled animals, that wicked blade gleaming evilly in the afternoon light.

The dog was tiring visibly, his great sides moving in and out like bellows. He was weakened from loss of blood.

Nicholas gave a sharp command for the dog to come to him just as the two disengaged.

But Bufón was too disoriented to do more than collapse on the ground, awaiting the cat's final killing pounce. Before the puma could spring in for his kill, Nicholas interposed himself. He flicked his knife toward the cat's throat, but only grazed him as the animal twisted agilely away. The man circled the crouching cat. Both were scarred veterans of many fights, wary, patient, deadly. Again Mercedes raised her weapon but Lucero was between her and the cat. Then before she could move around to take aim, the cougar sprang for her husband's throat and they went down in a blur.

Mercedes was silent, her throat parched bone-dry as she watched them thrash in the dust. If she had been desperate to save the dog, she was hysterical now! The big cat covered Lucero's body, ripping bloody furrows across his left shoulder. Her only chance to save him was to get close enough to shove the barrel of the shotgun into the cat's side. Holding her weapon steady, she drew closer.

The sharp yellow fangs sought his throat, but he blocked them and felt the agonizing sear as they sank deeply into his right arm. Using his left hand, Nicholas drove the blade in the cat's underbelly, sinking it to the hilt. Then he pushed it upward, through the intestine and deep under the ribs, through the lung and into the heart.

Fortune could feel the animal's death throes, could hear Mercedes' scream as she called Lucero's name, but she seemed very far away. The cat's deadweight pressed in on his chest, restricting his breathing. He shoved it away, panting and struggling onto all fours, then shook his head to clear his vision and stood up.

"Oh, Lucero, thank God, you're alive—I was so afraid." Mercedes flung her arms around his shoulders.

"Once you wished me dead in the war—does this mean you've changed your mind, beloved?" he asked with labored breath.

Ignoring his raspy jibe, she looked around frantically for something with which to stem the flow of blood oozing from the slashes and puncture wounds on his body. Her horse had bolted as soon as she had been thrown, leaving her afoot.

"You must lie down so I can tend your hurts." They sank together to the earth. He held her in a fierce possessive grip, as if hanging onto the very essence of life. She was life—his life, and he had almost lost her to a senseless accident in this dangerous wilderness.

"Why were you out here so far from safety, riding alone down a blind arroyo?" he snarled angrily. Without giving her the chance to reply, he savaged her mouth with his, then dug his fist in her tangled hair and pressed her face against his chest.

Mercedes could hear his heart slamming against the muscled wall of his chest, smell the metallic sweet scent of blood—his blood. Sweet Virgin, he could have died, slashed to bits, his throat ripped away by that cat! Of their own volition her arms enveloped him, heedless of the blood soaking into her clothes. Her fingers dug into his back, holding him as fiercely as he held her, affirming that they were both alive.

From the instant he felt her hands pressing him closer, her body trembling with fright and desire, Nicholas could not feel the wounds the cat had inflicted. Yes, this was desire—she could not disguise it or control it. A brush with death often had a way of sharpening a person's awareness of the life force within.

"You feel it, too, don't you?" he said, tugging on her hair, forcing her face to tilt up to his. Luminous gold eyes, darkened by passion, stared up at him in mute, stunned entreaty. And still she did not release her fierce hold on him, even when he rocked his hips against hers and pressed his hand against the curve of her buttocks.

Mercedes could feel the hard bulge of his erection pressing into her belly, into the sizzling inferno that had bubbled up so suddenly in the wake of death. From deep within her, some mindless instinct overrode all caution, tore down every barrier that she had striven to erect between them. Her hips rotated against his and she was rewarded by his low ragged gasp.

Nicholas pressed her to the ground, his hands frantically shoving her heavy twill riding skirts up. The stiff fabric resisted, bunching thickly around her thighs. Ignoring it he pulled her soft white cotton underpants down, tearing the tapes, abrading her delicate pale skin.

Mercedes did not feel his roughness as she undulated her hips, assisting him in freeing her of the restricting clothes. All the while, her arms clung to his shoulders, feeling the slickness of sweat mingled with blood. She pressed her mouth to the raw gashes, kissing them voraciously, tasting the salty tang on his skin.

Feeling the velvety caress of her tongue against his fiery wounds almost caused him to spill his seed before he could free himself from his breeches. He tore the last button on his fly free and yanked the tight pants down, then reached beneath her rucked-up skirts, desperate to feel her answering feminine heat.

Soft. She was so damn soft, and wet. But there was no time for the surge of exhilaration he should have felt at this hard-won victory. He moved her thighs apart and guided his throbbing engorged phallus into the slick waiting warmth of her body.

The contact was like the instantaneous combustion of lightning striking a pile of straw. Scorching rivers of fiery pleasure rocked her with his first deep plunge. She cried out his name as he filled her with life, penetrating deeper than he ever had before, moving with a relentless desperate rhythm that she no longer wanted to fight. Instead her hips rose up to meet his as she opened wider, greedy for this melding together. For the first time she wanted—needed—to join him in this mad mindless surfeit.

The glory of it built and built until she thought she would go insane from the pleasure. His lips pressed on hers, and he tasted his own blood. Then he plundered inside her mouth, insinuating his tongue around hers, thrusting above as he did below. There was a frantic life-affirming desperation in their ancient mating dance. They clung together, giving and receiving, panting and moaning in animal hunger that echoed a far more profound discovery than the mere ecstasy of copulation.

She needed him and freely gave in to it for the first time, allowing herself not to think but only to feel with her body—and with her heart. And so she climaxed on the barren, dusty earth with the taste of his blood in her mouth.

Nicholas felt her stiffen, her rippling convulsions squeezing his staff, wringing his seed from him in long wrenching spasms that seemed as if they would splinter both their bodies with the intensity. Then he collapsed onto her. All he wanted to do was remain this way, holding her so intimately to him, covering her with his body, feeling the soft subtle aftershocks of her first orgasm. Now he had bound her to him in a way Luce never could. Mercedes belonged to him.

She could feel his weight pressing her hard against the rocky ground. The surreal haze of pleasure was gradually replaced by an awareness of their vulnerability. The wetness of his blood began to soak through her clothes.

"Lucero?" She struggled to roll him off of her. Finally he seemed to regain consciousness, shaking his head to clear it, then raising up enough to kneel between her legs and pull up his pants. She scrambled up beside him, tugging her torn clothes into the barest semblance of order before she turned to him. He swayed on his knees, then started to collapse into her arms.

"Careful, my darling, don't fall," she murmured, lowering his big body to lean against an outcropping of shale. Dear God, now she could see that he was losing blood at a terrible rate. She needed something for bandages—her heavy riding skirts. The stiff twill would not give when she tried to tear it by hand.

"You need . . . my knife," Nicholas said, as consciousness ebbed and flowed from him in giddy lightheaded surges.

At once she scrambled over to the dead cat and pulled the blade from its gristly mooring. Ignoring the gore encrusted on it, she began to hack methodically at her skirts until she had torn free a long strip of the heavy cloth.

He could feel her hands tremble as she wound the makeshift bandages around his arm. A jagged bolt of agony restored his fading consciousness when she tightened the cloth against the lacerations. He swore an oath. "Don't panic now or you'll finish what the cat began."

"You were crazy, trying to kill a puma with a knife," she retorted, frantic over the amount of blood he was losing.

"I didn't try—I succeeded, at that and other things," he said, reaching up to caress her cheek. "If I hadn't fought the cat you would've shot Bufón, a poor reward for saving your life."

At the mention of his name, the shaggy dog raised his head and whimpered.

"At least he says thank you," Nicholas added, grinning at her through pain-glazed eyes. God, how pale and distraught her face was. Her eyes glowed like molten amber as she studied him, angry and frightened over the way he had risked his life.

"Lie still so the bleeding eases," she whispered.

"No need for such wifely concern. I've been cut up a lot worse than this and survived."

"I've seen the scars, Lucero," she said with a quiet shudder.

The two of them sat on the hard dusty earth, huddled together, staring deeply into one another's eyes, each reading more than the other intended to reveal.

"You must be in terrible pain," she said.

"It never hurts much at first. Shock, I suppose," he replied as his teeth began to chatter. "Always gets damned cold though."

With nothing to warm him but her body, Mercedes leaned closer and put her arms around him, trying not to cause him further hurt. He could feel her soft sweet breath against his throat and smell the lavender scent of her hair. He reached up with his good arm and caressed the silky curtain that spilled around her shoulders.

The gentle caress caused her to shiver along with him, but she was not cold, not cold at all. "Thank you for Bufón," she murmured.

"I only hope he makes it," Nicholas replied.

"He will. You both will," she answered, stroking his forehead, which had suddenly become clammy in the afternoon heat.

"Patrona!" Hilario's voice echoed over the clopping of hoofbeats as he and Gregorio rode toward her. "We found your horse at the mouth of the arroyo and knew something terrible had happened. I sent Ramón after help."

Weak with relief, Mercedes raised her head. "The *patrón* has been injured. Can you move him without reopening the wounds?"

"I can ride," Nicholas said doggedly, trying to sit up. The earth spun crazily and he collapsed back into Mercedes' arms.

"I'll rig a litter," Gregorio said. He dismounted and began to unfasten the bedroll on his saddle.

In a matter of minutes several more riders arrived. They carried their now-unconscious *patrón* and the big dog back to the house where Angelina was waiting with Rosario.

Rosario ran out to greet them, tears streaming down her cheeks. "Is my papa going to be all right? And Bufón?"

"Yes, child, but you must go upstairs and wait in your room while we tend them," Angelina said calmly, then issued instructions for the men to carry the *patrón* upstairs and the dog into the kitchen.

"Hilario, send a rider for the doctor in San Ramos," Mercedes ordered, then turned to the cook. "Set water to boil and tend to Bufón as best you can. When the water's ready, send it upstairs to me. Have Lupe fetch clean linens for bandages and bring them at once."

She turned and followed the litter with Lucero's unconscious body on it. She could still feel the sweet frisson of heat his touch had brought when they held each other amid the bloody carnage, but forced away thoughts of the savage passion that had preceded the tenderness. That she would examine later, when there was time . . . when she dared.

Don't you dare die, husband, she admonished silently. He was truly her husband, the man who had risked his life for her and her beloved pet. He was her protector, her lover. She would not let him die.

* * *

Mercedes leaned against the high back of the wooden chair and ran her forearm across her brow, wiping perspiration and a stray lock of hair from her face. All the while her eyes never left the unconscious form of her husband lying so still on the bed. She had needed every nursing skill she had learned from the sisters and from hard experience the past years as *patróna* of an isolated hacienda. The slashes across his left shoulder were deep and required many stitches.

She smiled grimly, thinking about the fine embroidery skills her *dueña* had drilled into her. The old woman would have been horrified to think a proper lady could actually sew up a man's flesh! But what would any *dueña* think of a woman who writhed in ecstasy beneath a man out in the open without even the dignity of nightfall to cloak them?

Turning back to the matter at hand, she forced herself to evaluate the extent of his injuries. The wounds had been raw and ragged but open enough to be cleaned with *contra yerba*, an ointment made of the leaves and roots of thistle for disinfection. Then she had covered his injuries with a thick paste of yarrow to clot any further seepage of blood. What really worried her were the deep fang punctures in his right arm. If the red streaking poison set in he would lose the arm, perhaps even his life, for few survived the ordeal of amputation, even with laudanum or ether to dull the pain during the horrendous procedure.

"You would hate being deformed, wouldn't you?" she asked softly in the silence. His perfect male beauty had been marred by numerous scars but his body was whole and strong. He was a horseman, who could outride any of his vaqueros, a man to whom the loss of a limb would be unmanning. She knew that, foolishly, he would rather die. She also knew that she would never let him die.

He stirred restlessly and she rose quickly, checking the drains she had placed in the wounds on his arm.

"Do you think the reeds will work?" Angelina asked. She stood in the doorway, a worried frown creasing her normally smiling face.

Mercedes had inserted small lengths of hollow reed in each of the punctures, hoping to let the poison drain out before the outer skin healed over. "I have read that doctors employed the practice on battlefield injuries with some success. If a bullet hole can be made to drain, why not the piercing from an animal's teeth?" She wrung her hands, then turned from Angelina back to Lucero, feeling his forehead for the heat of fever.

"I've steeped cherry bark. As soon as he awakens, we can spoon it down his throat. Let us hope it will prevent the fever."

"Thank you, Angelina," Mercedes replied softly. She then added, "Where is Rosario? Is she all right?"

"Since you would not allow her in here, she has remained by Bufón's side. Her presence seems to calm him. It's amazing that he is alive, but I have stopped the bleeding with yarrow and laid spiderwebs on his wounds. I think he will live."

"He saved my life. If I'd blundered onto that cat's lair in such close quarters, he would probably have killed me before I could've done anything." *But much as I love my pet, I'd give his life and my own for yours.* The thought sprang suddenly into her mind as she gazed down at the pale, still form of her husband.

"You are exhausted," Angelina said. "I'm going to draw a hot bath and dish up a bowl of hearty lamb stew for you. Then you must rest. Lupe and Baltazar can take turns watching over the *patrón*."

Mercedes shook her head. "I'll stay with him through the night. If the fever rises, he must be cooled at once."

"At least let me bring you food. You will do the *patrón* no good if you fall into a faint from hunger," the old cook admonished. Without waiting for a reply she turned to the door, adding, "I will send Baltazar up with a tray. You will eat."

Mercedes watched through the night, dozing on the large cushioned chair beside the bed. Near dawn she awakened to the sounds of moaning. He tossed restlessly in short jerky motions beneath the sheets, then called out her name. His voice was low, raspy and hoarse. She placed her hand on his forehead and found it burning hot.

The fever had begun.

Summoning Baltazar, she sent the elderly servant to fetch buckets of cool water from the well. Then she unfolded several large white bedsheets to use as soaking cloths. Through the day and into the following night Baltazar and Angelina assisted her in placing the sopping wet cool sheets across her husband's long body, covering him from neck to feet, holding him down when he thrashed in feverish delirium.

He spoke in brief disjointed phrases about the ghastly brutality of war which he had lived through, interspersed with bits about a woman named Lottie that made no sense at all. He also called for someone else—Luz, a Mexican woman's name, she was certain. Mostly he called for Mercedes. His voice was so weak and breathless that much of what he said was too garbled to be intelligible. The old cook and valet said nothing to the *patrona* about the fact that he spoke in a polyglot of languages—English and French as well as Spanish.

Mercedes was the only one who recognized all three but even she could make little of his fevered cries, other than to recognize how often he invoked her name. He never mentioned Innocencia. But who were Lottie and Luz? Probably some *soldaderas* he had taken up with when he rode with the *contre-guerrillas*. Still, some sixth sense, some repressed fear of what he might reveal caused her to dismiss the servants once the ravings began to grow stronger.

"*Patrona*, you cannot hold him down. He will lash out unaware and injure you," Baltazar protested, his austerely lined face haggard from lack of sleep.

"We have bound his wrists and ankles. The linen ties will hold," she said stubbornly, pushing them from the room. "Fetch more cool water and bring it to me. That is all I need." Her voice was firm, set. They obeyed. She closed the door, then collapsed against it for a moment, more frightened than she had ever before been. Could Lucero have become so used to speaking English and French during the past four years that he would lapse into it this way? Or had she made that savage surrender on the ground to a total stranger?

All the little things, the inconsistencies in his behavior during the past months surfaced again, nagging at her. He liked honey on fry bread when he had always hated it in the past; he read in Anselmo's library late in the evenings when before he had boasted never to have opened a book since leaving his tutors; his responses in church were careful, not repeated with the careless rote boredom he had formerly exhibited, even during their nuptial mass. And his hands, those marvelously skillful ambidextrous hands. He could employ left or right with equal ease in a myriad of small tasks.

Lucero had returned to her a better man than when he left, one who worked hard, cared for his daughter and was benevolent to starving peons. She and everyone else had come to accept that. But in the privacy of the bedroom, he was different. Mercedes blushed to remember her response to his touch. He had employed slow patience to win her surrender when she would not give it. After months of self-denial, she had finally surrendered. Was it because he was not the Lucero she had wed?

As a bride she had known so little of her husband, other than fear of his cruel mockery and shame over the careless way he took her and then deserted her for his mistress. She really had never known Lucero Alvarado at all—until now. And even as she was coming to love him, she feared he might not be Lucero at all, but another man blessed with his beauty, freed of his flaws.

"It cannot be," she whispered as she gazed down on his flushed naked body. Now every inch of him was familiar to her, every long hard muscle, every scar, even the scent of him. It had not been so before when he came to her only in darkness and then only for brief painful couplings before leaving her alone, feeling aching and defiled.

But now he was her mate, her love. She ran her hands gently over the crisp abrasion of hair on his chest, then down one long sinewy leg and back up. He was still too hot, too dry. Bending down, she tugged another wet sheet from the bucket where it soaked and smoothed it over his flesh, cooling and wetting him with life-giving water.

All the while she worked, she prayed.

Chapter 14

Nicholas thought he was drowning, attempting to thrash his way to the top of a pool of foul, stagnant water. Ice cold water. His teeth chattered and he shook, causing a searing arc of pain to shoot across his shoulder and arm. Then he felt the warmth of another heartbeat, another body. Soft heat enveloped him, small smooth hands soothed him. He could feel her body fitted against his, perfectly familiar as no other woman's had ever been. The fragrance of lavender filled his nostrils as he drifted off into peaceful oblivion at last.

Mercedes felt him relax. The chills that had wracked his body were over and he slept naturally for the first time in forty-eight hours. She had spent the second night lying beside him, at times throwing her own body over his to keep him from breaking open his stitches as he struggled against the linen bonds that held him fast to the mattress. When the chills began, she covered him with warm blankets, then stripped off her clothes and pressed her body against his to quiet him. Sometime during the night the fever had broken. She had removed the bindings from his wrists and ankles, and then she had drifted off to sleep herself.

Scooting over in the bed, she sat up and studied the man sleeping so peacefully. His swarthy skin was pale from his brush with death but still bronzed against the white bed linens. A beard stubble shadowed his jawline, giving his face a piratical look. Those troubling wolf's eyes were closed, the thick dark lashes swept down onto the high, finely chiseled cheekbones. She reached out and touched his face, letting her fingers feel the raspy scratch of whiskers, trace the elegant contour of his thin hawkish nose, glide over the smooth arch of a heavy black eyebrow. Sleep made him look younger.

Her hand moved lower, unconsciously seeking out the steady reassuring drum of his heartbeat as she pressed her palm against the hard slab of chest muscle. When her hand followed the natural pathway of the narrowing arrow of body hair that vanished below the covers at his waist, she withdrew it abruptly with a small gasp of recognition. She wanted him to make love to her, wanted to feel what she had felt lying beneath him on the hard rocky earth! He possessed her very soul now. Here she sat, completely naked in his big bed, gazing down lustfully on his equally naked body, caressing it while he slept!

"Don't stop now, beloved. You were just reaching the best part," his husky voice whispered. He chuckled when she gasped again and seized the edge of the sheet, pulling it up to cover her breasts. His eyes blinked open and he looked at Mercedes. She looked enchanting with her cheeks pinkened in embarrassment, her hair tousled and falling in tangles around her shoulders. Her amber eyes met his, darkening in accusation.

"You were supposed to be asleep," she said crossly, self-consciously running her fingers through her hair. It was a fright. She was a fright! After going without bathing for two days she felt sticky and filthy. A vile film pasted her tongue to the roof of her mouth. And yet he stared up at her with an intensity of desire that robbed her of breath. She could say nothing, do nothing but return the look and tremble.

Nicholas sensed her embarrassment. Before she could wriggle from the bed, he seized her wrist. "Please, don't go," he said. Then a stab of white-hot pain sucked the air from his lungs and he gasped out a surprised oath, looking down at the bandages swathing his right forearm.

"The cat sank his teeth in deep. Watch that you don't jostle those drains or you'll really feel some pain," she scolded, reaching out to check the wrappings holding the small pieces of reed in place.

"What the hell have you done? My arm looks like a porcupine's back."

"So far the suppuration isn't excessive and the punctures are draining nicely," she murmured with obvious pride in her handiwork.

He smiled in spite of the pain. In her haste to keep him from moving his injured arm, she had let the sheet drop to her waist again. Two high-pointed breasts stood out to perfection from the angle at which he viewed them. He felt the stirrings of lust begin to override the abominable aching in his shoulder and throbbing in his arm. "You've saved my life, beloved," he murmured, letting his arm drop onto her thigh where he could feel her trembling.

Mercedes felt his eyes on her, willing her to meet his steady gaze. She could not, but rather looked down only to realize the sheet had fallen. When she tried to pull it back up, he held it fast.

"Don't hide from me, Mercedes. We've known each other's bodies far too intimately for shyness now." Even as he spoke the words, he knew they were not true. There was so much left unsaid after her surrender out in the desert. "Everything has changed between us, hasn't it?" he asked.

She swallowed the lump in her throat and nodded, uncertain of what to say. *Are you truly the man I married*? she wanted desperately to ask but dared not.

"When I saw you afoot and realized you could have been killed . . . I knew that I couldn't imagine life without you." He studied her face warily as she continued to look away. Was she afraid of the passion she had finally felt or was it something else—something truly damning?

"What did I say when I was feverish?" he asked abruptly. Her head turned in surprise and her eyes locked with his. He watched her nervously moisten her lips with the tip of her tongue before replying. God, had he revealed his identity—that he was not Lucero Alvarado!

"Mostly it didn't make sense. You spoke of the war . . . and you called my name," she replied, evading the implication of his question, and the fact that he had spoken in two foreign languages with which Lucero had scarcely a nodding acquaintance four years earlier.

Neither of them said anything for a moment, but he did not relinquish his hold on the sheet covering her thigh. Then his hand began to move softly back and forth, caressing her.

"You're lovely, Mercedes."

"I'm wretched-looking, unbathed, haggard and thoroughly disheveled," she responded, unnerved by his scrutiny. What was going on behind those mesmerizing eyes? Did he suspect that he had said something incriminating while delirious?

"You're the very best wife any husband could ever wish for," he said quietly.

Wife. Husband. The words sealed a pact between them. His hand slowly loosened, then fell away from her as he drifted off to sleep once more.

They would never again speak of his feverish ravings.

Nicholas mended quickly after the fever broke. He awakened that afternoon, voraciously hungry and, much to Angelina's delight, polished off a bowl of lamb stew. Rosario bounded in as soon as the tray had been cleared away.

"Papa! They said you were getting well. I was awfully worried. Are you feeling better now?"

He patted a space beside him on the bed and she climbed up amid the pillows surrounding him and gave him a hug. "I'm feeling much better. How is Bufón?"

"Angelina says he will live even though he might run with a limp. You saved his life, Papa," she said with pure adoration in her round dark eyes.

"I'm glad. He saved your stepmother's life, you know."

She nodded gravely, "I don't ever want her to die—or you either." She burrowed against his chest and held onto him tightly.

A surge of empathetic warmth filled him. She had been alone and frightened, deserted by her mother in death, then taken away to an alien place by strangers. He understood what it meant to be a child afraid and alone, only he had never had anyone to worry about him, anyone who loved him . . . until now.

Stroking her shiny black curls, he said softly, "We'll never leave you, Rosario, I promise."

That is how Mercedes found them when she brought his medicine.

During the next few days as his strength increased, a new tension grew between Nicholas and Mercedes, subtly different than the intense sexual antagonism of earlier when he had teased and stalked and she had held herself rigidly aloof. He knew he had revealed something during his delirium. Yet she had chosen to ignore it. He had always considered that it was only a matter of time until Luce's wife would realize that she was sleeping with an impostor, but he had hoped it would be after she was expecting his child, when she would be powerless to speak out. But that was before he met her . . . and fell in love with her.

A foolish thing to do, certainly nothing he had ever planned to do, falling in love with his brother's wife. But he knew sure as the summer rains came that he would never give her up as long as he drew breath. Perhaps even though she did intuit his charade, she returned his feelings. But the scars Luce had inflicted on her were deep. She guarded her heart and had feared to yield her body until the savagely fulfilling sexual encounter they had shared last week. Perhaps her own response had frightened her almost as much as the thought that she had freely given to him what she had never given to Luce.

Before he had been patient, playing a waiting game, taunting her, teasing her untried body, arrogantly assured that one day she would surrender. They had moved past that point now. She had slept in her bed the past week, insisting he needed to rest without risk of her brushing his injured shoulder and arm. At first he was too weak to protest, but now he had mended well enough.

Determined, he threw off the covers and swung his legs over the side of the mattress. Until now Baltazar had been helping him walk. Today he would go outside under his own power. He stood up, grateful when the room did not tilt as it had the first time he tried to stand up the day before yesterday. Gingerly he made his way across the floor, holding onto furniture until he reached the window facing on the courtyard.

He called out to Lazaro, who was working at the well, to draw him a warm bath, then sat down on a chair to begin unfastening the bandages over his wounds. As he worked, Nicholas was flooded with memories of two days earlier when Mercedes had taken the curious little reeds out of the draining punctures. He flexed the injured arm, making a fist even though the exertion caused him to wince in pain.

They had been sitting side by side on the narrow wooden bench in the courtyard. "Are you certain it doesn't hurt that much?" she had asked dubiously. The flesh around the drains looked slightly pink but that was from healing, not suppuration. "There aren't any streaks of red."

"I'm relieved to hear it," he said dryly, "since I've no wish to have you sawing off my arm."

Her head shot up, a look of horror in her eyes. "You've actually seen that on the battlefield?"

His expression was flat as he choked back the memories. "I've held men down while it was done to them. Sometimes I think it would've been a greater mercy to put a bullet in their brains than to maim them for life."

"You'd hate that—not being perfect, wouldn't you?" she asked hesitantly.

Amusement replaced the opaque look in his eyes. "Father Salvador would scarcely concur that I'm perfect, but I do thank you for the compliment." With pure pleasure he watched her blush.

"I scarcely meant . . . oh, you know well enough what I meant," she said, flustered, then returned to her work.

"Ouch! Watch what you're doing," he groused as she fumbled removing the last drain.

"Serves you right for making me nervous," she replied.

"Do I? Make you nervous, Mercedes," he murmured low, leaning nearer to her, crowding her backward on the narrow bench. He could smell the lavender fragrance in her hair, the sweet essence that was Mercedes.

She leaned away, holding the small tweezers up like a miniature weapon. He could sense her trembling. The small pulse fluttered at the base of her slender golden throat. The sun was warm on them and he could see the dampness dewing her skin . . . imagine it trickling between her breasts below the modest neckline of her *camisa*. He reached up with his good arm and lightly touched his fingertips to her collarbone, tracing a pattern on the silky skin, then moving higher to brush that pulse in her throat. He took his fingertips from her skin and touched them to his lips, tasting her.

"Salty-sweet, very enticing."

"You describe me as if I were fry bread," she replied, breathless now, very still.

He smiled at her wit, still as acerbic as ever, but she did not return the smile. They sat there in the warm morning sun, gazing into each other's eyes until Lupe came out of the kitchen, her apron filled with parched corn, which she scattered, calling the chickens who flocked noisily from their roost behind the blacksmith's shed.

The spell had been broken then, but now Nicholas remembered her response, the still hesitant, half-hidden longing in her eyes. If it had been half-hidden, it had also been half-revealed. Today he would press her to drop all her defenses, to give him what he truly wanted of her—not only her passion but her love.

Gritting his teeth he pulled on a robe and belted it, then began to walk slowly across the room. It was midmorning. Rosario was at her lessons with Father Salvador, Mercedes was in the fields with Juan and Angelina was in her kitchen. He took his time, pausing to rest at the bottom of the stairs, then again on the bench in the courtyard. By the time he reached the bathing room, he was perspiring and weak, but it felt good to be up and about again.

He was used to forcing himself to function while injured. Often in his past life his survival had depended on that well-honed toughness. In the dirty business of war, often the wounded who could not ride with the troop were left behind to die.

This was a glorious day to live, he thought as he sank

beneath the warm soothing water and laid his head back on the edge of the tub, letting his aching muscles and the stiff tightly drawn slashes in his shoulder soak until he could rotate the joint freely. If Mercedes would only remove the damnable itchy stitches, he would have complete use of it. Baltazar brought him his razor, offering to shave off his bristling bandit's beard, but he wanted time to soak in peace and privacy, so he dismissed the servant with thanks. He worked up a stiff lather in his hair and dunked his head to rinse, noting the length.

"I could use a trim, but it can wait," he said to himself, lying back to imagine Mercedes' small hands, seizing fistfuls of his hair, pulling him to her for a fierce, passionate kiss. The image made him instantly rock hard.

Mercedes rode in and dismounted at the courtyard gate where Lazaro stood, ready to take her mare for a rubdown.

"Good morning, *Patrona*. I did not expect you back for several hours."

"My mare's limping. I think she may have picked up a stone in her shoe. Would you have Hilario see to her when he comes in?"

"I will take her to the stables right now, *Patrona*. Then I must hurry back to the bathing room. Don Lucero might need me."

"He's bathing?" she fairly squeaked. "How did he get downstairs and all the way across the courtyard—did you and Baltazar carry him?"

The old servant shrugged. "I do not know, *Patrona*. He ordered a bath. While I was filling the tub he walked into the room. Baltazar brought him some things but then the *patrón* sent him away."

"I'll see to him," she said with a nod of dismissal, then stomped across the courtyard. Of all the impossible, insane, stupid, dangerous things he could have done, this was the worst yet. What if the wounds reopened or he fell getting in or out of the tub? Sweet Virgin, he could pass out and drown in the bathwater! She began to run, frightened at what she might find.

As Mercedes neared the heavy wooden door, she slowed, half-afraid that she might again see that slut Innocencia in the tub with him. Shaking her head to dismiss her jealousy, she opened the door. He was alone, sitting in the tub. His hair curled in dripping ringlets, plastered against his nape, hanging over his forehead. He looked as beautiful as a Greek god, Neptune rising out of the Aegean in all his pagan splendor.

Those haunting eyes studied her hungrily. "Come inside. Bar the door." His voice vibrated in the stillness.

She stepped across the threshold, then turned, fumbling with the heavy latch until it fell into place with a loud thunk. The water made a soft rippling sound, once more drawing her eyes to him as he sat up, his arms braced on the sides of the tub. Small rivulets glistened as they ran down his chest and over his shoulders. The angry red wounds on his left shoulder and right arm were faded to a light pink now.

"You've soaked those stitches. They could become infected."

"Then remove them," he said, daring her. "I've pulled most of them out by hand. The water loosened them up. It feels good."

To illustrate his point, he skimmed his arm across the surface of the water, palms cupped as if he were swimming. The muscles on his shoulders and arms rippled sinuously. She knew they would feel iron-hard beneath the sleek wetness of his skin. The thought made her mouth go suddenly dry.

The teasing dare left his eyes now as he extended one hand to her. "Please, Mercedes, come to me, love."

She could say nothing, only do as he asked. A deep feral heat began to build inside her, radiating from her belly to her breasts, right down to her fingertips. Most of all it centered at the juncture of her thighs, in the hot dampness of that feminine place only he had touched . . . *unless he was not Lucero.*

Mercedes stopped suddenly a scant two feet from the tub, her eyes filled with anguish and confusion. Dear God, she desired this man, she burned to touch him, to feel his wet slick flesh, to smell the spicy masculine scent of tobacco and leather that blended so subtly with his own unique essence. She had never felt this way when they were first wed, never imagined the hunger that consumed her now. Why now? Why him . . . now, after all these years?

"Don't be afraid," he said simply, breaking into her thoughts. "I need your help."

"I don't doubt it," she finally managed. "You're probably too weak to stand without someone to steady you."

"I managed last week well enough, under far more adverse conditions," he reminded her.

Her face really flamed now as she recalled the way they had coupled on the ground like wild animals mating, blood-smeared and desperate. She had struggled to block it from her mind, but she could not, for the soul-robbing pleasure she had found in that brief and brutal coupling still amazed her—as if there were another woman inhabiting her body, a wanton, reckless stranger.

Rather than stand like a dithering fool in front of him, she sat on the edge of the heavy tub and inspected his injured shoulder. He was right about the stitches. Most of them had been soaked loose and pulled out, the flesh knitted smoothly without inflammation.

"I still see a few threads that should come out," she said, probing at the healing wounds.

He reached onto the bench on the other side of the tub and produced a small penknife. "I took it from your medicine bag."

She accepted the tool and began cutting the last of the stitches and pulling them out. A few had grown tightly into the healed flesh and she had to tug to free them. "You mend incredibly fast," she said, biting her lip in concentration.

"I've survived a lot worse, just as I told you. Nothing keeps me down." As he said the words he thought of his submerged body, rigidly hard for the past half hour.

Her eyes flew from his shoulder to the water, then instantly back. She knew he had caught the lapse. Quickly standing up and brushing off her skirt with an agitated stroke of her hand, she said, "There, you're all done."

"Oh, no, I haven't even begun yet, Mercedes." His voice was like warm molasses, thick and smoky dark with promise.

She struggled with her embarrassment until he added earnestly, "I won't be rough this time. I promise it will last longer . . . much longer."

His sexy smile could melt solid bone.

He took hold of her hand, pulling her to the edge of the tub, then turned the palm up and placed it against his lips. She could feel the rasp of his beard, the soft firm pressure of his mouth, a swift subtle flick of his tongue—ah, that wicked clever tongue. Would he pull her into the water clothes and all? Mercedes knew she would not resist him if he did. His voice, silky and low, with an earnestness that was quite opposite from his usual taunting drawl, broke into her heated thoughts.

"My razor's on the bench but Baltazar forgot my mirror. Have you ever shaved a man, Mercedes?" He knew she had not. Luce would never have possessed the patience for such an intimacy with her.

"I could slit your throat," she warned. There was an odd lightness in her breathy tone as the frisson of a thrill raced up and down her spine.

"I'll take my chances." He handed a square of homemade soap to her. "First you have to work up a thick lather and spread it over my whiskers," he instructed, taking her hands in his and rubbing them over the soap.

It felt incredibly sensuous, the slickness of the soap, the warmth of his roughened callused hands. When the lather was billowing out from between her fingers, he released her hands and tilted his head back, jutting out his jaw.

"Work it in good."

She complied, eager to touch him this way, openly, boldly, initiating the contact she craved. The soap glided over his lower face. His whiskers felt dense and prickly. She could feel the muscles of his jaw and throat move under her fingers.

The instant Nicholas felt the caress of her hands on his skin, he tensed, struggling to hold himself in check, wanting her to have time to learn the texture of his body as he had learned hers. When her eyelids fluttered down for a moment as she stroked his beard, he smiled to himself. The barriers were really coming down. He had feared after the last explosive coming together that he might have frightened her in spite of, perhaps even because, she had experienced her first culmination.

When her eyes opened and she looked down at him, suddenly aware of how she must have reveled in touching him, she grabbed a towel and wiped the suds from her hands.

He handed her the razor, saying, "Take your time, love. We have all the time in the world."

Mercedes held the shiny blade up in her trembling hand. "Perhaps this isn't such a wise idea," she said. "I might slip—anyway I like the whiskers." What had made her blurt that out?

He smiled. "If your hands were steady enough to sew up my shoulder, you can shave me."

"That was different."

"Oh? How?"

"You were injured. I'm used to caring for injured people but this . . . it's . . ."

"Personal? Intimate?" His voice was husky but it was not teasing.

Mercedes swallowed and met his eyes. "Yes, it is intimate," she admitted with less embarrassment than she would have imagined possible. She raised the razor once more and found her hand had not steadied. "What if I bring you a mirror?" she suggested. "There was one in that cabinet by the door."

"All right," he said calmly, watching the heavy skirt of her riding habit swish as she walked. This outfit was newer, of fine green linen. "I'll have to take more care with your habit than I did with the one last week."

Mercedes almost dropped the mirror. "Yes, you certainly will, else I'll be forced to ride around like a farmer's wife with my skirts hitched up, showing off my bare legs."

"Very lovely bare legs they are, too." He reached for her hand holding the mirror and adjusted it so he could see his face. "Hold it just like that. It might be easier if you knelt." He guided her to a kneeling position beside the tub. They were at eye level. Her hands still trembled slightly as she gripped the mirror, but his were steady as he ran the gleaming blade across his jawline.

Scrape. Scrape. The raspy sound was low and incredibly erotic. She had never seen a man shave before and would never have dreamed it could be sexually arousing.

It was. His strong brown hands plied the blade in long clean strokes, leaving behind pathways of smooth tanned skin. When he ran the razor up his throat, tilting his head to one side and pulling the skin taut, she swallowed audibly. The urge to run her fingers down his jaw, to feel the contrast after the scratchy beard had been removed, was overwhelming.

If she had not already been on the floor, she might well have ended up there. Her knees were so weak they would never have held her upright and her breathing had grown swift and shallow. He put down the razor and reached for a towel, briskly wiping the last traces of soap from his face.

"Care to try again?" he asked, prying one hand from its tight grip on the edge of the tub and placing it against his smooth cheek.

Could he read her mind? Before she could answer the question, he leaned out of the tub and swept his damp arm around her waist, pulling her toward him. His mouth met hers suddenly but there was no savagery in this kiss. Rather, it was incredibly gentle, light as the touch of an evening breeze, warm and soft. His lips brushed, stroked, then he rimmed the edges of her mouth with the tip of his tongue, outlining it. By now she was holding his face cupped between her hands. Her eyes closed as she drank in the delicate, delicious sensations, eager for more.

Nicholas obliged her, probing softly at the seam of her slightly parted lips, darting inside for swift little sweeps when she opened for him, then retreating, coaxing her to do the same. She learned quickly, daring to dart her small sweet tongue against his, to taste of his lips, to follow inside his mouth and meld with his tongue as the kiss grew slowly in intensity.

Her hair hung down her back in a fat shiny plait. He

unfastened the ribbon holding it with his free hand, then combed his fingers through the golden masses. Freeing the curtain of silk to fan across her shoulders, he stroked it and buried his hand in its lush thickness, then massaged her scalp, cradling her head as he slanted his mouth across hers at another angle.

Mercedes was lost to everything but this man who was wooing her with such patient skill. She ran her hands back around his neck and pulled him nearer, holding on to him like an anchor in a storm. And the storm was building slowly, like the rise of a desert wind that starts in small cooling eddies and then grows into a howling inferno that drives mountains of sand in its scorching wake.

Nicholas knew he was losing control. If he did not stop now he would pull her into the tub and rip off her clothes again. And he knew that was not how he wanted it to be this time. She trembled against him, clinging, kissing him back with such sweet fierceness that his heart nearly burst from the joy of it. Slowly he broke off the kiss, pressing his lips softly to her eyelids, cheeks, then trailing his mouth down her throat.

Mercedes could barely make out his low whisper over the beating of her heart and the short panting breaths she struggled to draw. He murmured against her throat, "Not in here, not this way. Upstairs, in our bed."

Chapter 15

Nicholas slipped from the tub and dried off in haste, then slid his maroon silk robe over his nakedness with unconscious grace. They walked hand in hand across the courtyard, pausing briefly at the well for him to rest.

"Are you certain—the fever?" her voice was breathless and tentative.

He smiled with his eyes. "I'm certain," was all he replied as he stood up and they resumed their walk into the house.

When they reached the bedroom, Mercedes became suddenly quite shy and self-conscious. She had been out riding for a short time and surely smelled of horse. Yet here she was, walking into their room with the deliberate intention of making love in broad daylight, while outside their chambers a house full of servants would be going about their chores.

Nicholas could sense her reticence as she stopped at the edge of their big bed, staring down at the newly made up covers. Silently he locked the door, then walked up behind her and placed his hands on her shoulders. He brushed her hair aside and his lips nibbled softly at her nape. He murmured against the side of her throat, "It's all right, Mercedes. No one will interrupt. Lupe's finished her morning cleaning." He smiled against her skin, adding, "Of course, we're going to mess her beautifully made up bed."

"Father Salvador is tutoring Rosario at the other end of the hall," she replied, mortified.

He did chuckle softly then, unable to help himself. "Then I'll just have to place my hand over those sweet lips when you become too noisy."

Her cheeks were fiery but he was standing so close, doing such maddeningly wonderful things to her body that she could think of nothing to retort.

He continued whispering seductive reassurances as his hands reached around her waist to the small covered buttons of her jacket. In a moment it fell open down the front and he slipped it off her shoulders. Beneath it she wore a sheer underblouse that revealed her small perfect breasts through the gauzy fabric. He cupped one in each hand, lifting them, his thumbs working tight magical circles around the nipples until she moaned.

Nicholas turned her in his arms and unhooked the waistband of her heavy skirt, letting it drop to the floor. Then he stepped back to look at her, clad only in sheer white cotton undergarments and her riding boots.

"I feel rumpled and dusty," she said uncertainly, seeing that old familiar hunger in his eyes yet wondering what it was about her that now made her so attractive to him.

"You're incredible." His eyes devoured every curve of her body, made all the more alluring by the scanty covering. "Sit down on the chair so I can remove your boots," he commanded.

Silently she obeyed, perching on the edge of the seat with her feet tucked demurely beneath the chair. He knelt in front of her and took one leg, raising it and pulling off the boot, then massaging her instep with those amazing hands of his. When he repeated the process on the other foot, she laid her head back against the chair and said throatily, "That feels wonderful."

"Only wait. It'll get much better," he promised.

And it did. His hands slid up the curves of her calves, stroking her quivering thighs through the sheer folds of her slip. Then he rose and offered her his hand.

"I'm not sure I can stand," she admitted. "My legs are trembling."

But she did stand, eager for him to continue his ministrations. He loosed the drawstring and slipped the underblouse over her head, tossing it aside, then put his mouth to her breasts, one at a time. She cried out softly, arching her back, offering them to his suckling lips. She even helped him peel her slip and pantalettes from her hips, stepping out of them and into his arms, reveling in the feel of the smooth silk of his robe against her heated nakedness. His hard erection probed her belly as they melded their bodies together, their kisses swift and breathless. He guided her hand down between them at the opening of his robe and placed it around his pulsing phallus.

How hot and smooth it felt as she stroked the length of it under his guiding hand. Her own boldness amazed her, she who had never dreamed that she was capable of fondling a man's private parts. When he gasped and murmured choked love words in her ear, a heady sense of power came over her.

He slid the robe off with a fluid shrug, then growled low, "Best we get in bed before I lose control, beloved." Leading her to the bed, he pulled back the covers with one hand and climbed onto it, never letting go of her hand. She followed, meeting him as they knelt together in the center of the large soft mattress.

Her fingertips skimmed gingerly across his injured shoulder. "You might reopen your wounds," she whispered, kissing them softly.

"You'll have to take care to be very gentle with me, beloved," he murmured, smiling as he positioned her back on the bed and leaned over her, lying on his side. Then he worshipped her with his hands and mouth, from the crown of her head to the soles of her feet, caressing, licking, nipping, exploring every nuance of her responsiveness, now that she had at last given herself permission to enjoy the pleasure he offered.

And he offered much. Each breast was molded in his lean, long-fingered hands, offered up to his mouth, which then traveled to her belly where his tongue made small feathery forays into her navel. He kissed her quivering inner thighs, the sensitive skin behind her knees, the curve of her calf and the arch of her instep, then retraced his way back up until his hands found the soft golden curls of her mound.

When he touched her there, Mercedes came up off the

mattress. The jolt of sensation was even greater, more acute, than it had been the last time. She would never have believed it possible. An ache, so keen, so tightly stretched built deep in her belly, radiating down her thighs as he teased and caressed her, avoiding that central locus of her pleasure until now.

"Oh! Please," she cried raggedly, begging for surcease, knowing now that he would provide it with his body.

Nicholas watched her toss her head back and forth. Her eyes were closed, her back arched. She dug her hands into the sheets, clawing at them, on fire. At last she wanted him as desperately as he had wanted her from the first time he took her.

"Yes, love, yes," he crooned, positioning himself between her thighs, preparing to slide deep inside. She opened for him and he plunged into the slick wet heat, throwing his head back in triumph as he buried himself completely. "Hook your legs around my back," he commanded as he began to stroke.

Mercedes obeyed, arching to meet each thrust, crying out in small whimpering, mewling noises, less than speech yet communicating more than mere words ever could. Her hands slipped up his arms which were braced on either side of her. Carefully avoiding his injuries, she locked her hands behind his neck and drew him down to her, eager for his kiss.

Nicholas obliged, resting his weight on his elbows and taking her eager mouth with his, his tongue thrusting in sync with his hips. *Make it last, long, slow, as good as it can be.*

But he had reckoned neither on her fiery arousal nor on his own still weakened body. All too soon he could feel her reaching the crest just as sweat began to sheen his flesh. He grew dizzy and her lovely face blurred before his eyes as he watched her convulse in orgasm.

Mercedes had thought nothing could equal the sheer physical thrill of the last time but this exceeded it—so prolonged, so tenderly built up to, it was the most exquisite sensation she could imagine. Wave after wave washed over her yet she waited, wanting him to join her, to feel the thrill of recognition when he stiffened and his rod swelled and spilled its seed deep within her.

"Please, husband," she whispered against the curve between his shoulder and throat.

Her soft entreaty was all it took to drive him over the brink and send him spiraling into the dark sweet whirlpool of release. Feverishly his body convulsed in unison with hers until the last tremors finally died away, like ripples in a clear lovely pool that became glassy and smooth, tranquil once more.

He felt ready to black out again and fought it, not wanting to fall on her as he had the last time. Carefully, he rolled onto his side, taking her with him, keeping her flesh joined with his.

They lay that way for some time, holding each other in silence, he too weak from his exertions to speak, she too overcome with the newness and depth of the experience to gather her scattered thoughts.

When he finally withdrew from her and rolled onto his back, she felt a sense of loss. *He's bound me to him irrevocably now.* All thoughts of whether or not he was Lucero fled her mind. The wonder of their newly discovered love displaced them utterly. Especially when he took her hand and raised it to his lips, murmuring, "I love you, Mercedes. You do know that, don't you?"

She stared at him, stunned, for she had not expected him to voice the words aloud. His expression was open, vulnerable. The expectant tension between them grew palpable as he waited for her to return his declaration, this man who had become the center of her life, turning her well-ordered existence upside down from the moment he had ridden into the courtyard of the big house all those months ago. This stranger. Yet how could he be a stranger when he knew the secrets of her body so intimately . . . and even those of her heart?

"I've surrendered everything else to you . . . Lucero. Why not admit what you must know I feel? Yes, I love you, too."

Nicholas noted the way she paused, emphasizing his brother's name. The flash of pain that seared his heart told him this was the price he would have to pay for his masquerade. *But you love* me, *not Luce*. He gazed deeply into her fathomless golden eyes, fearing that she knew yet was afraid to admit it. Silently he held her, pressing her head against his shoulder and closing his eyes. *Ah, Mercedes, my love, what are we to do*?

The invitation to the ball at the Vargas hacienda arrived the next day, hand-delivered by one of Don Encarnación's own riders. Mercedes watched her husband break the heavy wax seal with the Vargas crest on it and read the message on the expensive vellum paper.

"What is it?" she asked.

He handed it to her with an amused lift of one eyebrow. "An opportunity for you to dig out that scarcely used trousseau and show off your loveliest gowns. We're invited to a ball honoring the Prince and Princess Salm-Salm. A Prussian mercenary. I understand he's a particular favorite of the emperor."

"Did you meet him when you were at court?" She was mildly curious about the rumors she had heard regarding the emperor's lavish lifestyle.

Nicholas laughed dryly. "A lowly lieutenant in the guards scarcely travels in the same social circles as a court sycophant like the prince."

"Do you dislike him?" Lucero had always instinctively mistrusted foreigners.

"I've heard of him by reputation. A good professional soldier, but past his prime. God, the war seems so far away now—and good riddance."

"Then you don't want to go," she replied.

He grinned at her with a boyish charm that made him suddenly seem years younger. "Of course we'll go. I want to show off my beautiful wife, who has worked hard and deserves a chance to dance and drink champagne."

Except for a few brief trips to Hermosillo on business, Mercedes had not been off Gran Sangre since her betrothal. Her time for balls and other social events, while she was a young girl in Mexico City, had been few. The lure of music and gaiety was strong. "There's so much work to be done here," she began uncertainly.

"It can wait. A few days of fun and rest will be good for us both."

"What about your mother?"

"What about her?"

"She's been so ill. What if she takes another turn for the worse? She might die while we're gone."

He frowned, then shrugged. "She detests the sight of me. I'll leave her to die in peace. She has Father Salvador to watch with her."

"I don't think she's ever known peace . . . or ever will," Mercedes replied, remembering the last bitter interview. "Even Father Salvador fears for the state of her soul."

His eyes became wary. "Is that so? After a lifetime of prayers and fasts, I can't imagine why she'd be in any danger—if he disregards the hatred she's always borne her husband and son. Until now that hasn't particularly seemed a problem to him."

"He wants the two of you reconciled." For some reason Mercedes had struck a nerve and she was not certain why, but before she could worry about it further, he interrupted her thoughts.

"We've reached all the accord that's possible," he replied enigmatically. Then his mood changed swiftly and he took her chin in his hand, raising it and smiling. "Go pick out a ball gown, Mercedes. You'll be the most beautiful woman there."

In the weeks that followed, their lives fell into a new routine. Every morning the *patrón* rode out at daybreak while the *patrona* remained near the house overseeing the harvest, the drying and preserving of fruit and vegetables and the milling of the most bountiful corn crop Gran Sangre had ever grown, thanks to the spring irrigation. Lucero's horses and cattle, hidden in the secluded canyons, grew sleek and fat on lush grass fed by summer rains.

Every night Mercedes rode out to meet him, sometimes accompanied by his daughter. On occasion, if the camps where the men were branding livestock were not too far, Mercedes and Rosario would come at noon, bringing a hamper of Angelina's succulent food for a picnic. Everyone on Gran Sangre could see what a happy family they were now that the don had changed so much since his return from the war. They also remarked on how obviously Don Lucero and Doña Mercedes adored each other. Was not young love grand?

One morning only a week before they were scheduled to go to Hacienda Vargas, a lone rider dismounted by the copse of cottonwoods that wound around the bank of the river. Gregorio Sanchez had been expecting Porfirio Escondidas for several weeks. The young vaquero was waiting impatiently at the arranged spot when the Juarista arrived.

"You're late," Sanchez said. "We were afraid the French patrols might have caught you."

"Dressed like this?" Escondidas said with a laugh. He wore the frayed brown robes of an itinerant mendicant friar and rode an ancient mule.

"It is a good disguise," Gregorio admitted. "What word from the president?"

"I have instructions for Fortune regarding Vargas. Summon him to meet me here before daybreak."

"Why not simply go to the great house and beg alms? They would offer you a good meal and you could sleep in comfort for one night."

Escondidas shook his head. "Not with a Dominican priest living under the roof. These robes may fool soldiers and peons, but not him. He'd see through my disguise in a trice."

"Perhaps it is best you remain here," the youth conceded. "I'll bring you some supper."

Nicholas had been waiting for word from the Juaristas for some weeks, wondering exactly what in the hell they expected him to do at the Vargas fiesta. He was relieved when Gregorio had given him the message from Escondidas last night.

Slipping away from Mercedes before dawn had not been difficult. Although she did not complain, he had noticed that she had been unusually tired many afternoons over the past few weeks and slept soundly at night. After spending a restless night, he carefully slid from bed, covering her securely against the cool morning air. Her breathing remained steady and deep, undisturbed.

Taking his Remington from his desk in the study, he made his way down to the appointed rendezvous. Porfirio Escondidas was waiting when he arrived.

Fortune took in his ragged disguise with a sardonic arch of his eyebrows. "You have too lean and hungry a look for a friar. The fires of a revolutionary burn in your eyes," Nicholas said in English.

"But not in yours, Señor Fortune," Juarez's agent replied in his precise accent, eyeing the gun in Fortune's waistband.

"I'm not a Juarista. Only be grateful I'm not an imperialist either." Nicholas assesed Escondidas. His face was narrow and thin, with the finely molded features of a *criollo*. Fortune had always wondered what made any of the Mexican aristocracy support the republic, yet a significant number did.

Escondidas' keen dark eyes studied him from beneath pencil-thin eyebrows. "Why would you fight for those French bastards since you've become one of us now?"

Nicholas laughed cynically. "I fought for the men who could pay me—in gold, not pipe dreams."

"This is a republic with a constitution. That is no pipe dream, Senor Fortune. You're Americano. You grew up under such a government."

"I *was* an Americano. Look what it got them—a bloody civil war, the same as here. There will always be haves and have-nots. What made a *criollo* like you join the have-nots?"

"There are things more important than class or money, even than land. And perhaps you understand this better than you realize," Escondidas added with a slight smile.

"You didn't ride this far just to discuss politics, Escondidas. What do you have for me?"

"Soon the president will move his headquarters from El Paso and return to Chihuahua City. Hacienda Vargas is only a day's ride away."

"You think Don Encarnación and his friends are going to attempt an assassination?"

"It would provide their best opportunity. They must break the momentum of our armies quickly. Matamoros is now ours, also Tampico—two of the richest ports on the east coast. Our armies march inland to take Monterrey and Saltillo. In the west, Mazatlán and Guaymas will soon fall. The net tightens around the emperor. His wife sails for Europe to beg Napoleon for more help. General Bazaine has been ordered to return to France within the year."

As Escondidas ticked off the news, Nicholas' interest grew. "So, Carlotta and Bazaine are both packing. It would seem the imperial cause is in dire straits. Perhaps you've chosen shrewdly after all, my friend."

Ignoring the cynical jibe, Escondidas replied, "Everything could still be lost—without Juarez."

"He is the glue holding the republican factions together, you're right about that," Nicholas conceded, rubbing his jaw in consideration. "Without his leadership there would be a vacuum that no general could fill. They'd all fall to squabbling among themselves just as they always have, but do you think Don Encarnación would seriously consider a mere Indian capable of this feat of leadership?"

"Perhaps he has received encouragement from someone else," Porfirio replied. "We don't think it's anyone at court. The emperor isn't astute enough."

"Bazaine calls Maximilian the Austrian dreamer," Fortune said. "No, neither the emperor nor his studious little Belgian wife have any idea about the real conditions in this country—any more than the *hacendados* do."

"Our situation is greatly complicated by another fact. It would be difficult enough protecting the president along one thousand miles of wild back roads, but there is a spy in his ranks. Someone close to Juarez is sending information to Vargas."

Fortune's grin gleamed whitely in the dawn's light. "So, one of your fellow patriots isn't as selflessly noble as you."

"We need to know who it is and where Vargas' men plan to attack the president's entourage. In order to attract less attention, he insisted on a small escort."

"Escobedo doesn't exactly have troops to spare these

days with Miramón and Marquez on the prowl," Nicholas replied dryly.

"You will spend several days inside the Vargas home. You must learn about their plans and who the spy is. I know it will be difficult. After the things you have done since assuming Lucero Alvarado's identity, the dons will not trust you easily."

"I've been turning that over in my mind these past weeks. I think I have an idea about how I can twist my rather liberal actions to my advantage and win Don Encarnación and his friends over. We'll see."

"I will be in San Ramos when you leave Hacienda Vargas. Bring me word of anything you learn."

"And McQueen? Where is he while all hell breaks loose in Chihuahua?"

"Ah, Señor Fortune, surely you do not expect a man of Señor McQueen's talents to reveal that to such as you or me," Escondidas said with a laugh before he vanished in the trees.

After Nicholas had slipped away, Mercedes awakened slowly, aware of the loss of his comforting body heat. She blinked her eyes. Darkness, the thick impenetrable kind that comes just before dawn enveloped the room. A sense of uneasiness washed over her. It was too early to begin the day's work. Where would he go at this hour? How long had he been gone? Visions of Innocencia flashed in her mind, but she pushed them aside as foolish. He had well and truly banished the slattern from his life and spent every free moment with his family.

Wide awake now, Mercedes threw back the covers and slid her legs over the side of the bed. When she stood up a sudden surge of nausea washed over her and she bolted for the basin on the dry sink across the room, barely making it in time. Holding onto the marble top of the sink, she vomited the scant contents remaining in her stomach from the preceding night, then leaned back against the wall, pale and shaken.

She rinsed her mouth, careful not to swallow any of the water until her roiling stomach abated. After bathing her face with a cool compress, she donned a robe and sat down at her dressing table to consider the matter. This was the third time in the past ten days this had happened. Both other occasions had taken place after Lucero had left early in the morning, although not quite this early. As she thought, she ran the brush through her tangled hair, distractedly remembering how it had become such a mess. Lucero had unplaited it last night, burying his face in it, holding great fistfuls of it, pulling her to him.

Their lovemaking had become something she looked forward to with eager anticipation now. She was glad when dinner was over and Rosario had been tucked in. The two of them would exchange heated glances, making excuses to touch each other all through the interminable evenings. And to think she had once dreaded her marital duties. Now everything had changed so dramatically between them.

And it was about to change again. She rose restlessly, set the brush aside and walked over to the window. The sun was just rising above the distant edge of the Sierra Madre Occidental, outlining the mountains in a blaze of golden light tinged with deep fire orange and slashed through with purple and magenta. The birth of a new day.

If she had read the signs right, Gran Sangre would see the birth of its new heir early in the spring, the child Lucero had come home to give her. Would he be pleased? Once she had feared that becoming heavy with child would provide excuse enough for him to turn once again to his whore, humiliating her and leaving her alone now that he had performed his duty. She tried hard to believe he would not do that. This man loved her and loved children. He adored Rosario and would be overjoyed to have more brothers and sisters for her.

But will he still want to make love to you when you grow fat and shapeless? She massaged her temples with her fingers, willing the nagging fear to abate. At least they could go to the Vargas fiesta before her waistline began to thicken. Should she tell him before that?

"I must be absolutely sure," she murmured to herself as she began to dress.

But she knew the signs were almost certain. A month after Lucero had left Gran Sangre four years ago, old Don Anselmo had summoned the bride to his study and interrogated her in humiliating detail about her intimate bodily functions and dismissed her, furious to learn that she was not breeding. Mercedes had become forcibly acquainted, to her maidenly dismay, with all the symptoms of pregnancy at the tender age of seventeen.

When she entered the dining room, Lucero was already halfway through his breakfast. He looked up at her with a warm smile. "You're up early today. You've been sleeping later. I didn't expect you so soon or I'd have waited for you." His eyes studied her with concern as he pulled out her chair. "Are you feeling all right?"

"I'm fine. It was such a lovely morning I couldn't sleep any longer. You left earlier than usual." She waited expectantly for him to offer some explanation, but before he could, Angelina came bustling in from the kitchen with a pot of steaming fragrant coffee and a platter of fried eggs with spicy red sauce.

"Sit and eat, *Patrona*. You look pale this morning. You need more flesh on your bones—does she not, *Patrón*?" she asked, setting the platter in front of Mercedes.

Nicholas looked at her with concern. "You are a bit peaked, love. Are you sure there's nothing wrong?"

The rich oily aroma of the coffee filled her nostrils, combined with the spicy tomatoes and before Mercedes could reply, another wave of nausea struck her. Leaping up she gulped an excuse, nearly overturning her chair in her rush for the kitchen door.

In a flash Nicholas followed, finding her bent over the slop pail by the door. He knelt beside her, holding her shoulders as she was racked by a series of dry heaves. When they subsided, he handed her his handkerchief and helped her stand, then ushered her to a chair. Interestingly enough, Angelina had not come after him into her domain.

"Now," he said gently, pulling another heavy kitchen chair up beside hers, "don't you think you'd better tell me what's wrong?" He had a pretty good idea but was afraid to jump to conclusions, knowing how his father and Doña Sofia had hounded Mercedes about her possible barrenness.

Mercedes looked into his eyes, those dark magnetic wolf's eyes. Once she had thought them cold and predatory. Now they glowed with warmth, concern, love. Taking a swallow for courage, she said, "I was going to wait until I was more certain . . . but it would seem I am carrying your child, Lucero."

That name again. He must get used to it. She could never learn to call him by his real one, he knew. But at a moment like this, it hurt. He stood up and pulled her into his arms. "Beloved, I am overjoyed." Then he raised her bowed head and looked into her eyes. "Are you?"

She had sensed something bothering him. If he wanted the child, could he actually believe she did not? "Oh yes, yes, my love. I'm truly happy."

He studied her, a faint frown creasing his brow. She did seem genuinely pleased. "When is our child to arrive?"

"In the spring . . . early I think." She could tell he was figuring the date of conception and blushed at the broad knowing smile that followed.

In all probability she had conceived the day he had been injured saving her from the mountain lion.

Chapter 16

NOVEMBER 1866

Rather than be rattled like a maraca, Mercedes pleaded with her husband to leave the hacienda's ancient, ornate coach to gather dust in the stables. The journey on horseback would be infinitely more pleasant, an argument to which Nicholas "indulgently" bowed. After all, as a dutiful husband, he would be forced to ride in the coach and "rattle" along with his wife.

Six armed vaqueros accompanied Nicholas and Mercedes enroute to Rancho Vargas, leading pack mules laden with finery for the days of feasting and dancing.

"Have you ever met Don Encarnación?" Nicholas asked Mercedes as they rode.

"Once," she replied. A wary expression crossed her face as she looked at her husband. "Just before we were married. He rode to Gran Sangre to bring us a wedding gift, that ugly silver tea service gathering dust and tarnish in your mother's sitting room."

"I'd forgotten. It seems so long ago now, after the war and all that's happened," he added as smoothly as he could. Luce had told him nothing about her meeting with the old man, but he did know something about him. "Don Encarnación probably sent the silver wedding gift because he owns the largest silver mine in Chihuahua."

"I've heard he's fabulously wealthy."

He grinned. "Wait until you see Hacienda Vargas."

"He and your father were quite close once," she prompted.

He could feel her eyes studying him. Damn, there was no way to know everything about Luce's past! "They had a falling out many years ago," he said with more assurance, recalling that rather unsavory tale from his brother. "I think it was over Encarnación's wife."

"Doña Teresa? She's been dead for years."

"She was a real beauty in her youth. Apparently she caught my father's eye. I doubt she encouraged him, but it certainly placed a strain on the friendship. They had little to do with each other since."

"No wonder he was so grave and austere when he came to visit us," she said grimly.

"He was always a severe old goat. I'm surprised he invited us to this celebration."

"You're not responsible for Anselmo's sins, Lucero. Perhaps this is his way of bridging the rift in an old family friendship."

"I doubt it. More likely he wants every *hacendado* in Sonora and Chihuahua to turn out for his special guests. Encarnación was always full of himself, even more arrogantly class conscious than my father, who was too debauched and self-indulgent to ever be a *criollo* purist. On the other hand, I suspect that Encarnación might fight and die for a cause. I doubt my father ever would have forsaken his vices long enough to become involved."

"He certainly was angry when you left for the war," she said thoughtfully.

"Only because I hadn't done my duty by getting you with child first—once that matter had been attended to, I would've been quite expendable, I'm certain."

She had never before heard this bitterness toward his father. It startled her. Lucero had always been angry with his mother for her rejection of him, but he had worshipped the old don. "You used to imitate him. He was your idol."

"Idols have feet of clay. Sometimes a man has to grow up himself before he's able to see that."

Before she could comment further, Gregorio signaled that riders were approaching over the distant rise. Everyone reined in as Nicholas quickly scanned the surrounding open brushy area for cover. Little was to be had. Worriedly, he left his wife surrounded by the other men and rode ahead, pulling the glass from its case on his saddle and looking through it.

A dozen men quickly came into focus, well armed and superbly mounted. "We for damn sure aren't going to outrun them," he muttered beneath his breath. Then he raised the glass and looked again. He gave an oath of pure relief. "Leave it to old Encarnación to pull out all the stops for that Prussian and his wife." He rode back to Mercedes to explain there was no danger, chuckling. "Those aren't uniforms. They're wearing livery . . . private military livery!"

In a few minutes the patrol arrived to escort the guests into the broad valley where the Hacienda Vargas was situated.

"This is truly amazing," Mercedes said as they approached the enormous two-story adobe fortress.

The chapel alone was nearly two times the size of Gran Sangre's house. The compound had towers at each corner and the heavy wooden gate at the entrance bore the Vargas crest, a pretentious affair with Castillian lions on it. The whitewashed adobe walls and red tile roof were traditional for most northern haciendas, but this complex of buildings looked more like a miniature city than one man's estate.

"It's built like a fortress," Mercedes said.

"Encarnación's great-great-grandfather built most of it back in the seventeenth century. At the time it was the farthest outpost in the province of Nueva Viscaya," Nicholas replied.

A vigilant sentry in the corner tower observed the paramilitary escort as it approached with the hacienda's guests, then signaled for the massive mesquite wood gate to be opened. They filed into an enormous courtyard with three fountains and enough flowering shrubs and palm trees to cover half a dozen village plazas. Arched porticos ran the length of the interior buildings facing out on the courtyard.

Birds in brilliant plumage swung in cages from the porticos fronting the great house and hammocks were strung along the wall so the family and guests could while away warm afternoons in pleasant relaxation. Above the porticos a tiled verandah ran the length of the house, affording a splendid view of the interior of the Vargas domain. A huge gate opened at the opposite end of the courtyard leading into Don Encarnación's private bullring. Stables, corrals and tradesmen's shops lined the rest of the interior.

"It looks like something out of medieval Granada," Mercedes said as they rode across the courtyard.

Nicholas' eyes were on the welcoming committee standing at the main archway that was the entrance of the house. "I told you it was something to behold."

A slim old man with ramrod straight posture that lent his scant five-foot-four an illusion of height, stood on the stone portico shadowed by a frangipani tree. His face was deeply tanned, scoured by the desert wind, his hair thin and silver-white. The corners of a narrow mustache turned up as he smiled ever so slightly in a welcome that did not extend to his wintry blue-gray eyes. Don Encarnación Vargas was a spartan man in appearance and outlook.

"Welcome, Don Lucero. You've grown to be the very image of your father. I would recognize you always, even though we have not met in many years. I trust your journey was uneventful," he said, bowing stiffly to the younger man.

"We experienced no problems, sir, but were grateful for your escort."

"I expected you sooner. When you did not arrive I dispatched my private guard. There are Juarista banditti everywhere."

"We would have arrived sooner but my wife needed to rest at frequent intervals. I did not want her overtired. She is expecting our child in the spring," Nicholas said with pride as two of Vargas' soldiers helped her dismount. Turning, he took her hand and presented her to the don.

Mercedes made her curtsy in front of the hawk-faced old man, whose expression was so severe it appeared the furrows at the sides of his mouth were like grooves carved in granite. "I am honored, Don Encarnación, and most grateful for your hospitality." The way he inspected her, Mercedes was glad she had decided upon her less comfortable but far grander royal blue riding habit with heavy black braid trim.

"Welcome to Hacienda Vargas, Doña Mercedes, and my felicitations on the forthcoming birth of Gran Sangre's heir. My home is your home. I am certain you will wish to rest and refresh yourself before the evening's festivities. Viola will escort you to your quarters."

He snapped his fingers sharply and a small Indian girl appeared seemingly out of nowhere. She bowed nervously and gestured for the lady to follow her.

Nicholas raised Mercedes' hand and kissed it, then watched as she entered the wide arched doorway leading into the grand *sala*, followed by three servants carrying the bags which had been unstrapped from their pack mules.

"She is most lovely. Rather reminds me of my Teresa when she was young," Don Encarnación said. "She was Spanish, from the north in Galicia. The same gold hair and eyes."

Nicholas detected a wistfulness in the old man's voice for a brief moment, but then Don Encarnación's expression hardened again as he gestured for his guest to follow him along the wide stone portico. They bypassed the songbirds and hammocks. At the third door he turned into the house, entering a study which was lined with books and furnished with dark, heavily carved pieces. Heavy crimson velvet covered the windows and an old Castillian tapestry depicting El Cid in triumphal march hung on the inside wall. A full suit of Italian armor, probably Argonese, stood militantly at the side of the wall hanging.

Several men were clustered around a liquor cabinet, crystal goblets in their hands, laughing and talking. Fortune recognized Encarnación's son Mariano from Luce's description, a slightly plump man of forty or so, with light brown hair and slate-gray eyes, possessing his father's imperious manner, but not the iron discipline to make it convincing.

He turned, smiling broadly. His waistcoat buttons stretched across a thickening middle as he bowed the same formal way the old don had. "Lucero. Welcome. It has been years—you were but a stripling last time I saw you."

"As I recall, your chestnut mare beat my black rather

handily," Nicholas said, praying he remembered the story accurately.

"I've retired from racing to pursue more important matters now," Mariano replied, beaming with the remembered victory.

"My son is the imperial representative to the *alcalde* in Chihuahua," the old don said with pride. "Allow me to present my old friends, Don Hernan Ruiz and Don Patrico Morales and Don Doroteo Ibarra."

The men were courteous but somewhat reserved. With the exception of Don Hernan, they were all older, closer to Encarnación's age. They made pleasant small talk about their journeys to Hacienda Vargas and the ball that night.

"When do our guests of honor arrive?" Nicholas asked.

"Prince Salm-Salm and his wife have arrived, along with his aides," the balding Don Patrico replied.

"You will meet them at the festivities tonight. They are resting now," Don Encarnación added. "Perhaps you and the prince can exchange reminiscences of the war."

"I understand you fought for the emperor, Don Lucero. Do you know the prince?" Morales asked.

"I haven't had the pleasure as yet, but I have heard of his exploits."

"Why have you left the military, might I inquire?" Don Hernan's dark eyes swept Fortune swiftly, inventorying his obvious good health. The *criollo's* right arm hung uselessly at his side, a war injury of some sort, Nicholas assumed.

"Upon my father's death, the responsibilities for Gran Sangre fell to me as his sole heir. It was his dying wish I return home to rebuild it."

"I've heard some disturbing rumors. Of course, Sonora is a distance away from my home in Durango . . ." Don Patrico paused for effect.

"What my old friend is trying to say is there have been some absurd stories circulating about your coddling peons," Encarnación put in brusquely, his blue-gray eyes turning dark and flinty.

"How so?" Nicholas asked, taking a sip of his host's excellent port.

"By letting them go free without so much as a taste of the whip after they were caught butchering your beef," Mariano supplied as he poured himself a generous refill, then studied the man he thought was Lucero over the rim of his glass.

Nicholas shrugged philosophically. Now was as good a time as any to try his plan and see if it would work. "Yes, I let them go free—even gave them the damned dead steer. It was of no earthly use to me."

"But making an example of thieving peons is vital if we are to maintain our authority," Don Doroteo replied angrily.

"By making examples of the stupid savages, all we do is send them scurrying into the arms of Juarez and his damned rabble. I was only keeping them properly grateful for my benevolence," Nicholas replied with dripping cynicism in his voice.

"Juarez!" Don Hernan spat the word as if it were the vilest epithet he knew. "That filthy Indian upstart from Oaxaca, leading a band of rabble armed with rusty muskets and machetes."

Nicholas' eyes lost their cynical amusement and took on a steely glint as he spoke with such intensity that it riveted every man in the room. "That upstart savage's rabble have captured Mazatlán and Guaymas, effectively shutting off west coast shipping in my state. Matamoros, Tampico and Vera Cruz—our three most lucrative Gulf coast customs ports are in their hands now, too. Escobedo's army sweeps from Nuevo León into Coahuila and Diaz has taken the capital of Oaxaca, driving out the archbishop.

"Now I realize, gentlemen, that you are isolated here in the northwest, but I can assure you from firsthand experience of only a few months past, Juarez is gaining ground, rallying his forces."

"You can't seriously believe these godless republican scum will overthrow the monarchy?" Don Hernan said, aghast. "I saw them starved and beaten at Puebla in sixty-three."

"Starved?" Fortune's eyebrows rose derisively. "Yes, after they held out for three months under bombardment by a force ten times their numbers. They're fanatically determined to defend their constitution and that mesmerizing little Indian who holds up the scrap of paper as if it were the Holy Grail. They fight and they win—and now they have outside help. Juarez's wife has been welcomed by the damnable *gringos*. Do you know she was invited to speak before their Congress? That their government has been sending shipments of Springfield rifles across the border to arm Escobedo? My *contre-guerrilla* group confiscated hundreds of them this past year."

Fortune's eyes swept the assembly for dramatic effect. Several of the men were slack-jawed in amazement and Don Encarnación and Don Hernan were furiously angry. But Mariano? His expression appeared bland, almost unconcerned as he polished off another drink.

"So what is your point—that we should throw up our hands and let the land reform lunatics take our ancient heritage, divide up our proud haciendas among the peons in forty-acre tracts?" Don Encarnación asked, his dark complexion livid red beneath his tan.

"Hardly! But unless someone can stop Juarez, I plan to keep my options open. A smart man makes his own laws and acts to protect his heritage—if he plans to hang onto it. There is nothing I'd like more than to see Juarez out of the picture. Without him the whole rebellion would unravel into internecine warfare and we could pit one petty republican general against another. But with him as their icon, they won't be stopped until that infamous little black carriage of his rolls back into Mexico City!" He looked measuringly around the room as he took a generous swallow of port.

"What you're suggesting then is that we should eliminate the Indian," Mariano said as blandly as if he were discussing putting down a spavined old horse.

Nicholas shrugged. "I understand it's been tried already . . . unsuccessfully. Now I fear it's too late."

He casually walked over to the latticed doors and peered out into the courtyard, as if unaware of the implication of his words, but he could sense the silent exchange going on between old Encarnación and his companions. Were they all in on the plot? Probably. Mariano was a cipher though. The old don's son seemed as apolitically decadent as Anselmo had been. *I wonder . . .*

The gathering broke up shortly, ostensibly so the men could dress for the evening. Nicholas suspected Encarnación and his minions had probably closeted themselves to discuss whether or not to trust him, hopefully to invite him to join their scheming. All he could do in the meanwhile was keep his eyes and ears open when any opportunity to learn something presented itself.

Standing in front of a mirror in their suite, he inspected his appearance. He had dressed traditionally in the fitted short jacket and silver-trimmed pants of a *criollo*. The suit was black with a snowy white lawn shirt and white silk stock that contrasted with his swarthy complexion. The only color in his outfit was the brilliant crimson sash at his waist. He opened the door of his small dressing room and found Mercedes standing expectantly in the center of the enormous bedroom. She was surrounded by the lavish ostentation of frescoed ceilings, gold leaf wallpaper and Persian carpets, but still her slender figure dominated the room.

"Doña Mercedes, you are the jewel of the House of Alvarado," he said in a low growl of appreciation as he strode across the dark maroon and gold rug to take her hand.

Her gown was of deep violet silk, a stunning and dramatic color that overpowered most blondes, but with her dark gold hair and eyes, it only heightened her vibrancy. The plunging vee at the front of the dress revealed an enticing swell of pale gold breasts where an heirloom necklace of amethyst set in silver filigree nestled lovingly.

Raising the heavy stones, he placed his mouth on the warm satiny flesh, inhaling her delicate fragrance as he tasted her skin. "Lucky gems," he murmured, feeling her pulse begin to accelerate.

"I take it that means I meet with your approval?" She had let the maid Magaña labor over her hair until it was curled and piled high with silver and amethyst combs securing its heavy weight. One long soft lock draped over her right shoulder, begging a man's touch.

Nicholas could not resist. Taking the curl and twining it about his index finger, he replied, "I told you you'd be the most beautiful woman at the fiesta."

She laughed tolerantly. "You haven't even seen the other ladies yet. I met several of them in the *sala* earlier. Doña Ursula, our host's daughter-in-law, is quite striking," she said, recalling the raven-haired beauty with the flashing violet eyes.

He raised an eyebrow. "Mariano's wife? I'd expect her to be a bit long of tooth."

"His *second* wife. The first died some time ago. Ursula was forced into the arrangement last year, an innocent of seventeen, but she's become worldly wise now." The instant she said it, her eyes flew to his, realizing the implication. "Lucero—I didn't mean—"

"Shh . . ." He silenced her with a soft kiss. "What's past is past for us. Let's look only to the future."

"To the future," she echoed softly and took his arm. They headed downstairs to face the glittering assembly.

Nicholas said, "I understand there are to be pole dancers out in the courtyard and a formal dinner before the musicians strike up in the ballroom. Then fireworks to end the evening."

Her eyes lit up. "I've never seen pole dancers."

"It would seem Don Encarnación is really rolling out the royal carpet for his guests of honor."

As they strolled down the wide carpeted stairs into the main *sala*, Mercedes observed the brilliantly gowned and jeweled women. Here and there the glitter of gold epaulets and pure white of an imperial court officer's uniform stood out among the crowd. Most of the men were dressed in the same expensive and conservative manner as her husband, but to Mercedes, none filled out the fitted suit half so well as Lucero, with his broad shoulders and long lean legs. The brightly colored sash at his waist only emphasized his flat belly which felt as hard and sleek as all of his naked flesh. *Stop it*! *Here I am undressing him with my eyes in front of a room filled with people*!

They made their way around the room, being introduced

to various *hacendados* and their ladies, making polite conversation. Mercedes watched Doña Ursula, Mariano's bride, make her way to them in her capacity as hostess for the widowed Don Encarnación. Nicholas noted that the short voluptuous brunette was a beautiful woman who was well aware of her effect on men and knew how to use that effect.

Ursula Terraza de Vargas had chosen a dramatic silver-shot blue organza gown as a pale contrast to her dark hair and eyes. The décolletage of the gown revealed ripe heavy breasts and the layers of silvery ruffles on her skirts no doubt concealed plumply pleasing curves of hip and calf, but she was a bit fleshy and short of leg for his taste. Still, her slanted violet eyes were intriguing as she smiled at him with a predatory gleam in them.

"Doña Ursula, this is my husband, Lucero Alvarado," Mercedes began the introductions.

"My father-in-law has spoken of you. I understand you served in the Imperial Army. You simply must tell me all about it," Ursula gushed breathlessly.

Nicholas watched her curtsy and bat her lashes like the seasoned coquette she was, letting her fan open and close artfully against that overbounteous cleavage, teasing him.

"There's not much of war that's fit for a beautiful lady's ears," he rejoined smoothly.

"Then you will tell me of his majesty's court, for I know you were there—shall we say during the first waltz tonight?"

After she had excused herself to mingle among the other guests, Mercedes mimicked beneath her breath, "You *will* tell me of his majesty's court! A command performance."

"Jealousy becomes you," Nicholas said with a chuckle. "I find it endearing."

"Only give me no cause for it and I shall *remain* endearing," she replied sweetly, dreading the months ahead when she would put his love and loyalty to the test as she grew thick and shapeless in pregnancy.

Nicholas broke into her reverie. "I believe the guests of honor have arrived."

He gestured to a slender, dark-haired man with a rigid military bearing. At his side was a younger woman, voluptuous and as tall as he, with dark auburn hair and a bold yet merry-looking face. Both were colorfully dressed even in this flock of gaudy plumage. The princess wore red velvet, and enough diamonds to weigh down a smaller woman. Prince Salm-Salm was resplendent in imperial white and gold, his chest covered with a rainbow of ribbons and heavy gold and silver medals.

"If he steps out onto the verandah, he'll tinkle like a wind chime," Nicholas whispered to Mercedes.

"Jealous wretch." She giggled. "He's an imposing figure of a man."

In profile he was hawk-faced with a large Roman nose and high forehead. A thick set of muttonchop sideburns and heavy handlebar mustache covered his stubborn Prussian jaw. His hair was brown, dramatically accented by one silver streak swept back from his brow.

The royal couple—actually he was the second son of a minor German princeling and she was American—began to amble in their direction, champagne glasses in hand, making polite conversation along the way. Mariano Vargas escorted them.

"I think we're about to have a signal honor bestowed upon us," Nicholas said dryly.

Vargas introduced them with the same casual watchfulness Nicholas had detected earlier. Was this some sort of test? The Prussian's Spanish was halting at best, so they spoke mostly in a mixture of English and French. "It's an honor, Prince Felix, Princess Agnes," Nicholas said, returning the Prussian officer's formal bow.

Mercedes curtsied, noting the indulgent smile the formal prince bestowed so often on his wife, who was openly friendly.

While they talked, Nicholas still had the eerie feeling Mariano was measuring him. Vargas indolently drained his champagne, then signaled a waiter for a refill. What, he wondered, was the connection between the Vargas family and the imperial court? Did the prince know about the plot to kill Juarez? Was he perhaps the instigator?

Nicholas had heard the Prussian possessed a reputation

as a skilled politician as well as a professional soldier. The only way to find out if Salm-Salm was involved was to cultivate him. But Fortune had to be careful of how easily he conversed in French. If he betrayed too much fluency around Mercedes, she would note it. That he also could muddle along well enough in German would convince her that he was not Lucero. He vowed to confine his conversation to French and a bit of English and hope she would not pay attention in the noisy crowd, which was beginning to filter out into the courtyard for the pole dancers.

Mariano escorted the princess and Mercedes, allowing the prince to chat freely with Don Lucero as they made their way outdoors.

"I understand you served at court briefly. I think I remember you," Salm-Salm said.

"I was there only briefly, sir. You do me a great honor to have noticed."

The prince studied the hard-looking man with the scar across his cheek, then touched his own ruddy cheek where a similar thin white line disappeared into his whiskers. "A dueling scar from—how do you say it?—*in meinen unerfahrenen Jungen Jahren*."

"Your misspent youth," Nicholas supplied, then immediately realized his error when the Prussian nodded shrewdly. "I acquired my scars fighting as an irregular. I was a captain in the *contre-guerrillas* for four years. The men are an international mix. I had a Westphalian comrade who taught me a smattering of German." Which was true, only he had met Kemper while he was still in the Legion in North Africa.

"Most interesting," the prince replied, bemused. "You have far more facility with languages than I."

Nicholas' gaze moved quickly ahead to Mercedes, but she was engaged in animated conversation with the princess and Mariano and did not overhear the exchange. "War is a stern taskmaster. You yourself well know how a soldier's life and an officer's effectiveness depend upon understanding and communicating orders. More of the men were European and North American than Mexican."

"It's a strange business, this war." The prince sighed.

"But tonight we are here to celebrate," he said, his mood once more lightening as he looked from the five brightly attired dancers to the one-hundred-foot pole which they would eventually climb.

Don Encarnación, spying his special guests with the Alvarados, made his way to them. "I should have known two soldiers would find much in common—and your wives both speak English. How fortunate. But if I might tear you away for a bit, I have some other guests most eager to make your acquaintance."

Speculatively, Nicholas watched the old don and the Prussian prince vanish in the crowd, drawing the princess with them. Mariano remained behind with Mercedes and him.

"A most engaging man, Prince Felix," Nicholas remarked, waiting for a reaction from Mariano, but just then the entertainment started.

The crowd oohed and aahed in delight as the dancers began. They were elaborately costumed in harlequin suits of vivid red, blue, green and black with feathered headdresses and sequined masks, a peculiar blend of ancient Aztec ritual combined with European showmanship. They circled the pole in a dignified slow processional dance, then nimbly scrambled to the top of it, where each attached a rope to his ankle. Once this was accomplished, they flung themselves out into midair, one by one. All five of them spun in dizzying arcs round and round the pole while the ropes slowly slipped down toward the ground. Miraculously the ropes did not entangle with one another as the men went through all sorts of elaborately convoluted movements, flailing their arms, their free legs, and indeed their entire bodies to keep themselves in simulated flight. Drums and flutes kept a steady rhythm to which their stylized "dance" adhered. Finally, when they came within a few feet of the ground, each one landed deftly on his free foot and unfastened the ankle binding. The guests honored them with thunderous applause.

Smiling delightedly, Mercedes said, "That was absolutely incredible. They're as good as the circus acrobats I saw in Madrid when I was a girl."

Having rejoined their group during the performance, Ursula said archly, "That should make the Princess Salm-Salm feel right at home."

Mariano gave her a censorious look. For the first time seeming a bit nonplused, he explained, "What my wife means is that Princess Agnes once performed as an acrobat in the circus."

"That's where her 'dear Salmi' met her," Ursula whispered with poorly concealed delight. "She was a bareback rider in pink tights. It's really quite a scandal that she's received at court. My aunt Honoria says the empress dislikes her but the emperor won't hear of dismissing her. He—"

"Enough, my pet. The prince and princess are our guests and no one should gossip about the imperial court." Mariano's voice was soft but the look in his eyes was hard and glacially frigid.

Observing the exchange, Nicholas thought, *So there is one thing that can get you to show some emotion—your spoiled young bride*. The girl was obviously bored and piqued at her husband for thwarting her love of gossip. Perhaps cultivating her would be an easier way to find out what he needed to learn—if he could do so without having Mercedes claw his eyes out in a jealous fit!

Chapter 17

After the rope dancers finished, Don Encarnación formally introduced Prince Felix Salm-Salm and Princess Agnes to the local notables from Chihuahua and Sonora who had been invited for the occasion. The guests of honor led the procession into the dining room where a fifty-foot-long table of polished mahogany was set with Sevres china. Giant ice sculptures and masses of zinnias, crimson bell and dahlias were positioned at intervals along the table.

At the special request of the prince and princess, Nicholas and Mercedes were seated across from them and his aides. One, a young Prussian Junker, Lieutenant Arnoldt von Scheeling, made Mercedes distinctly uncomfortable although he did nothing overtly wrong. Indeed, he was the soul of punctilious courtesy, yet something in his manner disturbed her. His squarish face was pale-complected and clean shaven, typical of the North German gentry from which he came, but his light gray eyes reminded her of the outlaw Lucero had killed on the Hermosillo road.

"This war never seems to end," Princess Agnes lamented. "It really is such a trial for poor Max. Now that Carlotta is gone, he wanders about Chapultepec like a lost soul."

"I've heard that the emperor and empress are very close," Mercedes said sympathetically, recalling Ursula's snide remarks about Carlotta's contempt for Princess Agnes du Salm.

"Well"—Agnes leaned closer to Mercedes to speak in confidence while the men were busy discussing military matters—"she is frightfully astute and conscientious about matters of state. Max relies heavily on her judgment, but when it comes to matters of the heart . . ." She shrugged expressively. "He is a lonely man."

"How like a woman to attribute all a man's failings to his inadequate love life," von Scheeling said in ponderous Spanish. His tone was filled with patronizing amusement.

Agnes' eyes narrowed. "Oh, Max's *love life*," she emphasized the word, "is rather full. What he lacks is the genuine female companionship that transcends mere physical liaisons."

"Ah, a tall order, indeed. Tell me, Doña Mercedes," von Scheeling said, turning to her, "do you believe in transcendent love?"

Mercedes' eyes swept involuntarily from the taunting Prussian to Lucero, then quickly back. Her sense of unease increased when she realized von Scheeling had noted the troubled expression which quickly flashed across her face. "Perhaps," she replied enigmatically, meeting his coldly mocking gray eyes head-on.

"I do believe we have embarrassed the lady, Princess," von Scheeling said without taking his eyes from Mercedes.

"Then perhaps we should change the subject," Agnes replied to him. "Tell me about life on a great Sonoran rancho."

As Mercedes and Agnes chatted, ignoring von Scheeling, he was drawn into the conversation between the prince and Nicholas.

"It's difficult for us to imagine what life is like here in the north when we live in the safety of the capital," Felix said thoughtfully.

Nicholas replied, "Don Encarnación has his own militia to protect Hacienda Vargas from the enemy. Most *hacendados* aren't so fortunate."

"That is why the emperor dispatched the prince on this journey. We will see what must be done to eliminate the republican menace and we will deal with them," von Scheeling interjected crisply.

"That might be easier said than done." Nicholas' tone was mildly irritated. "The Juaristas have the advantage of fighting on home ground. They use hit-and-run tactics that are almost impossible for regular troops to combat."

Von Scheeling's face reddened. "You mean that they won't stand and fight like soldiers—they run and hide like thieves."

Nicholas shrugged. "A most effective way to wear down the enemy."

"And you are, of course, an expert on these guerrillas?" There was an unmistakable hint of insult in the question.

Prince Salm-Salm quickly gave von Scheeling a stern look, saying, "Don Lucero has spent many years fighting the rebels. He is more than qualified to speak on the subject."

The junior officer's expression was mutinous but he immediately subsided.

To smooth over the awkward moment, Fortune said, "I've fought the Juaristas for four years as a counterinsurgent. When you go up against them one on one, you learn to respect their abilities . . . or you end up dead."

"In Europe rabble such as this would never have been able to challenge proper authority," von Scheeling replied.

"This isn't Europe," was Fortune's silky reply. *Pompous young ass.* Von Scheeling had never fought in a guerrilla war. The Prussian was a court fop in a starched uniform, the sort he had always scorned.

So, obviously, did the prince. "The situation here is vastly different than General von Schlieffen's campaigns," he said dryly, observing the dangerous-looking Mexican's disdain for his brash young officer. He had always disliked von Scheeling, and of late, the fool was becoming burdensome. Perhaps Alvarado was just the man to relieve him of that burden.

"An excellent man, von Schlieffen. He would cut a wide swath through Juarez's so-called army," the lieutenant replied. "Are you perhaps familiar with his tactical genius?"

Fortune was. "The general has been your Minister Otto von Bismarck's tool to gobble up increasingly larger portions of German-speaking Europe. I believe he'll eventually tackle the French emperor." He ignored von Scheeling dismissively and asked, "What do you think, your highness?"

Mercedes heard bits and snatches of their conversation and realized her husband was discussing European diplomacy and politics like a seasoned statesman. Lucero, who had admitted never having read so much as a single book on history. She toyed nervously with the elegant orange liqueur dessert soufflé on her plate, too filled with apprehensions and unspoken fears about her love to want to consider this new inconsistency. Then, as faint music from the orchestra began to drift into the dining room from Don Encarnación's enormous ballroom, Lieutenant von Scheeling interrupted her troubling thoughts with an invitation to dance.

Guests were already filtering out of the dining room and down the hall, drawn gaily toward the sounds of a soaring waltz. Although she disliked the patronizing young officer, Mercedes felt an overpowering urge to get away from her husband at that moment, away from him and his witty, brilliant conversation with the prince. Smiling and taking her leave of the princess, she accepted the offer.

Nicholas watched as von Scheeling assisted Mercedes from her chair and solicitously took her arm, heading to the ballroom. He suddenly felt the insane urge to slap the lieutenant's hands off his wife's soft golden flesh. Jealousy, bald-faced and totally irrational, confronted him head-on, all the more absurd since he was certain that Mercedes detested the pompous Prussian officer as much as he did.

Prince Salm-Salm smiled shrewdly. "Perhaps we should not neglect the ladies or bore them with politics any longer, but adjourn to dancing. As an old soldier who has a right leg filled with grapeshot, I make an insufferable partner for such a superb dancer as my wife."

"What Salmi is none too subtly hinting at is for you to partner me in that delicious waltz," Agnes interjected with a merry laugh.

"It would be my great honor, your highness," Nicholas said, rising and bowing with a courtly flourish. The prince's American wife was a born flirt, but charming and amusing nonetheless.

While they made their way down the hall, she whispered

conspiratorially to him, "As you no doubt have heard, my accomplished dancing skills come as a result of my professional training. I was a circus acrobat who danced atop bouncing horses when Salmi met me."

Nicholas threw back his head and laughed. "Let us hope I will prove a smoother dancer than a circus horse, although I make few promises beyond that. It's been some years since I waltzed with a beautiful lady and never before with a princess."

She tilted her auburn head, smiling at the compliment as they entered the ballroom. A breathtaking expanse of polished hardwood floor was filled with couples dancing beneath the glittering lights cast by two immense crystal chandeliers, each lit with hundreds of candles. A champagne fountain bubbled at one end of the room and an orchestra worthy of the imperial court played at the other.

"I certainly didn't expect to see this sort of a display so far away from the capital," Agnes confessed.

"Most *hacendados* do not fare so well as Don Encarnación," Nicholas replied. "He can stave off marauding soldiers with his own private army, an army he's kept for the past thirty years to ensure that his silver shipments reach the American border."

The princess nodded in understanding. "And what of you, Don Lucero? How does your hacienda fare in these troubled times?"

"Now that I'm home, we'll manage. Mercedes did a splendid job while I was away. It was hard on her, not to mention dangerous, but she held two armies at bay and kept our people fed and sheltered, no mean feat in wartime." His eyes swept the floor automatically, searching for his wife's golden head amid so many dark ones.

Agnes fondly watched the way he looked at his wife. Young love was marvelous. Hell, love at any age was marvelous. "Perhaps it's time you rescued her from Arnoldt's clutches. He fancies himself a ladies' man, but in fact, he's a frightful bore."

"Ah, but first I must waltz with a princess. It may be my

only chance," he replied with a smile as they swept onto the crowded floor.

"You haven't had much time together, have you?" she asked shrewdly.

"The war has separated many families, even the emperor and empress, as I heard you remark earlier."

"I don't think they were ever quite the love match you and Doña Mercedes are," the princess said dryly. "Max is true to his Bonaparte forebears, a born philanderer. You did know he was Napoleon's grandson, didn't you?"

Fortune had heard the rumor about Maximilian of Hapsburg's mother having an affair with the son of the first French emperor. "He would seem more Bonaparte in his grandiose schemes," Nicholas conceded, then grinned. "I've also heard he pursues every beautiful woman at court. How does the prince keep you safe?"

"La, you are a flatterer. I am utterly devoted to Max and he to me, but not in that way. He's really rather like the charming but scandalous younger brother I never had."

Fortune arched an eyebrow dubiously. "Somehow I find it difficult to imagine you in the role of a stern elder sister."

Now it was she who threw back her head and laughed heartily. "Elder sister, yes, but stern, never. I find myself quite indulgent of his foibles." Her expression sobered as she added softly, "I only pray his grand adventure doesn't end badly for him."

From across the room Ursula Terraza de Vargas watched the exchange between the dangerous-looking young *hacendado* and the princess. How mysterious and heart-stoppingly handsome he was, with that aura of leashed violence always lurking just beneath his flashing smile. Don Lucero was completely unlike her own bland and stolid Mariano, who was as passionless as a monk, a man who never showed any real interest in his beautiful young wife unless it was to upbraid her for some foolish breach of social decorum.

After nearly a year of trying to gain his attention, she had resorted to taking lovers in secret, her only means of rebelling against his indifference and his father's social strictures. But she would not think of Mariano or Don Encarnación tonight.

No, not now when that vulgar American circus performer was making Don Lucero laugh in his wickedly sensuous way. No, indeed. Licking her lips in anticipation, she began to scheme.

Outside on the terrace, Mercedes breathed deeply of the cool, fresh night air, redolent with the perfume from frangipani trees in Don Encarnación's gardens. She walked quickly behind a copse of poinsettia and hugged herself, shivering. This was totally stupid, irrational. She had faced down Juarista bandits and fended off the advances of lecherous politicians, even held a French captain at gunpoint and made him back down.

"Why does von Scheeling terrify me so?" she murmured to herself. He had done nothing worse than pay her flowery compliments in awkward French and even more clumsy Spanish, and perhaps hold her a bit too closely while they waltzed.

It was those eyes, merciless and flat, like granite. She felt foolish for having made up a headache and excusing herself in the middle of the waltz like some flighty virgin, but she had to escape that dreadful sense of menace.

Lieutenant Arnoldt von Scheeling was a man who gave off the scent of death. Lucero had already had words with him and she did not want to be the cause of a scene between the two volatile, dangerous men. Far better to let her husband continue laughing and dancing, surrounded by female adulation.

The jealous turn of her thoughts was absurd, of course. Agnes du Salm was devoted to her prince, but that little cat Ursula seemed far more interested in Lucero than in her own husband. From her vantage point in the garden Mercedes could see in the open floor-length doors of the ballroom to where Lucero's tall elegant frame stood out half a head taller than any other man in the room. Right now he was bending low to hear Ursula whisper some flirtatious nonsense.

"I have no reason to be jealous," she repeated to herself like a litany, as she watched him dancing with the voluptuous raven-haired beauty. But what of when his wife grew fat and shapeless as she began to increase? She could not shake this nagging fear. Was Lucero really such a changed man after all?

"I've brought champagne to soothe your headache, *Liebchen*," von Scheeling purred in her ear.

She turned to face the Prussian officer with a startled gasp.

Inside, Nicholas whirled Mariano's spoiled young wife around the dance floor, his mind only half on her vapid conversation as he considered how to excuse himself so he could go in search of Mercedes. "You were saying, Doña?"

She pouted prettily. "You haven't heard a word I've said. Soon I shall think I'm losing my beauty."

"Never that. Don Mariano is the luckiest of men to have such a lovely wife," Nicholas placated.

"Him," she replied petulantly. "He ignores me as if I were invisible. I used to believe he had a mistress. Perhaps he does, but she is not a woman."

A premonition washed over Fortune as he inclined his head to hers. "Really? What then, Doña?"

"It is boring old politics, just as it is with his father. He is just as secretive, involved in some silly plot."

"Somehow I have never thought your husband and his father much alike," he prompted. "What makes you think your husband is plotting something?" All his senses were at full alert now.

"Hah! I followed him one night," she replied with an eerie glitter in her violet eyes. "For months now, every Saturday he rides away just after midnight. I was certain he was meeting a woman." Her eyes narrowed to slits. "But it was only another man, some rough-looking gunman. I sneaked behind a bush and listened to them discuss something about that Indian who still claims to be president," she said scornfully.

"Really. Surely you must be mistaken. What could a pistolero know of Juarez?" Nicholas asked, even as he calculated. Tomorrow night was Saturday. Would Vargas hold his assignation when the house was filled with guests?

"I don't recall any of it. I was so furious. If Mariano had

deserted my bed for another woman, that I could understand. But for political intrigues!" The young woman quickly quelled her anger, shifting tone. "I look for my pleasures elsewhere now." Ursula gave a seductive flutter of thick black lashes. She leaned closer to him, pressing her ample breasts against his chest, brushing them back and forth across his shirt studs tantalizingly. "Does that feel as good to you as it does to me?" she purred.

Just then, Agnes du Salm caught his eye from the opposite side of the floor, motioning him to look toward the gardens outside. She mouthed his wife's name. What in the hell was going on? The music ended and he made his bow to Ursula, glad of the excuse to end their increasingly intimate encounter before he was forced into an altercation with Mariano, dashing his hopes for gathering any useful information from Encarnación's circle of plotters.

When he reached the princess, she took his arm at once and smoothly slipped through the wide doors that opened into the courtyard. "Come quickly," was all she would say.

He followed her down the length of the porch, past the birdcages and hammocks, out into the lush concealment of the ornamental garden. Mercedes stood at the edge of a small fountain, daubing her lip with a wet handkerchief. Nicholas turned her to face him, taking the small lace square from her and holding her chin up to inspect it in the moonlight. A thin trickle of blood welled up from a cut on her lip and the bodice of her gown was torn at the right shoulder.

Mercedes shivered in spite of the flush of anger surging through her. She could sense Lucero's left hand gliding down his thigh, instinctively reaching for the knife he normally wore there, ready to use it on the man who had done this. "He did nothing that I wasn't able to handle."

"I can't wait to see the shiner Arnoldt will be sporting by morning," Agnes said cheerfully. "You really socked him quite neatly," she complimented Mercedes.

"Lucero—"

"You know I can't let this go," he said grimly, cutting off her plea, but she held tightly to his arm.

"It will only cause gossip if you call him out."

He looked at her with Luce's most coldly haughty *criollo* expression. "And you don't think having guests and servants see you with your gown torn and your mouth bruised from von Scheeling's mauling would cause gossip?"

His tone was sarcastic, almost accusatory. "Are you implying I encouraged him?" she asked, stung.

"For God's sake, I don't think for one minute that you encouraged him. Tell me what happened."

"I believe this is the best time for me to leave you two alone," the princess interjected. "Personally, I shall be delighted to see Arnoldt get his comeuppance. It's long overdue. Salm has wanted to challenge him for the past year, but he says it's considered bad form for a superior officer to kill one of his subordinates."

Mercedes' eyes flashed from the retreating Agnes back to her husband. "You might be the one who's killed!" She clutched his arms, digging her nails into his biceps even through the heavy fabric of his suit coat.

"Never fear, beloved, I've grown accustomed to dealing with men like von Scheeling, but I'm touched that you fear for me." He pulled her into his embrace, stroking her hair softly.

She felt so secure, so protected nestled in his arms. "He made me uneasy when we were dancing so I excused myself. I know now that fleeing the dance floor like a timid virgin seeking out her *dueña* was a mistake. I only whetted his appetite for the chase. He followed me outside on the pretext of bringing me champagne." She gestured to the shards of glass glittering on the flagstones a few feet away. "I asked him to leave me alone. When he wouldn't, I walked away, thinking such a direct insult would surely cause him to take offense and leave." She laughed bitterly. "He took offense, but he didn't go away. Instead he followed me here and tried to kiss me. I smashed my fist in his eye and grabbed one of the glasses he'd set by the fountain. Even throwing the champagne in his face didn't deter him. He's insane, Lucero."

She looked up at him with tears welling in her eyes. Nicholas could feel her beginning to tremble now, her earlier iron-willed self-possession deserting her as she relived the horror. "He grabbed me and I twisted away, but he held fast, laughing all the while. That's when he kissed me and cut my lip but I tore free and stumbled back, searching for a weapon. I saw the glass stem lying where I'd dropped it in our scuffle and I picked it up. When he was certain I'd use the jagged edge on him if he came a step closer, he shrugged and walked away. Agnes passed him on the porch and figured out what must have happened. She found me here, then went in search of you. I think she means well, but she wants you to duel von Scheeling."

"She's in luck. Her wish will be granted," Fortune said in a low furious rush of breath.

"He's dangerous, Lucero! I think he wanted this to happen—for you to challenge him. He wants to kill you."

"I'm not easy to kill, my love, as many of my enemies could attest—if they were alive to do so. Come, let me take you upstairs and fetch your maid to tend your hurts."

"Then you'll search out von Scheeling, won't you?" She stiffened apprehensively in his arms.

"What do you think?" he asked rhetorically.

"Then I'm going with you."

Her chin was mutinously set. He knew short of throwing her over his shoulder and locking her in their room, he could not prevent her presence at the challenge. "I suppose you have the right, but the women will gossip when they see you like this."

"I don't give a fig about gossip—only you," she said fiercely. "He might try to kill you some sneaky underhanded way."

He was touched by the concern, even fear, that underlaid her anger. Running his fingertips lightly across her cheek, he placed a soft kiss to her forehead, then knelt by the fountain to soak her handkerchief in fresh water. When he pressed the cool cloth to her lip she winced but did not pull away. Rather, her hand came up, covering his as they stood side by side in the courtyard, staring into one another's eyes, communicating silently. She entreated fearfully. He refused adamantly. Yet beyond the clash of wills love trembled and grew.

Finally she spoke. "I could not bear to lose you, husband."

"You won't, love. I know what a man like von Scheeling is capable of, believe me."

"Think of our child."

"I am. And I won't let my children grow up hearing their father called coward. You know our honor demands this."

She could read the finality in his eyes. "Let's go. I know he's waiting for you."

The Prussian was indeed waiting in the *sala*, surrounded by a number of *criollos*, holding forth on past campaigning glories, a crystal snifter of Don Encarnación's excellent French brandy in his hand. It almost seemed as if he had staged the scene.

The crowd of sycophants parted nervously as Fortune strode across the room. They looked from the cold deadly gleam in Alvarado's dark eyes to his lady, standing defiantly in the doorway. Her gown was torn, and she pressed a bloody cloth to her mouth, staring daggers at the Prussian. The soft murmuring died away when Nicholas stopped directly in front of von Scheeling.

"You know why I'm here, von Scheeling. Name your second and meet me at daybreak on top of the hill facing the mine entrance."

"So, the young lordling really is a fighter, even if he has quit the emperor's service," the lieutenant replied with a slightly drunken slur overlaying his German accent. He clicked his heels and bowed, causing a straight hunk of his thick yellow hair to fall across his forehead. When he straightened up there was a gleam of madness in his flat gray eyes. "I shall enjoy killing you."

Fortune smiled chillingly. "I suspect it is impossible for a dead man to enjoy anything."

"As the challenged, it is, I believe, my choice of weapons."

"Of course."

"Then I choose sabers—cavalry sabers." Von Scheeling's smile was slow and nasty.

The hushed room erupted with low murmurs and shocked gasps. This was certainly a breach of *criollo* decorum.

"But surely, Lieutenant, you cannot be serious. A duel is fought with foils or pistols," Don Encarnación said stiffly, his voice ringing from the doorway which he had just entered. "Gentlemen do not duel with sabers."

"I am not a gentleman. I am a soldier," von Scheeling replied in Spanish. In German, he added scornfully, "I've met no gentlemen in this lizard-infested wilderness."

Nicholas understood the insult but could make no comment without revealing that he spoke the language.

Don Encarnación and several other of the men around von Scheeling intuited the Prussian's hostility. The murmuring in the room quieted as the two antagonists faced each other. Nicholas knew why von Scheeling chose sabers. The Prussian thought he could use his heavier build to advantage and hack his opponent to pieces.

The smile that slashed Fortune's face broadened, but it did not reach his deadly wolf's eyes. "As you say, a saber is the true soldier's weapon. At dawn tomorrow we'll learn just who the true soldier is, won't we?"

Chapter 18

"You cannot just leave me behind as if I were a child, Lucero. They have no physician here. What if you're injured?" Mercedes asked as they entered their suite.

"You can't come with me, Mercedes. A duel is no place for a woman. When a man fights, the presence of his woman is a distinct liability, a distraction that can get him killed."

"I don't faint or have vapors," she said with asperity. "Oh, Lucero, you could be killed!"

"Thank you for your confidence, but I won't be," he replied with dry assurance. "I know how to handle von Scheeling. Now, let me see to your injuries," he commanded, deftly turning her to unfasten the hooks at the back of her ball gown. "After all, it's only fair, since you've tended mine so often . . ." She winced silently when he eased the torn gown from her right shoulder. An ugly bruise was beginning to darken her soft golden skin, the imprint from that bastard's hand. He felt a killing rage wash over him, building up like an ocean tide rolling in.

Mercedes heard his sudden intake of breath and felt his body tense when he saw the marks. They were tender but not serious. She turned around to reassure him. The look of icy fury in his eyes was utterly terrifying and at that moment she almost pitied von Scheeling.

"I'd like to beat him to death with my bare hands," Nicholas said in a low growl as his fingertips carefully examined her, sliding the ruined dress to the floor and unfastening her lacy undergarments.

"I've given you a good start on that task, Lucero. Agnes

says I blackened his eye." She strove for a light tone but he did not join in her tremulous smile.

Gently he touched the bruises, then pulled her into his arms. "When I think of another man putting his hands on you, hurting you this way . . ."

She could feel him trembling as he held her so protectively, possessively. "I'll be all right, Lucero," she whispered, looking up into that implacable, beautiful face of his. She traced the thin scar on his cheek. "You've suffered far worse hurts than I."

"But he would have raped you." There was a savage desperation in his voice as he realized Luce had already done that to her, and that he, too, had almost committed the same crime the night he had smashed in her bedroom door. "Oh, Mercedes, I'm so sorry, so sorry . . ." His mind shut down, unable to think of it.

She held onto him, intuiting that he was apologizing not only for what von Scheeling had done but for what he had done as well . . . or had he? Could this man be capable of the coolly amused brutality to which she had been subjected on her wedding night? *No, don't think of it, don't . . .*

Nicholas forced himself to regain control. "Let me get cool compresses to soak away some of the ache." He raised her chin in his hand and daubed at the blood dried on her lip. The sick fury began to churn inside him again. Trembling, he released her and walked over to the dry sink by the window. A porcelain basin and pitcher filled with fresh water sat on top of it. He filled the basin, then soaked a soft linen towel in the water and wrung it out. "Sit down," he said softly.

She obeyed, walking over to the edge of the bed, clad only in her camisole and pantalets. He pulled down the sheets and she leaned back against the pillows as he sat on the edge of the mattress and began to sponge her shoulder and arm gently. Taking one edge of the towel, he pressed it against her mouth, soaking the scabbed blood until it could be carefully wiped away. His tenderness brought tears to her eyes. Never in her life had she felt so cherished. He removed her undergarments as patiently as the most skillful nursemaid might undress a child. Then he applied the cooling compresses to all of her bruises.

"That feels wonderful," she said dreamily. "You make a very good nurse."

"On the battlefield soldiers have to tend their own wounds. More often than not there are no doctors and those that are available are usually butchers."

Her eyes filled with horror. "It must've been awful. Promise me you'll never go back to the war." Her hands seized his, stilling his gentle ministrations.

Nicholas could feel her nails dig into his wrists as she held onto him tightly, imploring him. With a ragged smile, he nodded. "I love you, Mercedes, and I'll always protect you. I won't ever leave you."

"I couldn't bear losing you. I love you too much." Her eyelids fluttered closed and she drifted off to sleep.

Nicholas pulled the bedcovers over her, then quickly stripped off his clothes and climbed in beside her, pulling her damp, chilled body against the solid wall of his heated flesh, but he did not think of making love to her, only holding her, keeping her safe from all the cruelties of this world.

Finally he slept.

In the middle of the night Mercedes began to stir restlessly, thrashing and crying out. She was in von Scheeling's vile hands again, twisting away from his lascivious mouth, unable to get her breath, to escape as he tore at her clothing.

Nicholas awakened at once and sat up, then reached out and pulled her in his arms, crooning softly. "Shh . . . it's all right. It was only a nightmare, my love. You're safe."

"Oh, Lucero, hold me." She inhaled his familiar scent, felt the hard, scarred contours of his flesh, heard his heart beating next to her own. She wrapped her arms around his neck and drew his face to hers for a kiss, murmuring against his lips, "Make love to me, please."

"Are you certain?" he asked hesitantly. "You're hurt." But even as he spoke, she pressed her breasts against his chest and opened her mouth, trailing wet voracious kisses, nips and bites over his jawline and across his shoulder. He could feel her desperation and it brought an answering hunger leaping to life like living flames, searing his loins until he ached to join with her.

Mercedes lay down on the bed, pulling him with her until he pressed her into the softness of the mattress with the weight of his body. Her bruises remained tender and ached, but she did not care about the discomfort as she felt his rigid erection between her thighs. Squeezing them tightly together, she heard him groan raggedly.

His hands caressed her with feverish intensity. In spite of her bruises, her body held tightly to his, undulating sweetly beneath him. He rolled onto his back, carrying her with him so that she straddled his hips. Her hair hung down, covering her breasts in a silky curtain. The softly curling ends brushed and teased his rigid phallus.

Nicholas raised her hips with his hands, cupping her buttocks, positioning her as he instructed, "Take me inside you."

Instinctively she reached for the hard smooth shaft, wrapping her hand around it. He groaned and arched his hips, thrusting eagerly as she guided the pulsing tip into the core of wet heat that throbbed with wanting him. Then slowly, ever so tantalizingly, she let him fill her, controlling her impalement. Her hips lowered, enveloping him, letting the utter sweetness of the joining carry away all thought of tomorrow and its dangers. For tonight he was safe here with her, loving her, pleasing her.

And the pleasure was intoxicating. Mercedes had never before been in control this way, able to set the pace, to move, twist and writhe in utter abandon. She experimented, rolling her hips slowly, then raising up and plunging down in a swift hard rhythm that had them both gasping for breath.

Nicholas reached up and cupped her breasts, teasing the sensitive nipples. They hardened into nubby points. He drew her down until the pearly globes hung suspended and he could take one, then the other, into his mouth and suckle them. As he did so, her hips began to move more swiftly. Lest he lose control and spill his seed too soon, he took her delicate pelvic bones in his hands and slowed the pace to a languorous, lazy ride.

This was such delicious bliss it robbed her mind of all thought. She arched her back, coming down slowly. The sensitive little bud at the center of her passion pressed hard against the base of his staff, stretching her, pulling at her until she was utterly lost.

Nicholas felt the sudden shuddering tremors begin deep inside her as she cried out, digging her nails into the muscles of his chest. Her sheath rhythmically milked him until he, too, could withstand no more. When his phallus swelled, spilling its seed deep within her, he came up off the mattress, so intense was the release.

Mercedes felt him stiffen and shudder as he climaxed. The final thrusting glory sent her spiraling into yet another series of fiery contractions that ebbed ever so slowly, until finally she collapsed onto his chest, panting and exhausted, utterly spent with ecstasy.

He cradled her in his arms as she nestled atop his body. Her mouth pressed soft, damp kisses against his neck and shoulders and she murmured indistinct love words. They lay that way for some moments, neither could have said how long, still intimately joined, simply savoring the life-affirming act of love.

Just before dawn, Nicholas slipped from the bed and carefully tucked the covers back around Mercedes. He dressed quickly and quietly in a loose, white cotton shirt and soft wool pants, clothing that would allow him maximum freedom of movement for the fight to come. Checking to see that she was still asleep, he pulled on his boots and started for the door, but then stopped with his hand on the knob and directed his gaze to his wife's tousled golden head snuggled amid the rumpled bedcovers and pillows.

His wife. Suddenly Nicholas felt the unexpected need to seal their vows before an altar, to give her his name. But he had no name to give, even though he was Anselmo's son. To keep her, he had to continue the masquerade, to hear her call him by his brother's name when he ached for her lips to cry out Nicholas instead. Damning himself for a fool, he slipped from the room, closing the door quietly behind him.

As soon as she heard the soft click of the lock, Mercedes

threw off the covers and sat up in bed. The sudden movement made her wince in pain. Looking at the discolorations from the bruises, she raised her left shoulder and rotated her arm, loosening up the tight, aching muscles. She should have used the broken champagne glass to castrate that wretch von Scheeling! Then her husband would not be risking his life to avenge her honor this morning.

Thinking of Lucero, she quickly slipped on a dark gray riding habit. There was not much time. If only things went as they planned. Just then a sharp rapping sounded on the floor-length double doors facing onto the balcony. She crossed the carpet and turned the knob.

Agnes du Salm slipped inside the room. "You're ready. Good," she said as her eyes swept over Mercedes' outfit.

"How did you get onto my balcony?" Mercedes asked incredulously.

The princess grinned. "I used to be an acrobat, remember? Climbing across the porch roof is a lot easier than balancing on one leg atop a galloping horse, believe me. I thought there would be less chance of attracting attention if we avoided the hallways. Come, I'll help you down from the porch. We can use the bougainvillea trellis to descend to the courtyard. I've bribed a stable hand to have two horses saddled and waiting."

"You are amazing," Mercedes said. "I'm so grateful for your help."

"Oh, pooh. It's the least I can do in return. After all, your husband is going to dispose of that swine Arnoldt, for which Salmi and I will be forever in your debt."

"I only pray the lieutenant doesn't harm Lucero in the process of his 'disposition,'" Mercedes replied, biting her lip.

"If Lucero Alvarado is half as dangerous as he looks, after this morning Arnoldt von Scheeling will be incapable of ever harming anyone again," the princess said with blithe assurance. "Come, let's get to our horses. I see the first streaks of light on the horizon."

* * *

The sun rose slowly above the jagged peaks of the Sierra Madres like a great molten ball of gold, spilling harsh yellow light across the shadowy landscape of the flat open earth on top of the hill. In the distance a hole gaped in the ground, with a crude wooden winch and basket situated above it, the entrance to one of the Vargas silver mines.

Nicholas rode up and dismounted in silence, accompanied by Prince Salm-Salm, who had offered to second him upon hearing of the outrageous insult his subordinate had offered Doña Mercedes. The two men studied the lay of the land and direction of light with the eyes of tactical professionals who knew the advantage such attention to physical detail can provide.

"Watch those loose pebbles over there. If Arnoldt backs you onto them, he'll use his superior weight and you will be unable to use agile footwork to counter it," the prince said, pacing around the site.

"That's why he chose sabers. He's sure he can back me into a corner and hack away until he wears me down," Fortune replied grimly.

The prince nodded. "Yes, that is how he would reason. He is a seasoned soldier. A Junker of the Prussian gentry, born to arms. As the younger son, he was left to seek his own fortune in the military, but there was some difficulty between him and his superior—over a woman. Arnoldt has always been—how do you say it?—terrible with women."

Nicholas volunteered no further German and the prince continued his story. "At any rate, he lost his commission in the Prussian army and became a mercenary. It has made him a twisted and bitter man, envious of those with titles and land, beautiful wives—all the things of which he feels he has been cheated."

Nicholas nodded. "That would explain why he provoked me into this duel." The irony of their similar circumstances before he had assumed Luce's identity did not escape Fortune. "Odd, Mercedes realized it, too. She said she was certain that he wanted me to challenge him." He shrugged. "I wonder why me, not any of the other *hacendados*?"

"Perhaps because he sensed you would be the opponent with the most mettle."

Felix du Salm's expression was bland but his eyes revealed curiosity and a certain wariness. Don Lucero Alvarado was altogether too experienced a soldier to have spent his life in Mexico and to have come to the profession of arms only a scant few years ago.

Nicholas grinned. "I have a trick or two up my sleeve. Let's hope I don't disappoint the lieutenant."

Just then the sound of horses climbing the slope interrupted their conversation. Von Scheeling and the rest of the group from Hacienda Vargas crested the hill. Don Hernan Ruíz, the embittered former soldier who had lost the use of his right arm in the war, seconded the lieutenant. They dismounted across the clearing and made their way to where Nicholas and the prince stood.

Von Scheeling's right eye was well-blackened and slightly swollen. Fortune studied it insolently but said nothing. The lieutenant flushed angrily and stared straight ahead, waiting for the formalities to begin. Mercedes had marked him well, Nicholas thought, fighting to tamp down the fury that rose inside him. He had fought over women on several previous occasions, but none of them had really mattered. None of them were Mercedes.

Old Don Encarnación bowed with grave courtesy to the prince and then turned to Fortune. "There is nothing I can say to dissuade you from this challenge?" he asked formally, adhering to ritual.

"Nothing whatsoever," Fortune replied in a flat voice.

"Very well, then. Are you ready to select your weapon?"

Nicholas nodded as Don Hernan opened a heavy velvet-lined case. Inside it lay two gleaming cavalry sabers. The curved blades of the weapons were heavy and lacked the balance of slender fencing foils. Fortune picked up each one and tested it with several swift clean slashes. "They seem to be identical. This one will be fine," he said, holding the second one in his right hand.

Ruíz bowed stiffly, then offered the remaining sword to von Scheeling.

"The duel is to commence when I give the signal and continue until first blood—or until the honor of the challenge has been satisfied," Vargas said, looking from the Prussian to Fortune.

"Blood be damned. I'll be satisfied when he's dead," Nicholas replied, his expression cold, harsh, deadly.

Von Scheeling grinned sharkishly, revealing large, square white teeth. "I will cut you to ribbons and let your blood soak into this barren accursed soil."

"Don't be premature, *mein herr*," Fortune said softly, his eyes once again lingering on the Prussian's black eye. "My wife would've cut you to ribbons with that broken glass. You backed down from her then, but there's nowhere to hide now."

Nicholas watched as the Prussian stiffened and his big meaty fist tightened around the handle of his saber until the knuckles were white.

Something in the Mexican's tone of voice warned von Scheeling that he was in grave jeopardy. But his foe was, after all, a *criollo*, the spoiled son of a rich *hacendado*, he reminded himself, not a professional soldier. He would kill Don Lucero, and soon after, he would have the haughty, golden-haired wife. Perhaps he would tell the *criollo* that before he finished him. Yes, he would indeed. The fine light of madness gleamed in von Scheeling's pale eyes.

Don Encarnación interrupted the tension building between the antagonists, asking, "Are you ready to begin?" When both men nodded, he made a chopping motion with his right hand and stepped back to watch the fight.

In spite of von Scheeling's breach in dueling etiquette regarding choice of weapons, the *criollo* onlookers were all eager to see this highly unusual combat. They had been raised on the blood sports of cockfighting and the bullring. Like the rest, Don Encarnación was inured to violence, yet the crackling aura of hate emanating from the combatants as they faced each other riveted his attention. His avidity was reflected in the faces of the other men who stood in a loose semicircle at the western edge of the hilltop. Several discreet wagers had already been made. Everyone watched intently.

None more so than Mercedes and Agnes, who crouched hidden and breathless in the thick mesquite at the edge of the clearing. Behind them lay a steep drop-off to the trail below, which they had scrambled up after leaving their horses hidden behind a stand of piñon pines.

Nicholas hefted the awkward weapon. Both men were about the same height, but von Scheeling was far heavier-boned with thick ropy muscles covering his arms and a wide barrel chest. He looked, Fortune thought grimly, like a German butcher.

Fortune had already mapped out his strategy. Now once again assessing his foe, he decided it just might work. Hell, it had better! He had received some excellent pointers in the fine art of swordsmanship from an old comrade at arms in the Legion, a former New Orleans fencing master named Andre Vichey.

He could still see the pursed-lip Gallic disdain of the old veteran who had explained, "No, no, no, Nicholas. The saber is not a gentleman's weapon. It is the cudgel of an oaf, a lout, fit only to slash and hack. Should you ever be forced to use this butcher's implement, your foe may well be physically stronger than you. Remember never to parry his strokes with the strength of your arm lest you tire in an uneven contest. Parry as you move around him in a circle."

Mercedes watched as von Scheeling drove Lucero backward with a series of blindingly rapid slashes. Her husband parried the brutal blows by sidestepping, circling to avoid the full force of the attack, but he continued to give ground. She bit her lip fearfully but made no sound. Her hand slid inside her skirt pocket, where she had concealed a Sharps .32 caliber four-shot pepperbox. The cool, smooth, ivory grip on it felt reassuring against her palm as she clutched it tightly.

God forgive me, I'll kill von Scheeling if I must to save my husband.

If he is your husband.

Mercedes squeezed her eyes closed for a second, willing away the awful suspicion, which had continued to grow as the months rolled by. The man she loved behaved less and less like the man she had married.

"Arnoldt is using his greater weight to press his attack," Agnes commented critically. "Salmi said he'd do that. Now if only that wickedly handsome husband of yours is fast enough to use Arnoldt's clumsiness and has endurance enough to outlast him. He does handle himself well," she added, watching the lightning speed with which Nicholas fended off von Scheeling's bullish attack.

Nicholas smiled grimly as he kept out of von Scheeling's reach, watching his foe's growing frustration. He was careful not to squander his strength by absorbing the Prussian's blows head-on, nor did he make sweeping offensive slashes, but rather used wrist action with the heavy blade, scoring a small nick here, a larger slice there, but von Scheeling seemed impervious to pain.

"Be as precise as the picador lancing the bull," Andre had said. Unfortunately, what Nicholas was faced with here was more Black Forest boar than Spanish bull.

Both men began to perspire as they moved in an arc, back and forth on the rough, rock-strewn ground. Several times Fortune almost lost his balance while avoiding von Scheeling's murderous assaults.

"You grow weary, *ya*?" the Prussian taunted.

"I grow bored, *ya*," Fortune replied, parrying an overhand stroke as he slipped to his own left. Although the maneuver had allowed the blades to make only glancing contact, he could feel a powerful shock surge up his arm into his shoulder. A few strokes like that parried flat-footed, and he would not even be able to lift the damned pig-sticker. He circled the smirking lieutenant, not attacking, not even wasting his strength with a feint. He simply waited.

Once again, the Prussian leaped forward with an overhand stroke, and once again, Nicholas slipped to his left as he parried. However, this time he countered, not with the classic cavalryman's slash to the head, but with a flick of his wrist. Quick as a striking rattler, the blade of his saber slipped over the Prussian's extended arm, leaving a deep slice in his thick shoulder muscle. At last von Scheeling winced, trying to counter with a clumsy backhanded swipe at his opponent's side. The blade only hissed through air. Fortune had already danced nimbly away.

Enraged, von Scheeling cursed, lunging recklessly after the faster man. This time the Prussian feinted an overhand strike but quickly turned it into a downward angling slash at Nicholas' right side. Caught off guard, the slimmer man was forced to take the full force of the blow on his own parrying blade. The shock wrenched his shoulder, and he could see by the gleam in von Scheeling's eyes that the lieutenant knew it. But once again, Nicholas made his stocky foe pay a price. His wrist flicked up and this time von Scheeling grunted in agony as the tip of Fortune's blade left a deep wound in his triceps.

"You think to have me wear myself out, don't you?" the Prussian asked in Spanish, his voice as mocking as heavy breathing would allow.

"I think to bleed you like the pig that you are," Fortune replied.

No one had ever mistaken the lieutenant for an intelligent man, yet even he was beginning to see that brute strength would not carry the day. It was time to change tactics. He began to slowly stalk his tormentor instead of charging in after him, taunting in mocking Spanish, "*Criollo* bastard! Do all of you dance the flamenco better than you fight?"

Ignoring the hissed rage of several young onlookers, von Scheeling lunged forward for what seemed to be another ineffective overhand stroke. Nicholas' blade came up to parry as he slipped again to his left. Then von Scheeling sprung his trap. He had maintained his balance by not committing his full strength to the saber stroke. Now he reached out and seized the wrist of Fortune's sword arm with his left hand, while driving the elbow of his own sword arm against the lighter man's jaw. Nicholas crashed to the ground, slipping on the loose rocks.

The Prussian hesitated an instant at the collective gasp of spectator outrage. Don Patrico and Don Doroteo actually stepped forward, half ready to draw their weapons in protest over von Scheeling's breach of the code duello. Fortunately, the small distraction was sufficient to clear Nicholas' fogged brain. When von Scheeling drove the tip of his weapon downward to impale his opponent on the rocky soil, Fortune rolled sideways, coming up on his knee and delivering a disabling slash to the side of the Prussian's knee.

Von Scheeling let out a grunt of rage, the sound of an animal in pain. Then he cursed and hobbled backward. Nicholas staggered to his feet. The lieutenant was covered with blood, but Fortune's right shoulder ached and he was having trouble focusing his eyes.

Christ, which one of us is in worse trouble? Fortune decided that he was, in spite of his opponent's bloody appearance. Time to try something different. He shifted the saber to his left hand, facing von Scheeling in a relaxed stance. Then, he delivered an insult—in quite intelligible German.

Agnes Salm-Salm had learned her husband's language and was used to overhearing an occasional vulgarity, having spent years as the wife of a professional soldier. But Nicholas' oath brought a flush of red to her cheeks.

"What did he say?" Mercedes whispered, her throat gone dry as she clutched the hidden gun.

"Well, it relates to Arnoldt's parentage," the princess equivocated. "Er, something to the effect that his mother was a woman of loose morals who had relations with . . . well, barnyard creatures. You can imagine the rest."

But Mercedes was too busy watching the enraged response of von Scheeling to imagine anything else at that moment.

The lieutenant's head snapped back as if he had been smashed in the face with a fist. With a bellow, he lunged forward. Nicholas caught the blow on the hilt of his weapon. The mighty Prussian's right arm had finally lost some of its overpowering strength.

Holding his foe's blade motionless with his own, Fortune stepped close. For a moment two pairs of hate-glazed eyes locked. Then, Nicholas drove his knee into von Scheeling's groin. The lieutenant doubled over and Fortune—like a matador—came up on his toes, aimed the tip of his blade, and drove it through the Prussian's back and into his heart.

Just like the bull after all, Andre.

Mercedes knelt on the hard rocky ground, numbly clutching the weapon which had proved so unnecessary. He had not needed her help . . . whoever he was . . . this stranger who used his left hand as skillfully as his right, who spoke not only French and English but obviously German as well. *I wonder what else he knows that a* hacendado *would not.* She could lie to herself no longer. Mercedes Alvarado carried the child of a man who was not her husband. And, God help her, she loved him. If need be, she would have killed for him.

"Come, we'd best be gone before the men find us. Salmi would be furious and so would your deliciously deadly Don Lucero. What a fighter he is," Agnes rhapsodized, unaware of her friend's turmoil as she tugged at Mercedes' arm.

Silently, Mercedes slipped away from the bloody dueling ground without saying a word. She did not look back.

Chapter 19

Mercedes paced in their bedroom, her eyes darting to the clock sitting on the credenza near the door. Soon she would have to face him.

Him.

He knew so much about the Alvarado family, the servants, everything on Gran Sangre, right down to childhood memories. Surely Lucero must have told him. No one else could have done it. But why would he? Could her love have threatened her husband's life? Sweet virgin, could he have killed Lucero? Certainly he was deadly enough. On several occasions now she had watched him kill with detached calculation. He was utterly ruthless and cool under fire, but he was also the man who risked his life to save Bufón. Lucero would never have done that, any sooner than he would have acknowledged Rosario.

Her lover was far more admirable than Lucero. Yet everyone believed he *was* Lucero. How could they not, when he was virtually identical?

"What a marvelous jest Lucero would think it—to send an alter ego to claim his bride," she said bitterly. Her husband had never loved her.

But he *does.*

And now he had planted his seed in her. There was some consolation in believing the next *patrón* of Gran Sangre would be as conscientious as his father, she supposed. But it did not solve her moral dilemma. She was in love with this man and she did not even know his name!

"If only I could seek solace from the Church, confess . . ." But she knew that was impossible. No priest, least of all Father Salvador, would believe her. They would think her mad. Or worse yet, what if they did believe her? She was guilty of lascivious adultery. Her penance would be contingent upon banishing her lover from her bed forever.

She buried her face in her hands and gave in to the stinging tears that had burned behind her eyelids on the ride back to Hacienda Vargas. *I'm lost, an irredeemable harlot, for even if I could betray his identity, I would not.* The thought of giving him up, of never feeling his touch or hearing his voice again, was more than she could bear. Mercedes longed with every fiber of her being to spend the rest of her life with the man.

And she did not even know his name.

When he returned to the room an hour later, Nicholas found her lying on the bed, still dressed in her riding habit. Princess Agnes had been downstairs smiling slyly at him, as if they shared a private joke. When she congratulated him on his victory, she had even used a few German phrases. He cursed himself as seven kinds of a fool for revealing his command of the language during the fight.

Now, seeing Mercedes' tear-streaked face, a tight knot of dread lodged in his throat. He moved silently to the bed and sat down on the soft mattress beside her. As she rolled up with a surprised look on her face, the Sharps slid from her pocket and lay gleaming between them.

He picked it up, recognizing it as the gun he had selected for her to carry as protection whenever she was away from the hacienda grounds. His eyes moved from the weapon to her face with a question unspoken.

"Yes, I was there . . . and yes, I would've killed him if I had to," she whispered brokenly.

The torment in her eyes felt worse than taking a saber thrust from von Scheeling. "I'm glad you didn't have to," he replied carefully, then held his breath as he waited for her to respond, perhaps to accuse.

Instead she flung herself into his arms and held onto him in desperation. "I love you so much, I'd do anything for you . . . anything at all."

Nicholas stroked her hair, burying his face in the soft

fragrant curls. "Hush, don't cry, beloved, please," he crooned.

Mercedes forced herself to calm down, then scrubbed at her eyes. "I must look a fright," she said overbrightly. "It's only the baby that causes these mood swings, or so the other ladies have assured me. It will soon pass, just as the morning indisposition will."

"You're utterly beautiful to me and always will be. I love you more than life," he said quietly, willing her to believe him. And to forgive him.

But he could never ask it, nor would he ever speak a word of what had silently passed between them.

After dinner that evening, when the ladies had excused themselves, Don Encarnación led the gentlemen into his study for fine aged port and Cuban cigars. All the men avoided mentioning the bloody and highly irregular duel they had witnessed that morning. Most were incensed with von Scheeling's slurs against their honor as *criollos*, but that one of their own should respond so viciously and kill him with such chilling dispatch made them distinctly uneasy. Conversation as always turned to politics.

"I've heard the republican rabble plan to attack Hermosillo," Patrico said, nervously puffing on his cigar.

"What is Bazaine going to do about it?" Doroteo interjected, directing his question to the prince.

Felix du Salm took his time swallowing Vargas' excellent port while framing his reply. His expression was bland, impossible to read. "It is difficult to say, gentlemen. As I'm sure you know, the general has not been given the additional reinforcements from Napoleon which he requested."

"Hah," Hernan Ruiz snorted in disgust. "The French perimeter contracts even as we speak. Soon they will be walled up inside Mexico City. All the outlying areas will be on their own."

"It was always Emperor Maximilian's plan that his imperial forces would take over when the French withdrew. One reason I am touring in the north is to gain firsthand information for the emperor as to how best to facilitate the military transition from French to Mexican hands."

"Then it is true that Napoleon the Third has ordered Bazaine home?" Encarnación asked shrewdly, reading between the lines of the prince's comments.

"It has been expected, although not for some months, perhaps another year or more," Salm-Salm said carefully. "French presence in Mexico was merely to facilitate setting up Mexican imperial authority."

"It seems to me the question is are you ready to assume that authority?" Nicholas asked, placing his comrade at arms in a difficult position. He needed to gauge the reaction of the *hacendados* to the prince's reply.

Salm-Salm's expression was grave now. "I will not deceive you with glowing reports of thousands of crack troops ready to patrol the length and breadth of a land so vast as yours. We do have the core of a fine army composed of loyal Mexicans combined with Austrian and Belgian volunteers sent by their majesties' families. But we need the support of men such as you—landholders with noble lineage willing to offer their swords and their wealth to sustain the monarchy."

"Many of us have already sacrificed greatly on both counts to benefit the emperor," Ruiz replied stiffly. His crippled arm hung limply at his side in silent testimony to his words.

As the exchange between the prince and several of the older *hacendados* continued, Nicholas observed in silence. Hernan Ruiz and old Encarnación most forcefully condemned the French for leaving the Mexican imperialists in the lurch.

Mariano remained, as did Nicholas, a silent observer, with a contemptuously amused expression on his face.

What game does he play? Fortune hoped he would soon find out. If Ursula Vargas had not been spinning fanciful tales, her husband would hold his secret rendezvous later that night.

The heated political argument among the *hacendados* grew more awkward as young Silvio Zavala, well into his cups, proposed a toast. "To crushing the ignorant peons and their Indian leader. We don't need French guns—or any other European help—to restore Mexico to her former grandeur!" The pale-complected young *criollo* searched the room, his glazed blue eyes skimming contemptuously from the prince to several of his aides, all Austrians, Prussians or other Europeans.

Several of the other young hotheads chorused agreement.

"Long live Mexico!"

"We'll stand Juarez and all his rabble before a firing squad!"

"The idea such trash should presume to a position of authority over their betters!"

Fortune listened to the bravado, studying the blustering arrogant young *criollos*. He was reminded ironically of the fiery words and contemptuous dismissals of the American Confederates who had visited Gran Sangre. Soon these untried, spoiled rich boys would face a brutal reckoning even more terrible than that which those seasoned veterans had experienced. For the first time Nicholas began to feel his spying mission against Vargas and his friends was not such a distasteful task after all.

Seething inwardly, Fortune turned to watch his comrade Prince Salm-Salm. The Prussian had no reason to conceal his anger. His eyes narrowed and he stiffened at the implicit slurs against the professional soldiers who had been unable to defeat the republican guerrillas. However, as emissary from the imperial court sent on a goodwill and fact gathering mission, he made no reply, only stood in stoic, yet lethal, silence.

Don Encarnación quickly intervened with a stern rebuke. His patrician features were cold but his pale eyes flashed with searing anger. "I am certain we all wish the Juarista rabble vanquished and the emperor ruling over a prosperous Mexico. However, our cause is ill served when young men who have not seen the hardship of battle speak so uncivilly of those who have. You are fortunate his highness does not choose to call any of you out. I am certain he could make short work of the lot of you young pups!"

After that scathing set-down, several of the older men clustered around the prince and his aides, making apologies for their sons and younger brothers.

Gliding to the corner where Fortune stood, Mariano said, "You seem to have become the Prussian's friend. Why didn't you leap to his defense?"

"A man like the prince is well used to defending himself, as your father pointed out," Nicholas replied dryly. "Anyway, I doubt Felix du Salm feels more than the usual irritation of a professional dealing with amateurs."

Before Mariano could reply, the prince approached Nicholas, extending his hand. "I must bid you farewell, my friend, for our party is scheduled to depart for Durango at first light."

Taking the Prussian's hand, Nicholas shook it warmly. "It has been a pleasure, your highness. I thank you for acting as my second this morning."

"Ach, it was my pleasure. It is really I who should thank you. Von Scheeling was becoming an increasingly dangerous liability. I am happy you disposed of him." He paused for a moment, his shrewd dark eyes studying Fortune. "If you should ever again want to resume the profession of arms, please come to me."

Their eyes met in understanding as they said their goodbyes. Mariano observed their exchange, saying nothing.

After his foreign guest of honor and his aides retired, Don Encarnación quietly spoke with half a dozen *hacendados*. Nicholas was not included in their coterie, but he overheard the covert invitations and decided to eavesdrop on the gathering.

While Encarnación closed the massive mahogany doors to his study, Mariano closed those facing out to the courtyard porch. They were sealed in for a serious discussion, Fortune decided, grateful that he could hear through the thin glass door panes. He leaned closer in the darkness. The shadows cast by thick poinsettias concealed him from the men in the brightly lit room.

The old don quickly got down to the matter at hand. "Well, you have heard it all but publicly confirmed tonight.

From what the prince has said to me in private, I am certain Maximilian's government is on its last legs."

"Bazaine's troops hold a small enclosure around the capital. When they pull out, there will be no effective force to take their place," Mariano added.

"Then do we act as the prince requests and give Maximilian our gold?" Patrico interjected.

"Bah, you speak like those young idiots," Encarnación said, fixing his wintry gaze on Patrico.

"Obviously, Don Patrico was speaking in jest," Hernan responded cynically. "Our charity begins closer to home, no matter if we like Salm-Salm. Anyway, he'll be moving on soon after the French."

"If he had any sense, so would that foolish young Hapsburg," Doroteo said in disgust.

"Whether he stays or goes is not important," Encarnación replied, cutting to the heart of the issue. Every eye in the room fixed on him then. "We can deal with any conservative government in the capital—even with a series of squabbling republican generals, as long as they keep their power struggles confined to the Valley of Mexico."

"What we cannot have is a strong central government united under that damned Indian. Juarez must be eliminated," Mariano pronounced succinctly.

"We've tried before and failed," Hernan said impatiently.

"We cannot afford another failure! Our families have ruled this land for generations. We are about to lose everything." Mariano Vargas was no longer the bored, half-drunken debaucher. His usually jowly and bland expression now blazed with passion. "Diaz's armies are sweeping out of the south and Escobedo moves from the Gulf coast menacing Monterrey and Saltillo. Juarez is the focal point, the unifying force holding the rebels together, bending them into a cohesive unit. Kill him and the rest will break up into squabbling factions, leaving the northern tier of the country to us." Greed and lust for power glowed in his eyes.

"Do you think killing Juarez will save the emperor?" Patrico asked skeptically.

Mariano shrugged. "Probably not, but whether or not

Maximilian maintains a toehold in central Mexico isn't important."

"As long as he's surrounded by rebel generals fighting over the spoils, he cannot interfere with our plans, nor can they," Encarnación added. "I have had my own small army assembled and ready for years, and I'm making plans to hire and arm more soldiers."

"Just think of it," Mariano said fervently. "We will carve out our own kingdom of the north. There will be no one strong enough in Mexico City to stop us!"

"It will mean the breakup of the nation," Patrico said, his voice uneasy.

"Yes, but it will also assure the preservation of our way of life, here where our family lands are located. If that republican rabble led by a lowly Indian succeeds, he'll see that the rest of his kind get the vote. They will break up our haciendas," Encarnación replied.

"What of the *gringos*?" Silvio Zavala interjected. "We have all heard reports that they plan to intervene and they sit on our very doorstep. Already they send arms to Juarez."

"All the more reason to kill him. Without him as their democratic figurehead, the Americans will give up on any hope of a Mexican republic," Mariano answered. "Invading would be like sticking their arm into the whirling blades of a windmill."

"To the death of Juarez!" Don Hernan raised his glass in a toast.

"Long live Mexico!" Mariano added with a cynical laugh.

Outside, Nicholas listened with bile rising in his throat. The bastards! The filthy treacherous bastards! *They don't give a damn about Mexico any more than they care about that blundering fool Maximilian.* Spoiled and selfish, seeing nothing beyond their own *criollo* world of class privilege and creature comforts, they would plunge the whole nation into anarchy in a vain attempt to hold onto a dying way of life. How many times in his travels around the globe had he seen the same thing? But he had never given a damn before.

Why do I care now? He had begun to think of himself as

a *criollo*, a *hacendado*, because he was an Alvarado who had at last come into his birthright, but now he recognized that his feelings ran far deeper than class or money. The country of his adoption had captured ahold of his mind, his very soul, and its only hope of salvation lay with that stubborn little Indian whose soldiers were willing to face down cannons with machetes. Could he do any less?

Nicholas listened as they fulminated against Juarez, but no details about how they would destroy him were discussed, only that Mariano Vargas would handle the matter through his allies in Chihuahua City.

Take your midnight ride, Mariano. I'll be waiting.

The night was brilliant with moonlight, a mixed blessing for Nicholas as he watched Mariano slip out of the family's living quarters and cross the wide courtyard. Once they were out on the open road, it would be far more difficult to follow without being detected. Vargas frequently looked around, as if sensing someone's presence. Or perhaps he was just naturally cautious.

Fortune watched him lead one of his father's palominos from the stable. Good. The bright gold horse would be easy to see. His own pewter stallion, in contrast, would blend into the shadows. He swung up on Peltre bareback and followed Vargas down the road toward Chihuahua City.

About five miles from the hacienda, Mariano turned off the road into a narrow, twisting ravine, covered with yucca and ocotillo. It could be a trap. Fortune waited at the opening for several minutes, concealed behind a ponderosa pine. Then another rider approached from the opposite direction and entered. The wide brim of his sombrero hid his face as he passed by Nicholas.

"How the hell am I going to get close enough to them to learn anything?" he muttered to Peltre.

The rendezvous site was only a few hundred yards inside, beneath an overhanging ledge of sandstone. Once he spotted both men's horses, Nicholas dismounted. Pulling the spyglass from his saddlebag, he climbed to the top of a small rocky promontory about forty yards away, as close as he dared come without the risk of being seen. Now, if there was only enough moonlight so he could see through his glass.

He could not discern their words over the noise of the wind soughing down the small canyon, but he could dimly make out the stranger handing a packet of papers to Vargas. The two men laughed and talked some more as Mariano offered his companion something . . . a cigar? When the man struck a match, his face was cast in stark relief for a moment, and an unforgettable face it was, too, with a great hawkish beak of a nose and thick mobile lips. He had shoved his hat back on his head and his face was framed by shaggy straight hair. No mistake about it, he was *Indio,* probably full-blooded. Before the match flashed out he turned in profile, revealing a long jagged scar that ran from his jaw all the way across to his right ear.

Fortune had seen lots of scars like that in his travels—the keepsake of a man who had cheated death by surviving a knife slash from behind. Someone had tried to cut his throat—and botched it. But whoever it was, they had marked him distinctively enough for McQueen's agent Porfirio Escondidas to recognize him.

Mercedes lay staring at the frescoed ceiling. The lush pastoral scene with Pan playing his flute as lambs danced did not soothe her. All she could think of was Lucero's absence. *Lucero.* She still called him by that name. What else was there to do? She did not know his real name and did not wish to, for in so doing, she would be openly admitting the dark passion locked so deeply in her heart.

Where had he slipped off to tonight? When he had joined her in their room earlier, he had been preoccupied and quiet, almost angry. He had assured her it was only the tense political situation the men had discussed after dinner which put him into such a state. Even then Mercedes was certain it was more complicated than that.

After they had undressed and climbed beneath the luxurious satin bedcovers, he had again made love to her with exquisite tenderness. Now it seemed impossible to imagine ever again spending a night alone, without his arms enfolding her, his warmth and strength permeating every fiber of her being. That was why she had awakened when he left.

Slipping downstairs after him, clad only in her nightrail and robe, Mercedes had been baffled as she watched him follow Don Mariano out of the house. After a few moments, their host's son rode away with Lucero still secretly trailing him. Unable to do anything else, she had tiptoed through the dark silent house and returned to their bed. Her pregnancy made sleep imperative and she dozed only to awaken some time later, still alone.

Several more restless hours passed. Mercedes gave up on staring at the ceiling and threw back the covers with an angry swish. *Enough*! She could not lie passively while he was out doing heaven only knew what. She yanked a plain dark day gown from the armoire and began dressing. At least if someone caught her wandering the halls, she would be decently clothed.

Nicholas followed Mariano back to the house, eager to see what Vargas would do with the papers he had received. Mariano did precisely as he had hoped, depositing them in a secret compartment in the ornate desk in his father's study. Then he poured himself a stiff brandy, doused his lone candle and trundled off to bed. In moments, Fortune was inside the study, using his penknife to spring the lock on the hidden drawer.

Spreading the documents before him, he inspected them carefully. Incredible! Troop movements of various Juarista forces were listed on one page with notations as to their probable ordnance and where they might best be attacked. Another described a substantial shipment of American weapons intended for the rebels, which would be sent across the border into Chihuahua next month. Apparently it was to be the Vargases' mission to steal them.

But the most crucial piece of information was the cryptic listing of Juarez's itinerary enroute south early in 1867. Again notations on the best places to spring an ambush dotted the margins, with questions about towns and villages in their locales.

Nicholas was so busy examining the evidence that he did not hear the door open softly, then close. He suddenly felt a prickle of warning skitter up his spine.

"Do you find my son's work interesting reading, Don Lucero?" The low angry growl of Don Encarnación's voice reverberated across the silent chamber.

Chapter 20

Nicholas dropped the papers back on the desk, cursing himself for his carelessness. His Remington was concealed on his hip. If he remained seated behind the desk—

"Please be so kind as to stand and remove your weapons," Vargas commanded crisply, dashing Fortune's hopes.

Slowly Nicholas stood up, facing the deadly old man whose ice-blue eyes stared pitilessly at him as he took his gun from its holster and dropped it on the floor. "This is very interesting reading, indeed. Just when do Mariano's men plan to kill Juarez—while he's enroute from El Paso or after he arrives in Chihuahua City?"

Encarnación chuckled. It was a cold, mirthless sound. "Now that the secrecy of our activities is in question, I imagine the deed will have to be postponed until we can learn how much the rebels know."

"About your agent in their midst?" Fortune asked, reassembling the papers into a neat stack and sliding them back into their hiding place. Somehow he had to deal with Vargas and escape undetected before anyone else learned that he had been spying on the conspirators.

The old don's silver eyebrows rose. "So, you've learned about Emelio, too."

"The Americans have a vested interest in seeing Juarez stays alive. They know about Emelio and they'll stop him." *If I can get the information to McQueen.*

"You disgust me, a *criollo*, *patrón* of a great hacienda, throwing your lot in with a band of common thieves, scum of the lowest sort. You're a traitor to your class." Vargas' expression was arrogantly contemptuous.

"And you, Don Encarnación, are a traitor to your country. In a feckless attempt to keep your class privileges, you'll see Mexico dismembered and destroyed."

Encarnación bristled. "I should shoot you down like the dog that you are."

"I don't think so," Fortune replied softly. "The shot will awaken your other guests, who would ask embarrassing questions." As he spoke, Nicholas inched his way around the desk and slung one leg casually across the corner, sitting on the edge of the heavy mahogany top. His hand rested behind him, fingers groping carefully for the heavy crystal paperweight amid the clutter. He would only have one chance.

The don shrugged. "I will simply say I mistook you for a thief in the darkness. A most regrettable accident."

He raised the pistol slightly but before Fortune could act, Mercedes' voice broke the silence. "No! You will not kill him!" She grabbed his arm and held on. He struggled to free the weapon, slapping her hard on one cheek. Mercedes did not relinquish her hold.

Nicholas dashed across the wide room but just as he seized Encarnación, the gun fired, the shot muffled by flesh. *Dear God, let it not be Mercedes*! But then the old man began to sink slowly to his knees in front of the horror-struck woman.

She knelt beside him, staring at the widening red stain on his chest with disbelief. "May God and all His saints forgive me, I've killed a man," she choked out, looking up at her lover. "For a Juarista spy, a traitor to the emperor!"

"You didn't kill him, I did," Nicholas replied. The pain of her accusation stung, but there was no time now. He pulled her to her feet, saying, "When I grabbed hold of his arm, I turned the gun so he shot himself. It wasn't you."

She was dazed with shock. "What are you doing?" He seized an expensive gold letter opener and several other valuables and stuffed them quickly in his pockets as he rushed her toward the courtyard door.

"Let whoever finds him think he surprised a thief. That's what Encarnación planned to claim when he shot me." Scooping up his gun from the floor, he dragged her through the doors, leaving them ajar. Already he heard the sounds of voices questioning the deafening report of the shot. There were only moments to get safely back to their room and the only way to accomplish it was by climbing the trellis on the balcony. He raced down the long porch past the hammocks and covered birdcages until he found a sturdy wooden lattice covered with thick bougainvillea vine.

"Hike up your skirts," he said in a harsh whisper, then climbed up several steps and reached down for her.

She and Agnes had done this to return to their rooms after the duel, but then she had been wearing a heavy riding habit and boots. The splintery wood cut into her tender arches through her soft slippers and the branches snagged the sheer muslin of her dress. She struggled to climb as he pulled her up behind him. Then he swung onto the tiled portico roof and reached down to help her up.

In moments the courtyard was dotted with servants carrying torches. A cry of alarm had gone up. Someone must have found Encarnación's body, but no one thought to look for the thief reentering the great house. They made it back to their room by climbing on the balcony and slipping inside just as a knock sounded on their door.

"A thousand pardons, Don Lucero, but are you and your lady unharmed?" a servant's voice asked from the hallway.

Nicholas mumbled as if awakened from a sound sleep, motioning for Mercedes to climb beneath the covers while he ripped off his boots and pants and yanked his robe on over his shirt. Rumpling his hair, he opened the door, bleary-eyed. "What the hell is going on?" he asked indignantly.

"I was told there was a thief in Don Encarnación's study and I was to make certain none of the guests were harmed."

"As you can see, we are perfectly fine," Nicholas said crossly, slamming the door just after the sharp-eyed servant looked across his shoulder to see Mercedes huddled in the center of the bed, clutching the covers up to her chin.

After the footfalls echoed down the hall, he turned back to her, dreading the accusation in her eyes.

"Why?" was all she could choke out. She remained perfectly still, holding the heavy bedspread over her body like a shield, her small hands fisted whitely against the dark velvet.

He combed his fingers through his hair and slumped down into a chair across from her, waiting to see if she would say more—accuse him of being an impostor as well as a spy. But she did not. Big, dark, golden eyes searched his face. Her expression was haunted and bewildered more than angry now. He decided the truth—at least a part of the truth—would serve him best.

"During the war I fought against the Juaristas. I killed them—hell, I butchered them. Not only the soldiers, but old men and beardless boys armed at best with primitive muskets that misfired more often than not. They used them as clubs. They used machetes against modern breechloaders and repeating rifles. They even fought with their bare hands. No matter how great their losses, they never surrendered."

"They're led by a band of godless men, liberals who want to abolish religion! Look what they've done with Church lands." Angrily she threw back the covers and climbed from the bed to face him.

"I don't think Juarez or any of the other republican liberals are godless or that they planned to destroy the Church."

"They confiscated Church lands," she continued stubbornly.

"Yes. In a misguided attempt to give it to the peons. It was hardly as if the Church didn't have it to spare," he replied dryly. "They own nearly half the farmable land in the country. Do you know who ended up benefiting most of all? Not the peons, who couldn't afford to purchase it even at the very cheap price for which it was offered. The great *hacendados* were the ones who grabbed up the land. So much for the imperial sympathizers championing the cause of religion," he scoffed. "Do you think they'll give it back to the Church any sooner than Juarez would?

"I listened to Don Encarnación and his fellow conspirators plot, Mercedes. They care nothing for the Church, nothing for Mexico, or that poor fool Maximilian. They only want to preserve their own wealth and privilege. They plan to assassinate Juarez and throw the republican camp into chaos, then break the northern states away from Mexico to form their own little kingdom."

She digested that information with growing horror. "It simply cannot be. Men of such stature, to betray their emperor, their nation." She shook her head. "I can't believe they are more treacherous than those vile rabble who plunder and kill across Mexico in the name of their republic. Juaristas are murderous bandits, cutthroats, the worst dregs of society. I've heard stories about how they rob travelers, loot haciendas and rape innocent women."

He gave a harsh laugh and stood up, pacing across the room like a caged jungle cat. "You think the imperials were any better? I fought with the regular army as well as the *contre-guerrillas*. Believe me, they're no different—except the imperials are better armed . . . and wear fancier uniforms." He turned slowly and stared into her eyes. His face was contorted with an anguish that hardened his chiseled features to stone. He spoke with tight-lipped fury.

"I've seen officers—fine *criollo* officers—take a republican town and then turn the men loose on the innocent civilians. That fat French pig Bazaine is as ruthless as Attila the Hun and he's loosed Leonardo Marquez. Do you know what Marquez does, Mercedes? He uses babies for bayonet practice!"

She was taken aback at his anger, but even more so with his despair. The horrors he had lived through were beyond her ability to imagine. "Isolated at Gran Sangre we heard rumors about the French, but I never credited them as true. They came as our saviors."

"They're foreign plunderers just as much as the Americans were in 1846. The French placed a pair of foreign wastrels on the throne of Mexico—Maximilian spends millions on castles and parks while the countryside is ravaged by war. He rides in gilded coaches lined with silk and ermine. Juarez, at least, would not squander what little remains of Mexico's wealth on personal aggrandizement."

"But he's an Indian, a man without a birthright, nobody. How can he aspire to such a lofty station?"

Nicholas recoiled as if she had spit on him. *A man without a birthright. Nobody.* An overreacher just as he was. "Juarez was elected under the constitution of the land. He has the legal right to rule Mexico," he replied coldly. His own dark eyes met the proud golden glitter of hers.

But you know I have no legal right to you, don't you, querida?

Mercedes studied him, realizing there was much more he had not said. "And so you switched sides, became a traitor to the emperor for Juarez. Have you done it only to stop Vargas' conspiracy or have you always sided with the republicans? How long have you been spying for Juarez?" She wanted to remain angry so she would not have to think about his real identity.

He did not reply to her questions, but rather posed one in return.

"Will you turn me in?" His voice was soft as he reached out to take a lock of her gold hair in his hand.

Against her will, she stepped toward him as he held the glistening curl, rubbing it between his fingers. Mercedes could feel the heat of his body, so lean and hard, scarred by this war in which he had now become the enemy. But he was still the man she loved, whose child she carried. When she had seen old Encarnación about to shoot him her heart had stopped beating. "You are my husband," she said carefully, still not daring to touch him. "I have killed a man to save you, so I suppose I'm a traitor now, too."

"So noble, my loyal little wife." There was a faint mocking irony in his tone, but the smile that played on his lips was bittersweet. "I love you, Mercedes. Believe that, even if you believe nothing else," he said as he pulled her into his arms.

She went willingly, desperate to feel the warm solid wall of his flesh, alive and whole after their terrifying brush with death. His mouth came down on hers and what began as a gentle kiss swiftly turned savage. He plied her lips with his own and she opened for him, meeting the glide of his tongue, digging her fingers into his hair and pulling him down to her, closer, closer.

* * *

Mariano Vargas closed the door to his father's study and felt the silence descend. He was at last alone. Staring down at the bloodstained spot on the floor where his father's body had lain, he considered what to do. Had the old man stumbled on a thief who escaped, as everyone surmised? Or was there a far more sinister reason for his death?

Crossing the room, he stepped around to the back of the big wooden desk and pulled open the secret compartment. The papers were neatly stacked inside the small drawer, just as he had left them . . . or were they? He carefully removed them and began to check the order in which they were placed. Someone had reshuffled two of the pages, he was certain.

Cursing softly, he replaced the papers and closed the drawer. Who could the spy be? A servant? Highly unlikely for all their retainers had been with the House of Vargas since birth. Mariano was certain of their loyalty. No, the intruder who killed his father must be a guest. Quickly he ticked off their visitors in his mind, dismissing all Don Encarnación's old friends as well as his own. Then he paused, remembering the hard-looking young Alvarado heir who had killed von Scheeling with such professional dispatch.

Mariano stroked his chin consideringly. Difficult to believe old Don Anselmo's heir could be a filthy Juarista, but who among the others was as much of a cipher—and who else had done such a foolish thing as let go two poachers caught red-handed stealing hacienda beef? He poured himself a glass of fine French brandy and sat down in his father's chair.

"No, it's my chair now," he murmured to himself, taking a slow sip from the glass and letting the mellow liquor roll around on his tongue. It was time to plan what he would do to deal with Lucero Alvarado.

By late morning word of the tragic death of Don Encarnación had spread through the hacienda. The fiesta ended abruptly and all the guests departed for home, leaving Don Mariano and Doña Ursula to their grief.

As they rode toward Gran Sangre Nicholas remarked to Mercedes, "Old Don Encarnación's only heir did not appear all that distraught to me. Everything in life seems to leave Mariano untouched."

Mercedes shivered, remembering the awful scene in the old man's study. She had killed a man for her lover. What else would she do for him? *I've sacrificed my very soul for him and I don't even know his name*!

Forcing back the unthinkable, she turned her attention to Don Mariano and his wife. "You're right about Mariano. I've never seen a man so . . ." she groped for the right word, "emotionless."

"Quite unlike his father," Nicholas said dryly, recalling Don Encarnación's legendary *criollo* temper.

"Well, his wife certainly displayed enough emotion and none of it appropriate. She was obviously petulantly angry that the great celebration she was to reign over had to be cut short."

Nicholas chuckled. "Just think, she'll have to wear drab black gowns for a whole year. She's not at all good at concealing her feelings. Mariano is . . . that is, if he *has* any."

At last she worked up her courage to ask, "What are you going to do with the information you've gathered?"

He did not look at her but stared at the horizon. Canyons lined with cedar corkscrewed off to the north while patchy stretches of tough desert grasses, now gray-green in the dry season, stood clumped over the widening valley that led toward the Yaqui River. A harsh, unforgiving land. Home. Finally he answered her question. "There's an agent for the president waiting at a prearranged place on Gran Sangre. I'll tell him what I've learned." He looked at her then, trying to read her reaction as he added, "I've seen the man who's betraying Juarez to the conspirators."

"Do what you must, I cannot prevent you."

"No, you cannot . . . unless you want to see me dead," he replied, his voice flat. What more was there to say? She held his life in her small hands, but even more precious than that was the future they could have together with the child they had created. Was it all to prove chimerical? A dream far beyond his reach? Nicholas feared and hoped at the same time.

They rode in silence while she studied their armed escorts, wondering who among the men raised on ancient Alvarado land might also be traitor to it. How blind she had been. She was probably surrounded by men who agreed with her lover's politics, for after all, they had far more to gain in the revolution than he did. But regardless of that, she knew in her heart that she could never betray the man riding beside her. She loved him above honor or life itself.

The following day when they arrived at Gran Sangre, Nicholas saw that Mercedes was taken under Angelina's care after the long ride. Although her bouts of morning indisposition had abated and she seemed in the bloom of health, he feared for the delicate woman carrying his child. Although they had slept together on the trail, curled securely like two spoons beneath the blankets, she had remained troubled and reticent since the violent death of Don Encarnación.

Once Mercedes was upstairs soaking in her bath while the old cook brewed her herbal tea, he headed to the corral for a fresh horse to make the short ride into San Ramos. With luck he would be there and back by nightfall if Porfirio Escondidas was a man of his word. Hilario greeted his *patrón* warmly but made no inquiry about the success of his mission at Hacienda Vargas.

"I will saddle you that fine black we captured last fall. I have been working him and I think you will be pleased with the results," the old man said with pride.

"Bring the black up. I'll get my saddle," Nicholas replied, turning to the long row of stalls where Peltre was peacefully eating now that he had been rubbed down. "Pity I can't ride you, boy, but you've earned a rest," he said to the gray, rubbing his nose as the horse observed him through liquid intelligent eyes.

He gathered his gear, checked his Henry rifle and repacked his saddlebags. San Ramos was a republican village but the roads were always dangerous for a man alone. Just as he swung his saddle off the stall bar and turned around with it hoisted over his shoulder, Mercedes appeared in the doorway.

She was dressed in a peach silk robe, her hair still damp and curling from her bath. Her arms were wrapped around her waist and she stood very still. Hesitant and nervous, she looked at him, so tall and forbidding, with the heavy saddle slung so carelessly across his shoulder. Alkaline dust from their long ride still coated his clothing and clung to his skin. Those steady wolf's eyes gazed at her hungrily, but he said nothing.

Nicholas could smell the lavender scent from her hair and ached to touch the damp softness of her skin at the open throat of her robe. A pulse beat rapidly and he could see her swallow for courage before speaking.

"You're going to meet the Juarista, aren't you?"

"I said I would. Time is crucial. Mariano may suspect he's been found out. He's no fool."

"But he is dangerous. Don't go. Please, let the war be over for us."

"I've already explained why I can't do that," he said patiently.

She took a deep breath. He was not her husband yet she gave herself willingly to him, had forgiven his treason, had even killed for him. And now he repaid her love by going off to risk his life for a cause and a man she could not begin to understand. "You told me you were sick of war, of the killing."

He could hear the plea beneath the accusation in her voice and it broke his heart. "I am, but the killing will never end if Vargas isn't stopped."

"Let someone else stop him. You said you would always protect me—never leave me to go off to war again!"

"This is different. I have to deliver the information," he replied doggedly.

"Send one of the vaqueros to meet your spy. I know there are men at Gran Sangre who are Juaristas."

"This is my assignment, I'm afraid." Could he dare to tell her about McQueen, about his bargain with the Americano? He longed to, but her next words squelched the impulse.

Stepping closer and placing her hands against his chest she said, "Please, Lucero, do this for me . . . your wife."

Lucero. Your wife. So, the unspoken charade must continue. The truth of his identity brought out in the open would destroy their fragile relationship. He could not bear that. "I love you more than anything, Mercedes, but there are reasons why I have to go. Reasons I can't tell you." *You know why I dare not speak of it.*

"No, you can't. And I can't forgive you for leaving me this way either. Go risk your life for Juarez. Join the enemy. I was willing to give up my principles for you, but I see you aren't willing to do the same for me."

She pushed him away from her and tried to run from the stable but he caught her wrist and pulled her back into his arms, more roughly than he had intended. "I can't abandon the republicans—don't you think I would if in conscience I could?" His voice was tight with anger now and his whole body felt stretched taut as a noose drawn around a hanged man's neck. He could feel her stiffening in his arms, frightened of his violence yet trying to hide her fear beneath a veneer of cool haughty control.

"Let me go," she whispered, biting off each word.

His arms dropped away from her. She spun free and ran from the stable. Nicholas did not go after her. What was there to say? As if his impersonation of Lucero were not enough to contend with, now they were divided by loyalties to opposing causes. He would deliver his information to Escondidas and pray once the traitor in Juarez's camp was dealt with that McQueen would not ask more from him. Once the little man of law had returned to Mexico City, perhaps he and Mercedes could rebuild their lives together here in the isolation of the north.

The ride to San Ramos went swiftly. It was a small, shabby village like thousands of others the length and breadth of Mexico. Dusty yellow adobe buildings squatted in clusters, blistered by the late afternoon sunlight. A mangy cur chased several squawking chickens across the bleak little plaza where a well promised relief for the traveler's parching thirst.

Nicholas rode up to the small cantina, the most likely place to find word of Porfirio Escondidas. Perhaps he was inside, seeking relief from the heat with a draught of pulque. Just as Fortune swung down from the big black stallion, a grimy youth missing several teeth smiled hopefully at him, brushing greasy strings of hair from his forehead.

"You are Don Lucero, no?"

Fortune nodded expectantly, then listened to the boy Calvo's directions. As Nicholas remounted, he tossed a silver coin to the youth.

Escondidas was camped about a mile outside the village in a dense stand of pines and junipers. Because of the untimely death of Don Encarnación, Nicholas was several days early. As luck would have it, Porfirio had just arrived that morning and instructed Calvo to wait in the plaza until a man answering Fortune's description arrived.

As he neared the dense brushy swale, he veered off the trail into a clearing in the undergrowth. It looked just as Calvo had described. He could smell the faint smoke emanating from a small campfire. As a precaution, he called out to Porfirio, identifying himself, and received an answering welcome.

The wiry little man was standing in front of his fire with a coffeepot in one hand. "You are early. I'd expected to spend several nights on the hard rocky earth. I am grateful. What have you learned?"

Fortune dismounted and took a cup of the inky black brew Escondidas poured for him. They hunkered down on opposite sides of the fire. Nicholas had almost finished his report on the assassination plan when a shot cracked the still twilight. Escondidas slumped backward as Fortune dove for cover while pulling his Remington from its holster. A hail of bullets followed him as he rolled behind a large boulder surrounded by scrub pines and sumac. He returned fire only once. With no time to waste seeing if Porfirio was dead or alive, he began to work his way through the dense underbrush, circling toward the place from which the shots had come.

Nicholas Fortune had spent the past fifteen years surviving in brutal hand-to-hand combat, crawling over terrain better suited to reptiles and rodents than to men. Twigs ripped his clothes and fallen pine needles punctured his skin but he noticed none of it. Moving with the silence and speed born of hard-earned experience, he listened for telltale sounds to reveal where the assassin or assassins had moved since suspending fire.

Then he heard the unmistakable sound of a boot crunching on loose gravel directly to his left. Darkness gathered. He knelt down silently, concealed behind a sumac bush. Then he heard the breathing, low and feral, coming from his right. There were two of them. He must get them both to one side of him lest he be caught in a crossfire. He selected several small stones, tossing them with a quick snap of his wrist in front of the man to his right.

"Julio! Here!" a voice cried out, moving toward the clatter. Julio grunted and emerged directly in front of Fortune's line of fire.

It took one swift lunge with his knife to bring Julio down, his throat slashed cleanly. Fortune quickly resheathed his knife and drew his pistol just as the other killer broke into the brushy enclosure. The pistolero raised his Colt with a startled oath but before he could squeeze off a shot, Nicholas had fired twice. The impact of the .44 caliber slugs sent the second assassin hurling back into the brush.

After checking to be certain both attackers were dead, Fortune made his way back to Porfirio, who lay ominously still by the side of the smoldering fire. Kneeling, he examined the wound in the young man's chest, taking a handkerchief and pressing it to staunch the bleeding.

"No use, it is no use," Escondidas rasped, his hand grasping Fortune's arm with amazing strength. "You have to get to Juarez, tell him what you told me. Stop the assassination."

"Where is he? How do I find him?" Fortune asked, as the blood continued to seep from his companion.

''Go to Arizpe. Ask for Martin Regla at the Three Owls Cantina. He will take you to Juarez.''

''Is the president still in El Paso?'' Fortune asked, aghast at the prospect of traveling over three hundred miles to complete his mission.

''Regla will know,'' Porfirio replied raggedly and began to cough up blood.

''What about McQueen? Why can't I give this information to him? He's the one who recruited me.''

''Your *gringo*, he is like the wind. No one knows where he is or when he will turn up. Go to Arizpe, quickly, before it is too late. Long live Mexico!''

With that, Porfirio Escondidas' head slumped onto his chest. He lay dead in Nicholas Fortune's arms.

Fortune cursed savagely. He could return to Gran Sangre and dispatch Gregorio Sanchez in his place, but it would mean the loss of another half day. And Sanchez could not identify Vargas' spy in the Juarez camp, nor had the green youth experience enough to be able to recount all the details Nicholas had learned or to clarify their tactical significance for the president.

There was nothing to do but to ride north as hard and fast as he could.

Would Mercedes ever forgive him for this desertion? The soughing night wind held no answers as he rose and began to kick dirt onto the campfire until the bright flames flickered and died.

Chapter 21

The night sky was studded by a million stars, as it could only be along the Texas-Mexico border. A cold wind gusted, raising small swirls of dust. Nicholas pulled up his collar to keep the stinging particles from his eyes. A thin quarter moon hung on the horizon. The night would keep his secrets as he rendezvoused with the man who held Mexico's fate in his hands.

Juarez's headquarters was situated at the outskirts of El Paso del Norte. Fortune had ridden for nearly two weeks to reach the border, guided by a succession of Juaristas, mostly taciturn peasants who doubtless wondered why a *hacendado* had sided with their cause. He smiled grimly as he approached the small rickety frame building, little more than a crude two-room settler's cabin. If only his compatriots had known who he really was and why he had taken up their cause, it might have broken their stoic mistrust.

A tall, cadaverously thin man with a badly pockmarked face stood sentry at the door of the cabin, his eyes flat and wary. "You are the *hacendado* from Sonora?" At Nicholas' nod of affirmation, the man stepped aside and opened the door. "The president has been expecting you."

The interior was spartanly furnished and amazingly clean considering the relentless scouring winds outside. The large table serving as a desk was the only piece of furniture. It was messy, covered with books, papers and documents. A small man with shoulder-length dark hair streaked with gray sat behind it drafting a letter by the light of a flickering branch of candles. Benito Juarez looked up and met the tall

Americano's eyes, then stood and offered a gravely courteous handshake.

"Good evening, Mr. Fortune, or should I call you Don Lucero?" His voice was measured and resonant. The president was a man used to weighing each word before uttering it.

"Since I 'volunteered' for your service only to keep Gran Sangre, I imagine Don Lucero would be more appropriate," Fortune replied, not without wry humor.

Juarez smiled, appreciating the irony of the situation, then gestured for Fortune to take a seat before reseating himself. "I understand you've ridden long and hard to bring me information of some importance."

"Porfirio Escondidas is dead. Ambushed by agents of Mariano Vargas, who is the real leader of the insurgents trying to kill you." Quickly and succinctly Nicholas outlined everything that had transpired at Hacienda Vargas, including the rendezvous between Mariano and the scar-faced man and the way Don Encarnación had died, concluding with the details contained in the papers he had found in the hidden compartment of the old man's desk. "I could look around your camp for the man who met Vargas," he offered.

"I already know who he is," the president replied gravely. The lines of his heavy features seemed deeper, his expression haunted by the betrayal. "Emelio Jarol. He was with me when I was governor of Oaxaca. It is . . . difficult to believe he could do this but time and war have ways of changing men." His liquid black eyes studied Fortune intently.

"If you're implying time and war have changed me, you're right. A year ago I would never have imagined being a landowner, much less a republican."

"And now you are both." It was not a question.

Fortune did not respond, but asked instead, "What are you going to do about Emelio?"

"Nothing, Don Lucero. Nothing at all—for now."

Nicholas stiffened, surprise and anger registering on his face. He was saddle-sore and too tired to think straight. "After nearly ending up bushwhacked with Escondidas and then coming all this distance, you mean to say you don't believe me?"

"What the president means, Don Lucero, is that we want Emelio Jarol to believe you never reached us with this information, that the conspirators' plans are still a secret. Then we'll tell him what we want him to know and use him to bait a trap for Don Mariano and his friends."

Nicholas turned around when he heard the familiar voice. "McQueen. I wondered when you'd crawl out of the woodwork again." He watched as the pale Americano moved out of the shadows and took a seat across from him.

"I thought you'd be an asset to us, Fortune, but even at that, you had the devil's own luck stumbling on those documents."

"Exactly how do you plan to convince Mariano Vargas and his friends that I never reached you?" Nicholas asked. A prickling sense of foreboding raced up and down his spine as McQueen almost smiled.

"You're going to disappear," McQueen replied affably.

"I'm going home to Gran Sangre," Fortune said firmly. "I kept my part of the bargain—went a hell of a lot of extra miles, in fact, to give you some very valuable information. Now I have a hacienda to run. Dozens of people are depending on me."

"Including the lovely Doña Mercedes?" McQueen's tone was mild but the implied threat was palpable.

Fortune stood up. "If you're planning to expose me as a *gringo* impostor, you're too late. She knows I'm not Lucero. So does his mother—and, rather obviously, so does Hilario." He walked over to McQueen, who remained seated, completely unruffled by the dangerous glint in Fortune's eyes. "I told you before, I don't take kindly to blackmail. And I told you I was through after I completed this assignment." His voice was soft and deadly.

Juarez, who had been observing the exchange between the two dangerous Americans in judicial silence, now stood up, tossing a sheaf of papers across his desk. "I have here, Don Lucero, orders for our march to Chihuahua City, beginning the first of the year. According to your information,

Vargas will strike after we leave the state capital, most probably near the Chihuahua-Durango border. If they believe you are dead, they'll go ahead with their plans—but if you return to Gran Sangre, they will change them. And"—he shrugged eloquently—"I might die. A small matter if it were only one man's life, but at this point in the war, I believe my death would throw the forces for constitutional government into disarray."

Juarez gazed serenely at Fortune.

"You have an annoying way of understating a case and still cutting directly to the heart of the matter," Nicholas said sourly. He felt for all the world as if he were the spoiled boy Luce, caught riffling the church poor box.

"Does that mean you'll remain in hiding while we arrange for word of your death to reach Mariano Vargas?"

Fortune sighed in defeat. With an oath he said, "Yes. But I want to send word to Mercedes that I'm alive. She's with child and I don't want to frighten her."

McQueen started to object but the president raised his hand. "I will send a trusted messenger to her." Benito Juarez, who had a wife and large family living in exile in the United States, understood how hard war was on women and children.

JANUARY 1867

Mexico City was still festive but the frenetic gaiety was born of desperation. Brilliantly uniformed French and Austrian troops still drilled on the Zocolo, but everyone knew General Bazaine had received his orders to evacuate the capital shortly after the first of the year. Foreign embassies for the most part remained open, but many European diplomats started sending their families home.

At Chapultepec Castle the court festivities took on a tense, somber undertone in spite of the more lavish and hedonistic displays at balls, masquerades and picnics on the castle grounds outside the city. With the prim censure of Carlotta now removed, Maximilian's sycophants celebrated in his lavishly redecorated palace as if each day were their last. And their days were numbered.

Eighteen sixty-six had waned to an inglorious close for the Empire of Mexico with all the major seaports on both coasts as well as every northern capital city falling to the Juaristas. In the south, the bishop of Oaxaca petitioned General Diaz asking what clemency he might expect if he surrendered, to which the triumphant Juarista general had replied, "I'll shoot you in your golden robes."

Then word from Paris reached the emperor that his wife had gone mad. Always driven and insecure, the empress had broken down in the midst of an audience with Napoleon III. She had been placed under physical restraint after a series of interviews with the French emperor and his Holiness Pope Pius IX. Maximilian vacillated. Should he fight on or should he abdicate and go to Carlotta's side? His indecisiveness left his courtiers in a quandary. Some were fearful, others cynically determined to take advantage of the "Austrian Dreamer" for as long as he lasted. After all, there was still considerable wealth remaining in the imperial treasury.

One such pragmatic individual was General Leonardo Marquez, a military advisor instrumental in persuading the emperor to stay in Mexico after the impending French evacuation. The Tiger of Tacubaya was a short, intense man with burning black eyes and a cunning yellow-toothed smile. At the moment, he stood surveying a sheaf of papers and gazing across the Zocolo from the balcony of the imperial palace.

"The way I see it, we have perhaps six weeks to wait before Bazaine leaves. Then"—he shrugged eloquently—"it is in the hands of the gods."

His companion threw back his head and laughed heartily. "You mean the imperial treasury will be in the hands of the tiger!"

Marquez regarded his young subordinate with desultory fascination. Tossing the documents he held onto the top of an ornately carved oak table, he prowled languidly across the room, approaching Colonel Lucero Alvarado, who had by now earned his own nickname, El Diablo. Luce had become a satanic figure who dressed entirely in black, riding a great ebony stallion through the hearts of Juarista villages bringing terror and death.

"You want to be rich, Colonel? And here I believed you had joined the imperial cause for patriotic reasons."

There was a sly teasing note in Marquez's voice that grated on Lucero's nerves, but he let it pass. The general was his key to escaping what was rapidly becoming an untenable situation. "I'm as much a patriot as you, my general," he replied baldly, raising a glass of fine French cognac to his lips.

Now it was Marquez's turn to laugh. "Well said. Why do we fight then, if not for love of Mexico?"

"Silver?" Lucero ventured.

Marquez poured himself a crystal goblet of the cognac. "I don't think so—at least not you. No, you enjoy the thrill of danger, the blood sport of war. You enjoy it far more than I and they named me the tiger. You are the very devil. What demons drive you, I wonder?"

Alvarado's voice was flat when he replied, "Best not to tempt the devil, my general."

"And the devil you are. Wrapping that Juarista general up in wet rawhide and letting the skin dry in the sun was an inventive touch worthy of me. The life was squeezed out of Aranga ever so slowly as it tightened."

"You were my inspiration," Luce replied dryly. "A pity the general didn't talk before he died. That silver shipment his soldiers stole from the imperial army would have been well worth recovering."

"There is a good deal more in Maximilian's storerooms, believe me. After the French are gone, it won't be long before his dithering will deliver him into the hands of his enemies. Already he's considering a strategic move of his 'Mexican Army' to Querétaro, a more defensible position against Escobedo's armies."

Alvarado noted his chief's thinly veiled gloating satisfaction. "And you, of course, concurred that the capital is unfortifiable and the best place to make a stand is at Querétaro."

"We couldn't let the republican rabble lay ruin to all these splendid buildings our emperor has refurbished. What if they bring up siege guns? The *gringos* have supplied them with some formidable weapons, after all."

"So, Maximilian leaves and his treasury remains behind . . . with you to guard it." Luce's smile was sharkish.

"Alas, I won't be able to convince him to let me stay, since he expects a great pitched battle and wants all his generals united under his command, but I'll find a way to return here when the time is ripe, believe me."

"You can assign me to permanent duty here." Luce waited expectantly for Marquez's response.

"I don't think that would be wise right now. You have acquired a rather, shall we say, unsavory reputation in central Mexico over the past few months. If you hadn't captured General Aranga, I would never have been able to secure your promotion."

Luce's eyes flashed dangerously as he stared at the shorter, older man. "I did no more to earn my name than you did yours at Tacubaya. You had an entire city decimated and turned the women over to your troops as spoils of war. I'm leading guerrilla fighters, desperate mercenaries who expect plunder. The emperor hasn't exactly been prompt with payrolls of late. Something about the Juaristas capturing too many of the supply trains."

The general waved his hand dismissively. "Yes, yes, so you give them their booty in the form of women and allow them to loot churches and local shopkeepers. Well and good, but you've been so efficient at your job the Juaristas have placed a price on your head. Your rather ingenuous method of execution for Aranga was the final straw for Diaz. The two men were old comrades at arms. I fear Diaz's army is moving north with alarming rapidity, and he has promised to personally see to your execution."

Luce cursed. "Peasant scum! Mixed-blood mongrels. We'll be long gone from Mexico with a fortune in silver before Diaz and his ragtag army ever reach the capital."

"Colonel, I see I must speak a bit more bluntly. At the moment you are a liability. Even some of my comrade generals on the emperor's staff would not mind seeing you stand before a firing squad. Capturing the enemy's generals is commendable. Torturing them to death is not . . . at least for some of the more 'civilized' members of Maximilian's staff. For now, I want you to retire someplace obscure. Someplace I can reach you when the time is ripe."

"I know the emperor has forbidden me to show my face at court." Luce's expression was bitter. "I didn't expect you to insist on my utter banishment."

"Hardly that, my boy, hardly that," Marquez soothed languidly. "I have great need of your peculiar skills. The treasury is well-guarded and your men are loyal only to you as well as being the most ruthlessly effective of the *contre-guerrillas*. I should hate to have some Juarista sniper—or anybody's sniper—pick you off before we're able to achieve our goal."

Luce regarded his mentor with interested black eyes, their irises glowing like molten silver. There was a pregnant pause. Then he replied with a careless shrug, "Very well. I'll return to my ancestral hacienda to while away a month or two. God knows it's isolated enough to be a perfect hideout. I wonder how my brother and my—or perhaps I should say *our*—poor little bride will react to my homecoming?" he asked with rhetorical amusement.

The year ended and a new one began with the rhythm of everyday life little changed on Gran Sangre. Crops were harvested and livestock fattened after the luxurious winter rains. Sonora settled once again into isolated tranquillity now that the Juaristas were finally in control of Hermosillo and Guaymas.

Mercedes arranged to sell a small herd of cattle to a merchant in Hermosillo for a tidy profit. The household ran smoothly. But everyone wondered about their absent *patrón*. His lady had been bereft since he had ridden away over two months ago. No one believed he had rejoined the emperor's cause, but they wondered when he would return.

All but Hilario and the Juaristas who worked at the hacienda. And Mercedes. She had received word that he was on the border with Juarez and that any reports she heard regarding his death were fabrications. She was to communicate with no one. Taking orders from the republicans galled every principle with which she had been raised. Yet to refuse might well sign her love's death warrant. That she could never do.

Mercedes sat in the library clutching the letter from him. She had read and reread it until the paper was crumbling. He had signed it, "Your husband." Nothing else. "It's almost as if he can't bear to use Lucero's name anymore," she whispered brokenly.

Who was he, this stranger who fought on the side of her enemies? And what frightening intrigue was he involved in that kept him away from his land—the land he had labored so long and hard to rescue from destruction? He was responsible for their well stocked larder, the sleek fat steers in the pasture and the splendid horses that Hilario and his men were preparing to sell as riding stock. And he was gone.

Will he ever return? The thought of losing him terrified her as she scanned the terse sentences on the frayed paper, trying to read between the lines once more.

> My dearest Mercedes,
>
> Please forgive me for not returning at once. I had thought to conclude my business in the north quickly, but it simply cannot be done. I bitterly regret our argument upon parting. Please understand that I had no choice but to leave. As soon as I can return, I will explain everything to you. Then you will have to decide whether or not you still love me. I pray for the sake of our child, as well as my own, that you will. You may hear reports that I have been killed en route to El Paso del Norte. They are false. I can say no more now. Only trust me for a little while. After that, it is in the hands of God. Never forget I love you.
>
> Your husband

It was a plea for her forgiveness—not only for joining the Juaristas, but for assuming Lucero's identity. There was no way to deny or suppress it any longer. Mercedes could not call him Lucero anymore either. He said he was going to explain everything when he returned. But did she want to hear his explanations? Could she bear to have out in the open what until now had been cloaked in darkness?

Mercedes tried to pray with little success. Like murderous King Claudius in *Hamlet*, she felt her prayers flung back from heaven. She was the most heinous sinner, hopelessly in love with a man who was not her husband, an adulteress who carried a bastard child—and loved it with a fierce joy that no child of Lucero's could ever have given her.

She should confess her sin to Father Salvador, but how could she? The priest would demand that she never again lie with her love, that she denounce him to the world. He would be arrested, imprisoned, shot. The very thought made her shudder. No, there could be no solace in the confessional for her. She longed for his return with a fervor that was sheer agony, yet at the same time she dreaded it.

Sleeping alone at night made her feel such desolation that she had taken to reading into the early morning hours before retiring. His magical touch, the heat of his body curved protectively around her, the blissful oblivion that came in the culmination of lovemaking—she missed desperately. But more than anything, she missed his voice, his laughter, his companionship. He was both lover and friend. And the father of her child—a stranger.

Her belly had begun to swell now. Angelina fussed over her, yet understood her grieving. Everyone waited for the *patrón's* return, eager to greet him with joyous celebration. Only Mercedes knew the reckoning that must eventually come.

Their bittersweet idyll was over.

Mariano Vargas reined in his horse and scanned the rocky terrain ahead of him nervously. His men had discarded the gaudy Vargas livery in favor of the drab motley clothing worn by *contre-guerrillas*. They were hidden at the mouth of a steep arroyo that transected the ancient caravan route called *El Camino Real*, old Spain's royal road stretching all the way from New Mexico to Mexico City.

A faint plume of dust in the distance indicated the

approach of a sizable caravan. Among the wagons and riders was one small black carriage. Inside it rode the man Vargas was sworn to destroy.

Hernan Ruiz, who was a remarkably able rider in spite of his shattered right arm, reined in his mount beside Vargas. "Can we trust that infernal savage Emelio?"

Vargas adjusted the glass he was peering through and sighted in on the column emerging on the horizon. They were out in the open on a stretch of flat barren brushland, easily visible through the looking glass. "I see Juarez's carriage," he said triumphantly, handing the glass to his companion.

"I still don't like this, Mariano. Your father—"

"My father is dead," Vargas said flatly. "Killed by rabble like the ones who ride with that Indian. But soon they'll all die, too."

"Including that treacherous Emelio. I don't trust any man who would turn against his own kind."

Vargas shrugged cynically. "We paid him well. A pity he won't live to spend it."

"And you aren't concerned about young Alvarado?"

"After the two men of my father's failed to kill him, I sent word to General Mejia, who was most interested to learn of a *hacendado* turned traitor to the emperor. His men saw to it that Don Lucero never reached Juarez. I received a full report on his death."

"Juarez's old companion Emelio Jarol is still in his position of trust, that much is true," Ruiz said caustically.

"Now all we need do is dispatch those armed banditti accompanying Juarez."

Ruiz smiled with veiled contempt. "Ah, Mariano, my old friend, you are far better at intrigue than fighting. It is I and our soldiers who will engage the enemy. You will only watch." He turned his horse and issued crisp orders to the armed column.

Hernan's contemptuous remark caused a deep crimson stain to darken Vargas' face, but he remained hidden behind the safety of the rocks while Ruiz formed up the men and prepared to fire on the approaching party.

Inside Juarez's coach, Nicholas Fortune rode, his legs cramped from sharing the small space with Lieutenant Bolivar Montoya. The young officer to whom he had shown hospitality the preceding year seemed not at all surprised to find the *patrón* of Gran Sangre working for Juarez.

Indeed, after spending the past weeks with the little Zapotec Indian, Nicholas was coming to understand how the remarkable man had held a republic together virtually single-handedly since 1857. Juarez was a man of unswerving integrity and the highest devotion to duty, tireless in his work, shrewd and patient, pragmatic when he had to be, but never one to compromise his principles.

The republic was founded upon constitutional law and he was merely its executor, a man of simple tastes and hardy endurance. Juarez inspired those same qualities in the people who followed him and fought for him. Fortune thought wryly that he would once have laughed aloud at the absurd idea that he would fight for free. Yet here he was doing precisely that. No, he amended to himself, he wasn't fighting for free, he was fighting for freedom.

"It is fortunate for me that General Diaz sent me to report to the president at such a propitious time," Montoya said conversationally as they rode along.

Nicholas regarded him shrewdly. "There'll be a promotion in this for you, I assume."

Bolivar shrugged. "Perhaps, but think of the opportunity—how often does a man get to impersonate a president?" He brushed an imaginary speck of lint off his black frock coat and adjusted the stovepipe hat on his head.

Fortune wiped the sweat from his forehead with his shirt-sleeve, for it was stuffy in the small coach. "You don't resemble him at all."

Bolivar grinned. "Do you think those assassins will get close enough to know before we spring our trap?"

"As Hamlet said, 'Timing is all.' That rocky ravine up ahead is the likeliest spot on the road. We have to hold them until our detachment can reach us to finish them off."

"This should buy us some time, I think," Montoya said, patting the Gatling gun on the floor between them.

The gun and Fortune had been hidden in the coach before they set out from Chihuahua City, where the real Juarez remained. Montoya, disguised in the president's clothes, face concealed beneath the turned-down hat brim, had publicly entered the coach for the next long leg of the ride to Durango. They were nearing the border between the two states.

Suddenly a shot rang out and the cry went up. Montoya flung open the door of the coach as it turned sideways in the road. Fortune leveled the multibarreled machine gun and opened fire on the large column of heavily armed men who sped toward them. The gun belched smoke and made a deafening noise in the confines of the carriage. Through the sulfurous clouds, the two men grinned at each other when the approaching riders went down in rapid succession like a stack of dominos toppled across a board.

Nicholas recognized Hernan Ruiz screaming orders to his men to retreat and regroup. "There's one of the ringleaders, but where is that crafty fox Vargas?" he muttered, studying the chaos outside. Then he saw a horseman emerge from the mouth of the arroyo and ride hell-bent in the opposite direction. Shouting at Montoya, Fortune jumped from the opposite side of the carriage, yelling, "Don't shoot me by accident, for Christ's sake!"

All around him the small detachment of Juarista soldiers who had accompanied the coach had taken cover behind what scant ocotillo and sage there was along the sides of the road. Some lay behind their felled horses which served as a breastwork from which to return fire. Their reinforcements had come riding from the east and cut off what was left of Ruiz's men, who were now pinned between the two bodies of soldiers, well outnumbered.

Fortune seized the reins of a horse as it pranced nervously after its rider had been shot from the saddle. He swung up on the animal and kicked it into a wild gallop, dodging between men who were now engaging in close combat with sabers and pistols.

"Come on, Mariano. It isn't sporting to leave your own party this way," he muttered as he cleared the fight zone and bent low over the bay's neck, urging the big horse to greater speed.

Vargas was well-mounted but not much of a rider, Fortune concluded within the first minutes of pursuit. The terrain was increasingly hilly and rough as they rode farther south. Vargas, afraid of the patches of catclaw and junipers alongside the road, remained on the carriage trail, but with each sharp rise, he lost ground to his pursuer.

Realizing that he was being chased, he turned to see who it was and blanched incredulously, then drew a pistol and fired. Bouncing on horseback, he missed by a wide margin. Don Lucero drew closer. Desperation drove Vargas to rein in and yank his rifle from its scabbard, but before he could raise it to take aim, his foe was upon him.

They crashed to earth when Nicholas leaped from his galloping horse onto Mariano, wresting the rifle from his grasp. The ground was hard when they landed, and Fortune was on the bottom, taking the brunt of the crushing fall against his right shoulder. Vargas rolled away, panting for breath, his eyes searching frantically for the lost weapon before realizing in his terror that he still had several shots remaining in the pistol strapped to his hip.

With a grimace he drew it and fired. Nicholas rolled to the left while at the same time drawing his own gun. Two more shots rang out. Vargas missed. Fortune didn't.

Scratched and breathless, his right arm still numb from the fall, Nicholas struggled to his feet. Another shot, this time from a rifle, echoed from the hilltop behind him. He felt the dull powerful jolt, familiar to him after all the times he had been hit before. *This one is bad, bad as I've ever taken . . .*

As Fortune crumpled to the hard rocky earth of *El Camino Real*, he saw Lieutenant Bolivar Montoya shoot Hernan Ruiz. The lieutenant would indeed be promoted after this adventure. Then while consciousness began to ebb slowly away he focused on thoughts of Mercedes. Her lovely face floated like a vision inside his mind. Only once before he died he longed to hear her speak his name.

Nicholas . . . Nicholas . . .

Chapter 22

Luce reined in and looked down on the old hacienda. His inspection brought a broad grin to his face. "You've been most industrious, brother mine." A herd of fat cattle grazed on the hillside and the corrals near the stables were filled with over a dozen splendid-looking horses, no doubt recaptured from his grandfather's Andalusian stock which had run wild during the war years. Even the big house itself had a fresh coat of whitewash and all the outbuildings, down to the peons' rude cabins, had been rebuilt and refurbished. Gran Sangre once again looked like a small prosperous kingdom.

"A pity the Juaristas will come and take it all away from you now that they've reclaimed the northern states," he murmured wryly. But that would be in the future—perhaps a year away. In the meanwhile, it was a good place for him to hide and enjoy life for a month or two until Marquez summoned him back to Mexico City.

The cry went up from down the road as he rode in. "The *patrón* has returned!" Their faces beaming, men and women called out, "Don Lucero!" Children ran up to his great black stallion, expecting to be greeted by name as was his wont over the past year. But he ignored them.

Riding arrogantly past, every inch the returning grandee, his eyes were fixed on the courtyard of the great house. So Nick was not at home and these fools believed he was his returning brother. A sly smile slashed his face as he thought of Mercedes. Would she know the difference? An amusing game. Idly he wondered how Nick had dealt with her since assuming his identity. How amazed everyone here would be to learn the truth.

Of course Nicholas Fortune had become *patrón* and might well resent the return of the legal heir, no matter that they had been comrades in arms and were brothers. And Nicholas Fortune was a dangerous man to anger. But then so was he. Would they fight over Cenci? Perhaps she would find it amusing to share two identical lovers.

Mercedes heard the outcry and was already on her feet. The basket of mending she had been working on dropped to the floor unheeded. Now advanced in her pregnancy, she had taken to resting in the afternoons, doing sedentary chores around the house. Would he think her shapeless and ungainly? Angelina had assured her she would grow a good deal more before the babe came, but her belly was visibly rounded now.

How could you not be beautiful to me carrying my child? His words washed over her like a soothing balm and joy deep and piercing set her heart to pounding as she ran toward the courtyard. Then something made her stop in the shadow of the arched doorway, watching him dismount. With a curt nod he handed Lazaro the reins, then strode toward the house. His expression was one of faint amusement, boredom, indolence.

Lucero!

"Miss me, beloved?" he drawled in a mocking voice, as his eyes swept over her from head to foot.

Wordlessly she stood rooted to the stone steps as waves of horror washed over her. Finally regaining her voice she managed to say, "Lucero."

"Yes, Lucero—your prodigal husband has returned at last, although I see Nick has attended to my husbandly duties in my absence," he replied, as his eyes fastened on her hand which rested protectively over the small swell of her belly.

Nick. Nicholas. So that was her lover's name—the man who had given her this child. The question leaped to her lips, *What is his name—his full name?* but she squelched it. Lucero would tell her in his own good time. She did not want him to know how desperately she loved the stranger with his face.

When he stalked closer and raised his hand to finger a lock of golden hair resting on her shoulder, Mercedes forced herself not to flinch. Lucero had always loved to play cat and mouse games. "Why did you return after all these years?"

Her eyes met his defiantly, darkest gold, molten with anger. "No longer the vaporish miss, are you? You've matured into a striking woman, Mercedes," he murmured, ignoring her question as his eyes studied the perfection of her aquiline features. "There's fire in you now. I can tell. I can always tell that about a woman. Do I owe it all to Nick?"

She slapped his hand away. "You're disgusting! You sent another man—a stranger—to pose as my husband!"

"And I notice you didn't refuse him your bed in spite of that fact," he replied dryly.

Her face flushed but she met his mocking eyes steadily. "At first I didn't know. You were gone for four years and we scarcely came to know each other during the brief weeks of our betrothal and marriage."

"Yet you continued to give yourself to him after you learned the truth, didn't you?" His voice was silky.

She ignored the taunt, fortifying herself with fury. "He earned the birthright you spurned, He did what you weren't man enough to do." The instant the words escaped her lips, she realized her mistake.

His lips thinned in anger and those black wolf's eyes glowed with a keen feral light. Then, abruptly his mood lightened and he threw back his head and laughed. "Nick certainly has a way with women. I wonder what effect he's had on Cenci? Is she by any chance pregnant, too?"

Mercedes knew he was waiting for her reaction, hoping to see hurt or anger. Instead it was she who laughed this time. "No. He found her overblown charms quite unappealing, as a matter of fact. She's working in the kitchens as a scullery maid."

Before he could reply to that startling bit of information a child's voice echoed in high piping notes from across the courtyard. "Papa, Papa, you're home! They told me you would come back to us!" Rosario ran into the shaded portico where the two adults stood facing each other with Bufón bounding behind her. The dog stopped at once a good four yards away from Lucero. His back ridged up and he let out a low rumbling growl.

"Oh, Bufón, don't be silly. This is Papa. You don't have to protect me," the child scolded.

If ever there had been the slightest doubt in Mercedes' mind about this man's identity, the animal's instinctive reaction would have quashed it. Before the dog attempted to attack Lucero, she juxtaposed herself between the two and issued a stern command. "Bufón, outside!"

Tail drooping, he turned and padded resentfully from the portico and down the steps.

Lucero looked incredulously at the child, noting her dark skin combined with the delicate features of a *criolla* and the unmistakable black eyes with the silver irises. "Well, I see that I left Cenci with a surprise before I rode away," he said, grinning. "I'm amazed my lady mother didn't banish her and her child."

Rosario stood between the adults, confused by her papa's words. Why didn't he pick her up and fly her around in circles like he usually did? Something was wrong. She found her thumb going back to her mouth for the first time in many months.

"Cenci isn't her mother. Rita Herrera was. She died in Hermosillo last summer."

"Amazing! Yes. I'd all but forgotten that Papa sent her away before we were betrothed. How does the child come to be here?"

Nothing the strange man was saying made any sense. Why did he look so much like her father? "You aren't my Papa," Rosario said, growing more confused and fearful by the moment.

"Your papa has been away a long while, Rosario. He's tired and—and he's been ill. You must let him rest now and we'll talk later," Mercedes placated, then turned and walked swiftly into the *sala*, calling for Angelina.

The old cook answered her summons at once, regarding Lucero with shrewd, troubled eyes. "Welcome back, Don Lucero." So this time the real Lucero had come home. Odd, but Angelina could not think of him as the *patrón*. "I have ginger cookies and cool lemonade for you," she said to Rosario, taking the child's hand. "Come and you can tell me about your lessons with Father Salvador while you eat."

As they disappeared down the hall, Mercedes turned back to Lucero and said, "Nicholas received word about Rita's death and didn't want Rosario raised alone in an orphanage. He brought her home." How strange it seemed to at last use her lover's real name.

Lucero lifted one eyebrow sardonically. "I'd never have thought a hardened mercenary like Nicholas Fortune would have a soft spot for children." He shrugged. "Maybe it's his own impending fatherhood. Where is he?"

Mercedes felt fear race its icy fingers up and down her spine in spite of the warm afternoon air. "He had to go away, to the border—to buy some breeding stock. We expect him back any time." Please, God and all the blessed saints, what would Lucero do when her love returned . . . if he returned.

A calculating expression washed over Lucero's handsome face. "I gather from the reception I received he's been gone some time. Perhaps some ill fate's befallen him. Will you mourn, beloved? For a man who's not your husband? For the father of your child?"

"You never gave a damn about my feelings before, Lucero. Why on earth should you care what I'll feel now?"

"Because you're *my* wife," he said coldly.

"Not any longer. You gave me away to a stranger. You arranged this whole thing, didn't you? You coached him about your family, the hacienda, the servants. He knew almost everything."

His mercurial mood shifted again and he smiled. "He's very clever. But still, I wondered if he could pull it off. It would seem he fooled everyone except you."

"Not everyone. Some of the servants know and I think your mother suspects."

"So the old crone is still alive. I'd hoped she'd gasped her last by now. A pity Papa had to die before her."

"He earned his death," she said coldly. "Doña Sofia will follow soon. She's taken a turn for the worse in the past week or so. Father Salvador has already given her the last rites."

"Ah, yes, that vile meddlesome old priest. The harpy in cassock skirts," he said bitterly. "So, he's taken to tutoring my bastard now, has he? Must've had a real change of heart. I'd never have believed he'd want to be in the same room with my get, even the legitimate variety."

"You're the one who's vile. What are you doing here, Lucero? Now that the war is going so badly for the emperor, have you decided to switch allegiance?"

He laughed mirthlessly. "If only I could. But then I'd have to rusticate here in this godforsaken wilderness, with only the brilliant entertainments of Hermosillo to entice me. You'll be relieved to hear I won't be staying long."

"Good. I'll have Baltazar draw you a bath. Dinner is at seven. You know the way to your room, of course."

"Of course," he echoed with a sharkish smile, then turned and strode casually toward the wide flat stairs that curved up to the second floor. Pausing with his hand on the heavy wrought-iron railing, he said, "Have Baltazar fetch me a decent brandy—that is, if there's anything left in Papa's cellar."

She nodded, then waited until he disappeared up the steps. The sick sour taste of bile rose in her throat. Sweet Virgin, how would she abide sitting across the dinner table from him? And how would she explain to Rosario why she could not join them as she always had before?

Rubbing her temples in misery, she started toward the kitchen, then froze in her tracks when another even more alarming thought occurred to her. What if he tried to claim his marital rights tonight? Without another moment's hesitation, she walked into the library and headed straight to the gun cases.

* * *

Dinner was hellish. Lucero studied her as she took each bite until finally her throat all but closed off. His eyes were so like Nicholas' eyes yet so different, for her love's glowed with passion while Lucero's held a dark feral cruelty. Heavy-lidded and slumberous, his gaze dropped from the curve of her breasts to her belly, then back up to her face, which was pale now.

She had chosen one of her most drab and demure gowns, a maize-colored batiste with the high waistline cut to accommodate her pregnancy. The sleeves were long and the neckline high, but there was no way to disguise the increasing heaviness of her breasts. She knew he was staring just to unnerve her. Defiantly she picked up her knife and stabbed it into the thick steak, carving off a long generous slice, then cutting it methodically into bite-sized pieces.

"Increasing seems to agree with your appetite," he observed, taking another sip from his wineglass. In spite of Angelina's excellent meal, Lucero drank more than he ate. Although he had already indulged in brandy during his bath, the wine he drank now did not appear to have an effect on him. "Don't *enciente* ladies usually have difficulty holding down their food?" he baited.

She took a bite of the succulent meat, chewed and swallowed, then met his eyes, knife and fork still clutched in her hands. "Only for the first month or so. After that we become quite voracious." She returned her attention to the meat.

He chuckled softly. "Whatever happened to the demure little miss I married?"

"A war," she snapped. "You rode away without a thought for me or the hacienda. You've never even cared about the vaunted Alvarado name."

He ran his fingertips around the rim of the wineglass, then took another drink and stared into the ruby contents swirling in the bottom of the crystal. "No," he said reflectively, "I suppose I haven't. I wanted to experience life, to have an adventure. Ah, beloved, what an adventure this war has been!"

Mercedes set down her utensils and studied him. His expression was eerily animated and his eyes blazed with excitement as he seemed to relive the fighting in his mind. *He enjoyed it*! "You actually get a thrill from killing, don't you?" she asked incredulously, remembering the shuttered loathing with which Nicholas always greeted any mention of the war.

He leaned across the table toward her, like a panther poised to leap. "Does that alarm you?" His voice purred with danger now.

She did not back off. "No," she said calmly. "It disgusts me. I've seen enough of war here in Sonora to know it's an ugly, cruel business. I've struggled to hold this hacienda together, against the rapacity of imperials and Juaristas. Soldiers! Bah, they're all banditti." Her voice was laced with contempt.

He leaned back indolently once again, holding the wineglass up in one hand, the wrist drooping languidly. But his eyes, lord above, those eyes glowed like live coals. "A woman of strong opinions, just like my dear *mamacita*."

"We're scarcely of the same opinion on any topic," she replied with asperity, forcing herself to ignore the aura of menace that surrounded him.

"Except your dislike of me—perhaps even loathing . . ." It was thrown out not as a question, but a taunt.

"I cannot speak for Doña Sofia." Her ambiguous reply answered itself. "Perhaps you should pay your respects."

"I will, in the fullness of time," he replied, his mood again shifting subtly.

Mercedes finished what she could of the excellent food on her plate. "If you'll excuse me, another trait of breeding females besides voracious appetites is that they tire easily." She rose from the table, but he did not rise with her or assist her with her chair as courtesy dictated.

Instead, he remained in the slouching pose, looking up at her. "Angelina will wonder why you haven't touched your flan," he said, obviously not caring in the least what any servant thought.

"I ate a good deal more than you did. Desserts are too rich for my palate. Good night." Mercedes turned and walked from the room in measured strides, spine straight, head held high. She did not look back. He made no attempt to follow.

Angelina would understand why she had little appetite. Eating the meat course was all she could manage in the covert war of wills she played with Lucero. Strange, now she called Lucero by name with ease when it had always come grudgingly to her lips addressing Nicholas.

Nicholas Fortune. An Americano? Most likely. That was the accent when he spoke English, not the distinct British pronunciation her mother had taught her. *I know his name but I know nothing else about him. Only that I love him.* Who was he and why had he struck such a bizarre bargain with Lucero? For the land? She would not have put it past Lucero to have told a tale about great wealth. Perhaps Nicholas had come thinking he would be able to live a life of privileged ease.

How ironic, for that was precisely what Anselmo had done, bleeding Gran Sangre dry for every last peso so he could while away the hours in Hermosillo. But Nicholas had worked harder than anyone to rebuild the hacienda. He loved the land and he had told her that he loved her. Could she believe him?

Troubled and exhausted, Mercedes was preoccupied as she made her way upstairs to tuck Rosario in. How would she explain Lucero's continued coldness to the daughter who loved Nicholas so? When she entered the girl's cheery little bedroom with its pink gingham curtains and brightly colored braided rug, Rosario was kneeling in front of the bed saying her prayers. Silently Mercedes paused in the doorway, not wishing to interrupt.

"Please, Lord Jesus, I'm sorry. I must've done wrong so that my papa went away. I don't know who the strange man is but he is not my papa. After my mama had to go to heaven you sent my papa to love me. Now he's gone. My lady Mercedes is good to me. If she were my mama, maybe I could bear to lose Papa. The good sisters said I must accept your will, but even you had a Mama and a Papa. Please let me have just one. I promise to be a good girl. Oh, and please take care of my real papa, wherever he is, even if he can't come home to me. Amen."

Mercedes felt the tears rolling down her cheeks. No one could ever find a child as bright and sensitive as Rosario. Lucero had been given a precious gift and he scorned it—a beautiful daughter who knew that he did not love her.

From his corner by her bed, Bufón sat with his tail thumping sympathetically, taking in the silent tableau.

Rosario stood up and started to climb into bed when she saw Mercedes. "You're crying. Has *he* been mean to you?" she asked.

"No, dearheart, he has nothing to do with this," Mercedes said, kneeling to take Rosario into her arms and hold her tightly. "I thought to wait a while longer, but perhaps this is a good time. Rosario, I know you'll always love your mama, but—if you would like—it would please me if you'd call me Mama. Would you like that?"

The child threw her arms around Mercedes' neck and hugged her with a small sob of pleasure. Hiccuping, she whispered, "Yes, I would, Mama."

The tentative yet hopeful way she said the last word brought more tears from Mercedes, who stroked the little girl's dark curls and rocked her back and forth. "Now, I think it's time that you were tucked into bed. I'll read you a bedtime story if you'll fall asleep immediately after. Promise?"

When Rosario bobbed her head yes, Mercedes chose a book from the stand beside the bed and leafed through it, then began to read as the child climbed beneath the covers and listened raptly. When she had finished the tale, she doused the candle, kissed Rosario on the forehead and began to tiptoe from the room.

A rustling of covers caused her to turn. The child was climbing quietly out of bed. "Rosario, you promised to go right to sleep," she admonished gently.

"Oh, Mama, I will. As soon as I thank our Lord for answering my prayer."

Unable to speak, Mercedes nodded silently and blew a kiss to her adopted daughter, then softly closed the door. If only Rosario had the rest of her prayer answered and her "real papa" came home!

She walked down the hall and entered her room. Still no sign of Lucero. Good. Perhaps he had gone in search of Innocencia. She checked the lock on the door adjoining their rooms, then slid the bolt on the hall door and walked over to her wardrobe. Slipping off the muslin gown and donning a nightrail took only a few moments. She approached her dressing table. The cushioned chair took her weight when her knees suddenly seemed to give out. After sitting and staring into the mirror for several moments, she unfastened the pins in her hair, picked up her brush and began to apply it with long soothing strokes.

The image of Nicholas coming up behind her and taking the brush from her hands rose unbidden. She could feel his hands, deft and gentle, as they tilted her head and plied the brush as sensuously as if he were making love to her. Often it had been a prelude before they retired to his big bed in the next room. The bed where her legal husband would sleep tonight. In the eyes of the Church he may have been her legal husband, but in her heart Nicholas was the one to whom she was pledged.

"I have to stop thinking about it or I'll make myself ill," she whispered, laying down the brush and massaging her temples with her fingertips. She stood up and reached for the snuffer to douse the candles when suddenly the door connecting the two bedrooms slid open.

Mercedes dropped the silver implement and turned to face him. "How did you—?" The question died on her lips when he held up an old key.

"My father told me he once used it to gain access to my beloved mother—not that he bothered all that often," he added bitterly. "She always was a cold bitch. What about you, wife? Are you still cold or has Nick warmed you up?"

Mercedes watched him swagger into the room, arrogantly

certain that she would martyr herself by acquiescing just because he was her husband. Now she could see numerous small differences between him and Nicholas. He was shorter, finer-boned. His body bore not a trace of the many scars her love carried. But more than any of the physical disparities, she could simply *feel* that he was the wrong man. She felt the Sharps in her robe pocket and cocked it. Then with an amazingly steady hand she withdrew it and pointed it at Lucero. "I'm a fair shot these days and since I've already killed one man and wounded another, I won't hesitate to shoot you."

The gesture with the pistol and her simple declaration were so casually matter-of-fact that Lucero stopped in midstride. Quickly he recovered his aplomb and crossed his arms over his chest. "Other men had no right to your body. I do."

"You gave up that right when you gave me away, Lucero."

He took another step, daring her. "You can't shoot an unarmed man."

"For you, I would make an exception. Your death would solve a great many problems."

"For you and Nick?" He chuckled. It was a low, nasty laugh. "You can't ever marry him, you know," he said casually.

"I can if you're dead. Just take one more step," she countered.

"It would be incest." She blanched and the gun wavered for a second. "You little fool, couldn't you guess? Why do you think he looks so very much like me? Where do you think those Alvarado eyes came from—my father's eyes? My daughter's eyes? He is my brother! You've fallen in love with one of Anselmo Alvarado's bastards! His mother was a *gringa* whore from New Orleans. He's trash, a nobody who spent his life as a hired killer. And now you're carrying a bastard's bastard. How does that set with a fine *gachupín* lady, eh?"

Tiny pinpoints of light burst before her eyes. She blinked them away but her knees felt liquefied. "You're the one who's a killer, not Nicholas!" she lashed out, letting anger purge away the shock, the pain. "You knew you were sending your own brother to live with me and you didn't give a damn!"

He shrugged. "Neither did he. You see, in addition to his other rather obvious shortcomings, Nick's also a heretic. What do you think Father Salvador would say about all of this?"

"Get out!" She raised the pistol and sighted in on his chest. "I'll shoot you where you stand before I ever again let you contaminate me."

Her eyes blazed and her hand was steady in spite of the rosy flush staining her cheeks. She would do it. Luce had developed that sixth sense of survival, gauging whether or when an enemy would pull the trigger. And to Mercedes, he was the enemy, no doubt about that. And no doubt, too, she would pull the trigger. Lord, she had become a magnificent woman in his absence. Great masses of darkly burnished gold hair framed her face and tumbled around her shoulders. Her skin was like golden silk, not the insipid white of the court ladies. And the female form revealed beneath her sheer night clothes was lush and full with rounded hips and heavy ripe breasts.

Mercedes watched him hesitate. Half of her prayed he would back down, half that he would not. She steeled herself to shoot.

He muttered an obscenity. "You're still a cold little convent girl, not worth risking a bullet for." With a mock salute, he turned back to his door, saying, "I'm going to look for Cenci. She'll welcome me to her bed with open arms—and legs."

With that crude remark he slammed the door. Shaking violently now, Mercedes lowered the pistol and sank onto the chair beside her dressing table, clutching the weapon with both hands in a white-knuckled death grip. *A bastard's bastard. Incest.* The child of their love was conceived in incest. In the eyes of the Church a brother-in-law was the same as a brother.

Hadn't she guessed the truth months ago? The resemblance of both men to Anselmo in his youth was as unmistakable as a brand. "I must have known deep inside me. I just couldn't admit it to myself," she whispered raggedly.

Numbly she set the gun on the dressing table, then took a sturdy chair over to the door and wedged it tightly beneath the knob so he could not open it without awakening her. The hall door had a stout iron latch secured across the inside which no key could open.

Nicholas had broken down the door and walked into her room. She had held a gun on him, too, that fateful night, but she knew that she would never have been able to shoot him, just as surely as she knew she would have killed Lucero.

God and all the angels help her! What was she to do? Even knowing who Nicholas Fortune was, she still loved him.

Chapter 23

"The vaqueros are celebrating Bazaine's withdrawal from Mexico City. Aren't you going to punish them?" Innocencia asked Lucero.

He raised his arms and clasped his hands behind his neck, reclining on his big bed in the hacienda. She sat up amid the rumpled covers, naked with her inky hair falling below her shoulders. The dark nipples of her heavy breasts peeped impudently through the tangled curtain. His mistress wanted something and it had nothing to do with politics. "Why should I care?" he asked, laughing at her pique.

"They are Juaristas! You have fought for four years for the emperor," she replied indignantly. "You are Don Lucero, not that *gringo* impostor who spies for the enemies of the emperor!"

"The emperor who's now fled the capital and holed up at Querétaro, waiting like a dumb sheep for Escobedo's army to close in and slaughter him," he said with a sneer. "Anyway, why do you give a damn what the peons do?"

"It's not those lowly farmers I speak of, but your own majordomo—old Hilario and his friend Gregorio. They are directly in touch with the rebels—they have all the news from the south before we do."

"Even if I were inclined to bother with them, my pet, I could do nothing. Here on Gran Sangre, the only person loyal to the emperor is my beloved wife. If I attempted to disrupt the festivities, I would suffer the same fate as poor Maximilian. In case it has escaped your rather apolitical little mind, my dear, we have lost the war. It's all but over. I expect that accursed little Indian to ride back into the capital in a few months' time. Then the peons across Mexico will hold the very reins of government in their coarse, grubby hands," he said in disgust.

Her eyes widened in amazement. Then her ripe lips set in a new pout. "Are you afraid of your own servants?"

His expression turned hard. "Don't push too far, Cenci," he said softly. "I don't give a damn about the servants. Why should you?"

"I want Hilario and Gregorio whipped!" she blurted out, then quickly subsided, fidgeting with the bed linens which partially covered her nakedness. "I overheard them talking last night . . . about me and you . . . and the *patrona*."

"I can imagine what they said about you replacing my wife in my bed these past weeks," he replied dryly.

"They called me a cheap whore—and they said insulting things about you, too. About how much better Gran Sangre was when the *gringo* was in charge."

He chuckled. "But aren't you glad he isn't any longer? My brother proved far more patriotic than ever I did." His expression grew speculatively amused. "Imagine, Nick working for a cause—a Mexican patriot. Good lord! How ironic."

"I *am* glad he is gone and you are back. He was crazy to prefer your skinny bitch of a wife to me!"

Lucero laughed mirthlessly. "She isn't so skinny anymore." He could see Mercedes' lush curves, sense the fire in her. How he had wanted to try her, but she was wary of him and allowed no opportunity for him to entrap her and force her to give him his husbandly rights. She was always armed and the servants were completely loyal to her. He had no doubt if she did not shoot him, almost any of them would do it for her.

What a splendid virago she had turned out to be! Luce tried not to dwell on regrets. Life was too short and Cenci too convenient. Yet the thought of Nick's baby growing in his wife's belly bothered him far more than he ever would have imagined—if he had bothered to think of the possibility when he gave her away, which he had not. His forehead creased in a frown. "I wonder how it would feel to bed my dear wife after all these years?"

Innocencia huffed. "You would not enjoy such a cold stick of a woman! Ignore her—just as you ignore all the servants."

"All but you," he replied lazily. "Did you know he wasn't me before you overheard him talking with that *gringo* in the stables?" he asked with amusement glittering in his eyes.

She studied him intently as he reclined on the big bed. His body was lean and hard yet virtually unblemished by scars, unlike his brother. Most of Fortune's scars were hidden, but one very obvious mark was missing on Lucero. "Of course I did," she lied. "But I wonder why no one else has asked what happened to that small white mark—the one right here?" She raised her finger and traced the outline of Nicholas' saber scar on Lucero's smooth cheek.

"People see what they expect to see," he replied with indifference. In fact, he had been amazed at all the changes Nick had wrought at Gran Sangre in the months since he had become *patrón*. Everyone had accepted his brother and now they accepted him, even though he knew they secretly wished for the return of his more benevolent sibling.

"You tried to seduce him and failed, didn't you?"

She dared not meet his eyes. He was playing games with her again, just as he used to do, but now there was an eerie frenetic edge to him that was far darker and more deadly than before he had gone to war. He had always been a little cruel, but now he frightened her at times. Still, he was her *criollo* lover, her passport away from the endless drudgery of being a kitchen maid on Gran Sangre for the rest of her life.

He reached up and yanked the sheet away from her, causing her to tumble forward against his bare chest. "I have better things to do than answer questions about the uncertain future, Cenci." He rolled on top of her and knelt straddling her prone body, then grasped his rigid phallus in one hand and a fistful of her hair in the other, pulling her head roughly to him.

Soon it would be time to leave. Now that the French army

had left the capital defenseless, he had only to wait until Marquez sent for him. They would rendezvous in Mexico City and ride away with millions in silver. Of course, Cenci was not included in those plans, but in the meanwhile, she was a lusty diversion. He gasped with pleasure as she took him in her mouth, then forgot about everything else but the moment's gratification.

Doña Sofia lay propped up by a mountain of pillows. The candles at the small bedside altar gave off a sweet smoky odor, further impeding her labored breathing in the close confines of her room. She had been failing the past several months. The end was near now. She could not even roll over in bed without aid. Servant girls remained at her side nearly around the clock, and Father Salvador came in to watch and pray with her every few hours.

Even though her body was giving out, her mind remained amazingly keen. She could hear far better than she could see. By pretending to doze, she learned much from the gossiping servants who came and went, whispering behind their hands while they watched the embittered old *patrona* die.

She knew Anselmo's bastard had returned from his unexplained absence and that Mercedes was increasing. She had also heard some disturbing rumors in recent weeks, rumors about the *patrón* no longer sharing his wife's bed, instead taking up with that trollop Innocencia once more. This news was puzzling.

Maids always took vulgar delight in the sleeping arrangements of their betters. The fact disturbed her only because she had been so certain he was besotted with Lucero's wife. Perhaps now that Mercedes' waistline thickened he was only showing his true selfish nature, much as all the Alvarado men before him had. Yet it nagged at her.

Mercedes did her Christian duty by paying brief visits to check on her every few days. As always, the exchanges were strained, even more so since their ugly encounter over Rosario. The bastard's bastard was growing visibly in the belly of her son's wife now. Perhaps that was why Mercedes seemed so listless and her eyes were haunted. Something was not right. Sofia could not die without learning what was going on in the hacienda which had been her prison for the past thirty-five years.

She reached up and pulled the bell cord. When Lupe appeared, she commanded the girl, "Send for Father Salvador."

Lucero had just returned from a cockfight in San Ramos, flushed with pulque and the pleasure of winning a modest purse betting on a big Shanghai Red who had fought with overpowering ferocity. Of course, the few measly pesos would pale by comparison with the fortune that would soon be his, but for now, it had been a pleasant afternoon's divertissement.

He sauntered into the entry hall of the big house, headed for the library and what remained of the *aguardiente*. After consuming it at a profligate rate the past month, he had almost finished the last of it. Grinning, he realized the timing was perfect. He would be ready to leave just about the time the liquor supply ran dry.

Father Salvador watched Lucero amble into the library, already affected by an excess of drink and in search of more. How had he made such a mistake in judgment as to believe this dissolute killer could be redeemed? When Lucero first returned home, he had seemed changed, as if the wartime horrors he had survived had purged the baser elements from his soul. Now the priest concluded he had been mistaken. Yet he did not choose to examine at all closely the reasons for his error in judgment, for the ultimate consequences of such a quandary would make him and Doña Mercedes both guilty of the most grievous sins.

Should he dare ask Lucero the boon Doña Sofia had requested of him? Sighing, he knew he must, no matter how dire the outcome. He had given his word to the dying old lady.

Lucero responded to the light rapping on the door with an expansive invitation to enter, then gaped in amazement when the priest entered. "I'd offer you a drink, but there's precious little left to share—if I were inclined to share, which I'm not, especially with you." He turned his back and poured a generous slug of amber liquid into a glass, then threw back his head and polished it off.

"I have come on a matter of some urgency, frankly against my better judgment," the priest began carefully.

"Are you going to upbraid me for carousing with harlots? For profaning the sacrament of marriage with my adultery? Perhaps I'm not the only one guilty," he said, turning to Father Salvador with an odd glitter in his eyes. *Did the priest know the truth about him and Nick*?

Father Salvador refused to acknowledge Lucero's dangerous drunken ramblings. "This is an ill time for us to speak. I'll return tomorrow."

"I'll not be changed tomorrow or ever, priest. You know that. And if you want me to return to Mercedes' bed, best you ask her why she refuses to perform her marital duties," he dared, relishing the horror the old man would feel when he had to face the truth.

"I did not come to speak of your wife," Father Salvador said sadly, knowing the breach between Lucero and Mercedes was irreconcilable now. He turned to go but Lucero's purring words stopped him.

"If not the young *patrona*, then it must be the old one who brings you to beard me in my den."

"We will discuss it on the morrow." The priest reached for the doorknob.

"No need. I've neglected my beloved *mamacita* even more than I have my wife. I should remedy the matter at once, lest it weigh too heavily on my conscience," he added sardonically.

"You have no conscience," the priest replied gravely. "May our Lord and his Holy Mother forgive you."

"I doubt they will. What hope is there for a son whose own mother could never forgive him?" he asked raggedly, then cursed and turned back to the liquor cabinet. He did not look around until the door closed softly behind Father Salvador.

When she heard the booted footfalls on the polished slate of the hallway floor, Sofia knew it was him, coming in response to Father Salvador's request. She had half hoped he would refuse. Interviews with Lucero or that other one were always quite taxing for her. And now her strength was waning so quickly. Be careful what you pray for lest you receive it, the old maxim said. How true.

Lucero opened the door without knocking and entered the room, blinking to accustom his eyes to the dim light of candles. "God's bones, but it stinks of religion and death in here." He studied the shriveled old woman whose emaciated body was almost swallowed up in the pile of pillows. "Your prodigal has returned, *Mamacita*. Aren't you glad to see me?"

Her lips thinned in a feral grimace. "Now I understand. From the day of your misbegotten birth, I have never been glad to see you."

A cold flat light glowed in his dark eyes as he neared the bed. "Then you know it is me this time, not my brother. When did you realize he was an impostor?"

She gave him a withering look. "He loves Gran Sangre. And he proved a more attentive husband to your wife than ever you did."

The barb struck home, which surprised him. He had cared nothing for his pale, frightened little bride, but after seeing her now, he felt a completely unnatural anger with Nick for making her passion blossom. "A wife I was shackled to for a dynastic alliance. I have no interest in her," he lied.

Sofia struggled to sit up. "You gave your own wife to a bastard—allowed him to sire his own bastard on her. The heir of Gran Sangre will be the product of a foul incest, forever cursed." She fought to regain her breath, then continued, "How do you think your adored father will feel about that?"

There was a bright flame of madness surging in her once-faded eyes. They glowed with pure malice. Lucero studied her in amazement for a moment. "You wanted Mercedes to lie with him, to have his child—just to spite our father."

Then the utter irony of the whole situation struck him. He laughed. "Your husband's dead and can know nothing of Gran Sangre's fate. Your obsessive hatred of Papa has always been your weakness, *Mamacita.* You can see nothing else because of it. You never could. Do you know what is transpiring outside the narrow confines of this little world? Juarez and his republicans have won the war."

"Then Gran Sangre is lost," she said without much interest. "That, too, would distress Anselmo."

"No, I don't think so. As you said, my brother loves the land—more than either of us did—and he's a survivor. You don't know him as I do. He'll stab men in their backs, cut their throats, do whatever it takes to hold onto this wretched birthright of his. The birthright I've given him. He wants to belong to it as much as I wanted to be free of it. And he will succeed. Whatever Nick sets his eyes on, he takes and he holds." *Even Mercedes*, some inner voice taunted him.

Sofia watched his expression as he talked about his brother. "You seem to care for Anselmo's bastard," she said curiously. "To love him?"

Lucero shook his head. "No, I don't love anybody. I'm not capable of it. You saw to that. But I do admire him, yes."

"Then he is *your* weakness. Beware, for he will prove your undoing."

A chill danced up and down his spine as he stared at her. "Best you have your lap-dog priest start lighting candles for your way to whatever reward you think you'll find in the next world. In this world, once that damnable Indian assumes power, Mexico will no longer be under the sway of Holy Mother Church."

She crossed herself. "God will never permit it," she said arrogantly, denying the unthinkable.

He laughed again, harshly, bitterly. "Oh, he has permitted it, believe me. Why else do you think I've come back to this hellishly boring hideaway? The emperor is surrounded at Querétaro, fighting his last battle. The imperial cause is doomed and the church with it."

"At least you've lost your war, too," she gritted out.

"Not quite." Now it was his turn to gloat. He placed his hands on the edge of the mattress, leaning down to meet her harsh glare head-on. "I've merely been biding my time here until the capital is left unguarded—and the imperial treasury along with it. General Marquez and I will loot it and sail for South America. Think of me when you gasp your last. I'll be living in sin with millions in Mexican silver to support my debauched lifestyle. How Papa would have adored the Argentine ladies," he added spitefully. "Too bad he didn't live to see that!"

Sofia felt the impact of his words like an avalanche, careening down on her, crushing the life from her. He was telling the truth. Her homeland was lost. Her church would be destroyed. The proper social order was being overturned. Savages and riffraff were lording it over their betters. And Lucero, who cared for nothing but himself, would betray his class and his church. He would flourish when all else was destroyed just as he said Anselmo's other son would. "Damn you to the same hell in which Anselmo roasts—damn . . . you . . . d-damn . . ."

Lucero stood up now, his arms crossed over his chest, impassively watching her eyelids flutter and her chest heave as she lost her battle to breathe. Soft choking gasps of ragged pain wheezed from her as she went into her death throes. He had waited a long time for this moment. Since his earliest childhood. Odd that when her head rolled lifelessly against the pillows he did not feel the satisfaction he had expected.

He reached out for the bellpull and gave it a yank, then walked silently from her chambers.

March 1867

Just to prove he could do it, Nicholas walked across the room in the army hospital in Chihuahua City. At least he could stand up straight when he took a step now, a feat he had been unable to perform for the past two weeks. He had been limping, hunched over as a Zocolo beggar.

"I see your recuperation is coming along nicely," Dr.

Ramirez said as he entered the austere hospital room. He was a quiet young physician with a thin serious face and expressive blue eyes, another *criollo* who had given his allegiance to the republican cause. He had also saved Nicholas' life, digging Hernan Ruiz's slug out of his side. "After weeks of watching you hover between life and death, it's good to see some color back in your face."

"I should have color to spare. All you've let me do since I regained consciousness is eat and laze about the hospital courtyard. I only wish I could've sent my wife word that I'm still alive. She'll fear I've been killed."

"You almost were. If that bullet had hit an inch higher or to the left, you would be dead," the doctor reminded him.

"Well, it didn't and I'm ready to get out of here at last. My hacienda and Mercedes need me."

"I don't think that would be wise after all you've been through. It's a long treacherous ride from Chihuahua City into the Yaqui River country of Sonora."

"I've been shot before. I know my own limits and I can make it."

"I realize you've been through a great deal in this war—but as a soldier you must know how unstable conditions are. The republican armies control the state capitals here in the north but they have yet to regain Mexico City or to deal with Maximilian and the remnants of his army. Bands of *contre-guerrillas* are still on the loose and brigands are pillaging everywhere."

"All the more reason for me to get home as fast as I can ride."

"That's precisely my point," the young physician said in exasperation. "You can't ride fast. Why, I'd expect you to last no more than three or four hours in the saddle before you passed out, fell off your horse and broke your neck."

Fortune shrugged. "I hate to appear an ingrate to the man who saved my life, but it is *my* neck, Doctor."

"You'll find he's a most stubborn man as well as a very poor patient," Bart McQueen said from the doorway. He stepped into the room, eyeing the bare whitewashed walls and hard-packed earthen floor. Besides the simple rope bed, a pine chair and a washstand with a chipped water pitcher and glass on it, the room was utterly bare. "I can see how a fellow used to the niceties of Gran Sangre would want to return, but don't you think it's a bit premature?"

Fortune's eyes narrowed on the bland-looking *gringo* who spoke such perfectly idiomatic Spanish anyone would have taken him for a Mexican. "My work for you is finished, McQueen. Hell, from what I've heard, the whole bloody mess should be over in a few weeks. How long can the emperor's forces hold out?"

McQueen shrugged, nodding to the young doctor who excused himself to continue his hospital rounds. Once they were alone, the Americano pulled up a chair and motioned for Fortune to sit down as well, then began to speak in English. "Maximilian's defeat is only a matter of time now that the French are gone." He laughed mirthlessly. "Do you know they blew up their ammunition dumps rather than trust giving them over to the imperials?"

"Small wonder there. The reactionary Mexicans Maximilian has surrounded himself with aren't exactly reliable," Nicholas replied dryly.

"The imperial army is deserting him piecemeal since the siege began. Last week Marquez broke out and made a run for Mexico City."

Fortune's eyebrows lifted in cynical disgust. "To loot whatever's left before Juarez's General Diaz gets there?" he asked rhetorically. "Who's remained with the emperor?" He had a fleeting thought for Prince Salm-Salm and his plucky American wife.

"Most of his court favorites have stayed with Maximilian. For all he's a bumbling fool as a politician—not to mention military leader—he does seem to inspire surprising devotion and loyalty in his subordinates . . . with a few notable exceptions."

"Leonardo Marquez being one. He's no surprise. The Tiger of Tacubaya would sell his own mother for the fun of watching the Juaristas tear her to pieces. Who else has come, willingly or unwillingly, into your net, McQueen?"

Bart McQueen came as near as he ever did to spontaneous

laughter. "How well you know me, Mr. Fortune. Actually, it isn't my net but the president's. His newest 'recruit' is an ambitious young colonel from a fine old *criollo* family, Miguel Lopez. Right now he's on the inside with Maximilian."

"And Escobedo's soldiers will soon follow?"

McQueen nodded.

"Then it's over," Fortune said fervently. As a professional soldier, he had never before been so glad of impending peace.

"All but the disposition of the royal personage. Everyone expects Juarez will put him on the first boat for Europe."

Nicholas shook his head. "No chance. You know how methodical *el presidente's* mind is—rather like the mills of the gods—it may grind slow but it grinds exceeding fine. He'll execute the Austrian."

McQueen's expression betrayed not a whit of surprise at Fortune's bald statement, although he knew shocked protests would pour out of Washington when news of the trial of an Austrian archduke was released. "No one should dare to execute a Hapsburg," he said without a trace of regret.

"Juarez will and you know it. Question is, if Washington tries to do anything about it, will you expect me to become embroiled in the mess? I've done my 'duty' for both governments. Now all I want is to go home."

McQueen measured Fortune for a moment, then said, "The Johnson Administration will lodge official protests but do nothing else except a bit of public hand wringing for the benefit of the European monarchs."

Fortune smiled sardonically. "How better to teach them to stay on their side of the pond?"

"You should've been in my business, Nicholas," McQueen said with what almost sounded like genuine regret.

"Speaking about those marked for criminal prosecution by the republic, have you heard any more about my brother? He seems to have vanished into thin air."

"As well he should. General Diaz has put quite a hefty price on the head of El Diablo. They'll run him to ground sooner or later—or more probably, he'll turn up from under some rock. Be careful on your return to Sonora. Being Lucero Alvarado isn't exactly a healthy identity right now."

"No one this far north knows about Luce. He did his raiding with Marquez in Diaz's bailiwick in the south. Much as I know he deserves it, I hate to see him shot. Perhaps he'll escape. He always did have the devil's own luck."

"Perhaps," McQueen replied noncommittally.

Mercedes watched through the kitchen window as Innocencia grabbed hold of Lucero's leg. He backed his great black stallion away, preparing to ride out of the big courtyard.

"Hah! Foolish woman, to think that one would take her with him. He has always been fickle as the wind," Angelina said scornfully. "He cares for no one, not even his own mother, God rest her soul." She made the sign of the cross.

"It seems like only yesterday we buried Doña Sofia," Mercedes replied, realizing that another fortnight had slipped away since her mother-in-law's death. And still no word from Nicholas. At least now Lucero was leaving. She thanked God for that. If the two brothers were to meet on Gran Sangre, blood would be spilled, she felt it in her bones. And in wishing that her husband would die and his brother survive, she was guilty of yet another in a long list of mortal sins.

All of the house servants knew by now that the man preparing to ride away outside was not the man who had returned home a year ago, the man who fathered her child, the man she loved. Even Rosario, in her innocence, intuited the truth. Yet no one condemned her as a fallen woman. She should be grateful, but since Nicholas had left her, nothing else really seemed to matter, only that he return to her safe and whole. *I, too, would beg and abase myself as Innocencia is doing—but only for Nicholas.*

She recalled Lucero's farewell to her earlier in the day. Dressed for travel, an arsenal of weapons strapped to his body, he had come into the study where she was working on accounts. Startled, she had inspected him warily, reaching for the pistol concealed in her pocket.

"No need for the gun," he said, raising his hands in mock

surrender as he sauntered closer. "I just came to say good-bye."

There was a strange look in those predatory wolf's eyes. Mercedes thought she saw a glimpse of regret, perhaps even wistfulness. For an instant he reminded her of Nicholas. Giving herself a mental shake for the absurdity of her fanciful imagination, she stood up and faced him, placing her hands unconsciously on her belly. "Where are you going?" *Will you ever return to usurp Nicholas' position again?*

"You needn't look so fearful for your lover and his child," he replied, reading her thoughts with chilling accuracy. "I'm leaving the country. After I relieve the emperor of some of his silver. Where he's going he won't have any use for it," he added cynically.

"I can scarcely wish you good luck then, considering your mission," she said wryly, feeling an unexpected pang of regret. If only he could have been more like Nicholas—if only he could have *been* Nicholas, their lives would have gone so smoothly.

"Always so dutiful and loyal, Mercedes," he mocked, smiling.

Her expression became grave. "Not really, else I wouldn't have fallen in love with your brother when I knew he wasn't my husband."

"What will you do when he returns?" he asked, curious in spite of his casual tone.

"I . . . I don't know," she said honestly. "You were right. We can't ever marry . . . even if . . ."

He threw back his head and laughed. "Even if I were so obliging as to die? Well, I hate to disappoint you, little bird, but I plan on living a very long time. If I know Nick, he'll keep you and the land in spite of the convent school guilt the nuns drummed into you."

"Perhaps. But that's for Nicholas and me to decide when he returns." *If he returns.*

"You know, it's a pity we didn't meet now instead of four years ago. I'd take you with me to Argentina, Mercedes."

"I wouldn't go. You'll never change. You'd soon tire of me just as you did then," she said without rancor. It was simply over, as if there had never been a marriage at all. A surprising surge of relief washed over her. "It's best you do leave now. Good-bye, Lucero."

He had bowed mockingly and then turned to walk out of her life.

Mercedes brought her attention back to Innocencia, who stood in the dust of the courtyard as Lucero's cruel words of parting rang in her ears. "Surely you didn't think I'd actually burden myself with you, did you, pet? I can buy your kind at every wayside pueblo between here and Durango. Once I reach Argentina, I'll have wealth enough to win all the women I want."

"I will not let you leave me, Lucero!" she threatened as he pried her grasping fingers free of his leg.

"You cannot stop me, Cenci. Since my brother is immune to your charms, find another—perhaps even one foolish enough to wed you." With that he kneed his big black stallion into a canter, leaving without a backward glance.

She crumpled onto the ground sobbing, then looked after him as his figure vanished down the road. Her eyes were dry of tears now, narrowed into glittering black slits. She balled her hands into fists and pounded the hard unforgiving earth. "You will be sorry you did not take Cenci with you, Lucero. Very, very sorry."

Gregorio Sanchez was surprised to see Don Lucero's mistress enter the stable, swishing her hips seductively. "Not gone half an hour and already you look for a replacement," he said scornfully.

"Do not flatter yourself, Juarista peon," she replied with disdain. "I've come to you on business. This far north have you heard of a *contre-guerrilla* raider called *El Diablo*?"

"So?" Sanchez prodded, "Perhaps I have."

"Lucero Alvarado *is* the infamous *El Diablo* who dressed in black. Still he rides his great black horse. The Juaristas in the south have placed a reward on his head. I will have it once you turn him in. He rides east on the road to Durango. From San Ramos you could contact the republican soldiers in Ocampo. I know you are one of them."

"Don Lucero is *El Diablo*? I do not believe it," he scoffed. "You only tell the lie because he has spurned you."

"Have your Juarista friends wire Durango and tell them *El Diablo* rides the road to their city. *They* will recognize him when they see him."

Chapter 24

Nicholas sat up gingerly, feeling the night chill from the earth that had seeped into his bones as he slept. Lord, but he ached. Dr. Ramirez had been right about the difficulty of the ride, but in a few more days he would be home with Mercedes. Wincing at the stiffness in his side, he rolled up and began to gather his gear together.

He disliked making camp along the trail while riding alone. The north was officially pacified, but it was still dangerous territory filled with roaming bands of cutthroats as well as remnants of *contre-guerrillas* making their way toward the American border. This stretch of the road was barren with not so much as a peon's *jacal* left standing after the ravages of war. Sleeping in the open, concealed behind some junipers was his only option.

He saddled the big black and carefully swung up on his back, then let the horse pick his way to the road. Just as he was going to turn onto the narrow twisting trail which cut across the mountains, he heard the unmistakable click of a rifle being cocked. A tall rider appeared from behind a copse of pines, followed by half a dozen others, who quickly fanned out in a semicircle around him. The men were dressed in shabby uniforms of the Army of the Republic of Mexico, but their weapons were shiny U.S. Army Springfield rifles.

"You are Don Lucero Alvarado?" the lieutenant asked.

A prickle of unease danced along Nicholas' nerve endings. He almost revealed his real identity, but hell, this was Chihuahua—word of the truth might reach Gran Sangre. Besides, the odds were better for a Mexican than an American, who would only be treated as an imperial mercenary.

"Yes, I'm Alvarado," he replied guardedly, "returning home to Sonora after fighting for President Juarez."

"We have witnesses in Durango who will identify which side you fight for, Don Lucero," the lieutenant said coldly.

"You think I'm the *contre-guerrilla* raider called *El Diablo*?" Fortune asked as warning bells sounded now that it was too late—if it had not already been too late from the moment they surrounded him.

"You've admitted you're Alvarado. I have little doubt the witnesses in Durango will confirm that you are *El Diablo*." Turning to his corporal, he signaled for the younger man to disarm the prisoner.

"If you take me back to Chihuahua City, I have witnesses who will swear I'm a Juarista," he countered as his guns and knives were efficiently stripped from his body and his hands bound to his saddle.

The lieutenant allowed himself a broad grin now, revealing a mouth filled with rotted teeth. "Ah, but Don Lucero, we are going to Durango and it is in the opposite direction. Let's ride."

Mexico City was in turmoil. When Bazaine and the French garrison had departed back in February, people were restive but the upper class felt, as long as the emperor remained with his Austrian and Belgian troops to impose discipline on the Mexican army, that the situation was still viable. Then scant weeks later, Maximilian and his armies had also deserted the capital.

Panic set in at once. Shopkeepers boarded up their businesses, embassies closed, sending their personnel to Vera Cruz for safety, and wealthy families returned to their country haciendas taking coachloads of valuables with them. Everyone in the streets went heavily armed. Few ventured out after dark.

Rumors of General Diaz's approach from the south with a large Juarista force circulated wildly, causing those who had prospered at the royal court to shudder with fright. Every imperialist sympathizer expected the worst, especially after General Marquez returned to the capital, reporting that a second Juarista army under General Escobedo had the emperor and his forces encircled in Querétaro, trapped and besieged. So hopelessly outnumbered were they that Marquez made no pretense of raising a levy to ride to their rescue. Instead, he set about systematically looting the treasury before taking flight at the approach of General Diaz.

When Lucero arrived in the city, he noted the deserted streets with unease. A gut instinct told him that he had come too late. The capital had been so ripe for the plucking that Marquez had not needed *El Diablo's contre-guerrillas* to help loot the government treasury.

It took Alvarado several days to round up his men from the cantinas and bordellos. Then they rode hard to catch up to the Tiger, whose tail he intended to twist. Riding breakneck over the mountains, they might reach Vera Cruz before Marquez sailed. Lucero would not abandon his dream of a rich life in Argentina so easily.

Lucero had been gone for nearly a week when the rider arrived with a letter from Nicholas. Mercedes was working in her flower garden with Rosario when Angelina hurried out to hand her the message. The seal on it indicated it came from Durango. With a sense of foreboding, she opened it and began to read. Angelina stood beside her with a worried look creasing her usually serene face.

"Is it from Papa? What does he say?" Rosario asked excitedly.

Pinpoints of light danced before Mercedes' eyes, then everything faded to black. Angelina's strong arms reached out to steady her when she crumpled the paper in her hands and blanched. Dear merciful God, he might die! And she had let him ride away feeling her anger. All over politics. What did *that* matter now? Let Benito Juarez rule Mexico and welcome, if only Nicholas lived!

"Are you all right, *Patrona*? Come, sit down."

Mercedes let the old cook assist her in sitting down beneath the shade of a sumac tree. Rosario huddled beside her in wide-eyed fright. "He's been imprisoned by the Juaristas in Durango. They think he's El Diablo, a *contre-guerrilla* raider who's done terrible things."

"But that was Don Luc—" Angelina stopped short, looking down at Rosario with a horrified expression on her face.

"The bad man who said he was my Papa? I *knew* he was lying even though he looked like Papa," Rosario said, then turned to Mercedes.

Mercedes held onto Rosario, stroking the child's head. "They're going to execute him, Angelina, unless we can reach an American named Bart McQueen. It may already be too late." She bit back the sob of hysteria rising like bile in her throat.

"I will fetch Hilario. He will know how to do this," the old cook said and scurried off in search of the majordomo whom she knew to be a Juarista agent.

By the time she had located the old vaquero and young Gregorio Sanchez, Mercedes was calmly seated in the library, drawing up a list of instructions for running the household in her absence. She handed them to Angelina when the cook ushered in the two men. "See that Father Salvador receives this. He'll be in charge of Rosario's education and overseeing the big house while I'm away."

"But, *Patrona*— the babe—you cannot—"

"I cannot leave Nicholas to die without going to him!" She turned from the cook to her faithful old majordomo. "Angelina told you Nicholas has been arrested for Lucero's crimes," she said without preamble, too frightened for her lover's life to even think of the propriety of openly admitting she had taken two men into her bed and carried the child of the one to whom she was not wed. "Do you know how to reach this Bart McQueen?"

"We will try, *Patrona*," Hilario replied gravely. "I will ride to San Ramos and wire Chihuahua City. There are men in the republican army who may know how to find the *gringo*."

Gregorio listened as they discussed the situation with an expression of dawning horror on his face. "I think Innocencia may know where Don Lucero has gone. It was she who betrayed him to me. I'm going to speak with her—wring the truth out of her, if need be! I will bring the real *El Diablo* to face that firing squad."

Hilario crossed himself. "Pray God he can do it. I'll wire Chihuahua about McQueen. He has great influence with President Juarez's generals."

"Nicholas rode north to warn Juarez about Mariano Vargas' plot to assassinate him. Surely your president can stop this travesty," she said desperately.

"He would if he could be reached, but he has ridden into the south where heavy fighting goes on now. His location is a well-guarded secret after the last attempt on his life. The Americano may be easier to locate through our spies."

"Who is McQueen, Hilario? How did Nicholas meet him?"

The old man looked uncomfortable, not knowing how much the *patrona* knew about the man to whom she had given her heart. "McQueen works for the American president, who wishes to see the Europeans out of Mexico. He has a system of spies across the country. Little goes on, even here in Sonora, that Bart McQueen does not know about."

"What hold has McQueen over Nicholas? Lucero told me Nicholas had been a mercenary fighting for the emperor."

An unreadable look came over Hilario's dark visage. "Perhaps nothing at all. A man can have a change of heart . . . the same as a woman, no?" The old man seemed to study the toe of his boot.

Mercedes felt the heat stealing into her cheeks. "Yes, I imagine that is true."

Within an hour, Mercedes was dressed for the long ride to Durango. She had bid a tearful good-bye to Rosario and received Angelina's pledge to watch over the child. Clutching a small travel valise in her hand, she headed across the courtyard toward the stables. She could see Father Salvador rushing to intercept her midway, a confused look on his face.

In the weeks Lucero spent at Gran Sangre, her love's trusted vaqueros, old Angelina and Rosario knew that the man who had been so good to them was not the real *patrón*.

She was uncertain just when—or if—the priest had discovered the truth. The circumstances of Doña Sofia's death had upset Father Salvador so greatly that he spent most of his time saying masses and praying for her soul. When Mercedes had ceased coming to confession and receiving the sacrament after her mother-in-law's death, he had made no attempt to censure her. Rather, the two of them had avoided each other, not a difficult feat in a house as large as Gran Sangre.

"Angelina gave me this," he said, stopping in front of her and holding the list of instructions for managing the household in her absence. "Where are you going, Doña Mercedes?"

She swallowed, willing herself to have courage. *How can I tell him I'm in love with my husband's brother*? "My child's father is being held in prison in Durango—the Juaristas blame him for Lucero's crimes. I'm going to tell them the truth."

The priest looked aghast. "And brand the child in your womb a bastard? You cannot!"

"Would you rather I let Nicholas die?" she asked in furious desperation.

Father Salvador sighed. "He was a good man, far better than his brother. Even Doña Sofia recognized it."

Mercedes gasped. "So, you do know!"

He smiled sadly. "How could I not? He had the Alvarado eyes. That was what blinded me to the truth at first. They looked so much alike in spite of their different behavior. I tried to tell myself that Lucero *had* to be the same man who left here five months ago. But after my lady's death—and the way this one provoked it, I knew there were two men. Also that the other was Anselmo's illegitimate son."

"I will not confess a sin for loving Nicholas," she said, choking back tears, realizing he already spoke of her love in the past tense.

"You are overwrought now. Best you rest for the sake of the child."

"I'll not rest until Nicholas is free. Please see that Rosario does her lessons." She rushed past him without looking back and entered the stable. A dozen armed vaqueros waited to escort her on the long grueling ride to Durango.

Nicholas paced in the cold gray cell, careful not to raise his bowed head lest he strike it on the cobweb-infested rafters. The ancient dungeon of a prison dated from the early colonization of New Spain. It had been built during a time when men seldom reached a height greater than five-foot-four. The dark, lichen-covered stone walls oozed moisture in the dank, vile-smelling heat. One tiny window in the corner let a feeble ray of sunlight in to illuminate a filthy straw pallet on the floor, which he shared with the cockroaches and other vermin. The first night he had awakened to find a rat skittering across his foot. After that, he slept with his boots on.

He had lost track of how many days he had been incarcerated. If not for the window, he would have no sense of day or night. It seemed ages since he had sent the letter to Mercedes. It was the only outside communication he had been allowed and he'd had to bribe a guard with his good gold watch to get it sent, at that. He had parted with his love in anger. She felt betrayed when he had left her without explaining his reasons. He had feared speaking openly about his identity, but now his one slim chance for survival was to have McQueen vouch for him, and the only means of searching for the American was through Hilario and Gregorio. He had been forced to explain in a letter what he had wanted to tell her in person.

Would she understand? Would she forgive him? The questions haunted him far more than the thought of his own death. As a professional soldier, he had come face-to-face with death many times over the past fifteen years. Chasing down Vargas he had come within a hairsbreadth of losing his life. But the possibility that he could go to his grave with the woman he loved hating him because he was an impostor and a traitor terrified him.

Damn, where was McQueen? The illusive bastard had seemed to materialize everywhere over the past eight months. Why did he have to drop off the edge of the earth now? The answer, of course, lay in the very fact that Nicholas was being held in a Juarista prison. The republic was saved and the empire doomed. The fate of mercenaries, regardless of their special "talents," was now of little concern. Soon, if he knew Benito Juarez—and Nicholas had grown to know him well during their brief acquaintance—Maximilian of Hapsburg, too, would stand before a firing squad.

"Small comfort in that," he said wryly. Just then the loud clank of the outer door being unlocked interrupted his melancholy reverie. A soft sound like the rustle of a woman's skirts drew near, followed by the guard's voice.

"You have half an hour, then I'll be back." He turned the rusty lock to Nicholas' cell door and swung it open. The heavy iron made a loud screeching protest, echoing off the dank stillness of the stone walls.

Mercedes' voice was soft as she thanked the man and stepped inside the cell. Dressed in an elegant violet riding habit which had been let out at the waist to accommodate her pregnancy, she looked lovely in spite of being dusty from the long ride. Her face was pale in the darkness and her eyes enormous as she strained to see him through the gloom. "Nicholas?"

Hearing his own name on her lips at last, even if her voice was hesitant and trembling, broke the trance of disbelief. She was here, the golden lady of his fantasies, warm, alive, calling to him. "Mercedes—you shouldn't be here," he protested.

"What have they done to you?" She was horrified. He was gauntly thin, with days of grizzled beard on his face. His clothes hung in filthy tatters and his eyes, Sweet Virgin, those glowing black wolf's eyes seemed somehow dim, clouded. Before her own fright and uncertainty could gain hold, she flung herself into his arms. "Oh, my love, are you all right?"

He could smell the sweet lavender fragrance of her hair, feel her soft body pressed against his, her hands fluttering over his shoulders and chest, her fingertips grazing his face as she examined him for wounds. He put her at arm's length, saying, "I haven't bathed in weeks. I'll foul you with my touch." *I already have.*

"Don't speak foolishness," she replied, her voice an anguished cry. "I was terrified you'd already been executed."

"If I'd had any way to reach McQueen without involving you, I'd have done it. If I'd known you'd do something as rash as come here in person, I wouldn't have written to you. The ride is long and dangerous, especially for a woman in your condition." He could see the swelling of her belly now. "How soon?" he asked as his hand pressed against her soft roundness in wonder. This was *his* child.

She shook her head, clinging to his arms. "The baby isn't due for several months yet. I'm fine. It's you—Oh, Nicholas, Innocencia did this! She turned in Lucero and they caught you instead of him."

"You know my name," he said softly, causing her to pause breathlessly. Her whole body stilled as her eyes searched his face.

"Lucero told me. You're Nicholas Fortune, an American mercenary he met in the war." She could feel his body stiffen. His hold on her shoulders tightened.

"Lucero returned to Gran Sangre?" *Your rightful husband, who gave you to me as casually as he gave me Peltre.*

She could read the unspoken question in his eyes. "I didn't let him touch me." She turned away then and paced across the cell, stopping in the narrow shaft of sunlight, which gilded her hair with burnished fire. "He . . . he tried but I kept the Sharps pistol you gave me in my room. I would have shot him. I think he knew it. He never bothered me after that first night," she said, daring to turn and meet his eyes again. "I love you, Nicholas. You are my husband. I don't give a damn about your politics, what you did before we met, nothing else!"

The cold, hard knot deep in his gut dissolved as she spoke. He could breathe again and his heart soared. She had forgiven him the deception and she still loved him in spite of the strictures of her religion, society, everything she had been taught since infancy. He crossed the cell this time and pulled her into a fierce embrace, enfolding her in his arms, burying his face in her silky hair.

"Mercedes, Mercedes, my love, my darling. You're the best thing that's ever happened to me. I've been so afraid that when you finally learned the truth, you'd hate me."

"I could never hate you . . . and I've known you weren't Lucero from the beginning. That first night you took me to your bed, it was nothing like it had been with him. I knew . . . but I couldn't admit it to myself."

"I wasn't certain when you knew for sure, but I lived in terror of losing you. Ah, Mercedes, I came to Gran Sangre for the land. I never expected to fall in love. But you were nothing like Luce described you." He stroked her hair away from her cheek and cradled her face in his hand tenderly.

She kissed his hand, then pressed it against her face once more. "Gregorio has gone after Lucero. The republican *alcalde* in San Ramos has sent word through their network of spies, trying to locate this Bart McQueen, but I don't know if they can. Hilario fears he may have left Mexico now that the empire is finished."

"You have to go home to Gran Sangre right now. You'll be safe there. Hilario and the others will see that Luce doesn't harm you. If I can, I'll come to you, but if not—"

"No! Don't even think it! I won't leave you alone in this awful place. I'm going to talk to the commandant. If I tell him you aren't Lucero Alvarado, he'll have to believe me."

"You can't do that." His voice was flat and firm. He could see the startled look in her eyes, but before she could say anything further, he implored her, "Think, Mercedes, even if the authorities here in Durango believed you—which is highly unlikely—what would it mean for you and our child? You'd be branded an adulteress guilty of incest and our baby would be born a bastard. No. I will not bring that disgrace down on you and our child. If McQueen can't get me quietly off, it's better that I die as Luce."

"I don't care about disgrace! About dishonor, about anything but seeing that my baby's father is alive and able to be there when he's born!"

"Don't talk crazy, Mercedes. You don't know what the

men in charge of prisons can be like, what they're capable of. Believe me, I do," he said grimly. "If they think you are already . . . 'blemished' . . ." His voice faded away as he blocked out the horror. "It was madness to come here alone. I want you safely out of harm's way and back at Gran Sangre to await the birthing."

A mulishly stubborn expression came over her face. Her jaw clamped and her eyes sparked. "I won't do it, Nicholas. You can't stop me from seeing the commandant and telling him the truth."

He took her by her shoulders, his fingers digging into the soft flesh with bruising force. "I forbid it, Mercedes."

She could hear the guard unlocking the outer door, then shambling up to Nicholas' cell. "You can do nothing to stop me—until you're free. And then it won't matter."

"It will matter if everyone learns what we've done," he called out as she twisted away from him and slipped through the door the grizzled guard held open. "Mercedes, I forbid it," he ground out.

She turned, looking at him with anguish. "You cannot, Nicholas, for legally you aren't my husband."

The heavy iron bars clanged shut in his face. She fled up the narrow stone steps followed by the jailer. "Mercedes, wait!"

But she did not. He was left alone in the gloom once more. The only evidence that she had not been a figment of his imagination was the lingering essence of lavender that hung sweetly in the damp air.

The office of Commandant Morales was small and tidy, as neatly organized as the short slender man facing her across his scarred pine desk. "I regret the circumstances under which we meet, Madam Alvarado," he said courteously, offering her a seat. "However, there is nothing that I can do. The military tribunal will make the decision as to whether Lucero Alvarado lives or dies."

"But the man in that cell is not Lucero Alvarado. He's Nicholas Fortune, an American. He isn't *El Diablo*."

Morales looked at her as if she had grown a second head—

and had not a brain between the two. "I realize this is most difficult for a gently raised lady, but—"

"I'm not having a case of the vapors, Commandant. Nor am I making up a story to save the father of my child," she replied, struggling to remain outwardly calm.

"You're saying . . ." His eyes darted involuntarily to her belly. Then his thin face turned a distinctive shade of fuchsia as he immediately looked back at her face. "That is, ahem—"

"Yes, that *is* what I'm saying. Nicholas Fortune is my child's father, but he's not my husband. They're half brothers who both bear such a remarkable resemblance to old Don Anselmo that no one can tell the difference . . . at first."

Morales began to shuffle papers from one neat stack to another, methodically evening the edges with his small stubby fingers. "This is most irregular, but even if what you say is true, I have no authority to release him."

"When does the tribunal meet?"

He tugged at the neck band of his crisp blue uniform. "Tomorrow. At ten."

"I will be here precisely at ten." She rose and nodded politely.

The officer scrambled to his feet and rounded the desk to see her to the door. Bowing stiffly he said, "I doubt if you can do much good, Madam Alvarado. There are several witnesses. One is a . . . er, a young woman who was raped by *El Diablo*."

Mercedes paled, but thrust out her chin determinedly. "Then she should see that Nicholas has a scar on his left cheek. Lucero has not a mark on him."

She knew he did not believe her. God and all His Saints, what if the tribunal did not either? If only those witnesses could discern the difference between Lucero and Nicholas—but when one was missing, the other could so easily pass. Many of the people at Gran Sangre did not notice the absence of Nicholas' scar when Lucero had returned. *People see what they choose to see. Just as you chose to do for so long.*

The scar! Dear God, what if Lucero wore a beard when he was riding with the *contre-guerrillas*? No, when he rode back to Gran Sangre, he had been clean shaven. But now Nicholas was not. Here in prison he had been forced to let his beard grow.

At daybreak the next morning, Nicholas was awakened when his cell door screeched open. He sat up groggily, wondering what was happening. Mercedes walked briskly into the small cell, followed by a fat, balding little man with a leather satchel and a burly soldier who carried a heavy iron tub which he set down on the floor with a loud thunk.

Fortune combed his hair out of his eyes with his fingers and looked at Mercedes. "What in hell is going on?"

"I found that in prisons, like in most other places, pullets do not roost so high that they won't come down for corn. I bribed the jailer to arrange for your toilette before you appear at the tribunal."

She gestured at another soldier, who trailed them into the cell, struggling with two steaming buckets of water. As he dumped them into the tub and left to get more, the bald man extracted the tools of his trade from the satchel, barber's scissors and a razor.

Suddenly Nicholas and Mercedes' eyes met. Both remembered the time she had attempted to shave him in the bathing room at Gran Sangre. Their expressions betrayed the heated longing the memories evoked. Her cheeks flushed as she placed her reticule on the floor and began to roll up the sleeves of her simple pink muslin day dress. He looked at the way the sheer folds of fabric gathered below her breasts, falling softly around the swell of her belly. His body grew rigid with desire.

It was as if she could read his thoughts. When her eyes met his again, the aching sweetness of passion infused her cheeks and deepened her eyes to the color of warm molasses. She watched as the barber shaved her love's face and trimmed his hair while the soldiers finished filling the tub with warm water. As the razor glided across his cheek with soft rasping strokes, her fingers curled at her sides. She trembled with wanting to touch him. *Only wait until they've gone.*

As soon as the barber finished, she paid him and the water

carriers. All three men left with the jailer. She smiled. "Now, strip off those filthy rags and let me bathe you. I've brought you clean clothes from Gran Sangre."

He watched, amused, as she took one of Luce's best black wool suits from the small trunk that one of the soldiers had carried in. "I had your shirt pressed. Hurry now, before the guards return."

He grinned rakishly in spite of his grave misgivings about her being in this hole. "If you're considering an assignation, I ought to warn you about the rats around my pallet."

A brief look of alarm swept across her face, then vanished. She concentrated on him as he pulled his filthy shirt over his head and tossed it onto the floor. A new angry red scar was forming on his right side. "What happened?" she asked as he favored the wound, wincing as he turned back to her.

At once she rushed over to him, running cool soft hands over his heated flesh, walking around him to examine the entry wound where Hernan Ruiz's bullet had lodged. "You've been shot again!"

"Souvenir of my little expedition to stop Mariano Vargas and his friends from killing the president," he said wryly. "The doctor thought I was lucky to be alive," he added with a mirthless chuckle as he began to unfasten the fly of his breeches.

Her mouth went dry, partially from fear that he had almost died in another battle, yet more because of the way his trousers slipped down his long hard legs, revealing his aroused sex, which stood up proudly as if begging for her touch. "Nicholas," she whispered, unable to stop his name from escaping her lips.

His eyes narrowed, burning deeply into hers. "I love the sound of my name on your lips. How often I wanted to hear it when I came into you and you cried out."

He spoke low and rapidly, as if he, too, could not stop the words from slipping out. In an instant Mercedes was in his arms, her hands clasped about his neck, pulling his mouth down to meet hers. "Nicholas, Nicholas," she breathed against his lips.

Then he claimed her in a sweet, savage kiss, holding her

tightly to him as his mouth ground down on hers. She opened for his tongue, tasting him eagerly, glorying in his stamp of possession on her as he plunged inside, mimicking that deeper, most intimate possession of all, which had created the life growing inside her.

Nicholas felt his ardor spinning out of control and knew he had to stop before he did take her in the crude filthy cell. Breaking off the kiss and holding her at arm's length, he struggled to regain his composure. "I wasn't exaggerating about the rats," he said raggedly. "I'm stinking filthy and this is no place for a lady like you."

"You can be such a fool at times." Her voice was breathlessly impassioned, but there was an underlying stubbornness in her stance as she gestured to the tub. "Climb in and you won't be filthy any longer."

"You're an amazing woman," he said with a grin, doing as she bid him.

Mercedes took the soap from the trunk and knelt at the side of the tub. She wet her hands and worked up a rich lather, then set to work, beginning with his freshly barbered hair. He leaned back under the able ministration of her deft fingers.

After she had finished sudsing right down to his scalp, she said, "Sit up and close your eyes so I can rinse." He leaned forward and she dumped a small bucket of water over his head.

When he flung his head back, his hair sprayed water around the cell, splashing her with droplets. "Now, you're wet, too," he said.

His double meaning was not lost on her. She held the soap clutched in both hands, billowing white lather foaming between her fingers as her tongue darted out and quickly ringed her lips, moistening them so they glistened softly, invitingly.

"You'd better put that soap to use before it all foams away," he said in a hoarse voice.

Mercedes reached out and began to work the lather into his skin, beginning with his shoulders and moving down his arms and chest. The slickness of her soapy hands contrasted with the springing hair on his arms and the thick pelt on his chest. Hard ridges of muscle tensed as she touched him, massaging in the soap, then using the abrasion of a washcloth to scrub weeks of prison grime from his body.

She moved to his back, careful of the fresh scar, then scrubbed his long legs one at a time. When all that was left was what lay beneath the water, she paused. Nicholas chuckled, a rich low baritone that filled the stark cold cell with warmth. "You know what to do," he teased languidly.

"Yes, I certainly do," she replied in an equally sensuous voice, leaning down and letting her hands glide beneath the surface of the water.

When she found him, hard and aching, he considered for one fleeting moment letting her give him his release that way. It might well be the last pleasure he would have in this life, but he could not allow that any more than he could take her in this vile, unholy place. What they had shared was sacred to him. He could never defile it this way.

"Give me the rag," he said abruptly, removing her hands from the water and commencing to finish the bath himself.

He would carry the memory of their lovemaking at Gran Sangre with him to his grave.

Chapter 25

The tribunal was composed of three judges, two of whom were soldiers and the third an official in the Durango state government. All were seasoned veterans who had seen the ugliest sides of this protracted and savage conflict. They sat at a heavy pine table with sheaves of papers dealing with the various cases they were hearing while this special court sat today in Durango. Then they would move on to the next state capital to make similar judgments. The law of the republic was already exercising its jurisdiction, even before the nation was wholly pacified.

Nicholas had been given an attorney of record, a local lawyer whose private practice in the city of Durango had fallen on evil days during the upheavals of the war. Alfredo Naya was elderly, taciturn and smelled of pulque when he arrived at Fortune's cell a few moments before they were due in court. Naya asked no questions, only identified himself and inquired if Nicholas was ready to face the tribunal. Fortune held few illusions that the lawyer would do more than stand beside him when the judges passed sentence.

When he was led into the courtroom, Nicholas was glad that Mercedes had arranged for him to make a presentable appearance. He had little doubt of the outcome, but at least he would face the death sentence with dignity, as befitted an Alvarado, not filthy and disreputable as the New Orleans gutter from which he had fled. If only she were not there to witness this. But Mercedes had insisted upon accompanying him, and since the court believed her to be his legal wife, they had allowed it.

My wife. She was, in truth, the wife of his heart and

always would be, just as he was the husband of hers. This would be horrible for her. Having lived for so long as a soldier, he well understood how the military dispensed justice in wartime. Swift and merciless. If she pleaded that he was not her husband and revealed that she had betrayed her marriage vows with an impostor and carried his child, what might that priggish little commandant—or even these stern-faced judges—think of her? Do to her? A handful of his vaqueros had accompanied her to Durango, but they would be powerless to help her if she was assaulted while inside the great stone hulk of the government building.

When she was escorted into the courtroom by a young soldier, Nicholas again exchanged glances with her, silently pleading that she hold her peace, but he knew from the golden fire in her eyes and the mulish tilt of her jaw that she would not do it.

A number of other people filed into the room and took seats on the crude wooden benches lining the walls, facing the judges. Two were well-dressed merchants, a third a village curate and the rest clad in simple, loose-fitting cotton clothes were obviously *campacinos*. Witnesses to Luce's crimes? Nicholas could only speculate.

One young girl, no more than sixteen or seventeen, was voluptuously endowed, exactly the type that would appeal to his brother. Her waist-length tangle of ebony hair spilled out from beneath a frayed blue *rebozo* as she stared at him with sullen black eyes that made him feel she was already walking on his grave. *Damn you, Luce*!

The judge seated in the center rapped a crude wooden gavel and surveyed the room with glittering black eyes. His face was fleshy, yet saved from being soft-looking by a great beak of a nose and a bulldog jaw of granite-hewn proportions. When he spoke, his voice filled the room.

"The accused will stand." His eyes bored into Nicholas, who stood facing the panel of judges. Naya stood somewhat unsteadily beside him. "You, Lucero Alvarado, otherwise known as *El Diablo*, are charged with committing rape, murder and common brigandry over the past year in the states of Durango, Zacatecas, San Luis Potosí and Aguas Calientes. How do you plead?"

The gray-haired lawyer looked at Fortune with doleful eyes, then turned to face the court, but before he could say anything, Nicholas replied, "Guilty as charged. Why don't you save the republic's money and pronounce sentence right now?"

"No! You cannot," Mercedes burst out before the startled judge could respond to the prisoner's remarkable statement. She stood up and walked toward the bench. "He isn't guilty. He isn't even Lucero Alvarado!"

"And how, madam, would you know this?" the judge with a drooping handlebar mustache and heavy-lidded eyes asked.

"I am Lucero Alvarado's wife, Mercedes Sebastián de Alvarado, and this man is not my husband."

The people lining the benches began to murmur excitedly among themselves, all but the young girl with the venomous dark eyes. The principal judge called for silence in his stentorian voice and the room quieted as all eyes fastened on Mercedes. The third judge said to her, "Please be seated, Madam Alvarado. You will be allowed your turn to speak—at the appropriate time."

With a look of pleading at Nicholas, Mercedes returned to her seat. The accused and his attorney were also seated and a series of witnesses was called to testify. Each in turn took an oath and told a similar tale, shopkeepers and tradesmen, farmers and merchants, all of whom stood by as *El Diablo* had shot innocent civilians before their eyes, looted their towns and villages and put their homes to the torch. One of the last to testify was a village priest who described how the infamous raider had ridden his great black stallion into the sanctuary of his church, where he instructed his men to strip the altar of its golden vessels.

Fortune's lawyer made no attempt to question the witnesses. Neither did the accused indicate that the stories were anything but the truth. Mercedes sat on the hard wooden bench, her spine stiff and straight although her back ached abominably. She tried to remain calm and impassive but the lace handkerchief in her hands was shredded before the testimony was done.

Then Margarita Olividad was summoned. The sullen-faced young woman stood up and swished her ankle-length skirts angrily as she approached the judges. She paused beside Nicholas and gave him an insultingly contemptuous inspection, then continued up to the table to be sworn in.

Like the others, she accused *El Diablo* of cold-blooded murder and theft but in addition, she also described the brutal manner in which he raped her. Then, with her black eyes blazing with hatred, she stood and pointed at Nicholas. "He has done this dishonor to me! Now he must die for it!"

When Naya made no attempt to refute her testimony, Mercedes could sit still no longer. "Please, your honors, if I might address the court, I think I could show that she is accusing the wrong man."

One of the military judges leaned backward with an impatient scoff, stroking his handlebar mustache while the judge wielding the gavel sat impassively, regarding her with an unreadable stare. Only the civilian judge appeared ready to consider her plea. The three men conferred briefly among themselves in terse murmurs, then regarded Mercedes.

"You may step forward and give your evidence at this time," the center judge intoned, then turned to dismiss the Olividad girl.

"No, please, your honors. Let her remain. I have some questions to ask her."

As she walked to the front of the courtroom, Nicholas watched, overcome with dread for the possible harm she might be doing herself and their child. She had changed from the simple cotton day dress into an elegant, deep-green linen suit trimmed with black braid. Her hair was bound up in heavy coils high atop her head and she wore a small black hat with a matching green plume. She looked every inch a *criolla*, *patrona* of a great hacienda, an Alvarado's lady.

Swallowing for courage, Mercedes approached Margarita Olividad. "I know you went through a terrible ordeal and were very frightened," she began slowly. "I, too, lived in an isolated place where soldiers and *contre-guerrillas* came to rob me . . . and worse. I was frightened also, but I was very fortunate to have a gun when a French officer trapped me alone in my home."

Margarita's eyes widened in surprise, but she said nothing, just watched the beautiful lady in her elegant clothes.

"I will never forget his face." Mercedes shuddered but went on. "And I'm certain you won't ever forget *El Diablo's* face either."

"He is the one," the girl said with a mulish toss of her head, glaring at Nicholas. "I will never forget those horrible eyes, black as hell but glowing like . . . yes, like silver!"

"Yes, this man has the same eyes as Lucero Alvarado . . . because he is Lucero's brother." Another outburst of murmurs rose. "Nicholas Fortune is the illegitimate son of my father-in-law, but in spite of the similarities to Lucero, they are two different men. Nicholas has been a soldier all his life. He carries many scars—scars which Lucero does not have—look at the scar marring Nicholas' left cheek." She gestured to Fortune, but Margarita was having none of it.

"You say the French soldiers came to your great hacienda," she sneered. "But you are a lady." She said the word as if it were a malediction. "If you had been so cursed as to have a man rip off your clothes and rut over you, you would never forget his face. Never!"

"Then you must remember that El Diablo had no scar," Mercedes said desperately.

"I saw his face." Margarita pointed to Nicholas again. "Him! Do you think the matter of one little white line"—she made a slashing motion with her finger across her left cheek—"is what I would remember when those devil's eyes were boring into me! You have not been raped. You could never understand."

Mercedes felt her heart hammer, then her chest squeezed so tightly that she feared her heart would explode. She fought back the dizziness that surged over her as the judge dismissed Margarita Olividad. "Please, your honor, she all but admitted that she did not notice whether or not her attacker had that scar which Nicholas Fortune bears."

"How is it, Doña Mercedes, that you came to know this man—Nicholas Fortune I believe you call him—if he is not your husband?" the presiding judge asked while his two companions looked at her with a mixture of pity and impatience.

"No, Mercedes. Don't—" A loud banging of the gavel silenced Nicholas' outburst.

Her eyes pleaded for his understanding. A look of such intense love and pain filled them that he sat down, defeated, unable to stop her from doing what she felt she must do. And her disgrace would be in vain.

"Nicholas Fortune is his name," she said, turning her gaze from her love and back to the judges. "He rode up to Gran Sangre last year, pretending to be Lucero Alvarado returned from the war. As Lucero's wife, I welcomed him, but I sensed that he was not the husband I had known so briefly four years earlier. As time passed, I became certain he was not Lucero.

"This man is kind where Lucero was cruel, educated and tolerant where Lucero was superstitious and provincial. Nicholas speaks fluent English and French, even German.

"My marriage was arranged by my guardian. I did not favor it nor did my husband, who left me to ride away to war after abusing me for three horrible weeks."

The presiding judge's eyebrows lifted, but it was the second one, the civilian, who asked pointedly, "If, as you say, your lawful husband left you four years ago, then whose child do you carry?" There was an avid glow in his heavy-lidded eyes as he waited for her to reply.

Mercedes raised her head proudly and faced him, one hand pressed protectively to the swell of her belly. "This is the child of Nicholas Fortune."

An uproar began at this point, led by the priest who sputtered, aghast, "You say he is not your husband but your brother-in-law, yet you lay with him! Incest!"

The judge's gavel rapped ineffectually as all eyes in the courtroom turned to Mercedes, some righteously hostile like the priest's, some pitying, a few merely avidly titillated and curious. Nicholas looked at her, his jaw clenched tightly, feeling every word of condemnation directed at her as if it were a stab to his heart. She gazed back at him with tear-filled eyes, shaking her head to indicate it did not matter what they said.

"I will have order," the judge barked. When he had finally restored silence, Mercedes continued in a strong, clear voice, "When Nicholas pretended to be my husband, I pretended right along with him that he was . . . for I wanted him to be, with all my heart."

I love you. Nicholas silently mouthed the words in English. She blinked back tears and did the same.

"It is obvious that this woman would do anything to secure her husband's freedom, even perjure herself for him," the civilian judge said to the presiding judge.

"We have heard enough testimony from eye witnesses to be certain he is *El Diablo*," the last judge added.

"No! You're making a terrible mistake. He is not *El Diablo*—he isn't even a supporter of the emperor," Mercedes cried desperately. "Nicholas risked his life and nearly died working for President Juarez! He is one of you!"

Before Mercedes could protest further, Nicholas stood up, saying, "Please, my love."

She looked over at him, her eyes wide and filled with pain and panic. He seemed so calm that she quieted at once, waiting to see what he would do.

Nicholas turned to the panel of judges and said with a patient smile, "You can see, your honors, that my wife loves me very much—and that she has a most fanciful imagination, although I confess that while I was fighting with the *contre-guerrillas*, I did learn a smattering of French and English, but I am who I am and she is *my* wife. And our child is quite legitimate, though the shame of being my heir may be more difficult to bear than bastardy." He looked over at her then, willing her to acquiesce.

Mercedes stood facing him, aching to walk the few steps that separated them and fling herself into his arms. But it was no use. All was lost. She knew it with dead certainty as she stared at him with jewel-bright, tear-filled eyes.

The presiding judge motioned for the soldiers who had escorted her into the courtroom to remove her. When the two deferential young men reached for her, Mercedes relented with a stifled sob, shaking off their hands and walking defiantly ahead of them to take her seat once more. She sat straight, refusing to let the stinging tears fall as the judge's booming voice filled the courtroom.

"Lucero Alvarado, you have three days to prepare yourself. At dawn on the fourth day, for the crimes to which you have confessed, you will die by firing squad."

Luce sat staring into the flames of the campfire, a dangerous practice he had spent the last four years avoiding. A man whose eyesight had been dimmed by the blaze could be especially vulnerable to a foe attacking out of the darkness. Yet so despondent was he that all he could see was the vision of *The Fair Lady* sailing out of Vera Cruz harbor.

He and his men had missed the ship by a scant hour. Just long enough for it to clear the breakwaters and head out to sea, bound for Havana, along with Leonardo Marquez and most of the Mexican treasury. So close. He had come so damned close, only to be double-crossed by the man who had been his mentor.

Nick would laugh at the irony of it, Luce thought bitterly. He had given away one fair lady and gone in pursuit of a far more fickle one, only to have it elude him after his wife also had abandoned him. In favor of his brother. A wise man, Nick, to put down roots, choose the winning side in the stupid little war. Of course, Nick would have been the first to warn him not to trust Marquez, but Luce's own arrogance had made him complacent. A fatal flaw in their profession.

Echoing his thoughts, Jorge asked, "What will we do now, *jefe*? With Diaz's army in control of Mexico City we have no hope of raiding any of the rich men who stayed there during the upheavals."

"I've been thinking about that. Once the Juaristas get

their hands on Maximilian, it'll all be over. Then their armies will turn their attention to us."

"We cannot split our group, *nein*," Otto Schmidt said stiffly, eyeing Alvarado with his crafty pig eyes.

"No, I don't intend to break up this command," Luce replied coldly. He had always disliked Schmidt, who had first served under Nick. O'Malley and most of the others who had been with his brother for very long had either been killed or gone their separate ways after Nick had ridden off to Gran Sangre. Of the originals, only Schmidt and Lanfranc were still with him and they were a mixed blessing at best.

"What do we do then, *jefe*?" Jorge asked again, waiting rather like a large, slow-witted dog, hoping for a pat but expecting a cuff.

"We'll keep on the way we're headed, north, where we're not known. We can reach the American border if we have help. I hear there are some rich copper mines in New Mexico Territory . . . and my English is quite passable now," he added, thinking of Nick. The help he had in mind waited at Gran Sangre.

The next day they rode to the outskirts of Durango. Luce had traded his black stallion for a far less distinctive but equally sturdy dun gelding. Still, unwilling to chance being recognized in a city which he had ravaged, he remained at a small cantina and dispatched Lanfranc and Jorge to the market to purchase supplies for the last long leg of the journey back to Sonora.

He spent the afternoon with the rest of his men sitting in the back of the run-down adobe building, sipping from a grimy mug filled with warm pulque and watching a fat, sassy barmaid flirt with the rough vaqueros scattered around the place. Jorge entered the dimly lit cantina around dusk and made his way through the gathering crowd to where his compatriots sat.

"You look pleased as a man who just slipped *turnera* in his whore's drink," Luce said, watching the peculiar gleam of excitement in Jorge's normally narrow dark eyes.

"You will not believe this, *jefe*, what we have just learned in the city." He waited as the barmaid swished over to the table and poured another round of foaming pulque for the hard-looking crew of strangers. "*El Diablo* dies tomorrow—before a Juarista firing squad. Poof!" He snapped his fingers. "Lucero Alvarado is no more a wanted man. He is a dead one."

Several of the men hooted with laughter along with Jorge, but Luce remained thoughtful, his expression unreadable. Gradually the others sensed his pensive mood and quieted.

"You do not like it—that Nick has been taken in your place?" Schmidt asked.

"I never did like Fortune," Lanfranc said, lobbing a wad of tobacco in the general direction of a cuspidor. "He was a bastard to work for."

Lucero looked at the oily little Frenchman as if he were examining one of the cockroaches that scuttled across the cantina floor. "He may be a bastard, but Nick is my brother," Luce said in a soft, dangerous voice. "I can speak ill of him. You cannot." He took a long, slow swallow of pulque as he reclined indolently, his chair tipped back against the rough adobe wall behind him. The *jefe's* eyes were slitted almost closed, but not a man around the table doubted that the *criollo* could draw his gun or knife and kill him before he could reach his own weapon. In sheer deadliness, Alvarado and Fortune were indeed brothers.

Slowly, a smile spread across his beautifully chiseled mouth. His front chair legs hit the hard-packed clay floor with a soft thump and he leaned forward. "I think *El Diablo* is going to stage a marvelous escape right under their stupid Juarista noses."

Jorge blanched and Schmidt scowled and muttered an oath in German. Everyone else watched expectantly. The big moon-faced Sonoran dared to ask, "*Jefe*, why do you wish to rescue him? With the *gringo* dead we can ride to your hacienda and live like kings. No one will pursue us. *El Diablo* will be dead."

Luce looked at Jorge with cynical amusement. "Live like kings?" he echoed with a laugh. "Do you honestly want to spend the rest of your life chasing down steers and wild horses? Sweating and breaking your back like a common vaquero? That is the life on Gran Sangre. Have you forgotten how boring it is in Sonora, my friend? The Yaqui River Valley is two days' ride from Hermosillo—even if we had silver enough to buy the pleasures of the city, which we would not. What my father did not already waste, the French and Juaristas appropriated."

Strictly speaking, Luce knew that was not true. There was some sleek fat livestock they could sell for a modest profit, the herds Nick had reclaimed and built up. Mercedes still had some jewelry and there was a smattering of other valuables in the old hacienda, but none of it would last them long. Money aside, Luce had shaken the dust of Gran Sangre from his feet nearly five years ago. He had been bored to death with life in the Sonoran backcountry then. His recent visit made it hold even less appeal for him now.

Of course there was Mercedes. He smiled wryly, realizing that she would cut his throat as he slept if he tried to reclaim the husbandly rights Nick had assumed in his place. But he did not want to reclaim his wife or his hacienda. The irony was in what he *did* want.

He wanted Nicholas Fortune to live. If ever in his desolate and violent life he had met anyone who understood him and gave a damn about him, and whom he gave a damn about, it was his brother. He had worshipped the ground on which old Anselmo walked, but he had always known the don cared more for *aguardiente* and cockfights than he had for his son. As to his mother and her priest . . . his expression hardened as thoughts of them flitted through his mind.

No, Nick was the only person alive he cared about, the only one who had ever really helped him, who had ever shown any genuine interest in him. He remembered the time Nick had saved him from the Juarista mob in Tampico. No, he could not let Nick die.

On a more cynical and pragmatic note, Luce admitted to himself that Nick had Juarista friends up north and other connections across the border. He rationalized that his brother would actually be a lot more useful alive than dead.

"Breaking Fortune out of that rock pile of a prison, bah!

It would be easier to steal Saint Peter's keys and ride into heaven," Schmidt said.

Luce grinned mirthlessly at the German. "I'll think of something after I do a little reconnaissance." He snapped his fingers as he stood up, signaling Jorge to come with him.

In a few hours he had formed a plan which he shared with his men. "We move tonight. No one will expect a rescue attempt only hours before *El Diablo* goes to his death. Hell, they wouldn't expect anyone to give a damn about him. First, I'll get in position. Then Jorge will signal for the diversion . . ."

Luce quickly outlined a variation on the method they had used successfully to pull off a series of robberies during the past year. That old familiar aphrodisiac of danger began to burn through his veins once more. Sweet Virgin, how he loved outwitting the buffoons who were in authority, no matter whose government they served.

Alvarado was so excited that he failed to see the silent exchange between Lanfranc and Schmidt.

Mercedes bribed the guard again to gain entry to the prison that night. Nicholas hoped that she would come, even though a part of him wanted her safely away from this sinkhole of death and desperation. But the moment she walked through the cell door, his heart leaped with the bittersweet joy of holding her in his arms one last time.

She had vowed not to cry. But it was impossible once she saw him, standing so straight and tall, her splendid love, penned in this squalid little cell until they would take him out of it one final time to slaughter him.

"Nicholas, oh, Nicholas." She set down the basket she was carrying and threw herself into his arms, holding on with all of her strength as he crooned soft love words in English and Spanish. Finally, getting her emotions under control, she raised her eyes to his beloved face, letting her fingertips trace across the fine white line of the scar on his cheek.

"I knew it would do no good to tell the truth, *querida*," he said in English. Somehow speaking his native language with her his last night on earth seemed fitting. He took her hand in his and kissed her fingers softly.

"I had to try. I'd sell Gran Sangre or deed it over to the commandant if he would let you go . . . but he refused," she said in misery.

Nicholas chuckled softly. "There is a limit even to Commandant Morales' venality. You may bribe him to gain entry to the prison, but not to let me escape."

"How can you joke at a time like this?"

He sighed, then asked tenderly, "What else is there to do?"

"I would do *anything* to save you, give anything."

"*Querida*, Gran Sangre is our child's birthright. We've worked so hard this past year to secure it. Always remember that."

"I shall try," she said raggedly, seeing the years without him stretch endlessly ahead of her. "For tonight, I brought us dinner. The food in this place must be ghastly."

"I've had better, but I'm used to as bad." His appetite was not all that great but rather than disappoint her, he would share this last bit of time they had together. There was one request he had to make of her with which she must comply.

Mercedes knelt beside the crude pallet, ignoring the stale smell of it as she spread a clean blanket over it, then opened the hamper to reveal a bottle of wine, a loaf of crusty bread, assorted fruits, a wedge of sharp yellow cheese, even a whole roasted chicken. "It's simple fare, but fresh and good. I spent the afternoon at the market in the square."

She did not tell him that was where she wandered about aimlessly in despair after her attempts to bribe Commandant Morales proved futile.

Nicholas sat down beside her and began to pour the wine into clay mugs as she set out the food on plates. "We'll have to break the chicken apart with our hands. The guard wouldn't let me bring in a carving knife."

"Imagine that," he said owlishly.

In spite of herself, she laughed softly at the comment, watching as his long strong fingers quickly ripped the plump golden fowl into various parts. They ate slowly, savoring each moment. Their last time together was far more precious than any food. She described all that had occurred since he rode off to join Juarez—Doña Sofia's death, how Angelina and Baltazar and the other people on Gran Sangre fared, and particularly she told him anecdotes about Rosario and how well she was doing in her schoolwork.

"She knew at once that Lucero wasn't her 'real papa,'" she said, explaining the child's intuition. "You are truly her father in every way that matters."

As her eyes filled with tears, Nicholas raised his mug for a toast. "To Rosario, and to my wife in every way that matters, as well."

With trembling hands she raised her cup to his and they both swallowed the bittersweet taste of tears. After she finished drinking, Mercedes put her mug down, saying, "I need a cloth. My fingers are all greasy from the chicken."

He reached for one small hand and raised it to his mouth. "I'll wash them," he said in a husky voice.

She felt a small shiver of pleasure when the heat of his breath caressed her hand, followed by the soft velvety rasping of his tongue and lips as he licked the stickiness from her palm, then took each finger and sucked on it.

Mercedes closed her eyes, storing up the memory to last her a lifetime. When he took her other hand to lave it tenderly, she reached for his, reciprocating. His large dark hand was rough against her mouth, yet it was always so gentle whenever he touched her. She kissed his callused palm and thought of all the hours he had spent working stock, letting the rough leather reata pull through his hands.

Gran Sangre is our child's birthright. And you won't live to see our child born!

She leaned forward, shoving the hamper to the side and took his face between her hands, pulling him to her for a kiss, leaning into his body, embracing him. *One last time, love me one last time, my beloved.*

Nicholas knew what she wanted, what he wanted so desperately himself, but he could not do it. Gently he held her shoulders and withdrew from the impassioned kiss with soft nips and brushes to her cheeks, nose and brow. "No, *querida*. Not here in this filthy place. There are rats and the guard could walk in on us. I have no way to protect you here. It's best if you go now before he or one of the other soldiers gets any ideas."

She felt the firm pressure of his hands holding her and intuited what it was costing him to break away from her as he had. "After you were gone, all I thought about was that you might die for your President Juarez, and I had let us part in anger. I realized then that I didn't give a damn for politics—or religion—for anything but having you come back to me. How can I lose you now?"

"You have this," he said softly, placing his hand on the swell of her belly. "Tell our child about me when the time is right, and tell Rosario that her real papa loved her very much."

She nodded through her tears. "Of course."

"There is one more thing you must promise me, my love."

There was a warning in his voice. Her eyes flashed warily to his. "What is it?"

"I don't want you at the execution tomorrow. Ride for Gran Sangre at first light."

"No! How can you ask it? How can I leave you to die alone in this awful place? Perhaps they've found McQueen. He might—"

"No, Mercedes, he isn't coming. I suspect he's already left the country. It's too late for me, but I can bear it—if I know you and our children are safe. The soldiers and the others in court will be in that crowd. There's no telling what they might do to you—how they might turn on you—after I'm dead."

"No!" She placed her hands over her face, trying to blot out the horrible images.

"I've seen it before. If anything were to happen to you . . . then my life has truly become meaningless. Live for me and remember me as I am now, not as a lifeless corpse lying in the dirt. Please, promise me, so that I can die like a man." His voice shook slightly with desperation.

She lowered her head, shuddering, gasping for breath. "I . . . I will send Hilario to bring you home to Gran Sangre."

"Thank you. I would like to rest there where my life truly began."

Chapter 26

Nicholas was awakened by the sound of shots and yelling outside in the compound yard. "What the hell is going on?" He looked out the window, which revealed only a small slit of sky with bright moonlight streaming in. Too early for his execution. What was the shooting about? Thinking it was probably a drunken celebration among the garrison soldiers, he lay back down, awake now, staring at the thick sooty cobwebs clustered around the dim outline of the rafters.

Just what a man needed, time to contemplate his imminent death, he thought wryly. Saying good-bye to Mercedes had been so taxing emotionally that he had fallen quickly into a fitful slumber at first dark, but now he knew he would not be able to return to sleep. Regrets for his life? There were many, but this past year with Mercedes and Rosario had made them pale. And he hoped in part that his work as *patrón* of Gran Sangre had made up somewhat for the sins of Nicholas Fortune.

He laughed at the irony of it. Nicholas Fortune, mercenary killer, had taken on respectability to redeem himself and claim a fine old family name. Now he was dying because he had become Don Lucero. And the real Luce had done things far beyond Nick's blackest sins.

"At least I'll be buried at Gran Sangre, near my family." He had never given any thought to leaving children behind to carry on his name when he was gone, but then he had possessed no name to bequeath them. Now he did, and in Sonora, far from where *El Diablo* rode, the children of Lucero Alvarado would grow up to be respected *hacendados*. Rosario would make a fine marriage . . . and the babe? If it was a boy, he would be the next *patrón*. The Alvarado line would continue. He took solace in that thought.

The sound of the outer cell door clanking open interrupted his reverie. Something was going on. He rolled off the pallet and flattened himself against the wall as his instincts sent warning bells clamoring in his head.

His cell door swung open with a loud crash and a harsh voice yelled, "Nick, where the hell are you? I've been to every cell in this row and nearly broke my neck in the damnable dark!"

"Luce!" Nicholas glided out of the corner and looked at his brother, who did indeed look like Satan incarnate, silhouetted in the narrow shaft of moonlight, clad all in black with his Alvarado wolf's eyes glowing like coals from the floor of Hell itself. "What in the name of God are you doing here?"

"What does it look like? Come quickly. I've wasted too much time already searching for you. Here—" He shoved a loaded Army Colt in Fortune's hand as he turned back to the cell door.

In moments they had threaded their way through the stygian darkness of the deserted cell block where Nicholas had been confined and raced up a flight of stairs. Dim torchlight now illuminated their path as they ran toward freedom.

Along the way they encountered several guards, disposed of in an inventive variety of ways. "Messy but effective," Luce said as they stepped over one corpse whose skull had been fractured by an enormous water crock sitting near his chair. They crunched across the broken shards of pottery and out into the compound yard where a rotund Mexican vaquero waited.

"Jorge, over here," Luce whispered as the two brothers hid in the shadows of a copse of yucca. From downstairs the sounds of an alarm being raised added to the confusion already rampant outside the gate where Alvarado's men had created the original diversion which had allowed Jorge and Luce to slip inside.

"How the hell are we going to get past the outer gate—or have you forgotten that little detail?" Nick asked tersely as the blood began to pound in his veins. He might yet live to see his child's birth!

A mocking smile twisted Luce's lips. "We have a small diversion planned. Jorge has gone to give the signal now that I have you free of that infernal rat's maze below."

"Rat's maze is the right term," Nick said, remembering the rodents he had fought off nightly since his incarceration.

"Schmidt and Lanfranc have planted enough dynamite to blow off the side of Chapultapec Hill. That should buy us time enough to slip past the front gate."

They waited, crouched in the shadows as officers barked orders and soldiers responded. The crunch of gravel echoed as men ran double-time across the courtyard and into the bowels of the stone monolith. Two armed guards passed so close to their hiding place that they could smell the cigarette smoke clinging to their uniforms.

"Where the hell is that blast?" Luce snarled with an oath.

Several more moments passed with more pandemonium all around them. "It's only a matter of time until they find us here. We have to make a move. When they brought me in, I didn't get to see much of this sty. You know the layout any better?" Nick asked.

"There's a narrow gate near the back we thought of trying—used to let in vendors. But I thought it was too much of a bottleneck."

"Schmidt and Lanfranc never did have much use for me," Fortune said grimly. "I don't think that blast is going to go off."

Luce knew in his guts that his brother was right. Just as he was about to agree, Jorge burst into the courtyard yelling, "*Jefe*! They have gone and taken the horses!"

A volley of shots rang out and the portly warrior pitched forward and lay still, a dark shapeless mass in the dim moonlight. A dozen soldiers entered the courtyard in pursuit, overrunning Jorge's body as they dispersed around the perimeter.

"Let's find that gate!" Luce stood up and started to sprint around the open area, using the shrubs and shadows cast by the arched portico columns for cover. Nick was right behind him.

They made it the length of the compound before an alert guard saw the movement and gave the alarm. Luce shot him without breaking stride. They rounded the corner, coming in sight of the gate.

Nick sprinted ahead and flattened himself against the wall, covering Luce. They dashed for the narrow grillwork. "We'll have to shoot the damn chain off of it," Luce whispered as they rounded the corner.

"I do not believe that will be possible," Commandant Morales said sharply as a dozen soldiers with their rifles fixed on the escapees stepped out from behind the portico wall and surrounded them. "I'd suggest you drop your weapons and raise your hands at once or they'll open fire," he purred, moving behind the wall of men who had formed a semicircle which cut off all hope of escape.

Luce swore with vile creativity as he threw down his pistol. Nick tossed his atop his brother's in silence. So much for the foolish dream of resuming his new life.

It was over. They were escorted back to the hellish cell from which Fortune had so briefly escaped. This time the way was lighted by two armed soldiers carrying torches.

Once they were inside the cell, Morales preened in satisfaction, walking around the prisoners, inspecting the much taller men like a small bantam rooster strutting in front of two fighting cocks. He stroked his jaw as his sharp dark eyes studied them intently. His gaze moved back and forth between the two men, observing each virtually identical feature. "The two faces of Janus. Incredible. So, your woman told the truth—at least about the fact that there *were* two of you. I wonder, does she belong to both of you? Tell me, do you share her?"

Nicholas lunged for the commandant and was met with a rifle butt smashing into his solar plexus. He doubled over as Morales continued speaking. "I think she would've offered herself to me to save you if she hadn't been great with your child," he said speculatively, looking at Fortune. "From that outburst of temper, I assume she is your woman—but is she *your* wife?" he added, turning to Lucero. "Did she tell the truth about one of you being a Juarista? And if so"—he paced back and forth in front of them, looking at the ground, then raised his head and stared at Lucero—"which one is it? You? Or . . ." His gaze shifted to Nicholas. "You? How shall I ever be certain that I've executed the right man?"

"You could always shoot both of us," Fortune rasped sarcastically. The bastard was just playing with them. After their aborted escape attempt and the guards Luce had killed, there was no way he would let either of them live.

Morales' thin face split in a beatific grin. "A capital idea." He chuckled at his own pun, then strode out of the cell, signaling the guards to follow him. "Best get what rest you can. Dawn will arrive all too soon."

As the soldiers' footsteps echoed down the corridor, Luce turned to Nick. "Execute both of us?" A sardonic grin split his face. "*Hermano*, you really are an Alvarado!"

"A dead Alvarado and now, unfortunately, you'll be joining me. I'm sorry your gambit didn't work, Luce."

Alvarado chuckled fatalistically. "Not half as sorry as I. Ironic that they're killing one of their own." As they sat on the hard-packed dirt floor, leaning against the clammy stone wall, he studied Nick. "Why did you switch sides? I was amazed when Cenci told me about it."

Laughing at the irony of it, Nick replied lightly, "Fortunes of war." Then he squinted in the darkness, pondering for a moment. "I guess I always did have a sneaky admiration for the way they fought. Hell, they had a cause they really believed in. Something I never had."

Luce shrugged. "I still don't."

"Why did you come in after me?" Nick asked, wishing he could make out more of his brother's face in the darkness. "You could've gone home to Gran Sangre in my place again. *El Diablo* would've been dead. You'd be free and clear."

"Free? Free to do what—rusticate on the land, work until my hands were callused and my back bent? No, *hermano*, that life isn't for me."

"You still didn't have to risk your neck to free me," Fortune prodded.

Now Luce's white smile gleamed in the dim moonlight. "Don't ascribe your newly acquired nobility to me. You have contacts up north. You could get me over the border, help me find another convenient little war somewhere—killing Apaches for the mine owners in New Mexico, whatever." He shrugged, dismissing the topic, which obviously made him uncomfortable.

But Nick couldn't seem to let it alone. After a moment or two of silence, he said, "Maybe you did it for Rosario and Mercedes and the baby."

"Maybe not," was the succinct reply. "I'm a selfish son of a bitch who doesn't much like women. Hmm . . . You know Nick, that's the God's truth and I just realized it."

"Having met Doña Sofia, I understand the reasons. My mother wasn't much of a mother either. She regarded me as a nuisance, but I don't think she actually hated me. Your mother knew I was an impostor. Guessed my paternity and thought it'd be a grand joke to let a bastard's bastard inherit Gran Sangre."

"I watched her die, you know," Luce said in a disembodied voice.

"Mercedes told me you were with her. I guess you wouldn't have run to summon help . . . she was beyond saving no matter who had been there."

"Beyond saving . . . just like me."

The sound of the damned echoed in his brother's voice. Nicholas felt a shiver and also an empathy. "Maybe we didn't grow up as differently as I thought when I first met you."

The silence stretched, more companionable now.

"What was he like?" Fortune finally asked.

Alvarado knew he meant Don Anselmo. "Bigger than life to a small boy. He lived for loose women, cockfights, the bullring. Could drink any man alive under the table. He knew how to live, our father. I bet he died in The Golden Dove with a whore in each arm. He took me there when I was fourteen and introduced me to a girl named Conchita."

Nick snorted. "You were a late bloomer. I was twelve my first time, but then I had the advantage of growing up in bordellos."

"I envied you that life," Luce said suddenly.

Nick felt poleaxed. "You had a name, a magnificent home, a father!"

"I said he introduced me to my first whore. That was the only time he really ever paid any attention to me . . . now I realize even that was more to infuriate his lady wife than to please me. I was the requisite heir. Every good *hacendado* has to have one, as you doubtlessly have learned by now. The Alvarado name was the only thing he ever loved. You're more Alvarado than either of us when it comes to the land. You actually sweat and bleed for it like our grandfather, something even our papa didn't do."

"I did it for her."

"Maybe. I think you did it for yourself, too," Luce replied, the old lazy mockery returning to his voice.

They spent the night alternately dozing and waking, talking about their childhoods, the war and the various women they had encountered. Neither mentioned Mercedes or the baby again.

The dawn was sullen and hot as if expecting the worst from the day. Mercedes had not slept through the night, nor arranged to leave the city at first light. She had not precisely lied to Nicholas. She had only told him she would see that he was buried on Gran Sangre. He had assumed that meant she had acquiesced to his wish that she not witness his execution.

In truth Mercedes was not certain that she could endure watching the gruesome spectacle, but neither could she ride away leaving him to die alone. She would be in the prison compound with her men, ready to claim his body as soon as it was over.

Shuddering to think of it, she felt a sudden surge of nausea. This time it had nothing to do with her pregnancy. Bending over the slop pail she was violently ill. When the wracking spasms passed, she climbed back onto the edge of the bed and sat, shivering in the still morning heat.

"I have to get dressed," she told herself, dragging her weary body up from the mattress and laying out a lightweight gown. It was lavender, the nearest thing to mourning she had. Once back at Gran Sangre she could dye all her clothes black, but Nicholas would hate that. He would want her to celebrate the new life growing inside her, not grieve for what they had lost.

"I will raise our children to remember you with pride and love, my husband," she vowed as she prepared to face the most horrible day of her life.

Nick and Luce watched the sun rise through the narrow cell window. Both were grimy with several days' beard stubble, their bodies unwashed in the heat, their eyes bloodshot from a sleepless night. Luce had bribed the jailer to bring them a bottle of cheap mescal, which they had taken turns emptying as the moon set.

When the sky began to lighten, the guards brought a priest to their cell. Fortune noted wryly that he was not the same one who had been a witness against him in court.

"I am to hear your confessions and dispense the sacrament of Holy Unction," he said, looking at the two eerily identical men's hardened piratical faces. He was old, his eyes shadowed and weary, his face creased with a fine crosswork of lines. The priest knelt and began to open the small leather box containing his stole and the oil of the sacrament.

"I won't be availing myself of your services, Father," Nicholas said, not unkindly. "I'm not of your faith." He did not add that after pretending to be Catholic for the past year he did not want to continue the subterfuge. "God will just have to take me as I am, I'm afraid."

The priest's eyes moved from Fortune to Alvarado. "And what of you, my son?"

Luce laughed cynically. "I'm afraid I'm further beyond the pale than my heretic brother here. All the prayers from Durango to Vera Cruz couldn't save my soul."

"Through the mercy of our Lord and the intercession of

his gracious Mother, all things are possible," the priest replied patiently.

"I'm a man whose own mother despised him. You'll forgive me if I don't count much on anyone else's," Alvarado replied.

"No man is beyond God's help . . . unless he wishes to be," the old priest remonstrated gently.

"Take his blessings, Luce. Perhaps they'll help you," Nick said, thinking of the writings of Blaise Pascal that he had borrowed from a French compatriot in Algiers.

Luce shrugged fatalistically. "By the time I confess all my sins, the powder in the soldiers' rifles will have lost its charge."

"I doubt buying us time will do either of us any good."

"Who knows?" Luce replied, turning to the priest, who motioned for the guard to take them to a private cell.

A quarter of an hour later, the guard brought Alvarado back. "The good father promised to pray for both of us," he announced to Nick.

"That didn't take you long. You must've omitted quite a bit," Fortune said dryly.

"Actually, once I began, Father Alberto was wise enough to realize that a general confession was required, else the commandant would come and drag me off to the firing squad before he'd shriven me."

"Commandant Morales is going to take us one at a time, the guard just told me," Fortune said. "He's afraid of the crowd getting stirred up if they see there really are two of us. Once the first execution is over, they'll disperse. Then he can take care of his second prisoner without any civilian witnesses. He has no authority to execute you without reconvening the tribunal and they left yesterday to hold their next session in Aguas Calientes."

"But since I killed some of his men breaking in here last night, he's going to shoot me anyway. Now the question is, who goes first?" An odd gleam came into Alvarado's eyes as he regarded his brother.

"Me, obviously. I am the firstborn, even if it was on the wrong side of the blanket. And, I'm the one they convicted."

* * *

Mercedes watched from the edge of the crowd. The mood was ugly. Many who had experienced the depredations of *El Diablo* had come to watch him die. Nicholas had been right to fear for her safety. She had covered her hair and swathed her face with a long gray *rebozo*. With the full cloak she wore, no one could discern that she was with child. If she was careful and remained in the shadows of the portico, none would recognize her as the wife of the convicted man, who had pleaded so desperately for his life.

Then she heard the drum roll. A loud growl of excitement spread through the crowd as the prisoner was led out into the big compound. *Oh, Nicholas, my love, my only love*! In the distance she watched his tall, slim body move with arrogant grace as he took his place against the stone wall, refusing the blindfold. He tossed several coins to the soldiers in the firing squad. It was an old Spanish tradition to bribe them so they would not aim for the face, but for the heart instead.

Without realizing it, her arms were clenched around her body as if she, too, were to feel the ripping agony of the bullets.

She closed her eyes and prayed as the command to fire was given. When the simultaneous explosion from six .58 caliber rifles died away, she opened them to see her beloved lying in the dust with a wide red stain blossoming across his chest.

Sinking to her knees, she huddled on the stone step of the portico, unaware of the chaos around her.

The compound was deserted now. The crowd of curious onlookers had been herded out and the gates once again barred. When they escorted him to the wall, he looked down at his brother's body lying sprawled and bloody in the dust. *The bastards left him there deliberately for me to see*. He cursed Morales again as he was told to stand by the corpse. Stroking his cheek, he looked bleakly at the dead man's façe—his face. If not for the scar, no one could tell them apart.

No one but Mercedes. He shrugged away the blindfold. "An Alvarado has no need of it," he said after paying the bribe to avoid facial mutilation. They had kept their word with his brother. Maybe they would with him, too.

Upstairs on the balcony overlooking the courtyard the commandant stood poised, ready to give the signal. His sergeant awaited the order to fire. Just as Morales raised his hand, the door to his office flew open and a *gringo* with sandy hair and colorless eyes stormed in.

"Morales, you'd better pray the man lying down there doesn't have a scar across his left cheekbone or else you'll be joining him by special orders from President Juarez." Bart McQueen's voice was deceptively calm, but his eyes cut through the commandant like ice-cold steel.

Morales blanched and signaled for the soldiers to lower their Springfields. "What is the meaning of this?" he demanded, noting the two men with the Americano who held his staff officers at gunpoint.

"You'll forgive me for not taking the time for diplomatic niceties, but if I'd let your secretary read the documents, the man I came to save would certainly be dead." He looked out the window to the two prisoners, one standing almost nonchalantly against the wall, the other lying beside him. "Who did you execute first—Alvarado or Fortune?"

The commandant did not doubt for a moment that he could be in significant trouble. "They decided it between them. I don't know." His voice was brittle and it cracked with nervousness as he spoke. When he began to read the executive order signed by Benito Juarez, Morales' hand shook and sweat beaded his face.

"Bring me the man who's left alive," he croaked at the guards, sinking onto the chair behind his desk. His legs would no longer support him.

McQueen gestured for his men, who wore the insignia of presidential bodyguards, to let the garrison soldiers obey their commandant's orders.

Mercedes followed the guard into the dimly lit room where Nicholas' body lay in its shroud of cheap canvas. When they returned to Gran Sangre, she would have him buried in fine linen. Her vaqueros walked to the bare table and started to pick up the body. Abruptly she commanded, "Wait. I want to be alone with him, for just a moment."

The guards and her men filed respectfully from the room. This was her last chance to say good-bye. After the long journey to Gran Sangre in the heat, the body would have decomposed. "At least they didn't hit your face, my beloved," she whispered as she pulled back the stiff cloth with trembling fingers and bent to place a kiss on his cold lips.

Chapter 27

"Commandant, that woman is outside—his wife. She's hysterical. What should I ?"

"I will see Commandant Morales this instant," Mercedes cried as she barged through the door into his office. "The man you shot is Lucero Alvarado! What have you done with Nicholas Fortune?" she demanded.

"You're supposed to be on your way home to Gran Sangre."

Mercedes whirled around with a gasp of disbelief. Nicholas stood behind the door, his face haggard and exhausted, yet he was whole, unharmed. She ran into his arms. The tears began pouring from her in torrents, all the tears she had forced herself to hold inside these past hellish weeks.

"Oh, my darling, my darling, I thought . . . I . . ." She reached up and caressed his scarred cheek, feeling the prickle of whiskers on the soft pads of her fingers. He was warm and alive, here in her arms.

Nicholas crooned soft love words, soothing her as he enfolded her in an embrace. She clung to him tightly, trembling like a frail palm frond in a hurricane. "I'm all right. They took Luce. He insisted on flipping a coin to see who went first. He lost the toss. Hilario got word to McQueen and he arrived in time to stop them from killing me, too."

She could barely hear him or make sense of what he was saying. All that mattered was that he was alive. "Then—then you're free? They'll let you go?" Her fingers dug into his arms as she searched his face for an answer.

"Mr. Fortune has received a presidential pardon for any and all misdeeds he may have committed during the past conflict. Benito Juarez will always remember the Americano who risked his life to save his adopted republic and its president," McQueen replied.

"You are free to go," Morales added stiffly, eager to have this whole fiasco ended and these two dangerous *gringos* out of his jurisdiction. Thank the merciful saints that he had executed the right man! The commandant did not doubt the foreign agent's threats, no matter how mild-looking his appearance.

Nicholas could see Mercedes was on the brink of collapse and feared for her and their child. "I'm going to take you home," he said softly, holding her close against his side. Then he turned to Morales. "There is one thing . . . my brother. I want to take his body back with us for burial on Gran Sangre."

Morales scrawled an order and handed it to the guard. "The body will be released to you at once."

The smoke from the campfire rose into the clear, cool night air. They had made good time that day in spite of Nicholas' concern for Mercedes' condition, then camped that evening near the Chihuahuan border. While the men stood sentry, the *patrón* and *patrona* sat in front of the fire. She reclined in his arms, leaning against his broad chest, feeling the steady thrum of his heartbeat.

"I can't believe the nightmare is over at last," she said, exhausted yet utterly content.

"It could've ended differently. If Luce hadn't tried to rescue me or if I'd lost that toss with his silver dollar . . ." He shrugged. "Odd, I wonder where he got an American lucky piece like that. It sure didn't bring him luck at the end."

Mercedes glanced over at the canvas-shrouded body lying in the dim light at the edge of camp. "Maybe he intended it to end the way it did."

Nicholas looked down at her, puzzled. "I was going to go first. As firstborn, it was my right. Something made him resist. He offered to flip me 'for the honor,' as he called it."

"He called heads you went first, tails he did."

A small frown creased his forehead. "How did you know?"

"The silver dollar was Anselmo's lucky piece. It was a gamester's trick coin he'd acquired in the United States. He gave it to Lucero years ago. Both sides were the same."

"Tails," Nicholas said with a bittersweet oath. "Damn, it was almost as if he knew that he could save me by going first."

"But there was no way he could've known that," she replied.

Nicholas shrugged. "It's strange . . . in war men get superstitious. After surviving for years, watching others die all around, a man can develop a sort of sixth sense . . . maybe he did know."

"Then he gave you the most precious gift anyone ever could," she said in a choked voice.

"We talked all night before the execution . . . we told each other things we never had in all those months we rode together. I may have been the only person he ever really cared about . . . as much as Luce could care about anyone."

"I never loved him, but I shall always be grateful to him. And I'll light candles for his soul."

"I have a feeling he'll need them," Nicholas said fondly, remembering Luce's rather irreverent manner of receiving the last rites.

"Of course, the state of my own soul may invalidate my prayers, at least in Father Salvador's eyes," Mercedes said with a sigh.

"You're a widow. If he won't marry us, we can travel across the border and be married in American territory. I know it isn't the blessing of your Church, but—"

She silenced him with a soft sweet kiss. "We've pledged our vows to each other. I need no other sanction."

But you would like the blessing of your Church, he thought to himself, troubled as he held her against his chest.

The wind blew, soughing softly through the willow trees and the air was fragrant with heady musk from angel's trumpet vines. It was spring in Sonora as the people of Gran

Sangre gathered to lay one of their own to rest. The soil, still damp from winter rains, was fecund with the promise of a fine fertile planting season. Among those gathered to pay their last respects were half a dozen women great with child, including the *patrona* herself.

Father Salvador read the words that consigned Lucero Alvarado to eternal rest. Nicholas held Mercedes' hand as they watched her husband's body being lowered into the earth.

After the graveside rites were complete, the silent assembly began to disperse, to resume their daily chores. Nicholas and Mercedes walked toward their carriage, his arm protectively around her shoulders.

"It will be all right, *querida*," he whispered soothingly in English.

"Father Salvador called you Don Nicholas. We've buried Don Lucero. Soon everyone will know,"

"Everyone on Gran Sangre had already guessed, some time ago." His tone was gentle, but the pain in her voice cut him deeply.

"But then it was different. They didn't *know*—they could keep to the fiction of addressing you by his name."

He had feared she would feel this way. "And so could you."

His words dropped quietly on the still morning air as he helped her into the carriage. Feeling his hurt she said, "Oh, Nicholas, you know it isn't that I love you any less. I could not love you more . . . but I am not as honest as Rosario."

"Hush, now. I never doubted your love," he murmured, holding her as he took his seat in the carriage beside her.

Upon their return the little girl had greeted the simple explanation about her "uncle" Lucero's death and the return of her "real" papa with the easy acceptance only a child can give.

"Perhaps we should have brought her today," Nicholas murmured thoughtfully, troubled at leaving the child at the house with Lupe.

"We agreed it would be best. He . . . he was not kind to her and she has no reason to mourn him. No one outside

Gran Sangre knows for certain whose child she is and she will always believe that she is yours. The young have such strong convictions, such faith . . . but I . . . I'm not that way . . . I'm just a weak and foolish woman."

"Rot! You are the strongest and bravest woman I have ever known," he said, taking her chin in his hand and lifting it so she met his eyes.

Her hand touched his cheek softly as she gazed into those fathomless wolf's eyes. "Everything will be all right. It's only the babe, making me weepy and foolish. Angelina assures me it will pass." She raised his hand to her lips and pressed a kiss against his palm. He returned her troubled yet loving gaze.

The sound of Father Salvador clearing his throat as he approached the carriage broke the spell. The priest studied them with his pale blue eyes, uncertain of how to broach the delicate subject.

Nicholas could feel Mercedes tense, and knew the priest's silent censure had cost her dearly since they had returned yesterday and arranged for Lucero's burial. "Thank you for what you said about my brother," Fortune said simply. *Thank you for what you did not say about me*, his eyes communicated to the priest.

Father Salvador nodded. "Don Lucero did a noble deed at the last, better than any of us expected of him, the Lord's work, no doubt. There is a matter of some pressing urgency about which we must speak. If I might meet you in the library after the noon meal?"

Mercedes could eat nothing, pushing the juicy slices of beef across her plate with a tortilla, dreading the confrontation to come with Father Salvador. She listened to Nicholas tease Rosario, drank in the musical peals of the child's laughter and watched as her love surreptitiously slipped bits of meat from his plate to Bufón, who lay beside his chair, waiting patiently. What a perfect picture of domestic contentment they made.

If only they could remain a family. But what would she do if Father Salvador demanded she stop living with Nicholas? Their relationship was a mortal sin, for he was her brother-in-law. Yet she knew with a fierce, sweet inner certainty that the love she and Nicholas Fortune shared was right and good. She would refuse to give him up. After coming so close to losing him in Durango, Mercedes knew that she could not live without him.

Sending Rosario off to play with the dog under Angelina's watchful eye, her parents walked silently down the long hall to the library. "Whatever you want to do, Mercedes, I'll do it," he said in a husky low voice.

She squeezed his hand. "You are the husband of my heart. I won't lose you, no matter what he or anyone else says."

The intensity of her voice stopped him. He studied her face and read the love in the depths of her golden eyes. A sudden surge of gladness infused his soul. "Trust me. I don't plan to be lost."

When they entered the library, the priest was waiting for them. Did he seem a bit nervous, uncertain? Nicholas again wondered at Father Salvador's request to meet them on their ground, not in his quarters, surrounded by all the trappings of his holy office.

"I don't know of any way to broach this delicately," he began without preamble, pacing across the carpet onto the polished hardwood floor.

Nicholas seated Mercedes in a high-backed easy chair, then stood protectively behind her. "I impersonated my half brother and took his wife. She is innocent in all of it, but it's my child she carries and I won't give the baby or her up, no matter what your canon law says."

"It is a troublesome matter. I have been praying about it and giving it thought for many weeks. I even wrote a letter to the archbishop who forwarded it to the Holy See. Now that Lucero Alvarado is dead, the issue is somewhat simplified."

"But my widowhood cannot loosen the blood tie between Nicholas and Lucero. Nicholas is still my brother-in-law," Mercedes said, confused yet daring to hope.

"Read these. Perhaps they will clarify the issue as I see it." The priest handed the documents to them. "These, of course, are copies in Spanish. The originals in Latin have gone to Rome. If you agree in your own good conscience that what I have petitioned is the truth, then you may sign such a declaration and I will forward it with all dispatch."

Nicholas scanned the papers quickly, his eyes skimming over the description of Lucero and Mercedes' arranged marriage, a union neither of them wished. She had earnestly tried to fulfill her duty but Lucero had shirked his, utterly disregarding the seriousness of the sacrament into which they had entered.

"If he had lived, it might have proven difficult to secure his signature on the petition," Father Salvador said as Nicholas handed the papers to Mercedes, then looked back at him.

"What you're saying, in effect, is that there never was a true marriage between them—that it can be declared null and void."

"Yes, that is how it appears to me."

"Then . . . then Nicholas never has been my brother-in-law—we could—" She broke off and looked up at him with a blaze of joy on her face.

"Only if you examine your conscience and know in your heart that you and Lucero never had a true marriage," Father Salvador explained.

Mercedes read the description of their relationship, outlined in stark narration. "Yes, what you say here is true, more than true."

"But will Rome see it that way?" Fortune asked, still unable to relinquish his cynicism. He could not bear to have her hopes built up and then dashed.

"Annulments have been granted for reasons of political expediency. In such a clearly moral dilemma as this, there should be no question. I've sent word to the archbishop about Don Lucero's death, which should greatly aid our petition. We should receive word in a month or two." The old priest's eyes moved to her belly, then were quickly averted as his pale complexion bloomed with color.

"In time for us to have our union blessed before our child is born?" Mercedes asked, knowing that she had an ally now, not the adversary she had feared.

"Yes, my daughter. I shall pray for a swift resolution."

"Where do we sign?" Nicholas asked, smiling at the flustered old man.

"I knew you'd come back to us," Rosario said sleepily as Nicholas closed the book of fairy tales and pulled up the covers around her. "I prayed every night for you. Why did you have to go away, Papa?"

He stroked her hair and placed a kiss on her forehead. "You know about the war." She nodded gravely. "I found out some evil men planned to kill President Juarez and I had to stop them."

"Father Salvador says President Juarez is a godless republican," Rosario replied, waiting patiently for further clarification.

Nicholas smiled ruefully. "Even such a staunch imperialist as Father Salvador would not condone murder, would he?"

"Oh, no! He would never permit that," she responded. She then asked, "Are you a godless republican, Papa?" Rosario did not seem particularly troubled by the possibility.

He chuckled at the resilience of youth—and the flexibility. "I am a supporter of the president, yes, but that doesn't make me completely irredeemable—or so your mama says."

"I'm glad." She yawned again. "Papa, does all of this have something to do with why you changed your name? The servants all call you Don Nicholas now."

"Someday, when you get a little bit older, your mama and I will explain why I had to use my brother's name," Nicholas said tenderly, tucking her in and watching as her eyelids fluttered closed.

"I suppose I shall . . . just . . . have to . . . wait."

Mercedes watched the child drift off to sleep as Nicholas walked silently across the room to where she stood in the doorway. Bufón watched them from his usual place beside the bed. As they closed the door, his tail thumped good night against the thick rug.

They walked arm in arm to their quarters. When they reached her door, he bypassed it, continuing on to his, then guiding her inside. Last night, upon their homecoming, the household had been in such pandemonium over the news of Lucero's death and Nicholas' return, that he had simply sent her to her room with Angelina to see that she drank a soothing sleeping draught and got some rest. He had made all the explanations and the arrangements with Father Salvador for his brother's burial, then retired to his own room much later.

Suddenly Mercedes felt shy and uncertain. It had been months since they last came together. She had tried to seduce him in that awful prison cell, but he had refused her. What if he found her body misshapen and ugly now? His voice, low and troubled, broke into her self-conscious thoughts.

"I told Rosario I had to use my brother's name. I couldn't tell her it was because I have none of my own. How will I ever explain it to her?" *Or to you*?

"You didn't steal Lucero's name. You have just as much right to the Alvarado name as he did—as Rosario does," she said, taking his hands in hers and drawing him to sit on the heavy oak settee by the window. Outside a night bird called to its mate and a brilliant Sonoran moon silvered the landscape with its glow.

"Sometimes I wonder which is worse—being Lottie Fortune's boy or finding out about the other half of my ancestry. If Sofia and Anselmo are what the House of Alvarado stands for, it's small wonder Luce ended up being the way he was."

"Not all the Alvarados were so bad. Even Lucero had some good in him at the end. I think I should tell you about your grandfather."

He looked at her with a startled expression on his face. "My grandfather Alvarado?"

"Yes. I never met him, of course. He died when Lucero was only a small boy, but he was a great *hacendado*—the kind who made the wilderness bloom with his own sweat and blood—a man like you. I've read about him through the diaries and letters of his bride, Doña Lucia Emelina Maria Nuñez de Alvarado." At his curious look, she explained, "When I was first brought here, there was little to do but become acquainted with the family I was to join.

Lucero didn't want to bother with me, nor did Don Anselmo, and Doña Sofia was hardly hospitable."

"I can imagine," he said dryly, waiting for her to continue her tale.

"Doña Lucia was only fifteen when she arrived. The place was little more than a frontier outpost then. Don Bartólome added both wings to the main hacienda as well as having the dairy, blacksmith stables and granary built. Most of the horse stables and corrals were his work, too. He imported fine Andalusian horses from Spain and improved the quality of the beef cattle, even introduced sheep to supplement the hacienda diet of beef and pork."

Nicholas listened as she described the labors of past generations of Alvarados, good men and women who loved the land and dealt fairly with it and its people. A new sense of pride and purpose infused him. "I realize now that we'll carry on their work. And our children after us," he said in a husky voice.

"Don Nicholas Alvarado and his lady, Mercedes," she said with a soft smile, turning into his embrace. "I always wanted to be like Doña Lucia, a pioneering wife."

"You've already proven your mettle, holding this place together all these years." He drew her into his arms, tilting her face up to his, brushing her mouth with his own until she opened her lips. His tongue lightly rimmed them, then stroked inside delicately, as if he were wooing his bride for the first time.

And she would be his bride, truly, as soon as the petition was approved in Rome. But for now, Mercedes only knew that she would pledge her love with her body and her soul.

Nicholas felt her response. Standing up, he swept her into his arms and carried her over to the big bed, which the maid had turned down for them. Like him, Mercedes had bathed and donned a robe before retiring. But hers was of soft sheer muslin, yards and yards of it. Gathered high above her waist, its voluminous folds concealed her pregnancy. The deep sea-green color enhanced her sun-kissed skin and golden hair.

He reached up and began to unfasten the small hooks holding it together, kissing her soft, sweet-smelling skin as he bared it. "You always have the essence of lavender clinging to you, like fairy magic," he murmured as his mouth grazed the pulse at her throat and it beat wildly for him.

Mercedes' fingers dug into his shoulders, kneading his hard flexing muscles, then pushing the loose satin robe from his chest. His mouth skimmed along her collarbone, then dipped lower to nuzzle the cleft between her breasts, which had grown large and heavy in the latter stages of pregnancy. She pressed her hands into the pelt of hair on his chest and let her fingers comb through it, loving the way his heart slammed against her palm.

She purred as his lips moved back up her throat and his tongue stroked around the edges of her ear, then she nuzzled him, snuggling her face against his heaving chest, teasing one flat nipple with her tongue until he groaned out an oath of endearment.

Nicholas slid her gown from her shoulders, murmuring, "It's lovely, but you're lovelier." Beneath the robe her nightrail was a pristine white, flowing batiste with a rounded neckline that clung to her full breasts. He slipped the buttons with deft fingers, then freed one pale milky globe, cupping it reverently in his palm. His mouth quickly followed, taking the nipple and drawing on it until she keened out her pleasure.

At once he withdrew the other breast and did the same to it. Mercedes could not have imagined the heightened sensitivity of her breasts during pregnancy. She gasped, then closed her eyes in bliss as he worked his exquisite magic. Her hands pulled at his robe, shoving it off his shoulders until he slipped the belt and shrugged it off. Beneath it he was naked. His body gave off a feral heat that made hers answer in kind as an aching wetness grew between her thighs.

But when he began to pull the voluminous gown up and slip it off of her, she seized his hands, stilling them. "Wait." Her voice held a husky plea.

Nicholas stopped, looking at her with a question in his eyes, his hands gentling as he whispered, "I never thought . . . is it all right to love you?" She was so frail and delicate looking, unlike the hardy *soldaderas* he had known. "Might I harm you?"

She shook her head. "No. Angelina explained all about what was happening to my body. I'm fine. Making love can't harm the child."

"Then what's wrong?"

"It's me . . . I've grown the past months since we were last together . . ."

He chuckled appreciatively. "I can see that," he murmured, cupping her magnificent breasts and letting his thumbs circle the upthrust nipples that begged for his mouth to suckle them.

"But I'm fat. My belly—"

"Holds my child," he said earnestly as one hand moved lower to cradle the swelling through the bunched-up cloth of her nightrail. "I can feel the life inside you—a life I put there. How could it not be beautiful to me? How could you not be beautiful? I want to see you this way, my love, to feel my child kick, to hold you both, to worship you with my body."

"Then how could I not agree?" she whispered raggedly, letting his seeking hands lift the gown up over her head and toss it fluttering to the floor beside the bed.

"Lie back," he commanded, pressing her to recline among the pillows on the big bed. Reverently his hands traced the trail which his eyes blazed, from her flushed face down her throat to her breasts. He cupped them and suckled them gently, then raised his head and let his hands move along the curve of her hips and across the swell of her belly, now fully rounded in the last months of her pregnancy.

A fleeting stab of fear touched his mind as he realized how slender she was and how great the burden she carried. Would the birth go all right? But then the baby seemed to provide the answer, kicking against his palm.

Mercedes watched as a broad smile spread across his face and he pressed his ear to her navel, listening. "He's a little hellion already," she murmured.

His hands massaged the taut skin of her abdomen and he

looked up at her and said, "How do you know he isn't a she?"

"Only time will tell for certain, but I do have an intuition," she replied, once more closing her eyes as he began to trail kisses around her navel and back up to her breasts.

One of his hands moved lower and found the soft wet heat between her thighs as she reached for his rock-hard staff that was prodding insistently against her hipbone.

Nicholas groaned as she stroked him. She whispered, "Please, my love, now."

He would not take her from on top, fearing he'd put too much pressure on her belly, but Nicholas Fortune was a man with an infinite sense of invention. Gently he rolled onto his side and positioned her with her legs raised, giving him access to penetrate deep inside the scalding heat of her body.

Mercedes arched up to receive him, wriggling her hips until his cries blended with her own, urging him to move harder and faster.

But he would not be hurried. Sweat beaded his forehead as he held himself under careful restraint, slowly sliding deep within her, then withdrawing in a gliding dance of such mind-robbing pleasure that they both gasped for breath.

Her hands clutched at him, one kneading his chest while the other dug into his hip, pulling him deeper inside her. Then, with a sudden animal ecstasy that took her utterly by surprise, the culmination began, like the shock wave of a great earthquake rippling through her body as she cried out, "Nicholas, Nicholas."

Even sweeter than the hot gripping contractions of her sheath, the sound of his name on her lips drove him over the edge to join her in the maelstrom of fulfillment. Nicholas Fortune had waited all his life for this moment. For the woman and the promise of their life together. He spilled himself deeply against her already-filled womb, knowing that this was the first but not the last child they would create together.

Slowly, reality reclaimed them. Insects droned softly outside the cheesecloth netting around the big bed. In the distance a coyote bayed at the moon and called to its mate.

One of Nicholas' prize mares whickered softly from the corrals and Peltre answered her.

"Life is good, so much better than I could ever have imagined before I met you," he said as he rolled onto his back and pulled her into his embrace.

Mercedes cradled his head against her breast and stroked his curly black hair. "Tell me about Lottie Fortune's boy," she whispered, kissing the errant lock of hair that fell across his forehead, making him seem like a youth once more. She wanted to know all of the tragedy and the triumph of his childhood in a foreign land, all the things that had formed him into the remarkable man she loved.

"I was born in a bordello in New Orleans. A very high-class establishment, according to Lottie. Her real name wasn't Fortune, it was Benson, before she ran away from her father to the wicked city where she survived as many beautiful women do. She became a rich man's mistress."

"Anselmo's," she answered, stroking his cheek softly.

"For a while, until he tired of her—or was summoned home to Gran Sangre to wed Sofia Obregón. I don't know which."

"Then he never knew about you." She was not excusing Anselmo's behavior. He would probably not have acknowledged Nicholas even if he had known.

He shrugged. "I'm not certain about that either, only that she lost her patron and was forced to find others to survive. Even selling her body was better than being with Hezekiah," he said with loathing.

She could feel him shudder and her heart ached for him.

"I'm glad you told me about Don Bartólome. Now I have one grandfather I can be proud of. Hezekiah Benson was the spawn of Satan. Ironic, that was what he called me when she finally sent me back to live with him on that miserable hardscrabble farm."

"How could a mother give up her own child?" she said aloud before she realized it.

"At the time I wondered, too, but as I grew older, I think

I understood. Her looks were fading from too much alcohol and the sort of life she led. She was on a downward spiral and knew it. I guess she figured a ten-year-old kid wouldn't last long on the streets in the neighborhoods we were inhabiting by that time. Or maybe she just wanted to get rid of me. Hell, I don't know. All I do know is life with Pap was pure hell."

"Pap?" she echoed.

"My grandpappy Benson was a farmer—or at least that was what he called himself, but he hardly ever tended his crops. That's what he had me for. Couldn't afford slaves so I chopped cotton. And had the skin beaten off my back when I didn't work to suit him. He wanted to be a preacher. Read the Bible every day—especially the parts about ungrateful children and the whore of Babylon."

"Your mother."

"My mother. He drove her away, then cursed her for leaving. When he wasn't spouting chapter and verse, he was drinking. Made him even meaner than when he was sober and that was plenty mean, believe me."

"He punished you for what he thought were Lottie's sins."

"He punished me for being born," he replied grimly.

Tears clogged her throat and trickled down her cheeks as she pictured Nicholas as a small boy with black curly hair, looking for all the world like a replica of his haughty Castillian father, a constant reminder to Hezekiah Benson of his daughter's sin.

"I took it for as long as I could, until I got big enough to fight back. By the time I was fourteen, I was as tall as him, but he was bull strong and sneaky mean. We had a few really nasty fistfights. I realized if I stayed, I'd end up just like him—or kill him."

"So you ran," she supplied.

"Back to New Orleans. Looking for my mother. Dumb, huh? She was dead and gone by then, so I took a job in one of the bordellos, emptying the slops and doing any other work too filthy for the adults. I filled out quick after that.

By the time I was fifteen, Pearly made me a bouncer. I'd learned to fight dirty from Pap, so I was a natural. Then I heard about this Frenchman recruiting for the Legion."

"The French Foreign Legion? So that's how you learned all those languages, traveled to all those exotic places you know about," she said with dawning understanding.

"Believe me, it isn't as glamorous as they make it out to be," he replied dryly. "North Africa was hot enough to make the Chihuahuan desert seem cool as London and the Crimea was so foul a cesspool, even the New Orleans slums seemed clean beside it. Most of all, I guess it was the war . . . always the killing, the stench of death. I was so sick of it all, of the rootless wandering, never belonging, just a nameless bastard who would end up some day in a nameless grave like all the others I'd met along the way."

"But you wanted something better," she said, curving her cool fingers around his jaw and stroking the faint bristle of whiskers.

"I found something better . . . better than the land, better than a grand family name, better than anything else on earth. I found you . . . so unexpectedly." He met her eyes and saw himself reflected in their warm golden glow.

"I can still remember the first time I saw you, standing in the yard outside the front *sala*. Your face was in the shadows cast by the portico roof. You looked so tall and harsh and forbidding, carrying enough weapons to stock an arsenal, marked by the war." She pressed a kiss against the scar on his cheek.

"You thought I was Luce returned."

"No, I knew you were different, from that first moment when our eyes met. I felt the thrill of that difference even though I didn't understand its cause at first. I desired you and that frightened me."

"And now that you know all about my sordid history . . . are you still frightened? Repulsed?" His hand played back and forth across her shoulder, fingers lightly stroking the silky skin.

She pulled his face to hers, framing it between her hands,

opening her lips for a deep soul-robbing kiss, as she murmured against his mouth, "What do you think?"

He had his answer as he crushed her in his arms and they tumbled amid the sheets. The specters of war and death were banished along with the shame of past deception. Nicholas Fortune was home at last, for good.

Epilogue

MAY 1867

"I do not care, *Patrón*, it is not fitting for you to be here. It is not the custom," Angelina said sternly, her big red hands planted firmly on her hips as she blocked his path in the doorway to his bedroom.

Another muffled gasp of pain issued from inside the room where his wife lay on their big bed. "I told her I'd be by her side, custom be damned!" He shoved past the old cook and rushed over to Mercedes.

She lay sweating, tangled amid the covers where Angelina and Lupe had just placed her after what seemed endless hours of walking up and down the long hallway. Nicholas had held her arm and walked with her, stopping each time a contraction seized her and she doubled up with the pain. While Angelina timed them with some infernal inbred female clock, he had stood rigidly still, feeling the agony lance through him with the impact of a saber slash to his guts. No, worse than any wound he had ever received in any war.

When the cook, who was also Gran Sangre's resident midwife, pronounced it time to put the *patrona* in bed for her delivery, she had closed the door in the *patrón's* startled face.

Now, dressed in a fresh nightrail, her hair braided in a fat plait lying across the pillow, Mercedes gritted her teeth in concentration, breathing in soft shallow pants as Angelina had instructed her.

"You will only be in the way," the midwife remonstrated.

"I've been through a dozen wars, Angelina, I don't faint

at the sight of blood," he replied grimly, not at all certain that Mercedes' blood would not be quite a different matter than his own.

Doggedly he pulled a stool up to the side of the bed and took his wife's hand.

Mercedes dug her nails into his palm, clutching the warm assurance of his strong, callused hand in her own smaller one. As the contraction eased, she smiled at him and said, "It really isn't that bad, you know."

"And you really are a terrible liar," he replied with tenderness.

Angelina applied a cool cloth to her forehead and nodded with satisfaction at how matters were progressing. "If you would be of some use, sponge her forehead with cool water between the pains," she instructed him. "It will not be much longer now." She turned to the door and called for Lupe. "Where is that girl with the things I told her to fetch?"

Nicholas and Mercedes exchanged a look of grave sweetness. "Father Salvador will be scandalized when he learns you were in here during the birth," she said.

"I may be of no use at this point, but at least I feel better if I can be with you."

"Your being with me is a great deal of use," she replied as another contraction began to build.

Nicholas held Mercedes' hand, bathed her perspiration-sheened face and refrained—with great difficulty—from asking Angelina how much longer it would be each time she checked his wife's progress.

"Ah, now, I think the little rascal is moving into place," the midwife said with satisfaction as her gnarled hands kneaded Mercedes' belly.

"It feels as if the whole Prussian army is moving into place," Mercedes gritted out, then looked at her husband's face, a stone mask behind which, she was certain, lay stark terror.

As the contraction ebbed, she said, "Father Salvador did a very useful and timely job, marrying us a scant three days before our child comes into the world."

"He kept saying the petition would come through in time, but I didn't believe him," Nicholas confessed.

"It's a miracle, but is it enough of one for you to let him baptize you?"

"I'm still thinking on that one. I had enough of religion when I lived with Pap."

Just then Mercedes arched up from the mattress as another sudden stab of white-hot numbing pain crashed down on her.

"Hold her, *Patrón*, yes, that way," Angelina instructed as Nicholas wrapped his arms around his panting wife. The midwife barked terse orders at Lupe, then reached down to pull the squalling red bundle of fury into the light of day. "It is a boy, *Patrón*."

"See, I told you it would be. Bartólome Nicholas Alvarado," Mercedes breathed in utter contentment. "Rosario will be so pleased."

"Now this *is* a miracle," Nicholas said reverently with tears in his eyes as Angelina placed his firstborn son, the heir of Gran Sangre, into his arms.

Author's Note and Acknowledgment

Ever since I saw *Sommersby*, I wanted to write *Bride of Fortune*. This story is for everyone who hated the ending of that movie or its earlier film noir incarnation, *The Return of Martin Guerre*. The writers of those screenplays viewed the theme of assumed identity in terms of honor and retribution. I viewed it in terms of love and redemption. Thus the relationship between Nicholas Fortune and Mercedes Alvarado took hold of my imagination.

In this story war is the crucible which refines my protagonists. But which war? What setting? Neither World War I nor the American Civil War met my needs. I wanted Nicholas to lay claim to a title and a great estate where his noble lady was sworn to provide their dynasty with an heir. The vision seemed almost medieval but not the characters as I conceived them. That's when the idea of nineteenth century Mexico came to me—the splendid feudal Mexico of Maximilian and Juarez where the rigidity of an Old World caste system clashed head-on with the revolutionary ideals of democracy.

Although the Vargas conspiracy in this story is fictionalized, the intense class hatred directed against Benito Juarez by many of the *hacendados* was very real. The Man of Law was in real life much as I have portrayed him in fiction, tenacious, shrewd and utterly incorruptible. The parallels between his life and that of Abraham Lincoln are remarkable: both rose from humble origins to their countries' highest offices; both were reviled as ugly and unprepossessing by their "betters"; and both were the driving forces which held together their nations during cataclysmic civil war. Juarez's wife and ten children spent the war years in exile in New York City. Mrs. Juarez actually addressed a joint session of the United States Congress in 1866 and received a standing ovation. Like Lincoln, Juarez died in office, although of natural causes.

After President Juarez's death in 1872, what Nicholas Fortune feared did happen. General Porfirio Diaz took over the presidency and Mexico became a dictatorship until his overthrow and exile in 1911. But the seeds of constitutional democracy had been planted in Mexico's fertile soil by Benito Juarez. It was left for his heirs to nurture them in the twentieth century.

Regarding the other historical characters in *Bride of Fortune*, Prince Salm-Salm and his daring American wife, Agnes, both remained loyal to Maximilian of Hapsburg until the bitter end. In exchange for her "darling Max's" life, Agnes even went so far as to offer her voluptuous charms to the young republican officer who held their emperor prisoner in the final days. Colonel Palacio honorably resisted temptation. On June 19, 1867, the "Austrian dreamer" along with two of his Mexican generals, the sanguine schemer Miramón and the honorable idealist Mejia, died before a firing squad. Virtually every government of Europe, as well as the Americas, protested Maximilian's execution, but Juarez held fast to the principle of law. The generals who deserted the army of the republic to follow a foreign usurper were clearly guilty of treason. In addition, European blue blood running red on New World soil was, in Juarez's eyes, not a bad deterrent to further Old World designs on Mexican sovereignty. Much has been made of the fact that Maximilian died well. Better for Mexico that he should have lived well. As for Prince Salm-Salm and his lady, they fade into history after surviving the Mexican adventure.

The ruthless butcher Leonardo Marquez's atrocities during the war inspired the development of Luce's character. Marquez actually absconded with millions in imperial loot. However, one of the most fascinating questions in Mexican history is what happened to that fortune. A highly ahistorical but entertaining answer is given in the film classic *Vera Cruz*. The Tiger of Tacubaya lived out his life as a pawnbroker in Havana and was finally allowed to return to his homeland, where he died an impoverished old man.

As for the American players, Confederates did immigrate to imperial Mexico, hoping to reestablish their antebellum social order. Matthew Maury, a brilliant scientist and embittered Southerner, actually served as Maximilian's Commissioner of Immigration. For him, as for most of the American settlers such as those depicted in *Bride of Fortune*, the adventure ended badly and they returned to the United States disillusioned.

Secretary of State Seward, who served both Abraham Lincoln and Andrew Johnson, recognized Juarez's government but went to great lengths to placate Napoleon III during the time the United States was rent by its own civil strife. Both administrations saw French recognition of the Confederacy as a more immediate threat than European encroachments in the New World. After the tide of victory turned for the Union, aid from north of the Rio Grande for the Juaristas increased dramatically. Spymaster Bart McQueen is fictional, but American agents like him were present in Mexico. Generals Grant, Sherman and Sheridan were outspoken in their support of the Mexican Republic as early as 1864. The latter two actually traveled into Mexico for talks with Juarez after our civil war ended. For the purposes of my story, I took the liberty of shifting the date when fifty thousand Union troops were deployed along the border from 1865 to 1866.

The civil war that raged during the French Intervention provided a glamorous backdrop, perfect for my embittered American mercenary and his half-English lady. The era was filled with elegance and violence. *Hacendados* lived in fabulous wealth like feudal monarchs while war raged on with savage intensity all around them.

Nicholas stepped into Don Lucero's life thinking to leave the fighting behind him and enjoy the privileges which he had long been denied because of his bastardy. He had not reckoned on falling in love with his brother's wife or being drawn to the Juarista cause. In spite of Mercedes' royalist sympathies, it was Nicholas' love for her that forced him to join the republicans. Their story is not merely about honor, it is about what ultimately makes men and women honorable:

the source from which they can trace their blood is not so fine a measure of their worth as is the cause for which they are willing to spend it.

In researching the rich tapestry of Mexican history I relied on the eyewitness accounts of Sara York Stevenson's *Maximilian In Mexico* for political events and Fanny Calderón de la Barca's *Life in Mexico* for social history and commentary on how the nineteenth century dons lived. *Maximilian and Carlotta* by Gene Smith and *Napoleon III and Mexico* by Alfred Jackson Hanna and Kathryn Abbey Hanna were superb secondary sources.

To capture the lyric, almost mystical beauty of the *hacendados'* way of life, Paul Alexander Bartlett's *Haciendas of Mexico* is unsurpassed for visuals and descriptive prose about the magnificent estates. On the other side of the coin, to learn about the earthy humor and richly textured lives of Mexico's lower classes, no one writes with more authority, insight or sympathy than J. Frank Dobie in virtually any of his works; I relied especially on *Tongues of the Monte*. For a first person account of nineteenth century travel in the northern states of Mexico, A. B. Clarke's *Travels in Mexico* is a cornucopia of authentic details and commentary.

As we developed this project, my associate Carol J. Reynard and I relied on kindness from many sources which we wish to acknowledge. The capable staffs of the public libraries of St. Louis and St. Louis County assisted us with our research. Carol and I could not have produced the manuscript of *Bride of Fortune* without "house calls" from our "computer doctors," Dr. Walt Magee and Mr. Mark Hayford.

My husband, Jim, spent the past six months of his retirement leisure tracking down bits of arcane information as well as choreographing action sequences and polishing dialogue in the manuscript. Our firearms expert, Dr. Carmine V. DelliQuadri, Jr., D.O., once again came through for us with some marvelous weapons for Juarista and imperial forces, even a gun for our *gringo* spymaster that was so bizarre, Jim accused him of inventing it.

Nicholas and Mercedes' love proved stronger than the divisive forces of civil war, betrayal and death and even provided the impetus for Lucero's surprising redemption. We felt our protagonists earned their happy ending. Please write and let us know if you agree. A stamped, self-addressed envelope is appreciated for replies. Happy reading!

Shirl Henke
P. O. Box 72
Adrian, MI 49221

Award-winning author of *Creole Fires*

GYPSY LORD
_________ 92878-5 $4.99 U.S./$5.99 Can.

SWEET VENGEANCE
_________ 95095-0 $4.99 U.S./$5.99 Can.

BOLD ANGEL
_________ 95303-8 $4.99 U.S./$5.99 Can.

DEVIL'S PRIZE
_________ 95478-6 $5.50 U.S./$6.50 Can.

MIDNIGHT RIDER
(March 1996)
_________ 95774-2 $5.99 U.S./$6.99 Can.

Publishers Book and Audio Mailing Service
P.O. Box 120159, Staten Island, NY 10312-0004
Please send me the book(s) I have checked above. I am enclosing $______ (please add $1.50 for the first book, and $.50 for each additional book to cover postage and handling. Send check or money order only—no CODs) or charge my VISA, MASTERCARD, DISCOVER or AMERICAN EXPRESS card.

Card Number____

Expiration date____________________Signature____________________

Name____

Address____

City____________________State/Zip____________________

Please allow six weeks for delivery. Prices subject to change without notice. Payment in U.S. funds only. New York residents add applicable sales tax. KAT 2/96